THE GHOST AND THE DARKNESS

BOOK 2 OF THE FALLOCAUST SERIES

VOLUME 1

QUIL CARTER

www.quilcarter.com

Cover by Quil Carter

First Edition

1530143284

978-1530143283

This book is dedicated to the Friskie, Jockster, and Daisy.

“Monsters are real, and ghosts are real too. They live inside us, and sometimes, they win.” – Stephen King.

A note from Quil regarding Book 2 and the best way to read The Fallocaust Series.

Ideally, I would love for my readers to see the companion books as a vital part of The Fallocaust Series. I decided to write companion books for The Fallocaust Series because I wanted the reader to see all sides of the story, and also see what motivates certain characters. The characters in Fallocaust are complex, and each of them have their own motivations and reasons for doing what they do, and being who they are. Some have enough motivation and reasons to fill a book… and so, I wrote them one. Though a companion book can stand on its own and has its own storylines that steer away from The Fallocaust Series, there is still that underlining connection to the main series. And the main series is written from the standpoint that the reader has read the companion book(s).

Though I realize there are people who will jump straight from Book 1 to Book 2 (I left you at a horrible cliff-hanger, I know). You're not going to get the full story if you do that. There will be references you won't get, plot spoilers that will be ruined once you do read Breaking Jade. And important characters that appear Book 2 that you should've already known about by reading Breaking Jade (like Sanguine and Jack for example).

So, think of Breaking Jade as The Fallocaust Series Book 1.5. If a certain site let me list it as Book 1.5 in the series I would have, but nooo numerical only apparently. Lookin' at you popular site that starts with A.

I would also like to explain how The Ghost and the Darkness is structured. Because of the size of this monster book, I have had to split it into volume 1 and volume 2. The book as a whole is over 400,000 words and because of that I won't be able to print the book in its entirety. Volume 2 is going to be released November 15th 2014.

Enjoy, and thank you for continuing this fucked up journey with me ;)

Sincerely,
Quil Carter

PROLOGUE

Twenty Years Previous

THE ASH WAS BLINDING, BURNING HOT, AND MIXED with embers that fell on the pacing shadow below like raining brimstone. It fell to the ground and thickened like fresh snow, leaving boot prints that framed every erratic footstep.

Greyson tried to inhale but his lungs filled with fire instead of fresh air, searing the soft tissue like he had opened an oven door. There was no air, he would have to find shelter soon or else he was going to pass out right there in front of the door.

Though the fear of his own demise didn't make him move. He looked up at the tall grey brick building and swallowed a sob.

No... no, I can't leave him.

"Lycos!" Greyson cried. He continued to pace, not knowing what else to do. He knew he was walking in circles but staying still was not an option.

"Lycos!" He felt his fists hit the brick building as if this desperate display of emotions would bring him back. But it was useless, Lycos would burn inside; this would be his tomb.

They had been so close.

Another explosion sounded from inside, bringing fresh tears to Greyson's already swollen red eyes. A strangled sob rimmed his lips and fell unabashed from his mouth, though with the next inhale he doubled over in hacking coughs.

So much smoke, as thick and black as oil. All Greyson could see were his own hands gripping the exterior. Hands that were so burned the skin had curled back like old paint, revealing red inflamed flesh underneath.

Greyson's head rose and he leaned his forehead hopelessly against the door frame. He closed his eyes and sobbed before sliding down to his knees.

Lycos was dead. Lycos was dead.

Greyson's ears rang as another explosion rocked the entire structure; he could feel the hot brick shake under his hands. The entire lab below his feet was probably collapsing in on itself; he wouldn't be surprised if the entire building fell under the hellfire.

"Greyson? Where is he?" a cold voice asked behind him.

How was he so fucking calm?! Greyson whirled around to face the towering blond man. The young greywaster looked up at him with tears streaming freely down his face.

"He's inside! Where the hell do you think he is?" Greyson cried. He put his hands onto his head and closed his eyes, his teeth clenching so hard he could hear them creak in his head.

Elish looked past him, his purple eyes incandescent amethyst against his white skin.

"Go to the plane." With the grace that only Elish could carry, he removed his cloak and handed it to Greyson, before disappearing into the thick black smoke.

"Elish?" Greyson hollered after him. His red flayed hands gripped the cloak like a security blanket, his mind jumping from one possibility to the other.

Greyson swallowed a frustrated scream before he turned and went towards the plane, his shaking footsteps threatening to spill him onto the hot ground.

The plane was a quarter mile away but it was still cloaked in a thin coat of grey ash. Greyson looked behind him to the burning building, wondering if this fire would melt the entire city. Kreig held many broken buildings, and with this heat…

Greyson took in a deep breath, ignoring the relief his lungs felt at the cooling air.

There was nothing to see, the building was in ruins. Black smoke was spilling from the door and through the vents. There was no way they would survive, not even Elish. He might be immortal but he had to breathe like the rest of them. His flesh would burn like any human's and it would take months for his carbonized body to regenerate.

And the baby – what would happen to the baby?

Greyson's entire body was trembling, his hands shaking with such a ferocity he could see pieces of skin fall from them and onto the ground below.

What now, what now? My heart... my heart is in there.

His father was right; he shouldn't have gotten tangled up with these people. They were not greywasters; they were not his kind.

I'm just a mayor's son, hoping to do a little bit more for this world than simply live in it and die in it. I just wanted to make things better for everyone, and look where it got me? Dad was right, care about Aras and nothing else.

But that's not me... I can do good, we can do good. Chance is just that... he's our chance. It might be a long shot, but if we do things right... he can put an end to King Silas's dictatorship.

What a foolish dream for a foolish greywaster.

Greyson's heart froze inside of his chest when he saw a tall figure through the smoke. His face twisted in a relieved sob as he ran towards them.

As Greyson got closer, the heartwrenching sound of a baby in incomprehensible agony reached his ears. The newborn was screaming so loudly every pause to gather breath made him choke.

"Lycos!" Greyson screamed. He ran until their silhouettes took shape before, in spite of himself, he took a step back.

Elish's blond hair was black with soot and ash; his milky face scorched and patched in inflamed burns. He was injured and badly, blisters already appearing on his swollen raw arms and chest.

But he was carrying...

Greyson took another step back as Elish swept past him. Elish was carrying Lycos in his arms, and in Lycos's own arms: the horribly burned baby Chance.

Greyson's boyfriend had his eyes half-closed. He could see his beloved boy's blond hair burnt to cinders, falling over his face like scorched grass.

The young scientist's clothing had been almost entirely burnt off too, but where the shreds of his lab coat ended and his peeling skin began Greyson couldn't tell, but he was alive and so was the baby.

When Lycos saw him his face twisted in agony. "The baby, the baby's burned. Greyson take the baby! Help him!" he begged. Lycos tried to lift his head but it fell back onto Elish's shoulder blade with a stifled moan of pain.

Elish jumped onto the plane and set Lycos down on the cargo hold. As Lycos's body shifted, Greyson saw a small little face. It was peeled and burnt, with blisters that swelled in front of Greyson's eyes.

Greyson couldn't contain the desperate groan. He kneeled down in front of Lycos as the plane door slid shut. He carefully took baby Chance from Lycos's arms and felt tears sting the tender exposed flesh on his face.

The baby's onesie was charred and burnt, revealing bright red skin underneath. Greyson carefully took it off the squirming infant, but turned away unable to handle what he was seeing.

Greyson had never seen such an agonizing sight.

Chance's eyelashes were burnt off, and so was his soft little frock of black hair. His eyes, black like an insect's, were rimmed with red, and tearing from the smoke and his wounds. Though only alive for not even forty-eight hours, his entire body was a ruin of charred and burnt flesh. The horrible smell was something Greyson knew he would never forget.

Greyson brushed his hand over the baby's stomach, and as he did, the baby's skin came with it. The child let out another painful howl; his body twitching and writhing from the burns.

Greyson felt the bile come up in his throat, and then a wave of nausea. He turned away from the both of them in an effort to compose himself.

Then Elish was there. With blistered arms, he picked up the child, and put a hand over Chance's mouth and nose.

"What are you doing!?" Greyson screamed as Elish's large scorched hand covered the baby's airway. "It's not tested! It's not tested!"

Elish's cold eyes didn't move, they stayed fixed on the infant as the little newborn raised a single balled hand in protest, his black eyes flicking around confused.

Greyson suppressed a sob and turned from the scene.

He felt Lycos put a hand on his shoulder in support; his boyfriend's skin scalding to the touch.

Then the baby stopped crying. Greyson turned when he saw movement and watched as the baby's arm fell limp to his side. After a moment, Elish removed his hand, and handed off the dead newborn to Lycos. Without another word, he disappeared into the cockpit, and the plane roared to life.

Beep... beep... beep...

Greyson brushed Lycos's burned scalp. He used to brush back those soft blond strands before they had gotten almost all burnt off, now he brushed back rough scabbed skin. But it didn't matter, Lycos was still handsome – even if he was a bit overcooked.

Lycos opened his hazel eyes. His blistered lips raised in a smile when he saw Greyson.

He can still smile.

"You're too nice to me." Lycos raised a hand and tried to pull on Greyson's short beard but it was still too painful to raise his arms.

Greyson leaned down and kissed the corner of his lips. "The salve and the IV seem to be doing a good job. Is your Skytech shit really that good?"

Lycos chuckled, but a moment later his face twisted in discomfort. It had been a week since the explosion and he was still in pain every day. He nodded though and motioned to his IV bag. "That's chimera juice I'm getting. They make it special just for us."

Greyson held his smile, though his heart ached to take Lycos into his arms. Every cell in his body clenched with frustration that he couldn't take the pain from him. He loved his chimera boyfriend; he wanted to protect him from the world.

"You're so brave," Greyson whispered. "What did I do to snag such a guy?"

"Got me drunk," Lycos whispered back. They both started to laugh, that was a night they both wished to forget.

Greyson reached over and pressed the morphine drip Lyle had been nice enough to set up for him. It seemed like Elish had his own mini-hospital in his skyscraper home.

There was a small knock on the door. They both turned and saw Elish's sengil Lyle in the doorway. He was holding a small bundle in his arms, a smile on his soft face.

"Guess who finally decided to meet the world?" Lyle said cheerfully, in the same moment there was a squeak from the blankets.

Greyson jumped to his feet as Lyle walked towards him. He handed off the bundle to Greyson and bowed before leaving the room.

Greyson looked down at the baby and felt his breath get taken away. The infant was brand-new, not a single blemish on his body. Greyson removed a button from his blue onesie, and with a finger he drew the soft cloth down to expose Chance's chest. Pink, soft, and smelling like baby.

The little fucker was completely healed.

"He's… he's perfect," Greyson laughed. "He works. You did it, a born immortal." He sat back down on his chair and gently put the baby into Lycos's awaiting arms. Like most people do as soon as they see a new baby, he immediately started talking to him in a high-pitched voice.

"Hey, Chance!" Lycos said happily. "How's my little man?"

Greyson reached over and drew the blanket back so he could get a better look. Chance looked wide awake, just like he had when he was still inside his glass tube. The baby's little obsidian eyes looking around the room trying to take it all in. Unlike normal babies, he could make out every shape, memorize every face, his eyes were already fully developed and sharper than any man's.

The baby's head turned to Greyson, though instead of crying like he usually did when he saw someone besides Lycos, his eyes seemed to widen further before he let out a squeak. Lycos *aww'd* in a state that Greyson could only describe as sheer bliss. He raised a partially bandaged finger and traced it over Chance's pale cheeks.

"He's perfect, just look at him, in every way he's the perfect little being. He doesn't even know yet just how long we've been waiting for him."

"Not as long as I," a cool voice said from the doorway. Greyson and Lycos looked up to see Elish enter the room.

The blond chimera looked different now but not at all less intimidating. The flames had burned his once trademark golden hair away, it now rested only a few inches below his ears.

But besides his hair, the remainder of his body was healed and new. As an immortal, Elish had put himself out of the pain with an overdose of morphine. Unlike the mortal Lycos, Elish could escape his injuries; besides his hair Elish looked like himself.

Like a gentle flow of water, Elish walked into the room and stood by Lycos's bed. He reached a gloved hand over and lifted the baby's chin with his pointer finger.

Chance didn't like this. He raised a small hand and wrapped it around Elish's finger.

"A suitable grip; I see he is focusing on faces already as well. Good, the vision enhancement took; only time will tell if the other enhancements were successful." Elish nodded approvingly. With a gentleness that was rarely seen on Elish, he pulled his fingers away from the baby's grip and started moving the digit back and forth. The baby's eyes were focused on it. "Is the bunker ready?"

Greyson nodded. "We're ready. Chance will have a good home until I can… convince my father to let Lycos in."

"You'll have two years. Whatever it takes either convince him or dispose of him." Elish's icy voice always gave Greyson the shivers. Every word from his mouth flowed like it had come from a cold lake. "And Chance is it? You do know the child will call himself by his given name once he starts to speak?"

Greyson nodded, secretly he hoped if they called him Chance enough it might stick. "You never know."

"And regarding the other matter… have you asked him yet?" Elish raised a blond eyebrow; his eyes focused on Greyson's pocket.

The greywaster flushed, feeling the small prickles of embarrassment rise to his face. He spared a glance to a confused Lycos and back to Elish.

He coughed in his hand. "No, not yet."

"I suggest you get it done before we leave for the bunker. There is paperwork I would rather have on hand, and I have someone in mind who can make it binding."

"Who?"

"Myself."

"What?" Lycos asked. He had the baby's hand around his own finger now; his hazel eyes travelling from Elish back to Greyson in confusion.

Greyson flushed even harder. He had wanted to do this in private, but maybe with Elish here to witness it, it might not be a bad idea.

With a hand that trembled for different reasons now, Greyson reached into his pocket and withdrew a ring.

"Since we have our son…" As soon as Lycos saw the ring his eyes started to well, with a mouth half-open from shock he stared at the small silver band with twin gemstones. "I was wondering… if you wanted to make this a family… and marry me?"

Greyson watched Lycos's face turn three shades paler; he looked like he was frozen in a state of shock. The greywaster took this moment to gently pick up his partner's hand and slip the ring over his finger, one of the few that weren't bandaged.

"Marry you?" Lycos whispered. He held up his hand and gazed at the wedding ring with such an unbelieving expression on his face it looked like he thought this was all a dream. "Elish? I'm allowed?"

Elish smirked. "You're dead according to our family, Lycos. You can marry whoever you wish."

Tears welled Lycos's eyes. He nodded and opened his free arm to Greyson. They embraced, Greyson trying as hard as he could to be gentle with his touch.

"I'll marry you, of course I will." Lycos's voice broke, and as they pulled away his eyes fell on the blond chimera looking on. "Thank you."

Elish gave him a small nod. "This is the first step in a very long journey. What fruits will rise from the ashes remain to be seen. In the meantime, just stay hidden and do what needs to be done to raise him."

Without another word, Elish turned to leave.

"Elish?" Lycos called after him, the bundle wrapped in a blue blanket still on his lap, cooing and grasping anything that came into reach. "What's his name? The name Silas gave him?"

Elish paused at the doorway, in that moment looking like a god in front of the pearly gates. The chimera's short hair had done nothing to stop the awe-inducing demeanor that always seemed to follow him from room to room.

"Reaver… his name is Reaver."

"Reaver…" Lycos whispered. He brushed his fingers along the baby's short black hair, soft silken wisps that only infants had. Even years later when the boy was old enough to push him away, Lycos, now Leo, would sneak into his room at night just to brush them away from his sleeping face. Sometimes playing his luck and holding Reaver in his arms, rocking him back and forth, giving the boy the human touch he so hated when he was awake.

But at two they became concerned, at four they were calling Elish begging for help for their child more feral than human. Reaver's engineering was taking over; he was becoming a monster.

How could he overthrow Silas when he was more animal than man?

But still Leo would hold him. Still he comforted him, even when the boy resisted any forms of affection. Reaver was his son, his boy. No matter what Greyson wanted for him, no matter what Elish's plans were.

Whatever you become, Chance, please – just be a good person.

But your dad will love you, regardless.

CHAPTER 1

Killian

IT WAS NUMB INSIDE OF ME. THE EMOTIONS I HAD ONCE so strongly felt had been chewed to ribbons by the events of the last hour. All I could feel now was my chest gently vibrating under the muffled roar of the plane engines; and the sinking feeling that the sliding doors closing on us had been the lid on my coffin.

The sound had been deafening. I had never been this close to an airplane, let alone inside of one. I had found myself temporarily stunned when Elish had thrown me into the cargo hold. My brain shutting itself down from any more stimulation in a desperate act of self-preservation.

It hadn't lasted of course. Only the warm hand in mine was stopping me from losing what remained of my sanity.

Now we were in the air. It was quiet, all but the talking. They weren't even whispering, I just couldn't process what they were saying now. My mind was at max-capacity and all my emotions had been left in a bloodied heap back at the north gate.

I felt something squeeze my hand; I squeezed it back more out of automation than comfort. I couldn't spare a glance to remember whose hand I was holding. My eyes refused to leave Reaver's body.

My boyfriend's throat was nothing more than a gaping hole, one that exposed veins, spine, and pink flesh, all shredded from the deacon's jaws. His low lip was missing too. I could see his white teeth, perfect as if he was still alive. Though his gums were colourless; his blood had been completely drained by the lacerations to his neck.

At least Perish had turned Reaver's face away from me. I don't know what I would do if I saw Reaver's black, lifeless eyes.

I wondered if I would be watching when the spark came back into them.

How could it be though? It was one thing to have Asher reappear but for it to happen to Reaver as well? The notion seemed outlandish and insane when applied to someone I knew, someone I loved – someone who I could see dead and cold only several feet in front of me.

How could it be possible that he would come back to me?

I clutched the hand I was holding tighter. Could I be the first person he saw?

"He is not dead. Like Silas he will mend and he will rise. If you are to cry, cry for the life you once knew. Do not cry for someone who can no longer die."

Elish turned and spoke those words as he brought me to the awaiting plane. Not for sympathy or pity, but because he had grown tired of my hysteria. Even though the words held weight, his cold impassive gaze did not falter or show any emotion. He had said it to me like he was chastising a child, before turning from the grisly scene around me, and taking control of the jet from his black-haired cicaro.

The same one I had seen years ago in Tamerlan and the same one I had shot in the arm the night previous.

I had been aiming for the ground.

So do I wait now? I wanted to touch Reaver, but I couldn't leave Reno alone. Or was it my own fear of feeling his cold grey skin that made me shy away from it? The fear that if I could confirm to myself that he was really dead, he wouldn't come back.

No, he had to have died before.

I felt my lungs tighten, making the breath in my throat retract. I remembered back to what seemed like years ago, when Greyson had choked him. I remember seeing the blood in his ears, and his glassy, dead eyes staring lifeless into the darkness.

Greyson *had* killed him.

My eyes widened. I gripped the hand even harder as the realization swept me with cruel indifference to my already shocked and damaged state.

I wonder how many times they had killed him. I wondered who else knew. Doc must have known, that I could confirm. He had been Reaver's personal doctor for years.

"Hey… hey, Iron Man, loosen up your grip a bit." For some reason even though I realized Reno had been trying to talk to me before, this snapped me back.

"Sorry…" I loosened up my hand and looked down at my ash-covered friend. Reno gave me a weak smile. He had his bullet proof vest off of him now, two of the bullets still imbedded in the links underneath. The one that hit his gut though was still lodged deep inside.

I made sure I wasn't putting too much pressure against the wound. I lifted it up and sucked in a breath, I felt tears spring to my eyes.

"You… you're horrible!" Reno whispered, trying to sound shocked. "You're supposed to tell me I'm going to be okay, like in the movies, not take one look at it and cry!"

I choked and laughed; I leaned down and kissed his forehead. "You'll be fine. Everyone I know is an immortal, so by default you must be too."

"He isn't," Perish piped up.

I turned around and gave him a withering glare. The scientist immediately looked down at the floor and sulked over to Reaver. I saw he was holding a blue blanket in his hand, Deek was walking with him, his tail low. He didn't like the plane at all.

"Wherever we land, we'll get you medical help." I brushed back Reno's damp bangs, his forehead was warm and clammy. "Skyfall has great doctors."

Perish tucked the blanket into Reaver's sides before he started dragging him towards the back of the plane. The sound of his blood-slicked body being slid over the metal made me feel nauseas. He left behind a brimming puddle of crimson red that continued to follow him as Perish dragged his corpse across the floor.

"We're not going to Skyfall," a voice said beside me.

Every head turned towards the front of the plane. The pet named Jade was leaning up against the doors to the cockpit, a small nylon case in his hand and a smirk on his face. The pet's eyes fell to Reno, then to mine. Without another word, he started unzipping the case.

"Mikey?" I looked down and saw Reno giving the pet a confused look.

"You're Mikey… how can you be Mikey?"

I smoothed back Reno's bangs, my mouth pursing to the side. Poor Reno was getting delirious. "That's not Mikey, that's Jade. He's Elish's pet."

I heard Jade give out a low laugh and the sound of boots tapping against the metal floor. "Reno knows me. Elish and I came to Aras twice. We had to go under assumed names. Reaver knows me well… he and Reno dangled me over the deacons' pens when I was sixteen."

My eyes widened. I looked at Reno who now had a smile on his face. "Those were some good times. I had no idea who you two were, Reaver neither. No wonder Greyson and Leo flipped shit on Reaver. We were fucking with chimeras." Reno gave a slight chuckle but grimaced under the pain.

"None of this fucking makes sense," I mumbled, not knowing if this revelation made me feel more secure or just nauseas. Like Elish and Jade meeting with my parents years ago, it seemed like these two had been planning all of this for a long time.

Planning on being the ones to deliver Reaver to King Silas. I wonder what kind of accolades and honours they would get for being the ones to turn us over.

I couldn't let that happen.

"It will, Mr. Massey." Jade smiled. I shuddered as I was reminded of his eerie pointed canines. He had metal implants in over half of his teeth.

I watched Jade hold up a pair of tweezers, before he gave me a wink. "Now brace yourself, you need to dig out your Geigerchip and snip off the ends. Same with you, Perish."

"Why?" I felt my gaze fix on those strange eyes, ones I knew I would never forget when we had previously met. Elish's personal pet, with brilliant eyes like a foxes, another genetic mutation at the hands of Skytech.

Jade as a whole was lanky with long arms and legs. His eyes were framed by shiny black bangs, which fell to the edge of his narrow cheek bone. His ears were small and almost pointed, with tips that stuck out over his hair. I saw several earrings too, all of them flashing with gemstones.

I immediately didn't care for him. He dressed in skimpy, tight leather clothes and a studded leather collar and cuffs. A lot like Asher's style choice which I didn't appreciate.

Though I think it was just his air that I disliked. His easy attitude contrasted my heavy emotions making me feel frustrated, and his impassiveness filled me with anger. If he was indeed a cicaro pet he certainly didn't have the air of submission, on the contrary.

Then Jade handed me a scalpel. A weapon. I stared down at it confused, my eyes widening as my mind raced with ways I could defend the three of us. But no, he was smarter than that and so was Elish. So what was going on?

"Because they have tracking devices in them. The Skyland models, including the one that Perish gave you."

Tracking devices? It was Perish's turn to get glared at. The scientist immediately looked away and started busying himself feeding Deek pieces of what looked like dried meat. I bet that was the sole reason he'd stitched that device into me. He wanted to track my every move, and make sure if I did escape, he could find me.

A sour taste filled my throat. My mind's tendrils drawing up the man I had known as Asher. His stalking and tormenting of me suddenly made more sense. I bet he had that information too. The guy had known my every movement. I bet he'd known where Reaver lived all this time.

My hatred for him boiled, and we were being hand-delivered to him.

Or were we?

In a casual motion, befitting only someone as crazy as Perish, I watched as he sat down on a metal bench and stabbed his collarbone with the scalpel. After a few smaller slices, he dug his fingers into the crater-like wound. Perish's fingers pinched together and he drew out the small, blue-tipped chip.

Wordlessly, he handed it to Jade, who took what looked like dog nail clippers from the case and snipped off the blue end. He handed it back to Perish before tucking it back in. The casual air in which they did this confounded and angered me.

Then Jade walked towards me and held out his hand for the scalpel. "Want help?"

I stared at him, my head running through a thousand different scenarios. I had the scalpel… I had a weapon.

The pet stared back at me, before I saw his yellow eyes narrow slightly. "If you're thinking of driving that thing through my neck, you should put more thought into it."

I shifted away from him, feeling oddly exposed at him seemingly ripping out my own unconscious thoughts, but he wasn't done. "You're high in the air with three chimeras, Killian. Why don't you just take that Geigerchip tracker out of you and stop looking at me like I'm the Anti-Christ."

Anger swept my mind, though I knew it was just a disguise for the fear I was feeling. "What the fuck is going on?" I snarled, in a voice that was unlike my own.

Jade didn't even flinch; he looked at me like I was a toothless Chihuahua baring its gums at him. He took the scalpel from me, and with his other hand he made the skin over the scar tissue of my last implant tighten. I let him; I had no choice.

I felt a pull, then a pinch and finally a snip of the dog clippers before he placed the Geigerchip back into my skin. Instead of stitching it like Perish had in Donnely, he held the wound together with two strips of tape and an adhesive bandage. When Jade had patched me up, he wiped off his scalpel and disappeared back into the cockpit without another word.

"Are you going to tell me why he doesn't want Silas tracking us, or are you going to hide all of this from me too?" I snapped at Perish, taking my frustrations out on the only one who would give me the reactions I needed to please my indignation and fear. Though it was a low hit, I was running out of patience, and if I was about to be gang-raped and murdered by a family of mutants I wanted to at least prepare myself.

Perish cowered and started to wring his hands together. He looked towards the cockpit then back at me.

Don't you dare. The look I gave him could curl paint.

With a muttered excuse, he got up and left me too. In my anger, I tossed a few curse words his way, ones that made even Reno say '*Killian!*' in surprise.

Then the tears came. I hugged Reno to me and started to cry.

And he was comforting me… I hated myself. I felt Reno put a weak hand on my shoulder, the blood soaking into his t-shirt leaving rusty paint strokes against my lap. "It's okay, babe. Let's just live minute by minute, okay?"

I sniffed and nodded, wiping the tears from my eyes. I put the pressure back onto his stomach. This was the second towel I'd had to get for him, but at least it hadn't soaked through. I think the wound had stopped bleeding, but if not at least it had slowed.

"You're not sleepy, are you?" I asked. I desperately tried to remember everything that Doc had taught me, but it was buried under the weighted debris of everything that had happened this morning. My mind was so shot, all I could see whenever I tried to pull something up was Reaver getting his throat torn out. Or the lifeless bodies of Leo and Greyson, completely blanketed by chalky dust, one slumped over the other.

Reno shook his head. I shifted him on my lap so I could start wiping the sweat and dust off of his face. His face was littered with small cuts and bruises from the mob that had taken us. Reno had defended me to the end; he took those bullets for me.

It had been horrible… a scene I never thought I would see, in a place I had always felt safe. The townspeople, with Redmond and Hollis leading, had found us. The deacdog trackers finding us as easily as a cat found the scent of meat. Reno and I had made it to the quad before they spotted us. The dogs barking, the mob yelling like they had when Reaver had held the town meeting to burn the convicts. It had been terrifying; I had felt like an escaped prisoner, being hunted like a raver in my own town. Only blocks away from my house.

I couldn't believe it when they opened fire.

They had shot him… they shot their own resident, a man whose family, for generations, had lived here. The cowards sold him out at the command of their king.

I didn't know then that Silas had killed Leo and Greyson.

I whimpered again and closed my eyes, refusing exit to any more tears. I was a man now, any kid that still stirred inside of me had been killed the moment I saw Reaver get partially decapitated.

I would have to be an adult now for what was about to come. Take it minute by minute Reno said, but I couldn't help but fear the short future ahead of us.

Reno stood a chance, I knew myself that I was doomed. Silas would never let me live, he would torture me for sure to get Reaver to obey him. Reno though, he hadn't done anything to make Silas mad. On the contrary, they'd slept together. It was a small chance, but maybe he would get medical care and be released into one of the districts. It wouldn't be Aras but he would be alive. With his charisma and charm, eventually he would be okay.

We wouldn't be though, especially Reaver. His newly discovered immortality only meant he wouldn't be able to escape Asher's clutches. The love of my life was damned to an eternity of misery and slavery.

Instead of the tears running down my cheeks, they seemed to recess inside of me. Burrowing down as a burn in my throat, a smouldering ball of fire that scorched me whenever I tried to swallow. My heart clenched so hard into my chest I gagged. I tried to internalize the pain but it only made my shoulders start to shake from my internal grief.

"Five… little ducks… went… out… to play."

As Reno tried to soothe me, I lost it. I held my injured friend close to me and completely lost my head.

For the next several minutes I was nothing but a crumpled heap of sobs and choking gasps. The only sensation I felt in my state was Reno's hand gently stroking my arm, sticky from his dried blood freshly wetted by my tears. I cried for Reaver, for Reno, and I cried for Leo and Greyson. I cried for my former life, now as fleeting as the dust we had left encompassing the north gate.

My lungs were on fire by the time I had cried myself to exhaustion. I didn't have a single tear left in me; I had been wrung dry.

"If you can gather yourself for a moment, it is time we spoke."

That voice…

I looked up and saw the towering figure that was Elish Dekker. With his long golden-blond hair that fell past his shoulders showing off a strong square cheek bone, and very unemotional purple eyes.

The cold countenance of the blond chimera's face cut into my raw and bleeding emotions. I felt myself angry at him. Like when Jade had challenged my biting tone earlier, no one seemed to care what was going to happen to us but me, and it was driving me crazy.

Then I remembered the day I had first met Elish, the calm visage he had given off, the impassiveness of his voice, the cool and placid demeanor. I bit my tongue as I remembered that this was who Elish was. To show emotion on his face was a rare thing, and rarer still to show someone sympathy.

So with that knowledge, I gathered up my courage and pressed down my wounded feelings. With Reno's help, I slipped him off of me. I gave him a blanket from the pile Jade had thrown us and rested his hand on the towel with the right amount of pressure.

"There is no reason for private quarters. Mr. Nevada will be involved in what will happen once we land."

I glanced out the window, the greywastes in full view below us. It was a breathtaking view in all respects, stretches of nothing but small black trees resting on rolling hills, houses, and layers upon layers of every colour grey you could imagine, swirled into one another like mixing paint. I had never seen such a view, and probably never would again.

"What's going to happen to us?" I stood tall and squared my shoulders. I tried to look intimidating like Greyson had taught me. My instincts to do something to help our situation temporarily winning out against the earnest reality that I was helpless.

Elish stripped down my armour with nothing more than an apathetic look. My shoulders slumped, and like he had many years ago, I let Elish look over every inch of my body with those frigid eyes.

"I have a house deep in the greyrifts; you will be staying in there while Reaver heals. Jade will be tending to your injuries, and Perish's as well."

I stared at him for a moment, not believing my ears. "We're…" Jade had been telling the truth? "You're not bringing us to Skyfall?"

"No."

I didn't buy it… but I had known about Elish back in Tamerlan; he had never been the kind of person to lie. He never had a reason to lie. He was Elish Dekker.

I couldn't take that risk though. "How do I know?"

Surprisingly, Elish's eyes travelled to Reno leaning against my leg. "Reno has met me several times before, and my cicaro. He can assure you of my allegiance with Greyson and Lycos."

There was a tense pause and I felt Reno shift around. "He's right, Tink. He was quite cozy with the mayors."

My mind exploded. A million theories and thoughts rushed through them like a stampede of bosen. Each one more crazy than the last. I felt like I was going to black out again. How much more could I take?

I wanted to sink down to my knees but my body seemed frozen right where that cold look had left it. I stared back at him, my eyes unwilling to focus on anything else.

His gaze was captivating, those purple shards of ice drunk my body whole and took me in without discussion or consent. I felt powerless as I stared back, but in a way that did nothing to quell my confusion, only amplify it.

There was something in those eyes that made my heart want to trust him.

Or perhaps I was just grasping at scattering straws, looking for whatever solace I could find in this flurry of fear and confusion.

No… it was more than that. It was everything that had happened leading up to this very moment. It was Jade dragging Reno towards the plane. It was Elish passively shooting the black deacon off of Reaver, then grabbing his corpse and carrying him to the plane like he was packing flour.

It was Elish walking over to me, his face unwavering at my strangled, choking sobs. He had picked me up by the nape of my jacket like I was a kitten and calmly told me to stop crying. He told me Reaver wasn't dead, not permanently dead anyway. Though that deep, cutting voice held no pity for me; he had told me to not grieve for someone who wouldn't die.

There was hell on earth all around me, right down to the panicked screams of people being ripped apart by the devil's dogs. All of this madness was hidden through billows of thick smoke and raining ash from the fires, from the explosion Reaver had detonated and the burning buildings around us.

It was in the cover of fog and ash that Elish took us, cloaking his calculated movements from the scrambling chimeras who were trying to shoot the deacons off of their king.

I almost heard the puzzle pieces click together, deep in the recesses of my brain. It was obvious now.

"You didn't kidnap us, did you? You rescued us."

The words left my lips and hung heavy in the air. For what seemed like hours Elish did not respond. Not even Reno had a smart, ice breaking remark to say back. I think he was staring in disbelief just as much as I was.

"The word for it is of no consequence. Call it what you will," Elish said finally. During the moments of silence I didn't see a single waver in that statuesque face. He was surely a man to be respected and feared. I had never known anyone who commanded such a presence. I had known Silas as Asher first, and I knew his inner mongrel, Elish presented himself with the air of a king, or even a deity. Without a single word you knew to bow, and bow deep.

But he was still a chimera… my Skyfall-taught respect for chimera authority only took me so far. He was still Silas's creature. I made a note in my head to never forget that. No matter what help he had given us.

"What about Reno?" I asked. I glanced down at my friend. Sure enough, he was looking up at Elish with both wariness and respect. I think he was just as blown away that we weren't being hand-delivered to Silas.

"I will be dropping Reno off at my skyscraper in Skyfall tonight," Elish said in the same passive, cool tone.

"What?!" I cried. My hands clenched. "You can't take him away from us. He needs me."

My strangled words bounced off of him like toothpicks against the Hoover Dam. Elish glanced down at Reno, giving the stained towel we had pressed against the wound a passing sweep of his gaze. Elish looked at me, his lips a thin line and his eyes as indifferent as ever. "Unless you are as skilled as my personal physician, and considering your age and the tremble in your hand I am assuming you are not, your friend will perish sometime in the next four days. Two if you try to extract the bullet so snugly nestled against his liver."

I sunk down beside Reno; I took his hand with both of mine. "He'll be in danger in Skyfall, won't he? How is this all going to get past Silas?"

"When my pet was lifting the plane for our departure I enjoyed the sight of two deacon dogs pulling his spine in two. King Silas will not be fully resurrected from his ordeal for the next forty-five to sixty days. In that time it will have been long established that Reaver, yourself, and Perish escaped without a trace."

"You'll be able to hide Reno from them? The ones who would recognize him?"

Elish gave me a very slight nod "Because of who he will become, I doubt anyone would recognize him. You didn't recognize this *Asher* as Silas, hm? Apparently there are people underneath those layers of dirt." The corner of Elish's mouth rose just slightly. The first time I had seen any emotion on his face.

I didn't trust that smirk at all. "What do you mean *because of who he will become*? Who'll he become?"

"My pet."

My mouth dropped open.

I saw Reno look at me, then at Elish in confusion. "What like a cat?"

"No." I swallowed hard; I put a hand to my neck as it ached. "You're…" A lump caught in my throat as I remembered just who I was talking to. This wouldn't be as bad for him as it would've been for someone like me or Reaver.

"God, that's perfect for you." I lowered my head and pursed the corners of my eyes with my fingers.

"What?" Reno's voice was just as strained and confused as he looked. I just shook my head, unable to hide the hoarse laughter on my lips. Reno was going to be a sex slave for a chimera. There was no better retirement for my friend, at least temporary retirement.

"It is merely for his safety." Elish's tone bit through my laughter like a lance through jelly. "I will not be reducing myself to greywaste carrion let me assure you, Mr. Massey." I cowered at the reminder that he indeed knew who I was.

Reno blinked, but nodded anyway.

"You'll be okay, just do as he says." I kissed his forehead. "You'll get to laze around his house all day, eating real food and watching TV."

"Do you have video games?"

Elish's facial expression didn't waver, but I got the feeling if he could show emotions beside callous and cold he would be giving him a very flat unimpressed look.

"My pet does."

Reno said a very small *yaay* and gave me a reassuring smile. At least he wasn't scared, I would've been.

I whimpered and wiped my face with my hands. "You'll bring him back?"

"Once he is healed I will return him."

My lips burned with the next question I dearly wanted to ask. I knew it would get shot down immediately, but the off chance that this imposing chimera would answer left me no choice.

"Why are you helping him?"

Elish stared down at me. He was at least two heads taller than me. He must've been at least six foot five. "My servant will be bored without my pet to tend to. Mr. Nevada will offer a suitable distraction."

I narrowed my eyes at him. I knew those words were only the skimmings of a deeper plan inside that genetically engineered brain.

I pushed him further. "Why are you helping us? Why did you save us?"

Of course it was useless to think that question would be answered. Without so much of a blink, he looked down at Reno. "Keep him quiet. My cicaro will be landing the Falconer soon; he's not as skilled at flying planes as he thinks he is."

My ears went hot as he turned and left us, gracefully walking back into the cockpit without so much as a dismissive glance. I clenched my teeth, my emotions translating nothing but annoyance and further frustration.

I didn't even want to believe we would be safe from now on. I was lying in the jaws of the beast, only a trigger word separating us from being torn to shreds by this ruling family. How could I calm myself and think of what we were going to do next when I was so helpless? Reaver was dead, at least for now, and my injured best friend would soon be taken from me. I was alone, the only companion I had now was an airsick deacdog. Even Perish seemed fully in Elish's mental clutches.

"Hey…" Reno's voice was strained with pain. He tried to adjust himself so he was sitting up. "It might not be much, but this situation is a step up from the one we left, right? We still have all our parts, and the one that doesn't apparently is just going to grow them back. Fucking asshole." Reno groaned as he succeeded in sitting up. "All those times he put us in danger. All the times he made *me* plant the explosives and he made *me* go into the ravers' den."

Sometimes I hated how easy it was for him to make me smile. I think the day he took something seriously was the day the world imploded.

I helped Reno sit up; still making sure the towel was over his wound. I noticed his leg was a bit… crooked though, but I didn't draw attention to it. I wouldn't be surprised if it was broken after the mob stomped on us a few times.

"You know what's really great?" Reno continued as the grey ash started dripping away from his face; his skin didn't look much different from the dust. I felt uneasy with how pale he was looking.

"What?" I prepared myself for another grudging smile. Around us I heard the plane's engine give a rev, and the gut twisting feeling of descent, like the elevators in Skyfall.

"If he ever makes you mad, Killian. You can beat him to death. He'll come back all fresh and clean. Brand-spanking new Reaver."

I chuckled, but inside my heart stirred. I… I never had to worry about him dying. Gosh, I was more worried about him not being able to die. What would Silas do to him? He could have Reaver forever.

But I had him now. I wasn't sure how fast this plane went, but from how quickly the greywastes had gone by when I looked out the window, I think we were deeper inside what had once been the interior of British Columbia. Even before the Fallocaust not too many humans lived in these areas, it was mostly just big trees and mountains. There would be no one alive out here, at least that's what I assumed.

We were three men from Aras now thrust into a game we hadn't even known we were playing. There would be no turning the system off this time. I had no choice but to play back.

The plane landed roughly, making me fly up in the air and making poor Reno groan with pain. I tried to get up to help Reno get off of the plane when I heard a teeth grinding sound of metal on metal scraping together. I shot up and ran to the window in the cockpit and saw us sink into the grey rocks we had landed on.

I watched in shock and amazement as the plane recessed into the ground. Soon the wasteland disappeared above us, and wires and metal beams took its place. The plane temporarily went dark as the sky vanished. We were underground.

Then a bright light that made me turn away from the window. I saw Reno looking just as amazed as me, sitting beside a sick deacdog who looked like he was about to throw up over all of us.

When my eyes adjusted, I looked back out, and realized we were in an underground garage. Or that was the only way I could describe it.

It was a large open room of metal reinforced beams, grey concrete, and stacks of boxes of all shapes and sizes. Above us I could see long strips of lights with coils of wire bunched up by white zip ties. It looked like we were in a warehouse that doubled as a garage.

I pressed my hands against the window and gaped at everything, trying to take in and process exactly where we were. Even if we had to stay in this room we would be happy. It looked so dry and new. I couldn't see any rust or paint chipping, even the concrete floor was clean of dirt and garbage. If I could imagine what Skyland would look like, it would look like this. It took my breath away.

I jumped as the sliding metal door opened. Jade jumped back onto the plane and started helping Reno stand. Though when I stepped forward to help him off of the plane, I realized Jade was directing him towards the cockpit.

"He's leaving already?" I swallowed yet another boulder growing in my throat. I knew Elish had to leave quickly, but the reality of Reno being so far away was devastating. I didn't want to trust him with Elish; he was my only friend. I wouldn't have Reaver in my arms again for god knows how long. I had no one to, well… cling to.

Jade put a blanket over Reno and handed him a bottle of water, and to my surprise he withdrew what looked like an IV bag full of blood from a plastic hinged case. As Jade pushed the needle into Reno's skin, he nodded.

"Elish is getting a few things, after he'll be leaving."

I bit my lip hard and made my way over to Reno. As the blood started to drip into his veins, I gave him a hug.

"You know, when Reaver first pointed you out, I really thought you were a bit of a weenie, but I think you're one of my favourite people now."

I choked back a laugh and squeezed him gently. "And I thought you were only his friend because you wanted to get into his pants."

"That's cute you think differently."

I laughed and wiped a tear away from my eye. Reno gave me another reassured smile. "When this is all over, if I don't get my threesome, I'm going at both of you with a chainsaw."

"Everyone has their price." I reached into my pocket and pulled out a very dirty, lint-covered Dilaudid pill and gave it to Reno. Without hesitation, he popped it into his mouth and took a drink of the water. It was the last one we had. Everything was hundreds of miles away in Reaver's basement, besides the heroin.

My face blanched. I put my hand to my mouth and looked from Reno to Jade. I felt dizzy enough to stumble back, my back hitting the door of the cockpit.

"What is it?" Reno suddenly became more alert when he saw the horror on my face.

I looked at Jade. "I need to talk to Elish. I have to talk to him."

Jade's yellow eyes looked at me inquisitively. "Why?"

"My… my cat, my cat is trapped inside Reaver's basement. No one has a key to get in there; no one even knows where his house is. He'll starve to death. He'll die."

I heard Reno swear, his voice sounded grim. I left Reno with his IV bag and started walking towards the plane's exit. My legs felt like jelly, my right leg kept bending funny with every step but my adrenaline was blocking whatever pain signals it was trying to send me.

My legs buckled and almost gave out as I jumped off of the plane. I looked around the garage area the plane had been taken to, trying to look for a door.

I saw Deek sniffing a box. "Deek!" The deacdog perked up and gave me a cautious wag of his tail. "Find Elish."

Deek raised his nose to the air, and with an excited shake, he ran towards Jade and sat beside him.

Of course he didn't know who Elish was, he was smart but he wasn't psychic. "No, that's Jade…" I said, trying to sound encouraging though my heart was being torn to pieces imagining my loving cat being alone and cold. I saw Perish walking out of a pair of open metal doors carrying a bag. "Perish, where is Elish? Biff's in the basement, we have to bring him here."

Perish's face fell; I saw his tooth bite down on his lip. "Poor Biff. I'm sorry, Killian."

My face crumpled, I pushed past him and found myself in a clean, beige-painted hallway. As I walked down it, I saw the concrete turn into a fine stone tile before, to my shock, I reached grey carpet.

"Elish?" Was that his title? I didn't know how to address this intimidating blond chimera. What had Dad called him? I thought it was just Elish or Mr. Dekker. If he was defying Silas though did he still want to be referred to by his master's last name? Fuck, my mind was swimming.

"Elish?" I called again. I glanced into what looked like a bedroom. I had to stop and stare at it for a moment, for the sole fact that my brain kept telling me I was looking at a magazine. The comforter was straightened out and colourful, the bed was perfectly made with pillowcases too. The night table was brand-new with the wood polish not even peeling in the slightest. And the carpet… my god, I felt like I was walking on cotton balls.

I turned away from the room to carry on looking for the blond man, but as I turned and went to take a step I walked face first into something hard.

I was knocked off my feet; I looked up to see what I had hit when my eyes connected with the cold violet icebergs.

Elish hadn't even flinched; me slamming into him was like the equivalent to a bird flying into a window. The chimera just stared at me like I was an annoying insect; his large, gloved hand holding a small black bag.

I shied away at his mask-like visage, feeling more small and cowardly with every passing moment. His eyes burned into me, as if asking why I thought it was so important to go running down the halls yelling my head off.

I cowered, feeling stupid, then I rose to my feet, my head lowered. I wanted to turn and run, heck, I wanted to hide. I could feel the heat of those purple flames. Fire and ice at the same time, but I had to save my cat.

"We left–" Just thinking about my fat tabby-spotted cat made the emotion rise up in my throat. I tried to control my voice wobbling. "We left me and Reaver's cat in his basement. It's a basement of a home, completely reinforced with concrete; no one knows where it is. He'll die in there. Could, I wouldn't be any bother, I would be quiet, please, please can you let me quickly get him? The house is remote. No one will see me, I promise."

I slunk down, feeling my head go hot under his stare. Never more did I feel like a dirty, out-of-place flea in a world I was quickly realizing I didn't understand.

"You will not be leaving this base."

I was too devastated to even cry. I managed a small nod before I stepped away from him to let him pass by me. Even though the hallway was big enough for him to walk around.

I pressed myself up against the beige walls, needing something to support myself as the reality of Biff's fate sunk in. At what point will my fat cat realize we wouldn't be coming home? At what point would he feel the first pang of hunger when his bowl ran out? How long would it take for him to die, wondering why we had trapped him inside?

I started to whimper, I held my hand to my mouth to stifle the tears. I realized as I tried to hide my face, that Elish was still staring at me.

"I'll be needing make an appearance in Aras; I was planning on doing it after my stop in Skyfall. However, if Mr. Nevada is familiar with the area and is of sound state of mind, I will go there first and allow him to gather a small amount of–"

I wrapped my arms around him. I have no idea why. It was one of those things you wonder many many years later just what the heck was wrong with you. I think I was just frazzled and had mentally reached my limit. Any sort of good news felt like the world to me at this moment.

If hugging Reaver was like embracing a rock at times, hugging Elish was like hugging the planet Pluto. I was too far into it now to recoil and run though, so I finished hugging him and pulled away.

"Thank you," I said quietly.

I felt an awkward hand pat my back. "It is of no consequence." Elish's tone didn't waver, but I saw a flicker of perplexity in his gaze that quickly diminished with an upturn of his eyes. I saw he was looking at something; I turned around and saw Jade staring at us, looking just as perplexed.

"Is Mr. Nevada ready?" Elish gracefully swept past me and started walking back to the garage with Jade

Jade gave me a fleeting glance before he turned around and followed Elish. I didn't have anywhere else to go, so I walked with them. I wanted to ask Reno to pick up several more things from the basement anyway.

I jumped into the plane and got my satchel bag. As Jade was helping Perish fuel the plane, I started writing down things I wanted him to bring. Before they were ready for takeoff I had handed off the list to him. Biff, Reaver's gun, Reaver's drug suitcase, the black bag he had of ammo and explosives, my guitar, and our clothing. I felt badly making Reno get all those things, but I was sure Elish would help him.

With a few more tears on my part, I said goodbye to my friend, my heart heavy and full of anxiety. I stood back and watched the platform rise; when it lowered the plane was gone.

I was alone now, with my dead boyfriend, the chimera who had kept me prisoner… and Elish Dekker's yellow-eyed cicaro.

"I'm going to put Reaver in his freezer now," Perish said. He had

Reaver slung over his back. "Killian, I will help fix up your wounds when I am done."

I gripped the door frame with my hands, feeling the sickening realization that I was all alone with these two. The chimera's pet and my crazy scientist… I didn't want to ask, but I hoped Reaver's… 'emergence' would happen sooner rather than later.

"I think Reaver's boy should just sit on the couch and watch a movie." Jade's tone was on the verge of mocking, for a brief moment I felt like taking a swing at him. "It looks like he's about to go Freddie Krueger on all of us."

I guess I was pretty transparent.

"Hah! I know who that is!" Perish said gleefully. I heard him start to walk down the hallway. I thought Jade had gone with him, but I felt a hand on my shoulder.

"Snap out of it, kid. You and Reaver are safer here than you were in Aras; Elish doesn't fuck around with these hidden bases."

I didn't turn away from the now lowered platform. I felt queasy and tightly coiled like a spring. I had no idea how I hadn't lost my mind yet.

"Okay, well, I need to close this door… we're letting the heat out. You can stay right there though, if you want."

"I… I…" I broke my gaze from the garage and took a few steps back. "I want my Magnum…" My hands went to my belt but it was gone. Jade had taken it when Elish had grabbed me, probably knew I was on the edge of shooting both of them.

The pet stared at me for moment, the door to the garage closing with a click. "Well, I don't think that's the greatest of plans, you're a bit serial killer right now. None of us have guns–"

"You have those teeth." I took another step away from him, in the distance another door closed. Perish was bringing Reaver somewhere, but where? I wanted to be with him. "I… I need something… to…"

I was all alone with them… alone with Perish who had once wanted nothing more than to have sex with me, and this pet who had once told me I would 'taste good'. Those impressions alone made the acid rise to my throat. Without Reno, or even Elish here to put down some authority on these two, I felt extremely vulnerable. They could do anything they wanted to me right now.

I wanted to go home… back to Reaver's basement, back to my cat.

"Killian… you don't need anything," Jade said slowly. "Elish brought you two here to keep you from Silas. You couldn't be any more safer–" The pet looked behind him and I think in that moment he also wished his master was here. "Why don't you sit on the couch, I'll give you a knife or something if it'll make you feel safe, and you can have something to eat and drink."

Whenever he opened his mouth I saw the flashes of metal. He had implants in his canines to make them sharp, cat-like almost, and behind them I could see smaller ones laid out in his mouth. Even with a knife that cicaro was a weapon himself. He could rip my throat out in a second…

But even though I wanted to huddle up next to this door until Reaver woke up, I knew I had to eventually move.

"Okay, why don't you go have a shower then? Get the ash and blood off of you. The door locks, all the doors in this place lock. How does that sound?"

I kept staring at those teeth, but with a defeated sigh I gave him a small nod. "Yeah, I can do that."

Jade nodded and gave me a wide berth as I walked past him down the hall; I guess he didn't want to spook me. I walked into the living room and looked around. Everything was clean and decorated with new unblemished furniture.

I found the bathroom and walked in, before making sure the door could lock. I tested the handle a few times before, with a forlorn sigh, I started to undress.

My mind was going to explode at any second… and I didn't know what was going to happen when it did. I needed something to help me through these events; I needed something to calm me down.

And there was only one thing I had available to me right now.

CHAPTER 2

Jade

I SAT DOWN ON THE COUCH AND BRUSHED MY BANGS away; the sweat dampening my hair was enough to get them to stay back. Once that blond kid was done with the bathroom I would be next. I showered every day back in Skyfall and I wasn't about to change now. Especially since I was completely covered in chalky ash and drying blood. I smelled like a corpse. Elish was going to have to dispatch a dozen sengils to steam this place once we left. It was going to be crawling with dirty little greywasters and their fleas.

I got myself some tea and placed it down on the wooden coaster. I reached over and grabbed the remote and turned the window on.

That was an odd word for it, but I didn't know how else to describe it. I took a drink and got up as the walls separated with a low whirring sound, revealing the vast and breathtaking landscape before us. It was like the council room back in the blacksands house but better. I always loved me and Elish's getaways here.

Sheared slices of granite framed each side of the bare grey crags around us, encompassing us like a horseshoe bowl. Only when the grey rocks joined with the haze of the sun did I lose where the dead and muted grey would go next. We were a hundred miles from the bottom of the cliff, three windows that looked invisible from any solid ground but to me they felt like the eyes of a god, or a great king looking out onto his burnt land. I always felt empowered when I stood so tall in front of the massive picture windows. I had asked Elish one night if he felt the same.

'Power is the greatest illusion, Jade.'

But the illusion of power was all I had ever had. So I didn't discard the feelings of being regal and refined, on the contrary, I enjoyed pretending. Even if I knew as well as I knew my own heartbeat that I was nothing, in all respects my boots still had slum grime stuck to them.

In the slums, when I had been walking side by side with my old boyfriend I had been the king of thieves. A regal light that, at my beck and call, could get me any illegal and smuggled good in all of Skyfall's districts. Now I reigned over no one, not even myself.

Though over the years my chains had become my comfort, a fact that still in the depths of night made me question my own sanity. I had been free in Moros, now I was bound in Skyland, but I was bound to Elish and that truth no longer bore down on me with thousand pound weights.

The shackles were ours, we were joined together, and together we faced all those who would want to hurt us. Over a year ago it was King Silas looming his threats over us, driven by jealousy and hatred over Elish's attachment to me.

Now he had shifted his eyes to another chimera, a chimera Elish had been following since before the boy had taken his first breath.

When he had gotten the call that Lycos had been captured it was as if his anger had extinguished the very light in the room. I had been helping Luca organize our plates for dinner and the action had made both of us quake in our shoes.

Something was wrong… and out of all the things to go wrong, something going badly with the secret in the greywastes was the most devastating.

Silas had Lycos, Silas knew, he had known for months.

Asher Fallon… that name stung my lips, and it burned my master's.

Now more than ever I was reminded just how much we had at stake going against Silas like this, once again he had blindsided everyone with his intelligence. Not only had he himself found out that Reaver was alive, he had snuck into Aras and duped everyone just to get a good look at his long lost partner.

I had, selfishly, wanted Elish to abandon everything right then, if only to keep my master safe, but to him there was no going back. The time had come now to harvest the seeds he had planted.

I just wanted Elish to be safe. It was like we were harbouring bombs within our walls.

Did my master really know what he was doing? Or was he scrambling to pick up the scattering balls that had fallen as soon as that phone call went through.

I pursed my lips as the questions started to sting my mouth like turpentine. The burn of the tea washed it away, and what confused thoughts remained the scenery helped distract me.

It was empty here, a desolate shell, so much rock, and the ground… just a bowl of ash littered with loose rocks and chunks of concrete from buildings long since burned or dissolved in the rains. This area was completely empty of humans, mostly since there seemed to be nothing to scavenge. It was a void, even of abandoned buildings.

Elish had told me the stories Silas had shared with him, about life before the Fallocaust. It was after our hours of lovemaking had died down, when I was in his arms, the darkness around us only broken by a faint warm light. It was when Elish was mine and no one elses. When he would tell me stories, answer my questions, and even ask me ones in return. I ached for those times with a thirst that no other sensation could quench.

It hadn't happened in a long while, since this all started.

I remembered one such night, when I had thought he had fallen asleep. Only then could I gather the courage to ask him. He was behind me, with his arms wrapped around my chest and my naked body pulled tightly to him.

"What did he tell you it was like, when he ended the world?"

And with the smallest intake of breath he had painted me a picture. Ash that stung your tongue like poisoned snowflakes and breaths of air that burned your lungs without fire. To this day those cities were uninhabitable. Nothing but graveyards of charcoal and ash, pounded to sediment under the hammer of time.

Then he would tell me of the fire. Of a world where everything was covered in white hot ash. From the cinders of thousands of burning buildings, to the bodies of already dead men baked in their carbonized skin. Some of the sestic radiation had been so concentrated it had made entire cities erupt into flames.

The hounds of hell had descended from a sky baked red from whole cities, twice the size of Skyfall, erupting into a white inferno as far as the eye could see. The heat was so powerful coming from the cities that they melted even the metal frames of skyscrapers.

When the fires finally cooled twenty years later, nothing remained but pools of melted steel. Soon ash covered these phantom remains, and now their locations changed from traveller's tale to traveller's tale.

But the flames of hell that wielded the power to melt cities struck few and far between, for the most part, everything stayed the same.

Well, unless you were living.

The sestic radiation that Silas had let off had killed, or driven insane, everyone that wasn't in what would become Skyfall. It mutated the animals, clouded the sky, and stifled the rain. It killed the plants and trees, or condemned them to an existence of stunted despair. It sucked the life out of all living things leaving them either dead or broken shells. Little grew in the greywastes but corpses, and even the greywasters harvested those. They ate friends and family alike without hesitation. Most too mad from radiation to do more than steal from and murder their fellow man.

Elish's cold voice had been so smooth, like he was reciting poetry or singing me an old song. It had made a frozen shiver run up my spine. I hung on his every word.

"Why did he end the world?"

"The world had already ended itself; they just quelled its suffering."

"They? Silas and Sky?"

"That's correct."

"And the sestic radiation did all of this?"

"That and the scars brought on by the war. Many bombs were dropped before those two had had enough."

"How did he cause it? Was it inside of him or a machine?"

I had turned by then and I had been facing him.

Elish's purple eyes were glistening gems but I saw he was relaxed, set at ease by our lovemaking. As soon as he left our room he would become my cold statue of white marble, but as for now, his body and mind were mine.

"It was him, but how he managed to kill the world I do not know – he never wanted us to know."

I felt the invisible string pull on my heart; he had been too busy to take me in quite some time. I missed the sex we had. Intense marathons that lasted hours, both filling me with a pleasure that brought me to my knees gasping and crying, and intense pain that had me scream for mercy.

Nothing could help the smile that came to my lips. In that moment my heart tugged towards him and I missed his cold touch.

The blond man of ice who had captured me in his snare and refused to let me go. Who looked upon my battered, bloodied body as I thrashed in my cage with a cold indifference. The dark times, the beginning years of my slavery with him had dimmed, overshadowed by what we had gone through together to get to this point. Those moments shone a beacon to the stars as bright as the moon, casting a shadow on the memories I had so deeply and brutally branded in my mind and flesh.

Memories I thought of fondly now, though I was glad I no longer had to dodge King Silas's hand, or the Crimstones' agendas, or even my ex-boyfriend.

I looked at my shackle scars, now a silver pink, then flexed my back to feel the crisscross scarred roads that told their own stories; ones that Elish would regularly get lasered off of my body.

Elish could be a cruel master at times; hitting me, fucking me until I sobbed. Or biting through my skin so he could taste the blood that drove every chimera wild. He was callous, unemotional and held in him a cruelty that still surprised me at times.

But my heart sang at the sound of his voice. And my body melted when he took me, whether it be a loving manner or not. My essence and my being belonged solely to him, and at the mere glance of those cold eyes I knew I was his pet and he was my master. Though we had become more than that long ago.

We had the rings to prove it.

I felt alone in the chasm of fire and ice in my heart and soul. My fear and respect for my master so intertwined with my love I no longer knew how to separate the long invisible strings. I just knew they drew me to him, and as I looked out into the vast rocks before us, I felt my heart ache from his absence.

"Make food."

My brow knitted together; I had been enjoying the quiet ambiance. Both Luca and I were used to the cold tranquility that Elish brought in with his presence. Even when he was gone and it was just myself and the sengil the only sound was usually the TV, unless I'd had a few drinks or a bump of something. This scientist brought an aura to him that was like lightning to the sensitive parts of my brain.

No... I take that back, not lightning, that wasn't flicks of light I saw, it was fractures. A glowing orb filled with thousands of tiny hairline cracks, ones that flared and split with different stimulants. At a distance, Perish seemed normal... but the closer I looked... yes, things were missing. He was damaged beyond anything I had ever seen or felt. There was something extremely off in this man's brain, like he was two different people shoved into one mind.

"Pet? I'm speaking to you."

Whatever sympathies I had for this brother I had never personally met dissolved with his condescending tone.

I turned around and narrowed my eyes at him. The scientist, unlike when Elish addressed him, didn't cower. I realized then we were going to have a problem.

I decided to quell our differences immediately. As Elish had taught me, you correct bad behaviour before it becomes habit.

"I am not your pet, nor am I your sengil. I am a chimera, like you." I adopted my 'Elish tone', one that had gotten me out of many predicaments. Our brothers often called me his little protégé just to annoy him.

Perish snorted; his light blue eyes seemed to mock my attempts at brazenness. "Don't bullshit me. You're Elish's cicaro."

My cool tone faded as my Morosian upbringing took over. "But I am not *your* pet, therefor... get *your* own fucking food," I snapped.

I stalked up to him, and like any slumrat worth his salt, I didn't stop until I was nose-to-nose with him. I felt a shrill jolt of adrenaline when I saw his eyes flick back and forth nervously, obviously surprised at my boldness.

But then they hardened at me, and I realized with an internalized laugh why. He was a bottom-feeding chimera just like me. Two pathetic fucks at the butt end of the totem pole. Struggling with the other scum suckers to grasp at whatever shreds of respect and authority they could scavenge and hold over one another. We were born genetically enhanced kings, only to be pounded down by our better, more advanced brothers. Now we fought over dignity like scraps of meat. There was no one lower than Perish and myself but perhaps Drake. And Drake didn't care to dominate anyone.

"You're Elish's whore. You put all the lipstick you want on the pig, Jade; you're a slavepet and you'll submit like one."

My insides boiled. I decided to yank out the only ace card I had, even if Elish had pretty much forbid all of us from mentioning it. "I am his fucking husband; you attended our shotgun wedding, did you not?"

"Elish said to all of us to never mention that again." Perish's eyes narrowed like he had indeed forgotten this fact, then he said haughtily, "You still have cuffs, chains, and collars. You're his pet."

"And not yours!"

"No difference. Now hop to it, pet. Food."

And with that my last straw was drawn.

"I'd say go fuck yourself…" I said through clenched teeth; my nose pressed against his. Our eyes were locked like laser beams, trying to burn the other one alive. I hated how at home I felt in this moment. It made me miss the dog-eat-dog attitude of the Moros slums. "But you're so much of a little bitch even Reaver's twink boy would be doing the fucking."

I was so shocked when his face fell that I took a step back.

Was he that easy to bring down? I was disappointed.

Perish's sky blue eyes looked behind me. I looked too but there was nothing outside the windows, just the first hints of darkness touching the steel grey sky.

"Killian's been in the shower for almost an hour." Perish wrung his hands together anxiously. What fire was in his eyes only seconds before had dimmed back to his shifty, inconsistent movements.

The mood was completely gone. I still felt cheated.

"So what?" I raised my hands and let them drop. I thought we were going to have a fight? I was looking forward to getting some hits in, feeling some pain. My adrenaline was rushing!

"Killian is very unstable; Killian's been through a lot today…" Perish looked around, his body moving as his head did until he had twirled himself into a circle. He took a step towards the bedrooms, then the basement, but with every step his mind started telling him to walk in the opposite direction.

"The… bathroom is to the left down the hall, near where the laundry room is…" I said. I spoke slowly in case he had a problem processing.

Perish nodded and rubbed his hands together. I felt shrill voices of anxiety hovering around his head, like he constantly had information fed to him whether he liked it or not. "Jade, Killian is very sensitive. You can act big all you want with me, but for Killian, and since Reaver is dead, please show him kindness. Killian is very sweet, but Killian is very delicate right now. Act like a chimera and not a gutter rat, okay?"

He said all of this like a huge run-on sentence. I nodded anyway, still confused but curious to this odd behaviour. Silas had really done a number on this guy; it was a known fact in the family that he was one of the worst treated chimeras in existence.

Perish started walking towards the bathroom, his hands still rubbing together. He got to the door and knocked lightly.

There wasn't an answer.

"Killian?" Perish whispered. He leaned his forehead against the door. I saw his eyes widen and fill with concern. "The… the light's off… Killian?"

Perish tensed his fingers and put his hand on the door knob. He twisted it, but it was locked of course. I had told the kid to lock it.

That little bastard must've been more injured than I thought. Elish was going to kill me if he died on my watch. He was the only thing that kept Reaver grounded. We needed him. "That's an easy door to get into…"

I ran to the kitchen and found a thin metal skewer. I shoved it into the hole in the door knob and heard a click.

I slowly opened the door.

It was pitch black. The bathroom was thick with left over shower steam and heavy with the smell of perfumy soap. I reached off to the side and flicked on the light, dreading what I was going to find.

My eyes immediately fell to the corner of the bathroom, where a naked little heap of blond kid was leaning against the wall, a fucking needle sticking out of his arm. Killian's head was off to the side, his eyes were half-open and glassy and his mouth slacked.

"Oh shit." I shut the door and quickly walked over to him. I bent down in front of the kid and slowly took the needle out of his arm. I tossed it into the sink and shook Killian's chin. "Wake up, wake up, you little junkie."

Killian's eyelids fluttered before his hazy eyes found mine. "No, I need… I need my Magnum."

"Are those the only words you can say?" I grabbed a robe and draped it over his shoulders. What a fucking piece of work, I should've made sure he didn't have any drugs on him when I frisked that gun. "I'm from the slums, dude. If you wanted to shoot some tar candy you should've just said it. No one here fucking cares."

Killian rose to his feet; he stumbled a bit but Perish helped him walk his little self to the living room. I grabbed that smelly bag he was always carrying around and got him a bottle of pop out of the fridge.

I tossed it to him and sat down with my tea. Then I started rooting around his bag for the heroin.

"You shouldn't snoop so much," Killian's raspy voice said. "It will just get you into trouble."

I couldn't help but laugh. That had been the first words we had exchanged with each other years ago, when Elish was firing his father and had left me behind to gauge Killian's aura.

"You remember me, huh?" Killian said. His hands shook as he tried to open the bottle, the soda bubbles started rising to the surface with each feeble attempt.

"Of course I do." Elish and I were involved in this more than Killian could possibly know. Elish had been pulling strings and arranging chess pieces for years. I had met Reaver before Killian had ever set foot in Aras.

I took the bottle from him and cracked it open before handing it back.

"Jeff Massey's kid, from Tamerlan. Of course I remember. Your parents died a year after coming to Aras, right?" The words left my lips before I realized that was a pretty awful thing to say; Elish would've slapped me upside the head.

Killian's face fell. He nodded and tucked his legs up under him; he looked like he was going to drown in Elish's robe. "Yeah."

This kid was so submissive and scared; he had gotten a lot worse since I had last seen him. I thought being around Reaver would make him strong, but then again this was all pretty fresh in his mind. Perhaps I was being unfair. It had taken me years to temper my body and mind under the hand of Elish, and that was with him actively training me.

I spent the next several hours trying to make conversation with the kid, but eventually I just gave up. He seemed just shell-shocked and almost catatonic. His movements were shaky and his eyes kept looking in all directions like he couldn't believe where he was.

Perish wasn't much of a help either, he was trying to force conversation on the kid even more. I think we were both hating the tension in the room, but Killian wanted to talk to Perish even less than he wanted to talk to me.

Finally the kid, after shooting up his last dose of heroin, put the empty ChiCola bottle down and shifted around on the couch. "I'm going to go to bed… where's Reaver?"

Perish shot up quickly, which made the kid flinch but the scientist didn't notice. "I put him in the freezer. I'll get him."

I watched the kid for the obvious reaction of shock over where we had put his boyfriend. The freezer seemed like an odd place to put a recovering corpse, but it was really the fastest way for him to heal.

"Why… why is he in a freezer? I thought he was in one of the bedrooms?" Killian said quietly. He looked behind him and I saw his fingers grip the sides of the robes. I swear that kid was going to snap at any moment, even with the tar candy in his veins.

Perish clapped his hands together and nodded his head. He walked in front of Killian towards the lower level of the apartment, where all the supplies were being kept, and also the freezer.

"Well, Killian," Perish explained in a happy tone, "during immortal healing the body heats up for several hours and then cools down. During this period of time, if you put them in cold temperatures it speeds up the recovery process."

I had learned this years ago with Elish; I knew all the tricks of the trade for immortal healing. I guess now that Killian was a part of the 'partners of immortals' club he had to start learning the ropes.

"Oh, alright…" Killian's small mousy voice said. "How… how long until he's back?"

"Let's see! I'll be right back, stay right there," Perish said excitedly. He disappeared through the side door that led down to the basement, his quick feet thumping up against the metal grating.

Killian stood there with the permanent worried look on his face. I hadn't seen him without that look since I had met him in Tamerlan.

He was so different back then, a small little soul with an aura like marshmallow fluff and bubble gum. I remember it had been yellow and white, and so happy. I had been jealous the first time I had seen it. Mine back then had been this cesspool of black misery and self-loathing, confused about my feelings towards Elish, and under constant threat because of Elish's own confused feelings towards me.

I didn't know what Killian's aura was like now. I hadn't checked. And until Elish told me I could, I wouldn't. The last time hadn't gone too well; I had been overwhelmed by the thirst to corrupt him, poison him, make what was crystal clear dirty and polluted. I had put my own aura against his and I was jealous as to how he looked compared to me.

I had wanted that… I had never been innocent, not even when I was a child.

Though Killian had nothing to worry about with me now, I had grown a lot since then. He was safe with me, and safe with Elish… it was only getting him to believe that, that would be the issue.

"When–"

I snapped out of my thinking and looked over at the boy. Still standing beside the couch, looking troubled at the couch cushions like it was them who had wronged him.

"–when is Elish coming back?"

I put down my teacup as I heard the footsteps of Perish start to go up the stairs. "Sometime tomorrow morning, I think. Since Silas is dead right now he is supposed to be running Skyfall, but Garrett and Joaquin will be more than happy to be head honchos."

The kid kept staring at me, and I think he wanted to trust me. I didn't know if he could bring himself to trust me though.

"What's going to happen to us?"

Now that was the million dollar question… I didn't know what was supposed to happen to him and Reaver. Elish had never told me. I just knew he was hiding him in the greywastes and that only Reaver could kill King Silas. All of this was unexpected.

"I don't know but Elish always has a plan," I said to him. "He's too invested in this to stop. He'll make sure you and Reaver are safe."

The boy nodded, and after that our attention was turned towards the basement door.

Perish was carrying Reaver slung over his shoulder, his usually shifty eyes bright to compliment the big smile on his face. I don't know what he was so happy about, he had been starved, beaten to shit, and just straight-out tortured by Lycos and Greyson. Maybe it was because the blond kid was near him again; Elish had told me he was quite enamoured with him.

"Okay, come here, sweety. Come look." I saw a pull on Killian's mouth at Perish calling him *sweety*, but perhaps that was just his thing. Either way, Killian shuffled on his mousy feet over to Perish as the scientist took Reaver into one of our spare bedrooms.

I walked in after the two, to see the dark chimera laying in all his glory on top of a brown comforter. There were faint wisps of steam rising up from his body like smoke; his corpse still adjusting to this new warm environment.

I heard a choke and watched Killian's pale face blanch further. He raised a trembling hand and put it on his boyfriend's cheek before I saw the first signs of him starting to break down.

I thought it was rather pathetic, Reaver was going to come back, but I knew this kid had been through a lot. I had been in this mentally fragile state many times with Elish, and I would've loved to have someone who understood what I was going through.

Anyway, Elish would want me to make nice.

I walked over to where Reaver's head was and cringed at the large gaping hole in his throat. I could see a hint of white from what I believed was his spine, and more shredded tendons than I could count.

I leaned down and went to pull his shirt down but I heard Killian's heart speed up as I did. I don't think Killian wanted me touching him.

"He doesn't have any other injuries…" Killian sniffed. His blue eyes were already glassy with unshed tears. "The deacon just got his throat."

And Elish shot the deacon after he did that, then he picked up Reaver and threw him into the plane; all of this under the thick cloak of dust and gunfire. It had been my job to grab Killian but Elish had to help me with that. The kid shrieked and squirmed more than a piglet.

Perish rolled back and forth on his heels. "Well, from what I've seen, Killian, Reaver will be back in four days. Maybe less, I am not sure. Each immortal chimera heals at different rates. Silas is a bit slow, Elish has always been fast. For me, I'm a bit in the middle. Every time Lycos killed me I tried to see how long it had been. Once they cut open my head and that was three days." The scientist gave Killian a smile, but it faded when he saw the distraught look on Killian's face.

The boy put the towel that had been wrapped around Reaver's neck back onto the wound, before kissing his fingers and laying it on his dead boyfriend's cheek. "I'm sorry, Perish. For what I did to you in Donnely, and for what Leo did to you."

"Reaver said you did it because you felt badly for leaving me. No one has ever cared about how I felt. I should be thanking you for caring about me that much. I care about you too." Perish looked up shyly before he reached down to the side of the bed and picked something up.

It was a stuffed Pokémon, a charmander to be exact. He handed it to Killian and rolled back and forth on his feet. "You can borrow him until Reaver wakes up."

Killian took the stuffed animal with a whimper. "Thanks, Perry. I hopefully won't have to borrow him for long."

What an odd friendship those two had going on. I wish I'd been a fly on the wall over what had gone on in Donnely. I'd have to get Killian drunk one day and ask him if they fucked. I didn't think so considering how attached Killian was to Reaver, but who knows; they seemed to like being unstable together.

After making sure Reaver was healing and recovering, we left Killian alone so he could sleep. I would be sleeping alone tonight, something that I had always hated. Hopefully by tomorrow I would have my master back to curl up beside. Even though he hadn't been away from me for long, it always seemed like the time just dragged on.

I just hoped that he was safe… and that everything was going according to whatever new plan he had in his mind.

CHAPTER 3

Killian

I HEARD THE SCRAPING OF HIS BODY BEING MOVED along the metal floor of the plane, leaving a streak of blood that ended at the cuffs of his pants. He was partially decapitated, the loose tendons and blood vessels hanging down, not a drop of blood wetting their shredded ends.

I stood over his body. I was in my bedroom and he was crumpled up on my bed. The same position he had frozen into when he died, with the deacon pressing down on his chest and the remains of his neck in the dog's jaws.

With milky eyes and a blood-soaked muzzle, the deacon licked his stained teeth. His lips rose in a snarl.

Reaver's eyes snapped open. He was lying in bed; I was standing over him, those black spheres glistened like the eyes of a devil.

Then Reaver rose to the sitting position, staring forward without a flicker of life in his eyes. His chest was still and cold, his skin the grey of an overcast sky.

He was still dead.

I shook my head, trying to shake away the growing feeling of unease.

No, no, he's immortal. He's alive.

I heard him mumble, but his throat was an open pit of red flesh lined with sinew and ropey veins. He couldn't speak properly. I could only hear rasping, hissing groans.

I felt myself frozen in place, my feet welded to the spot. I had no choice but to watch him rise to standing and look around the room. A glint of hostility in those obsidian eyes, polished clean but without reflection or even a hint of white.

It wasn't him… it wasn't Reaver. It was his body; he was walking and he was moving, but this wasn't my boyfriend. A different person was in him now.

Was this what it was like? Did the real person not come back?

I felt a bubbling cry form in my throat. I choked on saliva and felt my chest clench and shutter under the sudden gasp of air. I tried to swallow but my mouth was a dried lake.

Reaver was still there; I could smell him near me. His scent, gunpowder and burnt ash combined. The monster was here. My Reaver was dead.

But then I saw light.

I finally saw light.

His touch was so warm… like his hands had been resting over the fireplace; they were so soothing, so gentle. Oh, I had missed him so much. It hadn't even been that long but it seemed like forever.

So long since we had been in bed together; so long since he had been mine and mine alone. I had to share Reaver with Asher before I killed him, and after that we had been distracted with the aftermath.

But Reaver was mine… and in my dreams I wrapped my arms around him and let him hold me with every ounce of his strength.

Then I felt lips on me, soft warm lips that pressed up against mine with an urgency I didn't understand. I accepted them though and opened my mouth for him, feeling his tongue start to find mine inside my mouth.

His hands drew up my sides, before they slid down my pants.

It was then my reality started to slowly creep back to me, and like a cold chunk of ice had landed in my stomach, I realized that what was happening to me wasn't a dream.

With a start, my eyes snapped open, and I felt the man continue to kiss me, his hand behind my head drawing me closer and his other one massaging and pulling my dick. It was dark, I couldn't see a thing, but I knew that smell and I knew that mouth.

I pulled away from Perish with a gasp and a cry, and as soon as I heard his stumbled apology I completely and totally lost my mind.

Then there was screaming from me and apologies from Perish, and a moment later, the flick of a light switch to illuminate the transgressions that had just gone on.

"What the fuck are you doing?" I screamed. I picked up the table lamp beside us and threw it at him. It shattered against the wall only half a foot away from his head, showering him with blue ceramic pieces that fell soundlessly onto the floor.

"I'm sorry, I'm sorry… you were having a bad dream! I'm sorry!" Perish cried. He was only wearing cloth pant bottoms, the rest of him was bare. "I don't know why, okay? I just… I just…"

"What the fuck is going on here?" Jade was in the corner of my eye, his yellow eyes travelling first to me and then to Perish. He looked at the scientist and stalked up to him.

"What the fuck are you doing in here? Are you fucking kidding? Get the fuck out, you fucking psycho!" Jade roared. He grabbed Perish by the nape of the neck and started shoving him towards the door.

My mind couldn't catch up to my thoughts. I was stunned; I was more than stunned, I was terrified. I wasn't safe here; I wasn't safe with Perish and I wasn't safe with Jade. I was miles and miles away from home, with no one to protect me.

I had to get away from these people. But how? Reaver was dead… I had no one. I was alone with the scientist who had kept us captive; who had on many occasions came close to raping me… and Elish's chimera pet who I didn't trust at all.

Where was Reno? Greyson and Leo? My friends, the men I considered my family.

I was alone.

My breath choked in my throat, and with it I felt the anxiety reach a crippling point. A volcano that had been on the fringes of exploding finally shot out its first stream of magma. I was terrified, tired, shell-shocked… and done.

Jade turned around after Perish was gone. "Alright… tell me wha-"

"GET OUT!" I shrieked. I grabbed the digital clock that was resting beside the bed and threw it at the cicaro. Jade dodged it easily and put his hands up in front of him.

"Calm down… I'm not going to hurt you… the door locks, just–" Jade's voice was low, calm and unthreatening but it didn't matter. I didn't want him near me; I didn't want any of them near me.

I reached into Reaver's cargo pants; I knew where everything was in his pockets.

I pulled out the grenade.

Then I heard Jade swear. I turned to give him one last ultimatum when I saw the door slam and the cicaro gone.

As soon as I was alone in that room my brain snapped into survival mode. Without even thinking about what I was doing, I rolled my still resurrecting boyfriend off of the bed and pushed the box spring up against the door. Not feeling like I was safe enough, I piled both night tables onto it too, and then the two side chairs and dresser against it as well. I barricaded myself in as much as I could.

No one was allowed in. I had to be safe. I had to be safe… I wasn't safe anywhere. The basement was gone. Aras was gone…

When I had piled everything I could against that door, I collapsed onto the mattress Reaver was on and cried into his cooled body. Though it wasn't the same, it was all I had so I took it and I clung to it. Even if he smelled like blood and gunpowder… most of the time he smelled like that anyway.

The first thing I saw the next morning was Reaver's gaping neck wound, and the first thing I smelled was the odd smell of fresh flesh, like the meat packs we used to get from distribution.

At least he didn't smell rotten; at least… this meant Greyson and Leo were right.

He was immortal…

But I knew that, because I know they had killed him before, many times probably, but I just didn't know how it worked. What if there was a limited amount of time? Like how cats had nine lives…

I sniffed and wiped the sleep from my eyes before examining the wound more carefully. I was cautiously happy to see that I couldn't see his spine when I lifted up the flap of skin that was covering the worst of the wound. He was healing… could it really only be three more days?

Thankfully we had our own private bathroom. I had a quick shower and took some more heroin before curling up next to Reaver again.

There was a small knock on my door sometime around noon. I had been nodding off into zombieland the entire morning, pretending I was back in Aras, back when things were at their best. Biff was kneading my side and Reaver was letting me be close to him, even if I knew he preferred his own space.

Life was how it should be.

"Killian? I just need to know you didn't OD in there and die," Jade said at the other end of the door. He knocked on it again and I heard a sigh.

"I didn't," I murmured, not knowing if he could hear me or not.

"Alright… there's some good food in the fridge when you want it."

I didn't answer him and Jade left me alone after that. And even though my stomach was growling, I didn't take any of the stuff away from the door. The thought of going back out into the living room terrified me, seeing Perish terrified me.

I swallowed through the thorns imbedded in my throat. I could almost feel it piercing my stomach. I didn't even know what happened last night with Perish. He'd told me he had heard me having a night terror. When that used to happen in Donnely he would try and comfort me, but he had never kissed me like that.

I shuddered. I didn't know how I was going to explain that one to Reaver. He was starting to become cordial around Perish, now the kiss and the groping were going to ruin all of that.

But what did it matter? Perish was probably going to Skyfall once Elish came back.

As was my nature, whether I liked it or not, I started to try and justify Perish's actions. He had only seen me for a few nights since Greyson dropped him off in the basement… maybe this time I would forgive him.

No, not forgive him…

This time I wouldn't tell Reaver.

No, you kept enough shit from Reaver and look where you ended up? You'll tell him when everything has calmed down. A few days after he wakes up.

I sighed, hating myself as always, and snuggled back up against my corpse.

Just wake up, Reaver… please, wake up.

You're all I have.

Everyone else is dead.

Heroin was my only tie to sanity for the rest of the day and the night. With my friend heroin, I was able to sleep or just stare off into nothingness. It was my escape, and I knew how unhealthy it was, but in this moment, in this day… I had nothing else.

I couldn't hear anything but the murmuring of voices from the other two, and even that was kept at a minimum, besides a few times when they got into a fight. The bedroom I was in was the farthest from the living room at the end of the hall, and I think this place was soundproof from all the rock around us.

It wasn't until deep into the night that my stomach started to outweigh my fear of the situation I was in. I could get water in the bathroom but food-wise I didn't have anything. It had been over twenty-four hours since I had woken up to Perish kissing me, and besides a few bites of food beforehand, I hadn't had anything.

It sounded like they were both asleep… there were three bedrooms upstairs plus one room that was always locked. I assumed Jade and Perish were in those two rooms.

I wouldn't be long… I could get myself enough food to last me until Reaver woke up, then he could tell me what to do. Because I didn't know… look at where I was right now, I had nothing.

The space behind my eyes started to burn. I really didn't have anything.

I pushed the barrier off to the side until I had a foot of room to squeeze through, and put a shaky hand on the knob. I turned it and felt the door latch automatically unlock.

The living room was dark, the shades that covered the giant picture windows were closed and the rear projection TV was off. Everything seemed to be cautiously quiet, besides the electric fireplace that was still on.

My heart was pounding in my chest when I made my first step outside into the living room. I knew it was silly but I suppose it was just the instinctual fear of being caught. I had the same thing happen back in Tamerlan when I used to sneak down to steal cookies from Mom's cookie tin.

Drawing in a courageous breath, I left the door partially ajar behind me and tiptoed into the kitchen, keeping my ears out for any sound or movement. With my lack of other senses, I bet I could almost hear heartbeats like Reaver.

"Hungry are we, Mr. Massey?" a cold voice sounded from beside the fireplace.

I jumped a mile high, and when the living room light turned on I felt a percussion go through my chest. With my heart inside my throat, I turned and ran back towards the bedroom.

Elish was standing in front of my door.

I stopped dead in my tracks and looked up at him, before my eyes shot all over the apartment, trying to find anywhere I could hide.

"My pet would hide in my closet when he was feeling overwhelmed. You may do the same tonight, but as of right now… you will sit down on the couch and have a cup of tea with me." Elish stared down at me, his arms crossed over his chest.

I stayed there frozen in place, looking behind him to the safety of my bedroom, where Reaver was… where my heroin was. They couldn't get me there; no one could. I could be safe with Reaver and the grenade in case anyone came near me.

"No… I… I want to go back into the bedroom," I said anxiously. "I have to…" My heartbeat, already ripping through my chest, started to spread the anxiety throughout my body until I felt the first sparks of a panic attack.

"You will not cry, you will not whine. Get the tea mugs on the counter, pour the tea that is in the thermos, and sit on the couch. Your wailing will only waken my pet and not once in the last twenty-four hours did he leave the outside of your door." Elish swept past me and I turned around as he walked into the living room.

Jade was sleeping on the couch with a blue blanket pulled over him, looking as small and unassuming as he never did when he was awake.

I watched almost coyly as Elish leaned down and gently picked his cicaro up, with a gentleness I would have never thought he had. He cradled his almost full-grown chimera pet in his arms and gave me a glance as he walked down the hall where the bedrooms were.

"Now, Mr. Massey."

I lowered my head, almost feeling like I had watched something personal I perhaps wasn't supposed to see, and walked towards the kitchen.

I did what he asked and poured some of the brown tea into the two mugs he had laid out. I thought he perhaps had been wanting to have some with Jade before he fell asleep, but I saw a steaming mug already resting on the coffee table in front of the couch. I wondered if Elish had been expecting me.

When Elish came back he was holding a brown paper bag in his hand. He walked over with a sweep of his white cape and sat down.

The chimera cape… like Nero had worn. All the elite chimeras liked to show off their prestige. Elish most of all from what I could remember.

The chimera with long blond hair, dressed in silvers, whites, and greys, with purple eyes like two shards of amethyst. I could never forget the day I first met him.

And Elish had lost none of that dignity, poise or grace, even though, besides his cape, he was in a more casual white dress shirt and black slacks. He still looked every bit the chimera I knew.

He sat beside me and picked up the tea mug I had placed down, then put it to his lips.

I watched his every movement, my body twitching towards the bedroom as if trying to egg me on to just get up and run. I calculated the time it would take for me to lock the door, and wondered if he had the same chimera speed that my resurrecting boyfriend had.

"If I wanted to hurt you, I would have hurt you long ago, Mr. Massey." His cold tones always set me on edge, like I was forever walking a thin razor blade with him. "Calm your heartbeat, you are not amongst enemies."

"Where's Reno?" I whispered, my breath catching in the throat. "And Biff? Where's my cat?"

I couldn't help it, my eyes started to burn again. My imagination brought me to all different horrible conclusions: that he had never gotten Biff, that Reno was dead, that he was just keeping us here until Reaver came back so he could deliver us to Silas, take the credit for himself.

Elish didn't waver in his gaze. "Reno is currently under the care of my physician Lyle, and the cat is under the smothering care of my sengil

Luca."

My heart jumped. I looked up at him and tried to read his face, like Reaver could always read faces. But I wasn't Reaver, and I wasn't a chimera.

Reading my doubt, I saw Elish pick something off of his shirt and bring it to the lamp light above us. My lip stiffened when I realized it was a cat hair.

"He is a fat cat, white with spots that are brown tabby in colour. He was residing comfortably in Reaver's underground basement, resting on the black duffle bag Mr. Nevada and I also retrieved. Is that enough to appease your suspicions, Mr. Massey?"

I took a sip of my tea, my face flushing over the embarrassment of being called out over not trusting him, but I didn't think he expected anything else of me.

I nodded and replied quietly, "What's going to happen to us? You smuggled us out of that hellhole. You kept Silas from getting Reaver. What happens now?"

Elish opened up the paper bag. I peered inside thinking that that bag must hold all of our answers, but I realized it was only a hamburger wrapped in tinfoil. Automatically my stomach growled, smelling that the meat was real bosen, and I think I could see real cheese as well.

Skyfall food. Oh man, did I ever miss Skyfall food.

"All of this information will wait until Reaver successfully resurrects; all you need to know for now is that no harm will come to you or your partner. I suggest you eat, relax, and heal your body and mind." He handed me the hamburger and I took it a bit more quickly than would have been polite.

"Are you going to be staying here?" I asked after I had swallowed my first bite, it tasted like heaven. Human meat had nothing on factory-raised bosen.

Elish nodded. "Yes, Garrett and my brothers are under the assumption Jade was seriously injured during the chaos in Aras. It is not out of character for me to stay with him here as he recovers."

"Will Reno come back here when he recovers too?" I asked quietly, trying not to wolf down the hamburger, but I couldn't help it, I was starving.

Elish nodded and rose when I was taking the last several bites of the burger. “Reno can join you when he feels he has recovered enough, though that will not be for some time. He required surgery on his wounds.” The blond chimera looked towards my bedroom door. “There is a small side bedroom off of the master bedroom. You will be sleeping in there from now on. However with how hysterical Perish seems to be about his minor slip, I do not think there will be problems. We will help you move Reaver there tomorrow morning.”

I rose with him, and with a sigh, I followed him to the bedroom that had always been locked.

To my surprise, Elish opened up a keypad I hadn’t noticed before and pressed several numbers. When he opened the door I realized there was only a set of stairs leading down to a lower level.

I walked down the stairs with him. And though I couldn’t see what was in the rest of the room, I saw the master bedroom with a dim light on and Jade sleeping peacefully on the bed.

“Perish will not violate you again, you may roam the house as you see fit. I would expect this paranoia and need to barricade yourself in that bedroom has passed?” Elish said when I started to walk towards the spare bedroom.

My shoulders fell, and all I could do was nod. I just wanted Reaver awake so he could be my leader again. I didn’t know what I was doing… all I felt was just fear and sadness.

“Yes, sir,” I said quietly. In that moment, under his gaze, I felt like the fourteen-year-old boy in Tamerlan again. Though in the same thread, I knew he wasn’t going to hurt me, and I felt safe with him here now. He could control Jade and he could control Perish.

There was something else that was eating the corners of my brain, chewing through the barriers I had erected that prevented me from going off the handle. It was the dream that I’d had, the one where Reaver had come back… not himself.

“Will he be normal when he wakes?” I asked quietly, knowing that he probably thought that was an idiotic question. “He won’t be… different?”

Sure enough, Elish stared at me for a moment. “Different? Perhaps you should not watch zombie movies, Mr. Massey. I would steer away from the vampire ones as well."

I slunk down. "I just had a dream that he was evil when he woke up. I'd never… well, I don't know for sure but–"

"You saw him die when Greyson strangled him, and he also died on his way to rescuing you in that factory from what Lycos had told me. Did he seem different back then?"

Reaver had died when he was rescuing me? I didn't know that. He had never told me, but then again he wouldn't have known, obviously.

All I could do was shake my head no, and let out a tense breath. "I have nightmares a lot, just warning you… if I wake up screaming…"

Elish picked up where I had trailed off. "My pet has the same issue; there is medication he takes every day for it. I'll see about securing some for you as well."

Reaver had always threatened to medicate me, maybe that was a good idea. Before all of this I was clawing his face in the middle of the night. He would probably be relieved.

"Thank you, Mr. Dekker… I'll… I'll go to sleep now. Have a good sleep too."

The chimera nodded. "Good night then."

And I did sleep well; I hadn't slept this well in a long time. When I woke up the next morning I was undisturbed, in a clean bed and a brown room. It sounded like everyone was already upstairs.

I took my first hit of the heroin, showered, and was surprised to find one of our duffle bags resting outside of my door. I opened it and got out some of my greywaster clothes, which now seemed so ratty in this elite apartment

It smelled like home though, it smelled like the basement. I found myself bringing an old t-shirt of Reaver's up to my nose and just taking in the scent I had grown so accustom to. Wondering if, like the memories of Aras and our first couple months together, it would eventually fade.

But no… as long as Reaver was beside me, I would be okay. As long as he was safe and we kept him out of the hands of Asher.

I buttoned up a blue button-down with black cuffs, and put on the old cloth pants I still had from Donnely. Then, with a deep breath for bravery, I walked out of the side bedroom and into what I realized must have been Elish's private office. I guess that would explain why it was locked.

I resisted the urge to explore the office. It was lined with bookshelves full of books and little trinkets, but I didn't have permission and knowing Donnely there was probably cameras everywhere. Instead I shoved my hands into my pockets and walked up to the main floor of the house.

I walked into the living room to see Jade cooking breakfast in the kitchen, filling the entire apartment with the smells of arian bacon and frying potatoes. Two things I haven't had in a long time. Sitting by the dining room table was Elish, clicking away on his laptop and Perish who was–

–who was looking at me like he was about to burst into tears.

I looked away from him and walked into the dining room.

"Did you sleep well, Mr. Massey?" Elish asked. He was holding a coffee cup in his hand and the other was typing something on his laptop.

"I did, thank you…" I said quietly. "Please, sir, just call me Killian. Mr. Massey makes me sound so old."

Elish glanced up; I think I saw the faintest hint of a smirk on his face. "Very well, Killian, though perhaps you declaring yourself as old is convenient. When is your birthday?"

I stared at him for a second. My mind had seemed to be in anxiety-limbo for the past several days.

"Oh… not for several months," I said quietly. He must be leading to something because Elish knew everything. He knew when my birthday was.

"Yes, well, it's a fair excuse either way." Elish looked behind him to where Jade was flipping pancakes. "Jade, get the nylon case, everything else can stay on the plane. I do not wish for the boy or Reaver to have access to that M16 quite yet."

He got Reaver's M16 too? I wasn't sure where it had ended up. That was a relief, that gun was as a part of Reaver as his cargo pants.

Jade quickly returned with the nylon case and held it out to Elish. Elish didn't receive it though. He motioned towards me. "It's his, give it to him. His birthday might not be for a while but we can forget that fact this time."

I turned around with a look of sheer bewilderment. Jade seemed puzzled as well when he handed me the nylon case about the size of Elish's laptop,

"I didn't retrieve your guitar as requested. It's too bulky and there may be travel in your future. This one is more appropriate," Elish said casually as I unzipped the case.

I took out a small metallic plate, about two inches thick. It was something I had only seen with travellers coming to stay in Tamerlan. It was a Cilo guitar, a very expensive guitar that you could easily carry around. The body of it looked like an electric guitar but it was smaller and still functioned as acoustic. The spine part folded into the main part. The strings folded with the spine and would auto-tune once snapped into place. It was an amazing little instrument; the travellers could always make some nice sounds out of it.

"But…" I heard Jade say.

I looked up and saw Jade looking at the guitar, his upper lip almost disappearing into his mouth. "That was mine… Luca trained me how to play on that guitar."

Elish gave him an iced look, which made the cicaro take a step away from him, his yellow eyes still looking at the guitar.

"And you failed to learn how to play properly. I am sure Killian will be able to coax something out of that guitar that does not sound like someone is beating a bag of scavers," Elish said with a warning tone on his voice.

Behind him Perish laughed. Jade whirled around and glared at him, and at this point, I myself took a step back.

"Do you have something to say, retard?" Jade snarled, obviously taking his anger out on someone he didn't have to bow down to.

Unfortunately Perish, it seemed, also needed to vent his feelings, probably the guilt over what he had done to me. In a second, the scientist was on his feet, his small paperback laying forgotten on the couch.

"I have a lot to say, pet. Go back to cooking, slave!" Perish snapped, and to my surprise he pushed Jade. "Have you not learned to obey your master, slumrat?"

I looked over at Elish for help, but all he did was take another drink of his coffee cup before setting it down. Even when Jade pushed Perish back, making the scientist spring up and take a swing at the pet, Elish didn't move an inch.

"Killian, the pancakes are about to burn. Flip them and perhaps while we eat you can play a song on that new guitar of yours?" Elish said nonchalantly, right as Perish fell backwards, crashing into an unoccupied chair behind him. Then a moment later, Jade lunged at him and started smacking Perish in the face.

The blond chimera still didn't move; he only picked up his coffee cup to keep the rocking table from spilling it.

This… this was an interesting family.

CHAPTER 4

Jade

I COULD FEEL THE EXCESS OF THE SHEETS BALL under my clenched fists, damp and heated from me bunching and grasping them again and again. I buried my face into the pillow and opened my mouth in the swirling concoction of pure ecstasy and unimaginable pain. I screamed into it and bit down.

I chewed on the flannel pillowcase and pulled it, suppressing another groan. Behind me the pain was intense; a burning pressure that I knew would rip me apart at any second. Then the pressure withdrew, and as he separated our joined bodies I heard a cruel chuckle.

"So quiet tonight. Are you afraid Mr. Massey will hear you? You know these walls are soundproof."

"No." I managed to lift my head up enough to say that. I rested my head to the side and started trying to catch my breath. As I shifted my body, my legs brushed up against the wet semen that had shot out of me and onto the sheets underneath. I'd lost track of how many times he had brought me to climax.

I screamed as he thrusted it all the way in without mercy, but this time I didn't bury my face back into the pillow. I screamed for him loud and clear before clenching my teeth hard in my mouth.

"That's more like you." I felt him grab my hair and pull my head back. I panted and groaned feeling my ears ring with every thrust. It always felt like he was fucking my spine in this position.

The next orgasm made my legs collapse; I could no longer hold myself up. My knees slid on the bed until I was splayed out, my ass still up in the air. I put my face back into the pillow panting hard before inhaling sharply as I felt his body weight press into me.

"Perhaps I should get Perish in here?" his cold voice purred into my ear.

I gasped when he push a finger inside my already stuffed-to-capacity ass. I felt him kiss and suck on my neck before he gave it a hard bite. I cried out and felt my head go hot as his tongue ran against the bite mark; collecting the blood he coveted so much. "Or Killian? I'm sure he's never taken a man for himself before. I can get him right now."

I twisted my body away from his mouth and tried to turn to him. "You won't touch him. Reaver would never listen to you if he knew you made Killian fuck me."

A cold chuckle. I shuddered as he continued to kiss my neck, his thrusts slowing down to a slow rocking of his hips. "Indeed, don't think I didn't notice how tight you are tonight. Not one orgy in my household? Three virile, attractive young men, every one of them sex starved and you didn't even have one little slip? Not one blow job in the cover of darkness?"

"I'd never do that!" I snapped at him. I felt him wrap his frosted hands around my arm; I shrugged it away and continued to move away from his mouth.

"I'd never sleep with any of them, you know that," I said with my own ice in my words. I was annoyed that he would even think of me like that.

Another laugh. "I look forward to sampling the fruits of the greywastes. I would suspect Reaver would put up even more of a fight than you did. Mounting a feral greywaster would be a step up from fucking defiant slumtrash."

I felt my neck tremble as a growl reached my lips. This amused him. Elish's hand grabbed the bottom of my chin and he started speeding up his thrusts.

The thought filled me with anger. I didn't know what situation made me more pissed off, Reaver and Killian being touched by Elish, or Elish, my master and owner, touching them.

My teeth clenched and gritted, then I felt his fingers trace my lips, as if wanting to sample the anger himself. In that moment my rage outranked my beaten in obedience, and I bit him.

Elish only chuckled; he didn't remove his finger, instead he shoved another one into my mouth, both sideways so they were resting snugly in my jaws.

"This upsets you, does it?" he said in derisive amusement. "How does Killian's small little frame squealing under my body make you feel?"

I could taste copper; I must've drawn blood. I wrenched my mouth away from his static touch even though I loved the taste of his blood.

I felt my lips curl up in a snarl. "I'd kill him! You're m-m-mine!" I tore at the sheets as I felt him reach under and grab my testicles.

"I'll have to ask Silas how he compared to you."

"Hey, fuck off! That's too far," I snarled through a strangled gasp. I tried to wrench my hands back so I could stop him but a rattling of chains reminded me that was impossible. My hands were cuffed at my leather bracelets now; I didn't have enough slack.

He gripped harder and I continued to spit my poison, until with a few hard thrusts I came. Though the orgasm was nothing but a burning stinging pleasure from its prolonged and continued summons, but I still savoured every moment of it.

Then, with a gasp of relief, he released me from his grip.

I could feel Elish's aura burn brighter around him. He was loving every second of this. I bit into the pillow out of rage, chewing the cloth as his hips continued to rock into me.

"Tell me, maritus, how would Killian look when I am making him cum as I make you?"

My body burned from his cold banter, the defiance I still had inside me resurrected in a furious outburst that I knew would condemn me the moment it left my lips. "Reaver would kill you! I'd kill you. You're MINE!" I swore the moment the last word left my tongue.

I braced myself for the physical pain. I knew he was going to hit me, but instead the thrusts only quickened. I let out a surprised moan of pleasure as I felt his warm, electricity-laced hand touch my half-stiff member. Immediately my hips started to rise, welcoming his touch, but to my surprise he rose with me and put me on my back.

Confused over my lack of being hurt, I let him separate my knees and only clenched my teeth as he pushed himself back inside me. “I do love how much vinegar being here has put into your veins; you haven’t fought me this hard in half a year.”

I swore inside my head. Of course he wouldn’t touch Reaver or Killian. They had too much to offer him and getting Reaver angry would only make getting it more difficult. He was getting a rise out of me. If I could remember that he did this while he was doing it, I might save myself the humiliation.

Either way, I played into his hands; I always played right into his fucking hands.

I dug my fingernails into his back, the chains rattling behind me.

“Look at me,” Elish said.

I raised my eyes and met his; they were looking right at me. I glared at him, my mouth open in a continuous moan, seeing his golden hair around me tickling the sides of my face and my ears.

And this was the part that made me melt into him. My body shuddered as he stroked and pulled my member tucked into his free hand, the other supporting himself by my head. His blond hair all around me, trapping us within the domes of each other’s vision.

I welcomed his kiss with a tremble on my lips and a cold shiver of pleasure, touching and playing my tongue against his. I had hungered for that taste at night, to the point where I felt ravenous for it. The taste only I got of him.

Then with a low moan, barely a susurration on his lips, he filled me. The cold sculpted man shed his skin for a moment so brief your brain could barely process it. For a fraction of a second he melted into my arms too, and our auras seemed to become one brilliant blinding light around me. The purple and silver-black ripples of mine, combining with the white silvers of his own.

We were one person.

Then we separated and I felt the bed pull down beside me. I waited patiently on my back for him to regain his breath and take me back into his arms.

I heard my chains rattle as I put my hands behind my head, slipping into the dreamy tired state that only hours of sex and countless orgasms could drag out of you. I was exhausted, wet from sweat, and the seed I could feel on top of the sheets and down my backside. Satisfied though, and right where I belonged.

After several minutes passed in silence, I felt my chains get released, then a cold hand drew me in. He made his touch like that of an ice cube as he cooled my flaming body down.

I smiled and craned my neck; Elish indulged me and traced two fingers up and down the exposed side.

"Mm, I love you." I turned around and kissed him on his lips. Elish pressed back and drew me close to him.

"Reassurance? That's odd; I thought we were over this already."

My chest rose and fell, and I prepared myself for his laughter. "You just seem to be treating Killian pretty well, birthday presents, kindness… you've always been nice to him, even the first time we met him."

There was no scathing retort though, only a heavy silence that suited the atmosphere in the room, still thick from our lovemaking.

"Killian has always had a fragile mind, and requires a different approach than you would."

"Still," I said with a frown.

"You should know, Cicaro, Reaver will wake up soon, and when he does it will be Killian telling him not to murder all of us. Killian is the key to controlling the beast, remember that."

That made sense but I still felt the jealousy burn up my heart. I was so used to Elish being commanding and cruel to everyone who wasn't in his small circle of family, it rubbed me the wrong way that he was being this nice to Killian.

"True," I sighed and shifted myself closer to him; in response he tightened his hold on me. "Just don't be too nice. Remember what I said: I will kill any new pet you bring home."

He chuckled but was silent after. I didn't want him to sleep yet though, there was something else I needed from him, if only to appease my insecurities.

I huffed through my nose and pulled on his hand, which was still wrapped around my chest.

Elish let out a breath; he knew what I wanted. “Very well, maritus. I love you. Now sleep. Reaver will be awakening soon and I think we will need to rest up for the chaos that may cause.” I felt him rest his chin on top of my head.

I smiled at my small victory. I had been coaxing him to say it to me more often, but so far I had only gotten it out of him three times in the year he had started doing it. It was a win though and it filled my heart up with everything it needed.

I kissed his hand and closed my eyes.

In his arms I could sleep forever, but in those same arms not always was the sleep undisturbed. Frequently though, Elish would already be awake, because of my moaning or thrashing he was usually already up and petting my hair back when I would have my night terrors.

But tonight… no, this wasn’t a night terror.

I should have known what it was, but it had been almost a year since it had happened. So when I found myself getting out of bed and walking out of the bedroom, I didn’t know what was going on with me.

My temples started to pound. Oddly, I felt an electric shiver go up my spine.

Then a scream that immediately snapped my head into the direction of Killian’s bedroom. I felt a weird sensation behind my ears, a higher octave to the tones Killian’s screams were making.

I took the first two steps slowly before I broke into a sprint. My first thought being that Perish had found his way past the keypad, and he was trying to fuck him again.

When I opened the door and barged inside I stopped cold, staring at the darkness in stunned silence as I mentally hit a smoke-wall of emotion.

Killian’s aura was as thick as mud and the colours of a rotting corpse; I had never felt anything so horrific. I felt my own aura recoil and slink inside of me like it was some sort of living creature. I hadn’t had this reaction since I had felt Reaver’s aura, and before him, Silas’s. But theirs were filled with darkness this was filled with…

I had to get closer to him.

The door shut behind me, but my faded night vision made everything glow blue. I saw a twisted heap in the middle of the bed, Killian’s eyes half-closed and brimming. I saw his mouth twist open but no scream came out. Only his hands tensed tighter and his legs writhed in mental agony.

No… I turned and went to leave, my mind feeling overwhelmed and taken to its mental capacity. I had to escape from this aura; it was too much for me.

Two and a half years had turned a bright little sunbeam into… this? He emanated more heart-wrenching despair than the Fallocaust itself.

"Reaver?" Killian suddenly croaked.

I closed my eyes tight and ground my teeth as he pressed up against my soul. I felt him enclose me; wrap me in those tendrils of overwhelming sadness and fear.

I slammed my fist against the wall in frustration and turned towards him.

Like my movements were robotic, I walked up to the bed. With a pull of my own aura, I felt a flash of white-hot determination. I drew my own violet aura and pushed it against his own.

It was a feeling I had never experienced before.

The colours in the darkness were so tangible, yet I knew they were invisible to everyone else but me. Only Elish and some of the other chimeras could see their own auras reflecting in my eyes. Elish loved to watch ours, sometimes to gauge just how much I was becoming like him, other times to just watch during our lovemaking.

"You're aura is getting more silver strands; they make your eyes look like small galaxies."

I had smiled at him shyly, and rubbed my hand against his arm. "You're so powerful, yet you can't see it… look, just concentrate and you can see it lighting up your blood vessels."

Elish had smiled back at me. We were in bed again. I was tracing a finger along a pearly ripple waving its way up his chest before disappearing into his throat.

I could see his aura the clearest visually, but during day-to-day life I never saw or sensed them. It was something I had to concentrate on to make happen.

"Only in those golden eyes of yours I see them. I am not an empath like you." He raised a gloveless hand and traced it down my cheek; I felt it turn almost unbearably hot to iced cold in a matter of moments. "You know what abilities I was born with, the same ones you've been able to absorb."

I pushed my growing aura against Killian further and felt the first break in the thick smoke. I found myself physically reaching my hands out, until for reasons my mind couldn't justify, I put a hand against his face.

My mind lit up like I had taken a hit of LSD.

It was a flash, an injection of images like I was unloading a zip folder of short video clips. I saw them all pulse through my mind in rapid succession, each bringing their own fleeting moment of feeling.

I had felt this before…

So many horrible images, I couldn't grab onto one for long but I saw things that made my stomach turn. I saw Jeff Massey, infested with wiggling maggots and still alive, poor fuck. I saw Perish's throat open in front of me and spray blood onto my body, and I saw…

I furrowed my brow. I saw Reaver, a twisted snarling monster, chasing Killian with the realization that if he caught Killian he would rape him. They were in Aras, I recognized those building designs, this wasn't that long ago either.

And I saw the factory, that one almost brought me to my knees. The fear from that had lingered, a foul rib-shaking despair that rotted you from the inside out. This was before he found Reaver, before he had mental armour to put on.

But why was I seeing this…? I had only once seen into someone's mind, Elish's, and that was when I was incredibly ill. I'd had surgery done to prevent me from using this absorption ability after Garrett had told Elish it would eventually overload my brain and kill me.

I had to tell my master…

I heard a small sigh of relief; and a moment later, I was shocked back to reality with Killian's hand over mine.

I blinked and looked down; Killian's eyes were half-open.

"Reaver?" he whimpered. His voice was high and pleading.

You poor broken bird; they're going to destroy you.

Look at you… you small helpless little thing, writhing in your own internalized madness. A small songbird who happened to stumble into the clutches of a hawk.

A hawk that will not kill you, no, you will not be allowed such an easy escape. No, your wings will mend and he will break them again, until you are a crippled heap and he grows bored of such defective merchandise.

Silas is going to torture you until the sun consumes the earth.

You were a small beacon of light in the never-ending grey when I met you. A thirst for life and learning that seemed unquenchable at that age. You looked so much younger too. Now as I stare at that face I swear you aged ten years instead of two and a half. Not in your soft lanky body that any man would kill to touch, nor in your face that still made you look like a young teenager… but in your eyes. Those large spheres of a blue so deep if I kept looking I knew I would drown in them.

Jade?

What are you doing?

Lost eyes. The carefree spark of naive innocence had died in them, but at what point the images didn't tell me. I just knew everyone had been too busy to grieve its death. Now what child-like innocence he had was a shelled wraith, walking in a lost daze around a landscape that would never change, calling for colour but all they will serve you is red and grey.

Always red and grey.

What a cruel twist of fate. Not even two years after Jeff took you and left, did you return a shadow of yourself; a phantom blowing in the breeze, once full of the innocence, now you're an empty hollow shell hiding behind a polite smile.

No… not empty, you were full, full of the browns and greys of rotten carrion crawling with worms and insects. That embedded their small wiggling bodies into your skin and drove you mad with their movements. Your aura was covered in a layer of decomposed flesh, like the flesh you had knelt in when you realized *Asher* wasn't dead.

Put it down, Jade.

The things that king had done to me. In the darkness, with my and Killian's auras intertwined, I felt the atmosphere of that room in Skyfall I had gotten to know well: The Council Room.

The smell was a mixture of blood, sweat and the steel rods they had implanted in my head. Silas had drawn out each one as I screamed, feeling my brain inside of my head go haywire. My entire body was a ruin. I had been beaten, crucified, and the inside of my brain had been sliced and electrocuted to ribbons.

I sighed and felt Killian's cheek warm against my hand. I had been strong enough to endure the Ghost King. I was a chimera from Moros; I was born and bred to endure.

But Killian was no chimera; he would be put through what I had been put through but worse. This small little waif, as kind and sweet as they come. What a pretty piece of flesh to be passed around a family of rabid monsters just waiting to putrefy such innocence. Like a paint brush in a glass of water, a single dip muddles the crystal clear liquid.

Though this feeling I felt from Killian was no single dip of a used paint brush. The transparent water, reflecting sunlight and warmth, was now just a quagmire of mud and rot.

I felt inside my body a well of sadness and sympathy, one that overwhelmed even my advanced receptors. I could take the abuse. I proved I could. But this kid? Fuck. This kid didn't stand a chance. He would've been better off as Garrett's pet. At least if Silas had decided to grow jealous of the second born chimera's cicaro, he would be dead by now, just like his parents.

So much misery.

JADE!

I gasped as I felt a cold hand take my forearm and wrench it back, and with the strength of the pull, all of my lucid dreams shot out of my body.

I blinked, seeing only blue-tinged darkness around me, the blond kid laying just a foot away.

I was…

What the hell?

I looked down and realized I had been holding a pillow only inches away from Killian's face.

Then the cold hand was joined by another and I was yanked back from the boy.

"What the hell do you think you're doing?" Elish's frozen voice hissed. I blinked, looking bewildered at the pillow, not even able to answer his question.

The scene spoke for itself; I was about to try and smother the kid.

"I don't know!" I exclaimed, but a moment later, his hand clamped over my mouth. I felt Elish walk me back into our bedroom.

When he closed the door behind us I immediately took advantage of only one arm restraining me and I wrenched myself from his grasp. Anticipating getting the snot beat out of me I walked towards the bathroom to lock myself in it.

Elish had no patience for it; his mind was elsewhere. "I am not angry, Cicaro, and not surprised. However I expected this to happen differently."

"I had surgery to prevent this shit from happening!" I whirled around and said loudly. "I haven't been able to do anything beyond my aura reading since then. What the fuck!?"

Elish, to my surprise, picked up the chains he usually bound me with during our rougher sessions, and chained me to the bed. I knew why, so I didn't protest.

"Most of the implants Sid and Perish put in your brain were deactivated. I had it done as soon as I heard Silas knew about Reaver," he replied as he got back into bed.

I looked at him in shock; he hadn't told me that but maybe he hadn't wanted to.

"You will be nineteen soon enough. Old enough to become immortal if my hand is forced. The damage you'll do to your mind will be repaired by your first resurrection," Elish said. "I want you to start developing it, and your target is going to be Perish."

"What?" I lay back down on the bed and gave him a confused look. "You want me to keep letting it happen. What if I hurt Killian?"

Elish shook his head. "He will be sleeping beside Reaver and Reaver not let you near him."

"But why Perish?"

There was a pause, and I wondered if this was information he didn't want to give me.

"There is something inside his head that I need. This is a task I set out for you years ago, Cicaro, and as these seeds are coming into fruition, you must do as I tell you."

I looked at him and felt myself scowl in confusion, but I nodded and obeyed. I never had a choice in that. "But I don't even know how I do it, or what triggers it. How will I even know what to look for?"

"I have faith you will find a way. You'll know when you find what I need."

Always so cryptic… I wish I knew what was going on in that mind of his. What his plans were for me, and the other three. Elish couldn't hide Reaver, Killian, and Perish here forever, and eventually I would have to go back to Skyfall too where I belonged.

But still, in that same thread, my heart filled at finally being able to help Elish with this long cultivated mission. Even though it would be risky on my mortal brain, I had a gift that would help him. If I had to do some digging through Perish's mind to find information for Elish, I would do it.

I was the only empath chimera, the only one to hold these odd abilities. I couldn't let my master, my husband, down.

"I'll do anything I can to help you, you know that." I twisted a lock of his shiny blond hair in my fingers. "Have we had an empath like me before?"

"You are the second. The first one passed long ago… and without a doubt you will also be the last. They're too much trouble."

I scrunched my face, making my nose wrinkle in mock anger and tugged on the lock of his hair. In return he granted me a smile that made my heart melt to my feet. The rare smile, where I could see it in his eyes too.

In response, I leaned forward and we kissed. I was glad he wasn't angry at me; I didn't want to ruin our first time together in over a month.

"My parvulus maritus, such a docile thing." Elish's voice became a low purr, making a shiver go up my spine. "It is enjoyable to be with you here, after such a trying several months."

I moved closer to him, until my bare skin was rubbing against his. He stroked my back and I rested my cheek against his chest.

"It has. I missed it too," I sighed and rubbed his collarbone. "I hope Killian feels better once he has Reaver back. Silas destroyed him… his aura, it was like toxic sludge. He had been so bright and colourful before."

"Yes, all that is crystal clear will eventually be spoiled by the Ghost King, but his brilliant aura would've never survived the greywastes anyway. Killian will become stronger, and in time he will be strong enough to complete the tasks laid out for him."

"You really think that kid is strong?" I had my doubts.

"Yes," Elish replied back simply. "He is stronger than you would imagine. I did not send him to Aras just because he was pretty."

I looked at him. "Why did you send him to Aras?" My brow furrowed. I actually had thought he had only sent him to Aras because he was cute and innocent. Good flesh for the Darkness to consume, that and to get him away from Garrett.

"Because he and Reaver belong together."

"Like Silas and Sky?" Reaver was Silas's clone, and Sky was his boyfriend before he had killed himself. The other born immortal, a man who Elish had told me had been… a bit of a jerk.

"Yes."

I remembered back to when I had first heard Sky's name. I was half-conscious during the conversation I had overheard between Elish and Silas. Silas was saying how much he missed him, how much he had loved Sky. He even got Elish to promise they would find a way to clone him.

"Was Silas normal back then? When he had Sky?"

I pulled away a bit so I could look at him. Elish was on his side tracing a hand along my body. I was happy we got more time together, even though it was only because I had tried to smother Killian.

"I was not born yet, this was a long time ago."

"He never had anyone else?"

My blond chimera shook his head slightly. "No, we are his bishops, his pawns, his knights, and rooks… we are not his kings. He said if he was going to replace Sky, the man would have to be like no other."

And he got this man, only to have Lycos and Elish both steal him before Silas knew he existed.

"Yeah," I replied, "that's why he's pissed off about how things are turning out. His manufactured boyfriend loves someone else, hates him, and has the ability to kill him. I can see why he would be so upset."

"Mm, you're smarter than you look."

I gave him a smile, and kissed his chest before he drew me close to him. "Remember, I will be leaving in several hours. Reno is healed enough that I can deliver him to his new master. However I will not be long, expect me back this evening."

There was no stifling the yawn, but I managed a nod while I did. Skyfall was about a four hour plane ride from here on the Falconer, and Elish was still technically king while Silas recovered.

I got comfortable and closed my eyes, falling asleep to the feeling of him playing with the strands of my bangs.

And I stayed asleep.

CHAPTER 5

Reno

THE CRUTCHES I WAS GETTING USED TO, IT WAS THE slippers that weirded me out. I had never owned anything but boots, army boots if I could help it. Miller once wore sandals in the summer time and we beat him up for it. Slippers? They were like fluffy shoes that couldn't grip anything and when you ran they went *flop flop flop*.

I couldn't wrap my mind around Skyfaller logic.

I flip-flopped my sorry self into the sitting area of the apartment and sat down with a grimace of pain. The couches were fluffy and comfortable but the bullet hole in my gut wasn't letting me enjoy the fringe benefits of being Elish Dekker's prisoner. Walking was alright, but once I had to scrunch my stomach to sit down it felt like someone was skewering me with a flaming sword.

"Do you need help, Master Nevada?"

I jumped in my seat, my teeth biting through another wave of dull pain. Luca pursed his lips apologetically though that wouldn't stop him from doing it again.

Elish's servant maid, or sengil as we were supposed to call them, was like a little mouse, quiet and small. A mouse that sneaked unnoticed from room to room to see if someone needed him.

The kid had been glued to me since I had been dropped off, half-dead and leaving a trail of blood behind me. He had a patient and docile nature to him, and a soft face that told me him and Killian would've been best friends.

"Nah, I was just going to turn on *Simpsons*, want to watch it with me?" There was no hiding my loneliness anymore, I had been here for almost a week now and since then I had only seen Elish twice, and I hadn't even met my new master.

Yep, *new* master… I was a cicaro now, a chimera's pet.

I couldn't recall much, but I remember demanding to know where I was and where my friends were. Had I really heard that Reaver was immortal? What was this place? Everything smelled weird, and the objects around me I couldn't make sense of. I was in a hospital for only several people. It was small but full of medical equipment, and expensive-looking machines Doc would've smothered babies for.

I remember feeling myself start to panic. The older man in his late forties kept trying to calm me down but I couldn't settle until I knew what was going on.

I had blacked out after I'd rescued the cat. Elish had told me to stay awake, but once I saw the shadowed outlines of the skyscrapers, and buildings in the distance, my mind had started to get fuzzy.

And then he was in the doorway of the hospital room, and the doctor guy was gone.

I stared, my mind temporarily going blank. Elish had looked different in the greywastes, but now, in his element, he was a force to be reckoned with. I found myself gawking at him like a gobsmacked idiot.

I couldn't help it though. Elish was a towering sight; beside him the sengil's forehead barely reached his square jaw. He was tall and imposing, with long blond hair halfway down his back and a cold smile on his face. This dude was like a marble statue that seemed to permanently rest on a pedestal.

When Elish's eyes fell onto me, I felt my throat go dry. Even with logic telling me I was safe and he had helped me, I still cowered under those violet eyes. I hoped he was on our side; I did not want to become enemies with this dude.

"So what happens now?" I rasped when I had first saw Elish in the doorway. "Is Reaver awake yet? Have you heard anything?"

"Reaver will wake in the next three days, possibly four. As far as I know they are still doing well at my base," Elish's cold and imposing voice had said, it seemed to coat the room in ice.

"And the cat's okay too?" I asked. I felt a needle go into my arm, which I tried to bat away but Lyle the doctor held it firmly. I felt the instinct to thrash, but the old doctor's hand was gentle and his voice soothing, telling me I was getting worked up.

"Luca is taking care of the cat, you'll join him soon," Elish explained. "Eventually you'll also join your friends, but in due time."

The relief on my face was palpable, his stern but reassuring words loosening the knot in my chest with quick fingers. I missed my friends already, and it felt strange being away from them. I wanted to heal up and leave this place so I could help them. Killian was probably having kittens over Reaver being dead.

Reaver being dead. What an odd thing to say, but it also led to the question… one I didn't have the nerve to ask when Elish had let me silently slip into Aras to get the cat and my friend's things:

"So, you're on our side?" I asked, breaking my eye contact from him. I felt exposed under that intense gaze, stripped down and vulnerable and not in a fun way.

Elish seemed amused by this question; perhaps it was a stupid one considering everything he had already done for us.

"There are no sides; there is only what has to be done and what has to be prevented. If you need the solidarity to help you sleep though, yes, Reno, I am on your side." A small smile raised the corners of his lips, but his eyes were still cold. "Everything has worked out rather perfectly. I am impressed with how it all came together."

My face darkened, his smile seemed to mock every tear I had shed for Leo and Greyson, Killian and Reaver. I tightened my lip, refusing to succumb to the soothing feelings the sedatives were giving me. "Your chimera is dead, so is his partner. Killian and Reaver are hundreds of miles from their homes. How can you say that?"

Elish's face didn't move, not even a pull of his bottom lip. "Because Silas doesn't have Reaver or Killian. Or you for that matter. That is what Lycos and Greyson died for, to keep Reaver safe and hidden. He's safe now, and he's hidden."

I pushed down the hole in my chest, feeling the soft fabric tense under my tightening grip on the sheets. He was right when you consider the bigger picture but my heart was still broken from what had transpired.

I was a greywaster far from home and my friends, in the hive of the enemy. The big picture was too massive and far away from my vision to find much relief in it.

"It's amusing to me… not once have you asked of your own fate." To show his amusement I saw a sardonic smile creep onto his face. It did nothing to lighten his cold countenance; if anything it made my hackles rise. Elish looked even more sociopathic than Reaver and that was saying a lot.

"I don't care what happens to me," I said honestly, busying my fidgeting hands with the sheets resting over my bandaged and bruised body. The aching gnaw in my gut seemed temporarily silenced by the drug they had given me. "I just want to make sure Reaver and Killian are safe, and Silas doesn't have them."

Elish shook his head and tented his hands like a mage about to conjure a spell. "Silas is dead, and he'll stay that way for the next several weeks, if not more. Reaver and the deacons did a fair number on him. That will give me more than enough time to make preparations ensuring their safety, which you will be helping me with."

My eyes widened; Elish drank it up with a smile. "I see, now you're wondering your own fate."

I didn't trust that smile. It was out of place on his face, it just radiated sinister thoughts. "What do you need me for? Aren't I already your pet?"

"Oh, you are about to become more than that," Elish said quietly. "You want to help your friends, no?"

"I would do anything for them."

And with that I learned my fate. I learned just what his plans for me were.

"Reno, you will be going undercover for me, and you will be retrieving a certain keycard I am going to need. It's for a lab in a place called Kreig, where your friend Reaver was born."

I gaped at him. "Undercover? Like I'm going to be James Bond?"

Elish gave me that look, I think everyone knows what that look is. A pained, and almost pleading, look where the person tries to convince himself he didn't just hear that.

Elish chose to ignore me. "I left Skytech many years ago, so my rooting around the archives would bring attention to me I do not want. You'll get that card for me and give it to Luca."

I swallowed hard, feeling a prickle of excitement form in my stomach. I was going to be useful? I had a mission like Reaver and Tinky did? I had never been important before.

"How? How am I supposed to get in there? Like you want me to be a burglar or something?"

Elish shook his head and tented his hands with a thin smile. Then he told me something that I think I knew would change my life forever.

"I will be selling you to my brother, the president of Skytech, Garrett Dekker."

Back to my place on the couch. I stared at the white, spotless ceilings and felt Biff nuzzling my hand, which was hanging off of the couch. Luca was lying with his back against my body, taking care for his back not to hit my sore stomach. I played with his wavy blond hair out of habit.

Luca loved styling his hair, and at Elish's request, he had been let loose on me too. Elish wanted me to remain low profile while Silas was healing. I would get a new name that Garrett would give me, and an altered appearance.

I had wanted to dye my hair platinum blond but apparently it would clash with my darker features and look weird according to Mr. Beautician Luca. Instead Luca had tried silver hair dye on me, and with some hair clipping and layering, had styled me to look like quite the twink. With the hair dye to start off, and a pill I would take once a month, the colour would remain.

I wanted to ask if it would change *other places* I had hair, but Elish had been in the room.

To my delight, I also had gotten new clothes since I had been released from the hospital. I was too tall and lanky to fit into Luca's clothes but Jade's fit almost perfectly. So on top of being a silver fox now, I also had a wide variety of brothel-ready clothing. I felt hilarious wearing them at first, but now I had embraced the fact that under all that muck and dirt… I was fucking hot.

Reaver would've laughed at me, laughed until he cried. Killian might blush under my skimpy clothing but deep down the little knucklehead would like it.

I missed those two; every day I missed them more.

Until I went back where I belonged Luca would be my Killeaver replacement. He loved being touched. I couldn't blame him living with two Reavers. I might need to buy myself a servant, it was easier than finding a boyfriend. At least I wouldn't have to worry about him being the king of the greywastes like my last potential boyfriend.

I filed that thought away under *'Possible Solution for Loneliness.'*

"Is there any special chimera protocol I need to follow?" I asked after the show had ended, we were watching a commercial. Tomorrow I would be leaving this place and moving into Garrett's skyscraper, a towering building in the middle of Skyland affectionately called Skytower. The one I was living in was Elish's skyscraper, Olympus. Each god damn chimera (except twin chimeras shared) had their own palace in the sky. They really knew how to live it up here.

Luca shifted around a bit; he turned over so I could see his face. "Respect, just be very respectful. But being around you, you don't have to worry, you're very tame. Garrett will like that."

I snorted, amused at his choice of words. It was like he was talking about a pack of wild animals, which was true for some of them.

Though there were obviously a few wild animals still here. I poked a long silver scar on Luca's shoulder. "I've only seen Jade twice, but it doesn't take a genius to put two and two together. Elish beats the shit out of you guys, doesn't he?"

Luca's face whitened and I saw his green eyes go wide; he sat up and scanned the apartment. Most likely expecting Elish to be hiding in a corner somewhere with a whip.

"Listen to Elish, that's all. Jade doesn't and I, well, I'm just as sengil. I get treated well but sometimes I am disobedient, though Master Elish hasn't struck me in years." Luca rose and I sat up with him. I pushed my feelings of guilt down and decided to continue pressing him for information.

"What do you mean by that?" I asked curiously. I picked up my crutches and grimaced as I rose.

"Elish loves a challenge, Jade was a slumrat Morosian, but very popular in the slums. He caught Elish's eye and he took him as a pet and broke him as you would a wild animal." Luca slunk his head and picked up a duster he had put down when I had asked him to watch TV with me. He started to distract himself with cleaning, typical of the sengil. "Garrett is the president of Skytech; he's no Elish, not at all. I clean for him sometimes, or stay with him when Elish gives me leave. He's always friendly towards me, even though I am just a sengil."

I watched him in silence as he buzzed around the room with a thirst to clean that suggested it was more a disorder than a command.

More questions burned in my throat. I walked over to the dispenser and grabbed myself a glass of hot water for tea. Tea was everywhere in Elish's apartment, any kind you wanted. Elish was a complete tea fiend.

"And I have to find folders with keycards to get into Kreig?" I whispered, more to myself than him. I ran over Elish's instructions for me; I had done it again and again over the past several days. It was simple in theory, but right now it seemed so complicated it made my gut sour. Elish was depending on me.

Elish needed to get into Kreig, with Reaver and Killian. That was where Reaver was born, and there was information imperative to the plan he had been forming in his head for god knows how long.

'It all depends on you, Reno. Get the card key and give it to Luca if I am not here.'

My throat moved as I swallowed that information, like a jagged pill it stuck in my throat. I didn't want this to be dependent on me. I had spent waking nights in my bedroom worrying myself sick over the fact that this part of the plan was on my incompetent ass.

And it really was all up to me, it wasn't something Elish could do himself. Elish had stopped being involved in Skytech years ago, a very rough departure on bad terms (I think a lab explosion that supposedly incinerated their chimera brother might have something to do with it). If Elish started nosing around now, after Reaver's emergence, it would put a glaring spotlight on Elish that wasn't wanted. Especially considering he *was* hiding Reaver.

Therefore, I would soon be officially stripped of my title as greywaster and now I was Garrett's cicaro. It would show up on my census blood tests and everything.

Oh, how life can change so suddenly.

The next day was the day I would meet my new master. I took it all in stride, admittedly I was rather curious. Luca and Elish had both told me he was a friendly guy but a bit socially inept. He could close a deal and grow chimeras in microwave tubes but he was rather unlucky with men. Luca had even told me a story about how Garrett dragged him off to a fancy pub to make a waiter jealous when he scorned his advances… it had ended with the guy being shot in the head.

Shot in the fucking head.

Chimeras.

But I knew chimeras and I knew them well. So I was probably going to be a maid and a sex doll. As long as he didn't smack me around I was okay with that. I hadn't even stroked one out since I had gotten shot. Too painful and my head was swimming with too many troubles to think about it. It might be fun, chimeras were hot and they all had smoking hot bodies to make up for their inbred personality disorders.

I inhaled a deep breath and checked myself out in the mirror. I shook my head at the bizarre person staring back at me. Silver hair and bangs, a little past my ear and flipped out at the ends, and my eyebrows were manicured and shaped, giving my face a thinner more fancy appearance. If Luca showed emotions he probably would've cried when he was done with me. I could tell he was proud of his handiwork. I think I was a project to him. I wonder if he had done the same to Jade.

I saw movement beside me and I turned to see Luca with a box. I raised an eyebrow as it moved, and a moment later, I heard a mournful mew.

Oh, it's Biff… I hadn't thought about if I would be bringing him, I guess he was officially my cat now. I watched as Luca stuck his tongue out of the corner of his mouth to try and balance the crate, and gave him a smile.

"Do you want to keep him for now? I'm sure once all this shit is done Killian and Reaver will want him back, but that might take a while. Why don't you take him?"

Luca's face lit up at the same time Elish glided out of his bedroom, fixing his gloves back onto his hands; he was all dressed up and ready to go.

He gave us both looks as we turned towards him and narrowed his eyes suspiciously. I guess two boys and a moving box must've looked questionable to him. At this point Biff gave another sombre meow.

I smiled at him and gathered up all my charisma. "Elish, can the cat stay here with Luca?"

I took this moment to open the crate and pick up the cat; then I held Biff up to my face with a goofy grin.

Elish only stared at me flatly; probably counting down the moments to when I left his apartment.

"Would that please you, Luca? He's not a kitten, every request you've made has been for a kitten," Elish replied casually.

Luca's soft face lit up and he put his hands behind his back. "I don't mind. He's very well-behaved, Master, and his white fur will not clash with your furniture. He's lazy and calm… if – if it's okay with you…" Luca let the last part drag.

"Well, I suppose you finally got your cat then. Very well, he may stay, but the cat hair must be kept to a minimum." Ice Man looked down as Biff started hovering around his legs, meow-purring at him in a tone that almost made him sound like a hopper.

Behind Elish, and out of his vision, Luca broke his usual calm placid look with a big smile, even jumping up and down twice before he got his composure back.

"Thank you, Master!" Luca's voice raised a couple more octaves; then he ran towards Elish and started straightening up Elish's robes and shirt. He was vibrating excitement.

Once Elish was prepared to go, he said something quietly to Luca, who nodded and ran off. I waited by the door with my hands behind my back for something to happen.

When Luca returned a minute later he was holding something leather and studded in his hand. I felt my eyebrows raise and my mouth purse to the side when I realized it was a collar, not unlike what Jade wore.

Elish walked up to me in a strolling gait, and without a word of permission (obviously), he put it around my neck; then there was a tinkle of chains as he hooked on what looked like a leash.

He handed the leather handle to me and I took it. I don't know why but I immediately tried to pull myself with my own leash. I coughed, feeling it constrict my neck.

"Very suiting, Cicaro," Elish said, with a biting smile that suited his cold face like a tight-fitting glove.

I decided then even with the collar, I would always be Reno.

I growled at him like a dog and bared my teeth at him as comically stupid as I could. I saw the faint hint of a smile on Elish's face, so I took it as a win.

With a last fleeting goodbye to Luca, though not for long since he did come to clean and I would need someone to watch TV with, I left the apartment with Elish in front of me and we made our way to the elevator.

I stood in my own silence. My bags were already there, though I didn't have very much to my name. I was the only one missing now.

The next couple of hours would shape the next month or longer. Longer if Garrett wasn't the nice guy everyone had told me he was. No matter what though, I had to get into the Skytech office and find those papers, no matter what it took. My goal was clear in front of me; I knew what I had to do.

"Do you have any pointers for him?" I asked as the elevator started to descend to the lobby. Chimeras might not mind awkward silence but it always drove me nuts.

Elish was quiet for a moment, I tried to read his face but, of course, I couldn't. The chimera stared forward, his purple, cold eyes unblinking, and his long blond hair falling way past his shoulders, only shortening slightly to form long bangs in the front.

"Did you know my cicaro is an empath?" Elish finally replied. The elevator doors separated and we both walked into the large and elegantly decorated lobby. A young woman stood in the corner behind a black wood desk, tapping away at the computer until her eyes realized Elish was the one coming from the elevator. I watched as she stood up and bowed to him, even though she was ten feet away in a corner.

"No, I didn't. What's that?" I asked. I stayed a foot behind him as we walked across the lobby. I had seen Jade and Luca do the same and I decided to start practicing my pet skills.

"They can sense peoples' emotions. He is the only living chimera with this ability."

Neat, but I didn't know why that mattered. I'd love to believe that I was a chimera but I was just another Nevada asshole, I wasn't anyone special.

Elish continued, two armed thiens opened the black-framed doors for us, bowing as the chimera walked by. "Jade can sense peoples' auras, each person is a colour to him, a feeling. For example, mine is white and silver, his is purple, silver, and black… yours is red and black."

Was that a good aura to have? Chimeras could be so cryptic at times.

"You and Garrett are quite the match." Elish raised a hand and nodded at a man dressed in a black suit, I realized the man was standing in front of a car. My heart jumped with excitement. I had only been out in Skyland once with Luca to pick up my medication. Apparently I had a stomach ulcer, I blamed that on Reaver.

"Match? He's like a matchmaker?"

That notion seemed to amuse Ice Man. We both got into the car and Elish immediately raised the divider. I pushed down my inner excitement of being in a car and getting to see more of this massive, populated city and tried to hang on his words. Everything that guy said meant something, Elish was not one to say meaningless things.

"Jade called himself the same, and I agreed with him. He's already joined my brother Joaquin with a stray. He can see two souls that can blend, Jade handpicked you when we were in Aras to be Garrett's pet. He saw no greater pairing. Garrett, my brother, is a docile, kind man, but he can be shy, and though he is the president of Skytech he can have rather low self-esteem. He is hard on himself. I think your… *charisma*… will help him come out of his shell. Once that happens, request to accompany him to his office. When you get time alone, and you know for certain you will not be discovered, find the keycard and the folder I need."

I furrowed my brow as my mind processed what he had said. Then something occurred to me. I stared at him for a moment. "When you took that photo of me last winter, was that for Garrett?"

Apparently I was the most amusing guy on the planet. He kept that sardonic little smile, enjoying every moment of my confusion. "Yes, it was. I made certain to have Lycos know I would be needing you in the future. He made sure to keep you out of harm's way after it was obvious you and Reaver would never be partners."

There was a quiver in my gut that I couldn't shake. A feeling that would come and go whenever I thought about Leo really being Lycos Dekker. It was such a bewildering realization, especially since I would've never expected it. Now I thought back at every interaction we've had with different glasses on. Leo threatening Killian with a gun suddenly made a lot of sense.

"You've been planning this for a long time, haven't you?" I asked, watching the shops and green trees pass by in a blur. All these people in one place, and colours too; I had never seen this many in once area except on TV and doing acid. I hoped I could go and explore a bit more under my new master. Elish had me tight under his thumb. I was too valuable for him to let me go out alone.

"Yes, down to the very last detail," Elish murmured, "for quite a long time."

When I saw what was obviously Garrett's skyscraper, I started to feel nervous, which was out of character for me. I felt my hands tense around my sides. I scraped my fingers over the leather and let out a breath.

"The remote phone is in your bag," Elish said. The car pulled to the front of the skyscraper and stopped. "Call me, or if I am out of range, as the greyrifts are testy, call Luca. I will be going back and forth between the greyrifts and Skyfall."

"Okay," I said breathlessly. My heart was starting to become a nervous hammer.

My eyes widened as I actually heard Elish let out a chuckle.

I looked over in shock and saw Elish's face moving in a muffled laugh. "You're a man who grew up with the most vicious of all of us, and your heart shakes for our most docile? I am looking forward to your thanks. If things happened differently I could have given you to Nero just to amuse myself."

I smirked at him and raised an eyebrow, feeling a brave need to challenge his laugh. "I bedded your master, don't forget that. I got him to like me."

With a casual smile and a flicker of Elish's purple eyes, he looked up at me. His cold visage mixing in with the amusement he'd had on his face the whole trip.

"Another reason why you are suited for this task."

We both got out of the car, and in a dizziness of excitement and nerves, I didn't even remember going through the lobby, or the elevator ride up to Garrett's top floor apartment.

But the moment I saw Garrett Dekker… that I remember.

I heard the rattling of chains as Elish led me with the leash attached to my collar. I walked down a maroon-coloured hallway to a large double door guarded by two thiens. As soon as they saw Elish, they opened the doors and stood back with a single bow.

Garrett was standing by the door, his hands to his sides and his eyes staring forward with curious fascination.

I had never seen anyone like him.

Garrett Dekker looked like he had walked out of the 50's, down to a black suit and a red tie. And even though he was an immortal of over ninety years, he looked to be in his early thirties. He had short wavy hair that was combed to the side in a gelled flip, and a pencil moustache. His face was classically handsome and expressive, his eyes most of all. They were light green and large, deep set, and brimming with inquisitive emotion.

I noticed right away his face brightened when he saw us. I might've passed the first test.

Elish stopped in front of him and they inclined their heads to each other, before Elish introduced us in a casual, but bemused, tone. "Garrett, this is Reno Nevada from Aras. Reno, this is your new master, Garrett Dekker, President of Skytech, and Councilman of Skyfall."

I watched as he handed my chain over to my new master. As his soft and rather well-manicured hands took my leash, he gave me a beaming smile.

"It's a pleasure to meet you, Reno." Garrett's voice was cheerful but I saw a flicker of anxiety in his eyes. I could tell he was nervous. It was practically painted on his face – it made him rather endearing. "Thank you, Elish. Is he vicious?"

I burst out laughing, to the probable chagrin of Elish. I turned to Ice Man and grinned at him. "You should've gotten me a muzzle, or a spiked collar or something. We could've planned a hilarious entrance for me.

Maybe put some foam on the edges of my lips? You missed a golden opportunity, Ice Man."

Elish, as usual, paid no attention to my jokes; his eyes turned to Garrett. "I have a shock collar you may borrow, but it will be needed for his humour rather than ferocity. The vicious nature of the greywasters has been exaggerated, at least with this one. He seems to believe he is quite funny."

Garrett smiled and I saw a row of pearly white teeth, all of them perfectly straight. My bottom teeth were all crooked and I was missing a back molar. I envied chimera teeth. I always had wondered why Reaver had lucked out so bad in the gene pool.

"I like him already; I always knew I would," Garrett said happily. "I know you're in a rush, Elish, I won't keep you. It's just wonderful to finally have him after so long of a wait. Thank you, brother, and do give Jade my best. Pity he's injured and ill again, those winters just ravage that poor boy's lungs."

"Yes, well, what do you expect from a boy raised in Moros?" Elish nodded with a look on his face that almost hinted a wish to be a fly on the wall once he left. "I will bring by his papers once you choose a name. Enjoy."

The door closed behind him, and for a moment, we both stared at it. I think we didn't know what to do next.

Because I still hated awkward silences I turned to him and smiled.

"Well then, show me where my food dish is." I leaned back until my leash chain got tight. "And I also hope you bought me some squeaky toys."

Garrett looked at me, a bewildered expression crossing his previously shy face.

Then he started to laugh. Immediately I felt the tense mood break away like a hammer through a glass window. My chest felt lighter and a smile rose to my lips.

Deep down I knew I was in. Garrett put his hand over his face to cover the outward expression of emotion, and started to walk away from me shaking his head.

Unfortunately both of us forgot I was leashed. As Garrett walked away from me the leash pulled and constricted my throat. I gagged and stumbled forward.

"Oh god… I'm sorry… let's get that stupid thing off of you." Garrett spun around. I was pleasantly surprised to see he felt bad. Empathy on a chimera? This was an interesting development, even the empath chimera seemed like a bit of a dick.

Garrett unhooked the leash with a transfixing smile and he motioned me towards the living room. "This is your apartment now. I don't have a sengil like Elish, I am quite independent. I borrow Luca a few times a week for cleaning, and I usually eat out, or with my bodyguard Saul."

I started to follow Garrett into the large open living room. It had a similar layout to Elish's and the same elegant and antique furniture, even down to the marble top coffee table and brown rug underneath. Everything was neat and tidy, but not obsessive like Elish's. There were magazines on the tables, pictures in frames, carved wooden and rock sculptures, and a lot of things I didn't recognize.

His theme was mostly brown and grey, which baffled me. If I was a chimera with a trillion dollars I would've decked this place out in like bright blues and purples, you know cool colours we didn't see in the greywastes. Maybe some glow in the dark things and lots of black lights. My place would be awesome.

"I go to work at around nine, I come back sometime between five, and well, eight I suppose. But I'll come back earlier rather than later from now on, since I actually have someone to come home to. I was debating taking some time off until you get comfortable too." Garrett turned and gave me a smile; his eyes were bright. "I have all the channels here on the TV, and I purchased you a GameCube, Jade just loves his. I also have liquor you can help yourself to that. Do you drink?"

I picked up a *Popular Science* magazine and put it back down on the shiny table surface. I chuckled.

"We're all alcoholic drug addicts in the greywastes," I said, the corner of my mouth rising in a smirk. "This shit is all way too good for me; you could put a blanket on the patio for me and I'd be happy. I'm less maintenance than a goldfish."

I walked up to the windows that stretched across the city and looked out with a shake of my head. The view was breathtaking and I never got bored looking at it.

"I'll do whatever needs to be done to keep you happy and comfortable."

I folded my arms over my chest, one of the windows was open and it was making the room a bit chilly. Elish's apartment was always kept nice and warm, since Jade was so skinny a gentle breeze probably made him shiver.

It got cold being so high up in the air. We were the twenty-something floor up in Skyland, skyscrapers breaking and restored all around us, rising up like trees, and the roads separating the buildings like rivers through a canyon. I wish I hadn't been so dazed during my plane trip, that would've been awesome to see.

I sighed, hearing a clinking of glasses behind me, though I didn't turn my gaze. The city stretched out far past my own vision, until the grey buildings were nothing but haze; some with lights that twinkled at night but a lot swallowed by the darkness. This city was like nothing I had ever seen, even in movies.

I couldn't believe I was here.

"I'll turn up the heat, it is rather cold tonight." I felt Garrett beside me. He reached over and pulled the window closed, before handing me a glass of brown liquor. "It'll be weird for the first few days, I know that… but liquor cures everything, right?"

This was my kind of guy. I took the tumbler from him and followed him to the couch. We both sat down beside each other, the TV on in the background. The brown couch was comfortable, a soft fabric that felt amazing against my bare skin.

"Did you have a nice trip then?" Garrett was staring at his glass; I could feel his nerves and anxieties biting away at him. I liked it though, it made me see him differently. The other chimeras had really given their family a bad name.

"I don't know." I couldn't contain the chuckle, I hid it with a drink of the liquor. It was rum and it burned my throat like I had swallowed fire. I liked it. "I was dazed out. I got shot in the gut, three times actually, but only one hit and another one just half-hit, kinda grazed my stomach."

With amusement, I watched as Garrett closed his eyes for a second. I could almost hear him calling himself an idiot. "Right, right, my apologies."

I shifted close to him. I realized I already didn't like seeing him sad. Was Jade's empath abilities really this accurate? I was a pretty easy sell though, I kind of fell for guys who were nice to me rather easily.

I reached my arm over and chinked my glass with his. "Why don't you take a couple days off? You can show me around town a bit. I literally have never been past Anvil; this place is mind fucking me right now. You would be the perfect guide for me. Just you know… bring a Frisbee for me or something, and a tennis ball."

Garrett laughed and clinked the glass back. "You are a funny little thing. I remember Elish saying you were funny, but I didn't know what I was expecting once you arrived."

"You have to have a sense of humour when your best friend is Reaver," I said with all too much honesty. Inside I felt the pull of longing for my friends, even though I was giving Reaver a jab, but I was doing this for him.

That gave me a bit of a nudge to put on the charm, but I was finding myself not forcing it nearly as much as I thought I would. This guy seemed alright. "So far you aren't like your brothers. You are actually nice."

Garrett looked up at the ceiling as if he didn't know what I was talking about, but when I smiled, he did too. I liked his smile. I could see it in his eyes, unlike Elish whose smiles seemed like a door to more sinister scary thoughts.

Ugh, fuck you, Elish; you were right, or at least your little empath pet was right.

"When you say Elish told you about me… when was that?" I asked.

Garrett swallowed a bit. I didn't think this was a loaded question but he seemed embarrassed by it. "Um, well, almost three years ago since he first… well, told me about you."

Holy crap, I've been being stalked for that long? "Three years? Wow, you've been waiting three years for me?"

"Almost… two more like it, I'm sure." Garrett's ears went red, which I thought was kind of adorable. "It seems outlandish, yes, but his pet said we… well…"

"We're a good match?" The embarrassment on Garrett's face made him look like he was in emotional agony. It was cute.

The suave chimera nodded slowly. “Yes, I well… I saw your photo, of you holding some man’s head. I loved that smile.”

My head blanked for a second before it slowly started processing again. Lycos had taken a photo of me for records. How did it end up in Elish’s… ugh, that chimera knew everything, what a stupid question. “Bridley? After Reaver killed him? Wow, I was just a little kidlet back then. Elish is some sort of mastermind, eh?”

The mood of embarrassment hovering over Garrett seemed to break; he chuckled and nodded. “You have no idea.”

I moved myself a bit closer and leaned over to pour us more alcohol. I heard Garrett mumble something under his breath, before a hand traced my scarred arms. “You’ve had a rough life, haven’t you?”

I paused, and out of reflex, I retracted my hand. The scar he was talking about was obviously from being tied at the wrist unwillingly. It had been from Bridley. I had been tied in his house for days, naked, covered in every body fluid available, broken and helpless.

“You probably already know what that’s from too,” I said quietly.

Garrett shook his head no. He poured the liquor for us instead and gave my wrist a sympathetic rub, then a smile so overflowing with kindness it made my heart swell.

Because I wanted to be a good pet, I decided to steer away from the solemn subject. I put on a smile and swallowed the horrible memory down with the liquor. A routine that was not new to me.

“So tell me, what does a pet of Garrett Dekker do? Because if you don’t tell me I’m just going to start meowing randomly and scratching your furniture.”

Another laugh, I felt relieved I had turned the conversation.

The alcohol gave me an excited prickle in my stomach. I was starting to like his attention towards me; he looked at me like I was the only guy in the universe. Usually it was Reaver or Killian getting all the attention, I was just well… Reno the friend. It wasn’t like I was neglected or anything, I loved my buds, but they had each other. I had never had a boyfriend. I was always, well, I had been waiting for Reaver to come around before Killian came in. Then I had held hopes for Asher, but we all know how that turned out.

“Well… nothing like you’ve seen between Elish and Jade.” Garrett tipped his glass for the clear decanter I was holding. There were three of them that sat nicely in the middle of his marble coffee table almost forming a flower. Each one was half-full with liquid, two brown ones and a white one. I was looking forward to trying them all. I hoped he wasn't against drugs because my body itched for them.

"You seem to already be rather social and delightful, so the training isn't needed. I'd rather have someone with some personality who doesn't just agree with everything I say."

"I completely agree with you," I said with an honest nod.

"Thank you… really, when Elish said–" Garrett stopped as his brain clicked together the joke I just made. He playfully jab me with his shoulder. "You are a funny one; I really was expecting someone…"

"Feral and untamed?"

Garrett gave a small nod of his head. He put his glass down and reached over to the coffee table. I saw he had a stack of playing cards.

I watched in amusement as he pulled up the table and started dealing me Crazy Eights. "Unless you're hiding a darker nature, you aren't what I expected which is… well, good." He dealt the rest and handed me the cards. I wondered how he knew this was my favourite game, but I remembered that Elish seemed to know everything about me. No doubt this guy had been briefed on me. I wondered what else he knew.

"If I can skip the bitey feral part, I will. Elish came to our council meetings more than once with a bites, scratches, and bruises. It was fun to tease him about them, especially the chimera love bites."

I laughed at the thought of Jade being ballsy enough to attack Elish, and picked up my cards. "I like biting, so… don't skip too many steps."

That night after many drinks and many games of Crazy Eights, we both sat with our cards in hand playing Crazy Sevens. Why? Because screw you that's why, we were drunk as hell.

I slammed my card down, a jack of spades, but it fell off of the couch. I tried to get it up but I gave up after about three seconds.

Garrett laughed; his green eyes glassy. He leaned down instead and put the card on the table, before reaching his hand out to gently take the rest of my cards from me. "I think we should go to sleep before we pass out right here."

I agreed and rose to my feet, I stretched and yawned before I lost my balance and stumbled.

Garrett caught me and kept me steady. We had been talking for hours by now and I felt completely comfortable around him. The entire night I hadn't seen a single hint of malice in his handsome face, every smile was melting my heart.

"I like you." I looked up at him and poked him in the shoulder; he started walking me towards my bedroom.

The chimera, suave and classic in his little 50's niche, gave me a full smile back. "I like you, when you smile it's like you're a little otter."

Then in a bold impulse, fuelled by liquor and drunk-induced loneliness, I leaned in to kiss him.

Garrett's face turned. I recoiled back with my face flushing and pulled away from him. My ears went hot with embarrassment. I felt like an idiot.

He grabbed my hand and pulled me back with a playful protest. "Not with us so drunk. I won't sell you short." He smiled. His finger traced my lip. In that moment, the way he looked at me, I thought he was going to kiss me anyway. But with chimera restraint, he only rubbed the corner of my lip before he led me to my bedroom.

"Can I sleep next to you though?" Garrett hovered in the doorway after I had walked in and taken off my slippers. "Clothes on. I'm too drunk to attempt to change."

I beckoned him over with a sloppy wave, and flopped down on the bed. "Alright, but I'm too drunk for covers. Come 'ere."

I was in, I was in his pocket. I was doing everything Elish asked… and so far I couldn't be happier.

God damn, Jade might be on to something here.

Garrett laid down next to me and he turned the light out. I felt his hand slip into mine, and that was the last thing I remembered.

CHAPTER 6

Reaver

THAT COLD VOIDED DARKNESS. THE KIND THAT burned with fire whenever I drew an invisible hand out to touch it, like lava before it had been cooled to shining obsidian. It was all over me, wrapping its ethereal self around the glowing white core with the comfort of a blanket.

But it constricted, the void tensed and retracted until it coated my dead frame like a full-body mask, my muscles spasming and twitching with pain that made me scream in agonizing tones I didn't know my voice carried.

The fire became smouldering, but it still remained; it burned in my throat and seared away the saliva. I could feel the skin of my mouth slough off and fall to my tongue. I attempted to swallow but it was a piece of meat trying to slide down sand paper.

Time did not exist in this excruciating limbo, I had accepted many times in my torment that this was eternity, but in the next moment I was screaming and taunting death that he would never have me.

Then an icy chill, the first notion of temperature, a sensation I had all but forgotten. In the next moment, or perhaps the next year, I did not know, I felt the slow thrum of my heartbeat. A desperate low beat at first, but the longer I listened the stronger it got. It beat to a tune of a song I never heard, but every time I heard it, it seemed like an old friend greeting me on a sun bleached porch.

With a hand out stretched, I reached out my own; he laughed and pulled it back. I wasn't invited, not this time.

The man smiled, and as he did the corners of his eyes creased. He looked back at the house and said something to me, in a voice I had been hearing since the day he pulled me out of my artificial womb.

I opened my eyes.

I was staring at a wall of deep brown, with a warm incandescent light illuminating the room. It smelled wrong, and it looked wrong. Everything around me; what I felt, what I smelled, and what I saw, was alien.

The engine in my brain struggled to turn over; I felt a prick of anxiety and confusion as I tried to raise myself. This place smelled like the things in it. An odd way to say it, but that's how my mind processed it. I could smell the mattress, the bed, the lamp… in my basement I smelled myself, I smelled damp, gyprock, and cigarettes. I smelled the greywastes. This place was new; it wasn't touched by over two hundred years of rot and decay. It was… Skyfall.

I tried to sit up. I felt sounds around me but they were a garbled audio, a broken tape. I shifted my body so I was sitting up. The room spun.

"Reaver, love, stay laying."

I heaved my body up at that voice. My eyes fixed on the image, and as I stared, he came into focus.

Killian.

A deep and unsettling feeling built up inside me, filling my dry mouth with bitter liquid. The boy was giving me the softest, most relieved of smiles, but past his facade of calm I saw his fear. Behind the cut sapphire eyes I saw the stitched railroad tracks in his hairline and lips, crisscrossing like a crack through marble. With it, I also took in the fading bruises on his face, neck, and any place his shirt didn't cover. Like spots of black mould I saw them, healing but still prominent, still breaking up the white.

My eyes squinted, trying to erase such an uncomfortable realization from my groggy mind. When I opened them again, I heard a different voice.

Like a homing device, my eyes immediately shot to the direction of the voice. They focused like a scope and pulled him into view.

The pet! I felt my eyes blaze, my head lowered and my teeth started to grind together.

"Jade… Jade, get out of here," Killian's voice said hurriedly. I felt hands on my chest trying to push me back into a laying position. "Reaver… Reaver, it's okay. We're at Elish's."

"Don't tell him that!" Jade eyed me nervously. He stood his ground, but as soon as I swung a foot off of the bed, he turned and ran.

The prey started to run.

My eyes tracked him and immediately my brain told me to pursue. He was my only tie to the fucks that had killed my fathers and captured my boyfriend and myself.

The pet was toast.

I shot to my feet ignoring the hand that grabbed my arm in desperation. I found a snarl rim my lips as I yanked my arm away and burst out of the room.

My eyes scanned the area like a computer trying to recognize its location. I caught a flicker of black out of my eye and felt another rumbling growl move the back of my throat. I put my hands to my pants to try and grab my combat knife, only to realize I wasn't wearing anything but boxer shorts.

No matter, I'll choke him. I'll rip his windpipe out with my hands.

"Reaver! No!" I heard Killian scream. He grabbed my arm again.

The swirl of intense emotion filled my head with burned anger, but when boiled down my mind knew I was acting out of fear and confusion. But what faint trickles of realization I could hold onto slipped through my hands. All I felt was unhinged anger and the need to take it out on the people who hurt me, and killed my family.

And it was that anger that made me grab Killian and throw him to the floor.

With my shoulders hunched over and my chest heaving, I stalked towards where I had last saw the pet. I ran up the steps two by two and into a hallway with four doors, all of them open but one.

The black oil of violent emotions filled itself in every crevice of my mind. Ignoring the yelling around me, I threw my weight against the door.

It broke open and slammed against the wall with a deafening crack. I immediately heard frantic commotion, flickers of black and white, and a thick fear so intoxicating I stood there for a moment to drink from it.

The black pet. Dressed in fresh leather and a tight shirt, with ebony hair that shined against opal skin. He was cowering in a closet, his eyes wide in terror-stricken consternation. His heartbeat was a hammering in his chest, his body trembling like a leaf caught in a breeze. Oh, the fear made my chest prickle with electricity. My mind filled with dark, disturbing thoughts that would later on unsettle even my desensitized head.

When I opened the door I felt his fear ravage my insides. I grabbed him without care and whispered a word to him I didn't understand. In response, he thrashed like a stray cat being picked up by the scruff, and he howled like one too.

I dragged him out of the closet, but as I threw him onto the bed his pointed teeth found my arm. He sank them in and pulled out a chunk of flesh.

I backhanded him hard. He cried and fell onto the floor, a mist of blood staining the grey carpet underneath him. I slammed a foot against his back and picked him up by the collar. Without an ounce of restraint, I dragged him through the hallway. He was kicking, screaming, and howling words that became garbled under his panic; the room around us an eruption of activity but my eyes only focusing on the knife block.

I withdrew a cleaver and looked at it with a smile on my face. The shrieking around me melted into a pool of nothingness. I saw my own eyes through the flat mirrored side of the knife.

I was a demon; I was a Reaper back from the dead. My eyes were onyx pits, framed by loose strands of black hair that had been twisted into oiled locks. My face was grey, my lips tinged white, and behind the black slabs of coal, I saw nothing but my own madness.

I looked up at the boy I was about to butcher like a rat. I hadn't even noticed I was holding him off of the ground by the collar. I saw his hands grasping and clawing at his neck to try and get breath, his eyes wide and bugging out of his face, burning yellow spheres.

I gave his collar a twist, cutting off even more air flow. I shuddered as I felt his fear soak into my skin; an intoxicating almost tangible feeling like the last minute before an orgasm. Only his hot rushing blood would bring me to my peak.

Then, like a lightning strike, a jolt of incomprehensible pain ripped through me. My hands snapped open and I dropped the knife and the boy, who fell to the ground with a scream.

I whirled around, and out of my throat came a snarl I would more likely hear on an animal than myself. I focused on the blond man I recognized.

A chimera… I was surrounded by chimeras.

"Reaver, gather yourself. You're–"

I grabbed another knife and stalked towards him, my eyes looking up from under my brow. I was going to cut his hands off, cleave his pet's head from his body and sew it into his fucking stomach. What would chimera flesh taste like? I would dine on him.

But no… he was immortal; he would come back.

I needed blood that would stay dead, that would rot.

So when something grabbed me, grabbed the arm that was holding the knife, I whirled around, balled my fist and punched them right in the face.

The person fell, and I heard a gut-wrenching scream that snapped me from my morbid reverie, erasing the snapping jaws of a confused insanity I couldn't control.

My eyes turned with my body as I saw him kneeling behind me, holding his mouth, which was dripping blood. A sight that even the indistinct taunting of the dark shadows could not turn me from.

Killian's eyes were wide open in shell-shock. It was the exact expression I had seen on his face before I had died. Those deep blue eyes, the kind of blue you don't see in this world, unfocused, staring into the abyss; seeing something of such untold horror all he could do was scream in response. It was the look of someone who had just suffered the concussions of a reality his mind could no longer handle.

I dropped the knife and fell to my knees, not believing what I had just done. I had hit him; I had just hit my own boyfriend.

"Killi…?" I whispered.

He burst into tears and tried to shuffle away from me, but with every movement he made I shifted closer, wanting nothing more than to hold him and take the pain away, the pain I had caused.

I didn't know what was going on, or where I was… all I knew is he was hurting and once again it was my fault.

"Don't cry," I whispered to him. I reached out a hand to brush the blond strands from his eyes but I hesitated. In the same breath, I was taken back to the night in his bedroom, when he was screaming from a night terror. I found myself shying away, feeling like I had never touched him before.

"You're dead." Killian's voice was a whisper of agonizing loss, a strained tone that told of an inner struggle to even force himself to say those words. "You're not you anymore."

"I'm not dead." I pushed down the confusion and madness and touched his hair, then felt the warmth of his soft face against my hand. "I'm here, I'm me. I'm okay."

Slowly, trying not to scare him further, I drew him into my arms. I felt his frame shudder as I pulled him into me, and a small noise of relief. I closed my eyes and rested a hand on the back of his head. I held him in my arms, his quick heartbeat threatening to burst through his chest and into mine.

I heard the voice of Elish behind me, then the mumbled response of the pet. After Killian's heart had started to slow, I pulled away from him and wiped the blood from his mouth. He gazed up at me and I felt him search my face for any signs of hostility.

"Where are we?" Elish was here, the pet was here. Where the pet was, the master was, and if you followed the chain of leashes eventually you found Silas.

"Elish saved us. He helped Leo disappear with you. He's on our side; he hid us in the greyrifts." I felt him grip my sides as if he expected me to lose it again. "We're safe, I'm safe. Please don't hurt them."

My mind was still trying to uncoil the rat's nest of information, but emotion-wise inside of me was a cold lake of calm, a still winter night with ice just freezing the edges of the frigid moonlit water.

I stood, and he stood with me. I kept my arms around him as I watched Elish slowly remove the pet's collar, a ring of chafed red around his neck. The pet looked stunned into an almost stupor.

I felt a lump in my throat, a growing painful burr that grew as I scanned the room. It was only those two.

"They shot Reno!" Killian's voice was a strangled sob, breaking with every octave it climbed.

I tried to swallow, but the lump in my throat turned to ice. Everything was different now. Nothing smelled right; Killian didn't even smell right but I knew that wasn't his fault. It was like I had woken up in the *Twilight Zone* or something, maybe a different dimension.

"If this show is over and done with, please accompany–" Elish's voice was annoyed and biting, but how he felt right now was far from the realms in which I gave a fuck.

Without another word, I took Killian's hand and pulled him into the first bedroom I saw. I slammed the door and grabbed a duffle bag I recognized.

"Help me pack the bag… we have to leave," I said to Killian. My eyes shot in all directions looking for the door out of this place. I had already lost Reno; I couldn't lose the last person I had. I had lost everything; I had lost my life, literally and figurative.

"No! We can't," Killian's voice wobbled but I could tell he was trying to keep it steady. "We have to stay here, it's safe."

Wait for Silas to get me? What was this? A catch and release? My eyes tried to take in every strange and new object in this room. If I hadn't spent time in Donnely I would be even more taken aback but I was used to seeing new architect, electronics, and furnishings around me.

"Don't question this, Killian." I raised my voice. He shrunk away. I could hear Elish and Jade's muffled talking behind the closed door. "That blond-haired fuck is Silas's chimera; he's his second-in-command. He's going to fucking hand-deliver us to Silas. Are you fucking delusional?"

"He saved us, Reaver. He saved my life."

"To take all the credit himself… he could have warned us that the deal was going to go sour. He could've told Greyson that Silas was in that plane. Greyson, Leo, and Reno's blood are all on his hands."

Killian's hand lightly rested on my shoulder. "Elish left with Reno, to get him medical attention in Skyfall, far away from Silas. He left to save Reno's life. He was still alive, Reaver, Elish even rescued Biff."

"He's lying," I growled.

"He had cat hair on his shirt when he came back. He described him to me, hun!" Killian put his arms around me and sniffed. "Please, just calm down… let Elish explain it to you. You knew him before as James, right? Doesn't it make sense now? He's been in on it the entire time."

The prospect of trusting him filled my chest with malice, every shred of my hatred for Silas and the chimeras seemed focused on him.

But I couldn't ignore what Killian was saying.

He squeezed me, his hands still wrapped around my side and clasped around my chest. I heard a sniff and then felt his head rest against my shoulder. "I missed you… I missed you so much."

I turned around and we embraced, and the first trickle of warmth started to flow into my heart. I had missed him too, even in the voided darkness where only the white flickering flame could be seen. I had missed the touch I had once recoiled from.

"How long have we been here for?" I whispered, inhaling his scent, the soap smell he still had on him. Though that was no surprise, he smelled clean and this place was clean. All of it was neurotically clean, unlike my dirty basement.

"Over a week. Your throat had been ripped out… I've been here with Jade, Perish, and Elish. Elish has been running back and forth to Skyfall. Silas is resurrecting now, Elish says it will still be several weeks before he's back. He got massacred by the deacons."

I pulled away looking puzzled, even though my brain had automatically assumed he would come back, I remembered what Greyson had said to me.

–before they killed him.

I pushed that reminder down, and looked at Killian confused. "Greyson said only I could kill him… I killed him I ripped his throat out. Shouldn't he be staying dead?"

"It is not that simple," a voice said behind me. I turned around and saw Elish in the doorway, his pet beside him with a red welt appearing on his neck. "As I was trying to say, before you decided to brutalize your boyfriend and attempted to murder my pet, we are overdue for a talk. Shower yourself and eat something. When you are done, we will be meeting in my office."

My brain told me to challenge this patronizing attitude he seemed to have, but I held myself back and kept my mouth shut. I knew enough of

Elish Dekker, or James as he had been when I had met him a couple times in Aras, to know this was his character. Any other reaction would be odd for him.

"Where are we? Are we in Skyfall?" I said, not hiding my own cooled tones in my voice. I wasn't going to just lie down and show this chimera my belly. Leo's ally or not, he was a chimera.

"No, we are a four hour Falconer trip from Skyfall, hundreds and hundreds of miles inland," Elish replied. "Not a soul knows you're here. They are looking for you in the blacksands currently, though since it is me hedging the search, the party consists of three recruits and an elderly deacdog."

"Deek is here too, Reaver." Killian pulled on my hand. He had a faint smile on his face though his cheek where I had hit him was already starting to swell. "And he likes them."

"He liked Silas too."

Killian's face fell. I think he had forgotten that that stupid retard liked anyone and everything; he was a shit guard dog. "But he grabbed Biff, and he got your M16… and look, all your ammo is in your pockets. Love, if he wanted to hurt us he would have… please… come have a shower and we can sit down with him."

I didn't want to sit down with him, I wanted some cigarettes, drugs, booze… something to help me handle this cold new reality that had been unwillingly thrust upon me, but until I demanded drugs I would clean myself off, like the boy had suggested.

"This chat can wait for tomorrow, right now I need to get my head back," I said to Elish, who was still standing beside the doorway with his pet beside him.

The cold chimera nodded. "I suspected as much. Killian knows where the food is if you become hungry. You will be left alone."

And he left, not a protest on his lips or a veiled threat. I had to give him that small plus at least.

I soaped my hair three times and scrubbed every orifice of my body. After I stepped out I noticed my cargo pants and shirt and a pair of underwear all folded nicely. If Killian ever had to become a pet he certainly wouldn't be doing much different.

I smelled my cargo pants; they smelled like more soap, this house must be Killian's dream. I put them on and buttoned them, feeling my pockets I realized everything was still there, down to my grenade. My pistol was here and even my combat knife. The boy had been right; the chimera hadn't disarmed me.

Being armed made me feel better, but in the shower I'd had time to calm down my suspicions and try and make sense of this situation. If we were indeed prisoners of Elish there would be a hell of a lot more precautions being taken, and he certainly wouldn't have left his beloved animal where I could get to him. That kid had hung off of his arm when they had visited Aras.

But who I was still ruled with an iron fist inside of me. It took a lot of mental energy to silence the alarm bells telling me to take Killian and run. In my head I wanted to get as far away from this lions' den as I could, no matter what waited for us in the greywastes. Take our chances with the rocks and radanimals instead of seemingly waiting for my captors to come.

If I didn't have Killian I would have done that, but… I had him to watch out for.

I would hear Elish out… and base my decision on that meeting. He wasn't my captor, and I wasn't his prisoner. I was a greywaster, not a chimera pet or a sengil. I could leave if I wanted to and he couldn't stop me.

I opened the door, fully clothed, and walked into the living room and kitchen.

Killian was waiting for me at the end of the hallway; I saw two needles in his hand. I walked with him and he took me to what I guessed was his bedroom downstairs, the one I had woken up in.

I laid down on the bed and felt him prep my arm; I took a deep relieved breath as I felt the pinch of the needle. I hated how much I was liking doing drugs this way; I had never cared for needles before.

The rush was unbelievable; I let out a small groan and closed my eyes. I wondered why this was hitting me so nicely, then I remembered I hadn't done drugs in over a week.

When Killian was injected I felt him lay beside me. I put my arms around him and held the boy close to my chest.

"I missed you so much," Killian whispered. I heard him sniff and I braced myself for the tears. "I'm not scared here. Elish has been so kind to me, and Jade and Perish too. I don't know what's going on but it could be so much worse."

I inhaled the scent of his hair; he was slowly starting to smell familiar. That mixed in with the drugs almost had me feeling like I was home.

I would go back there eventually and take what is mine. I'm Greyson's son, I own Aras and if I have to execute every single fucking person in there, I'll get it back. I would love nothing more than to kill all of them and start fresh. Either way, they wouldn't get away with how they treated Killian and Reno. They were all fucking cowards. I would burn them all.

It was mine to take. Even if it took years, I would take back my town.

"Ouch… babe." Killian flinched. I realized I was gripping him rather hard. I released my hands. I felt him shift up, before my cheek warmed under his breath. "I'm so happy you're awake, I felt lost without you."

I closed my eyes, enjoying the warmth of the heroin seep into every nook and cranny of my mind, slowly unfolding the wrinkles in my brain one by one making it into a puddle of soup. In the embrace of the drugs I felt a small flame of confidence that perhaps we weren't as screwed as I thought. If I had Elish in my corner maybe he would just stick us in a cabin in the mountains, or we could stay here. I wouldn't mind that. I might go a bit psychotic if it was just Killian and I but… well, maybe we could adopt a pet. Killian could be that guy's friend.

No, I hated that idea… I didn't want to live in peace now, not until I could kill Silas and his creatures, not until I got Aras back. Then… then we could just go home.

My heart stirred… but if it meant Killian and I would be safe forever… isn't that what my dads wanted? For me to be happy and safe? But so much has changed now. And from the hollowness in my gut, I think inside I changed. Could I toss out my need for revenge for a simple life with him?

Who was I kidding… I suppressed a dry laugh. Elish hadn't rescued us to give us a better life. That blond douchebag had plans for me; one look at that imperious face told me that if you shook that arm, half a dozen aces would fall out.

Should I be a sitting duck waiting to see if a dog would emerge to retrieve me… or do I take the kid and run?

Run where?

Winter is here. The fucking boy doesn't even have a proper jacket; he'll freeze to death the first night.

My grip tightened, I swore in my head. I hated feeling trapped and helpless. Elish was a chimera; he was Silas's right-hand man. How did I know this wasn't another fucking game?

I really should've talked to Elish that night. I was an idiot for blowing smoke in his face. In that moment Greyson had just given me some disturbing news and I was feeling, well… a lot of self-hatred and the arrogance got to my head. I should've fucking talked to him; he might've given some sort of sign that he was going to be on my side.

Well, there was no time to feel sorry for myself. That angsty fuck died when the deacon ripped out his throat. I was the Reaper. I am amongst the elite and I had to act like it now. My top priority was making sure Killian was safe. At all costs. My fate wasn't a concern of mine; he was my only priority.

So we would stay here. I squeezed Killian and kissed his ear. Until his dying day I'd protect him. I would make another Fallocaust and kill everyone all over again if it meant he was safe.

"I'll never let them hurt you," I whispered to him. "You need to promise me, if they try and take me, you'll run. Shoot anyone who tries to take you. Promise me and mean it."

Killian shifted, I saw his eyes were red and swollen. They gazed at me. "I won't let them take you."

I brushed a lock of golden hair from his eyes. "Idiot, I'm immortal… I'll find you. They won't be able to keep me caged and they won't be able to kill me. I'll spend every waking moment trying to get back to you. We wouldn't be apart for long."

I felt him shudder underneath my touch. I rubbed his back. "Don't worry, I'll protect you. You know I will."

Those words stung my lips. I meant them, with every ounce of strength inside of me I meant them. But I knew the cards; I saw the hand I was holding. Elish had us right now, I was under his control and I didn't like it. Every bit of this situation made me feel like I was walking between razor blades. I had to tread carefully and be careful. I couldn't blow up at Elish; I needed to be patient. I had to gather information and see what was happening.

Everything was weaving together in a way that made me uncomfortable. I didn't want to be patient… I didn't want to wait it out. I felt like a tiger pacing his cage. How could I sit like I was on a fucking vacation? It was in my blood to rush in and get things resolved, do what had to be done. If I had been patient rescuing Killian, he would've been resting on some waster's shelf right now.

What would you do, Greyson…? I pushed the rising feelings of despair back into the hollow void. Greyson would've done what he had to do to keep his family safe. Like he had kept me safe all those years. He had put aside his dreams for me for my happiness. I didn't have a son, but I had a boyfriend.

Fuck… all those things Greyson and Leo had sacrificed for me, to keep me safe. I shut my eyes tighter and dared even a single neuron to make me feel something. I was a machine, I am the Reaper… *shit, shit, shit,* I can't deal with those two right now. I can't deal with what happened in Aras, I can't…

Why did I treat those two so badly the last few months I had them?

I wanted more heroin… but I didn't want to move. Instead I tried to shut down my mind, and enjoy the fleeting moments of comfort.

If Elish took me, if he offered Killian's safety I would take it. I meant what I had said to Killian, I would never stop trying to come back to him, and I would… I was smarter than Asher. He might think he was king but he had competition now. If I was him, if I was his copy, it meant I was as good as him and more. If he wanted to match wits with me and try and enslave me in Skyfall, he had another thing coming.

I felt myself slip into zombieland. Every time I surfaced from my dream world I smelled Killian and felt myself get lulled back into a half-sleep. I think the both of us needed this, especially him. He liked the contact and all that stuff, I was happy just having him near me.

In my lucid dreams I was killing Silas, no… he was Asher at this moment, his hair was still auburn. It was Asher in his greywaster clothes, the same clothes he wore when we got away from those ravers that night.

The night air was so prominent I could feel the cool taste on my tongue. So static and alive, buzzing with activity. The gut-piercing screams, the rush of being knocked off the bike and into the inky darkness around you. The smell of the dirt, the taste of blood…

I shook my head and dashed the memory from my mind. We were never in any danger really; we would both have come back. Greyson and Leo would've hid my corpse until I recovered and Silas would eventually have recovered in whatever mess of tendon and bone the ravers left behind.

Though they would've had to tell Killian, and perhaps the residents who saw it happen, or smuggle me out.

I wonder how many times I had died.

My brow furrowed. I pulled away and looked at Killian who was nodding off from his own hit of heroin. "Rubber fucking bullets… what an asshole."

The boy blinked at me and gave me a strange look; I just shook my head and sighed. How could I have been that stupid to believe that lie? Like the legionary carried around rubber bullet guns.

They had probably had a fine time bludgeoning me in the head to make it seem believable.

I kissed Killian's forehead, before drawing him close to me. I would hold him all night tonight, and I wouldn't push him away, even after he fell asleep.

Tomorrow was going to be a long day, this I knew.

The next morning I was up before Killian, which allowed me to scout out this strange base I was in. It seemed to be an apartment carved right out of the side of a mountain. The view was incredible, I could see for miles though all there was to see was the grey terrain and the black trees. Still though, it was amazing to be up this high, and safe too.

I had found the coffee pot and had put some on for everyone; I even managed to heat up food in the microwave, which was a plus. I'd leave the real cooking for the slavepet though, I just needed something in my stomach.

I was chewing on a piece of hard bread I had found, trying to get the remote control to work when I saw the deacdog perk up from his bed and look behind him.

I looked behind me too, and saw someone I never thought I would see again.

"You're a fugitive too, eh?"

Perish froze in place, he was still dressed in his underclothes and had an expression like he hadn't expected me to be here.

He took one look at me and turned around, but I think he changed his mind because he then turned right back around to face me.

"I'm sorry," Perish stammered.

I stared at him, wondering what he had to be sorry about. I liked that he was scared though, he *should* be submitting to me.

"What are you sorry for?" I swallowed down the bread and ripped myself off another piece.

Perish fidgeted, his eyes shifting from one direction to another. "I decided to tell you, so Killian didn't get the chance. He was asleep, and he was having a night terror… I tried to help him but I ended up kissing him. Killian screamed and got very very mad and barricaded himself. It's my fault, I'm sorry. I just so much missed him but… it won't ever happen again."

A cold frost swallowed up the casual air that the morning brought. I listened to the scientist's heart as it sped up like a revving motor, terrified at what I was going to do next.

I got up, and as I did he flinched. I walked into the kitchen.

"I don't know what came over me. I think… I think seeing him so scared. I just wanted…"

Perish was silent as he saw me grab a long knife from the knife block. When I turned around, I was almost surprised to see him still standing. He hadn't run like his ass was on fire yet.

"I'm… I'm–"

I grabbed Perish by the collar of his shirt and yanked him to my face.

"What makes you think you're allowed to touch my boyfriend now? My boyfriend, not yours, he was never yours." I lowered my voice, feeling his pulse jump like I had just injected meth into his heart.

His eyes continued to veer away from mine, but every time they did I jerked my hand and shook his chin, making him look at me.

"Nothing, it was… a personality fault. I understand he was never mine… but I miss him," Perish stammered.

I lowered the knife, and pressed the tip of the blade across the crotch of his cloth pants. He inhaled a sharp breath as I put a fair amount of pressure against it.

"If I ever catch you, or I think you are a danger to him… do you know what I will do to you? I will cut off your cock and balls and make you eat them. Then I will bandage you, sew you, and make you heal and I will never fucking let you die again. Understand that, Dr. Perish?" I said lowly, digging the blade in further until I felt it pierce the skin.

The scientist nodded. "Y-yes… I am… very scared of you, Reaver. I won't piss you off, I'm not stupid."

I nodded too, and as I withdrew the knife he let out a gasp and clutched his bleeding groin with his hands. I lowered the blade and took a step back.

"We have been more than kind to you, considering everything you did to us. I suggest you don't take my kindness for weakness, Perish."

"I won't."

I nodded and placed the knife on the side table beside me, the scientist rubbing his groin which now had a spot of blood forming on it. A part of me was tempted to cut it off anyway. If he had no reason to use it, why did he need it?

Instead I went back to my bread, enjoying the racing heartbeat and the nervous movements coming from him. "Why are you here anyway? I thought you wanted to go be with your master."

Cautiously Perish got up and walked past me, though he made sure to keep his distance. He made himself a cup of coffee and sat down on one of the chairs in the living room.

"I had to protect Killian, and when they were leaving Elish told me to come. I've been here ever since. Elish says they think I am with you two in the blacksands," the scientist replied. "I am going to go with you when we leave."

Leave? Couldn't be soon enough, but where it was I didn't know, and I wasn't going to ask him. I wanted it right from the source.

"I saw you with your arms shielding Killian. If you hadn't gone groping him afterwards you might've gained some brownie points with me," I replied, lighting a cigarette. "But I meant what I said, Perish… if you dare go near him again–"

Perish paled. He gripped his coffee cup harder and gave me a slight nod. "I won't, I won't."

I nodded back and blew the smoke out of the corner of my mouth.

A half an hour later Jade emerged, and behind him came Killian out of the shower. The pet started banging around in the kitchen, so I sat on the couch with Killian on my lap.

"You slept so quietly, not a single twitch." I handed him my coffee cup, smelling the shampoo in his hair. He seemed to look healthier; he had been eating well at least.

"Elish gave me medication to stop my night terrors. Jade is on it too; he has them as well," Killian whispered, though I saw Jade out of the corner of my eye watching him. I assumed he also had super chimera hearing.

"Well, you're not clawing my face off, that's a nice change," I murmured, taking a drink for myself. "When does Elish usually get up? I want to know just what is supposed to happen."

"I am already awake." I looked behind me and saw the chimera with the long blond hair, emerging from the doorway where his bedroom was. He was putting on his white gloves, his fancy chimera cape slung over his back.

He looked at me, and raised an eyebrow.

"You're looking better, or at least the crazed glint has faded from your eyes." His voice was always so cold and imposing, like woven ribbons of ice that set off a foreboding presage in my brain. I didn't trust this creature; his purple eyes had not even the flicker of emotion, and even worse his heartbeat was a steady drum. Not a single beat out of sync. This man's body language was a language I couldn't read and it was frustrating. But on the same note, every part of him that made me on edge and uncomfortable only meant he would be a formidable ally. I would rather join him than have to beat him.

"I'm feeling better, now that I have some caffeine and drugs in me," I said, keeping my voice a level tone. "Impressive place you have here."

Elish looked at me for a moment, the cold temperance steeling every feature on his face. A moment later, he gave me a nod and said to Jade in the kitchen: "Keep breakfast warm for us, Cicaro. Reaver, it is time we speak in private."

I nodded back and let him walk past me towards the second hallway further on. He was wearing a high-collared black button-down trimmed with a single strip of gold, and a flowing cape of the same colours. I could smell a fragrant almost spice smell to him and his clothing. It looked like this guy jumped out of one of the books Killian was always forcing me to read. If this guy had marched into Aras I would have thought someone had spiked my water with acid.

Elish flicked open a keypad that was attached to his bedroom door, and pressed in several numbers. I heard a hiss and a mechanical whine before he reached a white-gloved hand and opened the door.

I followed the blond chimera down the carpeted flight of stairs which led me to a large open room.

In front of us was a den combined with an office, and to my left were the doors leading to the bedrooms, including the one I woke up in, and a bathroom.

The office had a large wooden desk at the far end which had papers, books, and pens all obsessively organized with labels, colours, and small wooden bins. Behind the desk a tall and comfortable-looking computer chair, and further still, three filing cabinets. Everything around us was framed by four gyprock walls painted a silver white, all adorning different pieces of art.

I walked onto an embroidered rug which centered the room and tried to take it all in. The shelves on the far end caught my eye the most. They were full of books and objects I had never seen before but looked pre-Fallocaust. I could even spot several metal appliances with the sheen and smell that only new or well-preserved machines had. The kid in me wanted to run towards them and start taking them apart to see how they worked but I refrained, even though I thought I saw an espresso maker.

My gaze turned when I saw Elish take a seat on the office chair; he motioned for me to pull up a seat as well. I glanced to a row of several fabric chairs resting beside an empty fish tank and pulled one up.

I thought Elish was organizing a black folder, but when he opened it up and pressed a button I realized it was a laptop.

I had never seen one of those before. I stared at it almost feeling enchanted by the flickering screen as it booted. Computers were almost impossible to fix, laptops especially. This was probably the first and most likely last one I would ever see.

I sat there with my legs crossed, not moving and not talking as Elish clicked away on the laptop. A thousand burning questions were in my mind, but not a single one I was willing to offer up to break the cold silence between us. I would not speak first; he had called me down here to talk to me. I couldn't put into words why, all I knew is I couldn't blow this first real meeting between the two of us.

It was ten minutes of him tapping on the keyboard before he closed it with a small click. In that time I made myself used to his presence and the presence of the room. Though Elish had an air about him that made me feel like I was walking a razor's edge, I recover quickly. I would not make the same mistake twice. Meeting this chimera face-to-face had appealed to my reason and I knew what cards I had. Acting like a petulant teenager wasn't going to bring me anything but embarrassment. My fathers didn't die for me to spit in the face of the only man who could save me and my boyfriend.

"You are different than the snarling monster who awoken last night." Elish's eyes flickered from a beige file folder he was holding up to my own eyes. "Did your boyfriend calm you?"

"I am not the crazy beast you met those years in Aras, the one who attacked your boyfriend," I said soberly. I fixed my eyes on his and controlled every last twitch in my body. "I need no one to keep me calm, any normal person waking up to a chimera looming over him would react the same way. I am just more skilled to inflict harm than most."

A small smile raised the corner of his lips, though his eyes were still cold. "Indeed you are. You are an immortal chimera, with more enhancements and abilities than all of our brothers. You are indeed a ruthless killer, aren't you, Reaver?"

I realized in this moment I was talking to Elish for the first time, not James the traveller, or the blond chimera with Ares and Siris behind him. Real Elish, who had hidden me in the greywastes with Lycos; who had raised me with a goal in mind.

Silas's assassin.

"I am a killer, but I am no one's pawn, Elish. Silas's clone or not."

A sardonic smile spread across his lips. I had once thought he could never smile and now I wished he still didn't.

"Let us clear one thing up while we are alone, Reaver," Elish said in a casual way that made my eyes narrow.

"You are not just Silas's clone. We made you better than just a mere copy of an insane man."

I stared at him and raised an eyebrow. "You mean the chimera enhancements and all of that?"

Elish nodded. "Not just that though. You have a lot of the same characteristics and even physical features of a man who was King Silas's beloved. A man named Sky Fallon. Your hands, ears, nose, and *other places* were derived from what strands of his DNA we could recover from his O.L.S. You are subsequently a hybrid of the two of them. Silas's makeup but with a nice dusting of Sky's traits… enough to drive King Silas into insanity over not having you as his very own."

I stared at him for a moment. I didn't know how I felt about this. I didn't know who the hell Sky was. I had only heard mention of a boyfriend during my drinking nights with Asher. I didn't know who the fuck this guy was or even why he offed himself.

"So I am Silas's clone but you decided to be mean and create me as–"

"–as Silas's perfect partner. That is the reason Silas wanted to make you, to be his and only his for all eternity."

"Why not just create a clone of Sky then if you had some of his juice?" I narrowed my eyes at him, crossing my arms over my chest.

Elish tented his hands; I saw a smile edge up to his lips. "Silas has been trying to create a clone of Sky for years." Elish reached into a drawer he had open and oddly placed a electronic device, about the size of a small pebble, onto the table. "And every attempt failed. On top of that, with every attempt Silas ate through the only brain matter we had left of Sky Fallon. Eventually it ran out and the only bits we had left were secure inside of a small device we called an O.L.S. Which stands for Occipital Lobe Storage. This device keeps the brain matter alive and whatever neurons and synapses inside. Silas banned anyone from touching it, wanting to wait until the technology was there to know for sure we would succeed. I created you with help from strands of that O.L.S. Not just a clone of Silas, but a perfectly engineered boyfriend for our wonderful king. I succeeded, as you can now see."

My face darkened. "That will never happen."

Elish was still giving me that eerie smile. "Obviously not, and he will be dead before he can find out just what I have been creating under his nose."

"And that's my job isn't it? You want me to kill him?"

Elish nodded. "Yes, Reaver. You will kill him."

"I destroyed his throat; I did kill him. Why didn't that work?" Finally this question could be answered; it had been eating the back of my brain since last night.

The smile disappeared from Elish's face, the tips of his gloved fingers tapped together. "Because we do not know *how* you are supposed to kill him."

"What?" My voice became unnaturally hoarse. I gritted my teeth together, more upset by that news than the news of my makeup. "How can you not know?"

Not even a tightness in his jaw, not a single glint of emotion on that face. "Sky died long before the first generation came to be. Silas, of course, never told us. It is a mystery. One I intend for *you* to unravel."

"Me? Why me?" I dropped my voice and wiped my face with my hands. It wasn't like I was expecting killing Silas to be this easy, but I had hoped.

"Why you?" The thin smile returned. He leaned over and drew towards him a small black plastic device; it had buttons on it and a speaker. "Why not you?"

He pressed on the button and spoke into it. "Jade, send down Mr. Massey."

When his finger lifted off of the buzzer, I put my hand out as if stopping him. "All this bullshit aside, and before we both have to lie to keep Killian calm, I need to know… are we safe here?"

The chimera gave me a single nod, a lock of golden blond hair falling over his flawless face. "You could be no place safer."

"Besides this shitty legionary party you have in the blacksands, is there anyone else looking for us?" I leaned forward, almost rising from my chair. I had so many more questions to ask him, most I did not want to fall on Killian's ears.

Elish looked upon my advancement with cold indifference. He put up a hand and turned his violet eyes towards the sound of the door opening.

"No one, not until he awakens."

I looked towards the staircase and heard footsteps, so light they could have belonged to a child. I saw Killian's cowering little frame peek through the staircases recess, his eyes glanced over at us nervously, his hands clenching his sides. He looked terrified, like a child being called in by a ticked off parent.

"Sit," Elish's placid tone said.

Killian lowered his head in a submissive posture and grabbed one of the cloth chairs; he set it beside mine and sat down. I hadn't noticed how close he had sat on the chair until our shoulders rubbed together.

I opened my mouth to say more, when Elish's phone rang. He drew it out of his robes and held up a finger for us to give him a moment. His courtesies amused me, if I have a magic phone I wouldn't give a fuck who I answered it in front of.

"Hello, Garrett?"

Garrett? The president of Skytech, if I remembered correctly. I listened in as well as I could.

"Yes, he is doing fine, thank you for asking, and how is Otter doing?"

Otter? That's a stupid name.

"Indeed, I knew you would. Oh, did he now? Put him on the phone then. Yes, I would rather you leave without me asking. Indeed, yes." I was surprised when Elish looked over at me before standing up behind his desk. He motioned me over.

"Yes, Reno. He's – yes, he's right here."

Reno? My eyes widened in shock and I realized my mouth had dropped open, before I could demand it Elish handed me the phone.

I put it up to my ear. "H-hello?"

"BRO!" His laughter filled the phone; it started to loosen the rope seemingly bound around my heart. *"Man, you sound so different on the phone, like all raspy and sinister. Fuck, how are you, you immortal bitch?"*

I laughed, feeling the warmth come into my bones. I was so relieved he was safe. "I'm… I'm good… are you in Skyfall? Are they keeping you safe? Is that chimera fuck the one taking care of you?"

"Dude, he's like my master right now!" Reno hissed with another chuckle. *"I'm helping get some shit for you guys. He's a really awesome*

dude though but I haven't banged him yet, but I will soon, I promise."

Really now? I glanced over at Elish who wasn't even trying to pretend he wasn't listening in. I wondered if he was waiting to snatch the phone away if Reno said something he didn't like.

Well, he was going to be disappointed. I walked away from the desk, found their master bedroom and I closed the door.

"Alright, I'm alone, are you okay?" I whispered. I picked up one of their pillows and pressed myself up against the back wall. I knew Elish could hear as well as I could.

He chuckled. *"I'm not pretending, bro. I just need to hide 'cause Garrett doesn't know why I'm really here, and he's great, I don't wanna hurt him. Reaver... I think we're cool. It makes sense, eh? Him being so cush with Leo and Greyson? I mean... there is no going back, right, hun? This isn't home, it will never be home... but with the hand we got dealt – it could be so much worse, babe."*

I sighed and momentarily closed my eyes. I missed home. "I know, I just… I don't know what's supposed to happen now. What did you mean Elish has you getting something?"

"Keycard for Kreig, where you were born, my immortal Pop-Tart. Apparently Elish needs me to sneak in and get them because it would be suspicious for him to request that card. He hasn't told you this yet?"

"He was just briefing me when you called," I said, shaking my head, even though that was obviously a dumb thing to do alone in a bedroom. "I just came back last night. Killian seems okay though. I'm not taking him and leaving only because he seems to be returning back to his normal self."

"No, don't leave. The Legion and the chimeras might not be looking for you in the greywastes now, but as soon as Silas comes back they will be. Look, baby, I don't know... I'm just a dumb fuck but I trust them. I know I have shitty taste in men, but Garrett isn't like the others and he's Elish's best friend, on top of being his bro. I think these are like... the good ones? I don't know, man, but I trust them. Elish wants to kill King Silas, so he can't be that bad."

Hearing this from my friend meant more to me than Elish's words ever could, though I found this whole situation just frustrating. I shouldn't even be in a situation where I need to trust chimeras; I hadn't even known what the fuck they were before I met Perish.

But Asher had made it personal; he raped my boyfriend and he murdered my dads.

"Reno… if there's anyone listening on your end… if they're making you say this shit… just ask me if Killian is okay," I said quietly.

"But I actually want to know if Killian is okay... can't it be a code word like banana?"

"Sure."

"Is Killian okay?"

I really hated that man sometimes.

After a few more minutes of him telling me about his new master (he sounded like a giddy teenager), Reno handed the phone back off to Garrett and I handed it to Elish. I gathered Garrett would be led to assume Reno had been talking to Elish.

"How is he?" Killian whispered to me, tugging on my shirt sleeve.

"Happy… too happy for my liking. He's getting pretty cozy with his new master," I grumbled, looking over as Elish pressed the *end call* button on the phone.

"*New* master!? You sold him?" Killian's voice rose several octaves, but with a slight raise of Elish's gloved hand Killian's mouth clamped shut.

"I assure you, even though your experiences with my brothers have been rather one-sided, we are not all…" One of Elish's blond eyebrows rose, "bloodthirsty beasts."

I could see that, every one of those mutants seemed to contrast the next.

Elish pushed a file folder towards me. I opened it and saw a paper-clipped photo of a smiling clean-cut man in his early thirties. He had short black hair that looked parted on the side, with a suit and tie, a bowler-type hat sideways on his head, and a trimmed moustache. He was handsome like they all were, a thin face, manicured eye brows over large eyes, and to top it off, a cigar stuck between white straight teeth.

"Garrett Dekker, as you probably know, is the president of Skytech and a very prominent business man," Elish continued as I picked up the folder. The first page was a list of his stats, mostly body statistics. From his eye colour (green with yellow flecks) to his shoe size (9) even as far as his food preferences (liquor). On the next page I saw numbers and graphs I didn't understand, but I saw the words DNA so I assumed it was his chimera makeup.

"Somewhere in his house, or in his office, are the old passwords and cards to get into a lab in Kreig. I believe Lycos's office and a small area of the lab was protected and not destroyed by the explosion," Elish said. His voice seemed even more cold and ominous the further he went on. I realized with a hard swallow that this went deeper than I could have imagined. "I am of top council, I help run Skyfall and its surroundings, but when it comes to Skytech there is no reason for me to dabble in Krieg's files. Therefore, my probing would bring unwelcome questions from my brothers, and most of all, King Silas. I need to maintain my routine without waver, especially once he resurrects."

"Lycos's lab is in Kreig? So that was where Reaver was born?" Killian asked. He pressed a finger down on the raised folder so he could take a peek. I lowered it for him.

"Yes, he was born in Kreig, a large city further east inland. What I need from there is all the documentation regarding Chimera X. *You,*" Elish explained, glancing at me. "I will not send you to Kreig unless I know you can enter the lab safely. I will not send you on a fool's errand."

"Errand?" Killian's voice filled with questions, but Elish ignored him.

"Reno is already with Garrett and has been doing well; they're quite enchanted with each other as you could probably tell, Reaver," Elish went on, "As you know, your companion Reno has… *magnetism* and it mixes well with my brother's quirks. Needless to say, they're getting along well."

"You've whored out Reno?" Killian's voice climbed another octave.

"More like he's playing matchmaker," I mumbled, looking on the third page; this guy seemed to be a very flamboyant character. "Is he going to whip and beat my friend or is he actually going to treat him decent?" Shit, the moment those words left my lips I knew I should've swallowed them. I had seen the scars on Jade's body; I hadn't meant to make that a personal attack.

My eyes lifted from the folder to see Elish staring at me, if my words had any resounding effect he wouldn't show it. "The paper will show you that Garrett has low aggression, he is rather docile. His gift is with business, not so much interpersonal relationships."

"Why do you need Reaver's files?" Killian asked quietly, his voice decreasing to an acceptable level.

I decided to answer this one. "We don't know how to kill Silas; we just know that I can." I raised an eyebrow at Elish. "I'm assuming you think this information can be found in the lab research?"

"I am hoping to be able to dissect your makeup and see how it differs from that of a normal human and a normal chimera."

I put the folder down and pushed it towards Killian in case he wanted to take a look. "Do you have a file like this on everyone?"

"Yes."

"Even me?"

"Especially you"

My brow furrowed. I wondered what information he had on me; he had probably got a lot of it from Leo. Did he really have this much secrecy that he could have files on me out of Silas's reach? I could only hope the king was too busy playing games to notice what had been going on right under his nose. I hope for this, because it meant he wasn't as clever as I feared.

But what did he have on me? How much had Leo told him? These questions sat uneasy in my stomach.

I think he read my mind; he looked right at me and said without hesitation, "No, you cannot see it."

"Why… why are you doing this?" I turned, surprised at Killian's brazen question. He was looking up at Elish with his eyes wide and scared. I focused my hearing and noticed his heart rate had never slowed down.

"My reasons are my own, as yours are, Mr. Massey." Elish's voice was dipped in arctic waters, I felt Killian freeze. I knew that would be the last loose-tongued comment to come out of my boyfriend. The look those purple eyes were giving him could quench the flames of hell. "I will be meeting with you privately throughout my time here, Reaver. And if you have any questions do not hesitate to ask me. I am sure with what you have learned you have a lot. In the meantime, I encourage you to continue to enjoy my residence. But out of respect… do not smoke outside of your bedroom."

"What about other drugs?" The question slipped through my lips before I could stop myself.

Elish rose from his seat, I watched him for a moment before I rose as well, remembering this was his private office. Killian rose beside me.

"I have no issue with your drug consumption but my pet is only permitted to partake at my leave. He is a recovering addict and I wish to keep him that way. Even though he's a chimera, he has a weak immune system and falls into poor health easily," Elish said. I noticed his eyes were focused on Killian. I looked too to see what he was staring at. I cringed as I saw it right away.

Didn't that kid have long sleeve shirts?

"I would suggest you start weaning Killian from this heroin." Elish's eyes narrowed at the pink track marks going up Killian's lower arms. "The state of those in your possession is a direct reflection on you, remember that."

I hated my body the moment my ears started to go red. I tried to push down the humiliation bubbling in my throat but it was no use. My face darkened around the same time Killian cowered and tried to shyly hide his arms behind his back. His shoulders started to tremble from Elish's smouldering gaze.

"He's not my possession, he isn't a pet," I said in a level tone, desperately trying to hide my embarrassment over him. In my brain I justified it a many times over but my emotions were filling me with shame. "He has trouble coping with things; this helps him not break down."

"Yes, I have done similar, but he is safe now and it is time for him to start facing reality sober," Elish responded. "You as well, Mr. Merrik."

I opened my mouth to let out a more scathing retort but Killian pulled on my sleeve. I knew he knew me well-enough by now to know I was bordering on saying something that would cause friction. I practiced my social skills and closed my mouth.

Killian smiled at me. "We can try and quit together, hun."

I grunted and we both carried on up the stairs. A thousand thoughts inside of my head and a thousand more I pushed down.

CHAPTER 7

Reno

PLINK PLINK PLINK... WITH EVERY TAP OF THE IVORY keys I was only more convinced that I was a talentless hack. How the hell could Killian make all that music on that piano he had in Aras? I couldn't even perfect *Hot Cross Buns* without messing up at least twice.

What a job. In the greywastes we scratched a living from eating people and scavenging old pre-Fallocaust shit, in Skyfall they had enough free time to demand everyone learn instruments or textbooks. My new master had been adamant that I start learning some culture. Fuck culture; give me cigarettes, booze, sex, and drugs. I liked my greywaste culture, much easier than learning to bang a note on this over-sized xylophone.

I twirled in the chair a few times, watching Luca spin around into a blond blur complete with a pair of black cat ears held up by a headband. He was cleaning Garrett's apartment to give him something to do. He had already scrubbed every single surface in Elish's and was starting to get antsy and bored. Even Biff was getting tired of Luca petting him all the time. Biff had his own Luca-free zone, which was a tall window ledge above our heads.

"I'm Henry the eighth I ammm, Henry the eighth I am I am!" I sang as I spun around in circles on the swivel chair. I didn't know the rest of the song, so I just sung the rest of the tune with the same lyrics. When I was done I got up and flopped on the couch.

"I was about to push it back to clean under it," Luca said politely.

I sighed and slid off of the couch like I was suddenly made out of liquid and landed on the floor with a *thunk*. I splayed my arms out. "Drag me."

Luca closed his eyes and took a deep breath. I had been taking advantage of his sengil status. I had to shake up his little world somehow. He never left the skyscraper, and on top of that, he had to deal with Ice Man all the time or his snippy little pet that I now called Biter in my head. I was adding colour to Luca's otherwise dreary dreary life.

In all respects, I was doing him a huge favour.

Luca grabbed onto my hand and started dragging me off to the kitchen floor, his cat ears going wonky on his head. I *whee'd* just because.

"Since you seem bored, Master Nevada, would you like me to find a movie for you?" Luca asked kindly. I had been here for weeks now and never once did I get a single lost temper with him. It was infuriating, Reaver would have smacked the shit out of me if I playfully tormented him half as much as I did my servant (or petpet as I called him since that's what he was, a pet's pet).

"No, it's alright, Master Luca. Perhaps a cigar on the patio with some Cognac with a bowl of sour candies, yes?" I tried my best to mimic Garrett's voice. "But first hang up my pot pie hat. Be careful though it's an *artifact*."

Luca chewed his mouth, which in my books meant he was laughing in his head. He rolled his eyes and picked up the remote control. One day, one day I would make that little motherfucker laugh.

I heard a rattle, and looked up just in time to see none other than Garrett Dekker walk into the suite. Just like he had walked out of my last joke, he was dressed in a grey suit and a fancy hat with shiny black shoes I could see my face in. The suavey chimera had a cigar in his mouth, underneath a trimmed pencil moustache and sunglasses.

"Reno, my little otter, what are you doing on the floor? Lose something?" Garrett tilted his head to the side, towards Luca's hands waiting to receive his hat, and slipped off his shoes. He took a drag from his cigar as I got up and straightened out my pants.

"Just being a dick, that's all." I stretched and gave him a haughty bow. "How was work? Poison any school kid's milk today?"

Garrett laughed and gave me a quick kiss on the cheek.

The moment he laughed at my joke, only a few minutes after meeting him I knew why Elish thought of me to get this job done. "If you want that, I'll do it a thousand times over. Come. Sit with me on the patio. Luca? Some rye and some sweets, and perhaps today's bulletin? I left mine at work."

I shot Luca a *see?* look and followed Garrett out to the patio. Luca gave me another eye roll but his cheek was suctioned in like he was biting it.

Garrett sat down on his stuffed patio bench and I took a seat beside him in my favourite chair. The balcony was bloody incredible; it had heater things and a clear plastic cover to keep the heat in if we wanted. It got cold being so high up in the air.

The city stretched out as far as the eye could see, until the grey buildings were nothing but haze; some with lights that twinkled at night but a lot swallowed by the darkness. This city was like nothing I'd ever seen, even in movies.

The farthest away I had ever been was Anvil visiting my brothers and sisters. The biggest city I had ever scavenged was Sognir with Reaver. I didn't know how big it was compared to Skyfall because we never had a death wish big enough to climb a skyscraper to the top. Those were death traps, the floors were too sketchy.

I pulled the blanket resting on the chair over myself. It was chilly outside. In Aras we always dressed for the weather, but in Skyland sometimes I went all day without touching the ground. I dressed in usual pet garb, leather, tight mesh, and not much else. Today I had on looser leather pants and a slashed mesh shirt, my collar snugly under my chin, and my leather cuffs on each wrist. I looked hot as shit, but I couldn't help feeling my soul get sucked away every time I looked in the mirror.

Oh, would Reaver ever have a laugh at me when he saw what I looked like. My silver hair all washed and fancy, only my eyebrows were still black. I didn't really look like good ol' Reno anymore. I looked like the person Garrett referred to me as when he led me around on the leash: Otter.

It was his idea. He said when he first saw me the smile I gave him reminded him of a little sea otter. I looked it up to see what they looked like and I approved. At least my name wasn't cockroach, or donkey, or some other ugly animal.

Luca brought us our drinks, and with a bow, Garrett relieved him for today and he went back home to Biff and an empty house. I felt fortunate to stay here with Garrett. I was really starting to like the guy.

"You seem deep in thought," Garrett said through thick grey smoke. He was reading over today's bulletin. Skytech crap as usual; he lived for his work and didn't have a big social life besides parties to increase his image or bar hopping when he was particularly lonely. "Would you like to plan another day in the outlands?"

What a nice guy… we had gone last week after I seemed down to him. The outlands were just that, the outskirts of Skyfall where it was grey and rock, basically the greywastes. His way of helping me combat my homesickness was to have a date in my old home environment. I didn't miss the rocks and radiation though, I missed my friends and I missed my town.

And there was the lump in my throat. It was the town I knew I would never see again. Reaver would raze it to the ground if he ever went back there, and I would go where he went. So that chapter in my life was gone.

But Aras wasn't supposed to be a chapter; my family had been guarding Aras for generations. I was proud to have the job as field sentry passed down to me. Now it was on Vegas Jr's shoulders.

He better not touch my stuff.

"Nah, it's not that…" Well, it was that; it was always that. I took a drink of the rye and pursed my mouth; I wasn't used to liquor like this. That had been proven the very first night I was here. I still didn't remember what had happened, at least we'd woken up with our clothes on.

I picked up a few candies and turned them around in my hands. These were soft candies; not two hundred-year-old ones. It was so different. Everything tasted like what it should taste like, not old tin cans and stale sugar. "Probably just tired from the day, it's tough work teasing Luca."

The suave chimera smiled before he motioned me over and I sat beside him, then he pulled me over until I was resting my head on his shoulder. He put his arm around me and petted my new silvery hair back.

I gave him some mock purrs, it made him smile.

"I'll help find Reaver and his partner if it will make you smile," Garrett said, his voice soft like velvet. I had heard this promise before; it only went to show just how little Garrett was involved in his master and some of his brothers' activities. He didn't know how serious things were, to him there were no problems that couldn't be fixed with either money or power. Garrett didn't know how badly Silas wanted Reaver and Killian…

Garrett ran Skytech; he was elbow deep in the smooth runnings of several factories and all the labs in Skyfall and the greywastes. He was out of touch with the other chimeras and they left him alone because no one else wanted that job. It was more fun to cause terror and play games, running a city was boring. So they let him be. Garrett, Joaquin the curly-haired one, some dude named Teaguae and the twin ones who also had silver hair like me, Artemis and Apollo, those guys plus Elish were all on the council which ran Skyfall. Those bunch were the only ones that seemed almost normal, and in some respects, nice people but still chimeras. Elish made sure to remind me of that, deep down they were still chimeras and still had their odd quirks.

"No… you've already done a lot for me," I said quietly. My chest rose as I sighed. "How can you read my thoughts so well?"

He ran his fingers through my hair; it was getting longer but still only four or five inches past my scalp. I always kept it short before, but hell I might grow it out. I was kind of liking being silver and cool. "Your eyes always give you away. It doesn't take an empath to see you worry about them every day."

I guess I could be rather transparent. Though the guy had just gotten back from work, my problems were my own and a lot of them I couldn't bring voice to. I was a pet and it was my job to look cute and fulfil all my master's needs. I decided to change the tone and with a playful nip I kissed his cheek. "I'll be fine, just normal home sickness, but fuck it, I'm happy here with you."

I wish that was a lie…

Garrett pulled me closer to him and gently kissed the corners of my mouth, making my heart skip. I wondered if he could hear it. "Are you really?"

Inside my blood started to warm, whenever he got close to me I started to feel light like I was suddenly floating. "I am, I told you…" I poked his shoulder again with a shy smile. "I like you."

Then a smile appeared on that handsome face, making the corners of his eyes crease. "They painted greywasters as vicious insane little animals, but I must say…"

My body froze with shock as he turned his head and kissed me gently on the lips; his trimmed moustache tickling my nose. I pressed back and felt him put a hand on my side, when he pulled back he said in a whisper that made my head fill with even more heat. "I have a diamond in the rough."

God dammit... god dammit... I closed my eyes, my chest shuddering. *Dammit, dammit, dammit.*

That kiss had been incredible.

Then the guilt came, the deception rearing its ugly head in my gut. My feelings were growing for him; I was starting to feel guilty.

But I wasn't hurting Garrett, he just didn't know what Elish was doing. Eventually he would but it was too soon for him to know.

I wasn't going to hurt Garrett; it was nothing he wouldn't show Elish if he asked. It would just be weird for him to ask for something, and since Reaver, Killian, and Perish were missing it would ignite suspicion. Elish had to be careful right now. Nothing could be out of the ordinary with him.

It was a victimless crime, no need to feel badly…

"I hoped Elish charged you a lot for me." I looked up at him and felt my face flush. "I know he didn't give me nearly enough to have to deal with you."

He laughed his rich gut laugh, not the fake 'you're retarded, Reno' pity laughs I usually got, this guy honestly thought I was the funniest person in the world.

I knew why he did though, everyone else sucked up to him, were cautious around him, he was big boss man Garrett Dekker. No one was real in front of this guy, it was hilarious to see but also sad. Dude was pretty lonely, and even though he was well-known he was completely isolated. It would drive me insane to have no one act relaxed or normal in front of me. Unless it was his high-ranking chimera brothers and they all seemed batshit crazy.

"Elish rarely bribes us with money, he wants favours and information; my brother is fickle like that." Garrett smiled, running a finger gracefully down my cheek bone until it travelled to my lips. Then he leaned over and kissed me again, this time I felt his mouth part and his tongue meet mine. Another burning started to overtake me, and as my own hands started to stroke his sides, I knew I was going to need a cold shower before bed.

When he broke away I felt him chuckle, I opened my eyes and saw him looking back at me. "That empath sure knew what he was doing, am I the only one who is feeling these fireworks in my brain? I told you I wouldn't sell you short."

I felt my face flush, and I knew my cheeks were probably going red. "Elish might've made you wait, but I guess when he delivers the goods he makes sure it's quality stuff."

We kissed again, and this time, with a gasp I felt him slip a hand down my pants.

I looked around for Luca, before remembering with a relieved sigh that he had been freed for the evening. I gave myself into the sensation of finally being touched by someone who wasn't drunk or desperate, and slipped my own hand underneath his shirt.

"I know it's no chimera dick but no laughing when you see it, right?" I said before stifling a moan.

To my surprise, Garrett let out a laugh before hitting me on the shoulder.

"You blunt little shit, stop ruining the moment, I've been waiting for three years, shush!" he laughed. I grinned before we were drawn in for another kiss, now barely masking my moans as he rubbed my hard member in his hands. It wasn't taking me long to grow to full length; he had some skilled fingers on him.

"So what else happened in this fantasy of yours?" My mouth travelled from his lips to his prickly chin, then down to his neck. I locked my lips around it and started to suck, branding him as my own. I could be my own master if the mood took me.

"Things that would make you blush even more." I let out my first audible moan as ran his hand up and down the shaft. I opened my mouth to say more when suddenly we both heard a knock on the door inside the apartment.

Garrett retracted his hand and I let out a loud frustrated noise. “Don’t tell me you have to get that!”

My suave chimera laughed and leaned in to kiss my cheek. “If they made it up this far it’s one of my brothers and he will not go away. We have all the time in the world, lutra, patience.”

Fuck patience!

The next morning I woke up very clean from the twenty minute cold shower I had to take after me and Garrett’s ‘almost had sex but didn’t’ time on the balcony, one that was so joyfully interrupted by Teaguae Dekker. I was not impressed and I hoped that dumbass chimera knew that.

With a kiss on his cheek, I got up. I let the suave one sleep and after I got my morning coffee from Saul who, as usual, let himself in.

Saul was, well… Saul was great, and I think he hated me, but he was great either way.

Solomon was Garrett’s bodyguard and right-hand man for like the last ten thousand years. He was fifty years old, with a bald head and an angry grey goatee. The dude had eyes that told you he had not taken an ounce of bullshit in his life and he had no desire to start.

So naturally I had to take advantage of that.

“Morning, Sully,” I said. Even though I was still tired, I tried to make myself as cheery as possible.

Saul glanced up from his coffee mug; he had today’s bulletin in his hands.

“I’d keep that slap-happy look on your face, Garrett’s in for a long day.” He licked his fingers before turning the page. “Another worker got blended up in one of the factories last night. Third incident this year and he hasn’t sent the repairs over that he promised.” Saul took a bite out of his sandwich. He was a bachelor and that’s all he ate, any leftover dinner from the previous night got made into a sandwich. Today’s sandwich had lasagna between the bread slices.

Yeah, he was that bad.

“Too bad it wasn’t a rat meat factory, right?” I said with a chuckle.

"You could slap a label on it 'may contain traces of arian'." I laughed at my own joke, but Saul just ignored me. He didn't find me nearly as funny as Garrett.

"On top of that, Garrett's got meetings back-to-back. I'd go back in there and start doing your duty; it's going to be a rough one."

Do my duty? I stared at him blankly for a moment. His dead fish eyes stared right back at me before he shook his head and went back to the bulletin.

"Have you ever gotten your brain scanned, kid?"

"I've gotten it knocked around like a bouncy ball before, does that count?" I said opening up the fridge. We usually grabbed breakfast on the way to the office but I was hungry now. I liked having two breakfasts.

I grabbed a banana and sat down with my coffee, then I heard movement in the bedroom. I leaned back on my chair as I munched away on this weird yet tasty genetically engineered fruit. I liked it, but god damn did I ever puke up a storm the first time Garrett properly fed me. My body seemed to go into food shock. I had never had real cheese before and I had eaten a lot of it.

Back-to-back meetings... I took another bite. I had already checked the apartment and I hadn't found the papers Elish had wanted me to find. Garrett rarely took his work home with him, just his laptop and it wouldn't be on there.

But if he was going to be away at meetings all day...

If I was some sort of undercover secret agent this would be the part where I spin some classic lie as to why I wanted to accompany Garrett to work. Something so clever everyone watching would be so impressed, singing high praises for my intellect and daring; such a sneaky fuck going undercover to snoop through Garrett's office.

But well, this was real life.

"Garrett, I want to come to work with you today."

Garrett popped his head out of the bedroom, his hair slicked back and wet from the shower and his still dripping chest bare. "I'd love that! We'll order hamburgers for lunch."

So easy.

I pulled on my leash and made growling noises, sometimes if he left me in the car for too long I started to bark. Saul hated it and had threatened to shoot me like a dog on many occasions but Garrett still thought it was hilarious. I even had a bag of chocolate for treats, purely because he was buying into the joke just as much as I was. I'd even learned a few tricks.

I took my place in my corner as people came in and out to meet with him. I had a stuffed beanbag chair-thing in the corner, plus some handheld video games, and books to read. When the people came in they all got put away, and I had to stare forward looking invisible.

The men and women who came in were all shapes and sizes; I even saw several fat ones. There aren't really fat people in the wasteland; we kind of tend to eat them or they get left behind to get eaten because they're slow.

Garrett was in president mode. He was such a stern and formidable businessman it was fascinating watching him at work. President for a reason, Garrett took no bullshit and I watched in awe as he called out several people on lies or false facts. He knew the workings of Skytech in and out, no matter how much information his clients and workers had he always knew more. No wonder he didn't have a social life, he was too busy keeping up with all the work.

It did make me admire him and appreciate how loose and relaxed he was around me. Once again my mind pricked with amusement at how smart Elish had been hooking the two of us up. We seemed to feed perfectly off of each other, both of us at our best when we had the other one around. Jade's super aura magic really was indispensable.

I stifled a yawn as Garrett rattled on to Mr. What's-his-name and started counting the tiles on the floor. I was supposed to sit pretty but I got bored easily, I could never entertain myself by staring at walls like Reaver. I needed stimulus but at least I got treated nicely. To curry Garrett's favour everyone always complimented me and said nice things and I was okay with that. Sometimes I even got gifts. So far I'd gotten chocolate, a new Game Boy game and offers of a serval cat from Joaquin Dekker.

Then after we shared lunch, the person I had been waiting for arrived; the one with the hair up his ass about the blended factory worker. As I had hoped, he wanted to personally show Garrett the problems. The factory itself was on the island only several blocks away. I complained of an upset stomach from the hamburgers and some fatigue so I was left to my own devices in the office. After summoning Saul from his place near the entrance of the building, the three of them took off in a car, leaving me behind in the locked office.

As soon as I heard the door click a rev of anxiety started to turn over in my chest. The icy cold feeling you got before you did something stupid. I waited with an ear out for any sign of re-entry, and when they had been gone for almost five minutes, I rose.

The office I was in was really an entire apartment in itself. It was breathtakingly beautiful, in colours of ebony black and trimmed gold. The walls were marble and the floors so clean I literally ate off them. The art on the walls looked like little TVs too, that's how realistic they looked, and the furniture as well was restored with all the handles and knobs needed.

Back in Aras I had to jimmy my underwear drawer open with a butter knife.

Through my hours of sitting pretty, I had spotted several places I wanted to root through, mainly his filing cabinets. There was also a half-open door that seemed to lead to more storage.

I think I had my work cut out for me. I was looking for files way back twenty years ago and then some, since it took time to spit out a functioning Reaver. I knew I was looking for files on Kreig though, that would save me what would've normally taken me fifteen years to sort through.

Too bad Garrett wasn't obsessively organized like Elish obviously was, or it would've made things easier. Instead I was staring at folders and folders of half-labelled gibberish. Town names and lab names I didn't recognize, numbers that made no sense.

Oi, this was going to take a while.

The guys were counting on me though… this was my part in this big movie. I was the field agent getting insider info that would help our little rebellion become stronger. I couldn't fuck up my only job. Elish had hand-picked me for this.

Aw man, Garrett trusted me here though… I was only human, I still felt bad about it.

I flicked through the first door of the filing cabinet but I got the impression this was factory stuff since I recognized Tamerlan, which is where Tinkerbell was from. So I closed that drawer and moved on to the next one.

I only glanced in it for a moment before I immediately sensed I wouldn't find anything here. No, I can't see him keeping old files out in the main office.

My eyes flicked to the half-open door, and with a quick look around, I quietly padded over to it, my leash dragging behind me like a forgotten skip rope. I picked it up and tucked it into my black pants.

With a jitter in my veins that remained no matter how far away I knew Garrett was, I softly opened the door and flipped the light on.

My shoulders slumped as I realized how big the room was and how many filing cabinets were in here, wall-to-wall with stacks of paper that crawled up the ceiling like centipedes. This was going to take a while… at least it would give me time to think of a good excuse if they came back. Either I saw a rat or I had a headache and wanted to find some place dark. That sweet suave chimera would believe me; I had him wrapped around my finger.

Another pang of guilt… I banished it into my loyalty to my friends. They were counting on me.

I wasn't here to find a boyfriend. That was only a fringe benefit. I was here to find out how to get into Kreig; then Elish would take me back to my friends. That's what he promised.

I flicked through the files, starting counterclockwise. The first cabinet seemed more full of factory shit than Skytech research, but the third cabinet though caught my interest. The file folders were crimson red and labelled in black marker saying 'chimera information'.

The first file folder I had was for Artemis Dekker, with silver hair, royal blue eyes and standing a respectable six foot two. I thumbed through the next one which was his twin brother Apollo, and the next which was for someone I was familiar with: Garrett Dekker.

I pulled that one to the front and memorized the location, I wanted to look through it sometime and see if I could get some hints from it about things he liked. I skimmed through the rest, recognizing a few names but I didn't see Reaver. I did though find Lycos Dekker, it wasn't Kreig but it was close. I pulled it up and closed the file drawer; I sat down with it and started looking through it.

Lycos Dekker, born 193, blond hair, hazel eyes… I grazed through the stuff I already knew and to the back pages. It hadn't been updated that was for sure, attached to it was his death certificate, saying he had died in Kreig in 211.

I carefully looked at several attached pieces of paper on the folder but they were regarding his schooling, his teachers and…

My eye stopped on a familiar name.

Professor: Perish Dekker.

Facility: The College of Skytech, owned by Elish Dekker.

It was so odd to see the proof that Leo, the mayor of Aras, had been involved with these guys all this time, mind boggling really… and Elish owned that school, eh? I wonder if that's how Elish got involved in Reaver's creation. Those two definitely had some sort of history before that lab explosion.

I quietly closed the file folder, ignoring the strange feeling in my gut. The feeling that kept me up at night, knowing this stuff stretched back for years, long before I was born. It made me wary of Elish, even if I trusted him. I felt like a small fish in a big pond doing tasks that would impact the entire world.

I let out a breath and wiped the sweat from my forehead. While looking through folders I hadn't even realized I was stress sweating.

I decided to ignore it and move to the next file folder.

And the next, and the next until…

"There was a farmer who had a dog," I whispered as I opened the sixth cabinet. Inside were blue folders stuffed to the brim with white papers, the first one I saw was Donnely and that indeed was a lab. The second was Gosselin, which I knew had a lab years ago. *"And bingo was his name, oh."*

With a quiver in my gut that churned around until it formed a pit, all of this suddenly became very real. I could feel my pulse start to quicken and my chest start to flush with ice water. I pulled back the folders and when I saw Kreig my heart started to eat out of my chest.

I pulled it out; it was heavy. I sat on the floor and opened it up. I licked my dry lips with an even dryer tongue.

Chimera X

Scientists on hand: 1
  Lycos Dekker
Project name: Chimera X attempt 1 T-093C
  Failed at 3 weeks 2 days. No heartbeat.

Oh shit, Chimera X. That was Reaver's code name. I lifted up the first several pages and saw attempt after attempt fail. I wanted to look through those badly but I needed that keycard first.

More booklets of chimera info… I pushed it to the side and found a paper-clipped book of random numbers, none of which made sense. It was all math and science and that had only been tutored to me by Leo when I was younger, and schooling stopped at ten then you had to start apprenticing for a real job.

Then I felt something hard and square outlined the bottom of the booklet, I turned and saw a credit card looking thing stuck in a translucent plastic sleeve.

A keycard.

And because I was fucking unlucky, I heard a *thunk* underneath me as the elevator started to whir.

My heart immediately went into meltdown mode. I stuffed the keycard into my pocket hoping like hell Garrett wouldn't grope me before I got home. I needed to play it coy now, maybe fake a headache? Shit, I didn't know.

More elevator noises; I shoved the folder underneath the filing cabinet and ran out of the room, barely flicking off the light switch before I heard the doors open. I got to my pet bed and sat down in it with my head up against the wall, then I pretended to be asleep.

I could hear Garrett talking in a normal tone to someone, probably Saul. I closed my eyes and tried to relax my beating heart. Thankfully, I didn't think this guy had ninja heartbeat hearing like Reaver, but then again he could.

I heard him say goodbye and then a beep. I realized that he had been talking on the secure phone they all carried around, the chimera hotline.

I heard several beeps and then a ringing as the call connected.

"Jack, how's Juni doing? Good…" There was a pause and then a dry laugh; his voice was quiet. Not full of the cheer he had when it was just us after work, but low and serious. "Yes, you do know me rather well. How is he?" Another pause, I wished I could listen to the other side of the conversation. "Good, let me know as soon as he wakes up, the moment, alright?"

My throat tightened, he was talking about King Asher Silas. He couldn't know I was here, what would he do to me? Elish had said I would be far away from here the moment he woke up.

I… I shifted around and felt the small plastic card underneath me in my back pocket. *I have the keycard though. I will give it to Luca as soon as I can.*

"Elish is taking a leave of absence. His pet is injured and he's caring for him in one of those bases he has in the greyrifts, or the plaguelands, or something or other, not sure which one. No, no, nothing fatal but who's to know. I heard those deacons can look a man square in the eyes without looking up, terrifying."

You have no idea… my heartfelt funny having him talk about my old home. At least I had gotten to say goodbye when Elish had snuck me into Aras. It had helped me emotionally close the door on that life, and at least the cat wouldn't die. Fuck, it had taken every effort to carry all that shit with a bullet in my gut. Elish was of little help, but he was kind enough to hold the cat when he started to squirm around when the plane was taking off.

"Mine? He's splendid, tall and skinny, silver hair, yes. Otter. No, it's been surprising, I think the rabid nature doesn't stretch past Morosians, or perhaps Jade was just a rotten apple in the bunch. This one is quite extraordinary, funny and just good-natured. I'm growing rather fond of him." I beamed on the inside, feeling my ego get another stroke. I got so many compliments here.

But oddly, I felt a tingle go up my spine. I didn't know why until I heard Garrett speak, his voice had dropped to a strangle level. "No… I won't let him near this one."

This one…

"I know, I know what I have to do with him, and no, I don't like it, but… you know how our master is. I need to do it for his own good if I want to keep him safe."

What…? My heart dropped to my feet. I couldn't stop my brow from creasing; I didn't know what to do. I wanted to snap my eyes open and get an explanation out of him but I opted to stay silent and still. Maybe he would explain himself.

"Once he's had his fun, he'll be mine and if… if I play my cards right he'll let me have him. I mean… he let Joaquin have Jem, and eventually Elish was allowed to keep Jade…" Another pause. "I will tell him beforehand; this isn't just a pet… I won't blindside him."

Another pause, I could hear Jack's muffled voice on the other end of the line.

"I know, but Elish told me he was his friend. Silas held no ill will towards him. He might…"

Shit... shit... shit... I think I knew what this was about. It was what Garrett was planning on doing once Silas woke up, how to pass off Reaver's friend as his new pet without getting him killed.

I would be gone by then…

I clenched my teeth as I felt a surge of sadness burrow itself into my heart. I wish I could shut down my emotions like dear ol' Reaver; I was feeling shit I didn't plan on feeling. Look at the things he was saying about me… warning me about King Silas, going against the chimera code that King Silas was all our lord and master. Saying I wasn't just a pet, Garrett was planning for the future.

A future I wouldn't be in.

I heard the conversation wrap up and the phone get turned off, then there was a sad sigh that soon was muffled by cloth.

I opened my eyes and saw Garrett's head burrowed into his arms which were folded on the desk. He let out a huff-like sigh before he looked up.

I closed my eyes again but the image was still there, his big green eyes heavy with sadness and loss. The suave chimera was worried, his elegant countenance and caring attitude lost under the constant threat of his master. A genetically engineered super human and he still was afraid of Silas, all of them were firmly under his thumb.

Well, except for Elish… apparently someone finally got bored of Asher's bullshit.

I would never do it, I knew better, but I played with the idea of just telling him what we were doing. Telling him Elish was trying to find out how we kill Silas and stepping up to take over. Garrett looked like he was tired of it too; maybe him wanting to protect me would sway him to Elish's side.

But no, like I said I knew better, this shit had been going on for decades and I wasn't going to assume I knew the politics after only being here a few weeks.

In time he would… maybe we could be together then.

Gah, shut up, Reno!

It got worse though; there was a creak of his spin chair and soft footsteps. I could feel that he was standing over me. My heart shuddered inside of me, and a moment later I heard him whisper.

"I must be some sort of masochist…" There was a sigh and a soft hand was placed on my cheek.

I chose this moment to open my eyes; I tried to look sleepy. "Hey you, all done?"

As soon as he saw me wake up, his eyes became brighter. He gave me a smile and rose to his feet. "Finally, it took longer than I thought. Sorry to keep you waiting… let's go home." Garrett helped me to my feet and I gave a stretch for good measure. I picked up my leash and handed it to him and we both walked towards the elevator.

I was able to hide the keycard once I got home; it fit snugly in my backpack full of clothes. After we hung out together for a few hours, we took Saul and the three of us went down to the surface to get some drinks at the Penguin, a chimera-owned bar that was close to here. I had grown fond of it, and even though it was a bit too lowbrow for Garrett, or even Saul, he had started coming with me.

This part of Skyland was amazing; the roads had newer pavement on them, barely any cracks at all. The lamps worked too, and they lit up the streets with the help of the lights inside the various shops. Even when everyone had gone to sleep the lights remained on, illuminating the grey buildings and half-repaired shops.

Though there were still boarded up windows everywhere and abandoned buildings, just to remind me and everyone else that we were still in the Fallocaust. Not even rich elites and chimeras could erase the scars Silas had put on the world.

But it was still beautiful and even at night things were open. The bars never closed here, though shops were open from eight until ten. Uncle Carson closed his whenever it started to get dark, but he was always above the shop to help if you bribed him with beer. There really weren't any rules. I guess when there's competition like in Skyland you had to follow a few rules to get customers.

I took a long drink of my rum and coke (or ChiCola as it was called here, seriously, Chi stood for chimera), the atmosphere around me thick with smoke, liquor, and boy sweat. Saul was having beer and Garrett was drinking both with a cigar stuck between his teeth. He was having a discussion I didn't understand with his second-in-command, regarding purchase orders or some bullshit, I don't know, I was eyeing up a few cute guys drinking alone. One of them had fiery crimson hair that he had layered and gelled on his head, and narrow sinister eyes. He was hot. The shorter dude had blond curls and shiny brown eyes, both with muscular, smoking nice bodies. There really weren't many ugly guys in Skyfall, I think Silas had killed them all or maybe he sent their ugly mugs to the greywastes. We had a lot of guys in the greywastes who looked like dogs' asses.

Well, I must not be too horrible on the eyes if Garrett liked me as oppose to the hotter guys that seemed to be a dime a dozen in Skyland, even if I was nothing compared to a chimera.

The bar was abuzz with activity, and besides a few passing glances, everyone left us alone. I think it was more double takes that President Garrett was drinking amongst the peasant folk, or maybe it was my skimpy attire and the collar and leash on my neck. Either way, Saul seemed to be keeping them in check with his death eyes so they all left us alone.

I felt a hand on my knee; I looked down and saw that it belonged to Garrett. My glance fell to his face but he wasn't looking at me; he hadn't changed expression at all.

"No, Kordecht is already twisting my arm about switching to the synthetic corn syrup, I'm afraid he would blow a gasket if I suggested adding in the flour filler as well. I swear those miserable Morosians don't know the difference. Tact keeps them from dying, who cares about the taste? The greywasters have never complained."

I put my hand on top of his and squeezed it. I looked down at our hands together and felt the well of fear and guilt I had been feeling start to bubble back to life. I wasn't blind like Reaver had been when he slowly fell for Killian; it didn't take a kidnapping for me to recognize I was edging the danger zones with this guy.

The guilt overwhelmed me; I gave his hand a squeeze before I started to get up. "I'm going to the bathroom, I'll be right back."

I opened up the metal door to the men's bathroom and found a stall.

I sighed and sat down on the lid and wiped my face with both hands. I groaned at my own inconvenient feelings and sat wallowing in self-despair, the alcohol only fuelling the flames inside of me.

I looked at my arms, my wounds now scabbing with pink scars forming underneath, which were the remaining evidence of my greywaster struggles. If I would have had a magic genie lamp tell me this is where I was going to sit a few months ago, I would've sent his ass back to his itty-bitty living space.

I didn't think it would be this hard to do as Elish asked… I didn't bank on actually having feelings for the guy. God damn I feel guilty about leaving him… he really liked me.

And I liked him.

I jerked out of my stupor of self-pity as I heard the bathroom door open. I quickly took a piss and opened the stall to leave.

I stopped in my tracks as I realized the red-haired one and his friend were blocking the exit. The two dudes I had been eyeing up in the bar earlier.

"Excuse me, fellas." I went to push past them when I felt a hand on my shoulder. I immediately bristled realizing they were hostile. I took a step back and stood up straight. I felt the atmosphere in the room become dangerous. "Problem?"

They blond one's hand remained on my shoulder, his gaze was smouldering. Behind him I heard a click as the crimson-haired dude locked the door.

Yep… there was a problem.

"You were Elish's pet. I saw you with him so don't deny it. Where is Jade, why isn't Jade with him?"

I felt my eyebrows raise, who was this guy? I ignored the staticy feeling in the air and tried to play it cool. "I'm sure their business is not yours."

I took a step to walk past them when suddenly the blond one punched me right in the jaw. I was braced though, as soon as the fist connected with my face my own fist rose. I knocked the punk hard in the mouth, blood spurting from his lips as his tooth cut right through.

As my arm was extended, another blow hit the side of my head, courtesy of the red-haired fuck. A burst of light infiltrated my vision as my head snapped back. I felt it crunch against the hand dryer and dent in under the weight of the blow.

My legs failed me; I fell to the ground. I squinted hard as the room got bright and started to pulse in my head like a heartbeat. I tried to get up but I felt a kick in my stomach.

"You fuck, I was shot last month!" I snarled, coughing up a spray of blood; I had bit my tongue when I fell.

"Where is Jade? His pet? Jade. Where is he?" the crimson one hissed. I saw blue jeans as he knelt in front of me. Then a painful tug as he grabbed my hair; he kept wrenching my head up until I started to attempt to get to my feet.

"Hidden, he fucking got hurt and Elish is taking care of him," I coughed, tasting and smelling copper. My nose was bleeding like all hell; I tried to wipe it but it was like wiping a running tap.

The red-haired one shook my head, his teeth were clenched hard; I could see the entire outline of his jaw. "All he does is fucking get Jade hurt," he snapped. He grabbed my collar and shook me like a dog. "You, who are you? Why are you with Garrett now? Where's Elish?"

"It's none of your–"

He dropped me. I felt the cold tile hit the side of my face, smelling like bleach and dirt. I coughed and watched it become dusted with red, the world around me started to spin.

My face grimaced in pain as he kicked me for the sheer hell of it. I felt the first blow but the following volley was only pressure and the sickening thunk of heavy impact. My brain had shut it down. It was just a thudding rain of blows now on an already damaged and recovering body.

Then a window closed and I was alone in the bathroom, bleeding. I tried to sit up but I was stuck crumpled up on my side. Streaks of blood and boot prints were on the white tiled floor and my smeared hand prints from trying to right myself.

It took me many attempts and several minutes before I managed to stand. Blood was dripping down my nose like snot, leaking onto my prickly face and onto the floor. My mouth was full of it too from my bitten tongue.

I staggered out the door and took a shaky step before I collapsed against the wall. I panted for a second trying to regain my breath before I took another step, this one into the main area of the bar.

The entire bar fell silent.

Only the faded sound of music in the background, everything else was a hushed whisper, the eyes burrowed into me with shock and confusion.

I tried to take another step.

"Oh god, Saul! Saul!" I heard Garrett exclaim, his voice a high octave of fear. The moment I heard him I felt my knees give out, no longer feeling like they had to hold me steady since I was safe. I dropped and went to fall forward when I felt Saul grab me.

"Get the fuck out of the way. You there, help me with him. Garrett, run and get the car. You right there, go with him do not let him out of your sight. Now!" The tone that Saul barked those orders left no room for discussion.

I felt his rough strong hands keep me upright and a new set on my other side. "It was that red-haired shit, I saw him go into the bathroom with the blond one. Gio, get the thiens down here, get Ellis to call Garrett in the morning. He's going to want to talk to her."

The next few minutes passed in a daze, I just knew I was being dragged and that I couldn't move my feet.

Finally I think Saul got tired of dragging my ass and he hoisted me up into his burly gorilla arms. Then the cold feeling of winter outdoors, and with the slam of a car door, I was inside the vehicle.

Something soft was up against my nose, I tried to focus my eyes and

I saw it was Garrett's jacket trying to stem the flow. I moved my mouth to tell him to not ruin his fancy jacket with my blood but it came out mostly garbled.

"I want them found, Saul. I don't care if Ellis needs to send out every thien, I want them found." He sounded unlike himself, his voice was unnaturally harsh and the more he talked the darker it got. I heard the car quickly drive to the skyscraper. The driver, I could hear, was on his phone, I heard Lyle's name mentioned. Everyone was so busy, talking rapidly around me in angry voices. All because of me; I was so special.

Oh, the things you think of after you've gotten your head knocked around.

"Jade…" I murmured. I shut my eyes as a wave of pain shot up from my still healing abdomen, ripping up my back and ending in a burst of agony in my head.

I gasped, clenching my eyes even tighter. "And Elish."

"What?" Garrett's voice went down several tones. "Re- Otter, what did you say?"

I coughed into the jacket and sharply inhaled, it doubled me over into a coughing fit which seemed to rip my stomach apart with every desperate wheeze. I couldn't talk after that, the colour around my eyes swirling in spectrums that seemed to take my memory elsewhere. I fell into them and passed out, the last feeling I had was Garrett's arms holding me up.

I woke with the muddled warm feeling that only good opiates could give you. I opened my eyes but everything was a twisted blur around me, fuzzy motes of browns and reds that seemed to swirl every time I blinked my eyes.

My body shifted out of instinct, and I felt the soft new sheets against my skin which told me I was in Garrett's bed. I squinted and looked around.

I saw the back end of Lyle as he left the bedroom, just moments later Garrett walked in.

I could tell he was faking looking composed, his hands had a slight tremble, and from the thin jawline, I knew his teeth were clenched. But in the steel only reserved for chimeras, he carried himself with an air of confidence and control, even if he was a tornado of emotions on the inside.

The more I hung around chimeras the more I understood Reaver. Whether my best buddy knew it or not, he was definitely cut from the same cloth.

To go from having no family to having like a billion brothers varying from nice to insane.

Lucky guy.

My suave chimera gave me a kind and reassured smile and sat down in a fabric chair beside the bed. "How are you feeling?" He rested a hand on my damp forehead and brushed my silver hair back in a soft soothing motion.

With every ounce of strength I tried to pull my mouth into a smile, but a pain rippled through my lips. Of course, since my body is stupid, the *owe* I uttered made my lips stretch more; I felt them split back open.

Garrett sucked in a pity breath for me and dabbed my lips with a paper towel. "You're okay, just a bit tender. Lyle checked your bullet wound and nothing was re-opened or punctured."

"Did you find them?" I croaked. The hoarseness in my voice made him turn and offer me something brown. I drank it and realized it was cold apple juice. It made my face pucker.

His expressive eyes told me no, but his lips wouldn't give me any absolutions. "My sister is searching high and low for them. We will find them, I promise, *lutra dulcis.* Those two have no idea who they just danced with." I felt a small shudder as I heard the malice in his voice, a very interesting side of my suave chimera. Especially with that funny chimera lingo they spoke when they were feeling emotional. I hated that in my pain and muggy misery, I felt almost flattered and giddy that I had made him feel that strongly.

"The red-haired one, I think he thought I replaced Jade. He was pissed off and demanding where Jade and Elish were. He knew you guys."

A look of concern crossed his face, he thought for a second. "I know. I realized who he was soon after. He's Jade's ex-boyfriend. We had a lot–" Garrett stopped himself. After furrowing his brow for a moment, he shook his head as if dismissing whatever thoughts were running through his mind. "I've requested a meeting with my sister Ellis tomorrow. I'm going to bring you along if you're well-enough..." He sighed, before stroking my hair back and kissing my forehead. "I shouldn't have let you lure me to that pit. From now on we'll be frequenting better establishments.

I frowned, but with a sigh I nodded. "It just reminds me of home."

"Oh..." His green eyes were heavy; he drummed his fingers against his hand. "Of course."

I tried to think of something funny to say to him. That's what was needed, a nice quip or joke to quell the heavy air around us. I didn't like moments like this, silent tension between two people, it made my skin crawl.

"So are you going to give me a kiss or am I too gross for you now?" That was the best I could come up with.

Garrett smiled; he ran his hand to the side of my face and framed it, before he gently kissed my lips with his, opening the soft inlets and taking in my own. I shivered as I felt his tongue slip into my mouth and run along mine.

I lost myself in him, god damn these chimeras had pheromones or something. How else did greywasters and slumrats keep falling for them? I took him in, and we broke apart with my chest tightening.

"This won't happen again," Garrett said, the hard edge back in his voice. He stood up with a smudge of my blood on his lips and had his remote phone in his hand, clenched in a white knuckle grip. "We will meet with Ellis tomorrow."

CHAPTER 8

Reno

DURING MY DAYS OF BEING BEDRIDDEN, I MADE IT my personal goal to stop Garrett from smoking those awful cigars. I'd taken an inhale of one but had doubled over in a coughing fit to his amusement. They smelled like someone had compacted ten thousand old, dried-out cigarettes into one and then coated it with cat hair and wood ash.

My cigarettes mixed in the thick greenish smoke, the pale silver of my Skyfall quils lost within moments of it leaving my mouth. I had even tried to blow hard and push the smoke away but it was like soup. It lingered and stunk up the entire apartment. Luca choked this place with so much air freshener I was surprised it didn't set my Geigerchip off. I think deep down he was looking forward to going full-time back to Elish's. Mr. Obsessively-Organized-Sober-Ice Man.

But that being said, it was nice having him try to come home more often for me. It was a hard thing to juggle being the President of Skytech, a prominent social figure, and a good master, but he tried and he did a good job managing all his duties.

Unfortunately I had not been able to go back to his office; he flatly refused to even let me out of the skyscraper. The only time I had ever gotten a direct order from him. Jake, Saul's son, was stationed right outside the tower at all times on top of the usual thien security guards. I know he saw it as protecting people from coming in but when those combat armor-clad guys stood around there with their bushmasters strapped to their backs I couldn't help but feel like I was being kept prisoner.

But it was for my own good, though I was going a bit nuts being cooped up inside. Luca was my only companion besides my occasional lunches with Jake, at least until Garrett got home around six or seven.

I still had the keycard tucked into my clothes. I had debated calling Elish and telling him I had it, but I knew Ice Man was busy and he had told me to give it to Luca anyway. I decided to give it another couple of days before I called him.

Garrett held me closer and kissed underneath my earlobe. I snorted and scrunched my neck; I was ticklish as hell, something he had discovered, to much glee, since I'd met him. He knew all my soft spots, including ones I hadn't even realized I had.

We were relaxing on the couch in front of an electric fireplace, we had just finished dinner and Luca was clearing our plates. I was sitting on his lap as he half-laid on the couch, our TV with its Skyfall channels on in the background. We had real TV here though no new shows, just reruns of old pre-Fallocaust shows and news which was just fine with me.

After my show was over though he clicked the TV off. "I have a surprise for you, get dressed." Garrett shifted and I got up, my wounds now healed enough for me to be mobile. I rose and crossed my arms, raising an eyebrow at him as he casually started walking into the bedroom.

"What surprise?" This tickled my curiosities. Garrett though only gave me a playful shrug before he disappeared into his bathroom.

I narrowed my eyes at my suave chimera and got dressed like he asked. A half an hour later, Garrett came out dressed to the nines in a black suit and red tie and even sporting a cane. By this time my excitement had reached another threshold. I knew we were finally going out; it had been a damn week since the pub incident and I was dying to touch the actual ground.

I stayed by the door feeling like a dog about to go for a walk. Garrett's eyes shone at me with a glint of anticipation and happiness at my excitement. He opened the door and we left.

I bounced up and down not even hiding my glee. Garrett laughed lightheartedly at me and pressed the lit button on the elevator.

But when he pressed the button for the bottom floor… well, that was just it, he didn't.

"Floor two?" My brow furrowed. I narrowed my eyes at Garrett who has looking up at the elevator ceiling pretending not to notice me.

The skyscraper was a good twenty-storeys at least, but only about three quarters of them were in use by Garrett and his people. It was loaded with a ton of amenities I was free to use however. Weight room, kitchen, even a swimming pool which would be great if I ever learned how to swim. There were about twenty of Garrett's people who lived in the skyscraper including Saul, Jake, and other servants and workers.

There was a *thunk* as the elevator stopped on the second floor, and with that, a flutter went through my heart. The doors separated with a hiss revealing Garrett's surprise in all its glory.

It was a god damn bloody bar right on the second floor.

My mouth dropped open as Garrett grabbed my leash and pulled me in. The room was large and open like most of the floors I had been too. With light blue paint on the walls, still fresh and smelling wet, adorned with large paintings and trimmed with crown moulding.

I couldn't help but pause, my breath in my throat as I tried to take it all in. Even the atmosphere was that of a bar, smelling of smoke and booze and giving off that comfortable feeling that a pub did. There was even a bar man wiping glasses behind a brand-new wooden bar, with bottles of all sizes behind him stacked with varying levels of liquid.

And the main area, it even had god damn people in it. Everyone was ignoring us like bar patrons do, smoking and drinking with their friends, filling the hazy area with low voices.

"I know you miss going out," Garrett's voice said beside me, I could hear hints of bemusement. "So I decided to make you your own bar, *Otter's*. It's free to drink too," he said the last part with a chuckle.

He did this for me? My eyes swept from one side of the bar to the other, dark-stained wooden chairs, tables with a blue tablecloth adorning each, another electric fireplace in the corner with two overstuffed blue chairs. I had to chuckle at the absurdity of it all, all of this for little ol' me. Damn, just because he knew I missed the bar.

Like when he took me to the outlands, all of this to make me happy.

A very attractive looking waiter took us to our seats by the fireplace, bringing us each glasses of wine. I felt my mind swim but not from the drugs. The week since the accident had done nothing to stop the flames burning in my chest. Every day I felt my feelings for him grow, to the point now where I waited every evening for him to come home, and I felt a sense of absence and longing when he left in the morning.

As soon as the waiter left I kissed him softly and passionately on the lips. My hand on his side felt his body relax as I took him in. "I'm not worth all of this, you know. I'm a radiation-crazed greywaster, remember?"

Garrett made a dismissive noise and waved his hand. He leaned back and crossed his legs, and raised a wine glass to me. "Only the best for my cicaro, right?" He gave me a wink, which made my chest twinge. "Whatever you want, I'll get it for you, just ask." Garrett took a drink and put it down with a smack of his lips. "Which reminds me, take out those god awful steel pegs in your ears."

My hand automatically went up to my ear. I had three earrings in each, I liked my steel pegs. "Aw, really? Do you know how many ravers I had to kill to find matching sets?"

Garrett gave an animated shudder. "I saw a group of those once, in the blacksands I believe. How do you arians even survive in such a desolate place?" The president of Skytech reached into his pocket and I saw a velvet case in his hand. "To think of someone like you being in that world."

I stopped the frown before it could reach my lips. That was my world though and I still wanted to one day go back to my world. I missed the greywastes.

Garrett thankfully didn't notice, I watched as he held out the box to me. "I found my diamond in the wastes. It is only suiting you wear your status."

I gave him an inquisitive smirk and opened the box.

Well holy crap, he got me jewellery. My mouth dropped open as I realized past the pearl-size diamonds were little silver studs. They were earrings; six of them. One pair were white diamond; the other black diamond, and the other red.

"The red ones are rubies, real ones." Garrett took the box back and stood up. I felt him start to take my now very garbage-seeming earrings out of my ears. "The clear ones and the black ones are both diamonds, the backing is platinum."

"Thank you, you're making me feel like a king here. I'm really not worth this," I chuckled. Reaver was worth this, Reaver was a clone-chimera-Superman… I was just, a waster who got sold like a deacdog. I was nothing.

I wasn't even here to be his partner; I was here to get information for Elish.

When Garrett was done he reached into his pocket for a mirror. I sighed and held a hand out to stop him. "I'm serious, Garrett. I'm nothing; I'm a dime a dozen waster who was sitting alone in a cabin on a rock a few months ago, eating rat meat and snorting drugs. You know I'm not… I'm not worth this."

Cookie cutter replies were not Garrett's forte; he looked at me with a half-smirk and held up the mirror to me.

Three in each ear, white, then black, then red. "I don't care what you were," he said. "It's what you are now. You're my pet and that makes you deserving of every luxury and everything your heart might want. It doesn't matter who you were, you are mine now, *lutra.*"

I stared at my reflection in the mirror and took pause. I stared at myself, really stared at myself. Not the passing glance I had when I was fancying myself up or after a shower, I actually looked.

My soft, silvery hair that Luca loved to style, my now trimmed and shaped eyebrows that seemed to bring out my blue eyes. My face, healthier-looking and younger since I shaved every few days now, still oval-shaped, ending with a pointed chin.

The collar around my neck, leather and studded with red jewels, trailing off a thin leash of steel links, and my ears… now adorned with shiny gemstones, worth more money than I had ever made in my life.

Lutra… Otter…

My eyes closed. Reno Nevada, that was my name. I was a field sentry from Aras, my best friend Reaver was hidden in a safe house far away from here, in threat of danger every day, the same with my little Tinkerbell. I was a greywaster, I wasn't a pet named Otter. I had black hair, grey gaunt wasteland features, and permanent black marks under my eyes from too little sun, too much drugs, and a life of food with little nutritional value.

I don't think I even knew who I was anymore.

I thanked Garrett a million times and relaxed into the soft fabric, in response he put a strong and protective arm around my waist.

I listened intently as he rattled on about his day, what his plans were and anything he wanted to talk about. I felt a drowsy happiness as we talked. So relaxed, and content. The people who I still didn't know, coming and going with their drinks and food. Maybe he had offered free food and drinks if they would stay a while, add to the atmosphere I had missed so much.

My reverie broke though when I heard Garrett's phone ring. He gave a low groan, mumbling something I didn't pick up over the faint music and people chattering. I put down my glass, looking forward to him picking up the rest of his story when he was free again. Garrett was telling me in great detail about a centipod hunt he had been on several months ago. Giant centipede-type-things which sounded fucking terrifying. I had never seen one of those things around Aras but in our side of the greywastes we were more raver infested. It seemed around Skyfall and the plaguelands they had more abomination-type creatures. Probably since they had way more labs there, and apparently Silas found it hilarious to release breeding pairs into the wild.

My sense of contentment though disappeared as I saw Garrett's face fall. He read the screen of his phone with an ill look and glanced around the bar before taking the call.

My anxiety only intensified as he gave me a polite wave before getting up and taking the call out on the balcony.

I watched him pace, and make motions with his free hand, his expressive eyes showing a wide variety of emotions. I knew this wasn't good, and when he kept looking in my direction I had an idea who it was.

Someone had woken up early.

Garrett finally hung up the phone but he didn't immediately walk back inside. Instead he lit a cigarette and smoked it on the balcony, an opiate one. I had never seen him show any interest in them. He liked his hard liquor and his cigars; he was the most drug-sober person I knew.

I watched the blue ember make a swirl in the air as he flicked it over the side of the building. I saw him straighten out his red tie and walk back inside with a smile on his face.

But I wasn't stupid, I saw it in his eyes. "Do you want to go home?"

"Ah, sure." Garrett's eyes glanced around the room before he motioned to the waiter. Promptly the young man bought him his pot pie hat and his jacket. Then, with a tinkle of chains, he took my leash and we walked back into the elevator.

When we got into his apartment he immediately hit the liquor again. I was a pet so I kept my mouth shut about it. I changed into some less tight-fitting clothes and took it upon myself to get a bowl of candies and some soda to water down the rye he had just poured for himself, then I took my seat beside him.

"Silas has summoned us to Alegria," Garrett whispered. "His skyscraper, tomorrow evening."

My throat felt like it had been filled with small needles. I tried to swallow but it got stuck halfway down my throat and stayed there. "He's awake?"

Garrett gave me a slow nod, the tip of his mouth turned down, he looked grim. "He's angry… very angry that Reaver escaped."

"So he's going to take it out on me?"

Garrett took a drink of his rye; he shook his head as the rich brown liquid swirled in his tumbler. "He seemed amused that Elish gave you to me as a pet. He… well, he had good things to say about your nature."

That was a relief to hear, I had always acted normally around Asher. I hadn't minded the guy before he started trying to date rape Reaver. I mean even after he fucked me when I had told him no I was still civil. I don't think I had given him any reason not to like me besides being associated with Reaver.

"But… there is no doubt there will be questions," Garrett said.

I watched as almost instantly as his body language changed, like he was putting on his chimera shoes. He swirled the cup around and looked at me over his brow. "Reno, I respect your life before you came here. I hold no grudges against you, I have no reason to. I must know before we see him… do you know where Reaver is?"

I shook my head automatically as my heart did a flip in my chest. I pushed down my rising fear and the edging intimidation I felt at his tone.

In a matter of moments I felt myself humbled. I was in the presence of a chimera who was very much loyal to Silas.

God dammit, Reno, remember that.

"I passed out on the plane," I said. I was a terrible liar but I think I was doing a good job at keeping my composure.

"The next thing I knew I was in Elish's skyscraper with Lyle hovering over me. I… I don't even know if Killian is with him, or Perish." I shrugged and sighed, feeling a sadness wash over me that wasn't entirely put on. "I don't know anything."

I expected him to nod, or show some sign that he accepted my answer but those shards of green stone stared right into me. I shifted uncomfortably and dropped my gaze.

"Reno, I don't… I really don't care where Reaver is, or his boyfriend. It's taken me twenty years but I managed to separate my personal life from King Silas and my more… difficult brothers. I have no interest in this fight. I'm too busy running Skytech I can't play another one of his games." His cheeks puffed out as he sighed; he rubbed my hand and squeezed it. "I couldn't care less if you've been hiding Reaver in my closet all this time, I just don't want you to give him any reason to hurt you." His second hand clasped over his first and he gently shook my hand. "Do you understand?"

I couldn't bring myself to look him in the eye. It wouldn't be long now before Elish took me back, especially now that Silas was awake. It was going to break Garrett's heart. "I understand."

The longer I was here the more I did understand. I understood the cards Garrett was holding, and the cards Silas held as well. Silas was off playing his own little game of *Catch Reaver*, that's all he cared about. Garrett was just doing his normal routines running the companies; he had no interest in what his lord and master was doing.

It wasn't what I expected, but it made sense the more I thought about it. There was Skyfall to run and the trade routes and the block maintenance, it all didn't get done by itself. Some of the brothers had been raised for these positions and there they stayed, separated from the everyday chaos that was King Silas.

It was a huge world outside my cabin door, and the longer I was in it the more I was understanding just what it was about.

More or less I was understanding the Dekker family. There were almost three different worlds, the Skyfall world, the greywaste world, and the Silas world. Silas ruled all worlds but he only had an acute interest in his own. Sometimes they bled into each other but mostly I think *Asher* entertained himself with games and torturing.

Immortal people were scary.

I looked down at Garrett's hands, adorned with several silver and gold rings. I had memorized each of those bands now. I realized on his ring finger was a silver ring with three gems, a diamond, a black diamond, and a ruby. My heart hurt, recognizing the pattern and wondering if it had a symbolic meaning to him.

I placed mine on top of his, knobby knuckles and hands that would never properly play a piano, scarred but no longer rough from being a greywaster; my hands were soft and silky like any pet Otter worth their salt.

Otter... the words burned my lips but I didn't say it out loud. I leaned down and kissed his hand, and closed my eyes, wondering if I knew who I was anymore.

"I trust you."

I leaned forward to kiss him, and moments later with our tumbles forgotten I climbed on top of him. I slid my hand up his shirt and found his heartbeat.

Sure enough, it was a racing motor, and as I gently traced my fingers down his flat stomach I felt how tense he was. This alone put a doubt in my heart that his face could have never revealed to me.

But I pushed it away and let the taste of his mouth wash it down. In his arms I accepted whatever fate would come to me. Tomorrow before we left I would see Luca, and I would give the card key to him. If worst came to worst at least I had done my mission.

I just hoped it was enough.

The next morning, with a boulder inside my stomach I handed off the card to Luca. My petpet remained steadfast and neutral but I saw the frown in his eyes and I knew he was worried. Luca knew what was going on, thankfully though no one gave serventmaids a second glance. I knew he would get the information and the keycard back to Elish.

I was supposed to be gone by now... I swallowed, trying to dash the boulder inside me but it felt like I was dragging a dead weight.

Eerie enough, during the night Garrett had transformed himself. When he woke up the next morning he was very serious and almost cold towards Saul and Luca. I stayed well away from him and kept my joking down to a minimum. By afternoon I didn't think I'd said more than several words to him. Every time I looked to see what he was doing, he was rigid and seemed covered in prickles. I couldn't wait for this to be all over, just to see him relaxed again.

I decided to suck up and I practiced on the piano as he clicked away on his laptop and chain-smoked like a chimney. The entire time I watched a single stray black hair slowly free itself from its gel prison to eventually grace the middle of his forehead.

Time seemed to slow to a crawl, but in another way it came too quickly. Before I knew it I was in the car, my knee going up and down in a nervous twitch and my hands tensing around each other.

"Alegria," Garrett said in a cold voice. He stared ahead, I watched as his Adam's apple went up and down as he swallowed.

My heart pulled me towards him; I put a hand around his waist and drew him close to me before leaning my head on his shoulder.

"Reno..." His voice was so low it had a graveliness to it I hadn't heard before. "Listen to me, every word." He took a deep breath and started talking to me quietly, his own hand now on my knee clenching it. "I might have to say things I don't mean, and act in ways I won't want to. Remember Silas is my master, like I am your master. I have to submit to him, obey him, and love him." He took in a heavy breath through his nose. I got the impression he was trying to give a two hour speech with a five minute time limit.

"But what is more important is how you have to act. You are a pet now, you are submissive to me and to him, do not break your role. Do not give him a single hint that you're not submissive to him or he will *break* you until he feels you are." The way he said break made me shudder, it had a solidity to it that made me almost feel it. "Even if you forget everything else I've said remember that. If he doesn't feel you're obedient to him, he will break you down and, Otter, I will not be able to interfere or else he will only hurt you further. I am his creation, he is my master, and he treats me better than some of the others because I always remember that."

What have you gotten me into, Elish…?

The rhythmic motion of the car did nothing to lull my racing mind. Inside my bones rattled, like an earthquake that started in my head had spread to every cell in my body. I was tensed, nervous… nah, I was terrified.

The streets of Skyland seemed to separate for our vehicle, the commoners knew who we were. Master and pet, Garrett and Otter. They stopped and stared before carrying on their day-to-day lives. Full of shopping, full-time jobs, and the artistic culture that Silas had seemed to want to bring to Skyfall. Such a contrast from the greywastes, it still gave me pause more often than not. My life had changed so much… had Reaver and Killian's? Where were they now? Safe I hope and staying safe.

At least they had each other.

I got out and immediately my head rose to take in the towering skyscraper before me.

It was the most fixed up one out of all of them, every single window was still intact and most of them I could see filled with a warm light. The building itself was grey with black window frames at least twice as tall as Garrett's.

I tightened my jacket as I felt a shiver go through me, though it wasn't from the chilly winter air. I looked to see Garrett beside me but he made no move to warm or comfort me. He was in chimera mode, I could see it in his eyes.

I felt like a sacrifice being taken to the alter by an unwilling owner. It wasn't until my chain tightened that I realized he was leading me inside.

The entire entrance was glass, as I passed through the doors (opened by cute servants in tight little winter outfits) I noticed the glass was very thick, bullet proof I was assuming.

With my legs becoming more and more like dead weights I walked into the entrance area.

How it could be possible to make an entrance entry more fancy than Garrett's I didn't know. The walls were adorned with new blue pattern wallpaper split halfway down with black wood paneling. The floors were grey marble with black swirls which touched the corners of every room, there was even a god damn fountain in the center.

I recognized the creature in the middle, a scorpion, cougar hybrid. The same creature that Garrett had on a necklace made out of gold that always hung around his neck. They also called the symbol a chimera. I guess it was their mascot or something, I really hoped it didn't exist. A giant cougar with six legs and a stinging tail was nothing I felt like fucking with in the greywastes.

The lighting was dim, oddly warm, and welcoming. I felt an immediate sense of deception from just that. This was not welcoming, it was a lions' den. I don't know why but just the sheer contrast of what the welcoming area wanted to say and what it actually was shredded my nerves.

Killian… god dammit, he would be able to give me some pointers on dealing with the real Asher. Not the knucklehead I fucked senseless in my cabin, the real King Silas who tortured and raped him. I wish I had five minutes with him, I bet he knew what insects crawled under the king's skin…

A beep from an elevator and the smell of peppermint and anxiety. I automatically walked inside, and without a word spoken, we started to go up in the elevator. To the top floor.

My heart… I knew Garrett could hear it, I was sure Silas would be able to too. This notion made me steel my insides. Even if it was a band aid over an asthma attack at least it would serve as a reminder that I had to match my body language to my words.

Don't even bother playing it cool, he'll know.

Just pretend you're dealing with evil Reaver… no… just pretend you're dealing with Reaver after Killian dumped his ass and all he's done since then is grow more and more manically insane, and then add all the power in the world and like twenty super servants that fulfilled his every whim.

No wonder this guy was fucking nuts, Reaver would've started another Fallocaust by now.

I swallowed the razor blades seemingly lodged in my throat, and with that thought seeping its anxiety into my brain, I watched Garrett walk through the elevator doors.

I followed, but as soon as the doors closed behind me I couldn't move; my feet became welded to the spot as my legs began to tremble.

The apartment held in it a dark ambiance, rich brown painted walls with deep red carpet, a real gas fireplace in the center of the living room, framed by wall-to-wall windows of Skyland before us. Smelling of cinnamon and spices I couldn't identify, with ceiling lights on silver rails, halogen and warm, aided with black shaded table lamps that all matched.

The place was beautiful, but… but I still couldn't move.

I felt my leash tighten, though like a stubborn dog I didn't budge. Garrett turned around but I couldn't meet his gaze. My eyes were looking in all directions for *him*.

The apartment's darkness held shadows and in this moment the thought of Silas hiding in a corner to charge at me terrified me like nothing else. He was a phantom in my brain, King Silas was a ghost from a land far away; Asher was a raticater who I hadn't minded.

The two were not the same people.

"Reno… such a strange sight to see you… in my home."

I closed my eyes, hearing my breath come out of my nose in anxious huffs, bordering on hyperventilating. It was his voice but colder, like icicles would drip from their words if they were given the chance. I had heard that tone when he told me I had no choice but to be fucked by him.

My mind turned to mush, but in the relentless shifting of grey matter the resolution that kept replaying over and over was that I couldn't *not* act submissive, even if I didn't want to.

"Hey… Silas is it?" My mouth twitched a few times before I managed a smile. I looked down at my boots, still glued to their place. The leash was now slacked. "Good to see you."

"See me?" Silas whispered. I felt a dark presence press against me; I knew he was coming closer. "You have been avoiding looking at me… scared are we?"

My face recoiled as I felt a frozen hand brush against my chin; I didn't even realize he was so close to me until I felt that touch. Then I remembered Asher in Aras, he was stealthy, a ghost in the darkness sneaking from one place to another. The guy was a fucking wraith… and cold like one.

With a small upturn of his finger, my chin followed until I was eye to eye with him.

With golden blond hair framing his dark green eyes, Asher Fallon smiled at me, a sardonic, sinister smile that told me in volumes that this would not be an easy encounter.

"I… I like your hair…" I stammered.

I saw the silhouette of Garrett behind him but I wouldn't break my gaze and look at him. I kept them fixed on his eyes, deep green suns that burned my own in their sockets. I knew if I looked to Garrett for help he would feed on that immediately.

Asher strangely shushed me. He traced a finger down to my neck before it creeped back up. I shuddered as I felt his ice cold talons wrap my neck into his grip. He gave it a slight squeeze and shook it.

"Where's he, Reno? My *bona mea*? He's escaped." I felt his breath center on my ear as he hissed the last words. His head cocked to the side, and his emerald icebergs tried to find my gaze. It took me a moment to work my brain into looking at him again.

"Once the mob took us I didn't have a chance to talk to him, before I knew it I passed out. Elish brought me here. I… after a week or so I was sold to Garrett." My voice shook as his fingers tightened around my neck. My legs decided to work for a moment but they only made me step backwards until my back was up against the wall.

Silas loosened his grip until his hand was once again flat; in the same instant his touch suddenly became warm, almost hot. I furrowed my brow and craned my neck away from him.

How the hell was he doing that?

"Where would he be hiding?" Silas's voice suddenly became like honey. His warm touch soothed the frozen skin, however it did nothing to stop the hammer in my chest and my brain shooting warning flares throughout my body. My god, this is the exact way Reaver intimidated people. My worst nightmare was becoming his enemy.

"I… I don't know. For all I know he's hiding in the bunker. I didn't even get a chance to–"

"Garrett… undress him."

My body stiffened and tensed as he withdrew his touch; he stepped back as Garrett walked towards me. His face was stone, expressionless, and almost sterile. Like a robot he unbuttoned my top, then my pants. For not even a fraction of a second did he make eye contact with me.

I felt my neck go hot as he stripped down even my underwear. I pressed my bare back against the wall and hung my head, feeling too raw in front of them to make eye contact.

“Trimmed as well? Have you sampled his nectar already?”

“No, I have been wanting to wait.” Garrett was trying to keep his voice steady but the stammer gave him away. A gazelle that just took a step and revealed a limp. My chimera was scared which made me even more fearful.

I felt my head start to burn but I steeled my face and glared at the floor, determined to at least keep some of my greywaster pride.

“He is such a virile thing in bed, you will enjoy him,” Silas whispered. I felt a warm finger trace my short pubes then brush up against my very flaccid dick. “Love starved, that much was for sure. Did you notice that as well? He thirsts for attention; it was like he had a fever in his loins when he fucked me… though… we were both moaning for the same man.”

Same man... he meant Reaver.

“Reno… did you think of Reaver when I fucked you?” Silas whispered, his finger tracing the slit. They were still warm, almost uncomfortably warm. The tender flesh on the head of my penis was sensitive to everything; unlike these chimeras I wasn’t cut.

I felt the first twinge of hardness in my dick as he rubbed it. I tried to funnel all my energy into remaining soft but I felt my legs arch and stiffen.

“No,” I said through clenched teeth. I closed my eyes and felt him cup the head before he tugged on it.

“Oh, he’s telling the truth…” Silas whispered, warmth tingled on my neck, and I could feel his breath tickle the soft hairs behind my ears. A moment later, I felt his mouth lick my nipple.

“Lucky you, Garrett. He does like you.”

“Now… let’s try another question…” Silas’s tone dropped. “Reno, do you know where Reaver might have gone?”

I gasped as he nipped on the sensitive flesh, sending a wave of unwanted pleasure through my body. “No, I don’t.”

He stopped and withdrew his mouth from my nipple, his hand firmly clenching my half-hard dick in his hand. In the silence I opened my eyes and looked at him.

Silas's face was a granite mask, his eyes two knives that flayed mine as soon as they met.

He shook his head back and forth and clicked his tongue. "You're lying."

I gasped and let out a shocked scream as I felt an overwhelming jolt of pain spread from his hand to my penis, ripping up my back and pooling in my brain like lava. For a moment I stood on my tip toes until I fell to the ground, gasping and trying to stifle my own cries. I tried to get away from him but my legs were twitching and useless. I lay in pieces on the floor, crumpled on my side.

Then another one, this one on the back of my neck. It was like a white hot knife had driven itself into my last vertebrae and was being twisted around like a screwdriver. I felt every muscle in my body spasm and constrict as the burning electricity fried my every last nerve.

I heard Garrett yell. That alone scared me into a panic, my over-taxed nerves bordering on launching me into an anxiety attack.

Garrett, dammit, you said you had to remain collected!

"He doesn't know, Master, please!" I focused my eyes and saw Garrett on his hands and knees. His head was bowed. "Elish can attest to it, he saw it with his own eyes. Reno never got the chance to even see what direction Reaver went. He's just looking for a better life here with us."

Silas kicked him aside like a dog in the way and pressed a boot up against my neck. "Sing little bird, where would he be hiding?"

This is what he wanted from me? An idea of Reaver's location? That I could lie; I didn't know where the hell he was, just that it was several hours by plane and covered with rocks. But… I did know cities we scavenged, perhaps that would satisfy him.

I screamed again, my own agonizing wails mixed in with Garrett's. The suave chimera had lost his composure upon seeing me hurt.

We were both fucked, weren't we?

"Just tell him, Reno! If you know, tell him!" Garrett's strangled voice begged.

My head lulled from side to side, as my mind slowly returned I saw Silas looking down on me. “I want my property returned to me, Reno. I want Reaver, I want Perish and I want that squealing little defect Killian as well. You will tell me his hiding places.”

I coughed with his boot pressed against my neck. “I’ll tell you where we used to scavenge; he never had secret bunkers or anything. Fuck, man, I’m telling the truth. We… we scavenged a lot in Gosselin, Sognir, and Gaushall, maybe even Anvil. We also tried the outskirts of the Las Valleys, the canyons… the canyons fuck he could be in there. It goes on for miles, there are caves there.”

I heard Garrett give a sigh of relief; he turned away from me for a moment with his hand on his head. He was all nerves. His green eyes full of an unbridled fear I felt burrow into me. I wondered what I looked like to him right now, an animal being put in its place perhaps.

“Your pet is stubborn, Garrett,” Silas snipped, releasing his boot against my neck. “All this time and only now I get a real answer from him?”

He believed me? Oh thank god, I think my heartbeat was already jackhammering enough he couldn’t read me. Fuck, thank god.

“Do you remember how we enjoyed watching Elish beat Jade?” A smile spread on Silas’s lips that filled me with a gnawing dread. I lay there, naked and exposed, staring up at him. My cold chain hanging from my collar, weighing me down like there was an iron ball attached. “Do you remember… when I made Elish scream for Jade’s mercy?”

A chill fell on me when I saw Garrett’s face go several shades pale. “Master… I am not Elish… I… I have no issues admitting… my… my feelings for him. Just ask, ask me what you want to know. I’ll tell you. You know I am obedient.”

The king clucked his tongue and walked to the side of the room. I heard Garrett suck in a breath as he picked up something else. My heart fucking sank into my feet when I saw he was holding a small whip. “Tell him then. Tell him how you really feel.”

I tried to curl myself as small as possible, knowing it wasn’t any use to do anything. If I picked a fight or beat my chest right now I would only get broken down. I wasn’t Reaver, I was far from Reaver. I was just a dumbfuck waster who got caught up in this shit. I didn’t –

"I love him a lot. I love him already."

What? My eyes widened from shock, I looked at him in bewilderment as those words fell from his lips. Garrett squared his shoulders when he saw I was looking at him, and stood as tall as he could manage under the weight of Silas's gaze.

"That is very plain to see, love, it fills me with such an insane joy that you've fallen in love… for the tenth time." A bemused smile appeared on Silas's lips. I tried to mentally prepare myself for whatever would come next. "Tell me, what happened to your other lovers?"

My heart broke as I saw Garrett's lip tighten to a thin white line, but by his sheer will he stayed standing up straight, harbouring any pride he could muster. "They died."

"What killed them?"

His mouth twitched, I saw the hurt in his eyes. "Several killed themselves, you killed quite a few and… and I killed one."

"Mm, indeed… Garrett?"

"Yes… Master?"

"Beat him."

My mouth opened in a low cry. My arms wrapped themselves over my head and I continued to try and make myself small. I wish I had some clothes, even just socks, something to shield my body from what I knew was coming. I had never felt so fucking helpless.

"For… for how long, King Silas?"

"Until it ceases to please me."

Over my muffled whimpers I heard a dry chuckle. I looked up to see Garrett with his hand towards the whip but Silas pulled it back. "No, no, you're not Elish, remember? Do not whip him, *beat him*."

Garrett stared at him for a moment, before his eyes fell to me. Silas smiled and took a step back, his arms crossed confidently to his chest, the whip hanging down to his knees. Looking like the devil in a grey dress shirt.

Every game was different… every breaking in of a newcomer was different. I bet what he did to Elish and Jade were exactly suited for them. Tweaked and tuned to fit their individual personalities to induce the most suffering. Silas's game for Garrett was to hurt me, that would cause him the most pain. Not just hurting me, but hurting me with his own hands and physical strength

I wanted to mouth to him that it was okay, but I wasn't that stupid. If he knew it was okay Silas would only make it worse. He would switch to something even more damaging, even more mentally painful. I knew that fucking kid; that was Reaver through and through. I had seen Bridley after four days with Reaver, when he was still alive. My friend had paced around him like a cat with a dead mouse, proud as punch and flaunting his prize. That guy hadn't just suffered; Reaver had mentally destroyed him.

Yes, that was your advantage. I tried to draw up every single Reaver file I had. If this was him, if I was Reaver's enemy, what would he want? He would want to see me suffer and the person who loved me suffer. Reaver would drink my tears and cum to the image of my master's pain-filled gaze as he drew down each agonizing blow on my bruised flesh.

I let out a cry as I felt the first punch to my back, though it was more from surprise than pain. Garrett had nothing behind it. My suave chimera stood half-kneeling over me, his chest heaving up and down, a look of pure agony on his face. He closed his eyes with a frustrated yell and hit me again, this time on the shoulders.

A moment later I felt a cold chill, I looked up in time to see Silas crouch over me before he put a hand on my shoulder. "You're holding back from me, Garrett. Must I teach you?"

I shrieked, an electric energy burning every blood vessel in my body. I screamed so loud I felt my eyes bug out of my sockets. My body tensed and contracted in on itself so hard I felt my own piss run down my leg.

"STOP!" Garrett screamed. There was a release but my body wouldn't stop trembling. The remains of the electricity travelling invisible roads up and down my body, leaving behind its own aftershocks that, to my humiliation, made me keep pissing myself.

I tried to speak but my tongue was frozen to the roof of my mouth. I felt it open and close like a fish out of water. I didn't flinch when Garrett hit me hard on the chest, or again on the side of my face.

I tried to cough but it caught in my throat, a moment later I felt a blow to my chest that knocked the wind out of me. I started to inhale rapidly, bordering on an uncontrollable hyperventilating. Each breath was hoarse and ragged but still he continued to hit me.

Then everything stopped. I could hear their mumbling voices but I only caught the end of their conversation.

"I went so easy on you, you're lucky you've never given me any large troubles," Silas said crisply. "And if my mind wasn't elsewhere I might have made it worse."

"Thank… thank you, Master," Garrett croaked, his voice held a weight of sorrow that crushed my heart. I saw unshed tears in his large green eyes.

"Don't thank me, Garrett. I am not done with him. If I don't find Reaver in one of those locations mark my words, there will be a second visit." Silas took a step back with his hands folded behind him, giving him a deceitfully celestial appearance. His shining eyes fell to mine, and another sarcastic, knowing smile creased to his lips. "Keep him close, you never know when another one might decide to kill himself."

He turned and waved a hand at us. "You may leave."

Saul looked grim when we emerged from Alegria. He had Garrett's personal car waiting for him, this one with darkened windows and a lower profile. Where hopefully no one would notice us.

The old man with the stern face stood with his arms to his side looking forward, the door opened and waiting. Garrett got in without so much of a nod, his sunglasses covering his eyes, hiding any emotions he might be feeling. I didn't have anything to hide the welts forming on my face.

When we arrived home I stood there for a moment, wondering what was supposed to happen now. But when Garrett immediately went to the balcony with a smoke and a drink I gave up looking at him for guidance, so I took it upon myself to shower and change into clean clothes.

When I got out he was still out there, lighting one cigarette after the other and making himself one drink after the other from the liquor bottles left outside.

I fell asleep with my eyes watching the flaring orange ember, rising and falling every couple minutes.

Day came with me passed out on the couch, a blanket thrown over me. The apartment was empty, not even Luca was here. Garrett had gone off to work and there I knew he would stay until the evening, if he even came home at all.

I ordered in some food, even though I really wasn't hungry. My body felt raw and tender to any slight touch, during the night the red and purple welts had turned into black bruises, though they were nothing compared to the mental bruises I felt on my brain.

I poked my hamburger and potato fries; the smell that would usually make me salivate and act like a starved dog only made my stomach sour. I took two bites before giving up and placing it into the fridge.

This was a familiar feeling… one that was so imprinted in my mind I felt like drawing it up was as easy as clicking a file on a computer. I had woken up similarly when Bridley had fucked me. Though I hadn't been fucked just… beaten on by my master. Elish smacked Jade around, maybe I should just get over it.

I could get over it a bit quicker if Garrett would just look at me. He was ignoring me like the plague. I could understand if he felt bad but… why was he shutting himself away from me? I didn't fucking do anything wrong.

Maybe that was a chimera thing. Ignoring the person who had gotten hurt, even when the hurt guy would give anything for just a hug. Reaver had done the same thing when Bridley had did what he did. I had hated it, he just ranted and raved and threw shit when he had found me. Then after he went off for his two weeks of torture.

But that being said, Garrett didn't have someone to take it out on, he couldn't touch Silas. I guess he was just going to drink and smoke himself into a stupor and at the same time bury himself in work.

Sure enough… Garrett came home completely hammered that night.

My suave chimera was a mess, and though a good pet would support him and take care of him I was too pissed at him to really give a shit. I watched as he stumbled inside with a mumbled greeting, before grabbing more liquor and going to the balcony alone.

The entire day had been mental torture for me. I had never watched more TV or seen more movies in my life. I just wanted some distraction to get my mind off of what Silas had done to us. That was just a small bandage though. I didn't want to ignore it anymore. That was driving me crazy. I wanted to talk to him about it, get some fucking reassurance that he wasn't mad at me, maybe even get a hug. Not ignore it.

I didn't even have drugs, and my opiate pack of smokes was gone. I wasn't allowed out of the building to buy more, Garrett wouldn't let me.

My mouth twitched, I watched the dark silhouette continue to smoke, the tumbler resting beside him next to an overflowing ashtray. Garrett wasn't paying any attention though; he didn't care. Well, I wasn't going to sit around and drown my brain with more television, I needed to go out and get my mind really off of shit, at least for a while

I changed into normal clothes, and grabbed my jacket. I didn't hide any of this from the large windows that separated the living room from the large balcony. If Garrett wanted to stop me, at least it would force him to talk to me, to acknowledge my existence.

He didn't though, and with the press of an elevator button, I descended to the main floor.

The doors opened and I strolled through the elegantly decorated lobby. Ignoring the reception lady and the thiens holding their bushmasters. Surprisingly no one stopped me, maybe because Saul wasn't there to notice my escape. I adopted a face that said I was busy and on my way to something important and I walked through the doors.

Immediately I felt better. Once I was out of the eyesight of the thiens and the people hovering around Garrett's skyscraper I took a relieved breath of frozen winter air and exhaled a large plume.

It was nine at night. Everyone was out and dressed in fancy clothes with even fancier hairstyles, all of them walking by me without so much of a look. The elegant elites and the lower class visiting the shops, going to dinner dates or returning home late from work. In Anvil everyone was dressed in sweat-stained jackets and stitched together clothing from over two hundred years ago with boots held together with duct tape and rubber cement.

We were all poor in the greywastes. Even if you had three thousand tokens to your name you were still poor, because everything out there was used and old. You waltz into Aras with tight leather pants, clean fluffy hair, and a tight shirt two things will either happen to you: we'll make fun of you and then we'll scam you somehow, or within the week it'll be dirty, ripped, and stained and you'll start looking like a greywaster anyway.

But here… things were a lot newer, even though most of the clothes and shoes were pre-Fallocaust they had the machines to wash them well, and the shops to repair them. So much shit right at our fingertips.

Yet I would give it all back for my cabin on the hill. I felt like an ant in an ant farm. Like we were all Silas's pets, every single one of us whether it be Morosian or Skylander, we were ants and he could do what he wanted. I would rather be in Aras and free, better than waiting for the thumb to come down and squish you.

Poor Garrett, ninety years he's had to deal with this. I guess it didn't get easier. However my pity for him didn't extend as far as it would have for a normal compassionate and understanding person. Deep down inside I was resentful that he had decided to pretend I didn't exist.

Which is why I was going to go buy some drugs.

I shoved my hands into my pockets and walked down the sidewalk, lit in deceptive welcome with the shining shop lights, every small shop showing off their wares inside the warm store. They were tempting the rich and mocking the poor: big televisions, blenders, and coffee makers, even microwaves. All things my boy Reaver would have killed to open up and tinker with.

I'd show him around if he ever came here.

I glanced into the shop and saw a stack of what looked like waffle makers, that made me smile. I wonder what he was doing right now, if he was safe.

What would Reaver have done if he was there? He would have lunged and gnashed his teeth at Silas until they killed each other. But then again he knew Asher. He didn't know Silas.

No wonder Elish had finally had enough of this. I just hoped Garrett had the balls to come to our side when it was time.

Maybe since he had me he would… because if Silas had done to Elish and Jade what he had done to me and Garrett…

Perhaps that was the last straw for Ice Man.

I brought out my fancy, black metal charge card and slid it over to the drug store lady. As usual her eyes widened and she scuttled off to prepare the bill. This card was one of Garrett's and only chimeras or their partners or pets had them. I didn't know how it worked, I just knew as soon as I whipped it out everyone looked at me like I had just descended from heaven and they did anything I asked. I never had to pay cash for anything; I would be lying if I said it didn't give me a slight power trip.

I tucked my large bag of drugs into my jacket and ducked into the Penguin for a quick drink, though I scanned it first for the crimson-haired fuck and the other one. No one was there though. I drank a juice and vodka concoction, chatted it up with a few bar hoppers and went home. It wasn't much but I missed human interaction dearly. Even if all they did was bitch about work and their partners or kids. That's what everyone did in Melpin's anyway, so that wasn't really a huge change.

I came home without incident; my heart sank a little more into my feet when I saw Garrett was still outside smoking. He didn't care; he probably hadn't even noticed I had left.

I spread my drugs on the large coffee table and organized them. I had probably purchased at least a hundred tokens worth of hardcore and softcore drugs. In the dingy, less desirable areas of my mind it was clear I was doing this as a cry for attention. That and a growing ache to have my own vices to cope.

I had cigarettes of all varieties. They dipped them in anything they could here, from meth, to LSD, to cocaine, and opium. I also had straight-out sniffable heroin called china white, meth, cocaine, Dilaudid, Xanax, Valium and some shit I hadn't even recognized but it was on sale. Every fucking thing had the Dek'ko label plastered with warnings I don't think anyone read.

I got out my fancy metal Garrett Sebastian Dekker black card and cut myself up some china white. Then I scoured the kitchen until I found a straw and cut it to shape. With my drunken, not to suave, chimera continuing to pollute his lungs and his liver in his self-loathing I put on *Good Fellas* and took my first two lines. Then I grabbed a ChiCola and sat down to start enjoying my own unhealthy way of dealing with my issues.

As soon as the first wave of goodness came over me I closed my eyes and took in the incandescent frozen warmth that seemed to cradle my body. I let out a sigh, not of happiness or relaxation but relief. It was all going to trickle away, and what was left I would lose in the movie.

I pulled the blanket closer to me and burrowed my sullen feelings inside of it.

"You… went out?" I opened my eyes, the movie was half over, the drugs were warmth inside me. My eyes didn't look at him but I saw his black trousers in the bend of my vision. His voice was slurred like any normal drunk and he reeked of cigarettes and rye.

He must've taken my silence for confirmation; I saw a long, elegant, ring-adorned hand sift through my new stash of drugs. He picked up a package and opened it, before taking out a green pill. It was one of the ones on sale.

I followed his hand as he popped the pill into his mouth and washed it down with rye.

"You shouldn't take opiates with alcohol." I was shocked to see how hollow my voice was, it sounded like death was twisting each word that came from my lips.

Garrett's eyes were still heavy; he dropped the package and put his glass down. "You don't even know what those are, do you?"

I gave him a glance before I shook my head.

"It's Intoxone. It sucks all the alcohol from your bloodstream, the drug equivalent is Suboxone. Rather handy if you're overdosing. It was on sale, right?"

I nodded.

"I made it a law for it to always be on sale somewhere in each district of Skyfall. Everyone should have some around."

Funny, he was talking to me right now, what I had been craving since we left, yet I didn't know what to say back. My mouth felt glued shut, and my body stiff and cold.

A small silence fell on us, my eyes staring forward at the layout of drugs with Garrett standing beside the couch looking at me.

I couldn't meet his gaze. I had been waiting for him to say something to me for the past twenty-four hours, and now that he had I felt shy and uncomfortable, the memories of yesterday simmering to the surface with each drawn-out moment.

It was after about ten minutes that he spoke, and to my surprise his speech had returned to normal. The Intoxone had done its job, he sounded completely sober.

"I have done a lot of thinking, Reno."

I saw him move around from the window reflection and he took a seat beside me. His hands were clasped except for his two pointer fingers which tapped together. Hands that had grown used to always carrying around a glass and a cigar.

"Do you want to go back to Aras?"

I couldn't go back even if I wanted to, Garrett... Even the suggestion pushed a dagger through my heart. It just went to show how little Garrett knew about what had happened in my home. My uncle grabbing Killian, Redmond shooting me when I charged him... the horror and carnage we had left behind. I couldn't go back to that, not without Silas dead and my two boys by my side. I couldn't live with men who had turned their backs to us.

When this was over and Aras had been cleansed, I would follow King Reaver wherever he went, but right now – that was a fool's dream. So far and out of reach it was almost cruel to tease my mind with the notion.

"No," I whispered. I felt a small tinge of bravery and added. "Do you want me to?"

"Of course not!" My attention broke away from its hypnotic trance when I heard the shock and offence in his voice. I felt shame when I saw despair flood his green eyes. "I... I just..."

I watched him wipe his face with one of his hands and lean back on the couch. He looked defeated and tired, a sigh left his lips and he stared forward.

"I want you to be happy."

Things were too unsure right now for me to be happy, not truly happy anyway. The brief moments of happiness that I had gotten had been with him. How many more of those would I get before Elish collected me I didn't know. Maybe this experience with Silas would make it easier once I did leave.

I had never felt this conflicted in my life. It wasn't something cut and dry like being raped or dealing with Reaver and Killian drama. This was complicated. Many little fabrics woven into one big clusterfuck. I had gotten eyes deep in shit and I didn't even know where I stood anymore.

But there were moments of happiness, when I genuinely felt content, and they had all been with him. Having a drink with him and watching his eyes light up as he talked about all the work stuff I barely understood.

Or the sweet and kind things he did for me to make me feel more at home.

"I'm happy with you."

I saw the thin darkening of his jaw as it tightened, then his green eyes creased with inner turmoil. "You're not safe here; I'm going to set you up with a very nice place in Eros…"

"What!" I said loudly, the colour draining from my face. "That's it? Fucking honeymoon is over and now you're just going to put me away where you don't have to look at me? Fuck you!"

"It's not that, Reno."

"Yes it is!" I was getting more than just a little emotional. Fuck this shit with Garrett; it was making me understand Killian's outbursts. I hated that. "Is this why you're such a retard when it comes to personal relationships? Because once things get complicated you send them off to Eros? Fuck off."

Garrett's hands tensed, his brow was knitted together but his eyes were downcast. "You think King Silas is a *complication*?" His voice was low, almost bemused. "Everyone we love, he eventually takes away. Jade, Trig, Mika… every young piece of flesh is competition for him and he crushes any seed of competition we sew. You have a specific bullseye on you." Garrett's mouth twitched down. "I should… I was stupid to think I could make this work."

"I'm made from stronger stuff," I said flatly.

"You don't know my family… you don't know King Silas. You… you don't know how bad he can get."

I snorted. I saw him turn to me with an injured look on his face but it couldn't be helped.

"My best friend since I was four is your master's exact copy. You don't think I know your family or him? Please," I said incredulously. I didn't stop there though; my mouth kept moving like it had just been shot with W-D-40.

"If you would've just got your head out of your self-loathing ass and talked to me… I would've been able to tell you that. I know I look stupid, I know I act like a fucking joke most of the time, but you don't hang around with Silas Junior for eighteen years and not become a bit hardened to living with a maniac, and his boyfriend ain't much better. I…

I know what… being with you entitles." If Killian could do it, I could.

Then again he did dig up a dead body and lay in it.

"But…" Garrett looked completely taken aback by my small outburst, his mouth opened and closed a few times until he found his words. "What he did… made me do…"

"Yeah? And? So I got smacked around, so what?" I snapped, the anger started to burn inside me. I felt myself stand to my feet, my fists balled. I didn't even know what was happening to me, all I knew was I was getting pissed off.

"You've dealt with it for ninety years, why the fuck are you so broken up? I didn't even get a god damn sympathetic look from you, and here you are whining about how I am not happy, an entire day later? You know what would've made me happy? A hug, that would've been awful nice. It's fucking Reaver all over again. You self-hating little shitheads just go do what makes you feel good, because it's too painful for *you* to look at me. Selfish little fuck. Maybe this isn't fucking about *you*."

Garrett stared up at me, and I saw his shoulders slump. Fucking ninety-year-old super chimera looked like Killian in that second, sorrowful and guilty, but I wasn't done.

"I've been cleaning up chimera bullshit since I was a kid. I helped Reaver dismember a ten year old when he was eight, we ate every piece of him and no one ever found out what happened to him. So stop fucking treating me like I'm the dumb comic relief of some movie who can't deal with the real world or King Psychofuck. Alright? I know what Silas can dish out because I've been cleaning up broken dishes for years. So…" I clenched my teeth; I needed to end this before I completely went off the handle. I didn't have a fancy way of ending it so I made it easy. "So fuck off."

Somewhere in the last ten minutes I had forgotten I was a pet in front of his master. If I was Jade, I had a feeling I would've been knocked to the floor, but Garrett only looked up at me in shock, his mind trying to process every leaded word.

I got up and sighed with defeat. "You've… had a long day and rye isn't food. Did you even eat? I'll order you something." I started to walk towards the dial-a-sengil wall phone but stopped as he grabbed my arm.

I looked down in shock, his hand firmly grasped around my wrist.

"I apologize… I do forget where you came from, I admit." He began slowly, his lips forming every word carefully. "You… it's easy to forget because you're such a cheerful, kind-hearted person, I forget you came from such a horrible place. You hide your scars well."

It's not that horrible. It's my home. I'd loved my life. I couldn't help it, I felt defensive of my old life. It was a paradise compared to this biodome.

"But you're right, about… well… everything." If only they would listen to me when I first said it, him and Reaver. Why was I the chimera-to-human translator? I could see all of this shit plain as day but it seemed to perplex these guys.

Garrett continued. "You are made from strong stuff, stronger than I am," he said with a half-sigh and a tightening of his grip on my arm. "Business I can do, King Silas… he doesn't do this to me often, not very often at all. I think it's been ten years since he summoned me last in that way. Ten years since my last one died." A dry chuckle escaped his lips but his eyes were sorrowful. "I swore… I would never subject another man to my king, but look at me now?"

But Reaver will kill Silas... and you'll be free to be with whoever you want. Not now, but soon... and maybe soon enough that we wouldn't have to be apart for long. My chest burned for me to say those words to him, but I held strong even though it was painful. I wanted to give the poor guy some hope. That he wasn't just being a masochist… that there was hope for us.

I forced a smile and he loosened his grip. "If I can befriend and semi-socially adjust Chimera X, I can certainly handle a tantrum from his original here or there. Give me some credit, alright?"

My heart stopped in my chest as he rose, with a sparkle in eyes that had been drowning in despair for a day now. He put his hand behind my neck and I thought he was drawing me in for a kiss, but instead I felt the buckle of my collar loosen.

There were no words for the sadness I felt when he removed it. My soul felt as cold as my neck did without its leather band. I had gotten used to it in the past month. I was his, I was alright with that.

Was it over now? As quickly as it had started? I thought I had meant something to him, but maybe… maybe he fell out of love as quickly as he fell in. Maybe that's what it was like for immortals.

Garrett looked down at it and I did as well. I saw his fingers gently stroke the inner leather, probably still warm from my neck.

Then it slipped from his fingers, and fell to the carpeted floor with a soft thunk.

"Marry me."

My breath caught in my throat; I looked at his now free hands and then found his eyes.

Light green saucers, specked with yellow, very prominent over his pencil moustache and lips hiding a shy smile. He had such a handsome face, like he had walked out of a 50's sitcom, classically handsome and sophisticated.

He wanted to marry *me*?

I felt my knees start to wobble and he helped me sit down, my body still sore and tender from the previous night. I brought a shaking hand to my mouth and tried to breathe. I felt a supportive arm on my shoulder. He rubbed it.

What do I do… think, Reno…

I was supposed to go and be with Reaver and Killian once Elish collected me. I wasn't supposed to fall for him.

Had I fallen for him?

As I gave in to Garrett soft touch, I knew in my gut I had.

Well, I'd really done it this time. What was with these chimeras? I fell for the first one only to find out he had never felt the same way towards me. The second one I fell for… one of the most important people in Skyfall, was far from my home, my greywaste home, in a different world, bowing to my enemy.

I didn't know the future, so how could I make a decision? My two worlds were mixing in ways I didn't know how to handle. What if Reaver won and we went back to Aras? Garrett would have to stay here and continue to run Skytech, even more so if Silas was dead. I could never be where Reaver wasn't. He was like… my friend soul mate, I had to be where he was.

But I wanted to be where Garrett was too. Why the heck should I have to sacrifice Garrett for Reaver? He had Killian. I had… I didn't have anyone.

"This…" I swallowed the burning in my throat and tried to take in some normal breaths. "This has all happened very very fast." And yet with Garrett beside me, trying to soothe whatever inner turmoil I had, I felt my heart pull towards him. "You want this after only a month?"

"Time doesn't have the same meaning to me, and I've been waiting for you for three years, *lutra*." Garrett's hand moved up and he stroked my silver hair. "I'm old enough to know what I am feeling… and what I said to Silas was no admission made from duress… I love you, Reno."

Shit… shit… shit… my heart started to hammer. I think the only thing keeping it from bursting through my chest were my ribs. I was really feeling dizzy and a bit nauseas. The emotions were coursing through me like a hot knife going down a butter slide.

"I love you too," I whispered, barely even hearing my words. My own logic and reasoning dripped off of those words like water on wax. They had no place in my heart at that moment, I was a fool but I was unable to shut down the fire in me.

"I love you, Garrett."

I felt his forehead lean into my neck and a small relieved breath. I looked down with him as he slipped off a ring on his left hand, the same one I had noticed before.

But as I watched the silver band with the same gemstones that matched my earrings, I realized he had two. He had gotten another one; I hadn't even noticed. This had been planned; this wasn't some whimsy with him lost in the moment.

Garrett really wanted to marry me.

He slipped the ring on my ring finger; it fit perfectly which made a smile come to my lips. The endearing image of him measuring my finger while I slept briefly crossed my mind.

But a darker thought came, like a cloud of shade and shadows it descended on my mind and threatened the fires of joy that grew in me. I knew I could only do this if I made sure of one thing. The only deal breaker that would make me leave my chimera, no matter how much it hurt him and me.

"If I say yes, you have to promise me–" I turned my hand in the lamp light and watched the gems sparkle. "–and mean it. That you'll respect that I will always be aligned with Reaver. I will never betray him." I watched as every word that left my mouth made his smile fade. "If I ever have to ask you… to help him, even if it means going against Silas. You will."

Garrett looked sober, his lips thin and his eyes deep. It was several minutes of both of us sitting next to each other, his hand still on mine, our matching rings sparkling together in the dim light. Although the silence was a deafening weight on us, it wasn't awkward or at all forced. I wanted him to take all the time he needed because I had to have a real answer. Not an answer to make me happy, or to get me to make a commitment to him. This was my life and the life of my friends, and I couldn't be with him if his loyalties would always be to his master.

Finally he grabbed my hand, and when he spoke his tone was low and serious. "I meant what I said before, lutra. You could be hiding him in this apartment and I wouldn't care. I… I won't, and have never, gotten involved."

"But you *are* involved, because he's my friend and I love him, Garrett," I whispered, "and Killian too. I'm… Garrett, I think I'm asking you to choose sides." I stammered the last part, I had tried to word it so it didn't sound like that, but there was no denying it. "If it comes to it, if Reaver comes for him, or if Silas does catch him. Will you be loyal to Reaver? Would you help me do whatever it took…?"

Now it was his turn to look like he was going to throw up; Garrett looked positively ill. The chimera stared at me, I could feel the hurricane ripping through his heart and mind. Probably eating each other alive just like my own emotions had done to me.

Then he nodded at me, and a sad but full smile came to his lips. "My allegiance is with you, *amor*; always with you. Not Reaver, not Silas… with you and whoever you care about. If that's Reaver… I… I'm at your command."

My heart dropped, and in that moment the covers got pulled off of my mind, leaving my brain cold and exposed. As the gears starting turning freely, a new flood of realizations coursed through me with fierce fervour. I took off the rose-coloured glasses, and almost laughed at this situation.

Because I realized in that moment my goal had never been only to find the keycard for Kreig. No, that was too easy. I had a greater task –

one I'd never realized I'd been given until it hit me like a splash of cold water.

It was so obvious, you fool.

Here is your newest ally, Elish. Enjoy. I have the president of Skytech, and one Skyfall's most powerful figures in my palm, and as such… in yours. This was your plan all along, and it worked perfectly.

"I will marry you."

Well-played, Elish. Well-played.

CHAPTER 9

Reaver

THE WEEK SINCE ELISH RETURNED WAS, WELL, interesting. I thought it was amusing how everyone suddenly started walking on egg shells as soon as he emerged from the lower levels to mingle with the common folk. Jade especially, that kid did a complete metamorphosis as soon as that blond chimera opened the keypad door. Jumping up from whatever he was doing (usually wincing, Elish was a relentless machine on that kid's body apparently) and greeted his master with a head incline and squared shoulders.

I spent a lot of time in my room smoking, and out on the surface smoking some more. I had never smoked so much in my life but it helped me cut down on the drug use. Jade's cartons of fancy cigarettes never ran out, and once I found out which crate they'd stashed them into in the garage, I had helped myself to several cartons of each. I fit as many as I could in my drug suitcase and stuffed Killian's canvas bag, and my duffle bag of clothes, full of them.

During this time, Elish and I developed a mutual respect for each other. We didn't speak unless we had something to say, and I respected his rules of the house. I stayed on the sidelines and let the three amigos have their fun. Killian, Jade, and Perish had formed a shaky friendship based on drugs and video games but I mainly stayed in my room. I didn't want to be social; I had too many dark thoughts in my mind and I preferred to be alone with them.

I lit another cigarette, listening to the boys outside in the living room play an updated Mario Kart, from a game system we had never seen in Aras. Killian kept running in every half an hour to make sure I didn't feel neglected, and I didn't. There were too many people in this house for my liking and I wanted to be alone.

I had a lot to think about, and none of those things were good.

As the days went on, I just found myself getting more and more reserved. I was glad Killian seemed to be slowly healing, and though he still did heroin (and so did I), his mind was coming back. He was the boy I had remembered him being.

Me? I was still dealing with being not only the clone of a whackjob, but the fact that I had been engineered to be his partner. I had no clue how to handle that, so I just tried to ignore it. I was already seeing myself change as a person, and I really didn't need another reason to become more dark and isolated. In all actuality I think the old me got left in Aras, or perhaps it was the new me who had gotten left there, because after I had fallen for Killian I had started to open up a bit and come out of this thick shell.

Before my dumbfuck dads ended up getting themselves killed. Before they decided to hide my origins and immortality from me, and give me this task I had never asked for in the first place.

Fuck you two.

"Reaver, a word?"

I looked towards the door and saw Elish darkening the view I'd had of Killian playing his games; he was standing with a folder in his hand. I gave him a nod and rose from my bed, extinguishing the cigarette and following him towards the keypad door to his private quarters.

We walked down the stairs and both entered his office

As usual, I pulled up a chair and sat on the other end of the desk. In a flowing motion like he was dignity encompassed, Elish quietly sat down on his chair and tented his hands.

"I have the keycard, or Luca does anyway. I will be retrieving it soon," Elish began. He pulled open a shelf on his desk and withdrew a small black box. "Your friend is good at what he does. It seems my pet was wise to match those two."

I nodded; I had never stopped feeling apprehensive over Reno being in the chimeras' home base, but he was a greywaster… he knew how to take care of himself and watch his back.

"I have also heard back from General Zhou, who is currently regulating Aras. He has stationed guards outside of your street and Killian's house. Your houses will go untouched until you decide to take Aras back."

Legion in Aras? I didn't know how I felt about that. A part of me hated the idea but that part was the part of my heart that still considered Aras my home. In truth, the moment Redmond and Hollis betrayed me, the moment they went and captured Killian and Reno, they all became my enemies.

So fuck them.

"I will when this is done. You get Skyfall, I fucking get Aras. That's all I want."

A thin smile appeared on Elish's lips. How could a smile look so cold? "And what will you do with Aras?"

"I'm going to fucking burn them all," I growled. My emotions starting to play games with my tongue. I bit the corner of my mouth and forced myself into a more resolved posture. I looked up and straightened myself out.

I wonder if he had the same moral dilemmas of seeing me turn into a maniac that Greyson and Leo did.

"Oh, you will get Aras back. You can have the entire greywastes for all I care. My interests lie in Skyfall."

I nodded. "I suppose it's a good thing we're getting along so far. I guess we will be spending an eternity running the world."

Oh, he liked this. I witnessed a smile creep to his cold face. Running the entire world, I think that was Elish Dekker's plan.

"Another thing…" Elish said casually. "Are you aware of what day today is?"

I thought for a minute trying to count the days. "Friday?"

Elish quietly rose and walked past me; he turned his head and nodded me forward. Then in an easy almost kind tone he said: "Today is your birthday, Reaver. You're twenty years old."

Gah. I felt like I swallowed a knot.

"I'm not a teenager anymore," I sighed. My eyes lifted though when I saw Elish staring at me. I stared back before I started to chuckle; Elish smirked, the irony wasn't lost on him.

"Right, I'm immortal. I guess it doesn't matter anymore, does it?"

"For another couple years it will. Your papers in Kreig will say for certain but I was under the impression you would stop aging at the same time as Silas did. Twenty-four for both Silas and Sky."

I blinked, almost not understanding what I was seeing. With only a brush of his hand Elish pushed a bookcase aside revealing another door behind it. He opened the door which led to a white hallway. Elish walked into it, and with my mind full of questions, I followed him.

"I took it upon myself to get you a birthday present," Elish said casually.

I stopped and looked at him for a second, not hiding the bewildered look on my face. Elish didn't stop though. I jogged forward to catch up.

"You…?"

Elish didn't answer; he continued to take me deeper down the hallway before finally stopping in front of a steel, unpainted door. He had led us to an almost storage-type area. The halls were bare, the floor was pocked steel and there were security cameras visible, not hidden like they were upstairs.

"I think you will be quite pleased." The hair on my neck prickled at the frost in his voice; his facial expression only cemented in the reality that there was something huge through that door.

"Just delivered today, fresh." With a turn of a handle he opened the door and stepped back.

I eyed him curiously and put my hand on my pistol, more out of habit than feeling like I was in danger.

I took a step into the dimly lit room.

My body went cold; I couldn't believe what I was seeing. Strapped to two chairs, gagged, bound, and to top it off, a Christmas bow on top of each of their heads…

I let out a low laugh, but on my lips it could've passed for a growl.

… Hollis and Redmond.

"Happy Birthday, Reaver." I looked behind me and saw the most eerie foreboding smile on Elish's lips. His eyes were hard amethyst, and his tone held such a sinister foreshadowing it aroused my bloodlust in a way I had never experienced.

"I can kill them?"

To my surprise Elish took a step back, where there was another door. He pressed the keypad and opened it and I was immediately blinded by daylight.

However a moment later, it closed.

"Free them, kill them, starve them in here. They are yours to do as you wish. My gift comes with no limitations. Jade will clean whatever mess you make."

Elish tapped a small intercom by the door. "The door will lock behind you. You will need the code I gave you and Killian to access it and the door outside. If you need to contact upstairs, the intercom is available."

If Elish was trying to get me to like him, he was certainly doing a good job. Or perhaps he wanted to see just what the clone of Silas would do to them. Maybe he wanted to see for himself just how like his king I was.

He was about to find out, and something told me he would have a different reaction to it than Leo and Greyson would've.

When the door shut behind him, I turned around with a large smile on my face.

"Well… well… well…" I walked up to each of them and removed the sock gags in their mouths.

Redmond spat; Hollis started panting behind him. I realized his nose was broken and stuffed with blood. He must've had trouble breathing.

"What would you have done, Reaver?" Hollis's voice was strangled and hoarse. I thought I'd have a chance to taunt him before he got to that level of hysteria. "Tell me? King Silas himself was demanding them. You don't just fucking say no to him!"

"Save your fucking breath," Redmond sneered at Hollis, his eyes burned when they locked on mine. "Just die with some fucking dignity. You know as well as I do, we're walking corpses."

"Who shot Reno?" I yanked the thin nylon rope that had been holding Redmond's gag in and started winding it around my fingers. "And who beat Killian?"

"Carson, and Carson's dead. Your deacons killed –" I punched

Redmond in the face with my rope-bound hand. His head snapped back and a spray of blood spewed from his lips and onto Hollis. The former warden stared at Redmond with a look of horror; his mouth moving up and down as if his tongue was glued into the roof.

I unwound the rope from my hands and looked around the room. A small table was off in a corner, metal and sterile like the dim room we were in.

I walked over to it and picked up a screwdriver. I started wrapping the thin rope around it in a crisscross pattern. "Carson would've never shot his nephew."

"The only reason the mob didn't rip those two to shreds was because of me," Redmond sniffed, his nose congested with blood and mucus. "Silas didn't leave us a fucking choice! He would've burned Aras."

"You didn't even fucking wait for their bodies to go cold before you betrayed them and me. As soon as he shot Greyson, you dropped your fucking guns. You were the ones that fucked over Aras."

"Aras is surviving." I heard Redmond spit more blood behind me. "But you know as well as I do…" He spat again. I heard a plink noise behind me; I believe that was a tooth. "That we are the only people that can run Aras with Greyson and Leo dead. If you care for your town, you'll let us go. Not let it be run by Legion fucks."

I wrapped the second screwdriver as Redmond continued to plead. He tried to crane his neck over his shoulder to see what I was doing. "Reaver, I've known you since you were a boy. I did what had to be done to protect our fucking town!"

I started to whistle, tightening the pieces of rope until I had two separate weapons. I walked back to the two, and still whistling, I picked up the first screwdriver.

"Did you two see Leo before they shot him in the head?"

Redmond shook his head. Hollis though, swallowed hard and nodded. "I saw him."

"They removed his eye while they tor-"

Then Hollis started to plead loudly with me. I had to raise my voice. "*While they brutally fucking tortured him*." His whining lit a flame in my gut. I wanted more of it. I felt like a drug addict needing a fix.

At the height of his pleading and panicking, I put a hand on Hollis's face.

"An eye for an eye, but I require double restitution." I pinched his eye between my thumb and middle finger. It spun around frightened in its socket as I raised the screwdriver. "I'd stay still, lest I shove this through the socket and into your brain."

Hollis's mouth made a wheezing noise, like the air being let out of a balloon, as I dug the screwdriver deep into his eye socket. It never broke its gaze.

I jerked the screwdriver head towards me, popping the eye out. I grabbed it with my fingers and pulled the sinewy mess of veins with it. I cleanly sliced it from his body with my combat knife.

Warden Hollis groaned, his eyelid closing loosely like a curtain. He moved his head away as I released him; his eyes tightly shut and his tongue continuously licking his lips.

I turned to Redmond. His face was white as bone and his mouth open in shock.

"Do you really think this is what Greyson wanted for you?" he asked quietly.

His words bounced off of me like twigs on a tank. I put my hand on his face and repeated the procedure. When I had sliced it off too I looked at both the eyeballs in my hand.

I walked over and put them on the metal table, so they could see everything that was going on, and picked up the second screwdriver and rope I had made.

Then with another whistled song, I started to untie them.

They both stared at me in disbelief, neither of them brave enough to make the first move. Their remaining eyes stayed glued to my body, their heartbeats twin pounding drums. I observed drips of sweat mixing with blood, running down the foreheads of the two men, framing their expressions of terror and desperation.

"Did you hear that I am immortal?" I said to them, testing the weight of each piece of rope.

They both slowly nodded, though I was suspecting Hollis to go into shock at any moment. "The Legion knows you were the Raven all along as well."

I smiled and handed one rope to Redmond and one to Hollis. "Player

One, to your left. Player Two, to your right. On the go… we fight."

They stared at me. Their now singular eyes almost matching to make a pair. I spread my hands at both of them. "The rules are simple: only two will survive. You can both try to overpower me, but you'll need to trust the fact you'll be able to torture the code to get outside. Or… you can turn on one another. The dead one loses and the living one won't get killed by me. Take your places."

Redmond and Hollis kept staring. The former Warden Hollis blinked his good eye, and turned the screwdriver around in his hand. "F-fight? Each other?"

The malice that burned inside my chest flared at the growing fear in their eyes. I nodded with a smile and took a step back; I crossed my arms and craned my neck. "Who wants to stab me first? Or… are you going to go the more promising route?"

Redmond clenched his hand and at the same time bared his teeth at me. "I'm not playing your fucking game, Reaver. I'm not your puppet." He looked over at Hollis before dropping his screwdriver and its rope leash to the ground. The chief crossed his arms and glared at me.

He didn't even see Hollis coming.

With a lightning quick flick of his arm, Hollis swung the screwdriver like a knife. Redmond ducked, but not soon enough, the screwdriver grazed the side of his head, opening up his scalp like an overripe fruit. The force of the blow knocked Redmond off his feet, but as soon as he hit the ground his fingers reached for the rope. As Hollis raised his hand to stab him again, he forced the screwdriver up and got Hollis right in the gut.

I suppressed a shudder, and let the cold electricity in my chest flow throughout my body. I leaned up against the metal walls with my arms still crossed, enjoying the show in front of me.

The two men wrestled with each other, the screwdrivers exchanging blows that drew out trickles of blood, making the floor slick under their boots. They were my puppets, their strings wrapped around my hands.

I felt like myself in that moment, I felt like Reaver. I'd lost parts of me since leaving Aras. I'd lost my home, my family, even my smell. But now…

My lungs swelled as I inhaled deeply, the smell of blood so thick in the air I could taste the coppery metal. Their muffled swearing, groaning, and even the electricity in the room aroused my senses and quenched my thirst for revenge and carnage. The beast inside me was satisfied, but I wanted more. I wanted to push it. Redmond and Hollis were just a taste; my real feast would come when I stepped back onto Aras soil.

There was a loud scream from Hollis. I watched as Redmond lost his slippery grip on the screwdriver, the blue plastic handle sticking out of Hollis's neck.

Redmond tried to yank it out, but while he was struggling with it, Hollis swung his and tore a strip off of Redmond's cheek. As it hung loosely like hanging moss, I picked up Hollis's eye and popped it into my mouth.

Pop. My teeth bit down on the ocular; I always liked that sound.

They both stood, their chests heaving and their boots slipping back and forth on the floor, blood slicking the surface like ice, leaving a mosaic of painted steel.

Redmond stood with his screwdriver back in his hand, Hollis's legs buckling from the blood loss. The warden was bleeding heavily from several severe wounds. He was panting and wheezing, foamy blood dripping from the corner of his mouth.

"It's been a pleasure, Hollis. It's nothing personal."

Redmond clasped the screwdriver with both hands and swung it at Hollis's head.

It went all the way in, right up to the handle.

The warden's neck snapped back and he fell to the floor; his remaining eye rolling into the back of his head. Hollis started seizing, the foam spraying in choking coughs like an erupting volcano.

Then he was still.

I popped Redmond's eye into my mouth and bit down. I started a slow clap as the former chief stood over his friend, his shoulders shaking and his chest expanding with every ragged inhale. I swallowed the bitter, tangy meat and spat out the lens, those were always so tough to chew.

I walked past Redmond and put my finger on the intercom button. "Send down Killian."

"I want to leave!" Redmond's voice was strained and hoarse. He turned to me, his eye was ablaze in its socket, the other socket dripping blood down its closed lid. "Open the door."

I gave him a look of both disbelief and amusement. "Leave? Whatever for? You're my prisoner."

I saw Redmond's teeth clench, almost all of them since half his cheek had been torn open. He shouted at me, and as he did blood sprayed on my face and shirt. "I fucking killed him. I get to leave that was our deal."

This moment… this exact moment. Where there's still hope in his eyes, where he still thinks I'll let him leave. I live for these small, fleeting junctures. I can smell the fear; it's as potent as the blood around me. It's moments like these when I understand why they feared what I would become – No, what I *had* become. It's moments like these where I know I am the clone of the abomination who killed the planet.

I am the Reaper. I choose who lives, I chose who dies.

Unbidden, a knowing and sinister smile graced my lips. "Who do you take me for, Redmond? You really believe I carry myself on some moral pedestal where you think I won't deceive you for my own amusement? You're a fool. You two should've tried to overpower me when you had the chance."

As the words spilled forth Redmond's face fell. And when the last syllable left my lips, he charged at me, an anguished scream breaking the thick atmosphere of the room.

I dodged him easily with a sideways glide made smoother by the blood. Redmond wasn't as agile though; he slipped and lost his footing. He caught himself on the wall near enough to me that I was easily able to overpower him.

I held his hands behind his back and clenched them. I looked towards the steel door and wiped my boots on my pant leg for traction. I waited as I heard light footsteps down the hallway and Elish's muffled voice.

The door opened, Killian took one look inside and I watched his face turn to ash. His eyes first fell to Hollis but quickly met with Redmond's, then my own.

"Killian? Killian… he made a deal with me. He made a deal with me!" Redmond screamed, his words twisted in fear. Where was that bravery I had seen when I first came in? "Tell him to let me go."

The boy stared. He took a single step inside but paused, I watched as he lifted his boot up realizing the floor was coated in sticky red blood.

"It's up to you, Killian," I said to him, tightening my grip on Redmond's wrists. "They hurt you, they hurt Reno. It's your call. I'll do whatever you say."

I watched his face intently, wondering with sick fascination what I would see. I had gotten my fill as I saw the horror descend on Redmond's face, and earlier on Hollis's too. Whatever Killian decided to do was just dessert. My bloodlust was quenched; I wanted Killian to have a say in this one's fate.

The boy stared, not a word or the start of a word coming to his lips. Then in the same silence, he turned and left the room; the door closing behind him with a light click.

I stared, trying to hide my disappointment. Hearing the footsteps get fainter, I was about to loosen my grip on Redmond though when the footsteps stopped. A moment later they started to get louder.

The door opened again, Killian emerged now holding a thin but long object in his hand. Redmond saw it first, curses spitting from his broken mouth like water.

The boy didn't mince words; with an emotionally charged scream he swung the long piece of rebar towards Redmond's head. It connected with a sickening crunch, before it ricocheted back hitting the wall.

The blow knocked Redmond off of his feet; I let him fall onto the ground.

Killian raised the metal bar again and rained it down onto the back of his head. This impact broke Redmond's skull open like a watermelon; the next one exposed his brain and the third made it into pudding.

When he was done Killian dropped the rebar. The clang echoing off of the walls, the floor, and ceiling, sending vibrations up my legs. He stood in front of Redmond's corpse, his chest rising and falling with every sharp breath. I could see blood drops and spray all over his face and shirt, only moments ago clean and soft.

As Killian turned away, I saw a mixture of anger and satisfaction. His blue orbs burned into mine, not an ounce of malice intended but I could feel the hostility radiating off of them. An over-stoked stove, heated to boiling and spitting flames but still with unused fuel inside.

Fuck, look at all that blood on him… the sweat on his temples…

I felt a familiar throb in the back of my head, one that travelled all the way down to my groin. It burned like a small sun, sending electric impulses to all the wrong places. It was infiltrating my body and my mind, sending images to my head that made my briefs tight.

I don't know what came over me, but I grabbed Killian and pushed him up against the wall. I trapped him with one arm, my mouth pressed up against his, and with my free hand I grabbed his backside.

The inferno inside me flared to an unbelievable level as Killian passionately kissed me back, his own hand not shying away. He shoved it down my pants and grabbed my stiffening dick.

"Fuck…" I inhaled a breath; it had been an incredibly long time since I took him last, and with the bodies of our enemies around us, spilling blood and organs, I couldn't think of a better way to break us in again.

I undid his belt and dropped his pants to the floor, taking his hardening dick into my hands and rubbing it against my own.

Killian dropped to his knees in front of me, and with a wave of resolve-bursting pleasure, he started to suck on the crown. As my knees trembled and my boots slid, I shifted to a kneeling position on the floor, and watched Killian as he started eagerly tasting every inch.

Admittedly, since I hadn't even personally taken care of myself in quite a while, it couldn't have been more than five minutes before I started to feel the rapidly multiplying pleasure well inside of me. With one arm behind my back to prop myself up, and the other on his cheek, I came in his mouth.

When his lips found mine again we made out on the blood-soaked floor, him on top of me, grinding his hard penis into my recovering one. I could feel the back of my head resting against Hollis's cold leg, his blood pooled around his body, getting into my hair and my bent arm. I could feel the sticky mess everywhere around me, and fuck it turned me on in ways I couldn't believe.

I hooked the head of Killian's penis between my pointer and middle finger and started massaging the tip with my thumb, my mouth flexing and sucking on his neck. I could feel wetness grace the tip, I rubbed it into the slit and broke the seal on his neck.

I moved my mouth down and started licking and playing with his collarbone and Adam's apple. My hand sliding up and down the shaft of his cock with a soft but forceful caress.

Then, with a trembling moan made in between panting gasps, Killian's semen slicked my hand. I caught him as he collapsed into my arms, then, with a gentle roll, I placed him onto the blood-smeared floor.

With his semen as lube I eased myself inside him; he was tight, just how I liked him, but I was able to push through and bury myself to the base.

Killian gasped and dug his fingertips into my back. We locked our lips together as I clasped the back of his head with my hand; his legs now hooked over my arms. I started rolling my hips into him, our lips never breaking apart for more than a second.

The smell of blood and semen took me away, the flames of desire burning my body without a second thought. I felt every inch of myself on fire, wanting more and more of him. It wasn't enough. I wanted every part of him near me and under me.

It took every bit of my restraint not to do him hard, my blood burned to ride him with fierce fervour, claim him and own him, but I had done that once after I had burned the townspeople and now I knew my strength. Though my heart raced to take him in every horrible way possible, I kept my pace fast but cautious. Losing control in the throes of passion was different than losing control of the wild and morbid thoughts in my head. I remained steadfast.

Killian's low cries of ecstasy kept me in the moment and kept my mind from wandering as it had before. I felt his hot breath against my ear with every moan he made. I counted each one, analyzing their tones so they could tell me how fast or how slow I should go.

After a period of time his moans quickened. I could feel his hand by my stomach, stroking his own shaft vigorously, unable to restrain himself any longer.

I sped my own pace; I had already brought myself to the brink several times and my member was aching for release. I buried myself into his warm inner flesh, and when I saw the cum start to spurt from his swollen head, I gave myself the several hammered thrusts needed to throw me over the edge. I held myself up with a slippery blood-slicked hand as the pleasure overwhelmed me and stifled the cry on my lips, though it spilled through in a rattled gasp.

When I'd had a moment to regain myself, I separated us with an exhausted sigh and planted one last passionate kiss on my boyfriend's clammy cheek. Then I got up and started putting my pants on, feeling more than just a little sheepish at what we'd just done, and where we had done it.

I looked around the blood-soaked room, Redmond and Hollis both very dead, one on each side of us.

I smirked, unable to shake the coy grin on my face, and took a step towards Killian who was still catching his breath.

I stopped though when I noticed a buzzing in my ears, a low hum that broke up the silence in the room. I looked up and my eyes fell onto a camera.

Oh jeez…

I glared at it for a second, as if daring any one of those jokes to even bring it up if they were watching the feed, then I turned away and helped Killian to his feet.

We locked eyes for a second. His blue oceans were lit up and sparkling with the trickled remains of our passion. His mouth slightly slacked to accommodate his still heavy breathing.

I stared back and gave him a guilty smile. Killian kept his resolve for a moment before he flushed and returned my smile with one full of embarrassment.

He gave me a playful push. "You're crazy."

But the slick floor punished him for that push, Killian slipped and I caught him with a laugh. Then I hoisted the boy up, threw him over my shoulder, and gave him a smack on his ass. I opened the door and walked into the hallway, Killian laughing and hitting my back like he was banging a drum.

We took our boots off to keep from marking up Elish's carpet, and made our way up both separate flights of stairs.

Together we tried to slip into the main area of the house to make a break for the shower, but I should've known better. As soon as we emerged through the doors the shit-eater grins of Jade and Perish greeted us.

"Did you enjoy your birthday present?" Jade asked with a lewd grin. And with that comment, the hyenas erupted into laughter. I rolled my eyes and quickly ushered Killian into the bathroom, ignoring Elish's open laptop on the coffee table.

"I put the bows on their heads," Perish piped up.

"It's your birthday?" Killian said to me, as I quickly shut the door behind us, the catcalls only getting louder in the living room.

No matter if it is Aras, a closed off bunker, or Skyfall, men will never change.

CHAPTER 10

Reno

GARRETT WAS THE HAPPIEST I HAD EVER SEEN HIM. He was crowing over me as Luca straightened out my fancy clothes and did the last finishing touches on my hair. I looked like… well, I looked like I had just walked out of a fancy magazine.

My hair had been sprayed, flicked, and teased into wavy silver strands parted on the side, my face had been powdered and my eyes lined with black eyeliner. My clothing, chosen by Garrett, was a black vest and a crisp blue shirt underneath, my pants black slacks with a blue belt. I even got myself nice shiny shoes too.

"You look beautiful." Garrett beamed. He was dressed in his usual suit and tie, blue to match mine with a blue kerchief tucked into his pocket. He smelled like spice and cologne. I probably did too; Luca had been anointing me with many things since he had arrived. It was like Christmas for that guy, he was having the time of his life playing beautician.

It was my coming out party, if you could call it that. Our engagement had been announced, plastered on the bulletins, and now we were going to the stadium to celebrate. I was supposed to smile and wave and let everyone take a good look at me. The president of Skytech was getting married to a mysterious former pet; that was something to celebrate. As Saul pointed out with a chuckle it only came once every ten years.

Har har, Saul.

And what was Stadium? Garrett had told me the previous night with an eager smile that 'Stadium' was the place to be on Saturdays, the weekly execution of all the condemned prisoners of Skyfall. It was where Silas would pit their freedom against the three immortal brutes: Nero, Ares, and Siris. If they managed to kill one… they walked free.

Executing prisoners in front of a live cheering audience. Hmm… sounds familiar.

"Really? Burned them alive? Eesh!" Garrett shuddered as we made our way to the car; I had been telling him the grisly details of the execution in Aras a few months ago. He gave a shiver and we strolled hand in hand to the awaiting car. "I would not want to meet that man in a dark alley. He sounds positively insane."

I chuckled. I really missed Reaver, I wonder if he missed me as well. "He's really a great guy, people just see the dark parts of him but I've never had a more loyal friend. When it comes down to it, he would do anything for those in his circle."

"Silas is the same way." Garrett's lips raised in a proud smile, though it turned into bemusement when he saw the confused look on my face, topped off with a raise of my left eyebrow.

"Your experiences with Silas haven't been that great, yes, but just you see… besides the obvious things he does to us. He would burn the world to keep his creations safe."

"And in a constant state of fear," I muttered. I ducked into the open car door with a nod to Saul and slid across the leather seats. "He's not going to be at Stadium, right?"

The door shut behind us and Garrett took my hand again. "Of course he will be! The king would be present in his top chimera's engagement party."

I slid to the other end of the door and tried to open it. Garrett let out a rich laugh as he pulled on my hand. "Lutra, lutra, stay here. This is different, you'll see. A personal summons is night and day compared to an engagement party. I think you're about to be surprised."

I groaned and slid in the seat, our tinted windows showing flickers of the town going by as we drove deeper into Skyland. My stomach felt twisted into knots. This exciting evening had turned into a walk on death row in a matter of seconds. Maybe I would get a chance to jet without him noticing, though I didn't want to get too brash since I had only recently upgraded to fiancé.

I brought out my most useful manipulation tactic instead; I gave him the sad eyes and leaned my head on the back of the seat. Garrett only spared me a sympathetic noise before kissing my mouth.

He smiled. "Trust me. I'm ninety years old, I know his moods. We'll have fun; perhaps you might get to see one of my savage younger brothers get brutally killed. Wouldn't that make you smile?"

I grunted, but he was hard to stay mad at. I guess I was a bit safer considering everyone else would be around, including Skyfall people. I kissed Garrett back, but gave his lip a small nip. "I don't get the same joy out of seeing people die as you chimera boys. I'm a normal waster, just give me the bodies after so I can eat them."

I saw the stadium in the distance, which made my heart leap with anticipation. It was a huge round building with poles sticking up out of it like it had once been tented, however the roof was gone, leaving it open to the elements.

There was another thing that caught my eye though. "The ocean!" I exclaimed. I moved to the tinted window and plastered my face against it. I had only seen the outline of it on the top of Garrett and Elish's skyscrapers.

The stadium was ocean front, standing lit up against the grey dingy water like a stationary sun. It was giving the water a false sense of radiance, one that was lost during the day. The dead ocean varied from shit brown to greywaste grey, and it didn't reflect much… unless you counted sadness.

Around the stadium were buildings and sketchy back alleys, with a backdrop of skyscrapers that had never been repaired and sat in various states of ruin behind the glowing building. It was a contrast if there ever were one. The stadium was buzzing with people, dressed to the nines, with cigarettes and booze. Slummers and elites mixing with one another, filing into the stadium with an uneasy truce built only on the greater need to see the games. The mixing of classes seemed to fit the area of Skyfall we were in. An area with a brilliant stadium with millions of dollars of repairs in it, surrounding a city with a lot of dark remnants looming over like predatory ghosts, crawling with abominations that would even make

Reaver raise an eyebrow.

Saul pulled the car up, before hopping out and opening the door to us. Garrett stepped out first and I could hear the crowd around us abuzz with whispers and speculations. The president of Skyfall waved to the crowd, before he lowered a hand for me. I took it and stepped out.

The crowd had been cordoned off for us, by those velvety rope things that always felt funny. There must've been hundreds of them trying to get a look at us. We quickly walked past them, and I gave them a wave. A swell of importance that I had never felt before rushed through me like cold adrenaline; I squeezed Garrett's hand and started smiling.

"That a boy!" Garrett praised, shaking my hand. "Give them a smile and a wave; let them eat it out of your palm. You're my fiancé now, Reno. Drink it up; they'll love you for it."

So I did; the gathering of faces and the smell of cologne mixed in with the damp smell of the stadium giving me an almost intoxicating feeling. This place was a whole other world, but if I was going to be in this world… at least I was First Man of it.

After we had gotten inside the stadium we were ushered through many doors and climbed more than several sets of stairs.

The stadium had been repaired as well as it possibly could be. Fresh paint, new wooden trim, and stucco and tile wherever it broke off from concrete. I wanted to see the field though, that's where all the action was. I had been inside Anvil's old baseball stadium before and it had been breathtaking.

A lady with a gun ushered us into a large room with lots of food. I busied myself stuffing my face as Garrett mingled and talked to people I didn't know. Food was around. No time for meeting people; they had potato chips.

"Reno, come here for a moment," I heard Garrett call. I popped another chip into my mouth, and as I pulled my hand away, a kid about Tinky's age started wiping my hands off. I stared at him like he was crazy, but I noticed he had a collar around his neck.

I knew who he was as soon as I turned. A man about Garrett's physical age was standing beside him, tall and radiant with an amused, almost patronizing, smirk on his face.

The guy had silver hair, short and wavy, with some very flashy purply-blue eyes. His thin face was flawless, down to a short and narrow nose and full lips. He had Silas's eyes; there was no doubting he was a chimera.

"Reno, this is Artemis, my brother. He's President of Culture and the Arts. The sengil he has with him is Lance, who is Luca's brother."

Do I shake his hand? Bow? Do nothing? I took a leap of faith and shook his hand, hoping I didn't have too much remaining potato chip grease. I inclined my head as well and squared my shoulders. I was the fiancé of the president now. I should act like it. But who was I fooling?

"It's nice to meet you," I said with a cheery smile.

"And you too, Reno." Artemis inclined his head back and shook my hand. A mild shake but his grip was like iron; I felt myself wince. He seemed like a stoic but proper person, with fancy robes and capes like Elish wore. Hopefully that meant he was more sociopath weird, I knew how to deal with those types. "The others are waiting for us, including the king. Let's carry on."

The silver-haired guy walked through the doors, his pet, leash-less but obedient, waited by the door frame for all of us to walk through before he held up the end. Just last week that had been me there, now I was Mr. Important.

With the opening of the last metal door, the identical painted walls and grey tile disappeared into a long windowed hallway.

It was more of a tunnel though, closed off but everything could be seen from the patched-together windows, mismatching and welded into place with mounds of spot weld and rubber glue.

It led us in a straight line across the middle of the stadium floor, to a box that stood tall in front of the closed off arena. There were red plastic seats below us, stuck together in rows that circled the grey dusted arena floor, with only a shoddy chain-link fence separating them from the fighting.

As I looked around awestruck, I could see how the stadium was made up. It was obvious from the open ceiling and the dark shadows of the seating levels that time had not been kind to most of it.

What had once been the seating areas had been destroyed, stripped of anything of value, leaving nothing but broken concrete and rusted metal in their places. Those seats, I observed, must've been used to make the bleacher-type benches that circled the arena. The stadium in its prime would've been too big for even Skyfall; everything had been ripped up and rearranged to suit the needs of the Fallocaust. It was like a stadium inside of a stadium.

The bench-type seats were alive with people and adorned with strings of Christmas lights and old neon signs that read everything from beer labels to store adverts. People were already drinking, smoking, and leaning into each other to talk about things on their minds. I even saw concession stands lit up in the distance, advertising ratdogs, potato fries with cheese sauce, and packaged goods.

As we walked closer to what looked like an almost skybox-type area, there were several on the stadium floor from what I could see, the atmosphere hit me. I felt a shiver of adrenaline as we were led to our seats; the noise of the stadium-goers and the music blasting in the background making my chest vibrate. I was starting to get into this and I barely even knew what was going on. All I could feel was everyone else's excitement; the floor seemed to vibrate it with each step, alive in a continuous hum of energy.

The energy didn't dissipate in the slightest when I walked into the skybox.

The room had windows covering every inch of the wall, and from our palace twenty feet up I could see the arena in all its beauty below. It was covered in red dirt and greywaste dust, and was littered with footprints and dried blood. It was empty besides a microphone and stand.

"Ah, our guests of honour!" My blood turned to ice as I heard Silas's voice. I tore my gaze away from the windows, and for the first time, scanned the faces around me.

Silas was standing with two chimeras close behind him: a curly-haired pet with burnt orange eyes that did all but broadcast his genetically engineered status, and a tall man with black hair and eyes like blood, dressed in a suit with a red bow tie. The king, like everyone else, was dressed in elegant clothing suited to his style. A blazer over top of a tight, red sleeveless shirt that hugged his every curve, and tight dress pants tucked into long, silver buckled boots.

Garrett gave him a quick bow and I did as well. Silas strolled up to both of us, several other chimeras, including a few young ones, all of who I didn't recognize, behind him.

"Reno, you haven't met these ones yet." Silas gave me a smile that suggested we had absolutely no past together; he seemed in a great mood. He turned around and waved a presenting hand to the group of vampires. "This is Apollo, Artemis's twin." Well, that was obvious. The man was identical to his brother except his hair was long like Elish's. "He's the president of Dek'ko. Beside him, the older man, is his husband Jiro."

Apollo was either immortal or into incredibly older guys. Jiro was the oldest guy I had ever seen; he had to be at least eighty or more. He had white hair and wrinkly skin but behind the age he had a youthful, friendly smile.

Jiro gave me a kind wave, and as I watched him I noticed he was in a wheelchair. I smiled and bowed back to him. The thought that Apollo had loved his husband into old age twinged a cord in my heart; it was rather sweet, especially considering how that family seemed to function.

"This one is Drake, my personal pet but more than happy to indulge any urges you might get." Silas winked at me, before putting a hand on the red-eyed ones back. That man gave me a polite bow and a smile that made his eyes squint. "And this is Sanguine, my sengil and my loyal bodyguard. He'll also get you whatever you need, but you can't sleep with this one."

I couldn't hold back the confused look on my face. We were not friends, Silas, at least not anymore. Did you forget so quickly just a week ago you made Garrett beat on me?

Not showing the slightest reaction to my confused looks, Drake gave me a cheerful smile and a polite wave. That was the golden-haired one with the orange eyes, he was dressed well… I'd seen brothel workers with more clothes on. He even had a collar around his neck like me, except his had a silver dog tag.

"And this one with the crazy glint in his eyes is Caligula and beside him his partner Nico. Reno, you've seen him before, yes? In Aras?"

And there was the twisted dagger in my heart, the poison in my open wounds to sting me when my guard was starting to lower. I did recognize Caligula, curly black hair and eyes that looked unnaturally metallic. I remember he was stone-faced and threatening beside the brutes. Not a single eye twitch when the deacons had gotten released, just fluid quick movements and a shot that would rival Reaver's. That was one I would look out for; he wasn't immortal but he was fearless.

I bit down my emotions and gave them a curt nod of my head; I hoped Garrett would be proud of me for that. I would give anything to have Caligula and Silas alone in a room… well, if Reaver was there.

Caligula just glared back at me, I knew in that moment we would never be civil. He looked like a complete douchebag down to the snotty little sneer on his face. His boyfriend wasn't much better; he had slanty eyes like he was half-Asian, a square jaw, and a pissy look on his face. They were perfect for each other, they both looked like dicks.

"Everyone, this is Garrett's fiancé, Reno Nevada, former pet and former friend to our long lost brother Reaver *Dekker*. He's decided to join the winning team after stealing our lovely Garrett's heart."

Everyone gave me a nod and I stood there looking uncomfortable. I felt an urge bubbling in me to point out that Reaver never had a last name, and if he did it certainly wouldn't be Dekker, but I wasn't an idiot. Even if you hate the snake pit, once you're in it you don't start trying to step on them. The best way I had learned to deal with Garrett's brothers and King Silas was to just shut up and smile. Actually that belief had gotten me through a lot of hard times, including dealing with Reaver-drama.

"Enough introductions," Silas said. He turned and went to the window where a small radio was held. He picked it up and spoke into it. "We're here. If the others have arrived, let our games begin."

"I'll send up the little ones once the roster has been organized," a female voice sounded after several seconds. *"Are you going to send them out?"*

Silas laughed and held up the radio to his mouth, beside him Sanguine gave him another squinty smile; that guy was creepy as hell. "If they've been good, sure, tell the little shits I might give them their teeth."

Garrett led me to our seats. I saw a blue object beside me and noticed with amusement Lance had brought me the potato chip bowl I had left behind in sadness. I could get used to this treatment.

Reaver would hate me so much right now… but well, if this was all going to change soon I might as well soak up some luxury before I had to go home. Back to the world of ash and half-rotten rat meat. I was going to miss potato chips.

Another young man, who I think was a slave like Luca rather than a pet, stood behind a small bar in the corner, beside him another plate with appetizer foodstuffs, and bowls of soft candies and hard candies. I raided it and brought my stash to sit beside Garrett.

I heard him laugh, then a ring adorned hand reach in to grab a handful of two hundred-year-old candy-coated chocolate. He held them in his hand as he leaned over and kissed me. “For our honeymoon, I’m going to take you to the Dead Islands, to my vacation home. We’ll stay there together and do whatever you like. You just name it.”

The Dead Islands? Sounds romantic.

I kissed him back, feeling the knots in my body start to loosen under his warmth. “We could stay in a cardboard box for all I care,” I said, feeling my lips pull in a return smile. “Really, I’m not joking. I slept in a cardboard box once.”

Of course Garrett thought that notion was hilarious. He kissed me again. I glanced over and noticed Sanguine; he had his hands behind his back and was standing with a smile on his face beside King Silas.

“That one, he’s creepy. Why the hell would you make them with red eyes?” I gave a shudder.

Garrett laughed; he reached up and grabbed a piece of shelled candy. “He’s King Silas’s personal servant and bodyguard. He’s devoted to our king, in all ways. Sanguine is a lovely fellow.”

I shovelled more candy into my mouth. “I thought that was the brutes’ job… being his bodyguard.”

Garrett gave me a smile, before with a narrowing of his eyes, he looked at the servant. “Yes, they are, but King Silas wanted a bodyguard to protect him at all times. The twins and Nero, well, King Silas wouldn’t be able to stand them for long periods. Besides–” I blinked as I watched Garrett stick his tongue out of the corner of his mouth. A second later I saw a quick flash as he threw the candy towards King Silas’s head. It whizzed past my face like a small bullet; it had impressive force behind it.

There was the quickest blur of black, so fast if you blinked you would’ve missed it. My mouth dropped open as I saw Sanguine open his palm, revealing the red piece of candy Garrett had thrown. Without Silas even noticing what had happened, Sanguine flicked his crimson eyes up to Garrett and gave him a shake of his head with the same squinty smile. A moment later, he tossed the candy up into the air and caught it in his mouth, before turning his attention back to Silas.

"–he's quite good at his job, isn't he?" Garrett chuckled, before giving me a squeeze. "If Perish was still around I would've gotten him to make me one. He's a tiger in bed as well."

I gasped and gave him an elbow in the chest; he let out an *oof*, before putting his arms around me with a laugh. "One day I will show you just what I mean."

Then our attention was diverted to the arena. The lights above the small field turned on and focused down, before a voice crackled below us. I leaned forward and saw a tall older man with the microphone in his hand.

"Ladies and Gentlemen! Welcome to Stadium Night!" The crowd erupted into cheers; the lights flickered around like they were being controlled before focusing back on the man.

"Tonight we have for you–"

"Silas! Master Silas!"

Garrett and I both looked over as the high tones of a toddler came from the hallway. As the announcer spoke below us, two young boys ran into the large skybox. They looked to be about five years old. Both with long black wavy hair, but one with royal blue eyes and the other red, just like the sengil's. Silas must've liked the results. "We need our teeth!"

I watched with morbid fascination as Silas looked down at them with a smile. He adopted a look of confusion and waved them off, turning his attention to the arena below. The kids howled and jumped up and down, the red-eyed one started pulling on Silas's blazer. "We need our teeth."

"I don't know, have you been good? You've probably been little shits all day." Silas glanced down and shook his head. "Why would you deserve the teeth?"

One of the kids became dead weight as he hung on the blazer, making the jacket pull down off of Silas's shoulder. I could see the other chimeras around them chuckling and looking on in amusement. I was more bewildered, Silas looked, well… I'd sooner expect to see him throw the kids out the window than play along and tease them.

"We've been good! Please, please!" The blue-eyed one dropped to his knees and pressed the palms of his hands together like he was pleading. "We didn't get one spank today, not one!"

"Show us a trick!" Garrett called. He held out a cigar and beside him Lance lit it.

The two boys grinned and ran to the middle of the room. One of the little ones lay down on his back, and the other one stood over him, a leg on each side of his chest.

To the amusement of the room, the one on top, the red-eyed one, clasped his hands onto the laying one's hands. With a hoist, and strength a five-year-old shouldn't have, the top one braced himself on the blue-eyed one's arms, until his legs were sticking out in a perfect vertical point. Then the bottom one outstretched his arms, and as he did, the red-eyed boy raised his legs up into the air. He moved up until he was completely upside down, his arms extended onto his brothers and his little boots pointed in the air. A moment later, they both released their grip on their left hand, until only a single continuous arm held the red-eyed one up in the air.

Then the top one jumped off and raised his arms out triumphantly with a bow, the blue-eyed one also sprung to his feet with the energy only a child could have and also took a haughty bow.

Everyone applauded them, including me. That was fucking impressive.

Silas gave them a whistle; I could see real laughter and delight on his face.

This really was a side of him I hadn't seen before.

No matter… even if he showered the people below us in hundred dollar bills it wouldn't change the fact that he had killed Leo and Greyson, raped Killian, and had tried to steal Reaver. No matter what show he was putting on now, I knew the real face of Silas.

These chimeras were like bi-polar; it made me a bit sick wondering if Garrett had a side to him I hadn't seen yet.

The kids ran back to Silas, and to their joy and my confusion, Silas reached inside his blazer and pulled out two small sets of metal animal-like teeth, complete with very sharp little fangs. He gave the top and bottom set to each of them and they put them into their mouths.

"*Rrrrrroww!* Thank you, Master Silas!" the crimson-eyed one growled and gnashed his teeth at Silas's hand, the new murder teeth clinking in his small mouth. The king ruffled his hair, and with a boot in their butts, he sent them both back out of the room. They happily ran off gnashing their teeth and hooting and hollering like all young kids do.

Garrett laughed and took an inhale of his cigar; he elbowed my side. "Those are two of our youngest. Hunter is the red-eyed one, and Chaser is the blue-eyed one. Both of them are destined to be bodyguards, anything where they'll have to kill. They're type is what we call stealth. We have science, intelligence, stealth, and brute." Garrett leaned in, ignoring Lance beside him collecting the ash from his cigar. "Now with those two, we decided to raise them together. See how they feed off of each other? My first gen brothers and I were raised together, but after the second gen it became more sporadic. It was a lot of work raising so many chimera babies at once. We did surrogates for a few of them."

"Who's all first gen?" I asked curiously.

Garrett exhaled out of the corner of his mouth, making an effort not to get the smoke near my face. "Elish, myself, our only sister Ellis, and Nero, and later, Ceph, then Artemis and Apollo our first successful identical twins. Then Sanguine, Jack, and Valentine." Garrett smiled. "After the second big batch years would pass without a birth. It is now every five or ten years, some we surrogate out and some we raise within the family."

"Oh, more Reaver's? Wonderful," I said with a sarcastic smile. Garrett chuckled and kissed my cheek. We both turned our attention back to the arena.

Below us the crowd was going wild, cheering and hollering as two people in the arena went at each other with knives. Both only dressed in an undershirt and ratty cargo pants, they jumped around and slashed at each other. Red streaks and smears already spotted the grey marble of the arena floor.

As the first hour passed the chimeras around me started to get more and more liquored up, or as was some of their preferences, they smoked weeder or tainted smokes. That with Garrett's cigars filled the room with a brownish haze that reminded me of every bar I had ever been in, and Reaver's basement when we really got into our fun nights.

I watched as fight after fight took place, with small intermissions for performances with animals I had only seen in books or movies.

Everyone had a good chuckle at me when I had my hands pressed against the window when the lion came out. She was a slinky and quick female lion that could jump through hoops and go on sea-saws. They even threw her a few rats to kill. That was awesome to watch. She was Joaquin's lion apparently and her name was Nala.

Real original.

When we reached the tail end of the evening was when the condemned came out. Three of them this week apparently. Skyfallers set to die but could still regain a full pardon by taking on the likes of Nero, Ares, or Siris. One-on-one combat (though Garrett told me they did tag team when they felt like it) with only a knife between each of them as a weapon.

Garrett explained in his slurred speech that it was rare for one of the chimeras to lose. They usually only walked away with a slash or two which the doctor patched up. It was a literal fight to the death, but the brutes were the only ones who came back afterwards.

I watched, feeling content and fuzzy as Ares the chimera stood flexing his muscles to show off to the crowd. Beside me stood Apollo and Jiro, shrouded in a haze of smoke and saturated with the smell of alcohol and weed. Apollo was rubbing Jiro's shoulder as they both laughed and talked amongst themselves.

Further on in a partially hidden corner, Drake was at work between Caligula's legs, with Nico pumping himself into the pet chimera's backside; his pants still on him but unbuckled at the front. I felt a small twinge at that since I was still Reno, so I made a point to stop looking though the damage had been done.

I cringed as I watched Ares slash hard at the convict's throat; the guy was agile though and took a quick step back so it only grazed the flesh. The crowd responded in a hushed gasp followed by an even bigger increase in cheering and shouting. The announcer over the intercom praised Ares for his skills and said a few other things muffled under the room's atmosphere.

I yelped as I felt arms pull me down; I landed on Garrett's lap and felt him start to kiss my neck. I craned my head up as I watched Ares deliver a bone shattering punch to the guy's jaw. He fell onto the ground with a hushed whisper from the crowd.

Ares spun his blade in his hand, before, almost like a professional wrestler, he raised his hands to the crowd making a *bring it on* motion.

The mass of people fed into it and started chanting the brute chimera's name. I felt a pit in my stomach. It was no mystery what this action reminded me of. The same mass chanting I had heard when I ran into Aras, after I had been called down to help with the town meeting.

Reaver... Reaver... Reaver.

I rose up on Garrett's lap, feeling him brush my hair back tenderly. I wasn't paying attention though. I watched the thick and muscular chimera as he slammed his blade down into the convict's heart, before, with his arm moving up and down, he started to cut it out.

Even with the fun and casual smoke-filled atmosphere around me, I felt a cold sickening feeling. These small reminders of Reaver were starting to bother me more and more. Not because I missed my friend, and I did dearly, but because – they were all him.

The chimeras were products of Silas's genes, and so was Reaver. They were all alike, but in my wildest dreams I had never fathomed just how similar they were. Every time I was around one of these mutants they played out a childhood memory to a tee, well, the savage ones at least. Garrett, the silver-haired twins, and Elish were a bit more removed. I guess they were the intelligent chimera type. They weren't as in-your-face bloodthirsty but I'm sure they were just as psychotic.

I felt my shoulders slump. I dismissed the thought and hated myself for it but I couldn't help what I saw.

Reaver would've been right at home here. He would've loved these people. Did Leo really do him a good thing by forcing him to be normal and stunting the bloodthirsty fire we had all seen in him? The fight he'd had with Greyson was because he showed tendencies that Ares was doing to a cheering crowd right now. They made him feel shitty for feeling those feelings and even more so for acting on them. It was obviously a part of him that nurturing couldn't destroy. They had been preventing Reaver from becoming who he had been genetically engineered to be.

I watched as Ares pulled out the guy's heart and took a bite of it. He threw it off to the side towards the young chimeras, and I saw the two boys take it and take bites with their little metal teeth, cheering and hollering with glee as they smeared blood on their faces.

Yep, Reaver had done that too, right down to the blood.

My eyes fell to the closest thing to Reaver – King Silas. He was standing by the window, having a conversation with Artemis, holding an opium cigarette in his hands. Staring at the carnage below with his emerald eyes alight and focused. I saw him raise an eyebrow and say something out of the corner of his mouth before they both laughed.

Silas wasn't even paying attention to me; I continued to ignore Garrett's drunken advances as I watched him. Once again another side of King Silas. I had seen Asher; I had seen the Silas that took all the joy in the wasteland from torturing me and Garrett, and now I was seeing this relaxed king enjoying the company of his family with entertainment and food around us, complete with pets to satisfy our every whim.

"See?" Garrett purred with a kiss on my neck that made me shiver. I glanced to the corner of the room and saw Caligula nailing Drake to the grisly scene below us, Nico resting a hand on Caligula's shoulder, his eyes switching from the arena to their heaving bodies.

"This is my family. A personal summons like that from Silas is a rare thing for me, this… this is not. We're not all bad, lutra. We're not evil people like you greywasters paint us."

Not if you're a chimera and a part of the family… I said in my head, and there could be nothing more true. I watched with a grim look as Siris and Ares both started trying to pull the arms off of the convict. The crowd was going insane but I could hear the man's desperate screams over the noise.

We're not evil people.

Two months ago your master killed Leo and Greyson. My best friend's fathers, my mayors… and your brother. How could you forgive that so easily? How can you say this family isn't evil when they support and worship a man who raped and tormented a seventeen-year-old manic-depressive, a man who murdered his creation and his creation's husband in cold blood?

I sighed and turned away, but not before seeing the thin pink line around the man's arms start to spill red. Then, a moment later, red lights shone on the arena and the crowd of Skyfallers went insane.

I didn't want to look, I wasn't like them. I couldn't even watch when the convicts Reaver burned were still alive. I mean, jeez, what a way to go…

Reaver would love this, all of this… at least he would have if things hadn't turned out as they did. I had to rely on the fact that Greyson and Leo had known what they were doing when they stole Reaver. My boy had been raised for a greater purpose; he would become more than all of this.

Anyway, Killian could never be here… this place would wilt him like a flower. He was too soft-hearted and kind to deal with so much blood and carnage, and the intimidations of the chimeras and Silas. Even if I thought Reaver would be happy here, Killian wouldn't and we did what we had to do to keep Tinky happy, as well as Reaver.

There, I made it palatable for myself.

I decided to keep distracting myself with the gladiator-like fighting below me. I pushed out the dark shadows in my mind and tried to give myself into the atmosphere buzzing around us. To my grim amusement, and everyone else's, the next convict to go down was tied off and gagged.

"Watch this, love. It's hilarious!" Garrett exclaimed. He stood up straight and leaned forward with me. I was still sitting on his lap.

The crowd erupted into cheers as the two little ones ran into the arena; to my absolute hilarity they were dressed in little matching blue capes. They both raised their hands in the air like the brutes had done, and called in all the attention to themselves, like little professional wrestlers.

The next part though was just creepy, but also like nothing I hadn't seen before.

Hunter, with an agility that I had seen in Reaver, jumped onto the convicts back and took two tufts of his hair. With both his feet braced onto his back, he pulled the guy's head backwards exposing the soft of his neck.

Chaser, with an embellished twirl, took out the knife, before he balanced the tip onto his fingers and at the same time took a bow. He tossed the knife up into the air and caught it, before he paused and held his hand up to his ear and craned it towards the crowd.

"Bite bite bite!" they called. Garrett was laughing behind me and

clapping his hands. Every chimera was watching the show, and some of them started joining into the chant, raising their glasses or their smokes with their cheering.

Chaser threw the knife away, and with a flex of his hands and a cat-like pounce, he sunk his metal teeth into the guy's neck. I cringed and held my own throat as the blood squirted through his teeth. His head thrashed from one side to the other until the guys throat came out in a thick chunk of red flesh.

Well, that was enough for tonight. "I'm going to take a leak." I shuddered and got up.

"Aww." Garrett pulled on my arm, giving his cigar to Lance. "Come now, they were bred for it. They're having a grand time."

My skin was crawling; this was too much Reaver in one concentrated area. Reaver's crazy side had to be taken in small doses. "The smoke is making me a bit nauseas. I'm going to take a piss and get a bit of air. I'll be fine."

My suave but rather tipsy chimera frowned at me, but a moment later he looked past me and waved someone over. I looked and saw it was Nico, who had at some time during the fighting detached his dick from Drake's orifices. "Go with him."

I sighed. "I don't need a bodyguard."

Garrett waved me off like he was having none of it. "What happened last time you went to the bathroom alone? Come back soon, they'll be bringing out the last convict and Nero is always an entertainment."

I leaned down and kissed his flushed face and gave it a playful pat. He was getting so wasted. I got up and followed Nico.

I glanced behind me once and saw I was being followed by two other ones I didn't recognize. Chimeras or boyfriends that had trickled in during the fighting. We all walked silently down the tunnel and into the main part of the stadium. Everyone around us parting, and some even giving us bows and nods as we walked past. I would never get bored of that.

I went and took a piss; though when I emerged and was joined with everyone else we didn't head back. I looked questionably at Nico as he led us towards the lobby of the stadium.

"You like drugs, Reno?" Nico said in a voice that was accented;

though like all accents it was fake. They had died in the Fallocaust, but it didn't stop some of the arians from adopting them from watching movies. I guess they thought it made them unique, I thought it made them sound like yahoos.

"Of course I do, I'm from the greywastes." I chuckled looking over my shoulder. I paused for a second as Nico led us outdoors into the crisp night air. I shoved my hands into my pockets as the cold nipped them.

Nico looked from side to side and ducked us into an alleyway; he reached into his pocket and pulled out a baggy of powder.

"Master Nico, that's cocaine!" one of them gasped like Nico had just pulled out a severed head.

Nico scoffed. "Don't be such a wimp, Kay. It's good shit. You have no idea how hard it is to get this stuff. Clig has a nose like a bloodhound."

Aww, they're such cute little amateurs. I let out a snort-like laugh and they all looked at me.

"I have a thousand dollars worth of that shit at home, both my homes. You're getting all antsy for a gram? Give it here." I took the bag from Nico and dipped Garrett's keycard into it. I brought out some white powder onto the tip and snorted it. I shook my head and shuddered and handed it to one of the other ones, a kid with brown hair and big brown eyes; he had a silver studded collar around his neck.

He stared at me with wide eyes. Oh my god, it was like I was corrupting ten-year-olds. A moment later he took it and inhaled some. I could see his skin tense and his eyes start to water. I clapped him on the back, and he handed the bag to the one named Kay.

"What's your name? I didn't see you when I arrived," I asked, flexing my fingers as the burning drip fell down my throat. I felt my heartbeat rise as the coke kissed my brain.

"My name is Trig. I am Ares's pet. Nice to meet you, Master Reno." Trig bowed. When he raised his head I saw the small shadow of a bruise on his cheek bone, covered with makeup and powder. He was Ares's pet alright.

Nico rubbed his nose and jumped up and down on the spot; he shook his head and I could see the ripples of bliss go through his body. Finally the baggy got passed to Kay, and because peer pressure wins out, he took some too. So cute, I could be elbow deep in cocaine with the snap of my finger.

I outranked them now… hah.

After tossing the bag around one more time, we emerged from the alleyway and started towards the large lobby doors that would lead us back to the stadium. I looked on, amused at the drunken arians stumbling around, or sitting with bottles of Dek'ko booze in their hands. We were late in the evening now, and it was more common to see someone drunk or stoned than not. Everyone looked like they were having a good time; I could even see hookers of both types strutting their feathers in front of the entrance.

Suddenly a deafening boom rocked the building, shaking the ground under our feet.

Everyone froze in their place as the sudden noise ripped the night air around us. A moment later a second one, and to my horror, smoke started to pour out of the building.

Everything went insane in that moment. I felt Nico grab my arm and pull me away from the stadium, yelling something that I couldn't hear over the sudden onslaught of screaming. I followed him, tripping and stumbling as my eyes kept going back to the open roof of the stadium. Thick black plumes rose and disappeared into the matching night sky.

"We need to go to the safe house." Nico's voice broke the panic and dread that had started eating my gut alive. My attention snapped to him and I nodded, not even realizing I was holding Kay's hand too. All four of us were together. "Just run. The only fucking way we can help them is to get out of the way. Run!"

"Was that a fucking bomb?" The words left my lips in a shrill timber as the reality sucked itself back into me like a vacuum I realized what was going on around me.

Nico nodded, his head turning from one direction to the other while he ran across the pavement with us. Cars stopped in the streets as the people from the stadium started to flee.

The noise was deafening. I could hear the snaps of beams inside of the building, and as something inside came crashing down, I heard panicked screaming.

When we got to the other side of the street, Nico stopped; he reached into his pocket and pulled out his remote phone. I saw it was ringing, I hadn't even heard it under the screaming and panic we had left behind. As he talked on it, I looked behind me.

Everyone was spilling out of the building like ants out of a compromised nest. Darting off into different directions as the thiens tried desperately to control them. Smoke was still rising to the sky, but thankfully no other explosions had been heard.

Nico got off of his phone. "The bombs went off in the west skybox. Drake is injured and so are Artemis, Jiro, and Lance. We need to go now. The call got cut, I think–"

"Is Garrett okay?" Fuck, I used to carry a gun with me at all times, an assault rifle usually. Why the fuck didn't I have one now? I'd catch those assholes; I'd been catching troublemakers with Reaver since I was a kid.

"I think so." Nico was already several steps away from me. He wasn't waiting for us. I took a step towards the three of them, but my heart pulled me towards the stadium. Even if Garrett was immortal I couldn't leave him.

No… I have to be safe; he would be pissed off if I went back into the building. After a long sigh I turned away, though now Nico and the others were out of sight. I started to jog in the direction they had gone, down a dark alleyway full of dumpsters and trash-strewn edges. My heart hammering in my chest and spilling its anxiety all over my body.

Did this happen often? I turned a corner and started jogging down a second alleyway; this one had several doors on the sides with dimly lit lights.

I was halfway down when my own remote phone rang. I reached into my vest and pulled it out. The relief was palpable; it could only be one person.

"Are you okay?" we both said at the same time. I sighed from relief and I heard him too. I started to quicken my speed.

"You're alright? Where are you?" Garrett's voice said on the other side of the line. I could hear a loud commotion, and further back, people talking in hurried and angry voices.

I looked around, the other three were long gone. I started doubling back to where I came. "The alley, across the street. We went out for some fresh air when it happened. Nico, Kay, and Trig are ahead of me somewhere, going towards a safe house. I think I lost them though."

"One moment."

There was some commotion on the line and I heard Garrett talking. I heard Kay's name. I assumed he was telling whoever he was with that those three were out too.

I leaned against the cold brick. I heard a jingle and I realized it was my bracelets rattling together from my shaking hands. I tried to take some deep inhales to calm myself down. Garrett was safe, when it came down to it that's all that mattered. I kept trying to tell myself…

I saw a flicker out of the corner of my eye. I raised my head and glanced over. My body froze when I spotted a silhouette in the direction I'd just come in. It was someone standing beside a row of dumpsters.

Cautiously I took a step away from him, but as I did, he stepped forward. He was half-shrouded in the darkness, wearing ratty black clothing; I could see a remote clenched in one hand.

I took another slow step back and gave him a nod so he knew I could see him. My body tensed in on itself as he stepped forward into the light. The dim lamp illuminating crimson hair that still looked deep red even in the darkness.

Oh fuck…

"Garrett… Garrett…" I whispered, not taking my eyes off of him. "The red-haired guy from the Penguin. He's here… he's–"

"Get off the phone!" a sharp voice said behind me. I spun around and saw the golden-haired one only a foot away with a burly guy behind him. I looked back towards the crimson one and felt my heart lurch into my throat. He was holding a baseball bat in one hand and the remote in the other.

"What?" Garrett's voice was sharp. *"He's there? Reno hold on. Nero! Follow me, NOW."*

"Get off the phone…"

"He has a remote detonator," my voice rasped. "There are three–"

The golden-haired one hit me hard in the shoulder, making me drop the phone onto the ground. It split in half, the battery skidding off underneath the dumpster. I fell to my knees feeling a wave of nausea come over me.

The next blow was to my face, a flashing white light blinding my eyes, sending a buzzing heat to my ears. A cold sensation on my cheeks and bare arms told me I was on the cold pavement. I felt another thump hit my face which filled my mouth and nose with blood. I coughed, my body automatically trying to bring me to my feet.

The next cracking blow knocked me unconscious.

The greyrifts

"Garrett?"

...

"When?"

...

"I will be there by nightfall."

Jade thought it was a dream, a cold voice that tickled the outreaches of his subconscious. A conversation that he thought was just the last lingering chords of a recital before his mind would awaken to Elish beside him.

But when he woke up, the room was dark and Elish was gone, the sheets beside him disturbed and the pillow still holding the shape of Elish's head.

Jade sighed, thinking it was nothing but his blond chimera waking up early, but when he walked into the office, the laptop as gone… and so was his master.

CHAPTER 11

Reaver

I PULLED THE BLANKETS UP TO MY FACE AND TOLD whoever was stupid enough to turn the bedroom lights on in the middle of the night to kindly fuck off.

"Get up and get ready, we're leaving within the hour," a cold voice said from the doorway.

I pulled the covers down and looked towards the voice, trying to adjust my eyes to the light.

"What happened?" No need to mince words here, if Elish was in my doorway something had happened and something bad. "Is Silas coming?" I got up, ignoring the fact I was naked. If there was anyone in the world to not give a shit about that it was Elish Dekker.

"Get dressed and grab everything, now." Elish turned and left the room.

I stared at the door as it slammed shut, a myriad of questions flooding through my head, urging the rat in my brain to attempt to make sense of this. I looked down at Killian for help, but he just looked at me petrified

"Maybe he went to Skyfall and got the keycard?" Killian said quietly. The tone suggested he was trying hard to keep himself from panicking, but the anxiety was already chewing my gut.

"He wouldn't be that hurried…" I mumbled and lit a cigarette.

We both got up, and as we got changed we packed everything we had in our bedrooms into his satchel, my shoulder bag, and the black weapons bag.

When we walked out of the bedroom it was like we'd stepped into a different house. Jade and Perish were both running around panicked, both dressed in winter clothing and footwear. I briefly mused at how different Jade looked with clothes on; he didn't seem like Jade when he wasn't dressed like a slut holding an opiate cigarette.

My eyes scanned the room and focused on Elish who was typing away on his computer, an ear piece in his ear that was connected to his phone. He was out of everyone else's earshot, but with my hearing I could pick up the conversation easily.

"No. Shale, like the rock… is that right, Jade?" His eyes turned to Jade, who seemed to sense his master was looking at him.

I watched as the boy turned around and nodded. "Shale Eddik. He was raised in the orphanage like me."

Elish nodded and typed on his computer. "They're disposable. It's Meirko and Kerres who are the ringleaders in this – Yes, he's the one with the red hair."

I stopped halfway from tying my boots when I saw Jade's mouth twitch. His yellow eyes were heavy. It looked like he was almost avoiding me.

"What's going on? What happened?" I asked

"Jade, speak to Kessler. He wants apartment addresses and any family members you may know of." Elish took the ear piece out of his ear and held it out to Jade. Gently, Elish put the laptop down and stood.

He was dressed for winter as well: a grey wool long coat with untied tails that dangled below thick black pants and a white sweater. His gloves were black and lined with fur I could smell was real, and his hair was tucked into the jacket giving him a very un-Elish appearance.

His purple eyes fixed on us. The Cold One must've taken pity on our confused expressions because he motioned for us to sit down on the couches.

"There was a bombing at a chimera-occupied event last night." The calmness to his tones was deceptive; his face was holding the anger that his voice wouldn't submit to.

Elish looked pissed off.

Well, I wasn't; I hoped the explosion wiped a few of those fuckers off the planet.

"Reno, two pets, and a partner of Caligula were kidnapped, and we have reason to believe they're being held for ransom."

Jesus fuck. I took a deep breath, refusing myself to explode over this.

"You said he would be safe." There was no hiding the edge to my voice, my head felt hot and the anger was creeping up my chest. "Silas laughed when I tried to trade Killian for Jade, and he laughed again at trading Perish. I'm to assume Reno isn't high up on the chimera save list. So he's screwed then?"

"No." Elish shook his head. He looked down at his laptop and turned it to me. On the screen was an almost newspaper-looking document. I read the top. *The Bulletin* it said, this was some sort of Skyfall newspaper.

My heart dropped when I read the top headline.

President of Skytech's fiancé kidnapped.

Reno got engaged to that guy? I reached out to the touch pad and scrolled the page down, only for the page to reveal a photo.

I didn't recognize him at first; he looked so different. I heard Killian swear beside me and clench my hand. Probably also wondering who this guy was, since he certainly couldn't be my dirty greywaster Reno. The same guy who once preferred to wash his hair with flea shampoo 'just to cover his bases'.

My friend's hair was now all silvery, and longer than it had been before. His face was healthier and full, and holding a smile I could see wasn't put on. He was being led through a crowd by a strangely-dressed guy with a thin moustache and a tuxedo: Garrett Dekker.

"What do they want?" My voice was cold and unwavering; my only outlet for the helpless frustration boiling inside me was to squeeze Killian's hand. I quickly tried to scan the printing above and below the photo.

"Me."

That word seeped into my skin, leaving me cold. I glanced up at

Elish, wondering if now I would see some emotion on that face, but he was as collected as ever. "Jade? Perhaps you would like to explain why this has happened, and perhaps for my own amusement, tell them just why Kerres is still a problem."

Jade appeared in the corners of my vision. By this time I could hear the timer in my brain clicking down to the moment where I start flipping out and throwing shit.

Jade gave the phone back to Elish who was packing up the laptop now. He looked nervously at all of us, before lowering his head. "Kerres is my ex-boyfriend. He's… I, well, he's still determined to get me back, and he joined a terrorist organization to try and achieve that."

"Isn't it rather obvious that isn't going to happen?" I swallowed the acid starting to flow into my mouth.

"Yeah… yeah it is; he's gone kinda crazy…" Jade's voice was submissive and flooding with guilt. I followed Elish as he rose, and the blond chimera signalled for Jade to gather the bags. Behind us I saw Perish packed up with Deek beside him; he looked worried but was staying quiet.

"So what's going to happen now? How are you going to get him back?" I demanded. Without even a goodbye to the bunker that had been my bright little coffin, we all walked into the hanger.

I crossed my arms. "And most importantly: where the fuck are we going?"

"Kreig."

"Seriously?" I held onto Killian's hand and jumped into the plane. I felt bad for the kid, he hadn't gotten more than a couple words in and I knew he was just as confused as me. He liked notice when his life was going to change, but that was a luxury we had left behind months ago.

Elish opened the cockpit door and Jade walked in. I jumped out and grabbed my last carton of opiate cigarettes, even though all of our bags were full of them, and gave the hanger one last sweep. The dog was in, and Perish, Jade, Elish, Killian… the supplies were checked and the little belongings we had.

When I jumped back into the plane, the door closed behind me. Elish was still in the hanger, but he was holding a blue folder in his hand.

"I left for Skyfall an hour after midnight; I have already been there and returned. I have the keycard we need," Elish replied.

The metal-ribbed ground shook under my feet as the engine turned and rumbled to life, muffled and quieter than I had imagined in my head. A moment later I heard the teeth-clenching sounds of the gears turning, before the bunker house disappeared below us.

"And Reno? You're going to help save him, right? You're fucking immortal just… give them you and shoot them all or do your lightning touch." My feet started to move without me telling them and I realized I was pacing back and forth. I saw a cigarette out of the corner of my eye and took it, nodding a thanks to Killian.

"Reno is the fiancé of one of the most powerful men in Skyfall. They will not hurt him."

I gritted my teeth, a sour feeling filling my gut. "That stupid president brainwashed Reno and got him kidnapped, real nice fucking guy."

"Brainwashed?" I narrowed my eyes when I heard the amusement in his voice. "I assure you Reno is quite happy with his new fiancé, and the feeling is mutually shared."

"Reno likes anyone who pays attention to him," I snapped, my mind temporarily turned to mush as I said those words. I think halfway through I realized that I was mad at Reno. Mad for him agreeing to marry Garrett, and mad at him for–

No, no it wasn't that…

I swallowed, and realized I was hurt and perhaps a bit jealous. "Just… bring him back. Go get him and bring him back."

That was *my* Reno, no one else's.

"That's my intention, which is why I am leaving for Skyfall right now." Elish reached into his pocket and pulled out a folded up piece of paper. He handed it to me. I took it with a wary look and started to unfold it.

It was a map, albeit a bad one. It looked like something thrown together in haste. I scanned through it and Elish continued to speak. "I was planning on accompanying you to Kreig, but it goes without saying that plans have changed. What has also changed is that I have reason to believe this plane is being tracked. I'm dropping you off here." A slender finger pointed to a small red X, a few inches away I saw Kreig, and much farther away, almost off the map, I saw Skyfall Island. "I can't risk diverting my usual course. Silas woke up last week and he has eyes everywhere, some of which are blind to me. You will be proceeding on foot a several day walk from the city."

"Then what?" I asked, showing the map to Killian and Perish who were hovering by my shoulders. I could feel their anxious energy behind me, Perish's especially.

Elish handed Killian the small blue folder. "Perish knows where the building is and he will know how to get inside. Once you're inside, look for hard drives. I want all of them, every piece of software you can find. I'll come and collect you once Garrett and I have resolved this business with Reno."

"How long will that be?"

"It could be over a month, possibly two. I'm not sure, but right now the longer you are hidden the better. Use that time to help Killian's emotional recovery, and your own. I want no emotional baggage when I return."

"I'm going too?" Perish asked behind me, his voice was wavy and laced with nervous tones. "I'm not going back to Skyfall?"

Elish shook his head before he took the paper out of my hand with a gentle sweep, then placed it inside the folder Killian was holding. "Silas thinks you're with Reaver and Killian, you'll be answering to Reaver for now."

I smirked as I saw Perish's face light up, at least he could keep Killian busy. They could be emotional about things together. He could be the new Reno since mine decided to get himself involved in chimera politics.

"Another thing…" Elish's purple eyes shifted to the cockpit as if making sure the door was closed tightly. With a small downturn of his mouth he turned back to me, before nodding me over to the side of the plane, away from Perish and Killian's inquisitive stares.

"The others who were kidnapped… it's obvious what these terrorists are trying to do. The others were pets and the partner of Kessler's son. I think Reno was only captured because his engagement had only recently been announced, before then he was a pet like the others," Elish began. He smoothly folded his arms over his overcoat, done with such an elegance it always looked choreographed. "I am asking of you, Reaver, to, at least temporarily, assume ownership of my own pet. Considering this–"

I pursed the inner corners of my eyes with my fingers and groaned. Elish's violet icebergs cut me in half as I sighed and shifted my stance.

Elish continued, ignoring my display.

"–considering this involves his ex-boyfriend. Not only is he at risk in Skyfall, he is at risk for being taken as well, and rest assured… Kerres would rather Jade die than be with me."

"I'll take him but I really dislike him being called my pet. Can't he just be your pet and tag along?" I asked, feeling another weight of responsibility rest on my shoulders. I could hear the bones creak and wane inside my skull.

Elish slowly shook his head, for a brief moment his cold countenance slipped and I saw the smallest glint of apprehension in his eyes. The first non-cold emotion I had seen. Deep down, he really did love this kid.

I knew it.

"I would feel better if you had direct responsibility of him," Elish continued. "A companion would not carry the same burden."

There were more than a few emotions running through my head. But while my mind quickly sifted through them, one kept rising to the surface, pushing the others aside to dig itself into the grey matter in my brain.

Elish trusted *me* with Jade?

I wasn't happy with this; I already had Killian to look out for. Not to mention the fact that Killian listened to me, I didn't know if this pet would.

"I will." What was I getting myself into?

"And for your agreeance, I will not return until I have Reno with me. I will promise you that." Elish turned away from me and walked back into the cockpit.

I sat with Killian, who was flushed and looking pale, and threw a supportive arm around him, pulling the boy close to me. I was giving his back a supportive rub when I heard the first shrill shriek come from the cockpit. Killian jolted and looked to the front of the plane, his blue eyes wide and full of shock.

I kept rubbing his back. "Guess what? I got you a new pet!" I said sweetly.

Jade burst through the cockpit, looking like Satan in an overcoat. His yellow eyes immediately flared at me. "Don't even… don't you fucking even say anything, Reaver!" he snarled before he stalked to the other end of the plane, only to start taking the top off of one of the crates.

Because in the deepest fathoms of my heart I was an absolute dick, I grinned at him. "That's *master*, Cicaro."

The dark-haired pet's body shook from an eternal rage. I wondered what exactly he was angry about though. Being my new pet, or Elish ditching him with the fugitives. Like most chimeras, he had always worn his own mask in front of us, but now it was breaking from his face.

"Perish, mind the plane," Elish said from the door frame. Perish, more than happy to get away from this situation, got up and ran into the cockpit.

Then things got a bit real. I looked over and saw the crate's lid forgotten against the metal ribs of the plane with Jade standing behind it. He was holding a large knife.

"Very frightening, I'm the picture of fear." Elish stepped towards him, his tone biting cold and soaking with derision. "Put that away before you hurt yourself, or is that your intention? I thought we were over your penchant for masochism."

Jade's face twisted in an inhuman aguish; he brandished the knife at his master. I could see his boots shaking as he tried, with every ounce of control, to not break his brazen stance. "Fuck you!" he managed to scream, his voice seething with agony. "You said you would never leave me again! You promised me!" He held the knife up, and as he did, I saw his knees buckle more. I barely needed to tune my hearing to hear his heart thrashing inside his chest.

Elish took another silent step towards him, the closer he got the more Jade dissolved into himself. The cicaro sunk to his knees before bending forward in his own grief; his shoulders shaking and trembling with his body.

I honestly thought Elish would be moved by Jade's inner agony. I expected to see him take the kid into his arms and hold him, while admitting his love and putting a smile back onto his face, something to show at least a shred of empathy.

Heck, I felt bad for him.

But, as if to hammer in the cold indifference he had to people's suffering, he reached behind Jade's neck and removed his collar. With a soft jingling of chains he wrapped the leash loosely around his hand before he rose with the knife.

"You have no choice in the matter, maritus."

Without another word, with his pet shaking on his knees, Elish swept past me and Killian and went back into the cockpit.

Killian leapt up from me and put his hand on Jade's back. When Jade made no move to maul my boyfriend, I got up silently and walked myself to the front of the plane.

"Leave, Perish." I pointed to the door. Poor Perish, even amongst the people who were nice to him he still got bossed around all the time.

Perish sighed; he wasn't as snappy with my orders as he was with Elish's. He took off the co-pilot headphones and slunk out of the room. I closed the door behind him.

Elish didn't even look up, he stared forward as he steered the plane. I tried not to become lost in the breathtaking view we had of the sky, and turned my attention to him.

"I know your funny language. Maritus means husband, doesn't it?" I crossed my arms. In truth, I didn't know much of the language, but Killian had spent his time in the greyrifts apartment trying to learn it, and he'd told me what that word meant.

Elish's eyebrow twitched just slightly. "Silas likes crafting punishments to each chimera; my punishment was to marry my cicaro. However in all respects, he gets treated no different."

Interesting, it made sense. If he'd forced Killian and me to get married I would be a bit annoyed at how happy it would make Killian, but I wouldn't care. Equalizing this master and pet relationship would be torture for someone like Elish.

"Well, I don't give a fuck how you treat your pet, but give him fucking something. I don't give a shit that you need to be all cool and dead inside to keep up appearances, but give the kid something before you drop him off. He's obviously madly in love with you."

The blond chimera was silent, but I saw his hands grip the wheel a bit harder. "My cicaro knows me well; I do not have to say anything to him."

"Which is why maybe now you should. But what do I know, right? Him waving a knife around is an obvious window into his solid mental state." I smirked, but it faded when I realized Elish could see me through the reflection of the plane's window.

Suddenly a loud clang of metal sounded in the cockpit. Both Elish and I turned to the door, but as I went to open it, Killian was on the other side trying to get in.

"He fucking jumped! He grabbed a parachute bag and just fucking jumped!"

"Idiot!" Elish snarled, showing more emotions than I had ever seen on him. He pressed a button on the plane controls and rose before he ran past me. I followed.

Perish was gripping the steel frame as he tried to pull the door shut. Elish pushed him aside and looked out the open door, wind tossing everything around that wasn't crated or nailed down. I saw Elish's mouth move in a few curse words before he closed the door.

As quickly as it came, the wind died down to nothing as the cabin pressurized. With his face unnaturally angry, Elish stalked to the cockpit and slammed the door. Soon I was feeling the sickening sensation in my gut as the plane started to descend.

Killian was bawling his face off. I held him in my arms as he tried to tell me what had happened in a wobbling voice. I caught the gist of it, which was basically what I had expected: He tried talking to Jade; Jade got pissed off and grabbed a parachute.

I assumed he knew how to use it since Elish was landing the plane; I hoped we weren't going down to the surface to find a body. What an end for the poor little fucker.

I held Killian as I watched the mountains of the greywastes start to peak over the windows like a slowly closing jaw. As soon as the plane landed, Killian pulled away and quickly opened the door. He leapt to the ground and ran out into the open world before I could stop him.

Elish was out too, though the expression on his face made me stay several paces away from him. It wasn't a look of pure anguish that Jade had had, or even an expression of burning anger, but on Elish I knew it translated the same. It looked like he was forcing down an imminent nuclear meltdown with just his lips.

I saw Elish's eyes focus on one area blocked from my view by the plane. I jogged to that side of the plane so I could get a good look, mostly to appease my own morbid curiosity.

I immediately saw the remains of a white parachute, flattened against the grey rocks like a balloon with the air let out of it. Then, about ten feet away from that, Jade was walking away with his shoulders slumped and his body constricted on itself. He was alive though, but for how long I didn't know.

"Come here, Jade," Elish said sternly.

Jade's body tensed. I could see the faint rising and falling of his shoulders as Elish's voice hit his ears. He stopped but didn't move.

With Killian beside me I tiptoed over to where the action was, keeping our shadows hidden by the side of the plane. I motioned Perish over too and all three of us stood like hens watching it all go down.

"Is that collar really that important to you? It looks so uncomfortable." Elish's voice was a low but soothing temper, with only a slight air of being condescending.

Jade turned around, the anger was gone from his face. Now his yellow eyes glistened in the faint shreds of winter sunlight. "Get your digs in, make all the poisonous remarks you want and leave like we're all waiting for you to do. The moment you leave, I'm going, and Reaver doesn't give two shits if I follow."

"And where will you go?" Elish asked with an air of bemusement. "Going to farm rocks? Become a raver?"

"Anything's better than being shipped off for my slaughter."

I saw Elish's left eyebrow raise. He took a step forward towards Jade.

The pet didn't move, his gaze never left the rocky grey ground and his boots stayed firmly planted. He was defiantly standing his ground against the oncoming shadow.

"Slaughter?" Elish's tone turned curious. "Why would you think such an odd thing?"

I saw Jade's arms shake and the small white disks of his clenched knuckles. Jade turned his face away from Elish as Elish took the last step, until they were facing each other.

"You're leaving me alone with these psychopaths with my head slowly getting more and more fucked up. You're leaving me to die, aren't you?"

"You are such an idiot, maritus," Elish said with a smirk. He reached a hand out and I saw him caress Jade's cheek. "Is this what this tantrum is about? You think I'm putting you in harm's way on purpose?"

Complete and utter silence around us. Jade's yellow eyes burned into the ground with fierce anger before he jerked his hand away from Elish's touch.

"No, no, no, come here," Elish said under his breath. Only I could hear it, and possibly Perish.

Jade stood frozen and rigid, unmoving but obedient to his master's touch. I had felt that way when King Silas had touched me. I shuddered at the thought but buried it inside me.

Elish ran his fingers up the line of Jade's cheek bone, before he traced the pet's neck. I watched as Jade's steeled face started to show signs of wear.

The next thing that happened shocked me. I hadn't thought Elish had listened to me, but he cupped Jade's jaw into his hand and stroked his cheek with his thumb, before he leaned down and kissed him lightly on the lips. Then, as Elish pulled away, he took Jade's hand and I realized on the pet's bare hand I could see matching silver bands.

"I am not forcing Reaver to caretake you because I want you to die. If anything this hand I am being forced to play should tell you… I am doing the opposite. Skyfall is too dangerous for you, and any permanent damage to your brain will take at least a year, if not more, to become fatal. Really, mellitus, do you still doubt me that much?"

Jade's eyes rose; he looked at Elish sadly before I saw his lower lip tremble. A moment later Jade put his arms around Elish. I heard the girls behind me *aww* at the adorableness of it. I was just fascinated that I had actually gotten through to Elish.

Elish's overcoat-covered arms held his pet tight for a moment before he pulled himself away. A few very quiet words were spoken between the two of them, before Elish turned and left Jade standing there.

Elish noticed us watching him, and I heard an irritated sigh at the realization he did indeed have an audience. But like the cold chimera he was, Elish brushed it off and turned his violet gaze towards the plane.

"We're close enough to where I had planned to drop you off. Start bringing your supplies out of the plane."

When Elish was out of sight, Killian let out a shrill little squeak and pulled on the arm I still had wrapped around him. "Wasn't that cute!?"

"I'm not sure cute is the right word…" I started leading him towards the other side of the plane. "It just goes to show how special I am. It took me months to do what has taken him ninety years."

"Did you see their rings? Will you give me something nice one day?" Killian sounded giddy, riding on the emotional overflow he'd picked up by osmosis apparently.

"I fucking gave you a gun, didn't I? I even got you that stupid guitar you almost became food for." I turned around and saw that Perish had wandered over to where Jade was still standing. They were both speaking quietly to each other. Jade still looking dumbfounded and Perish jittering around like he usually did. I turned back and we both jumped into the plane, leaving our quips for after Elish left. I knew from my own chimera blood that if we brought it up around Elish, the next nice thing he did for Jade would take another ninety years.

Ah chimeras, genetically engineered to be super machine sociopaths but once we fall in love it's kind of like watching a fiery car crash in slow motion. It was cute in a way, though Elish's abuse of Jade's flesh and mind shouldn't be called such. It was a rather strange relationship, but I had hope for the statuesque and equally cold Elish. Hell, maybe I could keep helping.

Like Greyson and Leo had helped me with Killian. Huh, a greywaster-chimera relationship that had stood the test of time. They both really knew what they were talking about without me even realizing it.

Well that dampened my mood. I wordlessly started to grab our belongings, feeling the despair I had banished to the void threaten to claw out of my gut. Nothing I could deal with still two months later. Every time I was reminded of just how much of a shit son I had been… I immediately lost control of my emotions. The only solution I had was to stuff them down and lock them far away inside of me.

Drugs helped.

We didn't have that many things: a bag for each of us, and a large duffle bag with our food, water filters, and bottled water that I would switch between Perish and myself. Perish had been nursed back to his normal weight and appearance by Killian, and it seemed like he was in good shape. Even his brain had been turning a few more wheels the longer we were in the bunker. Though all of that would go out the window if he ever went near Killian again, but I think we had reached an understanding regarding that.

I was tossing bags to Killian when I heard a low roaring sound. I blinked and looked up at the sky. My face went three shades paler.

"Elish…" I said uneasily. "Do you hear that?"

Elish turned; he'd been in the middle of packing several things into Jade's bag. He took a step towards the plane door, then he paused. I saw his eyes narrow to small slits.

"That's a plane. Get everything and find cover. Do not come out until they're gone."

I grabbed my bags and split them between Killian and I. We both jogged to the other side of the plane and were met by Jade and Perish.

"The rocks." I pointed towards a small shelf of rocks that appeared to overhang at the bottom. "We're ducking under there until it passes."

Jade and Perish nodded soberly. With a cautious glance to the overcast sky, I handed Jade and Perish their bags and sprinted towards the rocks.

There was a collective seizing of hearts as we all heard the plane descend.

"They saw us! A chimera is in there," Killian whispered nervously. He clenched my hand in a death grip.

I heard Jade let out a snort. "No one else owns planes, dummy. Of course it's a chimera."

"Everyone shut up," I hissed. There was too much noise around me. If the chimera in that plane had enhancements like me, a single noise from one of these jokes and he would know where we were.

The boys quieted down. I tried to focus my hearing, but every time I did, their heartbeats drowned it out.

And there was another odd sound…

I tilted my head and tried to focus on it. I glanced towards Perish.

The scientist was staring ahead with his brow furrowed. I looked over at him and tapped him with my foot.

He jumped, and his heart did too. I pointed to my ears, just as I heard the second plane's engine cut.

Perish nodded and shifted himself in the dirt; he pointed to the ground.

He was right; the sound was coming from underneath us. I shifted myself back too, and as soon as I did, the weird noise got louder. This time Jade's hearing caught it, he looked at the ground and raised an eyebrow.

It sounded like shifting sand, a grating noise almost, or a continuous crackle of static.

Killian and Jade were staring at the two of us, knowing better than to talk. We could all hear the voice of a stranger behind us talking to Elish. If the two other chimeras recognized who it was, they weren't saying anything.

I put my hand down where I was sitting and felt the ground. I scowled when I realized the ground was vibrating. I moved my hand and started shifting the ash away. It was loose… looser than the compacted dirt usually was.

Black? My hand brushed away the last of the grey, revealing a rough black surface underneath me. I looked up to Perish and he did the same.

More black?

Suddenly Killian's heartbeat went crazy. I quickly turned my attention to him and saw his face had completely paled.

"Move…" Killian's voice was a strangled rasp. He slowly started shifting down from underneath the rock shelf. "M-move… move…"

I blinked, but with a pull of Jade's shoulder, all of us silently slid off of the mound of dirt under the rock shelf.

Then it started to move.

Immediately I drew my M16. I stood in front of the three as all of us took several steps back.

The dirt under the shelf started to vibrate back and forth, small grains of dirt flying up into the air as it spilled from the black shell underneath.

"Oh, fuck me," Perish groaned. "Well… um… we… okay, we need to get to the plane now."

Suddenly the shell lunged at us, and the last of the dirt fell back to the ground as it jutted forward.

It was huge, about the size of the deacdog and just as long. It had giant crab-like claws that snapped and snipped threateningly at me, and a large plated tail that waved back and forth, with a sharp and bulbous stinger poised and ready to strike. All of this behind a dozen black beady eyes that twitched in all directions as it caught us in its vision.

Yeah, fuck us… that was a scorprion.

I put the scope up to my eye and started to take quick steps back. There was no fucking place to shoot it. It was plated in armour.

"Reaver… we need to get back to the plane," Killian said behind me. He gasped and pulled me out of the way, just as the scorprion tried to jab us with its tail.

I swore. I took a quick look around and saw that Perish and Jade were already halfway up the shelf. I pushed Killian ahead of me before turning around and firing off a couple rounds at it. Without a moment to spare, I climbed to the top of the shelf, holding my arm out to make sure Killian and the others stayed behind me.

I could hear the ground shifting between its many legs as it tried to climb the shelf, leaving deep gouges in the ash as it effortlessly pierced through the compacted dirt. The insect was strong, but every creature had its weak spot.

I took a step backwards as I shot at it again, the bullets penetrating its dusted black armour, but doing nothing to slow it down. I narrowed my eyes and took a sideways step to try and find any vulnerability, but every inch of it was covered.

My body twitched to step closer, and I had almost convinced myself to when I saw one of the spider-like legs raise up and dig itself into the ash, followed by a second one. I fired off my M16 and watched helplessly as it slowly crawled its way up the steep ridge.

Behind me I could hear hurried voices, and the sound of a very pissed off deacdog who we had tied inside the plane.

There was no time for backwards glances. I ran to the edge of the shelf to try and lure the fucking insect away. I gave it a couple shouts but it ignored me, still digging deep rifts into the ash as it hoisted its large but clumsy body up.

It was an ugly fucking thing. Like a hand creeping through an ajar door, its spindly limbs scraped the ledge, wrenching its body up the shelf inch by inch.

I raised a boot and kicked it in the side of the head. In response, the stinger shot down beside me, missing my thigh by inches. I had forgotten about that fucking stinger. I raised my M16 and put the scope near my eye and shot a couple rounds into the bloated barb. I whooped as I managed to blow off a rather large chunk of it.

“Get back!” a voice commanded. It wasn’t Elish but I didn’t have time look.

Then a black blur jumped behind me and skidded down the shelf. Immediately the scorprion followed his movements and directed its attention away from the planes and the rest of our party.

I recognized that face, and I recognized the stupid moustache.

Garrett Dekker, my best friend’s fiancé.

Well, fuck him; he wasn’t going to have all the fun.

I skidded down too, to Killian’s shrieking horror. I dug out my pistol and threw it to the asshole and the both of us started leading the scorprion away from the group.

Garrett caught it, and as he raised a confused eyebrow at me, I gave him a glare in return.

“What? Don’t tell me you don’t know how to shoot,” I said to him annoyed. I already default didn’t like him, and I wasn’t going to start now. He had coveted my best friend and then got his ass kidnapped. This suit-wearing pretty boy wasn’t going to get off the hook by pretending to be a hero. I had already partially disabled the fucking bug anyway.

Garrett held up the pistol and shot it at the insect; I watched one of its black beady eyes explode into nothing. As soon as the pistol kicked back, Garrett’s hand was at his belt. He drew an almost identical pistol out and shot the next eye, all in a single flawless movement that rivalled the grace of Asher Fallon.

Oh, I see what he was doing… this was a competition was it? I raised my M16 and flicked its switch to automatic. With both of us rapidly running backwards, I unleashed a clip of bullets onto the scorprion’s eyes. Its tail still flicking and striking dead air only a couple feet away from us.

Then the dumb shit tripped over a jagged rock.

The suited idiot fell backwards with a *thud*, both guns falling from his hands. The scorprion lunged forward and I saw it flatten its back out, ready to sting him with what remained of its stinger.

Many thoughts flooded my mind at that moment, and I felt my legs stiffen in expectation to let Garrett get stung or snipped in half with its pinchers, but my future sight won out. The fact that this man did indeed know who I was, and was my best friend's fiancé, made me move.

Not to mention the fact he was also immortal, which meant the death would only be for my stubborn amusement.

The split second decision lifted my feet off of the ground. I leapt onto the scorprion's back and grabbed onto its tail.

That made it very very mad.

The insect thrashed around wildly, whipping its tail back and forth with ferocity. I clenched my teeth and held on, waiting for a break in its strength so I could grab my combat knife, but it whipped its armoured segmented tail around without rest.

"Reaver, let go!"

Killian!? My eyes tried to focus on where he was but everything was a grey blur, the jerking movements rattling my brains back and forth. I decided to listen to him though. I let go of the scorprion's tail.

I felt myself go airborne, the grey rocks and trees swirling in a circle as the scorprion's tail whipped me through the air. I tried to contort myself to land on my feet, but I wasn't a cat. I landed on my back knocking the wind out of me.

With a cough, I rolled onto my side – just in time to see Killian jump on the scorprion's fucking back.

"Killian!" I screamed. My heart constricted inside of me and started thumping uncontrollably.

Garrett had gotten to his feet; he had his arms out trying to distract the insect while Killian clung to its shelled back.

I ran over and grabbed my combat knife.

Before I could get to him the scorprion gave a thrash, slamming its left legs into the greywaste dirt. I could feel the ground vibrating under my feet.

Killian held on. I saw him reach into his cargo pants pocket and pull out… a grenade?

I held my knife and watched in awe as the kid pulled the pin out with his teeth and shove it into an open crater in its back, caused by our bullet holes. Then, just as quickly as he jumped on, he let the scorprion fling him off.

And this one did land on his feet.

"Move now!" Killian yelled to Garrett, before running towards the rock Garrett was in front of. I took several steps back before putting my hands over my ears.

I turned away when a burst of flame and black armour exploded into the cold air around us, then watched in bliss as the insect's body parts flew everywhere in a mixture of yellow goo. They landed all around me, covering the ground in a mist that held the faint aroma of damp fungus.

The series of thunks took me back to the time I had bombed the factory, the body parts falling onto the ground. I loved these sounds – just like the good ol' days.

When the last insect part met the ground, I turned and walked towards the creature. It was dead as a door nail, the back of it completely blown off and strewn across the grey rock.

I shook my head at Killian and tsked. The boy glanced up at me shyly before he looked away, probably expecting me to start beating him over the head with a stinger. Instead I flicked off a chunk of scorpion innards from his shoulder and kissed him.

"You're the only non-chimera here and you're the one to kill it? Where did you learn how to move like that anyway?"

The boy smiled and kissed me back. "Play to your strengths, right?"

I was about to answer back when my ears picked up Garrett breathing heavily behind me. I glanced over and saw him, his chest rising up and down in an attempt to calm the heart about to burst out of his chest.

Poor rich boy chimera wasn't used to a little action.

"You two make quite the team, Reaver." Garrett took a step past me and picked up both of our pistols, then wiped his sweaty forehead with his black blazer. Dude looked like he was a gay James Bond. "Stories about your heartlessness have been exaggerated it seems."

I took mine from him and sheathed it back into its holder. "If you don't find Reno those stories will seem like fairy tales. That I can promise you, *Garrett*."

With fascination I saw his jaw tighten. He broke his gaze, and with his head lowered, he walked past me towards the plane. He wasn't as hard to rattle as his blond brother apparently. Elish had been right, he was a docile one. These chimeras were every personality type on the spectrum.

"Why are you here and not looking for the fucks that kidnapped him?" I called after him. I started walking back to the plane. Killian squeezed my hand to try and get me to stop but my mind was already souring to Garrett again. "Why are you here?"

We both climbed the ridge; at the top, I saw the saucer-sized eyes of Perish and Jade and the cold face of Elish Dekker.

Garrett pushed past everyone and started making his way back towards the plane.

"Now, Elish. Say your goodbyes now," Garrett called without turning around. "Do what you need to do, but I need you in Skyfall this instant."

"Wait!" Killian, who had just grabbed my hand, jerked it away and sped after Garrett. I jogged after him, leaving the other three standing over the cliff shelf. "You're not going to tell Silas, are you?"

The chimera turned around. "I have more important things to handle right now. My loyalties lie to my fiancé."

Killian stopped as he got nearer to Garrett. I saw my boyfriend put a hand on Garrett's shoulder. "How was he? Was he happy? Please… he's our best friend."

I watched Garrett's face fall; I saw his eyes were tired and even swollen. Signs of despair that I knew Killian had picked up on. The boy probably figured it out as quickly as I did – that fuckhead did love Reno.

"He… he spoke of you two all the time…" Garrett stumbled. He looked behind Killian and to me. "Stories… he's proud of both of you… I…"

Garrett's eyes shifted over. I glanced behind me to see Jade only a few paces away. "I see what you were doing, Elish. Bravo. This was all so I would join your little rebellion, wasn't it? You've been stringing me along for three years, not because you wanted me to find someone, but to set me up to join you."

"Do you wish I had never introduced the two of you?" My feet automatically took me a few steps away as I heard Elish speak directly behind me.

Elish had his arms crossed, his face still giving away no emotion but the smallest of smirks. He seemed pleased with himself.

"You played me like a fucking violin, and you played Reno too," Garrett snapped, his thin moustache moved as his face twisted in an almost sneer. There had never been a man more unsuited for the greywastes. All the way down to his now dust-stained suit and tie. "And no, Elish, you and that empath cicaro of yours know that I don't regret meeting him. I love him. Which is why I need you in Skytower by tonight. Now, I need you. Elish… Elish, the whole fucking family is imploding over this. The whole island is talking."

"I will be right behind you, I already gave you my word," Elish said, his voice crisp and biting. "I would think a thank you would be in order? I hand-delivered your soul mate to you."

"Reaver Merrik's best friend! The best friend of Silas's fugitive clone?" Garrett exploded.

I snorted through a laugh, as I did I felt Killian's hand clench mine. I couldn't help it, it had just clicked with me. Elish *had* played him like a violin.

"It was never about Reno getting us that keycard, was it?" I chuckled and raised an amused eyebrow at Elish. "This was to get my best friend to bring the most powerful chimera to your side. You smart motherfucker."

Elish spared me an icy glance before looking back at Garrett. The chimera in the suit stared at me for a second before I felt his blood start to boil.

"Ninety years and I still fall for this shit." Garrett gritted his teeth together. "I don't care if you have to make yourself into a fucking cicaro, Elish, *you-will-fix-this*. I swear on our dead brothers, if Reno dies I will murder that little husband of yours, slowly."

"Hey, don't bring me–" There was a muffled *oof* as I think Perish hit Jade.

"Go back to Skyfall, Garrett. I told you, I will be right behind you."

The suited chimera gave him a stiff nod; he went to jump back into his plane when he turned around. Surprisingly, his eyes went to Perish. "It's nice to see you well, Perry. I look forward to having our chess nights again. And you, Jade, I am pleased to see you're well."

The scientist beamed and rolled back and forth on his heels. "I do as well, Garrett. Congratulations, Reno was very kind to me when I saw him."

When the plane took off, I caught a momentarily relieved look from Elish.

"I'm assuming that went better than you thought it would?" I smirked.

The look disappeared like it had only been a phantom, replaced by the stern mask.

"Garrett is the easiest one to sway; your friend Reno did a fair job." Elish passed a glance to Jade; the cicaro was untying Deek who was squirming to get to the scorprion carcass. "This ransom of the cicaros and Caligula's partner was not planned, and is something I need to remedy immediately. However, at least it's a distraction from you; that is a silver lining."

If it was anyone else I would have decked him for that quip, but I knew Elish and would expect nothing else from him.

"How far are we from Kreig?"

Elish started to walk towards the plane. I followed him.

"It is only a day, day and a half walk; you will see the shadows above the ridge to the east."

I followed Elish onto the plane. "Am I the only one here with an automatic weapon?"

"I took out a crate of weapons for the others," Elish said before handing me a briefcase. "My laptop is in there. Remember to transfer as many files as you can onto it and bring me Lycos's hard drives as well. Perish knows how to do that. What we need right now is as much information as we can gather regarding your creation. With Garrett's help, once Reno is found, we can figure out just how to kill Silas."

I took the briefcase and hopped off of the plane. "You're not coming back until you have Reno?"

"That is correct."

And that was that, soon we were all standing back as the plane rose up into the air. I took Killian's hand, but was happy to see it wasn't trembling. Perhaps he was as happy to be on the road as I was. We were back in our element, even if we didn't have a basement to come back to.

I gave Killian's hand a squeeze and turned around as I heard a crate open. With an excited squeal, Perish started taking out their assault rifles.

And onward we went.

CHAPTER 12

Reno

I WOULD DO ANYTHING FOR A CIGARETTE RIGHT now. I would do even more to see Garrett again.

The only thing I was sure of was that I was in a sewer, everything else had been a hazy blur… actually the last several days had been. A hazy gathering of memories and half-remembered dreams that all seemed to swirl into each other like mixing paint.

I had slept a lot, and usually fell asleep to Kay's crying. Trig and Nico were either silent or being held elsewhere. I could only hear the soft sobs of the little cicaro.

I inhaled the nose-curling scent of radrat shit and stagnant water and shifted around to a sitting position. The scars from my first time being bound had been chafed and now the silver streaks were rubbed raw and split open.

During my time in cold and dark isolation I counted water drops and listened to the radrats run the length of the pipes. I even tried out my imagination which was a light in this dark and damp seclusion. I'd never been one to have imagination. Reaver was the introvert. I let movies and video games decide my imagination for me.

I imagined being with Reaver and Garrett most of all. Those two had never even met but in my head we were all best friends, even Tinkerbell was there. We would scout and sentry, kill legionaries and hang out and do drugs. I dressed my fiancé up in waster clothes and even mussed up that slicked back black hair he was so proud of.

Those thoughts warmed the chill in my bones and quieted the hunger eating my stomach alive. They fed me worse than we fed our rats. Just half a square of a hard cracker-like thing they called tact. I had heard that word from Garrett; he was the one who distributed them to the Morosians.

The District of Moros… I wasn't sure if I was there but where else would I be? My captors had to be Morosians, if the crimson-haired one (named Kerres apparently) was Jade's ex and Jade was a Morosian, well, it wasn't hard to put two and two together.

My eyes burned as the door opened, light fucked my eyes in their sockets. I closed them and clenched my jaw.

As the footsteps clicked against the damp stone, I braced myself to get the stuffing beat out of me again. Usually they raped Kay before they kicked me around but he had been quiet for a couple hours now. That poor fucker slept a lot; he was the youngest out of all of us and the most pretty.

The scraping of boots on brick stopped and I squinted my eyes to see who it was.

"Memorize this." Kerres's tone spoke to me like I was a piece of shit on his shoe. Reaver would've made short work of this retard. I was looking forward to the day where he would be my bitch.

The crimson-haired Morosian unfolded a piece of paper and slid it towards me. "You can read, can't you?"

I wanted to spit in his face but they had bound my mouth with duct tape, mostly because that was all I had done the first couple days that they had me. Almost got my jaw broken too.

I stared up at the fuck, an idiot with a glint in his eyes that radiated batshit crazy. I wasn't sure what Elish had done to this asshole but he definitely had had his snow globe shaken.

My teeth grinded as he peeled the duct tape off of my mouth. "Read it, out loud and memorize it. If you don't, I'll shoot you."

I snorted, not even glancing down at the paper. "Get your pampered little ass out of Skyfall and live in the greywastes, buddy. You'll learn quickly that we're not afraid to die. Though perhaps all that hair dye has soaked into your brain."

Surprisingly Kerres narrowed his eyes at me. "Greywaster? Why the fuck are you Garrett's whore if you're a greywaster?"

Great, I wasn't in the mood for storytelling, but as much as I wanted to hock in this guy's face again, I decided to slip the knife and try and jimmy myself a door open. "My best friend is leading a rebellion against King Silas in the greywastes. I was shot, captured by Elish, and sold to Garrett, you fucking moron. We're on the same side."

The man's face tensed, and he paused for a moment before he composed himself. He rose to his feet and kicked the paper towards me.

"Memorize this; I'll be coming back for you in an hour."

And with that he left, though to my surprise he left the door open, letting light into the damp cell I had been thrown into.

I looked down at the scrap of paper, scrawled in shaky handwriting that rivalled that of a meth addict.

"My name is Otter…" Well, he already had that wrong. *"I am Garrett's cicaro. I'm scared, they've beaten me and the others badly, and I'm in fear for my life. Whatever you have to do please surrender Elish over to the Crimstones along with 10,000 tokens. The drop will be made in Sheryn Park five days to the minute of this videos release. Failure to comply will result in the execution of the cicaro Kay."*

I wanted to laugh but I couldn't over the poison rising in my throat; it was burning me with every attempted swallow. I was rather fucked.

We were all fucked… King Silas didn't do well with threats. Reaver had tried to bargain a cicaro's life for Killian and that had failed. There was no way he was going to exchange Elish for that little cicaro.

Poor fucker…

My eyes looked over the paper and I did memorize it, for no reason other than to take the heat off of me and the other captives. If I didn't do as this red-haired fuck asked, I would only get pummelled more. I wasn't an idiot; I had learned how people like this worked. Bridley had been the same way. I had fought him tooth and nail when he'd first locked me in his bedroom but eventually I just complied. Now I knew Kerres had my ass; I'd rather comply than get beat and then comply anyway.

An hour later he came back with the golden-haired one I had met before in Skyland, named Shale. They hoisted me to my feet and walked me out of my cell.

The sewers were dark brick, dripping water and radrat piss like my cell had been, with cylinder tunnels that stretched out and branched off deep inside of Moros. I could see cigarette butts and garbage on the floors, some of it slowly being taken away by the sewer current. The smell was god awful.

I walked, or limped rather, my movements nothing but half-hearted shuffles and the occasional stumble when they pushed me. My whole body was battered and bruised; even a molar had been knocked out of my mouth when they'd beat me with the butts of their guns. I hadn't broken any bones I think, but I definitely had more than a few internal injuries.

At least they hadn't raped me, that I didn't think I could handle. Kay got the brunt of that.

As my sentry instincts commanded me, I scanned and memorized my surroundings. But all of it was the same, long stretching tunnels of decaying brick, and the occasional bluelamp or extension cord plugged into old halogens.

If Garrett knew where I was… they could raid this place and find me. I sighed, wishing it was that easy, but I doubt if I started yelling my location while I was reading my ransom note they would release it. I was screwed, I really was.

There must be a way to alert him somehow. Think, Reno, think…

I had still been a teenager when Bridley had kept me captive, raped me, and beat me within an inch of my life. I wished so badly during those several days that there had been a way for me to signal Reaver. My best friend hadn't even known what was happening to me. I sometimes spent several days in my cabin without going to Aras or seeing Reaver. It was only when I missed a trojan caravan that he'd stormed up to my cabin ready to beat me himself.

He realized I was gone and put the pieces together quickly.

My thoughts were knocked out of my brain as Kerres roughly pushed me into a room.

Smart guy, this room didn't look like the sewer at all.

There was a video camera resting on a tripod, pointed at a brown chair and most interestingly: a coloured flag. I assumed that was the mighty Crimstone flag, the name of their terrorist organization. It had a green rock with red flecks in the middle, with a crimson background.

"Sit," Kerres commanded. He jabbed me in the back with his assault rifle.

As I sat down, I saw two other people I didn't recognize, a man and a woman, both also holding assault rifles they'd so conveniently pointed at me.

They'd watched too many movies… I looked forward at the video camera and shook my head. I didn't want to say the things on that paper. I didn't want Garrett to think I was scared, I wasn't.

I didn't fear death, dying was a part of the greywastes, it happened to everyone. I had buried a sister, a brother, and a father and I had eaten them too with my family. The threat of being killed was lost on me. In the end we all ended up as food. Our bodies helped our family and friends live another day and that was just life.

Think, Reno… think.

"Okay, record the video… tell us when you're ready, Vecht." Kerres glanced over and I realized that the man holding the assault rifle was now sitting in front of a computer. He was typing away on it with his tongue sticking out of the corner of his mouth. The kid looked like he was sixteen, brown hair and a rat-like face.

I felt the tip of Shale's rifle jab me in the temple. "We will shoot you, whore. We will do worse than that. I will fuck you until you call me baby."

"Go fuck yourself," I suddenly snapped.

As the butt of his gun hit me in the side of my head, I wondered why the hell I'd just done that. I'd been sensitive to threats like that, more Bridley issues, but I thought I'd outgrown those triggers. I guess not.

Someone grabbed me before I could slip off of the chair, but the damage was done. White lights collected in the corners of my vision and the room began to spin. I spat a mouthful of blood and grimaced as a wave of pain swept through my already tender body.

Fucking Morosians… fuck…ing… Moros… Morosi…

Mors… Morse…

Morse code, you idiot.

Morse code – Okay, do you remember it?

I closed my eyes pretending to be knocked out cold and racked my brain to try and remember my training. Every sentry attended this class;

Leo had hammered it into us.

Morse code, radio Morse code when you were in a situation where you had to secretly call for help.

I didn't have a radio but I could blink. Would those stupid chimeras even notice? I didn't know but it was the only thing I could do. I remembered enough Morse code to get by.

I felt a hand wrench my head up and a hard smack to my face. I opened my eyes and saw the red light of the video camera beeping.

My eyes swept my surroundings. Every piece of brick had been covered by their flag, even the floor had a sheet draped over it.

I could hear breathing behind me, and in the reflection of the camera lens, I saw two figures cloaked in black, holding rifles. They looked every bit like terrorists, even down to having black ski masks over their faces.

I blinked hard, trying to banish the shimmering lights from my vision. That was the last time I blinked, I didn't want them mistaking the Morse code for my eyes needing to be adjusted.

"My name is Reno Nevada from Aras…" My eyes flicked over to Kerres. I saw him frown, well away from the glare of the camera, but he didn't say anything. "And I am Garrett Dekker's fiancé."

M… for Moros. Two long blinks.

"And I love him very much."

S.

"Garrett, I'm scared. They've beaten me badly, and I'm in fear for my life."

E.

"Whatever you have to do, please surrender Elish over to the Crimstones along with ten thousand tokens."

W.

"The drop will be made in Sheryn Park five days to the minute of this video's release."

E.

"Failure to comply will result in the execution of the cicaro Kay."

R. Ending in two short blinks followed by a long one.

I saw the red light disappear, then a hard impact against my head. I fell to the ground and groaned; my face hitting the sheet-covered brick hard. After that, the next thing I remembered was waking up in the dark cell again.

My mind went a bit squirrely after. Though it more than likely was a combination of where I was, what I wasn't eating, and how many blows to the head I'd received. Either way, time melted to a depthless soup over the next several days.

The only thing that kept me from ranting and raving like a lunatic was the faint hope that one of the chimeras would pay enough attention to realize my blinking wasn't just from finally seeing light. As the time bled on however, I became more and more discouraged.

But I still had my hope, and the love for Garrett and my two buds to keep me going. I tried to channel Reaver and force myself to be strong. That guy had gotten through worse. He'd been chained up for a couple of weeks when Perish Dekker had imprisoned him, and at least I was sleeping.

Though he had good food, Killian nearby giving him love, and a warm room to stash himself. I was in a dank and damp hellhole, laying in my own piss and blood.

Well, that was your situation Reno… don't give them the satisfaction of seeing you upset about it. You've been through worse, at least you're still alive.

And as long as I was breathing, I was in a good place.

Like my mind was trying to relay the point to me, I inhaled a breath. My ribs ached and my parched throat tensed as the cold stale air filled my lungs. I coughed and spat out a wad of phlegm, before continuing to count water droplets.

Then there was a fuck load of yelling.

The door was thrown open, spreading light on me that was more a searing discomfort than relief. I immediately felt my body recoil, anticipating getting my ass kicked again.

Kerres was shouting; there was a flurry of activity around me. My body got grabbed and dragged and I felt the stale piss smell of my cell start to fade into the distance.

There was a rush going through my body, giving me enough strength to at least open my eyes to see the faces that belonged to the angry voices. I squinted and made out Kerres and Shale, and two more men.

How many Crimstones were there? Usually Shale fed me and taunted me; Kerres sometimes but only when he needed something from me. I wonder if Kerres had convinced them they had a higher calling besides him settling a grudge match with Elish.

Then Shale cast aside his usual muted but ignorant tone and let out a yell of rage. I was dropped to the ground where he proceeded to beat the living shit out of me.

Like he was underwater, I heard the muffling yell of Shale before I started to get dragged again. Kerres was shouting and snapping; I heard a fight break out behind me.

The fight faded and I was mercilessly chucked into another room. I landed on my side and didn't even make an attempt to move.

This place smelled better at least. I tried to inhale but ended up coughing up more phlegm, yellow slimy muck that stuck to my lungs like the black slime we saw on the bricks of old buildings.

"I checked you out… and you weren't lying. You are a greywaster."

Kerres grabbed my collar and pulled me up; I managed a sitting position and lifted my neck so I could look him in the eye.

"No shit," I croaked, barely recognizing my own voice. I sounded like a frog that had just been put through a blender, and I felt like one too.

Kerres lit a cigarette and took an inhale. He kneeled in front of me. "And you're Reaver of Aras's best friend too, aren't you?"

Yes, and he'll find you and murder you slowly. "Indeed I am."

"Reaver… the person King Silas is quite interested in finding…" Kerres let his voice drag with a creepy smile on his face.

The hair behind my neck bristled. I didn't know how he knew this but my educated guess was that Caligula's little boyfriend Nico had cracked. The other two were pets, Nico was a full-fledged member of the team, and Caligula had been there when King Silas came to Aras. Though the Crimstones looked to be made up of people from all districts, so maybe he had rats in high places.

I coughed and spat more phlegm. "I'm assuming your ransom video didn't go well?"

Kerres's jaw tightened and his dark eyes blazed. My hatred of him got the best of me. "King Silas won't trade any of us for Elish. You were stupid to think it would work."

The room became tense, the crimson Morosian looked down at me with disdain. It radiated off of him like a thick stench. Not just fear though, I saw desperation in his eyes which scared me more than anger ever could.

"You're right, Reno. He won't… but he will trade Elish for information on where to find Reaver."

I swallowed as those words left Kerres's lips, and as the silver smoke fell from his mouth, he lowered the cigarette and rubbed the ember into my bruised hand.

I clenched my teeth but said nothing more; I steeled my body and washed any outwards signs of pain on my face. I focused on the door knob behind Kerres, and dismissed any other sense around me.

"How am I supposed to know where Reaver is? I got shot in the gut and thrown on a plane by Elish and Jade, *your* Jade. I woke up in Elish's hospital, that's all I know."

I took in a rattling breath through my nose as he extinguished the cigarette on my arm, before taking my chin into his hand. Kerres clenched it, and lifted my face up so I was looking at him.

I hated it when they did that… made you look at them. Silas had done it… Bridley had done it. It was their wonderful way of trying to show you who was boss. Well, I had bosses already, and I didn't answer to anyone but Reaver, and maybe Garrett.

Reaver owned my soul, and Garrett owned my heart. Kerres owned my body and he could do what he wanted with it. I wouldn't say a word.

The asshole shook my chin in his hand; his smoke dusting ash on my face.

My ears picked up a strange crackling noise. I glanced down and Kerres did too.

He was holding a plastic electronic in his hand, with a blue lightning-like electricity bolt that shot between two prongs. I only saw it for a moment before he pushed it into my inner thigh.

The pain was nothing I had ever experienced before. An overbearing wave of electric shock that ripped through my body with such ferocity I felt like it was exploding my veins.

Immediately I felt my entire body clenched so tight my muscles spasmed.

I gasped. My mind had tried to swallow the tsunamis of pain but a scream broke my lips. With a rattled groan, the electric shock subsided and I was left a puddle of nothing on the floor, heaving and choking to fill my congested lungs with air.

"Where's Reaver?"

My mind jammed inside of me, the wheels stopped turning and all I could do was stare forward. A few moments passed before my lips moved.

"Do whatever you want. I can't tell you what I don't know."

There was no reason for him to suspect that Elish had saved Reaver, and that was what I would solely believe no matter what he did to me. I would never sell out Reaver, or bring down any hopes we had for killing King Silas. My life just wasn't that important. Reaver and Tink being safe, and King Silas getting raped and murdered, that's what was important.

I watched unblinking as Kerres's desperation filled him. A few minutes ago I was nervous about his desperation, but now I could be no more indifferent. If he was going to kill me for not telling him what he wanted, he could go right ahead. I wasn't selling out Elish's rebellion.

There was just nothing more to say about that.

"Everyone has their breaking points, Reno, and I will find yours," Kerres said lowly. He rose to his feet and dealt me a hard kick right to the back.

My mind went hazy after that, but I heard a click of the door as he closed it. Ignoring the burning pain in my inner thigh, and the still bruised and open injuries on my body, I shuffled myself back into the sitting position.

With blurry eyes I scanned the room I was in. To my amazement there was an old TV in the corner with bunny ears. I shuffled my sorry corpse over and turned it on.

It turned on… well, it looks like we got reception in this hellhole.

Good ol' Skyfall TV. I turned to channel three which was the news channel and wiggled the long antennas.

Like a slap in the face, my emotions came rushing to me. My heart hurt inside my chest when I saw my suave chimera standing beside King

Silas. It looked like they were holding a conference in front of Skytower.

He looked well physically, but it was an act, I could see it in his light green eyes. They were big, and staring, like he was doing everything he could to show unwavering confidence.

Behind him I could also see Ares, Siris, Artemis, Nero, and Caligula, each one holding the exact same expression: pissed off.

"We will not negotiate with terrorists; we kill terrorists!" Silas's voice was cold to a point where even I was surprised. "And any attempts at negotiation will be met with such action you saw today."

A man's voice narrated over King Silas. I realized this must've been recorded at another time. The TV switched to a view of a green park, with King Silas and Elish face-to-face with who I think was Vecht, the cicaro Kay, and five other masked Crimstones holding assault rifles. It was two chimeras against a fleet of men and women armed to the teeth.

My mouth fell open as I watched what happened next. With the male voice narrating, I saw King Silas take out a gun and shoot Vecht in the head, before both Elish and himself turned guns on the other Crimstones. A gun fight ensued that ended quickly. The Crimstones went down one by one, as bullets shot into King Silas and Elish without either of them flinching or batting an eye.

Kay wasn't that lucky. Before one of the Crimstones went down he shot Kay in the back. He fell down with his mouth open in a soundless scream. I felt my heart wrench for him. I had heard that kid sobbing in my cell just several days ago.

When it was over, with both of them bleeding but still standing, Elish and Silas walked from the park. The camera zoomed out to show them eventually getting into a black car.

"– Reno Nevada of Block Aras. The video was taken a week ago, and shows Reno pleading for the life of him and the other captives. All held at origins unknown." I grimaced at my own self on the television. Although it was neat seeing myself on the TV, I looked like absolute shit. I was half-dazed with blood streaked all over my body. My hair was getting black roots too.

But at least I was blinking. Yeah, at least I had done that right.

"Reno Nevada is engaged to Skytech mogul and chimera Garrett Dekker. Garrett Dekker had this to say:"

"Our family bends a knee to no one. My king saved your ancestors from the war and this is our repayment? Folly," my suave chimera said. He was being ushered into the building by Saul. *"Reno knows and understands that my family will not turn over Elish. I suggest to his captors they let Reno and the rest of the captives go, and take it as a lesson learned. The Dekker family bows to no–"*

I yelled and jumped back as two arms broke my view of the TV. They slammed into the television and pushed it off of the tray. I scrambled back as the TV crashed to the ground, the screen shattering onto the brick sending sparks and smoke up to the ceiling.

A blow to my face knocked me off of my feet. I fell backwards; the hands bound behind my back wrenching from their sockets making me clench my teeth so hard I thought they would break.

To my surprise and confusion, it wasn't Kerres, it was Shale. The blond-haired one with the brown eyes, the arrogant but quiet piece of shit who had spat on me more times than I could count.

Then he turned on me. I already had had my brain matter electrified so I didn't feel a single blow. A steady numbing essence had seeped itself through my skin, and though I was lucidly aware, I didn't feel any pain.

But when I tried to think… my mind didn't function properly. I recognized this feeling with grim realization, this had happened on day three of Bridley beating and raping me. I had woken up feeling different. Like I was always hovering just an inch over my body, the shell of me soaking up the pain and emotional torment, leaving my spirit free to watch, but out of pain.

Shale hit me, and through choking sobs he called me every name in his and my vocabulary. Vecht or one of the others must've been his partner – King Silas had shot his partner.

Then Shale grabbed my pants in a manner that filled my body with ice water. With both hands he pulled them down and over my shackled feet, exposing my bottom-half to him.

"You have to be fucking kidding me…" I whispered, a shudder of anxiety fluttering in my chest like loose moths. I automatically shifted away from him, licking my dry lips with increased dread.

Shale responded with a kick in my side, and a command that cut through my hazy mind. "Touch yourself… do it!" he snapped. The curly-haired fuck dropped to his knees. I realized his pants were off, an uncut dick with a gold piercing through the head being massaged in his hand.

My jaw became glued tight. I stared up at him, a surge of hatred mixed in with the nauseas memories filled my mouth like arsenic. My brain was being fed a constant noise of nails on a chalk board, or pinched fingers picking at a scab.

There was nothing in my mouth to swallow but pride, and that would stay on my lips.

Shale put a hand on my thigh and moved it between my legs; I gritted my teeth as I saw the desire in his eyes. He had been the main person who had raped Kay. I had heard him grunting and I had heard him commanding the teary-eyed cicaro in the same way he was me.

But he wouldn't break me; I wouldn't give into him. This was one situation where I refused to comply for my own safety.

Shale put his hand on my cock. I wrenched my cuffed wrists out to strike him, but the chains wrapped around my stomach stopped me. Instead the blond man laughed and dealt me a blow that knocked me to my side.

My desperate yell was muffled by my face being buried in the cold brick floor below me. I tried to move my shackled feet away as he raised my ass towards him, but he kicked my lower legs to the point of them being numb.

I pressed my lips together, my body going rigid. In response to the pressure behind me, I tried to shift away; but as he mercilessly skewered himself in me, my body froze and nothing but a gasping scream escaped my lips.

Without lubricant and without care, he broke me like he had a fever in him. My hands desperately clawed at the brick, trying anything to stop the horrendous pain ripping through my backside, up my spine and pooling like burning acid into my brain.

There was no pause. He ripped himself in and out of me without rest. I could feel the blood mix in with the burning pain as he grated flesh on flesh, susurrating on his lips a series of moans and grunts in tune with his thrusts. I only saw his left arm balance himself beside my face, and every once in a while, a curl of blond hair.

Then an unexpected change came over me; I stopped screaming and I stopped gasping. My forehead throbbed as it balanced my head against the brick, my hot breath coming back to me as I tried to control it.

The ripping continued but I forced my mind out of my body. The anger remained though. A seething, burning hatred that was a part of me now, a blazing inferno that wanted nothing more than to murder this man on top of me.

God damn, I was tired of being someone's victim.

Reaver had murdered Bridley, two weeks of torture, but Reaver wasn't here to kill him for me.

No one was here, I was all alone and a captive. I didn't have the luxury of being raped by a resident we could track down and deliver justice to. I was a hostage in a dangerous game.

There was nothing I could do. I was helpless. I was their fuck toy, their punching bag, and their ransom for Ice Man. Whose king cared more about where his nail clippings went than me.

The dark lurid thoughts, once just wisps of smoke, started to take shape, moulding into terrible forms that whispered even more terrible things to me. I had never imagined I would think such things. I wasn't a creative person, or a very smart one at that, but now…

This isolation had added a few more colours to my imagination spectrum.

What would my old friend Reaver do…?

In response, I completely lost my mind.

I wrenched my hand down and found my very soft dick. I started to stroke and tug on it, trying desperately to get the bastard hard. He'd never failed me yet, and if I could convince my mind I liked this, he wouldn't now.

Shale paused. "What are you doing?" he spat.

Ignoring my brain telling me I was insane, I shifted my body around. He let me and soon I was on my back. "It's been a while. Shut up and keep fucking me."

A wary expression appeared on Shale's face, but as I tensed myself, taking him in deeper, the wariness turned into lust. I grabbed my dick again with my shackled hands and let him pull my legs back.

It felt the same, but he was relaxing into me. He thrusted hard and fast, but at the same time he kissed and sucked on my neck in ecstasy. I moaned with his rhythms, all of it fake but he was too into it to tell the difference.

"Is that a piercing I saw?" I whispered into his ear before I let out a heavy breath.

Shale groaned. I could see his bare ass rising and falling behind his head; he was pushing my knees so far back they were almost beside my ears. "Yeah, can you feel it?"

"Mmm… yeah," I purred. "Let me play with it after. We don't have those where I'm from."

He didn't answer me; instead I clamped my teeth to my lip and bore the pain.

My dick was still flaccid in my hands but he didn't care. I had gotten my point across and now I had to literally take it until the end.

With blood spilling out during every ripping withdrawal of his dick, he finally came inside me. My mouth twisted and my teeth ground. There was nothing more sickening than having their cum inside of you. Bridley had filled me so many times I couldn't walk for a week afterwards.

Fucking Bridley… I had told myself this would never happen again, I had sworn to myself I'd never let another man touch me like this. Where was my chimera to come and save me? It's been almost a week since the video got into their hands. My Morse code had failed. They didn't fucking know where I was.

Shale withdrew himself from me, still hard and now streaked with blood and cum. He held it in his hand and looked over at me, his chest, holding several tattoos, shiny with sweat.

"Lick it… come here."

Shale grabbed onto the back of my head, and with his energy and my remaining steam, he hoisted me to my knees. He shoved my head down a few inches from the glistening pierced tip, then with his other hand he grabbed it by its base and put it to my lips.

My own blood and his cum… this will be fun.

I put my mouth over it, my face twisting under the taste. I took it in to its base, and suctioned it to the tip.

Shale took his hand away; I moved my mouth back down.

And then I bit.

I bit hard.

With a jerk of my head, I ripped his cock off and held it in my mouth like my prize.

A rush of blood sprayed over my face, before Shale screamed hysterically and jumped to his feet.

The blond-haired man looked at me with a wide and terrified expression before he dropped to his knees from shock.

I watched as he drew a hand away from the bleeding gash, ribbons of red blood streaming through his fingers like cascading spouts. When he saw his cock was completely gone he let out a high pitch wheezing groan.

I spat his dick out onto the floor, and swallowed the blood in my mouth. The glee was not lost on my face as I watched him moan and drag himself towards the door, babbling loudly for Kerres or someone to come and help him.

Kerres exploded into the room. His dark eyes fell on Shale; they widened and I saw his face turn three shades paler. As his eyes slowly rose to meet mine, I stared back at him, my face placid and void of anything. The scene would explain itself.

And here is where I die; I planned on taking as many of them down with me as I could.

Kerres looked at me with a glare weighted with hatred. He brought out his gun and I inhaled what I knew would be one of my last breaths.

"Kerres… I gotta go to the hospital, man…" Shale whined. I saw a clammy blood-soaked hand reach and grab onto Kerres's jacket, weakly pulling the cloth down. There was a pool of blood forming underneath him, and his pants had turned a darker colour near his backside.

"I'm fucking bleeding to death – Please, we gotta go…"

Shale sniffed, his head bowed and his shoulders shook from his own self-induced horror. He tried to stand, but under buckling legs, he fell back to his feet.

Kerres nodded to some people behind him, the woman and two men. They dragged Shale out of the door frame, and without a word, he closed the door.

Several moments later, I heard a gunshot.

CHAPTER 13

Reaver

THE TALL BUILDINGS, ONCE JUST A BLUR IN THE distance, towered over us like the canyon ridges I had been so used to seeing from our view in the bunker. Large derelict buildings in various states of decay, with rows of windows that were now only broken shards, all matted grey from years of baked-on grime. The only thing breaking the sepia tones were the small oily paw prints of radrats.

The buildings seemed to stare down at us, hollow but tall with a desperate air to them that begged us to make them whole again; but their souls were gone like the souls of the people who used to occupy them.

Now they were forgotten ruins, ones that glowed with the winter sun shining through their broken remains. These buildings were all around us, encasing our party so tightly it bordered on claustrophobia. Some even missing large chunks that seemed to have been sheared off with a giant knife.

Perish had pointed out the most glaring one to us. A large building, almost a skyscraper, with its front cut down like it had been flayed. Exposing segmented apartments now at the mercy of the elements, once office buildings or perhaps condos.

I tore my gaze away from the tall buildings and tried to focus more on what was on ground level to us, where the real threats would be. I could see old shops and stores, most of them boarded up, but some of them were wide open and exposed, going underneath the buildings like caves. There was lots of shaped concrete in this area, curving edges that turned down to undercover garages, and medians acting like barriers to shield the road from a fifty foot drop.

We were downtown, a place where the humans before us had the chance to design and sculpt everything to suit the trend at the time. Now though it couldn't have been more of a pain in the ass to navigate. If you wanted to get on the street below you, sometimes you had to walk an entire curve of road before it wound down to that street. It reminded me in a way of the broken onramps and highways we'd had northwest of Aras, just half-broken pieces of relics whose use had died with the radiation.

I jumped onto a concrete wall and scanned the area around me, and saw Perish out of the corner of my eye do the same. I couldn't see anything of use inside these shops though. Just a lot of crumbled plaster and the ghosts of shelving long ago covered in dust. However there was some variations to the greys around us, I also made out a few old skeletons, their brown skin dried to leather, stretched across their bones like saran wrap.

"This is what a real abandoned town looks like." My eyes never stopped scanning the looming, multiple-floored buildings and smaller structures around them. "Not like your obsessively clean town, Perish."

Perish and Jade were both dressed in black dusters, with AK 101's slung over both their shoulders. Perish decided to take it a step farther though. To top off his outfit, he had coveted the hat that had flown off of Garrett's head, a cowboy hat-type-thing but with smaller rims. The scientist looked like a merc now, though his movements were still jerky so he still reminded me of someone on meth.

"This town hasn't had people in it in a long time," Perish observed. He looked around at the tall buildings. I saw a glint of longing in his eyes, no doubt thinking about the lab he left behind in Donnely. "I haven't been here in a long time either."

I walked the length of the concrete block before jumping onto the sidewalk. I shook my head as I saw Killian opening and closing mailboxes and checking out the old payphones for change. The boy was dressed in one of my old jackets Reno had grabbed for us, and a blue sweater. He was even the proud owner of his own cargo pants now. Well, they had been mine, but since his stint with the scorprion I'd decided he'd proven himself enough to start loading him up with his own grenades and ammo.

"How much do you remember of when Reaver was being created?" Killian asked. There was a clink of metal as the payphone change stopper moved back into place.

Perish smiled at the question. It had been two days and a night since Elish had dropped us off. He not only loved talking to Killian, he loved even more being asked about his research.

"I came to help Leo after the last baby died. Lycos only had three more embryos left and Elish was getting mad mad mad. So I helped him with the baby and then I helped Elish with his two embryos. Lycos's baby died though, but that was alright… one of Elish's didn't and I helped transfer baby Reaver to the cylinder and helped keep our watch on him."

"Wait… really?" Jade, who had been dead silent over the last two days, spoke up. He was holding a cigarette in one hand and Elish's suitcase in the other. As soon as the kid realized his master had given it to me he decided to become its guardian. "Elish was responsible for figuring out how to keep Chimera X alive?"

The scientist nodded enthusiastically. "Elish was always smart, even when he was a baby. When he was four, he could already play piano better than me." Perish's eyes became focused, a sign he was trying to sort through the hive of information his brain was constantly throwing at him. Another thing the three of us had learned with Perish was to be quiet when he was doing this.

Sure enough, a moment later his features lit up again, like a halogen was going off.

"That's right." He nodded slowly. "The babies would die usually in the second trimester, which obviously meant they hadn't been cloned from Silas right. Elish came and he picked up the embryos and left. I left… I think… I think I left." Perish squinted and rubbed his head; he shook it as if trying to uncross the wires in his brain.

I watched as the scientist bit his lip, a pained expression on his face. "I'm sorry, I can't say."

I sighed; the mental wall had gone up again, typical for the retard.

Jade blew a puff of smoke out of his mouth; he looked curiously at the scientist before taking several quick steps towards him. The cicaro flicked his smoke before craning his neck to one side.

"You can say whatever you want; you're not on his side anymore."

Perish, a few paces ahead of me, shook his head vigorously. "No… no, I – can't – say. My mind tells me I can't. He hurts me when I try to think of it."

"So you have no idea how Reaver can kill Silas?" Killian's voice was sickeningly sweet. I knew he was pulling out a couple manipulation cards.

Perish shook his head, I saw some hints of apprehension in his eyes. "I wasn't involved in Reaver's kidnapping. I don't remember what happened after Elish left."

"Were you close to Lycos at all?"

His name was Leo…

The road we were going down echoed with Perish's laugh. To drive in his point, he pulled his shirt up, showing off his now scarred burn marks. Killian paled and looked away.

"No, no, Killian, look… Reaver can too. Too bad I can't show you how much cut up my head, or the welts and broken bones that healed. Was he my friend? Funny, funny. Lycos only had Elish as a friend, then Greyson and that was the end of that. He left us."

"Hey, shut the fuck up about Leo," I snapped, taking a step towards the scientist. "You were on Silas's fucking side, not ours. So take your licks and get over it."

Perish turned away from me, his jaw tight, but he didn't say anything else.

My mood plummeted; I felt my throat clench and a burning behind my nose. I mumbled an excuse to go scout and started walking towards an alleyway.

I ignored Killian's worried glances and walked away from the group. I knew they would be just fine; this place was empty.

When I was out of sight, I leaned up against the decaying brick and lit a cigarette. I took several long drawn-out inhales before I carried on.

Fuck, I missed those two.

What I wouldn't give to talk to them… I had been avoiding talking to

Leo and Greyson my entire life. Now I'd give my left arm to just sit down and have a beer with them.

I swallowed the growing lump in my throat and started walking to the other side of the barren alleyway. Nothing was blocking my way but a few fallen ventilation pipes.

I needed more drugs – that was all that was keeping me together right now.

"Hey, Reaver? I want to come with you." My mouth twitched to the side as I heard Jade's voice behind me. I sighed before I waved him over, not even turning around. The cicaro had been sulking and sad since his master had dumped him on me, barely saying a word unless spoken to.

At least I knew he would be quiet then.

I expected Killian to trail and then Perish, but I only heard the light footsteps of the cicaro. Killian and Perish would be fine; they had Deek with them who would alert them of anything, and I would be able to hear it.

Jade stood several paces behind me as we emerged from the alleyway and didn't say another word. This knocked my opinion of the kid up a few pegs.

The road in front of us was empty; it was obvious this town had been evacuated. There were few rusted out vehicles and no army vehicles to be seen. Only the looming ghosts of dead structures that did nothing but remind me of how small we were in this town, and how many things could be hiding from us.

The grass and plant life seemed to grow a little bit more around here too, which I think added to the decay of the town. Although it was still yellow, the grass was thicker and stronger than greywaste grass. More of it had forced its way through the concrete than usual, making breaks in the pavement that reminded me of the broken patterns that lay at the bottom of dried lake beds.

I turned to my left and saw the broken remains of several shops. Their windows shattered with pieces of glass still sticking up like upside down icicles, surrounded by plaster and the threads of a ripped up carpet. I clicked Jade over and started walking towards it.

"How are your eyes?" I asked him. I kicked a piece of the glass away with my boot and tested the raised platform behind the display window.

“Same as yours.” Jade tested the metal door handle; I could hear the rusted metal protest as he tried and pulled it. He looked into the store, and I saw his body stiffen. “Let’s go in. I need to talk to you about something.”

Oh great… he better not get all Killian on me. I might have judged him wrong.

Jade pushed the door the remainder of the way open and walked in. I followed him, keeping my hand in reach of my M16.

I coughed and so did he. This place was coated in several layers of dust and ash, with a faint odour of must and dirty socks that seemed to stick in your throat.

I took an inhale of cigarette smoke to get rid of the taste and started quietly walking up and down the aisles. This place, I suspect, had once been a corner store though not much remained. A lot of chewed up paper and plastic, radrat eaten I think. It covered almost all areas of the steel shelving, dripping down onto the shelf below in thick streamers.

I tried to unwedge a piece of the chewed up paper but with the dust and whatever dew had soaked into it, it was a solid mass. I lifted it up anyway and threw it on the floor. If needed be this would make excellent fire starter.

“Reaver, you know how I have that aura thing, right?” Jade was behind me, I could hear him start to rummage through the mounds of paper. There was an odd metallic twanging noise that sounded whenever you wrenched a piece off of the metal rungs.

“Uh huh.” I kicked away a few more bits of paper and motioned for Jade to follow me. There was nothing here, just the remains of paper packaging and plastic. No food at all. I sprinted out of the building.

“I’ve been picking up things that seem off… Reaver, stay still for fuck sakes, this is important.”

I jumped out of the store window display and started to sprint in the direction I knew Perish and Killian were going, before ducking into another shop.

Jade growled at me but kept pace; unless he wanted to get left behind he had no choice. I didn’t want to get too far away from Killian. I was only giving myself a few minutes in each shop before I moved on; loitering would only lag us behind and then we’d lose the group.

"There's something seriously wrong with Perish."

I stopped and turned around. I gave him the most 'are you fucking retarded?' look I could muster.

Jade's yellow eyes were white in my night vision, almost transparent against his eyeballs. He crossed his arms over his chest. "I've been seeing things over the past two days in him. It seems to almost explode in my brain when he starts talking about our brothers, his research, and most importantly: King Silas." Jade looked around the new shop we were in; an old restaurant with chewed up red benches and ripped out plastic tables.

His boots crunched against the plaster, the only noise besides his low-toned voice. "I've seen him… not just the Perish we know now, I think I am seeing glances of when he was normal. Just… hints of it."

"So what? I'm sure he wasn't born retarded." I tried to shrug it off. I walked through the restaurant dining area towards the bar, kicking a fallen lamp over with my boot as I did.

"*Elish was always smart, even when he was a baby. When he was four, he could already play piano better than me,*" Jade recited. Perish had just said that a few minutes ago when we were talking. I still didn't understand why that was a big deal though.

When I didn't give Jade the shocked reaction he so dearly wanted, I heard his boots grind into the dirty floor as he followed me.

"Reaver… how old is Perish?"

"Sevent- *Ohh.*" And there it was, the realization. I felt like the idiot in that moment.

I turned around and leaned my hands against the bar. The kid had my interest now. "Perish says he's seventy-one, but Elish is ninety, almost ninety-one. Basically Perish is lying about his age?"

Surprisingly the cicaro shook his head. He took a seat on a wooden bar stool and leaned his arms against the bar. "No, he isn't lying, that's the thing. Perish believes that's how old he is. Someone, I'd give you one guess who, tampered with his memory. That's what made him the way he is. I bet you anything the memories he lost was when he was normal."

Jade let out a breath, he slid off of the bar stool. "Elish wanted me to use my abilities on Perish, but I think Elish already knew this information. They all must have, unless Silas made Perish disappear for twenty years after first gen was born. Even more since Perish would appear to be the age he is now."

"So Elish wants you to dig in deeper and find out why Perish's head was buggered with? Why Silas did all of this?"

Now it was the cicaro's turn to look shocked. I started putting up bottles of vodka for us to share later, and also dug out a couple cans of maraschino cherries.

"You really think so?" Jade's tone held an edge of surprise to it. I don't know why, Elish was always up to something. For someone sick of Silas's games, he sure did enjoy playing his own.

I threw our findings into a bag and started leaving the bar. Jade trailing behind me with a troubled expression on his pale face.

"Elish was a part of the first generation… Elish, Garrett, Ellis, and Nero. If Perish is older than them… it means there was another generation before them? Why would Silas hide that from us? Elish taught me that Silas created the first generation on his own with the help of several scientists."

I felt my jaw clench, there was no mistaking that I had reached my threshold for this conversation. Talking about my chimera brothers always fouled my mood. They were a group of maniacs whose life goal was to make my life miserable and the life of my partner.

I decided to cut the tendrils of curiosity before I made it worse.

"I really don't care about all this chimera politics. I just want to find out how to kill the fuck and get Aras back. That's really all I want, nothing more. I don't want to be a part of this family."

"Well, Elish wanted me to sniff around Perish's mind for a reason."

"Then have at it, it's not my problem."

I hopped through another bare window frame, the cicaro still following me. "So you'll be fine if I keep trying to get information from his mind?"

I shrugged, not even bothering looking through this building; it looked like an auto shop. I jumped back out and started walking down the street. I wanted to meet back up with Killian and Perish now. I suppose we would be having energy bars, tact, and maraschino cherries for dinner tonight.

"You do what you need to do, bud. Like I said, I just want to find out this information for our cause and get the hell out of here."

I heard a crack as Jade opened a bottle of hooch and a shudder. "Alright, I'm going to do what I need to do to figure him out. That's why I am here in the first place apparently."

I turned around to grab the bottle from Jade when my face froze in shock.

Behind Jade was the most fucked-up-looking creature I'd ever seen.

It looked like a human, but it was a monster. It had a large, jutted-out jaw and a wide, lipless mouth with two small holes for a nose. Its eyes were nothing but shiny black slits and it was covered in soft, almost scale-like, grey skin.

It shuffled rapidly on all fours, its body swaying from side to side like a lizard's. It was coming towards the two of us, and fast.

I drew the M16's scope up to my eye; the cicaro only a foot away from me.

"Jade, fucking don't move," I said, making my voice an even level.

Jade's mouth dropped open; he looked at me in shock. I aimed my gun at the swiftly approaching creature now only twelve feet away from us.

I pulled the trigger and braced myself for the kickback. I watched as the bullet whizzed past Jade's shoulder and hit the creature right between the eyes, just meters away from where we were standing.

I quickly turned around, scanning the buildings around us. I took several paces and swore, feeling the hair on my neck bristle. There was something off in the air; it was starting to smell strange. The same smell that had seeped into the first building I had looked in: stale rot, dirty socks, and sweaty unwashed humans.

"Jesus fuck, I thought you were going to fucking kill me," Jade gasped, before turning around and seeing the creature. "What the fuck is–"

"Big rule, Jade," I snapped, my eyes trying to analyze every part of the overwhelmingly huge city around us. "Make sure there are none left and then ask stupid questions." My head jerked as I saw a flicker of grey in one of the apartment buildings, but it was just a tattered curtain.

I clenched my teeth and swore.

Jade held his AK 101 and started looking around as well, but a moment later, he shook his head as if dismissing the idea that there were more, and walked towards the dead one.

I hissed at him, and my hand twitched to shoot a few inches away from his head just to show him how stupid he was for going near it, but I refrained. I gave one last survey of the area before jogging up to fetch my pet. Even with the silencer on my M16, the city's building echo would give it away to the boys. Though in movies silencers were quiet little snaps of noise, in real life they still made a good racket.

"It's like a lizard human," Jade whispered, shaking his head in awe. The lizard thing lay dead on the pavement in a pool of thick blood.

I pulled Jade away but my eyes were still fixed on it. I paused for a moment to take this creature in; I hadn't seen something so fucked up since Perish's splices.

There was no doubt it was lab-made, and well-made at that. Its veiny arms and legs were bent in an odd fashion, assumingly to be able to move fast on all fours, and it had unnaturally long fingers and toes, like that of a frogs. All of this covered with tallowy-grey skin that showed off black veins like they were corpses.

Jade poked its lipless mouth with the barrel of his gun. Its jaw slacked, revealing several rows of needle-sharp teeth imbedded in pinky green gums; its tongue was even pointed.

Then another noise, almost like sandpaper being scraped together.

I turned around quickly. Sure enough, crawling out of one of the unboarded up shop windows, was another one.

A snarl spilled from my lips. I aimed my gun and was about to fire it when Jade's AK 101 went off in a different direction.

I sniped the one I saw first before turning to the cicaro, just in time to see another one of the lizard-humans stumbling forward – its right arm completely blown off. It started to scream and snarl as it twisted around on the ground, blood spraying from the arm stump like a hose. The human-like sound filled me with a grisly thrill but my attention was elsewhere. I had to warn Killian and Perish, they would be seeing them soon. I kept expecting to hear gunshots in their direction or the deacon dog's howls.

I aimed and finished off the second creature, by that time Jade had fired his gun again.

"Fuck, Reaver… there's three of them to the east; they're all around us," Jade called, his voice raising an octave. "Where the fuck did they come from?"

I looked around and felt my heart rise into my throat. Just in one direction I could see five of them crawling out of the windows, like spiders running out of a crack in the wall. They were way too good at scaling the side of the buildings for my comfort; they seemed to be quicker on the walls than on the ground.

"Reaver?" Perish's voice suddenly called. He sounded far away, at least a good block. We needed to meet up and find that fucking entrance to the lab, and quickly.

I tasted the air as I started to take several steps towards Perish's voice. The air had gotten colder and I could see shadows start to take shape from the towering buildings. It was going to be dark in an hour and I realized they were nocturnal animals. We had to hide and now, before this town started swarming with them.

"We're coming!" Jade yelled. He raised his gun and quickly shot two more creatures off of the building. I threw him a round and finished off my last several bullets, then refilled my own.

"I see six a block up. Should I take them out?" Jade asked. He was keeping pace with me; his hand gliding up and down his gun as he loaded the rounds with the ease of an expert. The Morosians were good with their firearms it seemed; either that or one of the chimeras had trained him.

"Stay near me and don't be a fucking hero. Perish and I are immortal, you and Killian are not," I said. I felt Jade's motoring heartbeat a pace behind me. "Protect Killian and yourself. That's your orders, Cicaro."

Jade suddenly gave a startled yell. I turned around just in time to see one of the lizard men land on the pavement dangerously close to him. It looked at the two of us with its sparkling black eyes and let out a nasally snarl, baring its rows of pointed teeth at us with a hiss.

I pushed Jade out of the way, and with the butt of my gun I hit the creature right in its jaw. The lizard man snarled and snapped at him, its now dislocated jaw slacked

I hit it again, making it fall to the ground in a tangle of limbs and gnashing teeth. The next blow I delivered split its skull almost in half.

I spat on it and turned back around before noticing I had knocked Jade onto the ground. The cicaro was holding his forehead, a small trickle of blood making a thin river down the concave of his cheek bone.

I raised him to his feet and thrusted his assault rifle back into his hand.

The cicaro looked around and gasped. "Fuck, they're everywhere…"

I turned around and felt the bile rise in my stomach.

They *were* everywhere. I looked behind me and could see at least three of them, continuing to crawl out of the windows of the looming, and now dauntingly tall and exposed, buildings. They weren't so fast that we couldn't out run them, but they had the numbers advantage on us.

No more fucking around, no more shooting them. We had to get the boys and fuck off.

"We need to run and now," I said. I grabbed onto Jade's shoulder and pushed the boy towards the road that would lead us to Perish and Killian.

Jade stumbled a bit but started running full speed towards the road. I was right behind him, but I ran backwards, mentally trying to determine how long it would take for each of the snarling abominations to come too close for comfort.

As I ran, I started to notice a lot of the creatures swarming where Jade and I had been. It was when one of the creatures raised a bloodstained, deformed face that I realized they were eating the dead.

"What the fuck are those things?" Jade's shrill voice suddenly sounded. I was about to tell him to shut up when he heard Perish answer back.

"Human komodo dragons, and yes I did create them, I'm sorry!" Perish gasped; he was out of breath. I ran to Killian and gave him a quick once over, but besides a racing heart and a terrified expression he seemed fine. Behind him Deek was driving off the ones behind them, where the lab was supposed to be.

"Where's this fucking lab?" I snapped. I whirled around as I heard the familiar sandpaper sound, and took aim at one peeking its scaled grey head through a broken window. With a shot in its neck, it fell down silently and landed twenty feet away from us with a sickening thud. I grinded my teeth as I saw several others lurking in an alleyway, their eyes glowing in the darkness.

"Follow me, it isn't far," Perish said, before he turned and started to run. "They're not fast, they're ambush predators, but there are many of them… they… they're very successful breeders. I didn't think that Silas would release them here."

"Is the city full of them?" Killian asked as Jade's gun went off. "They're fucking everywhere. Watch the wind-"

Suddenly Jade screamed. I whirled around to see one of the creatures jumping off of him. The lizard man snatched Jade's duster in its teeth and started dragging him away.

I kicked the grey-skinned creature in its face. It fell backwards, its arms and legs flailing like a tipped over croach.

I drew my combat knife and slashed its throat before turning to grab Jade. To my anger, another one had taken its place; it yanked and pulled Jade away as the cicaro screamed bloody murder. Both Perish and Killian had their backs turned, firing round after round into the half-dozen creatures sneaking up on us like a tidal wave.

I shot the one on Jade in the head and pulled the cicaro to his feet. "Perish, show us where it is. Run!" I pushed Jade as another creature fell from the window, kicking it in its head before throwing the snapping, slit-eyed monster against the wall. They were surprisingly light and their bones seemed brittle.

"There's a manhole cover a block up. It's marked with *Skytech* in white paint, under is a ladder," Perish said, before he fired off several rounds behind me.

A block up? We had to hurry, the night was sweeping the city with a fast pace and I knew from Donnely that the darkness would wait for no one. I grabbed Killian's arm and hit Jade's back as I turned to make a break for it.

Suddenly I felt something slam into me with such a force it almost brought me to my knees.

I felt an angry snarl spill from my lips as the creature dug its long fingers into my shoulders, before sinking needle-sharp teeth into my head. I thrashed around wildly, trying to throw the creature off of me; I could hear Killian frantically screaming something to Perish.

I could smell its rotting breath as its teeth gnashed against my skull. I tried to slam it up against one of the buildings but before I found my bearings, a gunshot rang. One that was so close to my ears I was surprised I could still hear at all.

The creature went limp and fell off of me. I immediately turned to Killian but he wasn't there.

"Jade has him. Run, fucking run, dumbass!" Perish yelled.

I stopped and stared at him for a moment.

Perish looked at me annoyed, an expression he'd never held for me before. He reached over and pulled out one of my clips and slammed it into his gun, before he held it up to his face and started shooting.

"Their bones are hollow. Leave it to me to make a point to make them light for sideways travel. I never thought it would come back and bite me in the ass." Perish shook his head and gave a shrug before he started letting out more clips.

Even in the chaos a chill went up my spine. The manic, busy movements, the hyper, rapid voice was gone.

He sounded… sane.

My attention turned when I heard a scrape of a manhole cover. I saw Jade jump in but Killian lingered.

"Hurry!" Killian called. The deacdog was still driving off the lizards with a chest rattling growl, and his hackles raised to make him appear even bigger than he was.

I could hear the nasally snarls and snaps of the creatures behind me. I tried to look up but was surprised to see that I couldn't, blood was now flowing freely down my face and into my eyes.

Okay, they're safe. I turned my attention away from them and started sniping the lizards as soon as they spilled from the alleyways and shops of the buildings around us; Perish beside me hitting the reptiles with flawless accuracy.

"Perish…" This was a long shot but I had nothing to lose. "Are you a chimera?"

The scientist gave me a puzzled look, his gun still on his shoulders. His eyes jutted back to the scope before he fired a round off, an echoing crack ricocheting off of the tall buildings.

"Of course I am."

"Were you born in a lab? Like the rest of us?"

I saw his eyebrow twitch. He shot the gun, and a moment later, he swore. I looked over and saw a pack of at least half a dozen, running as quickly as their deformed limbs could. More were crawling over the crumbling buildings, creeping down to the surface at angles that seemed to defy gravity.

"This isn't really the damn place, Merrik." Perish swore and ran ahead. I could hear Killian screaming at us to hurry; I had to get information from him though.

"Jade, close the cover, we'll be right there," I called behind my shoulder and ran after Perish. Obediently, and to Killian's continuous shrieks, the cicaro listened. I heard the manhole cover scrape before it landed with a *clunk.*

Perish had his large knife in one hand with the assault rifle tucked under his other arm. With a whoop that surprised even me, he started picking off every one of them.

But he was still Perish… I grabbed my own knife and charged at a lizard-human. Right as the little fucker was sneaking up on the scientist, I kicked it down with my boot and drove the knife into its head.

Wiping my own blood from my forehead, I kicked a second lizard away, just as a large-headed one took a chomp out of Perish's thigh.

The scientist didn't even scream; he growled at it with clenched teeth and raised his hand to hit it with the butt of his knife. The creature's mouth snapped open and it fell backwards with a flail of limbs.

"Perish, think. What's your earliest memory?" I said as I slammed my boot down on the creature's head. My eyes scanned every direction and I noticed the first tinges of my night vision; it illuminated the insides of the buildings.

My heart jumped into my throat, the building windows were alive like wounds chocked with maggots. I could see the pale creatures writhing and pacing the windows, waiting for the darkness to fall so they could trickle out like water.

I hit Perish on the arm and both of us started to fall back, our guns lowered but our knives ready. No time to waste shooting them now; we really had to get the fuck out of there.

"I… I… don't know, Reaver." Perish's voice was strained, his face taxed. I knew he was trying hard. I looked ahead, ignoring the churning mixture of anxiety and inquisitiveness in my stomach. I wanted to remain up here to drill Perish but I was also walking a tightrope. The only reason I was still out here was because we were both immortal. The mortal boys were safe inside, which was all that mattered.

I wiped the blood away from my eyes and bent down to lift the manhole cover and decided to try one last time.

"Think… Perish… earliest memory? Anything… what do you remember?"

Perish sighed, his light-coloured eyes squinting under his furrowed brow. He raised his left arm and dropped it as we pulled the manhole cover back.

"Fuck, Reaver. My own O.L.S holds a pretty important chunk of my brain. I couldn't tell you if I wanted. That little fucker is long gone."

O.L.S? The device Elish had mentioned to me; the one that also held Sky's brain piece.

I stared at him, my fingers frozen around the cover. "Silas cut out your brain? Why? What didn't he want you to know?"

"Sky, he didn't want me to remember Sky."

A flash of grey swept past my vision, and a split second later, Perish was gone. Without thinking, I grabbed my combat knife and lunged as the creature thrashed around, Perish's head snapping with it.

I heard his neck break.

CHAPTER 14

Killian

I STUCK CLOSE TO JADE AND FOUND MYSELF grabbing onto his arm. Not because I was expecting him to start running down the sewer we had just found ourselves in, but because I couldn't see a thing. I was the only non-chimera here, and because of that curse my entire world at this moment was pitch black.

The sounds of gunfire were deafening outside, and with the occasional scream of the lizards, it all blended together into an all-consuming assault on my senses. I wanted it to end; I wanted Reaver and Perish safe below in the sewers. But was it safe?

I felt the pet's warm skin tighten between my death grip. "What's inside of here? I can't see a thing."

Jade's breathing was quick, but not bordering on hyperventilating like my own. I felt his hand on mine, and a low whisper. "The walls here are damp brick, and further on, I can see it turns into two different directions. It's quiet down here; I don't think there's anything down here but us."

My sigh of relief was short-lived, a moment later we could hear Reaver's muffled voice shouting above us. I shifted to climb back up the ladder but Jade held onto my hand. "No, they're immortal, we're not. You popping your head up will only distract him."

He was right, I would offer nothing but turning his attention away from shooting those creatures, but I still felt useless. If anything, Reaver becoming immortal had put me on an even shorter leash with him. Now he could literally kill himself for me.

I jumped as the manhole cover slid off of the concrete, the scraping noise bouncing off of the walls and echoing down to the fork in the sewer tunnel. I looked up and saw the grey darkness above us, before it was eclipsed by a body.

"Take him, Jade, and get out of the way so I can jump down. Killian, Perish got his neck snapped." Reaver was out of breath. "I couldn't get the dog to come. He was too busy chasing them, but we'll get him tomorrow."

"Perish is dead?" A sense of dread washed over me, fearing for not only us but for Deekoi still out there. I had to trust that he would be okay. He was much faster than the creatures, and twice as big, so I knew he must be.

I stood by the ladder as Jade pulled the scientist down to the ground with a rough thud.

"It's only a neck break… wait a second." Reaver disappeared to shoot off several more rounds. He then swung his body onto the ladder and closed the cover with another scraping creak.

The smell of damp blood was all over my boyfriend, but smell was all I could sense. I heard rustling as Reaver put Perish over his shoulder, then I felt a hand on my head.

"Are you okay?" Reaver asked.

I nodded and I felt him take my hand. We started walking down the tunnel; Jade's clicking boot steps in front of us. The smell of musty damp and the usual stale rot of the world permeated my nose, crawling up my nostrils and laying itself right in the middle of my brain stem. It was an overwhelming stench.

"It's all flat ground, don't worry, just keep walking," Reaver said calmly, though he was still out of breath. I couldn't hear anything coming from Perish. "Jade? Do you have any idea where we're supposed to go to get underneath this building?"

"No… Elish said Perish would know." I heard Jade jog ahead, before letting out a long breath. "Did you really have to let him get his neck broken? Why did you two hang around up there anyway? You had a clean break."

I jumped a mile high as I heard one of the creatures above us give a shriek. Reaver tightened his hold on my hand. "You won't believe it… he was acting normal up there. Or what I assumed was his normal."

My eyes widened, even though it was still pitch black. I looked towards where I had heard Reaver's voice. "Normal? What…?"

As we took what I assumed was the only viable path in the sewer fork, Reaver and Jade both filled me in on the conversation they'd had before the lizard creatures had come. By the time they were done my mouth was dry, and my head filled with both awe and disbelief.

"He's not seventy?" I whispered, swallowing down the nervous pit in my stomach. I could hear Jade ahead of us checking what I think were random doors. They sounded old, the hinges long since rusted to nothing from the dampness of the sewers.

"Nope, he told me Silas cut out a piece of his brain. To make him forget those memories I am to assume. It was mind blowing how steady he was, it was like I was talking to a normal person." Reaver led me towards a door, before he stopped and I heard the sound of a bag unzipping.

"Reaver… I think we should keep it dark," Jade cautioned. Seconds later a blinding light infiltrated the pitch blackness I'd been walking in. "Radanimals will be attracted to that light… and it will also screw up our night vision. It's better the kid is blind than us."

Reaver shone the light onto the floor, then it became dimmer as he wrapped a green kerchief around it. Stifling the illuminating glow into what looked like a little green orb, he handed it to me. "I can't hear anything down here, but rest assured, if there's anything here they can already hear us. We'll be fine."

I smiled at him thinking about me, and turned the covered flashlight over to the sewers before sweeping it past Reaver; I decided to ignore the bleeding rag over his head. He was injured, but I knew if I drew attention to it he would shush me and tell me he was okay. Why waste the energy arguing with him? I couldn't see bone, brain, or guts so my Reaver was okay.

I shuddered as the glow shed its light on the damp brick, leaking water through rusted pipes which trickled down to a small river of muck and garbage. This place reminded me of some sort of brick tomb, and I could tell we were walking on an incline too. We were only heading deeper and deeper underground, and no one knew where we were going.

"No, left," Jade whispered.

I shined the light onto the ground and saw the eerie reflecting orbs of Jade's eyes, shining in the darkness like he was a wild animal; he seemed like one sometimes.

"Why? We're walking in a maze anyway. My gut says right." Reaver adjusted Perish, who was still dangling over his shoulder.

Jade ran a gloved hand along the mortar of the sewer's brick. "This has been repaired more recently. This is Dek'ko stucco; it doesn't flake like the others." The pet put a hand on the metal door handle and pulled it open. He looked in and sighed. "More darkness, but come here and smell… it smells cleaner, doesn't it?"

I was impressed at that; this guy seemed to know his stuff. I stepped back and started shining the light on the area I was standing in. The green glow shone against the damp brick walls until it was swallowed up by the darkness, for what could be seven feet or seven miles. Darkness had no boundaries.

Reaver took a step into the metal doors. "It doesn't smell better, it just smells different." The darkness of his jacket blended in with the tunnel he had stepped into, until I could see no more of him.

Since they were in the tunnel I took the green kerchief off of the flashlight. I jumped down onto the damp channel in the middle of the sewer and started walking up it.

I cringed when I saw a rat, ten paces ahead of the door Jade and Reaver were in. Its pink tail was covered in mud, and was bumping along the floor as it crawled away from me. I shone the flashlight past it and saw several more, staring at me with bright eyes. My feet took me towards them, but even with the kerchief off of the light, the darkness still devoured the beam.

"Squeak, squeak," I said. I dug into my pocket and broke off a piece of tact then gave it to the rat. As soon as one took a piece, others from all around started to come for their share.

I broke off another portion, feeling like some sort of rat king. Then I just got out the entire tact cracker and started throwing all of them crumbs, watching as I did, more and more little rats come out to eat.

"You're much cuter than our radrats," I whispered to them. "They're as big as house cats, but you all are so small." I gave a big chunk to a scrawny-looking one who wiggled his whiskers at me. He chewed on it with little teeth, his beady eyes shining up at me.

Then I felt an eerie feeling in the back of my brain, and as I looked away from the rats, I tried to direct my ears towards the dark pit in front of me and my community of rodents. With the rats squeaking around me, I shone the light ahead of where I was crouched down.

The heart inside of my chest gave one last normal beat before it plummeted to my feet. And as the beam of light fell on the grey skin and yellowing teeth of a deformed-looking lizard man, a string of nonsensical pleads to Reaver started to fall from my mouth.

This creature was different than the other lizards. In the brief, and all too fleeting, moments before I called for Reaver, I saw the thing crouching in a corner; its spine protruding like rocky ridges as it ate the top-half of a rat that was clenched between long boney fingers.

It had hair, black stringy hair, and small but glaring eyes that, unlike the lizards above us, had whites and pupils; it also had a nose and straight legs and arms. It was more human than I felt comfortable with.

I wanted to run, but I found myself frozen in fear. The only solid thought coming to my mind was that if I took the flashlight off of it, it would immediately attack me. Instead I kept the light fixed on it and tried to find a higher octave to my voice.

My tongue was glued to the roof of my mouth. I watched as the creature leaned down and took another bite of the rat's head, a sinewy strand of fur and tissue coming off of it. He didn't seem to see me, or the light, and if he did, he was ignoring it.

"Reaver?" I finally managed to faintly say. Suddenly the light began to shake as my hands trembled. I weakly said his name again, before a flicker of silver came into my vision.

I moved the flashlight over, and when the light scanned a half-dozen glowing eyes and the distinct sound of sandpaper scraping together, I found my voice.

"Reaver!" I screamed.

In the blink of an eye, Reaver was bursting through the door. I heard him call to Jade before he grabbed my shoulder and pulled me backwards.

"Jade!" he called a second time. He whipped me around and pulled me towards the metal door.

The next thing I knew he pushed me into Jade, then I heard the sound of the metal door slamming. I looked behind me, before to my horror, Jade took the flashlight and turned it off.

"The door latches into place," Reaver said hurriedly. "We need to find this lab quickly. I fucking saw a dozen of them out there. There is one in there that can stand too. Killi, are you alright?"

I was blind and I couldn't see a thing. My breathing started to become short as I looked around wildly, but without comfort or a moment to wait for my answer, Jade grabbed my arm and Reaver grabbed my shoulder and they started quickly walking me into the darkness.

I stumbled and felt Jade grab onto me harder, our collective breathing following us like our boot steps. I glanced behind me to try and see if they were following us but it was darkness, everything was just darkness. My anxiety flared as my mind started to power up senses that, at this point, I didn't want to have.

"Jade, how's your strength?" Reaver's voice echoed behind me. I could tell he was looking back towards the metal door. I did as well and heard the sounds of claws scraping against metal. I tripped again, this time almost falling on my face.

Suddenly I was being picked up, and with that, Reaver and Jade started to run. This act was followed by a crashing noise behind us, and more scraping.

I couldn't see anything, it was driving me crazy. I had to see where they were, how many were in this sewer. My mind was compensating for its lack of stimulation; my imagination was telling me there were thousands, just inches away from my face.

"Jade? Come on, fucking look!" Reaver yelled. I looked around wildly in my blind panic, feeling Jade's breath become laboured.

"We need to go to the surface, find a house or…"

"They're swarming the fucking surface!"

"They're swarming here too!" Jade snapped back. He turned around with me, and suddenly the entire underground sewer flashed like lightning as Jade shot his gun off with one hand.

They were behind us, dozens of them, and past the writhing, lizard-like movements I saw the tall, gangly silhouette of the standing one. He was lumbering back and forth as he followed the crawlers, his blank eyes staring forward with no expression on his hollow face.

They were coming closer.

"Let me down, I have a grenade!" I shifted to try and get Jade to drop me but he held on tight. He rained the creatures with bullets before he turned back around towards where he could see Reaver.

Their sandpapery movements and nail scrapes echoed off of the walls, infiltrating all of my senses and filling me with a sort of madness. I felt, in my limbo of incomprehensible fear mixed in with a streak of bravery, compelled to actually do something. The new feeling seemed to nullify as soon as it got to my limbs though. I was limp and frozen in the iron-locked hold of Jade.

I could hear them right behind us. The sounds were digging into my brain, pulling out every string of bravery I had and twisting them around their long, boney fingers. Not being able to see them was driving me the most crazy; every time Jade slowed down I could see them in my brain only inches away. Lizard-like faces, black slits for eyes… and the standing one, lumbering on like he was only following his friends. He gave me the most chills. He looked so human.

"Jade! I see a red light. Please for fuck sakes tell me–"

"It is. Run towards it. Run!" Jade suddenly yelled. He sped up and I started digging into my pocket to find a handgun, but the angle I was at was making it impossible.

I looked ahead instead and spotted the red light in front of us; I saw it disappear for a moment as Reaver approached it, then I was put down.

With the click of a suitcase, Jade got the keycard out of Elish's protective sleeve. Reaver and I took out our guns and started shooting the mass of writhing grey that came closer and closer to us.

When we were shooting I noticed something though, the tall one that had been eating the rat wasn't hissing or coming towards us. He was looking around like he was confused, following the group like he didn't know what else he was supposed to do.

That was odd… but then I remembered how he acted when I shone a light on him; he had ignored me completely. I'd been the one to hear and notice him; he'd just been there quietly minding his own business.

"Reaver, don't kill the standing one, I think he's blind. He's done nothing but follow the group; he didn't hurt me," I said over the gunfire. "Just leave him be, he won't hurt us."

Reaver gave me a look of disbelief before he shot another round into the crawling ones. I saw a fountain of blood appear where one of their eyes used to be. "You got to be fucking kidding me…"

"Please?" I pleaded. I heard him growl before he let off another round. The standing one was still swaying towards us. He was so close I could see a squirming rat clenched in his boney hand, its eyes bulging out like small raisins.

The fact that his head didn't explode meant Reaver listened to my pleas, though the ones surrounding him were dropping like flies, reduced to nothing but human-like shrieks and flailing twisted limbs.

Then the beep, the beep I recognized from Perish's lab back in Donnely. With a shout from Jade, we both fell back, until, with an audible sigh, the metal door locked and pressurized. I turned the flashlight back on and quickly scanned the white walled hallways, much like the Donnely lab, that surrounded us.

Reaver dropped down to his knees at this point and Perish's corpse slid off of him. I looked at him and cried out in shock when I saw part of his scalp had been ripped off of his head. Then a surge of guilt flooded to me for not noticing how bad it was before. The black had masked the blood that had been falling from his head wound, and Perish's body had hid the rest.

"Baby? Are you okay?" I put the kerchief over his scalp and held it.

Reaver's face was red and his breathing heavy. The energy it had taken to carry Perish, run though the cisterns, and fend off the kreiger creatures had zapped him.

Reaver gave me a tired nod and looked up at Jade. "Can you get power in this thing?" he rasped.

I shone my light at Jade but lowered it as his eyes squinted. "This is all shit Perish should know about… but I've turned on the power in our shelters in the greywastes so I have an idea. Just stay here until the lights come on; there's no way those mutants can come in here. We're absolutely safe."

Reaver nodded and I put some pressure on his head.

"Come here, sweety. I bet this place has a ton of bandages and antiseptic," I said.

"I'm okay, I just need to catch my breath... we didn't all get to be carried like princesses." Reaver smirked. I playfully gave him a nudge before I put my arms around him. He patted my hand before he rose to his feet and leaned against one of the shiny white walls. "We made it, that's all that matters. Are you sure you're okay?" He put a hand on my chin and tilted my head up and to the side.

"Yeah, I'm perfectly fine; I'm more worried about you and Perish..." I looked down at the dead scientist, his blood-streaked face turned to the side. I shuddered seeing that his eyes were still open, staring off into oblivion. "A neck break won't take long to heal, right?"

Reaver lit a cigarette and nudged Perish with his foot. "Not sure, I never asked Elish... the pet should know though. Fuck, I need a drink."

And at that cue, and with the vice around my heart unclenching, the lights turned on, then the sound of the vents above us as they circulated dead, twenty-year-old air.

I shut the flashlight off and looked around, feeling the anxiety currently coiled around my chest start to loosen. Not only at being inside and safe, but the entire place smelled like Donnely. And though my experiences there hadn't been positive, I'd felt safe there from the greywastes... just not safe from the person inside it.

Reaver, with the cigarette clenched in his teeth, started down the hallway and I followed him. I could see for the first time the smoke damage on all of the walls, though besides that I couldn't find any signs of fire. This place didn't look like it had survived an inferno; the labs underneath the building in Kreig must've stretched out beyond the walls.

I glanced in each of the Plexiglass windows, seeing an operating room, metal slabs lined up in rows like some sort of morgue, several bedrooms, and finally a living room-type area.

I directed Reaver to a cold musty couch, covered in a thick layer of dust but still holding an outline of an old magazine that had stayed where it was set down. I left him with his cigarette and met Jade who was coming back down from a narrow hallway off to the left.

"Where are we?" I asked him. He handed me one of our duffle bags which held medical supplies, and started walking towards where we'd left Perish.

"I don't know, but I can smell charcoal towards where the generators are, and there's a thick metal door where that smell is. I think this place was isolated from the inferno, perhaps in case they ever wanted to rebuild." I helped Jade drag Perish into the living room, then found a blanket to drape over him.

"Will we be able to get into the burned areas?"

The cicaro shook his head no, before he got out Elish's laptop and plugged it into the wall. "There would be nothing there, it's all incinerated. Elish told me this place had been locked off beforehand, by Lycos himself. When the alarms started going off, he pushed Greyson into this area and went into the labs to get the baby. Greyson escaped into the sewers we were just in, and Elish found him. Elish went inside through the actual building on the surface and brought Lycos and the baby back out."

I wetted a rag and started washing Reaver's wound. My boyfriend glanced up at Jade. "Why would Leo do that? Wouldn't I have just come back after I was burned?" He winced as I put antiseptic on his head, before he tilted his head up towards me. "Just put some loose stitches in it Killi, and then help Jade. Scalp wounds get infected quickly. I'm offing myself before bed."

I looked at him in stricken horror. Even with the knowledge he would be back by morning it still terrified me. But Reaver didn't have a single care to give over it. He turned his attention fully to Jade as the cicaro continued talking. Elish's remote phone was now plugged into the wall, and Jade's own medical kit laid out in front of him in a perfectly organized fashion.

"Actually yes, you would've come back," Jade said. He got up and walked to the other side of a divider wall and I realized there was a small kitchenette behind it. I heard him take something out of a cupboard. "With a thousand tons of rubble above you, and six inch steel doors trapping you inside, on top of that, no one even knowing you're alive. You would've grown up surviving on nothing but your own immortality, dying every couple of days from starvation or dehydration. You would spend an eternity like that, not knowing anything else."

Reaver froze and so did I; my hand still holding the rose-stained wash cloth.

"Seriously? Holy fucking shit," Reaver mumbled. "I never even thought of that, Jesus fuck. I guess I do still have shit to watch out for." My boyfriend winced as I put the first stitch into his head; his scalp was split open like an overripe fruit and I had to squeeze the two parts together to knit the thick flaps of skin back together.

Jade started bandaging his own wounds, mostly a road burn on his face and a few pocked bite marks on his leg. "When the Crimstones took me, their plan was to blow up a building in the West End with Elish and King Silas inside of it. If the skyscraper collapsed on them it could be months before we got the big machines to dig them out. I can't imagine being stuck in some place with no air, no room, and no stimulation, waking up only to die hours later." Jade let out an animated shudder. "I just hope they aren't planning an encore. Elish has enough on his mind taking down our Ghost King; he doesn't need this on his plate too."

A silence filled the room after Jade said those words. I busied myself stitching Reaver but I could tell he was deep in thought, thinking about Reno probably and this group that had apparently taken him. We had a lot to think about and a lot to do. I hadn't had a chance to explore this place yet. I didn't even know where the computers could be.

I moved onto Jade when I was finished with Reaver and gently peeled back his pant leg. Nothing I couldn't take care of; I'd cleaned and bandaged more than enough deacon and deacdog bites in Aras and these ones weren't much different. While I did that, Reaver started to explore the small apartment lab, his M16 in hand.

I wrapped the last piece of gauze around Jade's leg and gave it a pat. "There, I'll check on it in the morning and give it another clean. At least we have a good amount of time down here until Elish comes and gets us. It'll heal nicely."

Jade rubbed his leg and sipped the cup of tea he'd made for himself. Halfway through bandaging him the kettle I didn't even know he'd put on the burner started to whistle. He was a lot like his master in that way. Jade always had a mug of tea in his hands when he was in the greyrifts bunker, and when he was outside of the apartment, he had a cigarette.

I took my own mug of tea and started to walk into the kitchen to see if we had any old cans of food we could scavenge, but I hadn't even stepped onto the linoleum when Jade spoke.

"You were amazing as shit with that scorprion, kid."

I turned around, a bit taken aback. I noticed Jade was staring forward; his brow furrowed like it was physically painful for him to praise me in such a way. At least he'd stopped sulking like he had been on the way to Kreig.

"You're a… small, innocent, meek little thing who cries too much… but then all of a sudden you turn into this badass, jumping on the back of this giant radiated insect… you're like some sort of shapeshifter." Jade's yellow eyes glanced towards me. "Maybe your aura is toxic, weighing you down, but I think if you remained that little ray of sunshine I met in Tamerlan… you'd be dead by now."

I gave him a small smile, taking out some old dried pasta from a dusty white cupboard. "Reaver's trained me well, and he keeps me safe… but not safe enough that I don't learn some things along the way, even if he'd rather put me in a bubble."

Jade's brow furrowed even more; he took a sip of his tea and I saw his mouth twitch. "Elish was smart to hook you up with Reaver. If you would've been Garrett's pet… your life would've been easier, until Silas killed you of course, but you wouldn't have learned anything." He shrugged and got up, right when a chill went down my spine. The same one I got whenever I was reminded just how long Elish had been planning the events that were unfolding right now.

Well, at least the question as to who I was going to be sold to had been answered. I had always thought it was one of the cruel ones like Nero, but apparently it was the nicest out of all of them. I think I would've gotten along great with Garrett. But that was just another path I would never see the end of; my heart belonged to my dark chimera, the Scourge of the Greywastes, and the future murderer of King Silas.

I was counting down the days to when I saw Silas actually die… life would be a lot better after that, for everyone. Even some of the chimera family it seemed. I wonder how many of his brothers Elish had been able to sway. Garrett for sure, but what about the brutes? Or the other ones who ran the council in Skyfall? I know Elish wouldn't be doing any of this unless he had amassed at least a small following of his siblings.

"I'm going to start looking for those computers. You making us some din?" When I nodded, he nodded back, then motioned towards the suitcase. "I have suicide pills in there. Don't let Reaver convince you to strangle him or anything. Those pills will knock him out and by four am, he'll be fixed. Another grand Skytech invention." And with that, Jade disappeared into the halls, leaving me with the food and the dead scientist.

I was just dishing us up some meatless spaghetti sauce and noodles when both Reaver and Jade came in, snipping back and forth like they were annoyed at something. I served them their plates and sat down on the couch with Reaver; Jade taking the armchair.

"Well, this lab is safe, we have that going for us," Reaver said bitterly, stabbing the noodles and shoving them into his face since he still had the manners of a cave man. "But we have no computers, I dug up some lab plans in a dusty old office and it looks like on the other side of that metal door isn't fire and destruction, it's Leo's old office. The doors that lead to the blaze are way off on the east end, which explains why this place was so fire free."

I groaned, this wasn't good news at all. "Any idea how to get in?"

"Well…" I looked over as Jade started to talk, and noticed with a bit of amusement that he was carefully wrapping his spaghetti noodles onto his fork, in the neatest most mannerly way possible. The contrast between these two chimeras was fascinating and curious in so many ways. And since Jade was from the slums you could bet it was Elish that taught him these impeccable manners.

Jade went on, "Reaver's brilliant suggestion was to blow it up with C4, even if we're underground and there is tons of dirt and metal above us. My idea is to wait for Perish to wake up, and if he doesn't know… we can wait for Elish to come back and get us."

Reaver rolled his eyes; to him every problem could be solved with C4.

"That sounds like the best idea, once Perish wakes up we'll have more information." I looked over at the still dead scientist; I wondered if his body had started heating up yet. "Are you going to tell him about how he acted, Reaver? Or his real age?" I thought it would be important for us to start getting our stories straight.

Reaver nodded, already finishing off his food. "Yeah, I'm not going to lie to him and Jade wants to pick his brain a bit. If Perish starts getting that broken head of his to tick and realize shit is missing, Jade's job will be easier."

I felt a small jolt of protectiveness towards Perish, though I knew it would bring forth the scorn of Reaver so I tried to downplay it. "What job? You're not going to interrogate him or anything right?"

The cicaro shook his head no. "Nah, nothing like that, just an aura reading trick, like my matchmaking. Don't sweat it." Then he got up and took Reaver's plate, which surprised both of us, but I guess he was Reaver's pet.

"Get me some of those mariachi cherries," Reaver called after him, I assumed he meant maraschino. "And tea, Elish's fancy tea except put some vodka in it."

Jade shot him a look but kept his mouth shut, which made a smile appear on my boyfriend's face. He leaned over and said out of the corner of his mouth. "We're getting one of these once I'm king."

A couple hours later, we shared some opiate cigarettes and opiate pills. That was only the second hit today, so we were doing good with our cutting down. Jade ended up having some as well since his master had allowed it. I pointed out that there were some perks to Reaver being his temporary guardian.

Then we retired to our bedrooms. There were two from what we could find. I fell asleep beside Reaver with the help of the opiates lulling me into a deep sleep. I didn't even ask when Reaver was going to take that pill but I explained them to him before I fell asleep.

I just hoped I wouldn't have to wake up in the middle of the night next to a corpse, immortal or not, it still set me on edge to have him do it.

CHAPTER 15

Garrett and Elish

LUCA OPENED THE SLIDING GLASS DOOR, TUCKING his fingers into the thick wool blanket. He spotted Garrett leaning up against the railing, blue-embered cigarette in one hand and a glass of whisky and ice in the other.

The sengil pattered over on slippered feet and draped the blanket over Garrett's shoulders.

The president of Skytech took a drink of his whisky and let out a breath, a cold plume shrouding the twinkling lights of Skyland below him before dissipating into the cold night air.

"I wonder if he's cold," Garrett whispered. He turned around to face his brother who had trailed silently behind Luca, only his heartbeat giving him away.

"Do you think he's cold, Elish?"

Elish rested a supportive hand on his brother's shoulder. "The colder he is now the more he will appreciate when he's warm."

"What if he dies cold? In the dark? Thinking I… that I left him to be tortured by them?" The filter squished underneath Garrett's tightened grip. "It's been so long…"

Garrett flicked the cigarette and watched as it was swallowed up by the darkness. He turned and closed his eyes. "Why is this happening again, Elish?"

The blond-haired chimera stood with the warm apartment lit behind him, holding a glass of bloodwine in his right hand. He looked at his brother with an expression on his face that held no emotion.

"This will be the last time this happens," he replied, his own words holding a weight that suggested he had just spoken a volume instead of only eight words.

The same words hit Garrett, and as they sunk in, the man frowned. Then, with a shake of his head, he walked past his brother into the apartment.

Garrett stopped, as if trying to decide whether he wanted to pursue where the conversation was heading. But, whether it was from the whisky or just a need to talk about it, his own desires outweighed his past experiences and he pressed on. "Elish, you can't kill him… even if you do figure out how. He's our creator, and he may have his issues, but his family loves him. He has his moments but we've learned how to cope."

Luca trailed behind the two of them, closing the sliding glass door before pattering off towards his new cat.

"I refuse to cope, I refuse to bow…"

"He gave us the gift of immortality."

"And I shall take his as thanks."

Garrett let out a long breath before a clinking of bottles could be heard as he refilled his cup. "Once Jade is immortal I bet you will abandon this silly rebellion you're planning. This has always been about that boy."

"No, this is about someone in this genetically enhanced family of ours finally growing a pair of testicles about that Mad King. I know there is a way and it's right under my damn nose."

Garrett snorted, one of the few people in the world who could act as such in front of his dominant and prideful brother.

"Yes, we all know about Sky. I'm telling you it's bullshit. My theory is he was not an immortal. There's no way to kill us, brother, as much as you would like it. We're stuck with our little king." Garrett leaned up against the couch, completely ignoring the dangerous atmosphere that Garrett had managed to stir up around him. It wasn't like he was immune or not afraid of his brother's occasional violent moods, it was that the whisky was doing its work and making him quite loose of tongue.

"It's in Perish's head somewhere. However where it is I do not know.

I am counting on Jade to figure that out for me. I hold no faith that those hard drives will give us anything of use," Elish said bitterly, his cold purple eyes narrowed with thought. "I told them that finding those hard drives was their goal, but in truth, this all depends on Jade's abilities to see into our heads."

Absentmindedly, Elish reached into his pocket and pulled out Jade's remote. A small device that held the tracking chip buried inside of his pet's head. Not only did this device tell Elish his location, it also showed him Jade's health, radiation level, heartbeat, and overall physical health.

It was silent though, silent and offline… his cicaro was far in the greywastes and far out of range of the signal.

"You really think he'll be able to access Perish's memories? Like he did yours last year?" Garrett asked.

Elish nodded before tucking the remote back into his breast pocket, beside Jade's old collar which he always kept wrapped around his upper arm, underneath his shirt and hidden from view.

"Do you really think Perish knows how to kill an immortal?"

"I have reason to believe it was Perish who helped Sky kill himself."

There was a tinkle of a breaking glass as it slipped out of Garrett's hand. The chimera with the gelled back hair stared at Elish, the hand that had been holding the glass still shaking back and forth.

"Elish… you - you're not serious? Please tell me you're not serious."

"Not a silly plan now, hm?" Elish smirked sparing an upturn of his cold gaze.

Garrett took a step back as Luca appeared with a damp cloth and a spray bottle. He stared down at the sengil as he cleaned up the broken glass before the sengil ran off to get Garrett another glass of liquor.

"Please, Elish…"

"Do you want Reno with you forever?"

"Of course… I…" His face turned from stammering and flustered all the way back to annoyed. "You know what? I'm not answering that and I'm done with your damn mind games, Eli. I refuse to even discuss it while Reno is out there; all that matters right now is him."

Elish spread his hands. "I said nothing on the subject; you were the one to bring it up, dear brother."

Garrett took a fresh glass from Luca; he brought the liquid up to his lips, but the moment they touched Elish's phone rang.

The president of Skytech watched with a lump in his throat as Elish took the call outside. Perhaps it was Jade? He didn't know, it could very well have been. Elish had outfitted the young cicaro's phone with a blocker so the Legion wouldn't be able to track the phone signal. A call from a remote phone deep in the greywastes would immediately bring the Legion. It meant it was either stolen, or a chimera was out there somewhere becoming lost.

When Elish came back inside after ten minutes Garrett tried to read his face, but even though he knew his brother's every movement, every eyebrow twitch, and every shifting body language… he saw nothing.

"What is it?"

Elish looked at the phone and rested it on top of a console table. "That was Kessler. The signal from the broadcast was a dead end. We still do not know where Reno or the others–"

"No! No!" Garrett threw his half-empty whisky glass and it shattered against the wall, broken for the second time that night.

Garrett put his hands behind his neck and gritted his teeth. "Nothing? Fucking nothing then? We're back at square one?"

"I am afraid so."

Garrett sunk to his knees, feeling his eyes start to burn and sting. He shook his head and sniffed before backing himself up against the back of the couch.

Like a scared child, Garrett brought his knees up to his chest and wrapped his arms around them. He then rested his chin on his knees and looked at the grey carpeted floor.

"I want to be out there… why am I not out there looking?" he said after a few silent minutes had passed.

To Garrett's shock, Elish sat down beside him on the floor and offered him his glass of wine. A rare show of caring from his closest brother, who would usually just loom over Garrett and snip at him when he was at his weakest. Elish was not a man who directly cut Garrett down; his veiled words were more like death by a thousand paper cuts.

Garrett took a drink and Elish gently took the glass back. "When the same men kidnapped Jade, and I shared the same frustrations with you, you told me I was more useful here than another man on the field. We are smarter than the average man… or well, *I am* anyway."

There was a slight tug on the side of Garrett's face at his brother's attempt at a joke.

Elish went on, "We are most useful up here, planning and making sure no building is left unchecked."

"Silas has half the thiens looking for Reaver, Killian, and Perish…"

"But we have half our family looking for Reno and the others, and I would put more stock in them. They are enchanted with Reno's odd manner. They actually would like finding him… unlike my cicaro who I am sure they wished had stayed missing."

Garrett smiled this time, appreciative of Elish's attempts to lighten his sullen, frustrated mood.

"I suppose, yes."

"Even King Silas likes him, perhaps not as you would like… but he is amused by Reno. Really, I would think Reno has more help than Jade did, and perhaps Silas will not kill him right away when he returns," Elish replied casually. And as Garrett opened his mouth in aghast horror at the inappropriate mention of this fact, the cold chimera added: "And if I am king… you can have him for eternity, unharmed and happy with his chimera husband."

Garrett closed his open mouth and whimpered. "Hold me, I miss him so much."

Elish sighed and let Garrett lean against him. Elish put his arm around his brother and let Garrett shuffle into his arms. "I told my almost eighteen-year-old cicaro he was too old to be held, but how I can forbid him when my ninety-year-old brother needs the same comfort?"

Garrett sniffed. "You're a lot of peoples' support system."

"I know, which is why I do not begrudge you the comfort. I will not forget your aid while I was making my own decisions about Jade," Elish replied.

"You were a wreck."

Garrett looked up over his brows with a smirk; Elish spared him a half eye roll. "Perhaps for a day or so."

"Months."

Elish let out a breath but said nothing more on the subject. The two of them sat watching Luca in the kitchen chopping meat for the greywaster cat.

"I really love him," Garrett replied in a small voice. His eyes looking lost, like he was witnessing the saddest of plays get acted out in front of him. He always had large prominent eyes, ones which could break the heart of even the most steeled of men; large and full of expression and emotion, a trait that only he had carried when the first generation had been created. The other three, Elish especially, had struggled with emotions in general. Seeing them as weakness as they got older and something that held you back; a fault in their engineering.

But Garrett had always embraced his emotions. The soft-hearted chimera had made them his strength in a way, because not even Elish had the heart to be cruel to him anymore.

And with this thought in the cold chimera's mind, he gave his little brother's head a pat as it leaned against his shoulder.

"I know, brother."

"He's different than the others… he's so… different." Garrett took another drink of the blood wine before leaning his head on Elish's shoulder once again. "You know I didn't even sleep with him when I could have? If that isn't a testament…"

"Considering you bedded a sixteen-year-old dish-washer walking home from work once that is saying a lot."

Garrett lifted his head and scowled at him. "Don't tell him about that. He doesn't even know about us, or Luca, or that one time when you and Jade got drunk and…"

"Alright, it's time for bed." Elish started to rise. "And I have no idea what you're speaking of."

Garrett smiled and also rose. He looked down at his wine glass and twirled it until the wine started to swirl in a little whirlpool. "I won't do it until I marry him, just to show everyone how serious I am this time. I'll prove it to all of you."

Elish rested the glass on the coffee table and gave his brother a small shake of his head as he turned towards the hallway. "I know your feelings for him, it was my cicaro that matched you two. But if you feel the need to prove your love, so be it. Sleep now, we have a meeting with Ellis in the morning."

Garrett stared at Ellis's desk as his only sister and his oldest brother discussed the ransom demands for Reno, Nico, and the pets. He didn't raise his head even when they addressed him; all he could manage to do was stare forlorn at the piles of manila folders.

"They must have some sort of disrupters, the same technology they used to hide themselves when they kidnapped Jade," Ellis said. She was holding a red pen in her hands and was going over a map of Skyfall and the outlands, including Irontowers and Suicide Bay, all areas that they had once picked apart trying to locate Jade.

"There are so many abandoned buildings, hundreds possibly thousands for us to check, and as we learned before… they only need the basement of one building to hide their activities." Ellis shook her head and chewed on the end of the pen cap. "We learned a lot from Jade's kidnapping though. I would guess Milos's little brother Meirko will act the same as he did."

Elish looked down at the map, analyzing it with his deep purple eyes. His thoughts most likely were centered on when it had been him worrying about the fate of his pet.

"I have grown tired of Silas's leniency with the Crimstones. He lets them do as they will for his entertainment whether he admits it or not. While he's occupied with Reaver I want them eradicated once and for all," Elish said coldly. "They are slippery snakes who think they're more powerful than they are."

Like Silas? Garrett continued to stare at the edge of the desk. He wanted to say it, his lips almost moved to say it, but he remained quiet. Elish would wring his neck if he said something like that in front of their very Silas-loyal sister.

"I agree… and what we are going to do right now is cut off any and all media; all of the wanted ads we are running, all of the rewards. What information we could get from Moros we have already received. I want radio silence, and once it's quiet, we are going to put our best chimeras on the search. I want every building combed; it will be slow but–"

"They - they'll kill him." Garrett managed to raise his head to give them both agonizing looks. "They want the media attention; they want Skyfall to know they have something on us. If we all of a sudden make them feel like they don't have that power… they'll kill him."

Ellis gave him a glance before she slowly and subtly shook her head. “If the pets and the partners have to become fodder so we can stop this once and for all…”

“Fuck that!” There was a scraping sound as Garrett jumped up from his chair; he slammed his hand down on the table. “Reno will not become fodder! He is my fiancé!”

Ellis didn’t even flinch; she put down the red marker and rolled it towards Elish. “And you will find another one. You acted this way after the last one died and the one before that and so on. So will Caligula; he’s still young. They don’t have chimeras so this is the perfect opportunity to call their bluff, shut everything down and… Elish, he’s about to cry, can you deal with him? My patience is about spent over emotions getting involved in this.”

Elish looked over at Garrett whose face had crumpled into a look of unimaginable pain, his lower lip quivering in a way that reminded Elish of when they were younger. It was funny in a way how when the three of them got together the same story always played out. Ellis or Nero would upset Garrett and in turn Garrett would run to Elish so the older brother could deliver them a verbal tongue-lashing.

“I recall you being rather upset last year when the Crimstones bombed the buildings behind the precinct.” Elish crossed his arms; beside him Garrett slunk back down in his chair and stared at the folders, his light green eyes glistening.

“That’s different; Garren and Eve are half chimera.”

Elish waved a dismissive hand. “Sterilized half-chimeras with no abilities, no immortality, riding coattails or acting like imbeciles. I would think they are less important than the future husband of the second born chimera and president of Skytech.” Everyone had their weak spot and Ellis’s had always been her children.

Sure enough, there was the slightest pull on her lip. “I will not get into this with you, Elish. What it comes down to is that Silas will not give you up and all we can do now is try and smoke them out or wait for their next move.”

Garrett sniffed beside Elish. “Stop treating Reno like he’s just another notch on my bedpost, Ellis. I love him… he’s the one for me.”

“We went through this with Calvin just ten years ago and you said the same thing."

Elish decided to try and stem the tears that were quickly welling in his brother's eyes; he started packing the folders into his suitcase. "Well, this is the first time Jade has matched Garrett's partner and he's had great success so far. Garrett hasn't even bedded this one yet, he's waiting for marriage. Surely that means something?"

Ellis glanced up, and Elish could tell, even if she wouldn't admit it, that that did mean something. Garrett had always had low self-esteem, and growing up in the shadows of Elish, Ellis, and Nero had only accentuated it. Though Garrett was a grand chimera in his own right, he always felt overshadowed. His three siblings had an imposing threatening presence to them… something Garrett Dekker had always lacked. He seemed to fade into the darkness when he was around his fellow first generation.

Put him one-on-one with something though, and Elish's sensitive little brother lit up like the brightest star. Which is why he seemed to not only to attract men, but he seemed to end up getting burned by them as well.

Or by King Silas when he found out about them.

"Well, I won't lie, that does score him some points." Ellis was silent for a moment before she spoke, "But the plan doesn't change, Garrett. Even if Meirko and Kerres had kidnapped Drake or Timothy I would suggest the same course of action. If we keep giving them their audience, they'll put on a show. We don't want another incident over what happened with Jade's ransom video."

Garrett nodded and took Elish's handkerchief as he handed it to him. "But the family will keep looking?"

"Yes, Gare, they will…" Ellis sighed. "Stop… my god, stop staring at me like that. We'll do our best to bring him home."

Garrett gave her a sad smile. "Thanks, sissy."

After they had left Ellis's office, Garrett wiped his face with Elish's kerchief and sniffed. "Do you really think her plan is wise? To cut off our television promos and the media?"

Elish was silent for a moment, leafing through Jade's old notebook which he often did.

"Yes, I do. Because of you the Crimstones are getting even more attention than they did with Jade. You have a brand-new channel dedicated to finding Reno; they're loving the attention I would gather."

"But if it helps–"

"It is not helping, Garrett. We need to stop going at this as businessmen and councilmen and go about this as chimeras, as the genetically engineered men we are. I agree with her."

"I know." Garrett glanced out the window, watching the buildings go by as the driver took them back to Olympus. Garrett hadn't been back to his old skyscraper since Reno had been taken. It had been too painful to be there alone; he was no longer used to it.

"Will you be returning to Kreig soon?" Garrett asked.

Elish shook his head, still looking at the notebook. "I will remain here while this is all going on. They'll be safe in Kreig, and the more time that goes by that they're not found, the less enthusiastic the Legion will be to find them, and the longer Jade will have to crack Perish's head. I will not be returning until this is resolved. I promised that to Reaver and at this point gaining his trust is invaluable."

Elish ignored the smile that started to appear on Garrett's face, and ignored him as he leaned his head on Elish's shoulder. "You're staying because you know I need you. Thank you, Eli."

Elish let out a breath. "No, I'm sure I'm only staying to mediate our brothers and make sure things go smoothly. You have little to do with it."

But Garrett knew better, and he appreciated his brother staying on his accord. Garrett knew Elish missed his pet, but Jade was growing up quickly and he had his own task to complete. The only empath chimera in existence was a valuable asset to Elish, and the family as a whole.

Even if what he was doing could potentially kill him.

Garrett looked down at the notebook and smiled; though as soon as Elish noticed Garrett was looking he closed it and stuffed it back into his pocket.

"You're looking at his Pokémon drawings?" Garrett's smile widened. "You miss him a lot, don't you?"

"We're here…" Elish opened the car door, even though the car was still at a rolling stop.

Garrett laughed and stuffed the kerchief in his pocket, following behind his brother.

CHAPTER 16

Jade

WHENEVER HE WASN'T AROUND I HAD NIGHTMARES, nightmares of haunting auras and shadows that had never seen the light of day. Of blackness that was drained of colour, and a threat that scared me so much I refused to acknowledge it in safety of daylight.

My blond chimera had been my protector during these nightmares. Whenever I was in his arms, surrounded by those opal and silver hues, the creeping sepulchres of madness never came to me. He was my lamplight, my guardian… my everything. In our years together he had really become my partner.

But without him not only was the bed half-empty, but my heart was as well. We were two pieces of the same soul, intertwined and tightly knitted together to the point where sometimes I didn't know where my thoughts ended and his began. I knew him so well, as he knew me.

"Hot and cold, light and dark, black and white... we are opposites Jade, no one can deny that, but together we form a rather unstoppable force."

I hope doing this is making you proud of me, Master. We waited a long time, and you by yourself have been waiting even longer.

I can't believe these plans are finally coming into fruition, that we actually have Reaver in our grasp now. No Lycos, no Greyson… Reaver is all ours. And to both of our reliefs… he is malleable still, ready to receive your cold touch and become who he was born to be: your weapon.

But will you succeed? Or will everything you worked so hard to achieve turn to ashes in your hand. I refuse to believe for even a second that you haven't already pre-planned and analyzed every single situation that could arise. You are in control, you always have been.

But so has King Silas.

"Jade?"

I opened my eyes and saw the blur of Perish peering down at me, looking bedraggled and tired.

Stifling a yawn, I glanced up at him. "You're alive early. What's up?"

The scientist wrung his hands and looked around the room. "I don't know where to sleep. Is everyone survived?"

I shifted over and threw him a pillow. "Yeah, Killian and Reaver are fine. Reaver's dead in the other room after those creatures ripped his scalp in two. Just lie down beside me but keep to your side of the bed." The last thing I wanted was for Perish to sleep beside me but I also had a job to do with him. I had to put my personal feelings aside right now. If he tried what he had tried with Killian he would be needing to grow back his entire face.

Perish laid down on the other side of the bed. I saw him stare up at the ceiling with his hands behind his head. "This is kind of like my lab, but not. It smells old; my lab smelled clean and lived in."

I rolled onto my side and just watched him for a few moments, going over every detail of his thin but handsome face. "What time were you the happiest in your life?" I said my words carefully, trying to adopt the gentle probing tone that Elish had when he was trying to get information from someone timid.

I saw his lips turn to a smile, before an almost wistful look came over his face. "When Killian was with me, before he killed me. I was so happy then; it was wonderful to have someone so kind to me."

Not quite what I was hoping for, so I pressed further. "You're over seventy, there has to be more than just that."

"Seeing Elish forced to marry you was kind of funny."

I scowled at him, but when I saw the smile on his lips I reached out my hand and shocked him. Not enough to make him scream like Elish's thermal touch could do, but enough to make him jump.

This made the crazy scientist laugh though. With a grinning smile he said, "You know how funny it is when you see another brother get into trouble, right? Surely you know the feeling?"

I did, there was a deep down smugness inside of me whenever Elish would verbally tear apart one of his brothers, and even Luca; he was kind of like a brother to me. "I guess, yeah."

"Another happy memory is this one. It's not top ten, but since you're here, I'll share it. I was happy when you survived the surgery, and when I saw you with your new teeth put in."

I ran my tongue along my teeth, some of them my own, some porcelain implants and some, like my canines up and down, were steel sharpened to a point. When I had been kidnapped by the Crimstones and my ex-boyfriend, Milos, the old leader, had ripped out my implants; ones that had been pressed in over my original teeth, taking my teeth with them. They also beat me so bad that quite a few of them broke.

My family had repaired me. Not only giving me new teeth, but doing the surgery on my brain to keep my abilities from overloading and causing seizures, aneurisms, and eventual death.

It was a dark time in my life. I had gotten my head cut open and screwed up, that and being nothing but a broken shell I would've been useless to my family. But Silas had repaired me, and the doctor chimera Sid, and Perish as well, had fixed me up until I was past brand-new.

It was one of the first family-type things the other chimeras had done for me. My loyalty towards this crazy family had strengthened after that. I felt like I was a part of them.

Silas had left Elish and me alone after that too, everything was calm and I was enjoying being reunited with my master.

Until we got that call from Greyson.

Nothing was the same after that; Elish wasn't the same.

The next morning I woke up to the sounds of pots and pans and voices coming from the living room and kitchen. When I decided to open up my eyes, I saw Perish putting on a black t-shirt, his hair damp from the shower and sticking up. I said a mumbled good morning to him and found the shower myself, hearing Killian's high pitch greeting for Perish as I turned on the hot water.

When I emerged and did my ritualistic belting of my wrist and ankle cuffs and my leather collar, I put on my greywaster clothing and went into the living room.

Killian was washing the dishes and Reaver and Perish could be heard down the hallway. I assumed they were looking at the metal door that led into Lycos's office.

The blond boy gave me a smile and took me out some leftover spaghetti from the microwave. "I started heating it up when I heard the water shut off. I assume Perish left you alone since he doesn't have any bite marks on him."

I bit off a piece of toasted tact bread and ripped it off with my teeth. "I would have enjoyed a bit of chimera blood. Have they figured out how to break into that room yet?"

Killian handed me some tea and shook his head. "No, but Perish thinks he knows how. I hope you don't mind but he has Elish's laptop. He says he owned if first so he kind of pulled rank on all of us. He's going to hack into it."

I took my plate and quickly walked down the white hallways and towards the voices. Elish had everything on that laptop, and though it was all password protected, most of it inaccessible to even me, I still didn't want Perish to crash it or destroy it.

I walked in on Perish sitting down on the linoleum with Elish's black laptop on his lap. Reaver was standing behind him with his arms crossed, asking computer questions. To my surprise, Reaver was dressed in cloth pants and a zippered hoody, but when I tuned my ears I heard the washer going on in the background. Killian and Luca would've gotten along great.

The chimera greywaster looked up at me. His black eyes were sparkling with mischief, an expression that only broadened when he read the concerned look on my face. "We didn't look for you and Elish's sex videos, don't worry."

I gave him a flat look, ignoring Perish's giggling from around our feet. "Did you find yours and Killian's? After you killed Redmond and Hollis? Because that's one I know exists."

My chest rose as I enjoyed the fleeting moment of annoyance sweep

Reaver's face. But before I could fully capture it in my mind, he tapped Perish with his foot. "Find it and delete it."

"Oh, I'll find it, bro. I'll find it, and make copies of it, and watch it again and again…"

Perish squawked as Reaver dug his foot into the tender part of his side, though Mr. Maniac was laughing while he did it. He seemed in good spirits which surprised me greatly. He must've dug in the opiate bag, that or he was just feeling more in his element. Being in the apartment in the greyrifts, inside and unable to shed the blood he thirsted for so much, it was kind of like watching an evil flower wilt.

"I will accept that as my payment…" Perish did an embellished twirl with his finger before he dove it down onto Elish's keyboard. A second later there was a hiss and a snap before another loud metallic click sounded, then to my joy, a door handle popped out.

"Way to go!" I stood behind Reaver as he pulled the door open, but as a plume of dust that had been stuck to the other end of the door greeted us, I started to cough.

To my surprise however, Reaver closed the door again; a passing furrow of his brow that was gone before I could even blink crossing his face. He then raised his head and nodded towards the two of us, his face hardening. "Well, we got it open. Take five, Perish. Killian, are my pants done yet?"

I turned around and gave his back a confused look. Perish rose with the laptop which I quickly took from him. "You're not going in now?"

I followed Reaver as he went into the living room, sauntering around like we hadn't just had a major breakthrough. "Where are you going?"

Reaver grabbed his gun and slung it over his shoulder, I noticed then he was still wearing his thick army boots. "My dog is out there. The lab can wait, we have a long time to search through that shit."

I looked behind me at the door, my curiosity burning my brain. "Seriously? Come on, let's at least start bringing out the computers. I can do that without you anyway."

Surprisingly I saw Reaver's shoulders tense, before he whirled around and gave me a glaring look. There was something in that look, an emotion past those onyx black eyes that he wasn't giving voice to. "Stay the fuck out of that room. That's an order, Cicaro."

"Are you kidding?" I took a step towards him but Perish grabbed onto my shoulder. I jerked him away and stalked up to Reaver. "My master is putting a lot at risk for us to get those files and the hard drives. Who knows what might happen, even today. For all we know we could get raided, or those lizards could find a way in. I want them now to be safe."

My body jumped back as Reaver turned back around; it further tensed up as I saw his expression of blazing anger.

"I am your fucking master now, pet, and I told you to stay the fuck away from it. If you put a toe in that room I'll be delivering you back to Elish in pieces, got it?"

And just like that his happy attitude was gone, but as it plummeted into the brimstones of hell, mine was quickly following behind it. As my ears went hot, and all my previous bad experiences with Reaver rose to the surface, I pushed him with my hands. I felt the confidence flow through me. I wasn't the little teenager he dangled over the deacons' pen anymore, I was Elish's cicaro. I was a chimera and a fucking tough one.

"Fuck off, you're not my master. Go find the dog, I'm getting those files." As soon as the last words left my lips, Reaver went to grab my collar. I expected it though, Elish had handled me the same. Instead I shifted off to the side, away from his outstretched hand, and grabbed his hoody.

The dark chimera twisted around. He raised his fists to punch me in the face when Killian grabbed him. I took a stumbled step back and felt Perish grab me.

"Go, just go, hun, it's okay… he'll stay out of the room." I let Perish hold onto my shoulder as Killian whispered into Reaver's ear. Like an owner calming down a junkyard dog, his voice was low and soothing.

I saw the wild chimera's lip disappear inside his pursed mouth before he pushed Killian away and stalked down the hallway, a few tense moments later the door to the sewers clicked shut.

When the door closed Killian's shoulders slumped with a sigh. "This is going to be hard for him, Jade… let's just start going through files. I want as much of this done as we can before he comes back."

Oh? The little greywaster twinky was going above his boyfriend's head? I picked up my mug of tea and held onto Elish's laptop. "Why is it going to be hard on him? Are you trying to tell me that spaz attack meant something else?"

Killian opened the metal door, making a stream of light break up the dust motes inside; when he spoke it echoed into the room like he'd just entered a dark cave. "Leo and Greyson are on that video; he hasn't really said anything about them since they died. I think… it's going to be hard for him to see them."

I had forgotten about that. Well, not forgotten but I had been so busy just getting here intact I hadn't thought about it. Reaver had never wavered in his strength or power; he remained every bit a stone-faced badass. I assumed, I don't know, that the guy was alright.

Since I had the laptop, I followed behind Killian, sweeping my eyes across the old office. Then Killian flicked the light switch on.

The dust was thick over everything, and it was obvious that whoever had been here had had to leave quickly. There were papers on the floors, half-open filing cabinets, what looked like textbooks stacked on top of one another, and behind that, a computer monitor. Everything was grey under the dust but still maintained their distinct shape. They looked like corpses slowly rising out of their graves. All of it set me on edge.

I coughed into my sleeve, every step we made into this small area made the dust rise up like smoke. I permanently put my hand over my mouth and started to wipe off the computer monitor; Killian was already in front of the desk wiping off the tower.

It took some tinkering from Perish but eventually his face was bathed in the blue computer glow; he then flicked open Elish's laptop and started clicking things with his mouse. Killian and I continued to wipe off surfaces, the boy even going as far as to put some textbooks aside, for reading material I guess.

"Okay, I'm just going to back up all these files. Once done I'll take the hard drive and–" Perish paused for a second, so abruptly in the middle of his sentence it made Killian and I both look.

Perish knitted his brow together before his eyes shot up from the screen, to Killian's face, and then back to the screen. "Lycos… why does Lycos have…" I moved to the back of the dusty chair Perish was sitting in, and saw the mouse hovered over a single media file, labelled: Greg/Sky.

But that wasn't what got my interest. I looked to the side of the folder he had opened and saw a trail of over a dozen other folders opened and clicked. The first ones looked like they had been hidden in the program files, well away from prying eyes. No way Perish would've looked there first.

"Perish, how did you know where to go?" I asked.

The tension radiating off Perish was filling the room with his fractured aura, soaking into the dusty corners and creeping up the stained walls. As I tuned into it, I saw it fluctuating and pulsing, branching off before snapping back like someone had put their finger into glue. It was brighter than I had ever seen it; I could see each crack so perfectly I could take them into my hands if I wanted to.

"Greg…" Perish's voice whispered, a hushed sound that carried on it tones melancholy and longing. As I held my breath and tried to keep up his aura, my mind could practically hear the grinding sound of his brain trying to work. "Greg… Lenard."

That realization hit me like a Mac truck. His brain was trying to click out of its monotonous rhythm. I glanced up at Killian and saw he was standing completely still, being as quiet as a mouse. I put my hand on Perish and said to him slowly.

"Perish, what are you seeing in your head?"

The mouse still hovered over the media file. My mind filled with my own compulsive thoughts… to grab the mouse and click it, or tell him straight-out that Silas had been lying to him.

But instead… as Elish had taught me – I shut up and I listened.

The scientist didn't move; he stared at the screen until he clicked the video.

It took a moment to load, and in that time Killian managed to sneak to the back of the computer so he could watch too.

The first image I saw was of a young brown-haired boy, with a round face and glasses on. He wasn't a chimera; he was standing beside a slab-like metal table, in a well-lit room surrounded by windows. He was holding a voice recorder in his hand and he was talking slowly into it.

"Greg Lenard… I am here with Sky Fallon–"

I jumped a mile high and Killian gave out a startled yell as Perish jumped to his feet, and with an angry bellow, he pushed the computer monitor, letting it fall to the ground with a deafening crash, still connected to the tower below it.

"Perry!" Killian held out his hands at Perish, a pleading look on his face. "It's okay, you're fine."

The scientist let out another cry before he whirled around, his pale eyes two slabs of blue ice. "No, there isn't… I can't say! I can't say! Don't let him say!"

"I know, I know you can't, Perry, you're fine." Killian's voice went low and soothing but I knew the kid was in the danger zones. This wasn't Reaver, a wild animal who could be calmed by the soothed voice of his boyfriend. Perish was unpredictable and crazy. If Killian had forgotten that since his little lab excursion in Donnely, he was soon going to be reminded.

Sure enough, Perish glared at Killian, then lowered his head and took a threatening step towards him.

At this point I knew I needed to jump in, with his aura fractured and glaring around me, I reached out my hand to deliver the electric shock I knew would stun him.

But something else happened. Instead of the staticy jolt of electricity I was used to feeling, as soon as I touched the bare skin behind Perish's neck my mind lit up. In an instant, a firework-type flare coated Perish's entire body, and as it enveloped every crease and curve in its fireless flames it spread onto me, and went directly into my head.

Suddenly an influx of pressure rushed through my brain, filling every corner with such a weight I thought my brain was going to explode through my head. It was like a bag being filled with gasoline, it took every ounce of strength in my body not to scream from pain.

But inside that overwhelming pressure were small threads. Like flashes of salmon in a river, they rushed into my overtaxed mind, bringing with it memories that were not my own.

With my body tensed and my eyes closed, I probed it, dove into it, and like an injection of compressed data, they shot into my head.

Perish Dekker.

No, Perish Fallon.

He wasn't a chimera…

With a bellowing cry, the memory got ripped out of my fingers. I let it go, afraid I would damage his mind even more if I hung on, and as it slipped back into the torrent of confusion that was his broken mind, I found a single shuddering image tucked into the back. Like a box in a crowded closet, it glowed and summoned me.

That image was a part of something, a part of a closed off area of his mind. That area was different than the others, almost… like a different person was inside of him.

The person stared back at me, like he was both surprised and angry that I had met him here. A virus inside of his head that had been caught red-handed sifting and routing through things he had no business seeing.

The man looked like Perish, but in the same breath he seemed different. His aura was different shades of blue, whereas Perish's had just been fractured light.

It was…

Sky Fallon. His brother.

His twin brother.

This was the part of Perish's mind he didn't have access to; it was like the memory of his brother was preventing him from accessing it. But no, it went further than that, like Reaver had told Killian and I – Perish's brain, at least a small section of it –

"Was put into an O.L.S," Sky said quietly, his icy-blue eye seemingly sweeping my body, analyzing me like I was a strip of data. "Greg and I did it, to prevent Silas from ever finding out how I killed my own body. Perish helped me, and he knew."

"Perish once knew how you killed yourself?"

Sky nodded. "That information should die; Silas should never have that power. No one should."

"We want to use it to kill Silas."

Sky's pink lips curled in a smirk, a smirk that reminded me of Reaver's. That dark chimera definitely shared a few strands of DNA with this man.

"Indeed? It will not be easy to find Perish's O.L.S, but perhaps if you ask nicely…"

A ripping percussion of pain hit me like I had touched an electrified fence. My eyes snapped open and I immediately felt like my lungs were on fire. I took in a gasp, seeing the lab ceiling in front of me.

Then darkness again, and hands, several of them holding me down. I knew this feeling, it had happened before, long ago… though the hands had been Elish's and it had been his mind I had entered.

Elish…?

I let out a shuddering scream as cold water splashed onto me. I looked around wildly, confused and unaware as to where I was. For a moment, I thought I was back in Olympus, in Elish's apartment, back where I belonged and where I was comfortable.

Until I smelled the cigarette. Sure enough, I focused on the blue ember and saw Reaver holding an empty blue bucket.

Then Killian's voice beside me. "It's okay, Jade. Thank god you woke up; you've been in and out of it for hours. Are you okay?"

He put a towel over my head and rubbed it gently. I saw I was lying on the couch, the television flickering in the background. I grimaced and winced as my head gave a throb. I felt like someone was taking an axe to it. "Reaver? Front me some opiate powder, my head is splitting in two."

A book was put on my lap with half a dozen lines, but as I picked up the sniffer my arm was bumped. I looked over, still half-aware, and saw Deek the deacdog looking at me with our matching yellow eyes. I was happy to see that he was alright. He had done a good job fending off those creatures for us. And from the looks of the dried blood on his muzzle, he had had himself a party last night.

I inhaled the beautiful opiates and leaned back onto the couch with a hand on my head. "Where's Perish?"

Killian and Reaver exchanged glances, then Killian spoke. "He's locked himself in your bedroom. After that mind trick you did… he kind of lost it. I dragged you out and locked him in Leo's office and then Reaver put him into the bedroom. He's kind of shaken up with what you did."

That triggered the memories in my head. I tried to rise but fell back down as the axe in my head rained down another blow. "I saw Sky in his head. Sky and Perish were twins, identical twins, both born immortals. He's not a chimera, and he isn't seventy-one like we thought. I think they were both Silas's age."

Reaver and Killian both stared at me. I continued, "Greg Lenard and Sky; they removed Perish's memory of how to kill an immortal. They put it in a device. Reaver, the one Elish showed you, it's the same type: an O.L.S."

They both stared at me like I had just became one with crazy, each trying to process the information I hadn't even made sense of yet. But it was all there, all of it was there and it made sense. This was why Perish was so fucked in the head. They had removed a piece of his damn brain; that was enough to make anyone crazy.

Sky ordered it done to his own brother, and after Perish had helped him kill himself, Greg had done it.

I had to tell this information to Elish. He had to know we could put Perish back together… that he could be the one to figure out how to kill King Silas.

It had been done before. Sky had killed himself, and I knew the instructions were in that removed piece of Perish's memories.

"Perish Fallon," I said, more to myself than them. "That was his name. Sky Fallon and Perish Fallon."

This made Reaver's face change. His inquisitive black eyes suddenly became hard, and he said in a quiet but solid voice, "Perish. When he was normal for that brief moment when we were killing those lizards. He said he had a segment of his brain removed, he said it himself. I just…"

Killian's brow furrowed. "How can he be Sky's brother? Could they really remove over two hundred years of memories?"

I looked at Reaver, his face still hardened and creased in concentration.

"Everything Jade told us is true," he whispered.

Oddly he raised his hand and looked down at his palm. His eyes shot to Killian. "Remember?" He held his hand, palm up, towards Killian. "Elish told me he used some strains from Sky when they were creating me. He said specifically my hands, nose… some parts of me were taken from Sky as well as anything else that would make me Silas's perfect partner."

The boy's eyes widened. "And you and Perish's hands, the lines in your palms were identical."

It seems when an awkward silence descends, it brings a chill into a room, even if it was well heated. I felt that same chill sink into my bones, to the point where I outwardly shivered.

Then another flash of memory came to me. "Wait…" I paused and tried to gather the racing thoughts, hoping to snatch the right one. "Sky, he told me – he knows where Perish's O.L.S is, but before he could tell me I blacked out."

Reaver got up and took a step towards the bedroom Perish and I had been sleeping in, but paused when Killian made a nervous noise.

"Don't fucking coddle him, Killian." Reaver turned around and gave him a warning look. "He needs to give us some answers and I'm not going to stay here for months holding his hand until Elish returns. He obviously knows a lot more than he's letting on. Either he can tell me or I'll send the empath in there to do it."

Killian rose and crossed his arms, though that was as far as the little guy's defiance went. "I'm not coddling him; he requires different ways of getting information out of him and bashing the door in and wringing his neck isn't going to work!" Then he turned to me, I glanced up at him surprised. "Tell him. You know Perish."

I looked at the pair of blue eyes and then at the black ones and gave a dry laugh. "What so I'm the mediator now?"

Reaver seemed to bristle at the suggestion. I didn't understand why, but it became all too clear a moment later. "Reno used to be our mediator, or Greyson and Leo. We're running low on mediators." He looked behind him and I heard him take a weighted breath. "You have one shot, Killian; keep the door at least a bit open. No deep discussions, no heart-to-hearts, just ask him if he remembers where that O.L.S is."

Killian brightened like a bulb; he skipped up to Reaver and kissed his cheek. "Thanks for trusting me, baby."

I rolled my eyes but deep down it made me miss Elish. Though if I skipped up to my master and kissed his cheek he would probably think he'd shaken me one too many times. That being said, there were times when I was like that but it was rare, being around someone like Elish you learned to emulate him. Our soft-hearted moments were saved for the apartment when no one else but Luca was around, and of course… in the bedroom.

I got up, feeling a bit better since the opiates were singing to my aching head, and stood in the doorway beside Reaver. The dark chimera was tense; I could feel that even without my aura reading. I knew he was watching every movement of Killian, ready to jump in and save him from the unstable scientist hiding in the dark bedroom.

"He locked me in a fucking four-by-seven room, he molested Killian, attacked him… he kept us prisoner, and Killian still treats him like a kitten with a broken leg," Reaver growled under his breath. "So before you get on my case with that crazy fuck, sit and have a drink with me and I'll tell you just who that maniac is. He deserves me to go in there and beat him until he sings."

I didn't show it on my face but inside my mouth had dropped open. Perish was a person I had only seen passingly at my and Elish's shotgun wedding. Besides that, he was just the crazy chimera in the greywastes doing science stuff. I'd known about what had happened in Donnely, Elish had filled me in with what had gone wrong, but I didn't know the details.

I'd known he'd kept Reaver and Killian prisoner, but that was the extent of it.

The dark chimera was doing well then; if that was the history he had with Perish, I had to admire his restraint. That was one quality Silas did not have, and one that Elish had tried to instill in Reaver as he grew up. My master would be happy to hear this, hell *I* was happy to hear this.

I weighed my response as we both heard Killian's quiet and soothing voice inside my bedroom, when I spoke it was low enough that only my dear greywaster brother could hear.

"You can either force it in and deal with the screaming and the blood, or you can be patient and ease it in slowly and carefully. Both get the job done; only one will get you favourable results."

I kept my face serious as Reaver gave me a confused and somewhat pained look. "Are you comparing Perish to – you're a fucking weird one."

"Makes sense, doesn't it?"

Reaver shook his head but I could tell the words had gotten to him.

And with that, Killian appeared in the doorway, and the conversation between Reaver and myself was dropped.

"Perish remembered. He says it's in a place called Falkvalley."

Both Reaver's eyes and mine shot to the kid. "Falkvalley. Where the hell is that?" Reaver asked.

Killian looked at the ceiling as if that held all our answers, then he bit down on his cheek. "We're going to have to make a trip… to the surface."

"Oh?" Reaver raised an eyebrow. Killian nodded and we all walked back into the living room.

"Falkvalley… I think it's pre-Fallocaust. And I don't want to wait for Elish to get back to tell us where it is. Why don't we check out some areas, libraries or visitor's centers, and find out where it is? I know you're probably going to get claustrophobic here, love," Killian said.

A trip to the surface? I'd rather stay down here where the newly named 'kreigers' couldn't find us; I had grown used to being an inside pet. Usually when I went outside and into Skyfall I was leashed. But if we went during the daylight hours we should be alright, Kreig was empty and desolate before the sun set.

Reaver seemed to agree with Killian. "Alright, but only Perish is coming with me. Non-immortals stay in the lab."

The kid looked at Reaver stunned, and I knew a fight was going to break out.

"I am not staying in here, I'm going with you."

"No."

"Why not?"

Reaver rose from the couch. I thought he was going to the kitchen to grab a drink or something, but he just left the room. This must have been a common occurrence because Killian's face went red. I could see the angry energy radiating off of him.

"Reaver, for fuck sakes!" Killian called after him. "I am not your pet, you can't tell me to stay. I'm not the kid back in Aras; I can pull my own weight."

"Yeah, I know you're not him, but it doesn't matter… just drop it, alright?" Reaver was in Lycos's office. I could hear the echo.

But the kid was still not going to let it go. I nonchalantly followed him as he stalked out of the living room and down the hallway.

"I'm coming. We're partners, we're a team. I'm a greywaster,

Reaver."

There was silence; I could only see Reaver's arm as he turned on the computer tower in Lycos's office, before a flicker of blue light illuminated his face. He didn't answer back, he only waited for the computer to boot up.

I could understand Killian, and I knew where he was coming from. Elish was hard on me, but he was also extremely protective. Whereas once he used to let me go out and visit with Sanguine, or go for walks with Luca, after I was kidnapped and even more so after Lycos was taken, he literally kept me on a short leash. It had driven me crazy at times. I felt claustrophobic and worst of all… I felt like he didn't trust me to take care of myself.

In the darkness, with the smell of dust and old books around him, the dark chimera's black eyes reflected nothing but the welcome screen of the computer. A few feet away, Killian was holding onto the door frame looking at him, expecting an answer we both knew would never come.

"Babe… I know what you're feeling…"

Like Killian had just spat fire onto him, Reaver's black eyes quickly shot up from the screen and onto the boy's, making him cower in his spot.

"No, Killian, you don't fucking know what I'm feeling," he said coldly. "You really don't know anything. Why don't you leave the thinking to the person who does, and go make some tea."

Out of the mouths of socially inept chimeras.

Of course, Killian flipped out.

"Are you fucking serious!?" Killian shrieked. I took a step back, hiding my slender self into what I hoped was a blind spot.

"Make some fucking tea? I am a greywaster, Reaver. Without my help, Silas would've had you in Donnely and in Aras. Without me, you would've gotten killed by that scorprion!"

"And I would've come back!" Reaver shouted. He stood up and slammed his fist against the desk so hard I heard a snap from the wood underneath. "I would've come back! And you won't! I'm immortal, Killian, you're not. I already lost my dads and now you're throwing a hissy fit because I refuse to put you in needless danger? For what? To prove your worth? It's not worth it… just… get the hell out of the office.

I don't want to be around you."

"We live in a dangerous world, you can't prevent me from living life," Killian shot back. "Anyway, you're not my keeper. I can go if I want, and if you want to come with me – you may."

And with that he closed the door and walked past me, I saw his eyes brimming with unshed tears. He looked so sad and pathetic when Reaver hurt him, like seeing a puppy cower after you delivered him a kick in the ribs. It pulled on the remaining sympathies I had.

So I grabbed onto his arm and walked with him back to the living area. "You can't negotiate with immortals, Killian; they have different views on the world than us normal folk. In the scheme of things, does it really matter if you go or not? It's more important we find maps, you can prove yourself some other time."

The boy sighed. I was surprised at how quickly he gave up the argument, though whether that was a virtue or a curse I didn't know. Killian seemed to have a good head on his shoulders but he wanted to prove himself, which was a dangerous combination especially at times like this.

I felt badly for him though, I understood what he was feeling… and what made it worse was that Killian had almost been killed many times; Reaver had every right to be paranoid over him. Like it or not… one day Reaver was going to see him die, whether it be soon… or when he was an old man.

Now that was a heartbreaking thought. I would see him die too, and Reno, and all the other non-immortals, chimera or not. I was on the list to become immortal; Elish had made that decision for me over a year ago. Justifying it that it was time consuming keeping me alive, both for my knack of getting into trouble (or Silas's knack of trying to kill me), and my frail body that often succumb to sickness.

In truth, I knew it was because he loved me – he would never admit that though.

Killian and I let the chimeras do their own thing that night. I sat with the kid and put on some television then offered him drugs. Reaver stayed in Lycos's office, and Perish in my bedroom. The kid was good company and it wasn't hard to cheer him up, but the dark cloud seemed constantly over his head. That, and of course, the toxic thick cloud that constantly surrounded him.

His life had done a number on him but he was resilient, I had to give him that. Perhaps all that sludge that had poisoned his aura protected him from everything that had happened with him and his boyfriend.

Either way, there was no saving him now, he was fully in the jaws of the beast, we all were. All that mattered now was just how quickly they would close on us.

I could already feel them digging into my body.

CHAPTER 17

Reaver

"MY NAME IS DR. LYCOS DEKKER, CHIID 90034, YEAR 209 A.F, 09-23, the first video entry regarding Project Chimera X. All other entries beforehand are documented in Word and have been archived. As it stands now, we have received the fertilized eggs from Dr. Perish Dekker and Dr. Elish Dekker. These eggs are the exact genetic copies of our king Silas Dekker, with slight alterations to their outward appearance, and of course, the usual rounds of chimera enhancements."

He was so young; he looked more like a chimera in this video. Slender body, and a cute face that made him look like the twink he never was in the greywastes. There was no question why he caught Greyson's eye. Someone like that wandering into Aras could have a few things to look forward to: they'll immediately be claimed by someone, or they'll be passed around like a joint. Though since my blond father was a chimera, if someone did try to pass him around they would've ended up with half their skull missing.

Lycos the chimera… it was… harder than I thought it would be to see him as a chimera, he had always just been Leo. If there was any chimera in existence who bypassed my stereotypical view of them it would be my dear old dad. He probably had a majority of Garrett's DNA, since apparently he was Mr. Nice Guy.

My attention turned back to the screen as the camera started to turn.

"Shit... get away from the camera! Ah, whatever... this is Elish's documentations anyway. Alright, greywaster, say hello."

The camera panned over to my father, the very youthful Greyson Merrik, with a trimmed beard and a happy-go-lucky glint in his steely grey eyes. He laughed and gave the camera the middle finger. He was dressed in a weathered and stained brown jacket, with multiple layers of cloth underneath.

He looked… he looked like my dad.

"Hello! I fucking hate every single one of–"

"Greyson! Shut up! Oh my god... you're going to get me killed!"

So long ago, when there was still light behind their eyes… before their relationship became almost too difficult to handle under the addition of me.

They seemed happy… and perhaps I should have smiled. I should have felt a flicker of warmth in my heart to see them.

So why was my mood plummeting? Why were my emotions leaving me? I felt nothing.

Why did I feel nothing?

At that moment I decided to become a bigger masochist than I already knew I was; I clicked the file labelled *Baby X.*

"Say hi, Chimera X," young Leo's voice whispered. His voice was a higher octave and full of love. *"Say hi to the world."*

A small little baby inside of a watery tube came into focus. I was tucked up as small as I could be, my black eyes shining as I blinked sleepily at the camera. Man, was I ever small, just a little thing with a thin face and long, stick-like legs. I even had hair, just small tufts swaying back and forth in the water I was encased in.

I wonder if they wished they'd just given me to another family, or to Elish.

Leo's hand came into view, he gently tapped the glass, making me jump and look around. My eyes looked like little insect eyes; I could only see the whites when they jutted back and forth.

"Oh, I'm sorry, little man." I frowned as Leo's high pitch voice

sounded behind the camera. *"I see your hearing is good though."*

So happy right now, so content; they were bringing a baby into the world for their own selfish reasons. That poor little fucker in the tube had no idea what a shit show awaited him.

"He's... I can't believe it, but he's... he's alive. He's viable. The baby is seven months along now, so alert. I sleep beside him now, just to make sure he's okay. He barely ever sleeps. I can't believe it, just watches me come and go; his eyesight is impeccable. He's our little weapon; he'll really be able to do it. Can you believe it? You did it, Elish!"

Elish? Sure enough, a voice, like a cold river flowing through the darkest of nights, sounded out of view of the camera.

"Indeed... he is quite impressive, with his engineering he can survive at any time now, but I'd prefer you keep him inside the chamber until his due date. Mr. Merrik, have you started preparing your father for these new residents?"

"Ummm..." Greyson's young but still deep voice sounded. I saw just the corner of his arm as he crossed them. *"Stoen is still being difficult, but don't worry... we'll have two years to sort through that. I'll figure something out. I have too... this little weapon is too valuable to let my shit-faced father interfere."*

Little weapon? They kept calling me that. I suppose when it boiled down to it, that's exactly what it was. I was just a weapon to them, a tool to fight a battle I had never started. Maybe Leo had eventually formed some sort of attachment to me… but everyone else they only dealt with me because of what I could do.

The darkness inside of me was growing… and with every moment of that video, I felt it consume the sadness I'd had over the death of my dads. Where there had once been despair, longing, and guilt, there was only anger.

I was no one's slave; I was no one's weapon. The revenge I wanted was for Silas hurting Killian, betraying me, and killing my dads only because they were my dads and my family.

I was no saviour of the world.

I am the Reaper. I am not good.

Fuck both of them… they brought this on themselves, they started this. They brought Perish into Aras and they fucking brought Asher too. All I was doing was leading my fucking life but no, I had never been born free to them, I had been born with a thousand pound weight on my shoulders.

"Baby?"

I looked up from the computer monitor and saw my boyfriend peeking through the door… in my deep smoldering I hadn't even heard the latch click open.

I quickly turned the video off and clicked on a minimized aquarium game. I knew my boyfriend enough to know he would eventually come and get me.

"Can I watch too?"

My brow knitted together. I should've known my boyfriend enough to know he'd see right through that.

"No, I'm done."

Killian stopped at my tone. I was wondering if he was expecting me to start crying like some little bitch or something. "Let's go to bed."

The boy stayed in the doorway. "Do you… want to talk about why you're mad?"

I felt my hackles get raised. I turned off the computer and rose. "I'm not mad; don't do your psychology bullshit on me. Let's just go to bed."

He stayed in the doorway and didn't move when I made it clear I wanted to leave. "You were looking at their old videos… I-I miss them too… I just – can I see one?"

When he saw the look I gave him, he slunk back but still didn't move; he just stared at me with those huge starved kitten eyes. "I don't fucking miss them, and no… no, you can't. Now get out of my way."

The room went silent.

"How can you not miss them?"

I took this opportunity to grab Killian's shoulders and push him backward. He stumbled back before I stepped around him and made my way to the bedroom we had been sharing.

How could I not miss them? I did miss them but it didn't matter, that feeling was a small cup of water compared to an entire ocean. I felt so much for them besides just simply missing them. I hated them for the mistakes they made. I hated them for dragging an innocent baby into their plots. I hated them for bringing the chimeras here and putting my boyfriend in danger.

"Leave it alone, Killian," I said with a dangerous tone to my voice.

But the boy could never leave it alone, he had to talk about it, share his fucking feelings; try and eke out some more humanity out of me.

"But Reaver…"

"NO BUTS!" I whirled around. The kid took a step back but stayed inside the bedroom. "They're the reason why we're here. They're the reason why we had to run, why they're dead. Why would I miss them? I wasn't a son to them, I was a weapon, their *little weapon.* And once I couldn't do what Greyson wanted, he wanted to kick me out of town. I hated them. Fuck them, fuck Aras, fuck all of them, and you can shut the fuck up about it, Massey. Got it?"

His face fell but I had no sympathies for it. I had given him enough warning not to push me.

"Silas would have come anyway; he had your blood from Perish," Killian said quietly.

"Well, it was their fault for needing to hide me from the census," I snapped. "And their fault for making me have to be hidden anyway. I didn't ask for them to use me in Elish's fucking plot."

"It was either freedom in the greywastes, or slavery with Silas."

"I would've been his king, not his slave. He wanted me as a partner, not a cicaro, Killian." As the words left my lips I realized just how wrong it was to say that. I didn't mean it how it sounded… I meant it as… as…

Fuck, I didn't know.

But I did know how my boyfriend took it, because he took one horrified look at me and walked out of the bedroom.

Then the tears.

When I touched his shoulder, he shoved me away.

"Get the fuck away from me!" he shrieked, before rising to his feet and shoving my chest. "I'm so sorry Greyson and Leo stole you, so you couldn't have been with Silas right from the fucking start. I'm sorry they saved you from what HE would have made you into. You two were best friends right from the start, and obviously, it's a horrible thing now that you two are apart."

"Don't even say shit like that, Killian." My tone dropped. "All I am saying was they knew I was supposed to be his partner, not his cicaro or sengil. So don't make them out to be saints, I wouldn't have had a bad life."

"But you would have been just as bad as him. They saved you from yourself."

I snorted, and from that outward expression, I got a push in return. I was tempted to grab his hands to keep him from trying to start a physical fight, but I refrained.

"I am just as bad if not worse. Now I'm tired of fighting about this. You know how I feel about King Silas, and I'm still going to kill him, but only because of what he did to us. Not for some grand future plan. Just… I'm going to bed. If you want to be dramatic and sleep on the couch, go ahead." I turned around and walked back into our bedroom.

I got under the covers, and a few moments later, I felt the weight of the bed as he got in too.

When I heard his muffled crying, I took him into my arms and let out a breath.

"I miss them," he choked, before he turned around and started crying into my shirt. "And I miss Reno, and Biff. I miss Doc… I miss Aras."

"I know you do, Killibee." I rubbed his back. "I'll get you Aras back, just for you, I promise. We'll fill it full of stray cats and cicaros. Anything you want."

"Why didn't Lycos recognize him? Silas was in Donnely. Why didn't Leo know?"

I had asked myself the same question, and I responded with the conclusion that made me sleep at night. "I assume it was because he was covered in dirt and blood. He was dirty and caked in shit when you met him, right?"

I felt him nod.

"After that he was in West Aras and Leo was still giving Greyson the cold shoulder. I guess Asher just avoided him and Leo had too much on his mind." And, of course, the Ghost could remain hidden if he wanted. "It's pretty cool you killed him, right? My little murderer."

He kept crying, and I kept holding him.

"Don't let them take you. I know I keep saying it… but you're mine, no one else's."

"I know, Killi Cat. I won't."

"Promise?"

"I don't need to promise, it's a fact."

"Okay. I love you."

"I love you too."

I belted my M16's leather strap over my chest and hooked it into place, purposely going slow and purposely drawing out the fact I was going outside without my boyfriend. I even went as far as to ask Killian if there was anything he wanted me to pick up, cans of food, perhaps some textbooks; by the time I was ready to go out I could feel the heat on the back of my neck as he glared at me.

Jade, sticking to the shadows, refilled our cartridges and tucking them into his jacket.

Finally, savouring every moment, I glanced over at Killian clenching the couch, his face as straight as an arrow and his eyes glaring.

I then said nonchalantly, "Are you coming or what?"

The boy looked at me, probably to see if I was talking to Jade. When he saw me staring at him, trying my best to hide the grin, he said cautiously, "What do you mean?"

"Didn't you pitch a fit saying you wanted to come? Well, come on, grab some ammo. You'll be able to recognize maps more than I can anyway."

Killian's face brightened, before he scowled and pinched me in the arm. "Stop being such a jerk; you always torment me when you're bored."

"I torment everyone when I'm bored, so I'm going out to get unbored. Now grab your stuff and listen to everything I say." I glanced down at the deacdog, who was now sporting an old thick clothed jacket Killian had chopped and mended into a cargo carrier. We had loaded the dog up with ammo, knives, and some food. "Find radanimals. Alright, mutt?"

Deek looked at me with his stupid yellow eyes, but he was half deacon so I knew he understood me. One of the many vocal cues he was trained to respond to was 'radanimals'.

I slid the keycard through the door and let him out first.

The deacdog slipped through. I waited in the doorway for a few moments listening for any sound. With only Deekoi's panting echoing off of the walls, I motioned for the boys to follow me, taking my M16 out of its holder and clicking it to automatic. If there was one thing I had learned about the kreigers, is that for every one you saw, there were three you didn't.

Before the door closed behind them, I said under my breath, though loud enough for Killian to hear, "Guns out, no talking, no noise. Both of you are agile, use it."

They nodded, but something caught my attention. I looked down and saw that Jade was holding Elish's briefcase.

He noticed me looking at it and said quietly, "I won't leave it, not in this chimera den. Anything can happen. It's too valuable and it has all the files that were on the hard drives."

I would've rather he left it behind, but I understood his logic even though it was ridiculous. I didn't argue, only nodded before leading them down the dark cistern, Killian with his hand on Jade's shoulder to help aid him in the pitch darkness. Poor kid, a family full of night vision-enabled vampires and in darkness he was blind as a bat.

There was a joke in there somewhere.

Besides the smell of sour, damp wood and stale water, I didn't see any signs of the kreigers, besides their papery, white shit (which I realized was the stuff that had been covering the shelves at the stores me and Jade had stopped in), and the occasional bone from the scavenged remains of the dead ones we had shot. The place sounded cautiously tranquil, only the faded but reliable echoing drops of water could be heard.

The dog was sitting beside the ladder, and after leaning down and grabbing his collar, I managed to help him climb the ladder. As soon as he was outside, he was off to explore and mark every alluring building as his own.

The day was beautiful, though it could be pissing down acid rain and it would still be beautiful to me. It was funny to feel claustrophobic after the days I would spend in my basement, but this was different. I felt like a tiger in a cage down there, forced to stay hidden as the rats above me danced and played. After what had happened in Aras, and everything I had left behind, it was starting to wear down my last nerve to be kept in that cistern coffin. I wanted not only to be outside and free, I wanted to be useful.

With a deep inhale and the click of my M16 back into its holster, I started walking deeper into Kreig. Killian and Jade behind me and the dog running around ahead; his nose in the air and his legs barely touching the ground as he bounded around like a puppy.

Still the distrustful, empty calm that Donnely had, though there was more grass and it seemed the taller apartment buildings were closer together. We were right in the heart of these buildings, and from the old cities I had explored with Reno, I knew we were on the fringes of what could be called downtown.

Downtown meant there must be a map somewhere; this was a better bet than going to the areas behind the city in hopes to find a gas station. There had to be a corner store, a visitor's center, a hotel or something that would have a proper travel map in it.

The signs were all worn-out, dried and cracked like their paint was a skin that had been pulled too tight. The only ones readable were the plastic ones, and even those ones were mostly remnants of cracked plastic and loose electric wires. Some even face planted outside of their respective buildings, committing suicide without a single spectator.

In front of us was an intersection, with bent street and stop lights bowing towards each other, weak under the weight of age and uneven ground. We weaved through them and spotted an old bank with the windows wide open and yawning, and a video store that under old circumstances I would've been all over.

Instead we kept going straight ahead, to a road lit with the grey sun and trimmed with yellow grass, so thick it was even crawling up the trees.

I watched Killian like a hawk, every move he made had my attention; more automatic than on purpose, but I didn't trust the insides of these buildings. If there was one thing we all knew it was that somewhere deep inside those concrete caves were thousands of kreigers just waiting for the cold darkness of night. I wanted to wait until we had a good lead before we stepped foot inside any of those buildings.

We walked around for hours, and the few leads that we did have turned up nothing. Mostly corner stores and gas stations, I even got desperate and tried a library but the windows of the building, tall ones that stood the length of the walls had all been covered and welded shut. That was a last resort, I didn't want to make noise bombing a wing open.

The sun was still seen between the imposing buildings when I decided it was time for us to slowly make our way back. My mouth moved to announce it when Killian pointed towards a small building, sitting in the middle of a large parking lot full of buses. A can of fruit cocktail he had been sharing with Jade was in his hand. "Those are Greyhound buses; they might have a map in there to show people the routes they travel. We've seen more than a few buses on the highway when we were going to Donnely."

I didn't like the openness of the area, but then again, if the lizards started to come out I'd be able to see them a mile off.

So I whistled for the dog, which to my amusement made Jade look around confused for a moment before he realized what I was doing. By now I had perfected Perish's little whistle trick, I'd teach the kid how to do it later.

"Alright, the dog is a good enough sentry. Both of you are coming inside with me, guns out, flashlights on," I said in a tone I used to use with my old sentries.

There was a series of shuffling and metal against plastic before the boys got out the guns. I closed the distance between the fallen down chain-link fence and the parking lot, and leaned up against one of the buses to listen and smell.

The stale smell of the kreigers was old and the air tasted fine. With that on my mind, we walked up to the building.

It was a single-storey building, completely detached from the close-knit city that surrounded it. It had windows smashed open, or half-boarded-up with plyboard that had warped and bloated. The building wasn't in the best condition, but the roof had held its ground and that meant the papers below should be in readable condition.

Or so I hoped.

I put up my hand to stop the two from following me and kicked off the rest of the glass with my boot. Because my night vision wouldn't work when I was still in daylight, even if where I was looking was dark, I stepped inside and blocked as much of the window I could with my body.

Beyond the window I was perched on I could see almost perfectly preserved linoleum and the ghostly outline of several kiosks, racks of dusty papers, and a row of glass doors past that. They looked like they led to a partially-covered garage where I assumed most of the buses were.

After my ears revealed no imminent threats to me, I jumped down with a crunch of boots against brittle linoleum tile and started walking around the cold, dark area. My nose teased my brain with the stale and musty smells of home; that unmistakable aroma of over two hundred years of decay.

I first wiped off the layer of grime to have a better view outside. Through the windows I could see into a loading area, and to my unease a set of concrete stairs leading down. I didn't have the luxury to explore those places for kreigers though, so I quickly mapped out the building in my head, mentally jumping from open door to open door to make sure there was no place for the lizard men to hide.

When my mind deemed it safe, I clicked my tongue for the boys to come through the window. Killian remembered his cue and went through first, followed by the pet.

"We'll each take one of the racks, put the useless ones in a pile." I motioned to the two bigger racks and pushed them into the middle of the open room.

Jade took a row of pamphlets before tossing them to the floor. "We're near, or in, the Okanagan, that I know. So look for anything touristy, bus schedules… stuff like that."

I rubbed the rough and compacted dirt off of a magazine cover but it had become one with the paper years ago. Instead I opened it up and glanced at the still coloured pictures. Seeing brown hills and orchards full of fruit, boats with crystal clear lakes behind them and more brown and green mountains.

"Look… imagine that green outside. And the trees have white bark, some of them anyway." Like my habit of showing Killian bright colours, I pointed to the hills. Before switching over to a page I'd saved with my thumb, of a bunch of kids enjoying a water park. "And that. Hey, Jade, does Skyfall have a water park?"

The pet glanced over at the magazine and chuckled. "No, it's nothing like the magazines, but Skyland does have green parks and rivers, so does Eros. We have flowers too."

Flowers? I had only seen flowers in Perish's lab, besides maybe dandelions. It was a strange concept knowing they still existed, not to mention ones that grew out in public. If we had ever had that in Aras, they would've been picked and probably eaten by Reno or Miller.

Like the king had thrown away the green and blues of our now grey world, I closed the magazine and tossed it onto the garbage pile, and with that gesture, the three of us continued to look for a map.

It was tedious and messy work. As the sounds of fluttering paper continued to fill the hall, I found myself growing more frustrated. Every tossed pamphlet, magazine, and flyer seemed to taunt me. How can this city, once holding thousands of people, not have a single damn map of the area?

"I found a city map…" Jade sighed and held up what looked like a transit schedule; it unfolded in front of him, browned on the edges and wrinkled. I could see a small map with coloured lines going in all directions.

"Alright, I'm done with this… city maps aren't going to get us anywhere." I tossed the last pamphlet onto the heaping pile, and as I had done every several minutes, I watched the light beaming through the window. "Let's go back; we'll try another place tomorrow."

With the dog ever obedient, we made our way back to the manhole cover. Jade obsessively wiping the dust off of his hands and arms, and Killian with his nose in a stack of magazines he had put aside for himself. My eyes were on the open windows of the structures around us, hyper alert to pick up any movements and smells that would signal that the kreigers were waking up for their nocturnal search for food.

In the dark the city was theirs, but once daylight came it belonged to another type of darkness: me.

Suddenly though, my nose picked up something; it was faint but it was here… and out of place.

I stopped and said under my breath to Jade, "Do you smell that?"

It was loud enough for Killian to pick up; he lowered the magazine and smelled the air.

His face paled, and in the same moment, Jade's did as well.

"That's cologne…" Before the last syllable left the cicaro's lips, we all quietly sprinted to the side of a building, all of our eyes picking apart every inch of the area.

Immediately I grabbed the dog's collar and told him to stay put. His nostrils flexed but he didn't growl, the scent seemed to confuse him, and it did me as well.

"Could it be Perish?" Killian whispered.

Jade shook his head, and as I tuned my hearing away from the desolate city around us, I realized his heart was racing inside of his chest.

"No, only a chimera would be wearing cologne and only cocky ones at that. I recognize the smell, but I can't put my finger on who it is. We… Reaver, we can't go back to the cistern until we know they're gone. If it's King Silas, he'll have a keycard."

"Either way, I need to check it out." I nodded, feeling a liquid jolt of energy inflame my veins. I wanted to run and find the source, but I had two anchors on me right now that I had to keep safe.

Jade couldn't be seen with us, there was just no getting around that. Jade was supposed to be in the greyrifts apartment pretending to be injured; if one of the chimeras saw him it would be traced back to Elish.

And I couldn't leave them to find a place to hide. No way I trusted the boys to do that. There was only one place I could think of, one place where I might be able to stash them and the dog. Then I could quickly zip underground and grab Perish. I wasn't leaving Perish to the fate of whatever Silas had in store for him. Even if he acted like he was on our side, I didn't trust him to stay strong through Silas's coaxing. He loved his master, any praise from Silas and he would be jelly in his palm.

"I'm taking you two to that library we found welded shut. Find a way to get it open, then find a room you two can hide in. Don't go anywhere else, alright?"

Jade looked down at the map. "I can get me and Killian there. Fuck, I want to go with you…"

"No, I'm taking you there myself just so I know for sure you made it. While you're in there look for some atlases, you might as well. Killian, if anything goes wrong toss one of those grenades to alert me, alright?"

The boy put on a brave face, but when I leaned down to kiss his cheek goodbye I saw his lower lip disappear inside his mouth. "Don't let them take you… just promise me that."

At least the kid knew we had to make sure they didn't find Perish. Our mission was counting on what we could dig up in Perish's brain. Elish's laptop holding the downloaded information was good, but with what the cicaro had been able to uncover in Perish's mind, Perish was invaluable.

My heartbeat rose with anxiety over having to leave the boys. I didn't like being in this situation. I didn't just have one kid to protect, I had my boyfriend and Elish Dekker's little husband. At least Jade, from the stories he had told me, was more than capable of taking care of himself, and Killian had come a long way. But still, I didn't trust them on their own, there was too much that could go wrong.

But one hundred percent safety was a luxury we didn't have, something we *never* had. With our sneakers barely touching the cracked pavement and even the dog with his head lowered, we crossed the street and ducked behind a tipped over mini-van.

Jade checked the map and pointed to the left, we continued on.

Another noise came, this one made my teeth grind.

It was the confirmation I needed that the smell was no random occurrence, nothing that could be justified by some outlandish excuse like we were near a perfume shop. It was a plane, louder than the Falconer, that carried a low rumbling sound on it that bounced off of the tall buildings.

To my confusion, Jade's heartbeat shifted.

"That's a military plane," Jade explained when I made eye contact with him. "This could be normal patrol, but I won't bet my life on it. Just put that in the back of your mind, Reav. All military planes are marked with the Legion's cougar emblem."

I could steal that fucking plane… I might not know how to drive it but Perish and the pet could. No doubt military planes were hooked with tracking devices though; we would practically be gift wrapping ourselves for Silas.

Time went quickly as soon as we started moving again. I was impressed at Jade's stealth; the way he could land his boots without a sound rivalled mine. He had his attributes that's for sure, perhaps that's where he got his middle name: Shadow.

The library came back into view. A large building that before the Fallocaust had floor to ceiling windows and an umbrella-like roof. Now the windows were large sheets of metal and the roof its own death sentence. It was surrounded by flat ground at least, and trees big enough that they could climb and reach the roof if needed be. It wasn't perfect, but it was all we had.

We ran past what had once been a metal sculpture and ducked behind it. When my hearing picked up nothing but heartbeats, we closed the rest of the distance and started checking out the welded sheets of metal.

"Give me ten minutes I can have us in there." Jade stuck his fingers in between a sheet and the brick and pulled. Sure enough, with a shifting of material he was able to pry the weld apart.

That's all I needed. Though imposing and fortress-like from the street, it had its flaws on closer inspection. Welded or not, the sparse rains we did get had weakened the hold, and because the kreigers were too stupid to even realize this was a building, it had remained free of their presence.

With a quick check to make sure the boys had enough ammo, food, and knives, we quietly parted ways. Killian licking his lips out of nervousness and Jade adopting a look of calm control I had seen on myself on many occasions. This kid might've been a serial killer in Moros, literally armed to the teeth, but the greywastes were a different story; at least that's where Killian could fill in. With both of their brains at work, they would be able to survive; this wouldn't take long anyway.

But just in case… they had food and weapons. No matter what happened to me, they would be okay.

There was no justifying the looming cloud over my head though, the cloud that made me trust no one but myself with the people I liked and loved's safety. Even if I was trusting them with their own safety, no matter how much I tried I couldn't put faith in them being able to hide in the library without harm coming to them. I wanted to be there.

But what choice did I have? There was no choice, just the lesser of two evils.

My feet automatically took me towards the sound of the plane. My heartbeat background music to my straining ears as I struggled to hear any sound telling me I wasn't alone. The engine had cut out though, so I headed towards where we had walked past some parks. That park and a hospital parking lot were my best bet as to where they'd touched down.

Tension was in the air around me, however my greywaster blood was enjoying the feeling of some fire in my veins, bringing me back to my many excursions in the greywastes, most vivid in my mind when I had rescued Killian from the factory.

Apprehension and adrenaline went hand in hand during that time too. It seemed they were both devils sitting on my shoulders, trying to convince my chimera-wired brain to feel one more than the other. Needless to say though, their whispers didn't fall on deaf ears, I was able to push past the emotions and focus on the mission at hand.

And the first thing I needed to do was find out who I was dealing with.

Then I smelled one of my targets; the one with the cologne. I followed my nose and ran from alleyway to alleyway, car to car, until I spotted him.

He was dressed in a legion outfit, but he wasn't a grunt… his armour was black and grey, and he was wearing a blue cape with the cougar-scorprion-chimera-thing on it. At this point I froze and listened, not even daring more than a shallow breath.

That was a chimera.

He was walking with his assault rifle in his hand, a dangerous-looking one with a scope as good as mine. The man had a swagger to him I didn't trust, even with no one watching he was walking with confidence.

His black hair was slightly curly, that I could see… and his hands looked young, possible a teenager or in his early twenties.

I thought for a minute, eliminating all of the chimeras' photos I had seen from Elish's files. He had made me memorize every single one of them, and their abilities, while we were in the greyrifts, even going as far as to quiz me at random moments.

Though I didn't need a photo for this one, I realized I had seen him in Aras. I had seen his metallic eyes, like liquid mercury.

Caligula.

A chimera that technically belonged to the same generation as Jade and me. He was the adopted chimera son of Kessler and his non-chimera husband Tiberius.

Advanced hearing and sight, tough as nails, military trained though he had grown up in what chimera terms would deem a 'normal family'. Kessler had a soft spot for his family it seemed.

Which made the kid a viable option for kidnapping if it came to it. Caligula was mortal. I had already learned the hard way that Silas didn't negotiate with kidnappers, but Kessler might and he controlled the Legion.

"Dad?"

I jumped through an open door and slunk into the darkness, knowing he would be blind to the inside of these buildings unless he was staring right at me. I observed Caligula hitching his assault rifle behind his back. He then bent over, and to my grim surprise, he grabbed one of the sewer covers and scraped it off of the hole in the side of the street.

Then Kessler came out, thick-necked, burly body, with a buzz cut and an expression that permanently looked like he had thorns in his heels.

The Imperial Commander rose to his feet before grabbing a water bottle from his kid. "Nothing down there but rat shit. I really don't give a fuck what that king says, the entire lab is burnt, no one could be hiding in it."

So they were looking for the entrance to the lab? Perish had known where it was but it looked like no one else did.

"We'll keep looking, then we can tell Silas for sure that Reaver and Perish aren't there. It was probably just a random energy pulse or a shortage in the monitoring system. We had that once in Shockrock and it ended up being rats chewing the wires," Caligula said.

They had monitors to alert the Legion when electricity was turned on? I didn't even consider that.

"You're right, we'll keep looking. I have Gale and Willis on the east end and Tick looking around the old hospital," Kessler said with a soured look on his face. "Once it gets dark we'll break out the torch lamps. I think Perish once said the paint they used was reflective, but I'm still guessing they replaced the cover."

Well, that was the only information I needed. Leaving them to their back and forths, I started to sprint in the other direction, towards the cistern and hopefully to where Perish was sitting unaware.

Mentally my mind was playing an internal video game, mapping out the time I had until sunset and the important things we had to grab before we left to get Killian and Jade. Perish had no personal items anymore, and Jade kept his stuff neurotically folded and packed, awaiting quick exits like this. Killian's stuff was mixed with mine in our bedroom but that was just clothing and his guitar. The ammo bag was packed, as was our knapsacks of tact and water.

The smell of cologne dissipated the further I got from Caligula. No other legion members seemed to be around, but that didn't make me any less careful.

With nimble fingers and way too much noise than I was comfortable with, I slid down the manhole cover, and to my inner genius, I put it on upside down to hide the Skytech emblem on it. Sure Kessler was aware that we might have done that, but it still would make it less obvious.

I slid the card through the lab's door and ran in, but I immediately tripped over our bags. When I looked up Perish was just lowering the gun he had pointed at me.

"You have cameras up there too, I guess?" I asked hurriedly. I checked inside me and Killian's room but he had cleared it out. "Did you grab the hard drives?"

Perish put on our ammo bag and picked up several new bags he had packed. He nodded and motioned me over, his eyes shifting back and forth and his movements more jerky than ever. "I got everything. We have to go. Where's Killian and the pet?"

"I hid them in a welded shut library. We have to get them and get the fuck out of this town, it's going to be dark soon." Without a second glance, the metal door with the small green light closed behind us. I followed Perish into the cistern, and to my surprise, he led us in the opposite direction.

"What about Elish? We're supposed to wait for him..." Perish said apprehensively. He was moving fast, going from one direction to another in a way that made me believe he knew where we were going. I wanted to go out where we came, but I guessed this location would bring us closer to the library.

"We have two options right now: We meet Elish in Skyfall because Silas caught us, or Elish finds our chewed up bodies when he comes back with Reno. We have to get the boys to safety, once we're out of the city we can find out what the fuck we're supposed–"

I almost hit the back of Perish when he stopped dead in his tracks. I paused as well and listened.

Fuck, I knew that noise…

"Perish… where the hell are you leading us?" I hissed. I squinted my eyes but the sewer stretched out into darkness. Since my night vision was unable to make shapes out of nothing, it just seemed like a wide open black hole.

"I… well, this was a shortcut to the road the library was on… but um… I think this is a nest now. Let's turn around, okay?" Perish stumbled, his feet quickly stepping backwards.

But I didn't turn around; I got out my gun and continued forward. If it was a nest we could rain a few clips into them, or just cut the bullshit and pull a grenade.

With Perish grabbing at my jacket and making noises like a nervous mouse, I continued ahead.

I thought at first I had entered a large room covered in white mould. It was wide open, full of pipes as thick as truck tires and cisterns broken and leaking mucky water.

The echoing was what Perish heard and I could hear it too, like crickets chirping. A sound so low it itched your ears, and at the same time, automatically put you on edge.

White mould and… giant maggots? Curious more than I was wary, I stepped into the vast room, the crickets and the dripping water creating the oddest of melodies. My inquisitive nature brought me to one of the piles of maggots and I nudged it with my foot.

Some of this white was fungus… but there was a lighter shade of white with a strange texture…

What was it?

I put some pressure on my boot. It felt like I was hitting a water-filled sack. I pressed my boot against it harder until it burst.

My eyes widened. A kreiger fetus, or lizardling, whatever the fuck it was, twisted around in its broken womb, squinting its shiny black eyes before it gave a shudder and died.

Because I was, of course, still a huge asshole, I stepped on the rest of the eggs, spilling their writhing contents onto the dirty concrete floor.

I chuckled as I stepped on one's head, it made an amusing popping noise. I started gleefully stepping on more.

Though my fun was short-lived as I knew it would be. I started to hear the sandpaper sounds around me, and as I scanned the broken cylinders and the grate catwalks around us, I started to see them.

My eyes found Perish, clutching his rifle in his hands and looking up at the crawling kreigers with a blanched expression on his face. I walked over and nudged his shoulder to snap him out of his state. "Let's get the fuck out of here. Come on."

Perish didn't move, he was still staring up at the lizards, and like I had previously deduced, where I saw one I was quickly seeing three or four. They were all flashing reflective eyes at us, and serrated teeth that matched the colours of the egg pods and fungus that were tucked into every corner and crevice.

The kreigers were still slow, but fucking dangerous in numbers. And even if we would come back, it would be painful to be eaten alive, and the boys were waiting for us.

"No, they're behind us now. We were too slow." Perish glanced behind him before finally he started to move, though it was deeper into the cylinder room not back. "Follow me, don't ask dumb questions or smash the babies, just follow me, and try to cover me. Use silencer, mine doesn't have a silencer and it'll be heard by Caligula, Kessler, and their legionaries. Okay, Reaver?"

I nodded, and covered his ass as he started to hop over the rusted pipes, leaving streaks of red from the patina on his grey hoody and pants. I turned around and shot a kreiger slithering over the railing to my left, before I followed him on top of the pipe.

He was walking the length of the pipe which stretched across the large, high ceiling room before jutting up, joining three pipes on either side doing the same. I was amazed the pipes were even holding our weight. Everywhere I looked was covered in thick corrosive rust, even dripping down the smaller pipes and the rungs of the catwalk like miniature icicles. It was so broken up and fragile-looking I knew if I so much as waved a hand over the rough cancer it would flake off in my fingers.

But it held our weight and I literally had to run with that. With my hands outstretched and my back constantly being watched, I practically tiptoed along the thick pipe, only sparing a few moments to pick off the kreigers coming to close to me.

And they were rapidly approaching, and with them came their stale smell, accentuated more by not only their numbers, but the claustrophobic aura of this room. It was choking the air around me, making me feel like I was breathing in their own recycled breath; my lungs protested for fresh air.

Perish suddenly swore and took a step back as a kreiger landed on the pipe, and with him several more spilled over. Some hitting the pipe with a satisfying clang, before toppling down fifteen feet onto the sewer floor, a tangle of flailing twisted limbs and black blood; others though, hung on with their deformed fingers, clawing through eaten holes in the pipe and gaining a good enough hold to hiss and snap at us.

I aimed my gun and Perish stayed still. I picked them off with a spray of bullets; the colour of their blood and brains matching, almost perfectly, the corrosion they fell upon. Their heads seemed as frail as egg shells; it never took more than one hit to have their brains start to come out of their bald heads.

"Watch their blood. Don't slip," I called to Perish, looking up and watching the metal catwalk to make sure I didn't get ambushed; I wouldn't let that happen again.

I swore as I suddenly felt my boot go through a thin part of the pipe. I raised my arm to balance myself, and as I regained my footing, I looked down below us.

White, it was as white as if there was snow on the ground, though this snow was churning and hissing at us. No wonder Perish had led us to these fucking pipes, there were hundreds down there. Such a thick stew of writhing bodies, I couldn't tell where one ended and one began.

It was just like the rat pit in the Slaught House, except those ones were black. I wouldn't want to fall down there either; they would eat you like a raver, slowly and painfully. I wouldn't regenerate for fucking half of a year.

I heard the sound of metal against rust. I broke my gaze from the almost hypnotic churning of the kreigers, and saw Perish start to climb up the pipe, sticking his boots into the raised rivets and pulling himself up with ease. I followed him, watching below me a kreiger attempt to climb the walls to get us, but even with their deformed frog-like hands the walls were too wet.

At the top of the pipes were a set of stairs, but as soon as I stood up, I saw two kreigers hugging a narrow ridge that stretched the length of the adjacent walls. Standing almost erect like a human, they pressed their flat bodies against the brick, making their prominent spines jut out, permanently twisted and ridged like a frog's.

They fell, one after another. I lowered my gun to try and get my bearings; Perish already checking the top of the stairs. He gave me the all clear and I followed him.

"How much longer?" Another glance behind my shoulder. I could see the grey masses begin to navigate the pipes we were just on, hoping over each other like leapfrogs, the leader constantly getting replaced by the next one.

"Not long."

His tone caught my attention, and I hated the timing of it. He was using the same calm and sane tone he had used with me the first time we had been out chasing kreigers. But before I could think of calling him on it, he picked up the bag he'd been carrying and started walking down what appeared to be a concrete hallway.

"Don't shoot, as quiet as you can; we're underneath the reservoir now." Perish sprinted ahead and I took his flank, wanting nothing more than to keep shooting these abominations as they waddled and swayed closer to us, their mouths open and closing with a continuous thrum of hissing and snapping. The songs of the sewers, I wouldn't miss this soundtrack.

The hallway was dry, with many metal doors on each side. There was also spray-painted signs I didn't understand, and broken emergency lights dead and forgotten. None of this mattered to me, I needed to be out in the greywastes, not trapped inside these catacombs.

"Not this way, not this way…" Perish suddenly turned around. He grabbed my jacket and pulled me backwards.

The reason for this quick change in plans was apparent. Behind Perish I saw a kreiger leap through an open door, landing on the ground on all fours. He eyed us with a snarling hiss. Not a second later, another one emerged, and another one, until, like the ones on the pipes, they were all climbing over top of each other.

"Well, fucking where!" I snapped, too full of adrenaline to realize that we were getting trapped and quickly. I started opening doors but every one of them just led to a room, and I didn't trust the strength of the door to hold off an attack if they had the smarts to try and bash their way through.

Perish kept his hand on my jacket; he swore under his breath before taking a second hallway, halfway back to the pipe room we had just been in.

"Look, you need to tell me what we're doing or I'm going to just shoot them until they make their own path, Perish," I said angrily. Not only did I hate not having complete control of this situation, I hated that I was even *in* this fucking situation.

"That would be incredibly stupid, brother," Perish said calmly, but in his eyes I saw the fear he wasn't allowing to show on his face. His pale eyes looked behind him, and I knew he was seeing more. Every time I looked back there were more.

The sandpaper sounds had turned from a quiet scratching to the equivalent of a motor engine turned on inside a vacant garage, their screams the unoiled belt. I started looking up at the wire-strung ceiling hoping I would see a manhole cover, but it was concrete and brick, nothing else.

"Oh, there we go…" Perish let out a loud sigh. My head snapped towards him and I saw our saviour, a ladder leading up to a cover, and not only that, a rusted metal door.

We sprinted towards it, away from the stale stench and damp, rusted underground, and into the fresh irradiated air.

Perish wasted no time. He threw the bag down and climbed up, sliding the cover off before peeking a look at the outside world.

"It smells like it's getting dark; let's get the fuck out of there." Perish climbed up and disappeared into the city, the large reservoir to his left. I tried to close the door but to my inner frustration it didn't latch.

No time to bitch about it, within several seconds I was outside with him, shutting the cover and running through the gravely ground to where the road was. It wasn't until we found an alleyway that we took a moment to catch our breath.

A short-lived rest, it was going to be dark soon.

My chest gave a nervous start, creating a small ball of anxious electricity I tried to shove into the void. Suddenly Kessler and the Legion were a small blemish on my main goal right now, which was get the boys and get the fuck out. I had heard the General saying they were staying until after dark; I could only hope the kreigers got distracted eating them and left the four of us alone.

And with that, we started sprinting back towards the library.

CHAPTER 18

Reaver

WE HAD TO CREEP PAST THREE LEGIONARIES ON OUR way to the library, but they were blocks away and heading further from our destination. All three of them were walking dead, the plane was a mile into the city and I knew three legion-trained idiots wouldn't be able to fend off the invasion.

And they were coming… the air was already changing. I had to admit with a boulder blocking my throat that we wouldn't be able to get out of the library before they started to swarm. From what I remembered, it was about an hour'ish before sunset when the first kreiger had been spotted and I didn't want to delude myself into believing we could make it out of the city.

And even if we did make it out of the city, there wasn't some invisible barrier that prevented them from pursuing us into the greywastes. They were not smart creatures; even if they died under the daylight they would follow food.

Tonight we would be spending the night in the library. I had already concluded that.

At least, if we were lucky, we might have a front row view of some legionary getting killed. That might be fun.

To Jade's credit, the metal slab he'd unwedged from the brick didn't seem tampered with from the view from the sidewalk. I managed to hold it open for Perish before slipping in myself.

"Killi?" I said in a hushed voice, taking in the overwhelming sight of shelves upon shelves of dusty books. Further on, I saw many tables and chairs, stacked up to make some sort of half-hearted barricade.

Both of us walked between the bookshelves, our boots crunching against loose paper and shards of plastic from the broken light covers above us. Every area was completely covered in debris, from books to garbage, wall plaster and wires. This place was a pit.

I noticed as we walked past the dusty wooden shelves, that there were prints on some of the books. It looked like the boys had been here. Though I would've preferred they stay put, I *had* told them to find atlases.

Perish coughed behind me and reached a hand up to wipe a sign that had been stuck to one of the shelves. "Oh, Psychology… that's why Killian was here, he took some books. Let's find maps, where maps are they'll be." He was back to being normal Perish, his switches seemed to disappear as quickly as they came.

"I'll keep wiping down signs," Perish suggested. We walked into the next room, almost the same as the first but the tables and chairs seemed to be, for the most part anyway, untouched, just stacks of dust-covered books and material from the ceiling.

I gave him a quiet nod and looked to the floor for any tracks. I wasn't a bounty hunter though but I could see some shifting of debris. I was more focused on finding missing books, that screamed 'Killian was here' more than a footprint ever could.

"Killi?" I whispered again, and paused to listen, my ears picking up Perish wiping one of the signs.

"We're over here." My chest gave a cold shudder, relief flooding me from my head to my toes. I walked towards the voice, weaving inbetween tight isles of books until I came across a small barricade they had set up. Four tall bookshelves placed into a diamond, both of the boys inside with the laptop turned on.

As soon as Killian saw me he leapt into my arms. "Are you okay?" I didn't have time to answer though; he spotted Perish and I felt his chest rise and fall with relief. "Perry, did anyone see you? Are you okay?"

"I'm fine, no one saw us. We need to go… we need to go now, pack up the laptop," Perish said hurriedly, wringing his hands and almost jumping up and down in one spot.

I shook my head. "No we have to stay here tonight; I bet the kreigers are already coming out. We're moving to the roof and staying there until morning. Too many kreigers, and I spotted Caligula and Kessler checking manhole covers. Rest assured by the morning they would've fucked off."

"Clig?" Jade looked up at me, his eyes widened. He snapped the laptop closed and put it in the laptop bag with the remote phone. "His boyfriend got captured along with Reno. What the fuck is he doing here?"

They looked to me to lead them to the roof, but in truth, I had no idea how to do that, so I looked up and started trying to spot weaknesses in the ceiling.

"Unbeknownst to me, and apparently you, a signal was sent when we turned on the electricity. Caligula suggested it was a short, but Kessler wants to check the sewers to see if the apartment was intact or something. Either way, we're out of there."

I sprinted towards a missing chunk of ceiling and started to climb up the bookshelves; Jade took my lead and found another weak area.

"I had no idea; neither did Elish or he would've warned us." Jade stood up on the bookshelf and poked his head through the loose ceiling. The ceiling tiles were one of those push up ones, though at least the rungs they were resting on looked solid. "If they can't convince themselves it was a shorted signal, the kreigers will convince them to leave. Which reminds me…" Jade poked his head down and nodded towards his laptop bag. "We found an atlas of British Columbia. I'll show you when we get settled in."

At least we had that going for us, I slammed my fist up against the ceiling and hissed when it smacked up against something solid. "The awning overhang will make it impossible to get there from the exterior, I'd rather we put lookouts at the unstuck welding and camp in here." I sighed, not wanting to stay in a place I hadn't explored or mapped out exits, but I suppose I would have time to kill during the night.

I jumped down and so did Jade, hearing the floor crack and protest under our weight. "We'll stay here tonight. Unpack some guns, Perish, and watch the exit. Killian, get some food out and some beds. Jade, start looking for Falkland on that atlas. I'm going to scout this place out."

All three of them nodded and went off in their different directions. I was about to leave when I noticed Perish pushing the flap of metal open and looking outside.

"They're starting to come out the windows," Perish said, before, as quiet as he could, he let the metal cover retract back into place. "Take the dog with you; he really does not like those creatures. I'd rather him not near the opening. The kreigers have bad smell but very good hearing."

I clicked the dog over, who had been sniffing the covered windows with long drawn-out huffs, when he heard me he walked over with his tail wagging back and forth. "Good idea, keep an eye on the kids. I want to find at least two places we can take cover in if something goes wrong. Tell me right away if you see any of the Legion, especially a chimera."

I left Perish in charge of the door and walked into the darkness.

I spotted a flight of stairs and took them down to what seemed like a book depository, there were cardboard boxes, rat-chewed and roach-chewed, stacked one on top of each other and tables flipped over in the same barricade fashion we had seen upstairs. It was a large room, with a hallway leading to several others off to the left. No ceiling at all in this one, just hanging insulation and wires that hung down like rubber vines. It was that crappy push up ceiling that a lot of these government buildings had. As soon as one radrat ran across it, it usually collapsed and spilled its innards onto the floor below.

I wandered around, poking some of the bigger debris piles with the tip of my gun, hearing the dog occasionally sneeze whenever he tried to dig something out. The dust down here was incredibly thick, but that only meant the lizard men hadn't been down here.

Wandering from room to room, I found several places I could stick the boys if they needed emergency shelter, but nothing solid just bathrooms with locks. The dog ended up luckier than I did though and found himself a radrat. He gave me a start at first as I heard the squeal of him snapping its spine but when he came out proudly holding it in his jaws he earned a pet. I let him eat it in peace and let him carry the head up to the first floor so he had something to chew on.

The boys were dishing out cans of fruit cocktail and had opened small cans of Good Boy for us to eat; Elish's laptop was switched off but for some odd reason the phone was plugged into it.

I looked past them and saw Perish by the door. He had wedged open the flap of metal enough for him to look out of it, his assault rifle held securely in front.

When Killian saw me his face brightened, something that always made me feel good, I didn't even think he realized he did it.

"We found Falkland!" he declared with a smile. But as his eyes shifted to Perish, the smile faded, and was replaced with a nervous purse of his lips. "It's about a hundred miles, give or take, from here, northeast." He dropped his voice. "Perish… isn't happy. I don't think he wants to remember."

Jade's expression told the real story though. "He almost tore the page right out of the book." His yellow eyes flashed in annoyance. "And warned me that if I fucked with his head again he'd kill me himself. He really thinks he can fucking win a–"

I rolled my eyes and held up a hand. "We have more important shit to worry about then brotherly squabbles."

"It's not a squabble…" Perish spoke up, not even turning away from the small opening to outside. "They are my memories that I do not wish to share. No one asked my permission to go and get that brain piece. No one asked me if it was alright for Jade to start doing his empath thing on me."

I tried to hold back to snort but I couldn't. Even though I was just contemplating our improved relationship, I felt the words roll off of my tongue before I could stop them. "Maybe it's time for you to atone for all the horrible shit you did in this world, Perish. Do something to improve it rather than fucking it up with King Silas."

Perish glared at me, before turning back out the window. "Maybe I don't want to know what horrible shit I've done, Reaver?"

"Maybe this is a lot bigger than just what you want? Suck it up. Running from the inevitable won't help anything."

"Reaver!" Killian the rescuer hissed at me. He reached up and grabbed onto my jacket sleeve. "You're not helping, sit down and eat."

When Perish let out a scoff I felt my insides prick with annoyance. "Running from the inevitable won't help anything will it? Then call Silas to come and get you right now, Reaver *Dekker*, because if you think Elish's stupid plan will work, you're an idiot."

What happened next was rather funny. Killian leapt up and grabbed me, even though besides feeling like bashing his face in, I had swallowed his words without need for retaliation. I had never expected him to be completely invested in Elish's plan, the only reason I believed he was still with us was to be close to Killian.

As if to show just how off the mark Killian was with who he had to hold back, as he wrapped his arms around mine Jade jumped to his feet and stalked towards Perish. His arms open in the typical fighting stance of the slumrat Morosian.

"Say that again, retard?" Jade said loudly, arms open and back stiff.

Perish glanced up at him with minimal interest and said casually, "I'm saying Elish is an imperious, ego-maniac who has no idea what he's up–"

Killian let go of me, and as Jade raised his fist to deliver a street fighter-style punch to Perish's face, I grabbed his wrist and pulled it back. In response, and to my surprise, the god damn pet whirled around and sunk his little metal teeth into my hand.

"You little shit!" I snapped. I grabbed a tuft of his black hair and wrenched him off of my hand, before delivering a backhanded smack to his face, not hard but hard enough to snap the little feral animal out of his state. "Calm the fuck down, Cicaro, or I'll calm you down myself."

"Elish has been planning this for over twenty years!" Jade snapped, a trickle of blood running down his nose. "He's given up a lot to make this happen. Perish can–"

"I don't give a fuck what Perish can do. You're not here to become his fucking friend, Jade, you just have to live with him. Now go fucking sit and shut up, I don't need to deal with your god damn attitude," I snapped, feeling like I was channelling Greyson at that moment. I think I was slowly becoming him having to keep two mortals alive, one of them being a chimera that seemed to love getting himself into trouble. "That's an order. Go."

"Yeah, go pet, obey your master, you piss-eyed little lapdog," Perish said acidly.

"What the fuck!?" Jade thrashed his arms, trying to get out of my grip. "Fuck you, Perish Fallon. You're a fucking joke, that's what you are, a sad, pathetic, fucking joke. Elish treats you better than King Silas.

I'd treat him with some fucking respect."

"One blond monster for another," Perish said bitterly, his blue eyes were two slabs of ice. "What will change? Not much, especially since Silas will win. He's been here two hundred fifty-five years, Elish only ninety. Elish isn't as smart as he wants to believe he is. We won't win… all I'll have is new bad memories. What's the use? No use, just more pain." Those stone-cold eyes looked to mine, and with ours fixed together I saw a flicker of an inner pain not even the empath could see. "Why are you putting Killian through this? Can't you just enjoy him while you have him? I'm the only one who knows what's best for him it seems."

I immediately stiffened as Perish mentioned Killian; my throat felt dry, but he wasn't done.

"You only have another sixty years with him at very most, Reaver. Then an eternity visiting a grave. Why are you putting him in danger? You only have so little time before they die… so little time."

Those words seemed to knock me off of my feet. Jade took this moment to shift out of my loosened grip but he didn't attack Perish, he only stood beside me.

For reasons I didn't know, perhaps for my own protection I had never thought about it that way. We lived in the greywaste and death came hand in hand with everyday life. We all died one day; we all got eaten and chewed on one day… so we just never thought of it.

But my fate had been changed, I was now immortal… and as I took a step away from Perish's glaring blue eyes I realized for the first time… my time with Killian would only be a blink of an eye.

And what time I did have with him… I would watch him grow old. I'd watch him pass my physical age and grow into a man. I'd watch him become tall and strong, then slowly deteriorate, get grey hair, become slower… become an old man, lying beside a chimera forever stuck at twenty-four.

Suddenly I felt a black smoke creep its way into my brain and heart, settling down and coating my emotions like soot. It made my body standstill, and for a moment, I saw a future for myself that I never realized had become part of my destiny.

My insides stirred, my heart coiled in on itself. I felt like exploding, like an animal caught in a net, my body felt the urge to thrash and scream until I could change what was already written on my slate. In the permanent etched stone that no immortal hand could erase.

"I… I need to go for a walk." I didn't know what else to say. And though it felt outlandish to do this in the middle of the night, I had to get out of this situation before I lost my mind. Before my brain defaulted to the lowest setting of survival it had, I didn't want to regress. I had come so far, Killian had brought me so far.

I was going to see him die.

Even if everything went perfectly, and all our hopes and dreams for a new world came about, I was going to bury him and stand by his grave to watch over his bones. I would live my life without him – without my Killi Cat.

"Baby…" His sweet voice fell to my ears, but in this moment I couldn't look at him. If I did I might grab him and squeeze him until his body broke. Or kill Perish for implanting such a horrible realization inside of my head.

"I'm just… going to sit in a tree for a while…" I mumbled. "Don't let the dog follow me…"

Before the kid could stop me I lifted open the metal flap and slipped into the darkness, away from the chasm of swirling thoughts in my head. Ones that were eating away at my resolve, my resilience, and the steeled statue I had prided myself in becoming. I only had one weakness and Perish had drawn it up and smashed it in front of me.

My only weakness…

Killi.

I had watched King Silas and his brute shoot and kill Greyson and Leo in front of me. I had watched Garrett then steal my best friend, and now Perish was shoving in my face the fact that one day, whether tomorrow or in sixty years, I would hold my dead boyfriend in my arms. Everything I loved would be carried away; it was the first sting of my immortality I had ever felt.

This is what being immortal was about… watching those you loved die all around you. It had happened to Elish I bet, Garrett, and the other immortals…

And it had happened to King Silas.

As I jumped onto one of the black trees, ignoring the heavy stench of the kreigers around me, my mind uncovered a small kernel of understanding. A solemn looking glass into King Silas's mind, revealing what I suspected was a man who had watched generations of boyfriends, loved ones, chimeras and creations, some that he probably loved a lot… all die.

Was this why he was so insane?

Would I end up like him?

Of course I would.

I was him.

I climbed up the black tree, its bark bone-dry and shredding underneath my feet, like in my previous life when I used to watch Killian sleep. I climbed to a thick branch and perched, watching the ghostly white kreigers wander around the road and alleyways of the city, a parking lot and a large street away. They were haunting pale figures, their unaware movements like worms swaying back and forth. For the most part they were still, soaking up the moonlight with their heads raised like they were basking in the sun. Sometime they got into fights, other times they rushed over when one of them found a radrat or something new inside the buildings, but for the most part, they covered the ground and surfaces like a splattering of white paint.

My mouth moved to the cigarette I had lit, my mind deep in itself, churning over the question that had been my friend for months now.

How did I end up here?

Though now I said it differently, the tone of my inner voice was starting to become condescending, accusing me of taking risks I didn't need to take, and putting Killian in needless danger, all for a rebellion I didn't start.

I had never wanted to be king of the greywastes or Elish's weapon, or Greyson and Leo's for that matter. All my life my desire was to keep to myself, do my job and not be bothered… put in some random killing to satisfy that need inside of me and I was fine.

I was fine, Reno was fine, and Killian was fine.

This wasn't my fight and what had brought me to this city, to this tree, was that I had wanted to avenge Greyson and Leo's deaths… but when it all simmered down and I saw the residue that remained, the fact of the matter is… they all fucking started it.

I sighed, feeling angry at myself. I flicked the cigarette away and lit another one.

They didn't start it; King Silas started it when he decided to be a tyrant. I had heard those stories from Jade, what King Silas did to the chimeras' lovers; how he controlled them and tortured them when he felt threatened. Silas started it by becoming the insane lunatic in the first place. Elish was just the first one to snap.

This was for the greater good…

But as that echoed in my head, sometimes in Leo's voice, Greyson's, or Elish's… I found myself pushing their words away and gritted my teeth.

Because I wasn't good.

I am not good.

I am the Reaper.

All I care about is Killian. He's the only one that makes the warmth come to my veins, that makes my insides stir. Only him and no one else; I protect him, it's my job to protect him.

I am immortal and he isn't.

Fucking hell, I am no hero. I'm the opposite. I'd bomb Skyfall if it ever got into my hands, I'd force them into the greywastes so they could feel what it was like to live in this monotone hell.

I blew out the smoke, not realizing I had kept it inside of my lungs longer than necessary. When I did, I sighed and leaned against the black papery trunk of the tree.

If I am immortal, Elish is, Perish is, and Silas is… maybe this can wait. This can wait until… Killian is gone. I can spend every waking moment of my life making him happy with the time we have, and when he dies… then I can do it.

Time is now a road we no longer walk; we walk our own solemn road above the others, with a bird's-eye view of their lives from birth to death. We are nothing but deities in the sky watching them live and die as we continue our bleak journey.

That was my life now… Killian would only be within my reach for a short period of time.

Well… if Elish has been planting this seed for over twenty years, I can plant my own, take control of my own life and do what I think is best.

And what I think is best, is being with Killian where he won't be hurt. He is my responsibility and the love of my life. Silas will be there in sixty years like he has been the last two hundred and a half. Hell… when Killian dies I'll be insane from grief anyway, all the more fire in my blood to kill King Silas.

Sorry Elish… this is just how it has to be.

"I'm coming up, I need air too," a voice that still held shreds of youth called from below me.

The pet will find its master. Jade the cicaro always has to tag along. Well, it was better him than Perish or Killian. I still didn't want to see Killian and I might strangle Perish right now if I saw him. The pet knew when to be quiet; a few years with Elish had taught him to mind his manners.

I had to talk to him about something anyway.

So I shifted over on my branch and watched him skillfully climb the tree like he was half cat. Though that was explained when I saw he was wearing those steel murder claws on his fingers. Never go out unarmed I guess.

The cicaro looked up at our hazy grey moon and lit a blue-embered cigarette before tucking one behind my ear. The sapphire ember bathed his opal face in a cold glow, one that made his eyes appear green.

He was already looking older being in the greywastes, his face was covered in black stubble now and his once perfectly manicured eyebrows were back to their natural state. Even his clothes smelled like dust, though we had only been gone from the lab for a day.

I enjoyed my last fleeting moments of silence, enjoyed the crisp night and the foggy stars in the sky; I even enjoyed the kreigers crawl along the walls and the street. But I had to get this off my chest; I had to be free of this burden before I went back into that library.

I dashed the cigarette, watching the ashes rain down into oblivion, and took in a long breath.

"Tomorrow we're going back to the lab, I'm leaving you and Perish there… and I'm taking Killian and leaving," I said simply but firmly.

I saw the movement as his neck snapped towards me. To his credit he didn't flip out, there was no hiding the shock in his heartbeat though. It gave a nervous thrust before his pulse started to rise.

He looked back towards the buildings and swallowed hard. "He'll be at more risk in the greywastes. Silas won't stop looking for you."

"We're going far from here… past the greyrifts, past the Legion's power… I can survive on my own." I wonder if Leo ever wanted to do this with me and Greyson. Run away from Aras with the people he loved, to escape that insane king. Greyson would've never allowed it though; I was his hope, a hope for a better world.

I am no martyr though; they started this, not me.

"Into the plaguelands? They're called the plaguelands for a reason… anything past the greyrifts is just blight, disease, worse mutations, and lethal radiation…" Jade stopped when he saw the dangerous look cross my face. He switched gears in that moment and said in a silent tone. "He's got the best chance staying with us, being protected by me and Perish, Elish… everyone. You two won't survive long in the greywastes, and what life would that be anyway? Without a block to go home to… you've got nothing."

Frustrated, I threw my cigarette down but I didn't let myself show any more emotion. The cig bounced over the grey rocks, sending a shower of sparks into the darkness like fireworks… before, like my hope, they died in the night.

"He's crazy because everyone he loved died." I took the cigarette from behind my ear and lit it. "Killian, as Perish said, is going to die in sixty years. Why am I risking losing him? The chimeras involved in this are immortal, they can wait. Once Killian is gone, after he's lived a decent life… I'll do it, but not before that." I swallowed a well of guilt inside of me, and tried to convince myself I was the Reaper, but right now I was just Killian's guardian. "I… I should've left him in Donnely. Perish was right, he would've been safe there, forever. What do I offer him? A big chance of getting tortured, raped, and murdered by Asher. He's already done two of those things to him."

"That's just the life he has… Elish wouldn't have chosen him if he didn't think he was strong enough to handle it." Jade's tone still remained calm and level. "And you wouldn't be with him if he wasn't the kid he is now. He'd scream at you if he heard the shit coming out of your mouth.

Fucking everyone thinks that kid's weak, but he can be a little python when he wants. He ruined that radscorprion… just no one fucking gives him the chance to prove himself."

My thoughts only darkened and I spoke my realization out loud through a breath of smoke. "Yeah, the mortal keeps putting himself in danger and not hiding behind me now, I know. Look, Jade, I didn't tell you to argue. It's how it's going to be. Tell Elish to find me in sixty years and we'll go and kill Silas. You would've unravelled Perish's mind by then. We'll pick this up then… but I'm not risking Killian's life for something we both never signed up for." I shifted off of the tree and let myself fall. I landed on the ground with a *thunk* and started to make my way back to the half-lifted piece of metal.

"Silas will kill him, Reaver, and if you don't have someone on the inside, someone like Elish, keeping Silas away… he will find him, not just you, Reaver… him." The frosted silence of the night brought goose flesh to my skin, though nothing was colder than the words he had next.

"Whether you like it or not Reaver, you were born for a purpose. A purpose that Greyson, Lycos, and Elish decided for you. Only Elish is left now. If you decide to make my master's efforts be in vain, I can't predict how Elish will react."

I stopped in my tracks before I slowly turned around. "Are you fucking threatening me?"

There was a sound of his boots landed behind me, scraping against the grey ash and rock. I saw his yellow eyes flash, like that of a wild animal, as they reflected against my night vision. A chimera in front of me and a chimera looking back.

"Elish has been planning this for years with your fathers; he has risked a lot for this. Like it or not Reaver, Silas is coming for you and Killian. You can either fight it, and have Elish as an ally, or run from it with your tail between your legs, and have Elish right with Silas hunting you. My master is not a man of compromise, and you must not know chimeras well if you think he would let you go that easily."

My back stiffened and I felt a burn in my throat. But as I took a step towards him, the cicaro only flinched for a moment, before gathering the balls he must've gotten back from Elish.

"I do what I want. I am not his pet; I am not his weapon. My life is my own," I growled.

The pet kept his gaze with me. "Only greywasters are free, and you are no greywaster. You're a chimera; you are Silas's clone and now Elish's ally. Whether you bare your teeth at it or not Reaver, *Silas is coming.* Silas-is-coming, Reaver. Why the fuck are you planning on running from him? The Reaver I remember doesn't run from anything."

I felt like a fucking kettle boiling over, but all I could do to escape this frustrating helplessness sweeping over me was grinding my teeth and clenching my fists. Inside though I just wanted to break the kid's jaw for even daring to keep his gaze with mine.

"I am not running, I'm protecting Killian," I said coldly.

"Then protect him and stay with Elish… my master is a genius, a god of strategy… Elish will not fail; do you think he would have me here if he didn't believe you would protect us? He has faith in you and I do too, and Killian and Perish. If you run off with him now, you'll be on the run forever, always in fear. If we kill Silas…"

If I kill Silas…

"It will all be over." The words felt bitter on my tongue because they made sense and I didn't like that. I didn't want to find reason in his words; I wanted to protect my boyfriend in the only way I knew how: sheltering him from anything bad that was happening.

But now… danger was my own shadow, and no matter how far I ran, it was always behind me. That was the facts.

My heart harboured a painful ache, one that poisoned my brain and twisted my thoughts and feelings. Where was my logic? It was pulling me in so many different directions. A part of me had to protect the immediate threat, but the other side of me… the flame in my chest that maturity seemed to feed, told me the looming threat was greater.

What was best for him? Not me, not Elish, not Skyfall… what was best for Killian?

Because it had always been about him. Since the day I killed his parents I had claimed him as my own.

It was all what was best for him.

"I never had a choice, did I?" I whispered more to myself than Jade, and as I turned around I saw the cautious relief on Jade's face.

"None of us did," he answered soberly. "From Elish the oldest, to the younger ones, none of us have ever had a choice, Reaver."

I walked past him, and held out my left arm to receive another cigarette when suddenly… there was a scream.

Not just a scream…

"DAD!?" the voice shrieked… though this wasn't Caligula, this voice hadn't fully matured yet. The voice belonged to a teenager and a young one at that.

Jade and I both whirled around and looked past the parking lot to see a much different scene, one that had changed in only several seconds.

The kreigers were now moving. All of them crawling out of the black gaping windows and shifting their boney bodies down the brick to reach the ground. The ones already wandering around were making their way to an off-the-wall street; beelining towards the noise like the cry was its own homing device, much like they had done when they had heard us.

"That's Timothy." Jade's brow furrowed. He glanced behind him at the library before he watched the kreigers crawl towards the scream. "He's Kessler and Tiberius's youngest son."

"A chimera?" my tone dropped. I grabbed my M16 and started walking across the parking lot. I wasn't surprised when Jade grabbed my arm.

"This is how easily they can find you, Reaver, and they have bigger guns, more men, and advanced technology, remember that."

I shoved his arm away with a low growl and continued to stalk towards the screams.

"What are you planning on doing?" he said behind me.

What *was* I planning on doing? I checked my bullets and patted my cargo pants for filled cartridges. I was armed and well-armed, enough to fend off the kreigers if needed be, but I wasn't planning on them hearing me. I was dressed in black and nothing but added darkness to them.

"Hunting," I said lowly.

Another scream broke the cold night. I jumped over a median and used it as leverage to hop the chain-link fence that partially surrounded the parking lot, and with the sound of shifting metal, I could hear the cicaro brother of mine doing the same. I hugged the fence and kept my head down and my movements silent, only twenty feet from a group of kreigers quickly making their way to the road this chimera seemed to be on.

The closer I got to his screams the more I felt my chest fill with sparks of electricity, like a decaying heart renewing a dead heartbeat. There was no mistaking what I was feeling, the inner burn inside my heart that ached to kill, devour, and dominate, that demanded blood and the dying screams of the people who had done me wrong.

I could control it before, I had learned to control it, but now… now I couldn't.

The chimeras would pay.

They would pay for everything they had done to me.

For everything they had made me feel.

"Your smiling… why the fuck are you smiling?" Jade's voice said beside me, keeping the same pace as me.

I looked on, and felt the blood start to flow faster in my veins, lighting up senses that had lain dormant for months. I was breathing life back into the greywaster and handling emotions like I had done before.

With blood, with pain, and with terror.

I looked around at the kreigers, but they were more interested in the blood curdling screams and pleas coming from the road I was about to turn down. With Jade silent and stealthy beside me, they were either unaware of our presence or they just didn't care. This filled my blood with even more fire, and in spite of the fact that the friendship had eventually soured, being beside someone who could hold their own like Asher could was only acting as an accelerant.

And Jade just wasn't some random Morosian, I knew his past.

"They called you Shadow Killer in the slums, didn't they? Did Elish beat your bloodlust out of you, Shadow Killer?"

I sprinted across the road before leaping onto a mailbox and springing onto an apartment ledge. I started to hoist myself up but was surprised to see a blur of black land beside me with a sound of boots on brick.

Jade turned around and helped me rise to my feet, giving me a derisive smirk and a flash of cocksure bliss in his yellow eyes. "Are you trying to issue some sort of challenge towards me? It seems I am the one helping you to your feet." The kid smiled, his metal teeth shining in the moonlight, and as if to show me just who the Shadow Killer had been, he clinked his claw rings together and looked past me.

"Tim is a bitch, a fourteen-year-old little shit who never lets me forget I am nothing but a pet, even if I technically outrank him considering I'm 'Uncle' Elish's husband. If you stick with us, you'll have him and more. I can promise you that."

I didn't want to hear about that right now, I wanted to kill. Without acknowledging what he was saying, I turned around and started walking along the apartment ledge before rounding a tricky corner to find myself on the street that Timmy was on.

Sure enough, as I looked ahead I saw the figure of a tall, gangly boy with curly brown hair, holding a gun, which I assumed was out of ammo, in his hand.

I could see the whites of his eyes, he was looking behind his back wildly like a nervous bosen, running as fast as he could towards where he assumed his father and brother would be.

With Jade behind me, the Shadow and the Reaper… we quickly sprinted along the ledge. When the building ended we jumped down to an alleyway, still behind the horde of kreigers.

I looked around for another ledge to scale but the structures around us had no small awnings or ridges to run across. Instead the two of us stuck close to the building entrances, using the cars, telephone booths, and other debris to block our silhouettes.

"They're not interested in us at all," Jade whispered as we practically ran past a kreiger making his way towards the swarm. "As soon as they focus on a wounded target everything else is invisible to them."

This was valuable knowledge; if we ever got stuck I'd use Perish or myself as a bloodied sacrifice so the mortal boys could escape.

But if I was without those two… if I ever died in the greywastes, which would undoubtedly be more bloody and gory than a simple shot in the head, Killian would be alone and fending for himself until I came back.

Tim disappeared down another street, and on his heels a swarm of over fifty kreigers followed him. Slow but determined they hissed and snapped, accumulating more numbers with every building Tim passed. Like the boy was a drain and the kreigers water they all honed in on him, bearing their green gums and continuing to advance.

I passed a dead kreiger, riddled with too many badly aimed bullet holes, and a few paces later, a pool of blood that had the unmistakable aroma of chimera, almost like cinnamon. I glanced down and watched as Jade put his fingers to the pool and tasted it.

This kid was about as twisted as I was, though it seemed to be a chimera trait. Licking his fingers, Jade's eyes scanned the white wraiths climbing along the buildings. He opened his mouth to say something when a new voice filled the air.

"Tim? Tim?" My face darkened as I heard Caligula's voice. I nodded for Jade to follow me before I covered the next two buildings and ducked into the third, not far from where I could hear Tim's panicked breathing.

Jade was on my heels as I crossed the lobby ruins and ran up the stairs two by two. I got to an open door; dented and half blown off by what had once been an explosion, and sprinted down the junk-strewn hallway, looking into empty room to empty room until I found the one that I liked. Two-storeys up, high enough that they wouldn't be able to see us without looking but low enough to enjoy the carnage.

I had an idea, and that never boded well for the enemies within my line of sight.

I dropped to my stomach on the balcony and crawled over with my M16 in my hands. Without wasting time, before Caligula could spot him, I raised the scope to my eyes and focused on the brown-haired boy in my crosshairs. I squeezed the trigger and felt the kickback, then a moment later a satisfying scream.

My eyes found him, on his knees now, his left kneecap blown out. I grinned and shouldered Jade who was lying down beside me.

"Holy fuck, Reaver." Jade's voice shifted to a higher octave, watching with me as the boy screamed for his brother as he dragged himself away from the kreigers.

Then one of them finally got brave, or hungry, enough to attack. It tensed back like a spring before it retracted its neck like a snapping turtle and grabbed onto Tim's leg. The kid shot it back and kicked the kreiger in the head before struggling to get to his feet, panting and trying to yell.

Another one came from Tim's right, leaping on his back and slamming him down onto the ground, and like it had opened a bridge of confidence for the others, they started to move in on their kill.

To my disappointment though, there was a crack of assault rifle fire, and the kreigers scattered off of Tim like vultures. They slithered back a few feet before they mock advanced, arching their backs and hissing. Then another series of gunfire, each in quick succession, before the kreigers scattered further.

Caligula, the chimera brother of mine, had his fancy M4 carbine up, raining clip after clip on the lizard men. He was quick, with a confident stance that radiated a powerful and authorative aura that only chimeras could truly wield. He carried himself as I would've expected someone with his upbringing, something his brother had failed to grasp.

My mind ticked.

"Dad? I found him, over here!" Caligula shouted, turning only for a seconds before he ran to his bleeding and gasping brother; the boy's useless assault rifle lying forgotten beside him.

"You idiot, where are the others?" Caligula growled, grabbing Tim by the back of his shirt and wrenching him to his feet. He let go but caught Tim again as the boy's leg bent like it was made from rubber.

"Dead, all of them are dead. Why the fuck didn't Silas tell us these things were here?" Tim snapped, grabbing onto his brother for dear life. I could see his eyes were an odd brown orange colour, splotchy like some of the markings the cats at home had.

"I don't know… Dad?" Caligula dropped Tim and started shooting off the kreigers who were starting to get bold and come closer. He turned around and bent down to pick his brother back up.

And I saw my opportunity.

Jade looked over at my gun but didn't say anything. I wondered if he was worried about what Elish would think, or perhaps I had him wrong and he was disappointed he wouldn't get to rip a throat out. Either way, I was doing this my way, and my way involved more than just teeth and flesh.

I focused my M16 again and shot Caligula in the leg. The soldier chimera shouted from shock and fell to the ground.

I aimed again and shot his other leg.

"Those kreigers will get to Tim before I'll even get a bite." Jade's voice was amusingly bitter, like I had just taken away the sweetest of rewards. "I'll never understand how you can get fulfillment out of guns.

Teeth are just so… personal."

You want personal, Cicaro? You must not know me well.

"Clig?" Timmy cried. He put a hand on Caligula's shoulder just as a kreiger started to bite and pull Caligula's shoe. The kreiger jumped back and hissed.

The lizards were descending, becoming braver and bold as the man with the gun fell into a writhing heap, swearing his face off and holding his legs.

"Who's fucking shooting at us!?" Caligula snapped.

"I think it's Willis; I bait-trapped him. He's fucking dead when I find him! I'll rip him apart myself!" Timmy cried. And with that admission, I had to push down the laugh edging my lips.

"We're both dead, you little shit," Caligula gasped. His clammy face getting paler as the blood around his legs grew. Jade and I both flattened our bodies against the balcony as the chimera scanned the buildings for the mystery shooter, though his metallic eyes saw nothing but shadows.

Instead of panicking Caligula reached into his pocket for a handgun and gave it to Tim, just as the brave kreiger who had gotten kicked grabbed onto Tim's leg.

Caligula rose up and shot the kreiger before he started to drag his bleeding legs down the road. His brother trying to pull himself away; his own leg a lump of awkward, useless meat.

My insides stirred; my heart pumping wave after wave of grisly thrills throughout my body. It was overtaking me with such a torrent of murderous energy I didn't know if I could hold back going down there to kill them myself. Jade was right, I don't think just sniping them would be enough for me anymore.

"Don't kill Clig, Elish will be angry. We'll still need the Legion on–"

"I don't give a fuck what Elish thinks."

Why would he think I would? I wasn't Elish's slave and he wasn't my master. This was my vendetta, my payback. Not just to kill a chimera, but to pay Kessler back for all the hell he had caused Aras. Killian was almost killed because his legionaries wanted to make a couple tokens off of his liver.

I wanted to make him pay for everything.

"Clig? Tim?" Kessler called. We both looked up and saw the burly silhouette of Kessler as he burst out of an alleyway nearby, rifle in hand.

"Dad, our legs… Tim bait-trapped Willis and he got free. He's sniping us from one of the buildings. We can't fucking walk. Where are the others?" Caligula tried to shout over the assault rifle fire but his finger seemed permanently pressed on the trigger. He was sitting now, with his back leaning against Tim who was on his knees firing the useless handgun at the two dozen mobbing them only ten feet away.

Kessler fired a sweep of bullets into the ones swarming on Caligula, before running in front of his sons with a threatening bellow, opening his arms and advancing on them in a futile attempt to show dominance to the descending kreigers.

The lizards did scatter when he did this, but not a second after he did, they regrouped, crawling closer and closer.

"I'll carry you boys, don't worry, just cover my fucking back." Kessler gave his carbine to Tim before he leaned down to pick the boy up.

"Is he immortal?"

"Yes," Jade said under his breath.

I chuckled, and heard the cicaro suck in a breath like he almost knew what was coming. I looked into the scope again and found my new target, before firing off several rounds… I needed more than one bullseye for this to be effective.

The bullets burst through the soft area of Kessler's combat armour, making large bloodied holes appear where his arm would meet his shoulder; each one hitting their mark and sending its own firework of blood onto Kessler's neck.

The Legion General, the man whose army had been fucking with my people, bullying us, and murdering us for years, bellowed with rage, and like his son, he started scanning the buildings.

"Willis!? The Imperial General demands you fucking show yourself!" he roared, holding his arm as the blood gushed under his fingers.

But even if I decided to yell back, just for the sheer joy, there was no time for it. Caligula gave a holler as he jammed another clip into his gun and started shooting several kreigers trying to pull him into the black buildings around us. They worked together like a team, three kreigers, two on his left leg and one on his right, pulling him along like he was already dead.

Kessler shot all three of them, but no sooner had he done that did Tim's screaming sound behind him. The general, now using his left hand, pulled out a handgun and tried to shoot the kreiger dragging Tim towards the mob but he missed half of them, sparks flying as the bullets bounced off of the pavement.

I saw the sweat beading down his forehead; I saw the fear start to come to eyes I knew had only held brutality and power. I wondered when I'd see the realization of what I was making him have to do.

Your master told me I could only save one of my fathers. Now Kessler… which son will you choose?

"If you come down here and help me… I'll… I'll – Fuck, I'll promote you. You'll be in debt to the Dekker family. I command you to come down here!" Kessler ran and pulled Tim back. He dragged the boy towards Caligula before grabbing him too.

But his arm was useless, I could see his fingers not even tighten around Caligula's combat armour before they loosely let go and fell back against his side.

"Dad!" Tim screamed. He pulled the trigger of the carbine Kessler had given him but only a clicking sound filled the air. All the gunfire had stopped and now only the sandpapery shifting skin and the hissing of the creatures echoed off of the looming black buildings, mixing in with the chilly electric air. "They're getting closer!"

Inside my body the inferno grew, to the point where I thought I was going to have a full bodied orgasm. But instead of giving into my own physical pleasures, I watched Kessler turn around and freeze.

Then… then the climax.

Like his chimera mind had eliminated all other options, I saw the pain sweep Kessler's face. He bounded over to Caligula and picked him up with his still functioning arm. By now the boy was only half-conscious, blood pooling around him and splitting into several channels as it ran towards a gutter.

"Dad?" Tim's cries were full of agony. I turned from the delectable scene and saw Tim frantically hitting a kreiger who had latched onto his arm. Not a moment later, another one sprung out of the mob and snapped its jaws against Tim's side and thrashed the boy's body with its teeth, creating a squealing screaming noise from the boy I had heard many times before.

Kessler didn't turn around.

He threw Caligula over his good shoulder, his face holding anguish beyond tears. He secured his son with his arm wrapped around Caligula's legs, and shut his eyes tight as Tim's screams switched to a higher tone.

The tone of someone being eaten alive.

Kessler mouthed something… whether it was an apology or a curse word Tim's loud screams drowned it out. He took Caligula. And as the kreigers ran past him, no longer caring at all that he was there, he sprinted past his son, now being devoured by five kreigers and counting, then disappeared into the alleyway.

As soon as he was out of sight, I swung over the railing I'd been sniping behind and landed on the pavement below me.

One of the kreigers looked up at me and hissed. Without pausing, I walked over to it and bashed its skull in with the butt of my M16. It screamed almost as loud as Timmy was screaming as the side of its face got ripped off of its skull. When it was down, I started hitting the other ones; the remaining lizard men scrambling away from the boy's bitten and bloody body as I beat on them.

They lowered their heads at me and I felt teeth clamp against my leg. I raised my gun and shot it in the head.

"Help… help me…" Tim's weak voice cried. With Jade behind me kept the lizards away, I leaned over Tim and smiled at him.

The boy looked at me back before his eyes widened.

"You know who I am, Timmy?" I whispered.

As the kid, sweaty and covered in shining blood, stared at me, his calico eyes shot to where Jade was picking off the kreigers with his silenced assault rifle. "Help me… my family will–" He coughed a spray of blood and whimpered. "Help… help me… please?"

I chuckled and petted his dark hair back with my hands. Such a sweet little thing, my little brother, Tim Dekker. Only a year younger than the first time I had seen Killian.

Sweet, sweet little brother.

I leaned down and licked the blood that had just erupted from his lips. To my inner transgressive joy, his blood held on it the unique cinnamon-like flavour. I liked the taste of chimera.

I wanted more.

I licked it again and found myself almost moving to his lips, but instead they shifted lower… and lower, until I found his neck.

Jade gasped and swore behind me as I cut the straps of the kid's combat armour off, then the shirt he had on underneath. Ignoring the chunks of flesh the kreigers had ripped out of him I traced a finger down his bare chest and smiled at him.

Tim stared at me, his brown and black eyes bulging out of their sockets as I reached to my belt and pulled out my combat knife. His body was shaking, his pale chest with only small traces of chest hair, rising and falling under his own oppressing anxiety.

I held my combat knife in my hands – and stabbed it between his rib cage.

The boy screamed, and with that beautiful moonlit music gracing my ears like the quickened moans pre-orgasm, I dug the knife in and began to saw, splitting his rib cage apart. It was easier than I had expected, a quick saw, but not too deep, only to sever the fused-together bones.

I tried to ignore the fragrant hot blood spilling out of his chest and onto my hands and knife. Warm and wet, steaming in the cold… what I would give to bottle it and drink it every night before I fucked Killian.

Once I was confident I had weakened the flesh-covered bones seemingly clasped together like weaved fingers, I wedged my hand into the bottom of the rib cage and pulled it back with a sickening wet sound of tearing flesh and the snapping vibrations of breaking bones. Sound that I was no stranger to.

With a good pull and the high pitch shrieking of Timothy Dekker, still alive, I revealed his still beating heart.

Yes, I had never forgotten that I had wanted to do this.

One hand held back the hot slab of flesh and bone that had been his chest cavity, my other hand dropped the knife and reached in to grab his heart. The last image Tim's hazy eyes saw was me picking up the twitching, thrashing organ into my hands, connected with thick hose-like veins before bringing it to my mouth.

I bit down and found heaven in the greywastes.

Blood squirted into my mouth, down my chin and all over my face; the convulsing organ spraying pulse after pulse of warm blood with every desperate thrash. I swallowed the first piece whole, before closing my lips over the next bite as the heart inside my jaws slowly died.

I held it there and drank each pressured pump of blood until the once powerful spray of blood became a trickle… before it finally became still.

All of this only took half a minute, yet to me I was kneeling over the boy for several lifetimes.

I closed my eyes, his heart still warm and in my jaws. Right then, I was confused as to how I felt, until I realized I was tasting pure bliss for the first time in months. A chimera in his element, a bloodthirsty monster tasting the flesh he craved so much, and not just legionary this time, or the former councillor or officer in Aras… a chimera.

My little brother Timmy.

I breathed in the thick heavy scent of blood, and though I wish I could say I didn't recognize myself… the truth was I had just found myself again.

I shifted and realized my dick was rock hard.

I bit the thick blood vessels away from Tim's heart and took what remained with me as I stood. When I turned around I saw Jade, staring at me with his eyes wide, a dozen kreigers dead around him but several more quickly closing in.

"Keep them far away; they're not eating his body," I growled to Jade and picked up the kid. I was going to make a fucking statement to the Legion and to King Silas. I didn't care what it would mean for our mission for it to be known it wasn't this 'Willis' person to shoot Caligula and Tim. I feared no one, especially not King Silas.

I would store him somewhere safe, and tomorrow… yes, tomorrow I would have my fun.

After stashing the body of Tim Dekker into a closet of an old apartment building, Jade and I started walking back to the library, running along ridges and taking alleyways until we managed to lose the kreigers that were trailing us.

I was on top of the world. The intoxicating feeling was making me feel like I was floating, lifting me above my troubles and the worries that had been claiming me, and carrying me into the sky in a warm embrace. Oh, did I love the heavy smell of blood. I loved the taste of human flesh.

Perhaps it was because I felt like myself, the person I feared I would lose, though the only thing that had really been lost was my adolescent attitude. That had died with Leo and Greyson, and had been buried when I became the guardians of Killian and Jade. This new life hadn't killed the sociopathical desire to see people suffer, if anything it had only strengthened it.

What a thrill. I wish I could show Kessler and Caligula what I had done to their little Timmy… but no, no, do not rush it, Reaper. They will see… eventually they will see.

All of them will pay for what they'd done to me, what they had done to my family.

"They can't see us anymore. If we make a break for it we can get back to the library without them following us." Jade's voice was low but I couldn't read his tone. I didn't know if he was nervous with me now, apprehensive, or if this was just a normal day since he was used to chimeras. What it boiled down to though, was that he was still here, and he hadn't stopped me from eating Timmy's heart. That alone gave him points with me.

Yes, he was the serial killer in Moros… we were alike in more ways than either of us cared to admit.

He had never wanted this either. Jade had been a Morosian with a boyfriend, and I had been a greywaster with a suitable life. Nowhere in our past or our future did we wish to have become chimeras.

But we were chimeras, the torn apart mess on the pavement and the blood on our hands said that as clear as day. Whether I wanted to deny the realities that came with this knowledge or not, it didn't change the facts.

This was my family; I was but a resistant black sheep.

I offered Jade Timmy's half-devoured heart like I was passing him a post-sex cigarette.

The boy looked at me for a moment, before his eyes trailed to the heart of his brother. Then, like he had never had hesitation, he took it and tore off a good size chunk of it. I watched him eat it, and as he swallowed, I myself took another bite.

"I love our taste," he said lowly.

The blood ran down his chin, purple and shining under what moonlight the grey sky allowed us. And though I could never admit it, in that second the throbbing in my pants only amplified at how the cicaro looked right now. A slender thing with pale skin, brilliant yellow eyes and a face streaked with blood. I could see why Elish fucked him into madness every night; at this point if I was single I may have done the same.

I could… if… I wanted to.

Before my mind could tell me how wrong it was, I reached over and wiped the blood from his face before bringing it up to my lips and tasting it. My groin gave another throb, making me immediately retract and tear myself away from a very dangerous feeling. A new one that I knew came with my blood makeup, one I would have to watch from now on. It was common knowledge inside of me that I was not a sexual person, but when there was blood, murder, and agony in the air… that was the recipe to get to the inner lust of a chimera.

And if there was one thing I knew chimeras liked doing – it was fucking each other. Who else could bear our stamina? That had been proven with Killian time and time again.

Shit, Killian. I closed my eyes and clenched my teeth. With my boyfriend's trusting face in my mind, I shook my head free of those thoughts.

I took control of myself and pushed the feelings away, and like an orgasm, it faded back into the depths of my mind and reality quickly replaced it. I grabbed onto it and thrusted myself back into the moment, feeling my ears go hot at the mere suggestion of putting a move on the cicaro chimera, makeup or not.

I quickly walked home, the taste of blood in my mouth.

CHAPTER 19

Jade

"JADE?" KILLIAN LOOKED UP FROM THE TEXTBOOK he was reading but I grabbed the laptop and walked past him. If Reaver wasn't right behind me Killian would've followed me, would've asked what was wrong and why my mouth was lined with blood, but his boyfriend was there and he could tell him.

I had to talk to Elish; I had to warn him about what Reaver just did.

"Reaver? Are you okay?"

Depends on what okay means to you, kiddo.

I turned on the remote phone; my throat heavy with the taste of blood. No matter how many times I swallowed it was like I was swallowing liquid metal. I had missed that taste, however I knew I shouldn't have tasted it tonight.

Is Elish going to kill me for not stopping him?

Don't be an idiot, Jade, you couldn't have stopped him if you wanted.

That aura… fuck, Reaver's aura got fucked up when he wasn't around Killian.

It shifted like a spectre in the darkness depending on how he felt. No one's aura, none of the people I'd ever read had an aura that would change right in front of my very eyes. Sure peoples could change, mine had many times, but it was a process that took months…

Reaver's… seconds. I could see his self-control kick in; I could see him fighting with his cardinal desires. A fight he had always been destined to lose.

My eyes closed for a brief moment and I took a deep breath.

I should've known better. If chimeras started acting frenzied around blood and death of course Reaver would do the same… only amplified. I had never seen it before in him though, I hadn't expected him to take it this far. Not just killing Tim, but the morbid, creatively horrible way he did it.

I shuddered and started clicking around on the laptop, hoping beyond hope that I could connect with Elish's remote phone and be able to talk to him.

So I could get an earful because I was sure he would blame me for this. The Legion would be coming undoubtedly, and soon.

Do we leave? Elish, do we have to leave Kreig now?

My heart dropped when I saw the *no service* signal on the cell phone. Deep down I knew it would be hard to get a signal in this stupid place but I was still holding out hope. Maybe if I went outside? No, not with the kreigers outside. They didn't have Timmy's remains to feast on; they would be pissed off at being bilked out of a meal.

I rose and started walking around the library, trying to be as quiet as I could so Reaver and the others wouldn't hear me. They would be too interested in hearing Reaver's story about murdering Tim; they wouldn't be looking for me.

I wiped my bloodied mouth with my jacket and held the cell phone up into the air. When that was pointless, I took the laptop and started walking around the abandoned library to see if I could get a signal.

The halls were dark and even in my stealth I was still crunching against loose gyprock and the remains of the ceiling above me. What was once tucked tight into the rafters of the roof were now their own little alarm systems beneath my feet. Everything made noise, though with luck the only person they were alerting would be me.

I couldn't go any higher. All that was above me was wire, insulation, and probably lots of radrat shit too.

But I had to call Elish… I just needed to talk to him, hear his voice, even if I knew the entire conversation would be him verbally destroying me.

I closed my eyes and let out a long breath.

I heard something crunching down the hallway but I kept my eyes closed anyway. I could tell by their footsteps who was coming, Killian had small light movements, Perish was a normal saunter, and Reaver was… like me, silent as a ghost.

"Jade?"

I opened one eye and saw Perish leaning against a cracked wooden beam. He had a blue bag over his shoulder and was looking behind me at a bookshelf I had parked myself in front of.

Perish looked around the room. His eyes never seemed to be able to find mine; they were always wandering around like they wanted to take everything in.

"Yeah, what's up?" I said.

Perish clenched his hands and rubbed them together; I saw he had a blanket slung over his back. "Reaver and Killian went off to…" His brow furrowed, obviously Killian was off getting pounded. "The dog is out hunting and I was just exploring, seeing if maybe I can find some science things." Perish glanced down and opened the cover of a book before he let it fall in a puff of dust. "Are you staying here for the night? In this room?"

I shrugged, I wouldn't be opposed to sleeping in the little hovel Killian and I had made. Reaver would be sexed out and probably asleep, but I didn't want them to hear my conversation with Elish; actually I didn't even want them to know I was trying to call him. Reaver had his sonic hearing, better than mine was, and anywhere I ducked into… if he wanted to listen in he could.

Perish must've read my mind. He took the blanket that was thrown over his shoulder and gave it to me. "There you go; I'll be keeping watch all night and probably after Reaver will. If you hear anything come get me, okay? I'll tell them you're here, but don't worry, Tim was an asshole, right? I hated him… he's better off gone. Okay, have a good sleep."

I guess he wasn't one to outstay his welcome, with those parting words the scientist turned around and left the small room I had found myself in.

I bundled myself into the fleecy blanket and lay with the laptop open in front of me. To pass the time I played solitaire, a game my master loved to play, and then mahjong, another one of our favourite games.

It was so quiet here, and unlike Elish's skyscraper, it wasn't a comfortable silence. My ears were focused and strained, trying to listen for any sign that those lizard things were going to break in and eat us.

Well, if they did break in they'd eat Reaver and Killian first; I was probably okay.

So I closed my eyes and tried to get some sleep. I didn't know what our plans were for tomorrow, if we were going to risk it and go back to the lab. I was hoping Elish could tell us what we were supposed to do; he always knew.

My dreaming was interrupted some time in the middle of the night by a strange sound I didn't recognize at first, but it was shrill and loud. In response, my eyes snapped open, and as I looked at the illuminated remote phone screen, my heart jumped inside of my throat.

A desperate cry broke my lips and I picked it up. With hands trembling so badly I almost dropped it, I accepted the call and brought the phone to my ear.

"E-Elish?" I croaked. Without wanting to, I burst into tears. I felt a well of shame inside of me. I didn't realize how much I wanted to be with him until I knew he was on the other end of that phone.

"Where are you?" Elish's voice wasn't welcoming or kind; it was sharp and straight to the point.

I sniffed. "I'm... I'm at the library in Kreig with the others... when are you coming to get me?"

Even though he couldn't see me, I cowered when I heard him let out an angry noise. *"Why the hell are you still in Kreig? Did one of you fools not kill Kessler's son? Are you that moronic you do not remember that Jack collects the remains of our brothers? He's on his way there, you insufferable imbecile! It's your job to relay your knowledge of the chimeras to the greywasters! Get the group out of there; I have already delayed him as much as I possibly can. NOW, Jade!"*

"But... Master..." I stammered, a cold rush of anxiety ran through my veins.

"No, Jade. Get out of Kreig. I'll find you with your track-"

Then a long drawn-out tone – the call had dropped.

I sniffed back the tears and slammed the remote phone down onto the blanket. Then in my anger, I shut the laptop off and packed it up.

But there wasn't any time to cry, even if hearing his voice had made me miss him even more. I had to wake the others up and get us out of Kreig.

Jack was coming… the chimera we called the Grim. I knew Jack well; he was like Sanguine in that he had pointed teeth like him and an eerie disposition. He also had a device that told him whenever a chimera had died. So if the dead chimera was immortal Jack could collect their bodies and make sure they didn't remain in the custody of those who killed them.

This wasn't the first time I had to run from Jack and probably not the last. Now though, so much more was at stake. Jack would, of course, recognize me and he would recognize Perish. We had to go and get as far away from Kreig as we possibly could.

The prospect filled me with dread and more anxiety, but I had to push it into the back of my mind. I had another job to do, and my master was relying on me.

Once the laptop was packed up with the blanket, I made my way down the cold and dark hallway, not even bothering to mask my footsteps. I followed the crumbling walls and half-askew doors and found our small makeshift camp.

As soon as I stepped into the room I saw Reaver sitting beside the flap of metal, as usual an ember glowed near his mouth.

"Reaver? We have to leave." I quietly walked past the dozing Killian, Perish off in a corner near the deacdog sleeping too. Inside my guts were stirring. I wanted to yell it and wake everyone else up and get them moving, but I'd rather tell Reaver first.

The ember moved from his mouth, I saw his shining black eyes narrow. "You've been crying and you look half-asleep. Go back to sleep, crazy."

I shook my head. "No, it's not that. I was able to get a short call in to Elish. We have chimeras, Jack at least, coming."

I saw him raise an eyebrow at me. I don't think he believed that my phone call hadn't been a dream. "Jack? Silver hair, black eyes… pointy teeth like Sanguine, right? I can take him, go back to bed."

He's humouring me… he's not taking me seriously. I shook my head and tried to form my words slowly. "Reaver, I'm awake. Jack collects the dead. The chimeras, besides me, Elish, and I assume Lycos took out Perish's death-trigger… the rest have signals that go off when they die. Tim died. Reaver, we have to get the fuck out of here right now. Silas could be with him. Fuck, Sanguine could… they'll smell me. They'll find the lab…"

I saw his expression change from bemused to serious. Then, as the words sunk in, I saw the hardness return to his face. He stepped away from me and called out. "Perish?"

A tired voice sounded from beside an upturned table. "Yeah?"

"Is Jack coming for Tim?"

Like a rocket going off, Perish threw his blanket off and jumped to his feet. "We gotta go. We gotta go."

The anxious energy that suddenly filled the room made it impossible for me to tell Reaver 'I told you so', in a matter of minutes we were all quickly repacking our stuff. All with bed head but in our usual clothes. Unless you were safely inside of a block, nightclothes were a thing of the past.

"Who's Jack?" Killian asked me, wide awake now but with his blond hair sticking up in all directions. He was helping me fold up the few blankets we had.

"He comes for dead chimeras and we have a dead chimera…" I said grimly, zipping up the duffle bag and throwing it over my shoulder. Reaver was already outside, and the first hints of sunlight were peeking through the metal-covered windows.

I followed Reaver but stopped when he did. I watched him take a long drag of his cigarette.

"Well, I will have a surprise for him when he comes…" Reaver said quietly, then he glanced behind him. My chest shook slightly when I saw the thin smile on his face.

"You… you went out after?" I dropped my voice, wondering what he had done to Tim's body.

Reaver smirked and shrugged, before looking behind me to where Killian and Perish were emerging. "Nothing much, just a hello." He nodded towards them. "Let's go."

I swallowed hard, holding a scathing remark on my lips. If he would let Tim's body get eaten by kreigers we could still pass this off as it being Willis who did it… but now…

"Let's go." Reaver said sharply to me as if reading my thoughts. "That's an order."

I sighed… and did what I was ordered.

Soon enough, we were out in the crisp winter air. A few more months and it would be spring, but right now we were in January and it was freezing fucking cold.

I tucked my fingers into my jacket and walked behind Killian, with Perish leading us out of the city and Reaver doing a quick scout to make sure we were still alone. The kreigers had all gone back into their nests by now and the city had fallen into its eerie calm. One that seemed so false I could almost taste it on the air.

I would not miss this city, but in a way it felt like I was leaving yet another part of Skyfall behind, a part of Elish.

When Reaver gave us the all clear we started to sprint. We weaved around congested roads and downed power lines, following the scientist at a steady pace as we made our way to the outskirts of the city.

We followed Perish but Reaver kept branching off. He came back twenty minutes later and discreetly handed me a bloody plastic bag.

I stared at him.

"That's…"

"Just his liver. Iron is good for you, Cicaro." Reaver gave me a smirk. "Ever taste chimera before, Jade?"

I shook my head, though in all respects I was curious as to how we tasted. I put the bag into my own bag and we carried on.

It was an hour of sprinting between the tall buildings and cracked roads until we were cutting through grey rocky lawns and climbing over burnt debris. The apartment buildings and double roads were far behind us, becoming only memories in the low haze that had crept in from a lake I couldn't see. Ahead of us, I saw grey hills and strips of roads that disappeared into the distance, accompanied by sporadic black trees to which they had made friends with. But for the most part, everything was concealed by the uneven terrain, cloaked in the grey sun with the thick fog guarding it

Because of the decreased visibility in front of us, there could be a small town fifty miles ahead, but from my line of sight it was all a canvas of broken monotone.

Reaver led us to a house with a sunken roof and a wide open door. We took shelter in the covered half of a living room; the other end exposed to the elements and bogged down with ash that had crept through the windows. I took a seat on a rain-warped plastic tote and heard it rattle as I shifted around on it.

I got up and opened up the tote, only to find it full of human bones. "Who wants to make soup?" No one found that as funny as I did.

Reaver went off to sentry with the dog, and I stayed with Killian and Perish to make us all some quick tact sandwiches.

Tact was the staple food in Moros. The base of it was human stock and flour so it tasted like a hard cracker, it was packed full of vitamins, minerals, and all that health shit so the Morosians wouldn't die from malnutrition. It also came in a sweet variety we called sweet tact, which instead of human stock there was corn syrup. I lived off of this stuff; it was all I got as a kid until I had learned how to steal.

I hadn't lived a great life in Moros; the woman that Garrett had given me to at birth (I was switched out for a stillborn) was a crazy woman with mental issues and a drug problem. She tried her best though and I still miss her sometimes.

But the life I had led had prepared me for what I was dealing with now, if I had been born and raised with the family I might not be able to adjust to desolation again, but this was kind of an old hat. Starvation was my friend, cold misery my brother, and the lump of anxiety in the pit of my stomach a disease all Morosians inherited.

I'd had it rather good for the past few years though. Elish always kept the apartment toasty warm and Luca had catered to my every need, the food was plentiful and the tea hot.

I missed that skyscraper… and the people in it.

I missed Elish… I wonder if he missed me; it didn't sound like he had missed me.

My hand brushed over my wedding ring, before, with a forlorn sigh, I turned to help Killian make some sandwiches.

The kid was just finishing up, and rubbing his bare hands together which were pasty white and shivering. Perish was beside him layering some canned Good Boy onto bread, beside a pile of dried flesh which would satiate the dog until he could dig up a radanimal to eat.

I picked up my tact and took a bite out of it. It tasted… interesting. Bosen cheese and canned human meat, it was a mixture of crunch, mushy, weird textures in my mouth that made me miss hamburgers and potato fries.

An idea popped into my head. I put the sandwich onto the palm of my hand and put my other palm on top of it. Then, with Killian eyeing me like I was out of my mind, I brought up my aura abilities and tuned it towards one of the abilities I had absorbed from Elish.

My tongue stuck out of the side of my mouth as I concentrated on my hands, bringing out a burning hot touch that immediately started making the tact smoke. Then with a cackle I closed my hand and watched Killian's eyes widen.

"Toaster… you're a cicaro toaster," Perish chuckled. He reached over and hovered his hand over my own cupped hands before pulling them back. "I love seeing your abilities work; I engineered you perfect. But not much, remember your head can't handle as much. Use it to warm yourself not toast sandwiches, idiot. It hasn't started fading yet?"

"It's starting to but I have another few days." I took a bite out of my smoking sandwich. "And I might be an idiot, but you're going to enjoy cold food."

Killian seemed more interested in my hands than my sandwich. He reached over and brushed the crumbs off of my hands before putting his little icicles into my palm. "You can absorb other chimeras' abilities right?"

I nodded and made my palms warm; as soon as he felt the fluxuation in temperature he smiled and let me cup his hands. "Can Reaver do things like this?"

Why was he asking me? I looked over at Perish, assuming he would be the one to know but he just shrugged. "Elish and Lycos were in control of Chimera X. I only assisted them on physical traits and faulty gene removal. All them."

I put my half-eaten sandwich on my lap and cupped Killian's ice cold fingers into my hands and warmed them up for him. "I don't think he can, it seems only Silas, Elish, Sanguine, and maybe two or three of the others have that gene. I only can because I'm an empath and apparently it kills me a little bit every time I do it."

Killian's blue eyes were still bright though. He smiled and I felt him wiggle his warming fingers. "But he's Silas's clone! So he can."

The scientist looked amused but I couldn't see why, in all respects what the kid was saying made sense.

"No silly. King Silas isn't a chimera, he's a born immortal. Most of Silas's enhancements came from science, same splicing we used in our chimera babies. He'd kill himself and we'd do surgery on his healing brain. After he mastered these abilities, he got the idea to make the chimera babies, so we started on that." Perish scowled and I knew why. Perish had realized, as we did, he'd once again confirmed to himself his real age. "Now Silas has them all but I am not sure if they gave all of them to Reaver."

The scientist then paused and pointed a finger at me. "They are dangerous; you need to stop doing tricks. Didn't your master tell you to stop?"

Elish told me to stop but he also told me I had to unravel Perish's mind.

"He also did surgery on me to force it to stop." I shrugged and absentmindedly touched the scars I could still feel on my head, I had many of them. "Did your surgery have a time limit on them then?" Perish and Sid, two chimera doctors, had been the ones to cut my head open.

Perish nodded, then glanced up as we all heard a crack of rotting floorboards; Reaver must be coming in from his scouting. Killian jumped up with Reaver's two sandwiches.

"I did, and no it doesn't. He must've shorted the implant himself; all it would take was an electric pulse in the right areas. He probably did it himself so you can fuck around in my head." Perish said the last part with a certain level of bite; he was still sore towards me for what I had uncovered inside of his brain.

"Oh no don't get up. I'd hate to tear you away from holding Jade's hands…" Reaver said with a mouthful of food. He sat down on a pile of compacted dirt and gripped Killian's left hand in his before squeezing it.

"More useful of a talent than his aura trick." Then Reaver looked over at me and Perish. "There is a small town about ten miles from here,

I'd rather us find a basement or something there to hide in for a couple days. Once we're there we can contact Elish and tell him where he can find us, if he didn't go with Jack on his recovery mission."

I nodded, though the thought that Elish was near both filled me with joy and fear. He sounded really pissed that Tim had been killed. I hoped he didn't take it out on me.

The more I thought of it though, the more I realized Tim dying by Reaver's hand was kind of a good thing.

Tim was a necessary casualty and Kessler had his heir anyway. Reaver had almost left with Killian and killing the boy had solidified him staying with us. Giving Reaver a chimera to kill, letting him express some of that inner transgressive behaviour, was both a strategic move and a forced move on my part. Once Tim's panicked screaming had hit Reaver's ears I knew he was done. The kid was toast. Chimeras had killed Leo and Greyson, and Kessler's Legion had been harassing Aras for years.

Still, those were two different worlds that had interfered into each other's territories. Greywaster world and the Skyfall world, and though Elish and myself were on Reaver's side, we still lived in the Skyfall world where Kessler was a wildcard, not an enemy.

If Kessler ever found out it was Reaver who had killed Tim… we would lose that ally forever, no question. When Elish ruled Skyfall and Reaver the greywastes, we would need the Legion to keep the public in order. The last thing we needed was a war with our own army.

How have I been doing so far? So badly I wanted to ask Elish this, but even if he was beside me, dressed in the greywaster clothing we had worn to Aras, I knew he wouldn't tell me. His praise was rarer than sunbeams but just as warm, warm enough to make you crave it during cold times like this.

Now his angry voice filled my head… telling me I was an idiot for not remembering that Jack would be coming for Tim.

We ate together, me and Killian listening to Perish and Reaver planning the easiest route to the small town Reaver had spotted during his scouting. We were going to go off-road near a small grove of trees where we could break up our silhouettes if we saw anyone above us, or on the ground.

A small search brought up nothing but some pieces of silverware Killian tucked into his bag. All the plates were broken and the fabric chewed through. Five or ten more years of rain and this house would fall into itself like the others. Decay came slowly to the greywastes, from both lack of rain and the radiation, but even with the short rainy season decay still rotted the bones of houses. Soon they would fall, and like an injured animal, as soon as they fell, the greywastes would take them.

The ash was so dry underneath my feet it had its own unique crunch to it. I adjusted the duffle bag slung over my back and wished once again for the warm apartment in Skyfall. If I had known my times of comfort were fleeting I would've enjoyed it more.

Reaver kept branching off into different directions, climbing small crags or scaling to the top of tipped over buses or semis. It wasn't a rare sight to see him shielding his eyes and surveying where we had been and where we were going, the deacdog not far behind, loyal to his master.

There was nothing to see though, the greywastes stretched on. Or were we still in the greyrifts? I didn't know; through eyes that had only seen the dark windowless buildings of Moros, or the bright rebuilt skyscrapers of Skyland, everything seemed to look the same. Grey tones without colour, broken up only occasionally by a leaning house or an acreage too far into what had once been a field for us to explore. It was grey and it was quiet, so quiet I could hear all of our heartbeats and could now recognize each person's individual tone.

How long until Falkland? It was impossible to tell from the atlas we had found, but Killian had ripped out the page and now it sat snugly in one of Reaver's many cargo pants pockets. He had said it would take us over a month to walk there with flat road and good weather, and neither of those things were ever promised.

Too far for us to go on our own, but then again, I knew we couldn't be near Kreig anymore. Maybe we were safer being on the road, I knew Reaver wouldn't be able to cope with being a sitting duck for long.

And what would we find in Falkvalley? A small town, a block with a name we would all recognize? Or perhaps nothing but an O.L.S unit tucked into a dilapidated dresser. All of these doubts made my shoulders slump just a little bit more, and I wished once again for Elish to be here.

I missed those protective arms, I missed sitting on his lap and falling asleep, even if he would tease me that I was too old for that now.

I was almost eighteen, just one more month; my teenager years were as fleeting as my mortality.

"A plane is landing…"

Like Reaver's words were audible nightmares, my inner daydreams shot from me. All of us jerked our heads up to the sentry standing on top of a stone bluff, his stance solid but his hands twitching towards his M16.

I turned to the shadows of Kreig behind us, and saw with Perish the small dot circling the city. Like a fly hovering around fruit, it moved around several taller buildings before we watched it hover in place.

It was late afternoon now and we had been walking since the grey dawn had broken the east, more than enough time for Kessler and Caligula to go to Skyfall or Cardinalhall and report what had happened.

"Keep our speed up… if we hurry we'll be in the town within the hour," Reaver said, before jumping down off of the bluff. Immediately he took the bag Killian was carrying, though his eyes were still fixed on the shrouded city. "Nothing we can do now but move. Let's go."

Killian's face had already gone three shades paler; he stuffed his hands into his pockets, unable to tear his gaze from the distant city we'd left behind. "What if they come here?"

Reaver had already turned around, his pace a brisk walk. Perish wasn't too far behind.

"I'll tell you if it happens. Come on, we're exposed out here with nothing to hide ourselves in."

I walked beside Killian, with Perish lagging behind as he usually did; always covering Killian's flank as Reaver pushed ahead. He was guarding the mortal non-chimera like everyone seemed to want to do.

The sprint towards the small cluster of houses was quiet, the silence only broken up by the occasional update from Reaver who was, now more than ever, climbing anything that would give him a better view. There was little to update though, the plane had landed and there it had stayed.

We followed the road now, passing cars that sat where they had died, just shells of red corrosion sometimes stuffed with fabric and dried grass from abandoned radrat nests. They lined the streets like planted coffins, houses on either side doomed to tend these graves until time ceased going forward.

I looked behind me as Reaver and Perish both broke off into different houses. Killian was beside me with a fast heartbeat and a throat that swallowed his fear every several minutes.

With eyes that barely blinked, Killian watched the city in the distance, keeping close to the telephone booth Reaver had told us to stay beside. I knew his fears were not for himself, but for his black-eyed boyfriend and the king that stalked him. I wondered if he truly grasped the reality of what would happen if Silas ever got Reaver.

We walked into the small town, still keeping dead silent, but as we diverted from the main road I felt a change in Reaver's dark aura, a fluxuation of unease that was suddenly matched with Killian's. My eyes swept the small suburban structures around us, single-storey ranchers both standing and fallen, all surrounded by twists of metal and thick barked trees; some trees acting as such solid barriers they enclosed the front yard like a thicket.

"This town isn't abandoned…" Reaver said under his breath. He gave Killian a sideways glance before he walked closer to the boy, shielding him as much as he could without making it obvious.

I smelled the air and tried to tune my hearing, the nervousness starting to claw up my stomach and into my throat. It was faint, so faint only a chimera could smell it, but it was there: smoke, and the vague aroma of dried sweat and dirt.

The deeper we got into the town, the more obvious it became, animal bones stashed in corners and tire rims charred black from use. Every sign we saw brought another surge of nerves to the group, until finally it was enough for Reaver.

We were all holding guns by now, and with a quick check to make sure Killian had enough ammo he brought us to a small two-storey house. "Perish, stay with Killian… Jade, you're coming with me."

Me? He usually stashed me with the mortal boy. I resisted the urge to show pride in being trusted to scout with him, and gave him a serious nod, fingering the handgun on my side and making sure my combat knife was snugly beside it. Though with the pride came the fear. This wasn't Moros and in no way my element, but it was a hell of a lot better than being hidden in the house with Killian like I was a lion cub.

"Perish… if anyone comes near this house shoot them, no matter what Killian says, alright?" Reaver whispered.

Killian normally would've given him a look for that comment, but the boy was too worried. Perish didn't speak, only nodded, before putting a hand on Killian's back and directing him into the house.

When they were gone we started down a road with deep fissures that separated pavement from ash, splitting the road open like fresh wounds. Like Reaver, I tried to follow my nose towards the burning fire, but the faint smell of smoke seemed to have combined itself with the usual musty smell of decaying houses. It sank in everywhere, imbedding itself in every porous location, muddling my sense of smell and making it almost impossible to pinpoint its source.

"We'll stay here for tonight and move on tomorrow." This made my head jerk towards Reaver, his tone suddenly switching from a hushed whisper to a normal even tone.

"If there are people here, we'll tell them we don't mean them any harm."

Then I heard it, a slight shuffling in one of the buildings, and out of the corner of my eye, a movement in one of the windows that disappeared like a silverfish in daylight. I realized then that we were being followed; Reaver had probably known since we had entered the town.

"Well, we have lots of food to share either way… and booze." I shrugged, feeling an itch in my fingers to just bring out my assault rifle and start shooting. But by now I knew Reaver, I had known Reaver since we were young teenagers; he didn't need prompting to open fire on people. I had to trust his cues and follow his lead.

The tension radiated off of us, Reaver was rigid, his black eyes fixed beams of dark energy. I knew what he was waiting for, for them to make the first move. We had to play human, with human ears and human senses, even though the both of us could hear the people shifting around the houses, like cannons going off in an open auditorium.

We rounded a corner, hugging the far corner to give us as much visibility of the next road as we could. I was glad he did too, when we crossed a two-lane intersection we were greeted with two people holding guns.

Two men, dressed in dark greasy clothes mismatched and sewn together in a half-assed fashion. Immediately they drew their guns, just as the people behind us made themselves known. A weak attempt to ambush, with one whistle the dog would be here, and Killian and Perish.

"Now looky what we have here," one of them said, pointing his scuffed assault rifle right at my face. "Funny how fate just ends up working out, eh? We could get a lot of money for you two."

Reaver stared at him, before glancing behind his shoulder at another man coming out of a house. "Well, we're not rats, so I am assuming you're slavers. Is this your base or are you migrating?"

The man pointing the gun in my face chuckled; he was missing one of his incisors and his tongue had a thick scar on it like someone had once tried to cut it out.

"Brash one, isn't he? We're slavers, and who are you?"

Who *were* we? Reaver would sort that out, and he did, without missing a beat. "My name is Merrik, this is my personal slave Mikey. We also have a deacon dog which helps protect us from people who would do us harm, and two others with better-looking guns than the ones you're carrying. We intend to spend the night here and carry on in the morning, unless you have a problem with that? Which I am half-hoping you do."

Fucking hell, please do not have a problem with this… I didn't want to be in the middle of a gun fight.

"Merrik, eh? Merrik with a slave, interesting." I saw the one pointing his gun at Reaver lower it slightly, but the one on me didn't budge. "You look rather well-groomed for a traveller, Merrik. Are you a legion deserter?"

"No." Reaver looked over at me; I was still staring at the gun. "Lower your guns and I can tell you over a drink. I am not hostile yet, but keep pointing a gun at my pet's face and I will become a problem quickly."

"You need to watch your mouth boy or –" Suddenly there was a sharp laugh, both Reaver and I turned around to see a man leaning up against the warped patio deck.

He looked at us over the rim of a black dust-stained panama hat, and smiled a smile that I was immediately wary of. It was a natural smile, not forced or brought on to enforce a false sense of calm. It was a natural grin. And since there was, to us anyway, nothing to smile about… I didn't like it.

"Stop sticking guns in people's faces. Does that motherfucker look like a face you wanna fuck with?" The man, probably in his thirties, sauntered up to Reaver and me, as he did the other two lowered their guns. "They're healthy, and they have Skyfall eyes. The last thing I want is a legion bug up my ass – Who the fuck are you two?"

Reaver didn't take his eyes off of him, and like the man had, Reaver looked him up and down. He had brown hair hidden under that brimmed hat, and a faded brown leather jacket unzipped over several layers of shirts.

Though Reaver's observation of this man was only physical, mine could be more. I tuned my aura and brought up the colours surrounding him.

Grey and orange, an interesting combination and deceptively heavy, but most greywaster auras were. For a slaver he wasn't necessarily bad, but as slave-driving arians went he wasn't a thick cloud of shit either. I didn't trust him, obviously, but I also had the reassurance that he wasn't going to kill us. At least not before Reaver's mouth gave him a reason to.

"I already said as much as I want… I am Merrik and this is Mikey. We–"

I cut in; I didn't need any more reminders that Reaver had no social skills. Not to mention he now didn't fear death.

"We were chased out of Kreig by those lizard things. We're tired and we need to rest before we bugger off. None of us give a shit that you're slavers. We just need a night or two to crash."

The man tilted his head up as he gave me the once over. "Yellow eyes. You two are Skyfallers, eh?"

"I am not a–"

"We're defectors and the two others are greywasters," I answered before Reaver could finish his sentence. "Just travellers, that's all. Are you going to let us crash in one of these houses or not?"

"You mentioned booze?" The man eyed us with a certain glint that any man who lacked good swill had. I had the same glint whenever the drugs came out.

Reaver put his bag down, and with that gesture everyone raised their guns. He didn't care though; he opened the bag and took out two bottles of vodka. "There, that's all you're getting. Deal or not?"

I never understood how greywasters communicated; it wasn't a way I was used to. Sometimes I swear they could stare at each other and grunt, and by that gesture alone they could figure one another out.

Either way, the man, who I now assumed was the leader, nodded towards Reaver and picked up the booze. "We're clearing out once we fix a few malfunctioning collars anyway. We don't own this shithole, we're just squatting. Sure, Merrik, you camp in a house for a few nights." He handed the bottles to the man who had been pointing the gun at me, and held out a hand towards Reaver. Reaver stared at it for a moment before his social skills kicked in. He took the slaver's hand and shook it.

The man grinned; his light green eyes alight with curiosities over these two newcomers and their vodka. "My name's Hopper, and I won't bring you any trouble if you bring none to me."

"And if you step a foot inside our house or think you're quick enough to take us as slaves… you will find more trouble than you could ever imagine," Reaver growled, grabbing the slavers hand so hard he flinched.

Hopper laughed and all I could do was shake my head.

Killian needed to teach this boy some social skills.

CHAPTER 20

Jack

The Previous Night

JACK RAN HIS GLOVED FINGERS OVER THE SMOOTH polished wood, braided in such a beautiful way over the banister of King Silas's bed. He had always loved this bedroom, though a few of his chimera brothers have come to dread their summons from the Ghost King.

Well, only Elish and Jade. Everyone else quite enjoyed it.

Satisfied and content, Jack looked over at the king, sleeping soundly after more than a handful of hours in each other's embrace. He would be asleep for the next five hours, and as always, Jack was free to go when he was ready. His summons from King Silas were no out of the ordinary thing, like Garrett, Artemis, and Apollo (which he loved requesting together) or the younger generations, usually two weeks didn't go by without that phone call.

"Oh, doesn't he just look so adorable while he sleeps." Jack glanced up to see his brother Sanguine casually saunter into the room.

The sengil-chimera, with black hair that brushed his jawline, a thin face, and two blood-red eyes strolled up to the bed holding twin glasses of wine. When Jack made eye contact with him he smiled, revealing two rows of pointed teeth.

Jack returned the smile showing his own serrated teeth. They were some of the only chimeras to be born with such an enhancement. Chimera Ds as they had been labelled, though most of the time they were called as they referred to themselves as: the demon-chimeras.

"Yes, our king who killed the world… I swear if he wouldn't rip off my face, I would hold him like the little darling he is while he naps." Jack brushed away a loose strand of wavy blond hair from the king's face and took the glass of wine. Then, as he took a drink of the coppery liquid, he rose to a sitting position on the bed and drew the flannel sheet over his slender naked body. "He has been a rather rough customer as of late. I can tell he is wanting our greywaster chimera in his bed. I suppose besides you and Nero I am the best candidate for giving him the rough fuck he needs. God knows Elish is dodging every invitation he can right now," Jack replied.

Sanguine seemed amused by this; he swirled the blood wine in his cup and took a long drink. "Well, since Elish's pet is recovering in the greyrifts it's no wonder his mood is soured. He–"

Both of them paused as a quick pulse of beeps could be heard, a noise Jack had been hearing since he had been given the job of Grim Reaper, or Grim as they called him.

"Drake? Juni was tossing the ball for him on the roof. Perhaps he chased it off the edge again?" Sanguine said bemused, tilting his head towards Jack.

Jack looked over at the sleeping Silas before raising the wristwatch-type device on his hand.

His face paled, he almost couldn't believe what he was looking at. "My god, Sanguine… it… it was Timothy… Timothy's dead."

Sanguine's brow knitted together, but that was all for the emotions on his face. Casually he took another drink before twitching his mouth off to the side. Then the demon-chimera's eyes flickered towards the king, though whatever thoughts Sanguine had inside of that head, he kept to himself.

"Should we wake him?" Jack asked, leaving the sheets behind as he rose and stretched, his naked and firm body showing rosy patches and small welts from his tryst with the king.

Sanguine shook his head, not hiding his hungry glances at his brother's body. "No, he has enough on his mind right now; I'll break the news to him. I believe Elish has the only Falconer in the city right now. All the other ones are searching for our dark sibling."

Jack turned to address his brother, when with a light push, Sanguine tipped him back over onto the king size bed. He glanced up with a raised eyebrow, but before he could answer, Sanguine pressed his lips against Jack's.

The Grim kissed him back before trying to rise, but the sengil pushed him back down. He blinked, but was silent as the red-eyed chimera grabbed his legs and pushed them forward so Jack was half lying down, then he pressed his knees back.

"What in hell are…" A pleasurable rush flowed through him as he felt Sanguine's talented tongue start to tease his opening. "I need to go, you idiot. Put that tongue back where it belongs."

But the sengil didn't move from his position; his hands gripped Jack's knees as his tongue licked and flicked the tight area.

Jack heard a suppressed chuckle before Sanguine gave it a long drawn-out lick. "Mm, I taste our master on you. Was he the one to do the fucking tonight?" The Grim shuddered as his chimera brother reintroduced his tongue, then without fully realizing he was doing it, he started to pull his own legs back.

"You'll wake up our king. Get off of me now." Jack shifted his body back up, but once again Sanguine pushed him down. This time though, the sengil removed his tongue and crawled on top of him.

"Mmm, no, I don't think so."

Jack smirked; he grabbed Sanguine's bowtie and pulled him down into a kiss. "If you're wanting a tryst, you can have me once I return, or call Drake. I need to get going to Elish's to get that plane."

"Our brother isn't getting any deader." Sanguine winked, letting his tongue travel up Jack's neck. "Now… you can either follow me into my bedroom, where–" Jack gasped as Sanguine positioned his ass over Jack's hard cock now grasped in his hand. Sanguine pressed down, but not enough to break the tight seal. "I can ride you properly… or I can do it right here and wake up our dear king."

Why now, you stupid sengil…? Jack shook his head but kissed him again, his member growing and twitching under the sengil's grasp. There was no denying these advances weren't completely unwanted, but really – now? When he had to leave?

But Sanguine was correct, Tim was not getting any deader, and would a little longer be that bad? He could make up the excuse that he was still satisfying his king, that job took precedence over all anyway.

So with a long drawn-out sigh, Jack rose himself to the smirking-glee of Sanguine. The next thing Jack knew he was being pushed onto the bed with the blood-eyed chimera crawling over top of him with a devilish smile that only their own genetics could truly wield.

Jack grabbed onto Sanguine's hips as he lowered himself onto him, clenching his serrated teeth and grunting as the Grim's dick broke through.

"This is all on you if I get into trouble with–" Jack's teeth clenched as Sanguine lifted his hips before roughly pushing down, Jack's entire length sinking into him.

And that was the last words Jack spoke. Sanguine leaned down and claimed his lips once again, rhythmically pushing himself up and down on his chimera brother.

Sanguine smirked to himself in his head, wondering how pleased Elish would be at this so carefully calculated distraction. His blond brother needed all the time he could get to hide Jade and the others, and what was a better distraction than sex?

The black-haired chimera nipped on Jack's neck, and in response, his brother grabbed his backside to push him in deeper. Jack was into it, and if Sanguine wanted he could have him for hours.

And perhaps that is just what Sanguine would do.

The Grim found his clothes and started putting them on with an internal chastise of himself. "Once again you will get me into trouble. Do you think I should wake the king?" It had been two hours since Sanguine had dragged him to the bedroom, and he was starting to feel the first pang of guilt over indulging himself rather than doing his duty.

"Unless we know for sure, we will not bother him." Sanguine's voice sounded relaxed. He was splayed out naked on his black and red comforter, his hands folded behind his head. He seemed to blend in perfectly with the comforter and his own black tree bed frame. Black and red were a part of that sengil's being, from his appearance all the way to his clothing and decoration choice.

Jack stopped, the sleeve of his tailed Victorian coat half on his body. He eyed his brother with his shining black eyes, before narrowing them slightly. "Are you sure? But if it is Reaver… Kessler and the other two were going to Kreig to check out a sudden electricity power up, were they not?"

"For all we know Tim fell through some rotten floorboards, either way, I am to assume they have his body back in Cardinalhall." Sanguine absentmindedly ran his hands down his pale but well-toned body, tracing his abs with a smirk. Though at the display Jack glared at him, as if daring Sanguine to try and initiate another session.

"And anyway, if we mention even that prospect… losing Reaver in Aras has enraged him enough. I don't want to plant a false hope in his head." Sanguine rose and wrapped himself in a black silk robe. He followed Jack outside the bedroom door and into a long hallway, the dark living room off in the distance. "He's testy enough right now as it is and I'm the one that bears the brunt of his cruelty."

The last button got done up on Jack's coat, and after fully dressing himself he took a glance in the mirror.

Behind him Sanguine had his arms crossed, his red eyes suddenly troubled and his mouth a thin line. The sengil to the king didn't have an easy life, but this was his life and Jack had his own duties and responsibilities.

Jack's responsibilities were to collect the dead and the immortal dead, sew any wounds that might interfere with their recovery process, bathe and dress them and wrap them in silk. He had his library where they would recover, and once they awoke, Jack's job was complete. This was the reason why he was created; he was the collector of the dead, the Charon in the River of Styx. A job he prided himself on doing well.

And in all respects, his job was not to argue with Sanguine or argue with what was said to Silas or when. So with that, Jack left Sanguine to his duties and casually made his way to Olympus, Elish's Skyscraper. If there was one thing he and his brothers had learned during their immortal existence it was to never over-step your own duties. If there was fallout from this, it would be on Sanguine's head, not his.

With his sengil Juni beside him, Jack walked out of the elevator and into the hallway of Elish's apartment. The mood was always different in this skyscraper when Jade was gone, the empath chimera always brought a bit of sparkle to the atmosphere of his cold brother Elish; it was odd to have the boy absent for so long. The tension could be cut with a knife, especially since Elish refused to bed anyone but his little husband now. It was once a common joke that perhaps Elish wouldn't be so uptight if he got a blowjob every now and then.

It wasn't only Jade's absence that had soured Olympus, there was, of course, the ransom of that greywaster boy. Garrett had been moping around in Elish's apartment for months now. It was a gloomy time for their family, but as long as they weren't dying regularly it was a quiet time for the Grim. It had been enjoyable, he had lots of free time to paint, work on his books, and read. And really, that was all Jack needed out of life.

Luca answered the door with a surprised look. He bowed and turned around. "Master, it's Master Jack and Juni."

"I know," a cold voice sounded. Jack strolled in and saw Elish beside the large picture windows of his skyscraper, a mug of tea in hand and his remote phone in the other. "Tiberius called me; he's in the medical wing of Cardinalhall. Kessler and Caligula are seriously injured and Timothy is dead and still in Kreig."

Still in Kreig? So they left his body there? Jack's eyes widened. He walked over to where Elish was, hearing Luca in the background fixing him his own mug of tea. "And? Was it Reaver?"

Elish took a sip of tea. "No, Caligula suspects a legion soldier that Tim bait-trapped didn't take too kindly to the act and escaped. You may not find much of Tim's remains but, of course, they would like some of him recovered. It seems an underground spring, plus the radiation pulse after the fire, had an adverse reaction to some of Perish's creatures. A species of lizards crossed with humans apparently, and they ambushed them." He took another drink. "I will accompany you to collect his remains."

"The company would be nice; Kreig is a good three hours away, is it not?" Jack took his tea from Luca, and with a bow, the sengil headed off to make small conversation with Juni. The two were good friends.

"That is right." Elish still hadn't taken his eyes off of the horizon, though it was darkness in front of them, the sun would not rise for quite a while. "The Falconer is ready to go; we will be stopping off at Cardinalhall first. Timothy's chewed-on corpse will not be going anywhere and the irradiated lizards are nocturnal. We will head there when the sun has risen. Luca, Juni, stay behind. Do as you will but I want no trace of it when I return, am I understood?"

Oh of course, when sengil boys were left alone with a clean house and nothing to do they would indeed get into mischief. Sure enough, both Luca and Juni flushed before mumbling agreeance to the cold staring eyes of Elish. Ones that knew exactly how the mice were going to play once the cats went away.

"Jack, have you spoken to Silas lately?" Elish asked him when they were high above the greywastes, the flickering lights of Cardinalhall in front of them and Skyfall hours behind. It had been a peaceful and quiet trip. Elish had always been the silent type, and since he had the biggest hand in Jack's upbringing Jack had taken on more than a few of Elish's characteristics. They were both tranquil, quiet people; they talked inside their own heads, not so much out loud.

Jack, who had been trying to catch a few moments sleep, opened one eye to him. "I was in his company when I got the alert on my watch. Dozing though, I had just fulfilled a personal summons."

"Did he hear your notification?"

Jack opened both eyes, aware of the tones on Elish's lips. The cold chimera had something else on his mind and Jack knew it.

"No…" Jack said slowly. "Sanguine did though, but I left the king sleeping where he lay. Why, Elish?"

"I would rather he not know of this until we know what happened. For him to go off into the greywastes right now would be taxing on him. His mental state has already been compromised over the re-emergence of Chimera X."

A heavy silence fell over the cockpit as the lights of the legion military base blanketed the inside of the plane. Jack could see his brother's deep purple eyes reflect the artificial lights in front of them.

"You think he'll take his anger out on your little husband again? Do not take me for a fool to have me believe you worry about his health. Come now, brother." Jack's full lips split into a smirk, before he felt the jolt of the plane as it started to descend.

Elish didn't answer, which was typical for his oldest brother. He was silent when the plane landed, and silent still when Tiberius Dekker, Kessler's non-chimera husband, came sprinting up to them.

"Get back in… we… we need to get him out of that fucking city." Tiberius's voice was a strangled choke, and though no tears could be seen on the stoic man's face, his eyes were full and rimmed with red.

Elish held up a hand. "I must speak with Kessler before we depart, Tiberius. Unfortunately there is nothing we can do for your son now. I would like to hear their stories so the family can act accordingly."

Tiberius, a man with short brown hair and a thin beard, shook his head, his lips pursing. "Kess is conscious. He refuses to be dispatched to heal until he knows Tim's remains have been returned. Clig isn't… he… fuck, Elish, we don't think it was Willis. Kessler thinks it was that fucking clone. They're saying he snipered their knees and shoulders. He… he was deliberately making it so Kess couldn't carry out both of them, I am sure of it. I want Silas on the phone… he has to know this."

Elish shook his head. "Let me talk to Kessler first and we can take it from there. Jack, go to Kessler, I need to make a phone call."

Tiberius didn't seem happy with this but he obeyed. Leaving Elish behind in the hanger, the two of them went into the base.

The base was a converted industrial factory, set in the middle of a flat plain surrounded by sharp grey mountains. It was the main base for the Legion and had been in use since Jack was a child. He had been here many times, and many times more to collect bodies. It didn't happen often, but every once in a while Kessler or one of the other immortals accidently got blown up or shot in some sort of vital organ.

Jack quietly followed Tiberius down the long concrete hallway, passing legionary with their heads bowed and generals and sergeants alike who gave them their customary nods of recognition. That had always been a rule when there was a chimera in their presence, the family was royalty after all and no one dared not show the utmost respect, especially those with a more… intimidating appearance.

Jack ran his tongue along his serrated teeth and smiled wryly to himself. Though Sanguine had always had internal issues with how King Silas had created them, Jack had embraced the fear he stuck in the hearts of the common man. He quite liked that every non-chimera seemed to be absolutely terrified of him.

Tiberius led him through several long hallways, until they passed three legionary guards holding assault rifles. As soon as they saw the silver-haired chimera and the Imperial General's husband, they nodded and took a step back. Jack let Tiberius enter the room first.

"Well, bullet wounds do heal quickly. I am surprised they didn't put you out of your pain –Are you going to put in a request to make Caligula immortal after this?" Jack closed the door behind him with a light click; Tiberius already making his way to his husband's bedside.

He turned around to see Kessler laying in a hospital bed, staring forward; his grey eyes hard and his face stone-cold and emotionless. In that moment, Jack decided to back away from his immortal brother. The Grim was never one to sympathise with those who suffered from a death in the family, perhaps he was a bit desensitized to it all after so many years. Still though, Kessler was family, and the man did love his sons more than anything.

"He made me choose… I didn't see it in that moment, Jack, but he did," Kessler said quietly, his eyes not moving from their locked position. "I realized… this was no act of a scared legionary, unwilling to die for his king… this was the clone, Jack, this was Reaver's work. I know this because Silas would have done the exact same thing."

It was the clone? Interesting… but Kreig was hundreds of miles from Aras, how could that be possible? It had been a couple months, yes, but still, this clone was shaping up to be quite the incredible specimen. Jack was looking forward to meeting him, to be able to get a taste for who this born immortal was. Surely he was a magnificent beast for his own king to be so enamoured with him.

A killer of all things…

"You know what I also realized?" Kessler shook his head; he wiped his face slowly with his hands. "There was this sniper near Aras, we called him the Raven. For the last five years he would roam around and snipe our men… that was him too I bet."

"To think that Lycos was alive this whole time," Jack replied with a smirk. "I would give him a round of applause if he still lived. To have hidden our little dark chimera all this time? It's too bad how it ended. I would have wished for Silas to have tried to rehabilita- What are you doing?" Jack blinked as Kessler rose to his feet, pulling the IV out of his arm and grabbing a thick wool sweater that had been slung over a hospital chair.

"Kess!" Tiberius exclaimed but with a hard look he was quiet.

"We're leaving, Jack, this is personal now. Reaver killed my son and has been terrorizing my men for years. Elish will try and stop me and I will have none of it. Come with me. Tibbs, stay behind and try and delay Elish from following us – Now, Jack."

"But the creatures–"

"Are nocturnal and the sun is already rising."

Jack raised an eyebrow. Elish ranked higher than all of them, but his own duties technically ranked first, and collecting Timothy's remains was Jack's job. However he did wish his brothers didn't boss him around like some sort of sengil. But what was there to do? Being the silent observant type that Jack was had affected how his brothers treated him. If it made the chest thumping chimeras happy to order around their Grim of a brother, let the babies have their candy. It was easier that way.

But on the other hand, Jack did love to stir the pot, if only to passive-aggressively poke and prod.

"Elish will not like this," Jack responded in an almost sing-song voice, and with that, he smiled. He almost liked the chaos this move would cause; it was a break in the monotony and the dreary gloom that had been on the family. Watching the heated exchange that would undoubtedly come with Kessler's actions would be an absolute joy to witness. Especially since Jack had done nothing wrong personally.

A brother getting disciplined was such a delight.

Kessler let Tiberius stick a couple more bandages on his wound before Kessler batted him away. "Elish is in charge of Skyfall, the greywastes are mine. Let's go, good luck dealing with him, Tibbs. As I said, try and delay him as much as you can."

"I am not looking forward to it… but okay, for Tim." The stoic-faced general nodded solemnly. "Just bring our boy home…"

Once again carted from one location to another. Jack sighed internally but followed his brother to their plane. *Juni is at Olympus having relations with a cute little blond sengil and here I am dealing with family drama. Oh, the life of a sengil, it definitely isn't all bad, is it?*

This time, to his drowsy relief, Jack was able to sleep on the next plane ride. By now he had been up almost all night, only catching a cat nap here or there. Once he got home he planned on rewarding himself with an entire day in his tower, ordering his favourite food and perhaps ordering some new paints and canvases. The greywastes did not offer much but their grey-black rolling mountains and twisted trees always inspired his imagination. He could give the painting to Apollo perhaps; it was his and Artemis's birthdays soon.

Jack heard muffled sniffing. He opened his eyes to see Kessler gripping the steering mechanism for the plane hard. He was holding back his emotions as they flew over Kreig, and Jack could only hope he could keep it together until he was dropped back off at Cardinalhall. It was always so awkward when they cried; especially the more brutish ones who usually kept their emotions in check. Jack never knew what to do with himself, so he usually just ignored it with every fiber in his body.

With a yawn, Jack rose once the plane had been turned off and checked the device imbedded into his wristwatch. Every other chimera that had the death-trackers planted in their brains were alive, so after this hopefully he could go home.

"We – we left him on the street off to your left," Kessler said quietly, his voice thick with emotion.

The both of them stepped off onto the cracked concrete; the street Kessler had parked the plane on holding three-storey structures on each side. All of them intact but their siding had been stripped, revealing the bones of steel beams and mortar stained a hundred shades of grey. This street must've been in the industrial part of the city, or a lower-income one. The buildings were full of gaping windows, open and declaring their defiance to the elements. A perfect place for these so called *reptile men* to hide in. What a wonder Perish's splicing was; to think they survived off of small vermin, water, and radiation. Though perhaps the water had allowed the growth of fungus or something similar. Irontowers' sewers were full of fungus, most of the prey radanimals there lived off of it.

Jack glanced around, scanning each window for any movement, but as Kessler had said these creatures seemed to be nocturnal. So with that putting his mind at ease, he followed behind the Imperial General, now scanning the long double-lane streets. Not for the splices, but for this clone he had yet to meet.

"Oh look, moss… interesting, it seems they have a fair water source," Jack remarked, running his hand up a still standing light pole. He looked at his hand as he retracted it and rubbed his fingers together. Wondering what mixture of green and brown paints he would need to mix to make such a colour. "This place has so much water. The town will decay faster now but perhaps one day you can turn this into a block."

Kessler didn't answer. He was several paces in front of Jack, his head bowed and his shoulders tight. Dressed in only a wool sweater and a pair of thick cloth fatigues, he didn't look like the Imperial General he was. This made the silver-haired chimera a bit put off; if the clone was watching them he certainly wouldn't get the right impression of his family.

Jack followed and checked his watch again. He pressed several buttons to pin-point the location of the death signal he had received. To Jack's surprise, he saw the small red dot flashing to his left, down a small street they were about to walk past.

"Kessler… the street to the left is where I got the signal, not this one." Jack jogged over to the small single-lane street, void of the tipped over rusted cars and debris; it turned onto the suburbs from the looks of it.

"I can see where we left him and he isn't there – Fuck, I hope he didn't try to crawl to safety… I can't believe I actually–"

Jack didn't need to ask why Kessler had suddenly stopped talking; the reason was right in front of both of them, half a block down the street.

Strung up on a light pole.

Kessler gave out an anguished cry and broke into a run. Jack stared for a few moments longer before following him, his eyes going in all different directions trying to figure out if this was an ambush or not.

As Jack got closer, he found his steps start to slow, until they stopped altogether. He stopped and stared at the scene in front of him, and even though he had been collecting the dead for decades, Jack felt a cold nausea in his chest he had rarely ever felt.

Tim Dekker was hanging off of the street lamp, his chest exposed and the cavity empty of all but his dry ribs; though it was not rope that had been used to dangle the young chimera over the lizards, he had his own intestines wrapped around his neck. Semi-dried coils of peach-coloured guts, with black flecks that were flies buzzing around to lay their eggs in his brutalized and mutilated corpse.

Tim swayed there in the windless city. His chest cavity was open to the flies and his calico-coloured eyes staring off into oblivion and the young teenager's pasty chest a ruin from quick knife-work and eager teeth. Tim's entire body had been brutalized in the most beautifully artistic way.

Jack took a step closer and saw a pool of Tim's innards below his feet, already drying and sticking to the cracked concrete. The Grim tapped the pile with his foot, and with that gesture, a cloud of flies flew up into the air.

Good dependable greywaste flies. Not even winter stops them from consuming the dead.

The smell was interesting, the same stink of a freshly butchered corpse about to turn under the cold winter sun, the noise was even more interesting, but not unique in the least. It was the noise of thousands of insects buzzing over a soon-to-be disappearing meal – and, of course, Kessler muffling his own agony.

What a beautiful scene, breathtakingly beautiful.

Yes, this man is King Silas. Reaver's not just sending us a message; he made us an exquisite sculpture while he was at it.

Jack took a step closer and reached a hand out to touch the boy's boots. "Ah, yes, this would be the work of our clone, wouldn't it? Silas will be happy to hear tha-"

"I'LL FUCKING KILL HIM!" Kessler suddenly screamed. He whirled around and took several steps away from Tim's dangling corpse before whirling around and dropping to his knees. The Imperial General let out an agonizing scream before slamming his hand down on the pavement, tears falling from his downturned head and staining the ground.

This would make a unique painting... I shall remember this scene.

Sanguine's birthday is in the spring, maybe I will give it to him.

No... no, I want to keep this one.

"He could have saved him... he's... these are not fatal bites...

Reaver killed him. LOOK! He, oh fuck, did he take his heart?"

There was a sickening thunk as Kessler pulled Tim down to the ground, and with a moan, the Imperial General put a hand on Tim's chest.

"It wasn't cut out… his heart was chewed out of his chest. What kind of fucking clone is this?" Kessler groaned. He shook his head and sniffed, before raising a hand and brushing it against his son's cold, dead face.

"Well, they call him the dark chimera for a reason… he is Silas's clone after all," Jack answered back calmly, looking around just to make sure this clone wasn't peering at them from one of the crumbling buildings. It would be in his nature; Silas would have done the same thing. He got a grand amount of pleasure watching people experience the pain he inflicted on them.

"Silas was not born evil; Reaver's worse than he is. This isn't the work of a fucking chimera, he's… he's something else." Kessler's tone dropped. "I do not know what Lycos created… but I will see him encased in concrete for all eternity for this."

Then the Imperial General rose to his feet, a new fire inside of his eyes. As Jack looked on, his hands folded behind his back, he watched as his brother got out his remote phone, and after a few buttons pressed, Kessler put it to his ear.

"I want Tiberius here, and I want every legionary we can fit into the planes scouring the city and towns surrounding. Reaver Dekker did this and he cannot be far."

CHAPTER 21

Reno

IT USED TO BE THAT ONLY WHEN I SLEPT DID I SEE them. Now they were a constant companion to a mind that didn't know how to cope with a reality that didn't seem like a reality at all. I didn't know what was happening in that lump of tissue behind my eyes, I just knew inside of it I saw Garrett, Reaver, Killian… inside I saw Aras, my mom and dad, my siblings, and sometimes I even saw Asher.

Mostly I saw my three boys. I forced them to support me in my own mind, but even my delusional self turned their confident praise into worried glances.

I thought chimeras were supposed to protect the ones they loved?

I had two chimeras who I loved and where was I now?

Locked away like a quarantined rat, though it was because I was too valuable to them to kill and too violent to expose to light.

All alone. All alone and now I knew they were no longer looking for me.

Kerres had made sure of that and Meirko too. I had met Meirko the other day. They had shown me the news station, happily reporting on Grant Dekker's newest factory in the borderlands. They would be making Dek'ko brand chocolate bars now.

I had gotten replaced by chocolate bars.

They were going to be called SnapBars, and the mint flavour: Snap-Mint.

Congrats?

There were no more twenty-four hour promos on us. No news reports, no media attention… it was like we had never gotten kidnapped in the first place.

Had Garrett forgotten about me? Had he given up?

My eyes closed and I tried to imagine I was somewhere else, perhaps doing something fun. I did this often. My imagination was my life now.

Sometimes I imagined my mouth tasting the soft flesh of Shale's dick, however it didn't salivate like Reaver's did at the irony taste of blood. It soured and grimaced, wishing for something better, even if it was just a drink of muddy irradiated water.

Kinda sad. Why couldn't I be some smuggled chimera black-market baby? I was just good dependable Reno… who now ate rats and licked the brick walls of my cell to get water.

The president of Skytech's fiancé Reno Adrian Nevada, brick licker, rat eater… dick biter.

Heh.

I couldn't wait to tell them what I did. I bet they'd be proud of me.

There was shifting outside of my door, light scratching of the rats making their way through corroded pipes. Small little claws that made a noise that had been my background music for as long as I can remember.

That and screams… Nico's screams, I think Trig was dead.

I knew Kay was dead, or at least paralyzed, getting shot in the spine would do that to a boy.

Maybe since the important ones were dead, they had abandoned their search. I wasn't that important… I was new after all.

This thought made my lower lip tighten and my eyes started to well. I didn't like where my emotions were going but I was starting to cruelly tell myself that Garrett had abandoned me. That I was too much trouble.

It wouldn't be like an immortal being kidnapped… I was just an idiot greywaster…

A tear rolled down my cheek but I wiped it away, and even though I was all alone… I told myself it was just the sweat stinging my eyes.

No media, no news… no search parties. All quiet.

No one was looking for me anymore.

My eyes took me to a greasy rat, just a shadow of movement out of the corner of my eye. I froze my body and slowed down my breathing as it sniffed around the door, where his rat friends had been scratching.

I was leaning up against the damp brick, my clothes clinging to my body like a second skin. I had lost a lot of weight already and I was hungry as fuck. So I watched him through the greasy silver hair that fell over my eyes like I was a starved cat, and waited for him to come closer.

Then, with a flash of movement, I had him. I wrapped my fingers around him and as he whirled around and sank his filthy teeth into me I dug my finger into his neck and snapped his spine away from his skull.

My own teeth then found his head and I ripped it off, without wasting time I drank the still warm blood from his body, cringing at the taste, before pulling his loose fur from what little meat it had.

I was more animal than Reno now, but I had been raised in the greywastes and it was nothing I hadn't done before. Though radrats made a better meal than their miniature counterparts.

So many things in this world were called rats: subhumans, big rodents, little rodents. I had even heard Lyle refer to Jade as a gutter rat… was I a greywaster rat?

My eyes squinted as the door opened, and even though I was still holding the limp rat in my hand, I looked up to see who was coming to beat on me next.

To my surprise, or as much as my mind could still feel that emotion, two people were thrown into the cell with me. They stumbled and fell to the ground, their arms shackled behind their backs.

My eyes travelled to the crimson-haired man in the doorway. I opened my dry mouth to ask the bitch for some fucking water, when he turned around and stiffened his stance.

"I did. Shut the fuck up or I'll shut you up!" Kerres snapped. He threw a brown sack into the hallway and slammed the door, but the conversation could still be heard from outside. "I don't care what he says, and I'm not scared of him. Tell him to fucking talk to me about it if he has a problem with how I've been handling this."

There was muffled yelling.

"And they aren't fucking looking at all now, are they? I didn't hear any news segments, did you? They don't fucking care about them anymore. I told you we should have fucking waited until we could kidnap Jade again."

Rub it in a bit more Kerres… rub it in a bit more…

"–No, we aren't getting Elish for these fucks. I know that now. And no I–"

A shifting of clothes and a groan distracted me. I looked down and saw Caligula's little soldier boyfriend Nico and beside him: Trig.

So the fuckers were still alive?

The angry voice of the red-haired fuck faded, and as it did, Nico shuffled to a sitting position and leaned up against the brick wall. Trig seemed dazed; he only lifted his head and let out a whimper.

I extended my hand and offered Nico a bite of rat.

Caligula's boyfriend's face was filthy and his angular eyes were dull, but he looked at the rat and took it with one of his hands, before bringing it up to his mouth and ripping off a bottom leg.

"Thanks," he croaked before handing it back. I offered it to Trig but he shook his head.

"Even rat tastes good right now," Nico grumbled.

I tried to smile but my lips felt like lizard skin. "If we were chimeras this would probably fucking taste like chocolate."

I tipped the rat above my head and tried to wring some more blood out of it. A few cold drops spilled into my mouth which I swallowed

"If we were chimeras they would've found us by now," Nico whispered bitterly.

Like a thousand needles, those words pricked all of my sensitive, raw places. The fact that he shared the same sentiment I had made it all too real.

I lowered the rat and started peeling the skin off of it. Then I placed a hand down on Trig's shoulder to give it a rub; the kid's whimpering had only gotten more pronounced since Nico's admission.

"Nah, man… that's not it. They're looking for us." I didn't believe my own words and Nico knew it.

Sure enough, as I glanced at him, I saw his expression was hard.

"Do you know how replaceable we are, Reno?" I lowered my head as he said this. "All of us, especially you and Trig. Mortal pets to immortal beings. They don't give a fuck; I fucking don't even know what they did to Kay."

That's right, only I saw the news station that showed the shootout between the Crimstones, and Elish and Silas. "They shot Kay. He's dead."

Nico only nodded; his chest rising and falling over a blue jacket, half the seams torn and frayed, covered in rust-coloured blood and who knows what else. Like me, his fancy Skyland clothing had fallen to the state of most greywaster attire. I wish they made me feel more at home but I just felt sick over it. I wasn't in the greywastes… I wasn't home.

I hadn't even figured out where home was before all of this shit went down.

My cheeks puffed as I let out a tense breath. Absentmindedly, I kept rubbing Trig's shoulder. The kid was a typical cicaro, thin-boned and skinny, submissive and polite. Not like Jade at all, but I guess Elish liked them bitey.

This kid though… he reminded me of a weaker version of Tinky, and I say weaker because Killian had come a long way since Reaver had first pointed him out to me. Killiboy was fucking badass now. This kid… not so much.

With the conversation at a lull, or perhaps our energy just drained, I leaned back and chewed on the small rat bones, trying to get as much of the marrow as I could. There wasn't much there to begin with though.

When Trig was finally able to right himself, he shifted between me and Nico and brought his knees up to his chest, sniffing every once in a while to stave away the damp which seemed to make our noses either congest or run.

"Kerres says the media stopped reporting on us – Do you think it's true?" Nico asked after a while.

I didn't want to but I nodded. "Yeah, he showed me on the television. It's all silent and the Legion has apparently pulled back all their forces."

Nico nodded, no expression on his face. He waited a solid minute before he made direct eye contact with me. "We're escaping tonight… just so you know."

I paused, the rat with its skin peeled down like it was a banana, halfway up to my mouth. I had been savouring every bite of the little rodent.

"What?" What the fuck else could I say to that?

Nico leaned his head back before looking over at Trig and me. The kid was staring at the metal door, his hands wrapped around his knees and his chin resting on top of them. It didn't even look like he was acknowledging what we were saying.

"You were a greywaster, right? I am General Zhou's son, who's keeping those scum Aras residents in line after they sold you out to Silas." The man's voice dropped at this admission, right as mine was rising in my throat.

My old home – No, no, I can't feel anything regarding Aras. Like Nico had said they'd betrayed me; they'd tried to fucking kill me and Killian. I'd almost died from that gut wound. Fuck all of them, even my own uncle had sold me out.

"You know how to live out there, you know how to survive – not to mention you're Reaver's best friend, right?" Nico let this drag, before I saw him glance down at Trig. "But if this little shit slows us down, I'm slicing his tendons."

Trig looked up at him before lowering his head down to his knees. "They'll come for us."

"No, they're not, and Meirko is telling Kerres to execute us. We're too hot for the Crimstones. Too much press has already been reported on us, and too many eyes are out looking. They want to kill us and abandon the mission. Elish isn't getting handed over for anyone and they're finally realizing that."

A queasy feeling was quickly replacing my depression. I tried to force down the dread this information brought, but it only seemed to fuel it like gasoline.

Instead I analyzed Nico's face, and saw no fear on his odd features. In return, he gave me a look that told me there was a reason he was a chimera's boyfriend.

I stared back and mouthed the words slowly. "And how are you planning this great escape then? We're in a fucking sewer; we're locked in a room with nothing."

Nico rose to his feet before sitting down with his back to me. I watched with curiosity as he flexed his back, making several bones in his back pop. "Every legionary has a shiv implanted in them, mine is in my shoulder blade. I can't get it out. Get it out and give it to me and I can get these handcuffs off. We'll escape while Kerres is distracted with

Meirko."

"Why can't you get it out?" I lifted up my own shackled hands and helped him take his jacket off. I knew the answer as soon as I saw it.

His right hand had been taped with duct tape. I hadn't noticed it before.

"Like any soldier worth their salt, I use my body as a weapon. They have had first-hand experience with that," Nico replied.

I put a finger on his shoulder blades and immediately felt the small hard piece of metal resting underneath an inch long silver scar.

I tried to pick at it to see if I could get an edge but Nico tensed his back. "Just bite, chimera style, bite through the skin and then withdraw it."

Geh, that was the last thing I wanted to do. I was really getting tired of being reminded how much of a chimera Reaver was. I wonder of my sweet loving Garrett had this side to him.

Instead of bitching though, I held onto the small glimmer of hope that Nico had given me and pinched the scar between my fingers. Then I lowered my teeth to it and bit through the tight piece of skin.

Nico grunted and swore. I felt my teeth connect with each other and the sensation of something square and hard. I withdrew my mouth, spitting out the blood that had started to trickle. Then with my fingers, I drew out a small flat piece of metal and handed it to Nico.

"Handy but disgusting… how is that supposed to help us anyway? You think you can slice a throat with this weak piece of metal? It's as flat as a keycard."

Nico rubbed the shiv onto his jacket and turned himself around, shaking his head. "No, I'm unlocking these cuffs, then I'm fucking murdering the next person to come through those doors. Then we grab the weapons on them, and fucking run."

Grab weapons and fucking run… If I didn't have the knowledge that this Meirko asshole wanted to cut their losses and kill us, I would've kept my ass where it belonged. But now a whole new sense of urgency was on me. So I watched Nico go to work on his cuffs. Not just watched though, I learned.

He took the small bit of metal and wedged it into the locking mechanism of the cuffs where the raised notches were, then secured it in place. Then, with his free hand grasped onto the cuffs, I heard him squeeze them tighter, and at the same time, shifted the shiv in further.

My eyes widened when I saw the cuff give a bit of slack, and when he pulled off the first one I was fucking gobsmacked. “Seriously? I’m getting one of those fucking implants.”

“I’ll do it to you myself.” Nico glanced behind him before starting on his other cuff. He didn’t need to though, I was watching that door like it was a ticking time bomb.

Several times people walked past, making all three of us jump and anticipate a shadowy silhouette in the incandescent light, but besides fast talking and arguing, they left the three of us alone.

With each click of the cuffs coming loose, a chill filled the air, a certain taint to it that seemed to fill every molecule with electricity. I could feel it in my chest and soon in my veins.

But I never let it overtake my nerves; my hands were steady and only my heartbeat gave away the energy I was feeling inside of my chest. Reaver had taught me that. I had been in many bad situations with that man; he had taught me to stop being scared.

Easy for him to say, he was immortal…

The last click came from the cuffs around my left hand. I got up and stretched my arms, but I was so weak I had to lean up against the wall to keep from whiting out.

Nico did the same. I heard him take two inhales before more snapping of stretching limbs.

Trig was still on the floor, he looked scared. “I’m not going. Ares will come for me.”

There was a squeal and a sob as, to my surprise, Nico hit the boy over the head. Then he grabbed a tuft of the boy’s hair. “Listen to me, you little shit, Ares isn’t coming for you, just like Artemis never came for Kay. We’re on our own now and we can’t rely on them. Even if they wanted to get you Silas will never negotiate with these fucks. Are you going to come with us or should I kill you right now?”

The boy whimpered and my heart broke for him. I kneeled down and rubbed Trig’s head with a confident smile. “You little Skylanders are so soft. Come on, buddy. I know it’s scary and shit and it might seem easier to stay here… but they’re gonna rape you, kill you, and eat ya. At least this way you have a chance to go back to Ares, where he will only rape you. Isn't that worth the risk?"

The boy stared at me dumbfounded, like he couldn't comprehend the odd string of words coming out of my mouth. But as they sank in, his eyes shifted from mine and he gave me the slightest nod. "It is better… I heard Kerres too… Meirko wants to get rid of us."

And that won't happen. I gave Trig a supportive pat and helped him to his feet. Unlike Nico and myself he didn't have the weeping broken skin that had been rubbed raw underneath our shackles, the timid cicaro hadn't struggled at all. He still had an odd gait to him however, there was no denying what that was from. He and Kay had had a few features to them that Nico and I did not.

It was nice to get out of those shackles. I rubbed my hands, though it was like I was brushing back damp tree bark. I put my nose up to my wounds but I didn't smell rot yet, at least that was something to be happy about.

"What's our game plan, Nico? Just literally smash and grab?" I turned to the black-haired soldier. He was rubbing his hands as well; the shackles hanging out of his pants pocket. I tucked mine into my own too; we might end up needing them in the future.

Nico gave me a nod before walking up to the door. I watched him run a hand down it, before he pressed his ear against the dented metal. "They'll be feeding us in five hours, it's always between six and eight. Until then, we're quiet. If we're lucky, we'll catch some more intel."

And so we played the waiting game. Nico and I walking around the cell to try and get the circulation back in our legs, and Trig sat silently, only speaking when spoken to and only walking and stretching when one of us prompted him. I had my doubts if he would get out of this alive, but I had to try. If Reaver could see something beyond the innocence and weakness of old Killian, I should try and do the same.

When the voices started to come back, Nico and I got into position. I was on the right wall, he was on the left. They would see me first, and once they did, Nico would strangle them with the handcuffs.

However the plans we had talked about in hushed voices dissolved when we heard how many people were coming for us. I swore inside my head, and like the good sidekick I was, my eyes fell to Nico.

"Put your cuffs on loosely, there are at least four of them, play it by ear," Nico hissed. Then with a hurried jingle, we started making ourselves still look bound. "This would be a fucking suicide mission. Four is too many and one of them is Meirko."

Just as I was clicking the last notch into place, the door opened. With all three of us sitting against the wall, the artificial light filled the room.

Yep, four people…

They yanked all three of us to our feet and marched us into the blinding lamplight. I kept my hands pressed up against my stomach to hide my loose handcuffs.

"Where are you taking us?" Nico demanded, before, with an *oof* and a *crack*, I heard them hit him. No more questions were asked after that.

Not because I didn't have many of them, but because I wanted to be conscious for this escape. I had to be on my toes, and leave my delusions inside that cell where they belonged.

So I started looking around for some kind of weapon I could use, anything sharp I could pick up when things got messy. I could use my teeth like a chimera, but I don't know if I could do that much damage. I didn't even know where to aim; Reaver had been the freak show not me.

We were led into another room, though this one was twice the distance as the one Shale had raped me in. It seemed like a far away room for some dirty deeds. I hoped Nico knew what he was doing because I really didn't fucking know.

When we were shoved in the room, I saw Kerres in the corner with his arms crossed, a pissed look on his face; and a brute looking man with black hair and too many scars. That was Meirko in all his glory, a sour-faced shit who was the brother of the old leader.

Meirko was dressed in camo with a cigarette in his mouth, a vertical scar running from his cheek all the way to the left corner of his lips. I wouldn't put it past a chimera making that scar, and this fucker looked like he held grudges.

"Bunch of pretty little fairies, huh?" Meirko growled. He walked up to Nico and put a hand under his chin. "Except for you. Wrong place, wrong time, chew toy? Did you know your mommy offered us under-the-table money for you? Silas executed her when your own dad ratted her out. It was on the TV."

I froze, anticipating Nico spitting in his face or doing something, but he was a statue. He was standing as still as he could on his weak legs, staring forward with not a bat of his eye.

Meirko smirked and walked over to Trig. The kid was staring at the floor with his lips pursed inside of his mouth.

"And you, pathetic little pet. No one has offered anything for you, you're not even asked about. All it is is the fiancé and the boyfriend. How does that make you feel, slave?"

Trig turned away as the cigarette smoke blew into his face. I thought he was going to stay silent like Nico, but instead he raised his head and said in a mousy voice: "Ares will come for me. Ares loves me."

Meirko laughed, the same with the other three who had brought us in. Hell, even I internally laughed at that. Ares was a brute and they didn't love anything. Those fucking dudes were hardcore socio-fucks; they didn't love anything outside of rape and torture.

"No, you little shit, no one is coming for you. Which is why we're not even going to tape your execution. It would be a fucking waste of film."

Suddenly, in a flash of steel cuffs and dirt-stained bodies, Trig was trying to punch him. I swore and took a step back as the three who had been holding us jumped on top of the little cicaro, and started wrenching his body away from the leader.

Then Nico ripped his cuffs off.

And this was it… this was fucking it.

Taken by surprise, Meirko was pushed into a metal desk. He crashed onto the ground like a rolled over barrel, spitting booming curses as the others grabbed Nico.

I jumped in at that moment. Not knowing what else to do, I pushed one of the Crimstones holding Trig and grabbed his gun.

Not mincing movements, I shot him in the head before finishing off the second one; blood splattering against the brick walls as the chaos in the room reached critical mass.

Something grabbed my arm and twisted it. I whirled around to see Meirko holding onto me, his eyes ablaze and his mouth open, screaming shit at me I couldn't hear over my other senses.

I raised the gun, pointed it under his chin… and pulled the trigger.

But there was only a click.

There was only a fucking click.

Meirko took me and threw me up against the wall, but as the force of the blow knocked stars into my vision, I saw Nico behind him raise the butt of a handgun and slam it down on the Crimstone leader's head.

When Meirko went down, Nico took one look at me and wrenched Trig's arm. I didn't see it at first but he had the pet's hand in his. "Take him and run. If he's slow, leave him behind."

I didn't know what the plan was; I just knew no one was shooting at us anymore. I nodded and took Trig from him before the three of us burst into the long damp hallway.

Which fucking way? No one knew, I didn't know and I knew the other two didn't. I ran deeper into the dark cisterns, not wanting to risk running into any more of these fuckers.

It didn't take us long to run out of light, the strings of battery operated lights fading into the distance like the flood lights of Aras. We were in almost complete darkness.

Where was my chimera with his night vision? Just three fucking useless humans. Why couldn't they have kidnapped at least one chimera? Even the one that acted like a dog would've been able to do better than us.

I could hear the two boys breathing on either side of me, and like me, as the darkness coated us like a thick, stifling blanket, their movements slowed down. Soon we were just walking, bumping into each other with our hands outstretched, feeling the damp brick for any ladder or door that would take us to the surface.

No cold metal, no door to break up the long formless sewers we were trudging deeper into, all I could feel was brick, fucking brick. It was on either side of me with a trench in the middle that never missed an opportunity to trip one of us. Trig went down the most, and after that it was me. The water tasted like rat shit, and what bits went into my mouth when I fell I was sure were fucking full of disease. I swear if I got rescued just to get like trideath or quadeath or quintdeath or whatever the more worse versions of trideath were called… I'd be pissed.

"Anything?" I whispered to Nico, trying to keep my voice as low as possible. I had a hand on his shoulder and my other firmly clamped around Trig's.

"No," Nico murmured. I could feel his duct-taped hand sliding against the brick. "But there has to be an exit here somewhere. Just keep your hands out, let them be your eyes."

Then my hands lit up.

I sucked in a breath and swore with vigour inside my head as a flashlight illuminated my bloodstained hand. Immediately I grabbed Trig's wrist and memorized the path of the sewer tunnel we were running through. With my newfound bursts of adrenaline, I started to run down the dark tunnel, our sneakers splashing through the trench in the brick, making such a racket I wondered if the fucks above us could hear.

"There they are!" I heard Meirko shout. I gritted my teeth together and jumped onto the narrow and slippery brick ledge and pulled Trig's small frame onto it too.

The boy's hand was dripping sweat, or mine was dripping on him. I was able to get a hold of him though, and used my own mental map and the flashlight beams to try and make some sense out of this underground maze.

My mind didn't react when I started hearing gunshots, or when they pinged off of the walls dangerously close to my head. I made sure I had the boy and I fucking ran.

"It's only Meirko and Kerres," Nico said out of breath. He was running along the opposite edge of the trench.

Nico's eyes narrowing as he glanced behind him. "Just watch for a place to duck into. If we can disable their–"

Suddenly there was an audible crack of gunfire and he disappeared from my vision. I stopped and jumped over the trench that divided the middle of the sewer and grabbed his arm.

Nico clenched his teeth and looked down at his bloodied leg, Meriko and Kerres's boots coming closer behind us, with flashlight trails waving across the ceiling of the sewer. He looked up at me, and to my surprise, he shoved my hand away.

"This isn't a fucking movie, Reno. Take the kid and run. I have no heroic speeches for you, fuck off and run. Tell Clig… just make up something nice."

I stared at him blankly for a second before I looked down and saw the bullet hole that had pierced his upper thigh. A wound that could've healed, but under the Crimstones… if it rotted, he was fucked.

The boot steps came closer, as did the splashing and the pinging of bullets. I knew in the milliseconds it took for me to gape at Nico Zhou that any one of them could be hitting me next. I didn't know how many bullets they had, or if they were also packing assault rifles.

Reaver said to never be a hero, to never care, but me having to stand up, take Trig and leave that fucker behind… I knew I'd never forgive myself.

But I did it.

I did it because I was scared, and I did it because I couldn't go back into that room.

I never said I was a hero, and I never wanted to be a hero. I was some fucking sidekick that was always bailed out at the last minute by his Superman.

Kerres shouted behind me, and another flash of light illuminated the twisting corners of the sewer.

There was a fork, a split in the path. My heart jumped in my throat and beside me I heard a relieved gasp from Trig. I gripped his hand harder and we took a sharp right, before tripping over a raised piece of concrete.

This tunnel didn't have the rivet filled with water like the main one did, it was different… made out of only brick. I didn't know if that was a good sign but I took it. Me and the kid climbed onto it and ran into the darkness. My own nose picking up dry must and mould, leaving the damp rat shit behind with Nico.

We ran, blindly but quickly, we ran. No more light beams to be seen streaking across the ceiling and damp brick. There were no noises either; as we ran deeper into the sewer system they faded like the light and became nothing but an echo in my mind.

Only our panting and quickened steps.

"We're going to die in here," Trig whimpered beside me. I wasn't sure how much time had passed since we left Nico behind but we were both exhausted, tired from running and tired of relying solely on adrenaline resources. We had barely eaten during this captivity; we had nothing left.

"I'd rather die here than die in front of a camera," I growled, squeezing the kid's hand harder. "In the fucking greywastes we never went anywhere outside of Aras without a gun. I swear when I get home if Garrett–"

I let out a yell of shock as I ran right into a brick wall, smashing my nose against it and my forehead. I swore loudly and colourfully, before I laid an enthusiastic punch against the brick wall to show it what it had done. I didn't care how stupid that was, that fucking hurt.

I turned around to start to grope the walls for a different direction when I slammed up against something else.

This wasn't solid though. Swallowing the second curse on my lips, I touched the cold metal and hissed my glee.

It was a fucking ladder!

I jumped on it like it was a hot blond boy and climbed to the very top. With Trig's excited breaths below me, I felt for the lid and pushed up on it.

My eyes squinted at the cold winter daylight. For some reason I was sure it would be night time, but in the sewer it always seemed to be permanent midnight.

I scraped the manhole cover off to the side and scrambled to the top, before standing and helping Trig up and out of the sewer. It was colder out here, or perhaps it was just the daylight making it appear colder.

I closed the lid and looked around for something to drag on top of it, or at least some people that could help us, but there wasn't a soul in sight.

Just empty streets, no cars, no rusted twists or metal, no fallen light poles. Everything was standing in desolate greys and blacks, a ruin like the greywastes, but in the same way, also preserved.

I looked around. "Where are we?"

Trig and I jogged to a small alleyway with a dilapidated chain-link fence blocking off the next road. I saw the young cicaro look around at the monotone buildings that surrounded us.

"Cypress, it's an abandoned district west of Moros, near the West End," Trig gasped. He paused for a second to lean against the wall to catch his breath, but there wasn't time for that. I would make this kid run until he collapsed and died.

"Do you know where Moros is?" No one in Moros had remote

phones, those were for chimeras, but there had to be a thien there somewhere, someone to radio Ellis.

Trig looked around, his dark eyes going in all directions. I waited to see that light bulb moment when he told me exactly where we were but there wasn't anything, just his usual petrified look that seemed suited for his soft features.

"Trig?" I looked to my side, trying to ignore just how sick and beaten down this poor little fucker looked. "I at least need a direction…" Why hadn't I looked at a fucking map of Skyfall? Why hadn't Garrett taught me something about this stupid place?

"The ocean… we should go towards the ocean," Trig said quietly. He raised a shaky hand and pointed to a break in some of the taller buildings. I could see white sky and nothing else behind them, whereas behind me it seemed like an expanse of broken ruins and a maze of roads.

I nodded and started to quicken my walk when a searing pain shot up from my gut. It filled my vision with a white heat and I felt myself sinking to my knees.

I grabbed my stomach before lifting my stained shirt up. I swore as I saw a red swelling around my stomach, where my old bullet wound had been. Something had torn inside of me when Meirko had kicked me.

I looked around and tried to size up the double and triple-storey buildings we were walking past. From the white orb in the sky I wagered it to be around three, it would be getting dark in a couple hours.

But we had no blankets or anything and it was fucking winter.

"STOP!"

With my hopes and dreams of being in Garrett's arms before the sun rose falling to dust and ashes in front of me, I stopped with Trig and turned around.

I expected to see an unstoppable force of assault rifle-wearing people in camo, but instead it was only Kerres.

The red-haired man did have an assault rifle though, and a crazed glint in his eye I saw the day Reaver came back from Donnely; the one that screamed *stay the fuck away!* The gun was raised to his face and his movements were like he had bricks on his feet. He was stalking towards us, a wet trail of boot prints matching our own.

"Kerres… come on…" I raised my hands, one with a cuff still

dangling off of it, and talked to him in a soothing voice, like Killian had Reaver. "It's over… let us go, man."

Kerres's gun shook, his eyes were almost bugging out of his head; he was fucking crazy. "No! Fuck you, no. I'll get Jade back. Garrett would exchange Jade for you. He'll betray Elish, he will!"

Oh, this isn't going to end well… fuck, fuck, fuck. Jade wasn't even in Skyfall right now, not that Garrett would ever do that. He loved Biter and his pissy little attitude problem.

"Maybe… maybe he will. Why–" Umm… fuck. "–why don't we call Garrett and… and find out? Got a radio?"

That was all I could come up with?

"I'm not stupid, Otter!" Kerres screamed, my pet name echoing off of the high buildings. "Just…" He dug into his pocket, one hand still pointing the assault rifle at me, and tossed two pairs of handcuffs at us. They skidded along the cracked grey pavement and came to a stop right by my feet. "Put them on, PROPERLY! You fucking greywaster. You make one wrong move I swear I will kill Trig. I will fucking kill him in front of you!"

I stared at him; I wasn't going to do that. That was the last thing I was going to do. I wasn't going back down there. I couldn't go back down there, not when we were both so close.

"DO IT!" Kerres screamed at the top of his lungs, and I saw tears, the desperate tears of a maniac, stream down his face.

Then behind Kerres I saw a black silhouette, and a voice I had never wanted to hear again.

"What the fuck do you think you're doing?" Meirko boomed. "I said get them and fucking shoot them. Your screaming is going to alert every fucking radanimal out here!"

The Crimstone leader looked pissed off; Kerres was still giving everything ahead of him the death glare.

"Look at me, soldier! You might've been Milos's little protégé, but you will–"

In a second, Kerres turned around, and before the last words spilled from Meirko's mouth, the front of his skull blew off, spraying a slurry of bone and flesh onto the empty street behind him. He fell back with a sickening thunk, a large piece of skull becoming detached and rolling to a nearby curb.

I stared, stunned and welded into place, seeing the crazed Kerres's shoulders heave up and down as we all watched the blood start to run towards the gutter.

"Put – on – the – CUFFS!" Kerres whirled around and shrieked.

Without hesitation this time, I leaned down and picked up the handcuffs, pushing one pair into Trig's trembling hand. Now both of ours were trembling. I could barely get the fucking cuffs over my wrists with how hard they were shaking. This kid was fucked in the head, he had lost his mind… and I knew I had no other option than to do what he said.

Then Kerres walked towards us. I put up the cuffs to show him I had done what he asked but he only poked the tip of the assault rifle into my side. "March, walk, go!"

"Where are we going?" I asked, turning around and letting him lead us. Well, this was a step up from the sewers. I assumed since he just murdered Meirko I no longer had to worry about us going back to the Crimstones.

"Outskirts of town, in the greycoast, out of this fucking town… several of those cunts are still alive down there!" Kerres yelled. He didn't seem to be able to control his voice anymore. It was fluctuating from normal tones and then to shrieking yells like he was a radio with a busted knob.

"The fucking greycoast? Out of Skyfall?" The rest of the large island Skyfall was on was a desolate wasteland and entirely abandoned. No one was allowed to settle there, Silas's orders.

I tried to look behind my shoulder at Kerres, if only to attempt to make a human connection with him, but he jabbed me again with the gun.

"You should be fucking thanking me, Reno," Kerres continued to babble on. "Meirko wanted to kill you… they were going to kill you three down there. You're too dangerous. They had been searching Moros and the north end of Cypress. But no… they haven't checked here yet."

He directed us down one of the main highways, further on it turned into a bridge over another highway, then sloped down until I could only see hazy grey blurs in the distance.

Skyscrapers.

If I could run to the border… or a port or something… thiens and legionary guard the port and regulate the merchants. They are always heading back and forth from the factory towns.

For once I wanted to see a legionary, my old archenemies. I never thought that could be possible.

You are in a better position, Reno. At least instead of knowing you're going to die, you have a tiny tiny chance that you can sway Kerres.

When we were halfway over the bridge, Kerres still muttering things under his breath every once in a while, I decided to try and play nice.

"Kerres, you know if you turn us in to Garrett… and tell them it was you who shot Meirko, he won't kill you… he'll just be happy to have us back."

"I don't care about me, I want Jade. I want Jade away from that sadistic fuck," Kerres snapped back, using this opportunity to shove the tip of the gun into my back again. Beside me the staggering and whimpering Trig gave a jolt forward; I assumed Kerres had jabbed him too.

"But… Jade isn't even in Skyfall, he's somewhere in the greywastes," I said calmly. I opened my mouth next to tell him that perhaps he should let Jade go, but then I realized I was fucking retarded. So I pulled a card out even I didn't know was hidden.

"The guy I loved ended up hooking up with some little blond pixie kid – they're like madly in love now."

"Reaver?" Kerres's tone dropped down to normal.

I nodded. "I fucking love that guy with every ounce of me. We grew up together, and I know him better than anyone else. I knew him enough to believe he wasn't capable of loving anyone, even if I was so in love with him." I sighed, wishing all of this was just manipulation, but I had never been able to say it out loud. "Then this new kid comes to town, and the next thing you know Reaver goes all weird and starts to follow him."

I looked around and saw the city start to thin out, buildings more spaced apart and more areas that seemed to be old parking lots or houses that had been torn down a long time ago. "And the next thing I knew… they were in love, and good ol' Reno was left being the third wheel."

Kerres was silent for a moment, and our footsteps and exhausted breathing were the only things audible around me. I tried to count my steps, just as something to distract my mind from having a gun in my back.

"I took care of Jade since he was nine. We were inseparable. That is until he tried to rob a chimera mansion," Kerres responded, before telling me to turn right at an empty intersection.

"Elish rescued him apparently, and got Jade in his sights. Jade was gone and when I got him back… he wasn't the same, Elish had already brainwashed him."

Brainwashed him? Jade didn't seem brainwashed or robotic at all, quite the opposite. I wonder if this guy was as in denial as he was crazy.

"Looks like we both got burned by our chimera lovers, eh? They're a different type of breed those ones. Even Trig is like us, right?" I nudged the kid, trying to get him to say something so he could form his own bond with Kerres. It could end up saving our lives.

"Ares will come for me," the boy responded quietly.

"HE – IS – NOT – COMING – FOR – YOU!"

I jumped a mile high as Kerres screamed this at the top of his lungs, before he struck the kid in the back with the tip of his gun. Trig cried out and grabbed his back. I steadied him with my hand.

"No… no, no one's coming for us," I said quickly and calmly. "Whatever you… want to do, you can do." I squeezed Trigs shoulder to try and keep him quiet. I didn't trust this kid to know what he should be saying to this whack job. He could connect with him in a different way.

"No, Jade will come… Elish will bring Jade," Kerres said quickly. "I'll be able to see him, and not just on the TV. If he sees me… he'll remember how great it used to be between us."

"Kerres…" I said slowly. "If you let me call Gar-"

Trig screamed as a crack of gunfire exploded just a foot away from my ears. I screamed too out of instinct, and whirled around to see what he had hit, *who* he had hit.

I looked down.

Blood… lots of blood, coming from my upper leg. I stumbled back, and with that, it gave out and spilled me onto the pavement.

Then the pain came rushing to me, ripping up my leg and spine and pooling in my head like an exploded volcano. I clenched my leg and screamed, blood spilling through my fingers. Trig beside me, screaming.

Always blood, always screaming.

CHAPTER 22

Reaver

WE STAYED AROUND THE SMALL FIRE WE LIT IN THE living room, warming our hands as the winter air chilled our backs. Day two of hiding inside of this shanty town, seeing the helicopters and planes hover around Kreig.

But they hadn't come here yet, we were lucky in that sense. In all directions there were small ruins of towns where we could've been hiding. So hopefully they had a lot of places to look before their eyes turned to this location.

I stayed close to Killian, making sure there was always a spread of red coals near him so he could get the most heat. Out of all of us he was the thinnest, especially since Perish had died and come back. He looked almost normal now.

This kid didn't need to be on the road, especially in the middle of winter where we were all freezing our asses off. He needed a warm basement and someone to make sure he stayed healthy.

Now look at us.

I looked down as Killian slipped his little icicle hands in mine. I squeezed them, wishing I had the thermal touch that Jade had so I could at least warm them properly.

There was a shifting of blankets and I saw Jade lying on his stomach with Elish's laptop in front of him. He was clicking away with the screen bathing his yellow eyes. Behind him was Perish giving unheeded advice on how to make the remote phone give them the Skyfall Network.

They were trying to contact Elish through the network, trying to find a proper signal that the remote phone wasn't giving us. I knew nothing of computers, they were hard to fix and a pain in the ass to carry home. All of my old computers just ended up being piled in the first floor of my house.

I rubbed Killian's hands and he smiled at me. "I swear you just make them colder, Mr. Fridge."

"Well… if we can find a town or a block or something, we can buy you some better winter gloves. These Skyfall ones are shit once they get wet." I raised his hands to my mouth and blew some warm air onto them.

"Stop fucking touching the screen!" Jade snapped. I looked up and saw Perish poking something on the screen of the laptop before the pet batted his hand away.

"I wasn't, I know computers more than you," Perish snipped, removing his hand and sitting back down on the wooden chair he had found in the basement. "Where is this signal? You said he called once, so why isn't it going through now?"

"I don't know, it's just not finding the signal; it's all these fucking mountains around us," Jade muttered. "What if he is out there looking for me?"

"He isn't; he's in Skyfall pretending you don't exist."

I was quickly growing to hate their constant bickering; they acted like brothers those two. It really made me nauseas to know Elish was going to make Jade immortal. It meant I literally had eternity to listen to those two bitch and snip at each other. Perhaps once we figured out how I was supposed to kill immortals, I could do a bit of spring cleaning.

That thought alone put a smile to my lips.

"Hey, Skyfallers!?"

Everyone looked up and towards the barred shut door, but it only brought annoyance not terror. It was Hopper, I recognized his nutfuck voice. He had left us alone all day yesterday, though we could hear his slavers squawk whenever they got whipped. I was hoping they would've left by now.

I got up and heard the sound of my M16 being picked up but I put up a hand as Perish handed it to me. "He's not dangerous, he's just an idiot.

He knows better than to try and enslave us. I'll see what he wants."

I lifted the large two-by-four we had barred against the door and opened it up, immediately seeing Hopper several feet away clutching a bottle of vodka in his hands.

"I thought I said I would shoot you –"

"– If I stepped foot in your house. Yeah, I heard you, and I'm not. I thought of inviting you to our campfire but you're a suspicious little bitch so I assumed you would say no."

Well, he was right about that.

"So I decided to come here and offer you fuckers some real flesh. You just gotta tuck with me and my partner."

"No."

Hopper tilted his head back in an animated manner before looking to his side. I looked too and saw a young boy hiding in the shadows. I assumed that was his partner or perhaps just a slave he had come to fancy.

"Hear that, Churro? They don't want to drink with us." Hopper raised the bottle back to his lips.

The kid stayed in the shadows and said back to him, "I wouldn't want to drink with us either."

"But we don't have guns or knives or anything on us…" Hopper picked up a green bag I saw was sitting on top of a fallen fence and brought out a wrapped bloodstained package. It was obviously meat.

My stomach growled. We had finished off the liver that morning (fucking delicious) and now we were back down to tact and canned shit. I wouldn't mind a little bit of arian meat.

"That's too bad, since I'm drunk and bored and our other slavers are too busy looking after our slaves. I guess we'll just give the meat to the dog who has been sleeping by our fire pit for the last two hours."

I really hated that deacdog sometimes.

Killian appeared beside me. He popped his head out and gave Hopper a smile. "You look half-cut."

Hopper waved a hand at him and chuckled. "Your boyfriend is refusing good arian meat, boy. He seems to be the anti-social type, eh?"

Killian's pulse gave a jolt and I knew he wanted that food as much as I did. We were greywasters, we had a taste for human flesh.

I sighed and walked onto the porch before my boots hit greywaste dirt. "Let me see that meat. I want to make sure you didn't put any fucking roofies in it."

Hopper laughed again and unwrapped four hack-jobbed arian steaks. They looked fresh enough and smelled fine. "You can get your metal-mouthed pet to take a chew, or I can bite it myself and you can wait half an hour. Though if you think I'm dumb enough to enslave Skyfallers you're nuts. Half o' you look downright fucking insane."

At least he was smart. I picked up one of the steaks and took a bite of it. It tasted normal enough.

There was no harm in it; his small slaver group had only five members holding about two dozen collared slaves. We could overpower them and their cracked and rusted guns. I wanted to give Killian a few good meals anyway.

"Alright, just you and the kid, but you keep your hands where I can see them." I took the meat and stood back as Churro walked into the dim bluelamp light. I realized as he came closer that, though he looked like a young kid, in all actuality he was just short, probably in his late twenties with a thin beard and narrow eyes. I could snap him in half with just a poke of my finger from the looks of him.

Hopper and Churro walked into our house to Jade and Perish's surprise. The two immediately started eyeing our rifles which we had piled by the door. Without asking, Perish pulled his chair up to the door to guard the rifles while I gave the meat to Killian to start cooking.

"Want me to just cut strips and we can fry them? We found those coat hangers, we can wrap the handles in leather so they don't burn our hands," Killian suggested. He immediately gave up his chair to Hopper and pulled up a chewed up wing chair for Churro. Always the hospitable host, I still hadn't taught him to be rude.

"Sure, that would be easiest. Mikey, help him." I grabbed the bottle from Hopper, mostly just to see if he would let me take it, and took a drink. I handed it back and shuddered as the fire water burned my throat.

"I… I might as well. I still can't…" Jade paused, catching himself before I had to interrupt him. "I still can't get this thing to work." He sighed and closed the lid before helping Killian with our dinner.

Hopper whistled and nudged his boyfriend with his toe. "Why the fuck don't you make me shit?"

The kid, or not-a-kid rather, the short guy, glanced at him with a look of disinterest. "Because you can make your own fucking food?"

Hopper smiled and rubbed the short guy's brown hair. "I'm going to beat the snot out of you once we get back to the house."

Churro shook his head in a way that suggested this threat had been made many times before. I kept my eye on the both of them but their heartbeats told me they were relaxed.

I still didn't let my guard down and I wouldn't either. I had learned many times over not to be taken in by nonchalant, at ease strangers. Perish had taught me that one.

I glanced to my side and saw the scientist sitting on the chair by the door, his arms crossed over his chest. He wasn't watching the two slavers though; his eyes were on Killian and what he was doing.

My boyfriend eventually came out with a plastic margarine bucket we had found full of meat strips and a dump of salt on the side for us to dip it in. This was five star food for us. We dug in and started roasting them over the fire.

"So when are you guys heading out?" Killian asked. He was leaning against me wearing my leather gloves with the fingers missing; he had kept burning himself on the coat hanger.

Hopper, who was passing a cigarette between him and Churro, chuckled at the question. I was already disliking that dry laugh, not for any other reason than the fact that I didn't like any of them.

"Tomorrow. We're taking the slaves up the highway," Hopper said with a shrug. "What about you?"

Before I could tell Killian to shut up, he piped, "We're looking for a place called Falkland."

Hopper's eyes widened. He glanced over at Churro before letting out a laugh. "Falkland? Like Falkvalley? Buddy, we're heading to a town that hugs that place. Melchai. Fuck, we stop there after Melchai to load up on booze after we get our payday."

I stared at him and narrowed my eyes. I reached into my pocket and pulled out the piece of paper I had ripped out of the atlas and handed it to him.

I pointed at Kreig and then Falkland many miles away. "Is this where it is?"

Hopper leaned towards the fire to get a better look at the small text on the map. He nodded as he blew the smoke out of the corner of his mouth before handing the piece of paper back to me.

"Yep, that's the place," Hopper said. "Shitty map though, it's not accurate at all for the Fallocaust. Are you heading that way too?"

"It's none of your business."

Hopper shook his head and spoke with the cigarette still between his lips. "It might get a bit awkward when we say goodbye and start heading in the same direction, buddy. Because you would be smart to take the Coquihalla Highway to cross the mountains. I'll have a good laugh when the ravers and the carracats pick you off one by one though. You ever been up this way? You do know what's out there, eh, Skyfaller? Or how to get there?"

My face darkened, and as Hopper saw the expression on my face, his clown-fuck smile faded like the smoke coming from his mouth.

"If you call me a Skyfaller again, your meat will be the next on that coat hanger. I am not a Skyfaller; I am a greywaster from a greywaster block. Understand me, slaver?" I said lowly and quietly.

Everyone else around me was silent, even Killian was tense in his place. I didn't think there was a single heartbeat in the room that hadn't sped up the moment they heard the tone in my voice.

Hopper looked at me before he decided to play it casual. He was smart, any attitude from him and the slaver company would need a new leader. "Alright, you win, greywaster. I suppose a Skyfall boy wouldn't have made it this far. But you can't tell me that yellow-eyed little fucker is a greywaster. Those eyes don't happen naturally."

"He had an eye infection when he was younger," Perish suddenly spoke. "He's my younger brother. Mikey contracted acute melotonitus, which affected his iris pigment, so his green eyes turned yellow."

The slaver stared at him like the scientist had just spoken in tongues. I was confused at first too until I realized Perish was deliberately tossing around confusing words.

"Oh alright, well, fair enough," Hopper said with a perplexed look. "So… you four have some pretty big ass guns on you… would you be interested in–"

"No," I said flatly.

"We lost a few of our guard to ravers, and a few more to legion back near Marble. If you are heading towards Falkvalley anyway, what about we hire you two as guard and the young guys could be cooks?"

"Nope."

The slaver stared at me but, not being able to handle awkward exchanges, Killian tugged on my sleeve. Though to his credit he didn't question my decision in front of the slaver but I knew he was considering the idea.

I had never liked slavers, arian slaving was illegal in the greywastes and any men he lost to the legionary were his own fault. Raticating was legal because it was mostly just bolt gunning ravers, but capturing arians was just plain illegal in King Silas's eyes.

Now I never gave a shit about the shoddy laws of the greywastes, but it still made you look twice at the fucks.

Hopper seemed to take the hint, or he realized I was pretty close to kicking him and his boyfriend out of our house. So he switched the conversation to casual bullshit and laid off the request for hiring armed guards.

Instead he told us stories I didn't care to listen to, and bantered with his boyfriend which I found grating and annoying. I would've loved nothing more than to sit on the roof and watch the greywastes but I didn't trust him alone with the boys. Even with Perish and his assault rifle and Jade and his dragon teeth, there was just no risking it in the greywastes with these people.

The icing on the cake was when Killian brought the Cilo guitar out and started playing a song that Hopper recognized. He gave his cigarette to Churro and started singing along which was… which was just great.

By midnight I was smoking my tenth cigarette with Killian leaning on my shoulder as we watched Perish slowly fall asleep. He had switched places with Jade a few hours ago and now the cicaro was on the porch with his own AK 101, making sure the town stayed clear.

"Well, we should be heading back." Hopper rose and stretched, flicking the last cigarette butt into the red coals of the fire. "Keep in mind what I said, about being guards. In a way we would both be getting free escorts, and I would toss a few coins towards the little ones for their chef work. I get it, yeah, don't give me that look, evil one." I didn't know what look he was talking about, because I hadn't stopped giving him this look the entire evening. "Just stick the bug in your bonnet while we both make our way through the Coquihalla Highway."

I spared him a nod and moved my shoulder so Killian could wake himself up. "Alright, thanks for the meat. Keep your crew away from the house."

The slaver nodded, and with a creak of slowly rotting boards and the scrapes of greywaste dirt, he was out of the house and out of my sight.

I saw Killian yawn and look sleepy beside the fire.

I yawned too, and raised my voice to call to Jade. "Wake me up in a couple hours, Jade. I want watch a few hours before sunrise."

"Reaver…" Jade's excited voice sounded from the deck. I watched as he ran inside holding the lit up laptop in front of him. "It's connected. I don't know how but I got a signal. It keeps connecting and disconnecting and it's killing the battery… but I got it."

Killian gasped and rose to his feet but I was already standing beside Jade. The cicaro sat down on his bundle of blankets and put the laptop on his lap.

I could see the little computer icon showing it was connected to the Skyfall Network, then a series of windows started loading. One of them was Elish's personal email.

"I bet he's already cheating on you," I said with a smirk. "Look an email from… Juni. That's a cute name, maybe–"

"That's Jack's sengil and cicaro; he dictates Jack's emails for him." Jade shot me a dangerous look. "I'm just going to write him an email telling him we're heading for Falkvalley. He'll probably pick us up on the–"

"Reaver!" Killian suddenly exclaimed. He pointed towards the screen but as he poked it Jade smacked his hand away. The kid didn't calm down though. "Look, read the subject… it's from Ellis. She's the Commissioner of the thiens."

I leaned over Jade's shoulder and my jaw hit the floor. "*Crimstone ransom video*? Click it."

The little pointer thing scrolled over and clicked on the video. I waited as the swirly thing went in circles but became impatient. "What, is it fucking broken? Why isn't the video coming up?"

"It's buffering."

"What's buffering?"

"It's loading."

"Why? The Nintendo takes two seconds to load, make it fucking go faster!" I snapped. I leaned down and put my hand on the mouse and started clicking the video link again. Like he had done to Killian, the cicaro hissed at me and shoved my hand away.

"Because we're hundreds of miles away from Skyfall, it's a fluke we have a signal right now. Just be patient, Silas has like three satellites in the air now, it takes a while." Jade smacked my hand away again.

I growled, but before I could complain more a video window popped up. I could feel Killian tense up beside me. I slipped my hand into his, knowing that what I was about to see probably wouldn't be good.

"Just… remember: he's still alive. Elish would've told us if… you know," Jade said quietly, before pressing the play button. "Don't smash the laptop if you see something you don't want to see. Meirko's brother pulled my teeth out with pliers while Elish and Garrett watched."

This gave me pause, but there was no time for those words to have much of an impact, as the last syllable left Jade's lips, I saw him.

He looked like shit… of course he looked like shit, that didn't surprise me. My god though…

What the fuck had he done to his hair?

Killian whimpered beside me and I squeezed his hand harder, in that moment, Reno looked up at the screen and I felt my heart give a jolt. I never thought I would see him on a screen, like he was on television or something… it still looked like he was staring right at me. His blue eyes bruised and glassy and a look on his face that was so… defeated.

What the fuck was happening inside of my chest? It felt tight… I suddenly felt uncomfortable in my own skin. It itched and I felt the urge to just jump out of it, keep running until I made it to Skyfall.

I had to fucking save my friend.

"I need to get him…" I swallowed a lump in my throat. I turned and went to walk out the door, not knowing where I was going, just knowing I couldn't watch this.

"My name is Reno Nevada from Aras…"

I closed my eyes, my teeth clenching with such a strength I could feel them squeak inside of my head. Desperation filled me, and even though Elish had told me what had happened to my oldest friend, it suddenly became very real to me.

"I am Garrett Dekker's fiancé."

"No you're not!" I whirled around and snapped at the video. I stalked over to the laptop to shut it but Killian stopped me.

"It's okay, baby. He's alive… he's still alive," Killian whispered. I could see his eyes were filled with unshed tears.

"He's not his fiancé… if that fucker loved him, he would have him… back. He would–" I put a hand on my head and clenched my scalp; my teeth grinding back and forth. My eyes shot to the screen and I saw it zoomed on his face. Fuck… he looked–

I would have never let this happen to him. I had been guarding that fucking dipshit since I was two. I would have never fucking let them kidnap him.

"Sit down… Jade turn it off…" Killian put some pressure on my shoulder, trying to get me to sit on our bundle of blankets, but I shook my head.

My eyes looked over at the screen, to Reno still talking. I took in a deep breath and tried to find the steeled resolve I had lost as soon as I saw my silver-haired friend. The Skyfaller Garrett had forced him to become.

But he wasn't a Skyfaller; he was Reno Nevada, the field sentry and my best friend.

I kneeled back down beside Jade and watched him talk, watched his mouth move even though the volume was on low, watched the scared and defeated look on his face; every detail of my funny little friend.

I missed him, I never thought I would miss that fuck, but damn… I was so far from home, so far from the world I had grown up in.

They had fucking guns pointed at his head… I swear the day I meet those mother–

"Wait," I suddenly said.

Jade and Killian both looked at me. I motioned towards the mouse. "Rewind it…" I narrowed my eyes as I watched Reno's face, every muscle movement, every blink…

I knew him more than anyone did. I knew his body language and–

Jade rewound the video to the very beginning and it started to play again.

Holy fuck.

An electric jolt went through my heart and I felt it shoot cold water through my veins. I couldn't believe what I was seeing. I couldn't believe that fuck was this smart.

He was blinking Morse code.

I looked around wildly, Killian and Jade giving me the most crazed look they could. I reached over and grabbed Killian's bag and took out a folded up piece of paper.

"Pen… pen, Killian," I said sharply and gave him the bag. I turned back to the video. "Rewind it again."

"Why?"

"Do it!" I snapped. "He's blinking Morse code; it's where they're holding him."

Jade once again reset the video, and as it started to play again, Killian handed me a pen. I started writing down the Morse code he was blinking.

M Sewer.

"M? What's M? I showed the piece of paper to Jade; my pulse was racing. I felt such an adrenaline rush go through me I couldn't contain it. I felt like I could run to Skyfall right now and rescue him. I wanted to, fuck, I wanted to. Man, the look on his fucking face…

Jade grabbed the piece of paper and looked at me with wide eyes. "M? Moros sewers? It must be in Cypress where the sewers are more intact, that's an abandoned district that bleeds into Moros. I… we have to get a hold of Elish before the battery dies on this thing."

"How much of a charge do we have?" I demanded. Killian was rubbing my back in a pathetic attempt to keep me from flying off the handle, but it wasn't working. I felt such a rush at figuring out this message, but in the same vein, I had never felt more useless.

Jade clicked off of the video and immediately started typing out an email. "The connection is coming and going. I'll type this out and try to send it."

"Hurry!" I rose and started pacing, feeling like a wild animal more than anything. I wasn't used to feeling helpless and every time I did it drove me up the wall. I just wanted to scream at the top of my lungs right now. Not only did I have to see my best friend beaten with a gun to his head, but now I knew where he was.

Leo and Greyson had hammered Morse code into our heads, mostly for radio though. None of these chimera fucks had noticed he was trying to tell them something… but I did. I knew him better than Garrett ever would.

I didn't share my property… My teeth clenched even harder.

"Is it sent yet?" I whirled around and snapped at Jade. The kid was hunched over the laptop, his fingers busily clicking away a message.

"No… not yet…" Jade replied. He rubbed his hands and let out a sigh. "It's… buffering. The connection is really spotty and the roaming is sucking up our cell-"

Jade's face went dark and a fraction of a second later the cell phone beeped its swansong.

"Did it send?" I couldn't control the sound of my voice. Killian once again grabbed my arm and squeezed it, but a haze was starting to come. I yanked my arm away but he grabbed it again.

"I… no… it… it…" Jade's face went pale. He was scared of me… scared of how I would react. Jade was afraid of me.

I tried to push down the frustration I was feeling, but I felt the anxiety and desperation pool inside of my chest, gathering every stray strand of bad feelings I had inside of my body to cluster them into one pit, like a volcano on the fringes of erupting.

"We'll find a town," Jade said quietly. "One that we can charge the batteries in. If Elish doesn't find us first."

What about the lab? We could go back… I sighed not even bothering to bring a voice to that option; the lab was crawling with legionary now.

"We'll ask Hopper tomorrow," Killian said calmly. He was rubbing my arm, soothing… soothing like Reno always had to do. He hated seeing me upset; they all did.

I felt like I was about to lose my mind.

"I… I need to go for a walk," I said quietly, and when Killian gripped my arm harder I shoved the emotions into the dark void and kissed his cheek. "I'm… I'm okay, at least someone knows where he is – It's further than we were ten minutes ago."

The kid looked at me suspiciously but he nodded and kissed me back. "Don't be long."

I was never one to have bad dreams… that was Killian's thing.

But tonight was different.

There was chaos around me tonight.

Smoke, deacons, Killian screaming behind a wall of crumbled brick and burning ash but I couldn't get to him.

I turned around and saw them, coated in grey ash that stuck to their skin and caked on the orifices they were bleeding from. They were looking at me pleading, begging for me to do something.

Do something, saviour of the greywastes.

Greyson reached out his hand; his other one clutching Leo to his chest.

Leo was dead, he wasn't looking at me – He couldn't look though, they'd cut out his eye and the other one was closed in its eternal sleep.

"Reaver… help him. He's your father… help him!" Greyson pleaded, his face dissolving into his own grief.

My heart jolted. I bent down and put a hand to Leo's cold cheek and met my dad's gaze with mine.

"Help him, Reaver."

"I… I can't," I stammered. "I don't know how."

"He's dead… Killian's dead," Greyson cried. He looked down as I gave him a confused look, before I looked down as well.

It wasn't Leo anymore.

My little blond boyfriend's eyes had been removed, and his tongue cut out of his mouth. He was lying motionless in Greyson's arms; his mouth split open to make room for the tubes. Not a sound from his lips or a loving gaze from those two sapphires.

So blue.

The type of blue you just don't see in this world.

"Killian?" I shook him. I put my hand on his chin and tried to shake his head but as soon as I put pressure on it his jaw started to come off in my hand. It broke away from his skull like it had been made out of plaster, crumbling between my fingers.

"One day… one day, *bona mea*," the slippery smooth voice I would never forget hissed in my ear. "He'll be dead, and once his last breath leaves his body… I know you will finally be mine."

I gasped and jolted before I immediately felt a hand retract from my shoulder.

"You need to get up… don't wake up Killian," Jade whispered beside me. The fire was nothing but dying coals, the whole living room had grown cold. "We have company, but… don't flip out, just don't wake up Killian."

Immediately my body turned to ice. I got up, making sure not to disturb the kid, and grabbed my M16. "What is it?"

Jade was holding his gun in his hand, and though his face was calm, his heartbeat was not. "I heard voices and I snuck out to check them out. Legion came in from the west area of the town and they're on their way to Hopper's camp."

Dread washed over me, we had to get out of here now. I turned around to wake up Killian and Perish when Jade spoke behind me. "I know you want to run but they have a Charger plane now, Reaver, which has heat sensors on it. It's off in the distance not near the town but if we run… there are no structures further north for us to hide in. We need to stay."

"We can't stay!" I snapped at him, but I decided not to wake the kid. I gritted my teeth trying to figure out what to do next.

"Stay here with the boy and wake up Perish. I'm going to scout this out," I said quietly, clipping my M16 to the holder on my back. I took a step towards the door before I stopped. I had to cover all of my bases, no matter what. "If I don't come back, don't move from this house until Elish gets you. If you have to physically restrain Killian and chain him to something you're allowed. Got it, Cicaro?"

Jade looked stricken and pale with fear but he gave me a nod. "Of course."

I had nothing more to say. I slipped into the night and got as far away from the unassuming house as I could, crossing the street and running across the backyards of a row of bungalows. In the distance, I could smell the distinct smell of burning treated wood. I followed my nose, weaving between the structures, mentally analyzing which path would be the quietest.

Every loose piece of wood, every fallen over wall or hidden chain-link fence could easily be heard by a chimera, and for all I knew, Caligula or Kessler could be in this group.

Finally I saw the faint glow of light and the sound of voices talking quickly. As I hugged the edge of a two-storey house, I peeked down the street the slavers were on, and saw my marks.

Six legionary, nothing I couldn't take on. But if there were six, there was probably another dozen standing guard near the outskirts of the city, or possibly looking around the town.

I turned and walked behind a shed before climbing up a tree and jumping over the fence that separated the yard. The yards behind these houses were all clear and most of the backdoors unbarred.

I had to get closer to hear this conversation.

To my luck, the house I had eyed up as a good spy point had their backdoor open. I snuck in and lightly climbed up the stairs before finding another window and pulling myself onto the roof.

The roof was solid enough and the shingles in place. I dropped down to my stomach and lizard crawled to the peak of the roof. I pressed my back against a crumbled chimney and tuned in every bit of advanced hearing my chimera engineering had given me.

I used to think I was just born special…

Well, I suppose I was. I just thought I was some rare person, not a genetic clone of my mortal enemy.

Immortal enemy.

I swallowed down the bitterness of my own masochistic thoughts and put it in the void where that dream of my dads and Killian had been banished to. I closed it off.

"– their names are Reaver Dekker, Killian Massey, and possibly another chimera named Perish Dekker, two black-haired, the teenager Killian has blond. These are royalty, chimeras, do you know what a chimera is, ashmonkey?"

Well, it looks like they found us, though whether the idiots had figured out it was me who killed Timmy, or just the patrol Elish said was after us, I didn't know. It didn't matter in the end, legion soldiers were looking for us.

I wonder if their plane was the reason we were able to get that connection to the Skyfall Network. I wish I could pull one aside and give them a note to give to Elish but, of course, that was a fucking stupid idea.

I unclicked my gun from its holder and positioned myself and the rifle. I got Hopper in my sights and readied myself to blow his head off the moment he mentioned we were here.

"Yeah, I know what a fucking Skyfaller is –" I got his head in the crosshairs and rubbed my finger gently against the trigger. "– and we've been here for four days and we ain't seen shit. You wanna look and check our slaves? Or every one of these shitty shanties? Go ahead, you got your damn bribe. Let us get back to sleep, bessy."

I narrowed my eyes and withdrew my twitching finger from the trigger, just in time for the legionary to deck Hopper right in the face.

The slaver leader was knocked to the ground and around him the several other soldiers started laughing, before the one who hit him kicked him in the ribs.

"That's Officer to you, radhead, better than some shit sucker like you. Now you got another smart ass name for me, waster? Huh? You got something to say?" the officer sneered.

There was so much anger inside of me I could feel my shoulders shake, as soon as I killed Silas I was going to eradicate the Legion and replace it with my own. I would shred every single one of those big-headed fucks.

"Nothing to say," Hopper grimaced holding his stomach; his eyes were shut tight. "Nothing to say at all, Officer."

There was another kick and the group laughed some more before turning to the others. "I've had enough of this shithole. Take the slave and turn on the truck."

I noticed a young man with a shaved head and a probably short future being held by a legionary recruit in the darkness. The legionary followed the others once they walked past him, and trailed behind with the bribe. I suppose everyone had their price and arian meat was good meat. Silas didn't feed the lower-ranking legionaries well, so they usually turned to shadier means to feed themselves and afford luxuries like cigarettes, booze, or drugs. In all respects, the shaved-headed man's fate would be similar to the one my boyfriend had almost suffered.

Except there was no factory town for him. He would be nothing but bones and shit by tomorrow evening.

And if I wasn't careful, that could be our fate now. They were in the area, scouring the greywastes for me, Killian, and the mad scientist. We would be fucked if they caught me, and Elish would be fucked if they caught Jade. Not only did I have to get the hell out of here, and further away from Kreig, I had to do it without anyone finding us.

We could start walking to Falkvalley, the mountains would hide us well – I didn't want to leave without telling Elish, but I knew I had no choice.

Though that brought its own slew of issues.

Four people travelling together with no purpose would be suspicious, especially with Jade's eyes and implants. The legionary would pick us out if that plane flew by.

But –

I sighed and wiped my face with my hands.

– they wouldn't look twice at a slaver caravan… and they would be going near some towns I would think. We could branch off and charge the Ieon… get that message to Elish about Reno.

One thing was for sure, we were sitting here with our thumbs up our asses currently, and I had shit I needed to do. Not only find out what was locked inside of Perish's head, but now I had the responsibility to save Reno too.

It seemed like it was my job to save everyone now… I used to only care about myself.

Hopper rose with the help of Churro and an older man with a handlebar moustache.

The man with the moustache said to him in a gruff voice, "You know those three were the ones they were looking for, Hop."

Hopper picked up his hat and put it on his head. "We're going to need help crossing the Coquihalla anyway, and those four are going to need help too. If the evil one doesn't agree to be our mercs now, they will once they encounter their first urson. We'll be following them neck to neck once they get to the highway, there's only one road."

"I suppose you're right, we need all the help we can get if we're going to make the delivery to Melchai." The moustache one sighed and looked behind his shoulder. "I'm going to follow the legionary and make sure they leave the town. Go tell the fucked up one what happened, if he sees that the legionary are close he might just go with it now."

So I was the fucked up one and the evil one – I didn't mind that.

And with that, everyone but Hopper left.

I jumped down from the roof with a soundless thunk, and started walking down the street that would take me to Hopper's camp.

In all honesty, what Hopper said made me, if only a bit, more comfortable with mercing for them. If Hopper would've said he had some sort of moral code, or that he just did it to spite the legionary, I would've suspected that he had somehow spotted me, or knew I was pointing a gun at him. That was suck up talk not realistic greywaster talk, and certainly it wasn't slaver talk. No, this guy wanted something out of us to further his own agenda, getting to Melchai in one piece. Perhaps we could come to some sort of agreement.

Hopper glanced down the road, before doing a double take when he spotted me.

"You look like a fucking demon."

"I get that a lot," I said lowly. I decided not to mince words. "You know who I am, don't you?"

He didn't look surprised, even if he was an idiot he could put together that I had been listening.

"I know who three of you are. You're chimeras, huh? Well, I had you pegged right, you are a Skyfaller," he smirked.

I really hated being called that, but instead of telling him to go fuck himself I needed to secure what I wanted. Do the opposite of what Reaver would do, like Doc always said.

"I was raised in the greywastes, I am not like them. I overheard you, and we'll do it. Perish and I will be your mercs, Jade and Killian can do medical and cooking. Perish and I will work for the food and ammo, but with Jade and Killian we need money." I would rather do merc work with Jade, he was more capable than Perish, but I needed to keep that little shithead safe. Perish was immortal, Jade was not.

The slaver nodded, a half-smile on his face. "I would be more than happy to have a couple mutants on my force. You'll get your pay when we sell the slaves." He walked up to me and held out a hand. Though a handshake in the greywastes was supposed to be worth something, it was only so for the few moral people you came across and I think the last one had died in Aras.

But I shook it, because there was nothing else to do, even if it meant little to me. One wrong look, one wrong move, and Hopper's caravan would be extinguished.

And I knew he was thinking the same thing about me.

"Reaver?" Hopper called to me as I started to walk back to the house we were staying in.

I turned around.

"Why are they looking for you guys?"

"We're mercs, not your friends, Hopper," I said without missing a beat. "Just let us blend in and do our thing, and make sure your men know to leave my boyfriend and my slave alone."

"Fair enough." Hopper didn't seem happy with that but that was just too bad. We weren't a happy caravan bringing rainbows to the greywastes. I was a merc for a group of slavers.

I didn't like it, but there was nothing more to be said about it. This was our best bet to get away from Kreig and the Legion stalking our heels. I had to take that risk, and if things went bad… I would just kill every single one of them.

Being immortal had it perks.

CHAPTER 23

Killian

I CARVED OFF A THICK PIECE OF SKIN AND TOSSED IT towards Deek, who raised himself up on his hind legs and caught the flesh in his mouth. His teeth flashed as he chewed the thigh skin, and when he was done, he looked at me with hopeful eyes, waiting for more.

Jade was beside me, who happened to be a very bad cook considering he was a cicaro. But after my light teasing he had explained to me that in Moros, there really wasn't that much in the way of meat.

Meat was pretty much all we ate in the greywaste, meat and canned goods.

"Alright, that's the slavers' food…" Jade wiped his forehead and slid the heaping pile of trimmed rat steaks off to where Chomper was waiting with the grill. The former cook of Hopper's slave caravan, a gruff guy with a thick handle bar moustache and narrow but bright eyes, didn't give up control easily. Even though he was happy for the help, he had made it clear that he would still control the flames. I suppose that made us prep-cooks, or that's what they called them on the cooking shows.

I opened one of the totes and wrinkled my nose before grabbing the bag of meal that was the slaves' food. It was Ratmeal, which pretty much explained itself. A powered substance that had all the nutrients you needed to feed the rats. It used to come from Anvil in big condensed blocks, and would expand four times its volume when water was added. Since Aras was a block controlled by King Silas, Aras got access to the

Ratmeal; it was how we could feed the rats and the block without it costing more money or resources than they were worth. It was also spiked with a growth hormone so the rats would grow faster, which also made it not fit for arian consumption.

It made me sad that we were feeding this shit to the arian slaves, but I guess they only had to stomach it until they were sold to Melchai. Hopefully not being on it for that long would save them from the worst of side effects.

I brought out the scoop and scooped it into the cleaned tote full of a couple inches of water. I sprinkled it in and watched as it expanded in front of us.

Jade dipped a finger in but made a face as he tasted it. "This shit makes tact look like fucking ice cream sandwiches. Well, let's go feed them."

We carried the tote over to the slaves, and like Reaver had hammered into me, I didn't make eye contact with them and I didn't engage them. He had told me this over and over again and had even suggested Perish help Jade instead of me. But Reaver was off scouting a few abandoned houses about a mile away and couldn't stop me today.

We had been on the road for three days now, three days without seeing a legionary or any sign of the helicopter. I didn't like Elish not knowing where we were, but I knew if we stayed in or near Kreig, eventually the Legion would find us.

So we stuck with Reaver's plan and we went with the slavers – though I really didn't like them all that much.

Hopper was a nice guy, and Churro and Chomper weren't that bad either, but they gave off an atmosphere I wasn't comfortable with. There were some others that never missed an opportunity to talk down to me when my boyfriend, or Perish and Jade, weren't looking. They all just seemed like a pack of bullies to me.

But I kept my nose clean and did my job, if Reaver decided this was our best bet for staying safe, I trusted him.

"Okay, food time…" Jade called, and immediately I heard the sound of chains rattling. Every slave got their own bowl they used for the duration. They drank with it and ate with it. I think that was the only items they were allowed to have besides the clothes on their backs.

I watched as the slaves, about two dozen of them, all rose up from their places with their bowls in hand and their slave collars firmly around their necks.

They were all dressed in rags, puffed jackets with slashes leaking synthetic padding, jeans with tears and holes in all places, and some with blankets so threadbare you could see their clothes underneath. Their shoes were horrible too, smelly brown sneakers reeking of body odour and old feet, most with laces made out of dried intestine or grass that had been weaved together.

I felt horrible for them, which is why Reaver didn't let me look at them. Like me, these people had once been free, though unlike me, their fates weren't as sealed. Reaver reassured me that these men and women would be sold as house slaves or brothel workers. It was still a shitty life, but at least they weren't going to be used for meat or fois ras.

But it only lessened the sting of empathy a tiny bit. I wondered if their families knew what happened to them, or if they even cared. If Reaver hadn't been watching me would anyone have cared when I disappeared? I bet it would've taken until tax day for them to notice I was gone.

I sighed, hating that my own thoughts could bring me down more than what was happening around me. At least now I had Reaver and my friends, and although things were complicated right now… we were still alive.

I ignored the men's voices behind us, all of them clambering over the cooking steaks, and focused on ladling the mush into the slaves' bowls. The poor arians could smell all that good food and all they got was this shit.

None of them even said thank you, they were too worn-out and weak to do anything but give us all hollow looks. I looked away… and didn't make a face or wrinkle my nose at them. I wanted to treat them like they were people, that was the least I could do for them.

After the last dirty hand held out their cracked plastic bowls for me, I turned with a downcast sigh and picked up the now empty Ratmeal tote. With Jade beside me, wiping the white meal off of his hands, we walked back to the food tent to get our rations of steaks.

I saw that Reaver's special mostly raw steak was off to the side resting, it had only taken a few days and already everyone had learned my boyfriend. Like in Aras, they kept their distance from him. Reaver had that air about him that everyone seemed to understand within the first hour of meeting him. He wasn't a man to cross and the salt-of-the-earth slavers could sense that about him right away.

It must've been a greywaster thing, though unfortunately it didn't completely bleed down to Jade and me. They respected us but we still got bossed around a lot, mostly when Reaver was out of earshot.

"Oh, it's Twinkles and Sunshine!" Hopper said with a grin. He seemed to have found it hilarious to call Jade, who was usually stone and even-faced (no doubt a trait learned from Elish) such a nickname. I tried to tell him it was because of his yellow eyes but I didn't even believe me.

My nickname was rather obvious, it rivalled Reno's nickname of me 'Tinkerbell'.

Hopper picked up his steak with his hands and took a chunk out of it, before talking with his mouth full. "We'll be heading towards the entrance tomorrow, while we're on the highway it's half-rations. Usually we snag a wild biigo here or there at least. Skytech released some chipped ones to feed their precious little carracats."

I wonder if Perish's ears were burning, but I think he was taking the opposite area of the camp. I'd have to ask him if he was responsible for the carracats. I had never seen one before but the slavers kept talking them up as being something we all wanted to steer clear of.

"What's a biigo?" Jade asked. Like me, he now was eating his steak with a knife and fork. We really stood out here; it was obvious we were from Skyfall.

"What it sounds like," Hopper laughed. "A fucking big ass goat, with twisted horns that half of the time end up gouging into their own faces. Taste like butter though, I tell you."

I gave him a polite smile, before my eyes wandered to the dark silhouette I could see in the distance. My boyfriend walking on the collapsed roofs of the houses, jumping from one rotten pile of debris to the other.

I hoped he would come back soon, even if he was only gone for a few hours I always missed him. I had been worried about him lately. I know he had to be my greywaster while we were with the slavers, and not the boyfriend I got to myself in the basement, but I still missed him. Ever since Greyson and Leo had died, and the chaos had happened in Aras… it just seemed like he was slipping back to his own dark world.

He never talked about Leo and Greyson either, and whenever I mentioned them, even offhand he got annoyed at me. He didn't want to talk about it, and I understood why… but well… I wanted to talk about it.

The silhouette disappeared behind one of the houses and I went back to my food with a worried sigh and a tooth on the corner of my lip. I wished there was some goal, something I could look forward to, a time where we could be safe and comfortable together, but there wasn't. We had no home, no basement, no comfort… and none in our foreseeable future. Our main focus in life now was staying away from the Legion, and while we were at it: trying to fix Perish.

Suddenly there was a shout behind me, towards the stakes the slaves were tethered to. I turned around and saw an older man trying to take a bowl away from a younger one. The young one was pulling it back as the old man yelled at him to let it go.

"That's your problem. You two fed 'em, you break up the scuffles," Hopper said behind me and Jade. I sighed and got up with him, leaving the rest of my food behind.

"Give it here, fucking retard!" the old man spat. Then, with a hard yank, he wrenched the bowl free, but not before all of it spilled onto the ground.

The old man swore. "You spilled all of it. Happy with yourself? Food's for the ones who'll survive the journey. They're wasting food on little maggots like you!" With a toss, he threw the bowl at the kid's head.

The kid didn't even yell back or defend himself. He only stared blankly at the tipped over dish before backing towards the stake he was tethered to, a defeated and sad look on his face.

"What's going on here?" I raised my voice and tried to sound as dominant as I could, reminding myself that I was their superior, even though it knotted my stomach that that was the situation I had found myself in.

"Nothing!" the old man said, the sound of moving chains around him as he leaned against the post. "You hear him complaining? No? Then nothing!"

Wow, I hope they fucking ate this guy.

Though the most my authorative nature gave me was a dark thought towards the man, Jade was different. He walked over to the old man and kicked him in the side, making him yell out and fall over onto the greywaste ground.

"You talk to him with respect or I'll beat it into you, slave," Jade snarled, or Elish Jr snarled anyway. "Now you can apologize nicely, or you can apologize screaming, your choice."

The old man looked at Jade in a way I knew he would never look at 'Tinkerbell/Twinkles', with respect and fear. Maybe one day, but today was definitely not that day.

"Sorry," the man said simply, and Jade nodded in acceptance. He turned around and motioned me back, but I wasn't done.

I looked down at the younger one, who actually looked older than I had initially thought. His body was slight and frail though, and I had a suspicion this wasn't the first time someone had tried to steal his food.

"Was that your food?" I asked him.

He stared up at me; he had dirty blond hair that fell over his face in unwashed locks, and dark grey eyes. There was no question he was weak and sickly. The old man might've been right on him not surviving for very long.

The young man nodded, before giving Jade a sideways glance.

"Jade… get him more…" I said to him.

Immediately Hopper, who'd obviously been watching the exchange, said loudly, "We ain't making more. If he wants food he should fight for it."

I gave the slaver a dirty look but he was already gnawing on the rest of his steak. I could have, and maybe should have, walked away at that point, but I didn't.

"Do you want some of my steak?" I whispered to him.

The young man gave me a shocked look, like I had just spoken a foreign language to him, before he nodded slightly. I was glad Reaver was away so he couldn't stop me from engaging with him. This was why I wasn't allowed to look at the slaves.

"Jade?" I whispered so Hopper couldn't hear.

Jade looked down at the boy, and to my surprise, he nodded. He started walking towards our plates, so I turned my attention back to him.

"What's your name? My name is Killian."

Surprisingly, he said nothing back, instead he started making a weird gesture with his hands.

I blinked at him, so he did it again but slowly.

I still didn't get it… it wasn't until he kneeled over and started writing in the dirt that I understood.

He was mute.

I am Chally. He reached over and took my hand before gesturing slowly. The first one was in the shape of a C, and then the rest of the letters, most not as easy as just making them with his hands, followed.

"You can't talk?" I kneeled down beside him.

Chally shook his head.

"Where are you from?"

Chally started writing on the ground again. *Tintown.*

Maybe I could…

No, Killian. No…no… no, Killian.

"Were you kidnapped?"

Chally shook his head, and made the motion like he was handing me money.

"You were sold?"

He nodded.

Poor kid… I looked up as Jade came back with the remainder of his steak. He knelt down and handed it to him.

"He's mute, Jade. Look how thin he is… he was sold in Tintown."

Jade mouth twitched. I knew he would be in my corner about this slave. Jade was technically a slave too, he must have empathy for these types of people.

"Why were you sold?" I whispered, just as Hopper started yelling at us to stop talking to the slaves. I ignored him, he wouldn't get past barking and he knew it. I was Reaver's boyfriend.

I looked down as Chally continued to write.

I got too old.

Oh man…

I looked over at Jade, who I think in that moment had also had enough. He pulled up the steak that Chally had been tied too, with

Hopper cussing at us in the background.

"Get up, you're coming with us," Jade said, and we both helped the boy to his feet.

"What the ever-loving fuck…?!" Hopper yelled.

Jade held up the thick chain the boy had attached to his leg and said very coldly to Hopper, "I am purchasing him; he's my slave now."

Hopper threw his hands up and let them drop to his sides with a loud smack. "He ain't fucking for sale! Put him back where you damn well found him!"

Jade pushed the confused kid towards me and stalked up to Hopper. "I am a chimera and it's within my right to purchase any arian, greywaster, or rat of my choosing. I am buying this pet."

A hush fell over the camp. I could see Chomper and the others stop eating to watch the new show playing in front of them. Even the slaves behind us had stopped moving, their chains were silent.

Hopper glanced behind him, and when he turned back to Jade, his head tilted to the side. "You might be a fancy-bred mutant, but in my camp… you're a cook and our help, and cooks don't buy pets. Are we really going to have a problem here, Sunshine?"

Jade's lips pursed, and though I was no aura reader like him, I could see the anger radiating off of him. "Yeah, we are. Unless you sell me this kid, I'll make sure he's–"

Hopper shoved him backwards, and in a flash, the fuse on Jade's temper lit and exploded.

I ran from Chally and grabbed the back of Jade's collar as he pinned Hopper down and started punching him; the slaver swearing and spitting at Jade as he raised a fist and slammed it into Jade's head.

The other slavers were around us but Jade wasn't having any of it; with a beast-like snarl he whipped back and sunk his trademark sharp teeth into one of their hands, his own hands clenched around Hopper's throat. It was chaos, all around us was chaos, yelling, screaming, and from the feral pet himself: the same insane snarling noise.

Then I was shoved away, I fell to the ground and was relieved to see it was Reaver who had gotten me out of the dogfight. He ripped Jade off of Hopper and away from the others and glared fire at the slavers.

"What the fuck is going on here?" he demanded, still holding onto

Jade's collar.

Hopper rose and wiped the blood away from his mouth. "Your feral dog attacked me when I refused to sell him a bought slave. I'd take a fucking stick to that brat. He's too young to have that big of balls, especially for a slave."

Reaver turned around. Jade had his arms crossed and that defiant look on his face.

"What the hell are you doing? Don't fucking pick fights with greywasters, you moronic fuck. They don't play by your Skyfall rules. You're lucky Hopper didn't order them to shoot you."

I decided to jump in; I knew Jade wasn't going to handle this in a good way. "It was my idea. He's really weak; the other slaves keep stealing his food. He's a mute; he can't even scream or defend himself, please?" I wanted to grab his arm and cling to him until he let me buy Chally but I kept my distance. He hated showing affection in public.

A cold shock rushed through me as his eyes got dark. He looked at me and his face didn't soften.

"Killian… I told you not to look at them," he replied back slowly.

"Someone was hurting him and stealing his food," I protested. "It's not like we asked for him for free. We'll pay for him."

He was still glaring at me and I shrunk under his gaze. A moment later, he moved, only to grab my arm and pull me towards a small hill of rocks that had been sheltering us from the northwest.

When we got behind it I continued to cower, for good reason.

"What the hell are you trying to do?" he hissed.

I slunk down with my back against the rock and murmured, "He's disabled; he's sick… what's the big deal?"

Reaver hissed and turned around, before grabbing his hair and turning back around to face me. "Are you trying to get yourself killed? These are slavers, Killian, slavers! You and Jade are fucking lucky Hopper is easy-going or they would've shot both of you!"

But Hopper is easy-going… if I was scared of him I wouldn't have even asked…

I don't think.

"He wasn't going to…" I said, but I gathered my nerve and got back to my point. "Reaver, I want to buy him. He's a nice kid; he got sold in

Tintown. His name is Chally–"

"No, Killian," Reaver said sternly.

My mouth dropped open and I felt my eyes brim to my own embarrassment. "They're selling him anyway! I'll pay double, I don't care! I can't just watch him suffer."

My boyfriend shook his head; I could see the vein in his forehead bulging out as he got more and more upset with me. There was nothing I could do though. I would trade Reaver being upset if it meant I could save Chally's life.

"No, no and don't ask again. The answer is no. I am not opening up the floodgates for a fight with these fucks. Without them we're walking targets; we need to blend in. Don't jeopardize your safety for some fucking retard!"

"He's not a retard!" I suddenly raised my voice, making him hiss at me to keep it down but I didn't care. "He's a fucking arian human who got sold like I did. He isn't a rat, Reaver! Jade will pay for him if my own work pay isn't enough."

"Keep your fucking voice down!" Reaver snapped. "I have enough on my plate right now. I already have all of you and getting that message to Elish about Reno, and just getting a hold of Elish to let him know where we are! I am not buying into your fucking pity party for weak creatures. I let you keep the fucking cat, I let you keep the fucking dog, and so fucking help me I let you keep the fucking scientist. I've given you enough leeway with your penchant for bringing home defects!"

My lower lip started to tremble, and I could feel the hot tears on my face. I felt so awful for Chally. I didn't know what to do. I was so powerless.

I guess my boyfriend decided that he had said his piece; he turned around and started to leave.

As he did, I felt a funny feeling in my gut… the apprehension and anxiety I got when we had fought about Asher so many months ago. I hated it when he just left me alone after we fought, left me to suffer in my own misery. I felt like he was leaving me now, telling me how it is and then taking off to go be a slaver-mercenary.

Though it wasn't like before, because he wasn't the same person as he was before. Ever since Kreig he'd been quiet, reserved, and stressed out; only putting on a show in front of Hopper and the other slavers when necessary.

"He wouldn't be your problem," I said quietly, "he would be Jade and mine's."

"And you're my problem, so he's mine too," Reaver said lowly. "I already said my piece, Killian. No slave, don't look at him, don't talk to him."

"SINCE WHEN ARE YOU MY FUCKING MASTER?" I suddenly exploded, surprising myself with this outburst. I didn't even realize the way he was ordering me to not buy Chally had been wearing down my nerves. I think he'd just grazed the very first live nerve ending. "I am your boyfriend; I am not your fucking pet! I'll buy him if I want." I stalked past him, but as I did, he grabbed my shoulder to pull me back. I jerked my arm away from him and walked back to the camp.

"Grow the fuck up already, stop acting like a brat!" Reaver stalked after me. "We're not in Aras anymore, you can't–"

"I know I am not in Aras, asshole!" I whirled around, my face flushed from being so angry. "Because of *your* fucking family none of us are in Aras!"

Reaver stared at me for a moment and I knew I had gone too far.

I didn't know what to do though, I was too mad to apologize. So I just stared at him like an idiot wondering if I was going to get a smack across the face. If he did, I wouldn't hold it against him.

"Killian… I am trying to remain calm." Reaver took a big inhale and closed his eyes for a second. I was shocked that he hadn't exploded. "Do not piss off the slavers; do not look at the slaves. Right now, our mission is to not get captured by legionary, and to try and get to Falkvalley, or at least get as far away from Kreig as we can until Elish comes, not to adopt pets."

And with that, he turned around and headed back to camp. I followed behind, wiping the tears from my eyes, trying to ignore the slavers chuckling around the campfire… all of their laughs directed at me.

I walked past the area where the slaves were being kept, past many stakes in the ground with rusty iron chains attached. They were talking in low voices too, though most of them didn't speak… not from being mute, but because Hopper didn't let them talk.

I spotted Chally, and my heart lurched when I saw he had a red patch on the side of his face; it was quickly becoming a welt.

He looked at me and shifted his eyes away, then moved his entire body so he was facing away from me. He hated me now, I had gotten him into trouble… once again I had tried to help and it ended up backfiring on me.

That night I curled up in my sleeping blankets and listened to the guys outside the tent laugh and carry on. Even taking a few minutes to openly tease me as Reaver went on his patrols, but eventually Hopper told them to lay off. Probably because Perish was glaring at them or something; he was always camp guard when Reaver was patrolling. They were both never gone at the same time.

Twinkle's tantrum, that's basically how they referred to me and Reaver's fight. They also laughed and teased Hopper over him getting rabies from the feral dog, who was pretending to be asleep in the bedroll on the other side of the tent. I bet he was seething too.

The whole situation just rotted my gut, and I realized in the cold air of the greywaste night that it was getting harder for me to pretend I was okay with being companions with slavers. It was illegal for one; even in the shitty lawless greywastes it was illegal, though no one ever cared. The fact of it was these were not good people; if they were slavers, they were slavers for a reason.

Jade understood… he was a slave too, and he felt the same way I did about keeping people captive. Perish wouldn't of course, he had done the same thing in Donnely; he experimented and fed his splices with arians.

The tent flap opened and I heard Reaver tell Deek to stay near the entrance, then the clinking of him taking his gun holder off of his back.

A few moments later, he got into the blankets and put an arm over me before he shifted to spoon me.

I shoved him away.

"No, don't even try it," Reaver said flatly. "It's freezing outside and you need the body heat, you're skin and bones."

I let out a breath through my nose but let him push my back up against his chest. I felt him draw me in tight and rest his forehead against the back of my head. I would never take for granted him actually wanting to be near me. At least there had been some positive changes to this new, darker Reaver… he wanted me around him more.

So I shifted around so I was facing him and buried my face into his neck.

"I'm sorry," I whispered to him.

Reaver sighed and petted my hair back. "You wouldn't be my Killian if you didn't have a need to help everyone. Just… not this time, Killi Cat. I have enough stress worrying about you and Reno."

I nodded and he kissed my forehead before resting his chin back onto my head.

"He kind of has the same skinny blond boy look as you though…" Reaver murmured. "And he doesn't talk either. He's like a better, more tolerable version of you… Killian 2.0, now without a voicebo-"

Reaver squawked as I dug my fingers into his side before he laughed quietly and kissed my forehead again. I raised my head and kissed his lips with a smile and settled in to sleep, hearing Jade snicker from his bedroll.

CHAPTER 24

Reaver

WE WOKE UP TO A COMMOTION THAT MORNING.

I left the boys in the tent and walked out into the tense atmosphere around the camp. I glanced around and saw the majority of the group a quarter mile away hovering over what looked like…

"Is that… a dead slave?" Perish said beside me. He shielded his eyes from the glaring grey sun and furrowed his brow.

My mouth pursed to the side. I was half-hoping it was the mute kid just so Killian could put his pet wish to rest.

I wasn't that lucky though. I could see the dirty blond-haired kid leaning against the pole he was shackled to, staring off into space like most of the slaves did during their resting times.

"Chomper… what's going on?" I walked past the moustached cook who was stoking the fire.

"It looks like a slave tried to escape last night." Chomper glanced up before throwing a thick cut up two-by-four onto the flames. "The spikes activated on his collar, and once that happens there's no going back."

Perish's heart jumped but I gave him a warning glance to keep his pride in his head; I assumed he was the one who designed that collar. Must've been a newer model, from what I remember the collar he had put on me would explode once activated.

"I'll check it out," I said, before motioning Perish to follow me. I walked out of camp and towards the gathering of slavers, all of them, especially Hopper, talking in quick and angry voices.

When the slaver spotted the two of us he raised his hands as if pleading with me to explain to him what had happened. "Are you kidding me? Really? Why would he even try running? We explain to them very carefully, even the stupid ones understood it!"

"Who was watching over them?" I asked, walking past Hopper and taking my last steps towards the corpse to give it a better look

My teeth clenched as I looked down. I realized it was the old man who'd apparently been harassing Chally, with blood stuck to his neck and dried onto the cold ground below.

Suddenly this morning surprise had turned a lot more personal.

"Tabbit was but he fucking fell asleep. I don't understand it, that ol' man was pretty fucking well-behaved." Hopper spat on the body and gave him a good kick in the side. "Well, that's food then. For fuck sakes, Melchai pays two hundred a head. This is –" Hopper let out an annoyed noise before he kicked the dead slave again out of sheer frustration.

"Maybe mute boy scared him," one of the men, a dark-skinned one named Jimmy said with amusement. Though with a withering gaze from Hopper he shut up. Hopper wasn't in the mood to make jokes which was odd for him.

"Whatever… I'm fucking flogging Tabbit for falling asleep and this fucking slave is coming out of his pay. Reaver… get your boyfriend and the pet to help Chomper chop him up before he starts to stink. I'm making myself a fucking drink." And with that, Hopper pushed past us towards the camp.

Well, I wasn't needed here. I turned around, leaving the blood-caked old man to his fate, and made my own way back to the camp.

As I walked I looked down at the footprints, freshly pressed into the greywaste dirt. This area was compacted and the dirt had a lot of rocks in it, but I could make out the slave's path just by his shoe imprints. They had shitty shoes, and the rest of us all wore army boots or the equivalent.

Something interesting caught my eye as I analyzed the prints; they were made in a way that told me he had been running. But why run? Why make a break for it when you knew your collar would go off?

The answer made my throat tight. I came across a disturbed rock and a partially flattened thatch of grass, and found another print… from someone else running.

Only this was an army boot.

I wiped my face with my hands and closed my eyes… this I didn't need.

The slave hadn't made a mad dash for freedom… he was chased.

Quickly I kicked the boot print so it mixed back in with the dirt and stalked towards the tent.

It could only be one person. There was no way it would've been Killian, this had serial killer chimera written all over it.

I walked into the tent and was greeted by Killian brushing his teeth and Jade lacing up his boots.

Anger flared up inside of me, searing my gut and lighting the fuse on my temper.

The pet looked up at me as I stalked over to him. He let out a surprised yelp as I grabbed his collar and yanked him to his feet.

"Reaver!" Killian shouted behind me but I ignored him

"Had fun last night, Cicaro?" I said in a low voice.

Jade gave me a bewildered look. "W-what?"

I wasn't in the mood to play games. I twisted his collar making his hands clench his neck as it started to restrict his breathing.

"I know what you did last night. If you think I wouldn't find out you're a fucking idiot. If you dare pull a stunt like that again, I swear on your husband's life I will give him back a fucking unic. Got me?"

"What the fuck are you on? I was right here–" Jade gasped, craning his neck back to get proper air flow, "–sleeping. What are you talking about?"

Then Killian's hands came and took my arm. "Put him down! Tell us what happened."

I growled but listened to him, though I was so pissed off I felt like chaining Jade to his own fucking stake out there. I was trying to get our hunted and wanted asses as far away from Kreig as I could, and these two dumbfucks were trying equally hard to get bullets in our heads.

"That old man that was harassing your newest defect was chased out of the camp last night and his collar activated," I hissed as Jade massaged his neck; his breathing laboured and his eyes still partially bugged.

"Those slaver idiots think he made a break for it, but I found boot prints. I would've woken up if it was Killian, not to mention he couldn't scare a fucking kitten. It was you, wasn't it, *Shadow Killer*?" He had become a serial killer in Moros and now he was putting his fucking steel claws back on.

The kid's heartbeat was already racing. I couldn't gauge his honesty by that, but the look he gave me was trying to tell me he was innocent. Unfortunately for him I knew better.

"I was here the whole fucking night. Perish was sleeping almost right next to me!" Jade snapped before turning to Killian. "Let's talk to Chally, see if he's–"

"You are not talking to him!" I yelled.

Both of them stopped in their tracks, staring at me like cornered toddlers. I clenched my jaw before turning away and stalking out of the tent.

After a quick breakfast and my eyes never leaving those two clowns, we packed up and continued on our way. In front of us I could see the mountains of the Coquihalla Pass coming closer and closer into view.

I stayed behind the caravans, which were two carts being pulled by bosen and were full of our supplies, and made sure we weren't being followed. Behind the caravans, the slaves were walking freely with their slave collars firmly attached to their necks. Perish was in the front with Hopper and Jimmy, and Churro was taking our flanks.

Another reason I was behind the group was so I could keep an eye on Killian and Jade. Both of them were sitting in one of the caravans playing a card games, waiting for the time to come where they could start preparing food.

On top of the other things on my mind, I now had the kid to worry about too. One wrong move from that maniac cicaro and we could all end up shot. Perish and I could get out of that pretty easily, but the pet and the boyfriend would be screwed.

And I couldn't put Killian in any danger… he was in enough danger as it was.

Like my heart was attached to a battery, I felt an electric percussion run through it; the old feelings I'd had back in Kreig were coming back with a gnawing vengeance. Perish's words had never really left my mind though; I'd just been too busy running from the Legion.

Though the pain I felt, that one day I would bury him, was still there, it was overlapped by the immediate danger we were now in. We had no block I could shelter him in, no reinforced basement. We were surrounded by people I didn't trust, and the people I did half-trust were turning on me.

Fucking hell, Jade – Elish, your cicaro better not fuck this up for us or put Killian in danger, or I swear...

I sighed and inhaled a deep breath to try and break the tension in my chest, then kicked a rock for the deacdog trailing beside me and watched him chase it. That stupid dog loved rocks for some reason, when we were on a break he would usually just sit and lick rocks unless I had a job for him. I told him it would fuck up his teeth but whatever... not my problem.

Then there was a quick movement to my right, near where the slaves were walking. My eyes shot over automatically and I saw the slave kid on the ground.

I walked past him. He was on his knees, his head bowed.

"Get up. You get too far away and your collar is going to shoot six sharp prongs into your neck," I said to him acerbically.

Chally looked up at me with big eyes like an owl and a pasty grey face. He nodded and scampered to his feet before shaping his fingers at me.

"I don't understand that shit, just walk faster," I said, before turning when I heard Jade's voice.

The cicaro was walking towards us holding a water bottle, Killian peering submissively from underneath the canvas tent, a spectator to something I knew he was in on.

"Cicaro..."

"It's my water." Jade handed the bottle to Chally with a smile. The kid took it with shaking hands. I saw his lips were so parched they were peeling like shedding reptile skin.

Then the pet glanced at over at me. "Go back to the group, Chally. Keep the bottle."

At this remark, Chally lowered his head and went off back to the shuffling slaves, water bottle in-hand.

"We need to make our detour soon, Reaver. Tabbit says there's a town coming up, off to the west. Hopper is avoiding it, but with its layout over the mountains we can stop there and take a shortcut to catch up with them," Jade explained. "The road branches off towards Mariano, the closest non-block town. Hopper says they'll have electricity for sure so we can charge the Ieon and possibly even get a signal to get Elish to pick us up."

"Don't you have some sort of tracking chip? Why can't Elish just find you now?" I said. I had tried to push down my frustrating over not being able to tell Elish where Reno was. He could be dead by now because we were stuck with these slaver assholes.

Jade shook his head. "No, I'm way out of range. If he flies overhead he can catch my signal, but I wouldn't trust him being able to find me right now."

My mouth gave a twinge and I realized I was clenching my teeth. "When is this town coming up?"

"Three days Hopper said. The highway we are about to walk on will branch off. We can get some better supplies there too." Jade glanced over as Chally finished the water in the bottle. "And some water purification tablets if they sell Dek'ko products there."

My eyes travelled to Killian who was still avoiding my gaze. I debated for a second whether he would be able to make the trip with how fast I would be walking, but there was no way I was leaving him alone. Jade was a different story though. No doubt the Legion would be checking out towns for us, and though they weren't looking for Jade, his eyes stayed in people's minds.

I could get away with it though, and Killian as well. We were Skyfallers, and though my eyes were unnaturally dark, they weren't purple or yellow like some other chimeras.

We had been on the road for several days now, with Kreig nothing but a memory in the distance and a vast expanse of grey in front of us. Hopper had been right when he told us the pass was going to be a challenge. I could see the mountains in front of us, a barren expanse of crags, trees, and sharp inclines that rimmed the twisted highway. There was nothing to be had in that landscape. No scavenging, no houses, even the cars seemed more rusted out and skeletonised than they were in the lower elevations. No one lived up here before the Fallocaust; this was just a road through a mountain that would hopefully lead us to Falkland.

And as I thought of that stupid town, I felt my mouth fill with a bitter taste. There was no reason why we had to walk to Falkland; we should be in one of those fancy planes. The only reason we were walking with this caravan now was to blend in; so if a plane or a legion caravan came strolling on through, we wouldn't draw attention to ourselves. Fate just happened to have our decoy heading in the same direction we needed to go.

Elish had wanted us to get the hard drives and we got them… now we were just running from a group of fucks I used to take immense glee in shooting. All of this going on while I had the knowledge where Reno was, an obvious code that apparently these chimera idiots didn't catch.

But no, I had the info and I was useless. I was just running now.

Running… when the fuck did it get that bad? I never ran…

Perhaps because I never had a reason to run. I always had the confidence that I would be just fine. Now I knew I would always be fine, but it wasn't me that was important anymore.

My eyes travelled to my blond boy, having a silent conversation with Jade who was now holding Chally's empty water bottle. That kid was so sweet, so sweet it was fucking driving me nuts. I wish… just until we were safe from the Legion, that he would steel that soft heart of his. He had to be selfish right now, for us. In the end, it was just the two of us… he couldn't save the world.

I walked up to him, and as he gave me a confused look, I leaned over and kissed his forehead.

He giggled and pinched my chin. "I thought you were coming to yell at me some more."

I shook my head, but bit back a retort that would probably start a fight. "As long as you don't bring home any strays I don't need to yell." I took the hand he had on my chin and kissed it, making him blush. "It looks like I have to make a trip, and there's no way I'm leaving you alone with this new penchant you have for pissing off people with guns. You and me are going together; the pet and the scientist are staying behind."

Jade made an angry noise. "I'm not staying behind. I need to–" When I held up my hand for him to be quiet, his protesting turned into an annoyed growl but his comments stopped there.

Killian's eyes widened though. "I get to go too? Jade says it's a day's walk… are you sure we should? Elish might be able to pick up Jade's tracker, it'll just take a while longer."

"We'll be fine if it's just the two of us. I wouldn't mind scouting out the pub and seeing if the Legion has started asking around. All we need is a charge for the Ieon, warmer clothes, and some water tablets, and we can make our way back…" I shrugged and leaned over to see past the edge of the cart. I saw Hopper and Tabbit walking side by side with their guns on their backs. "I need a few days away from these clowns anyway; they're starting to grate on my nerves."

And they were, I was used to a quiet basement… a place that I could retreat to when I felt like there were too many people around me. I didn't have such a place here. The only break I got was when I was off patrolling, and even then I couldn't relax because I didn't want to leave Killian for too long. We would be alright; I hadn't seen any sign of the Legion since we left that shanty town.

Killian gave me a sunny smile; I think he was looking forward to the break too. We hadn't had some alone time together in a while.

I cleared it with Hopper, and after that it was set, I was going to be able to escape this caravan and get a couple days with just me and my boyfriend. I needed it.

"– You know what? If you can pick me up a new fucking pair of goggles, I'd be your best friend." Hopper drew the goggles he had on his head down to his eyes and squinted, I could see the outside of them were sand blown and covered in thousands of small scratches. "But you need to be back in three days. We'll be halfway up the Coquihalla by then, and if you take the cross-path we should sync right up with each other. The caravan would take ages with the rocks, but you and Twinkles should make good time."

"We'll be quick. At least we haven't seen any sign of the Legion," I said quietly. "I'll listen in at their pub and see if I can get any intel on their activity. Do we have any other towns besides this one until Falkland?"

Hopper shook his head before he stumbled over a loose rock. He gave it a kick to show it he didn't approve of it tripping him and turned back to me with a muttered curse. "Nah, not unless you start going west once you're out of the mountains. Where Falkvalley and Melchai are is up near the plaguelands. No one goes up there, which is why they pay out the nose for slaves."

"What for?"

Hopper chuckled before kicking another rock out of the way. "They sacrifice them, they're a superstitious bunch. They think it makes their crops grow better or some crap. They have fucking amazing farmland but it's bullshit, obviously, but whatever… we are–"

We both paused as the very familiar sound of Killian bursting into tears could be heard.

I closed my eyes for a second, took a deep breath, and fell behind a few steps so I could address this.

Sure enough, Killian's face was dissolved into tears. When he saw me he buried his face into his hands and shook his head. "They're going to kill him?"

The lead slaver nodded solemnly. He twitched his mouth to the side but that was it for his sympathies. "Sorry, little Twinkles, we're slavers, we ain't the Peace Corps."

All around us the slavers were giving us glances and snickering to each other. Jade on the other hand was stone-faced, staring forward with a silence to him that made it all too known he was screaming in his head.

This I didn't need… this I *really* didn't need. I wanted to just kill that stupid little mute right then and there to save having to deal with the fallout of Killian's newest realization.

Really though, I suspected as much. Slaves were usually sold as either free labour, sex workers, or food, rarely ever did they get sold as maids. Only elites could afford an arian as a maid, and from Jade's stories about Elish's sengil Luca, they trained those little creatures from toddlers.

I put a hand on Killian's shoulder but he jerked it away. I didn't give a shit though so I put it back on.

I rubbed it and said as gently as I could, "Killi… we can't save them all."

The boy looked up at me, his eyes red and full of tears. He stared into me with such emotion I felt my cold dead heart give a flicker of empathy.

"Please, Reaver?"

I hated the pull that kid had on me at times.

"He's-not-for-sale," Hopper piped up beside me. "I told ya, he ain't for–"

I shook my head and swore oaths under my breath, but I had an idea… and it might just be a happy medium.

"Look, what if we take the kid with us to Mariano, and we'll sell him to some nice elite that will probably use him as a sex slave or a maidservant… if you think that's a better life, Killian." I let out a sigh and glanced over at the mute who was kicking a rock for Deekoi. "In return, I'll bring you back a healthy slave to replace him from the town, and get you your stupid fucking goggles for free. How's that?"

Hopper opened his mouth in a way that told me he was about to disagree, but he closed it as soon as his slow slaver brain caught up to him.

He nodded and put his goggles back over his head. "Alright, Merrik, you got a deal. You get the mute and I want a healthy arian in return."

Killian let out a squeal and I felt his arms around my neck. I grimaced as he planted a kiss on my cheek. Then he seemed to remember my hatred for showing affection in public, so he settled for a beaming smile. "Thank you, thank you, baby. I won't forget this."

I wouldn't let him.

CHAPTER 25

Reaver

CHALLY RUBBED HIS NAPE; HIS LONG DIRT-CAKED fingers grazing over the swollen, rash-covered flesh of his neck. Hopper had taken his collar off a couple of hours ago and he kept putting his hands up to stroke where it used to be, as if not believing what was actually going on.

When he saw me looking at him, he smiled, and signed something to me as he moved his mouth. I could read his lips though.

"Thank you," he signed and mouthed to me.

I glared at him and his smile disappeared. "Don't thank me; you're probably going to wish you were dead once we sell you to some fat elite with a cactus-dildo fetish."

"Reaver!" Killian elbowed me in the ribs. I reciprocated by digging my hand into his side making him give out a squawk.

We were all in pretty good moods considering everything. I was happy to be on my way to Mariano to charge the Ieon. I had to get that intel to Elish as soon as I could. I was also happy to just be away from Hopper's caravan, and to a lesser extent, Perish and Jade. Those two grated on my every last nerve.

Killian, of course, was just happy I decided to save Chally from his fate, and Chally was obviously happy to be temporarily free. Those two seemed to be getting along rather well, which was okay, I guess.

"Reaver!" My inner thoughts were broken by Killian's laughing voice. “Look…”

I glanced over at the grubby little mute kid and watched him make like he was holding a knife. He then stabbed his pretend knife into his clenched fist before his hand made another shape.

“Fascinating.” I looked back to the greywastes but the giggle-buddies started laughing.

“He’s killing an *E* then an *N*. Kill-*E*-*N*. That’s how he signs my name!” Killian said.

I let out a breath through my nose. “So when I finally cut out your tongue to stop you from nattering at me we can still communicate?”

Killian smiled at me before shaping something to Chally.

They both burst out laughing as they glanced back at me.

My mouth dropped open. “Are you fucking kidding me? What did you say? You can’t talk behind my fucking back!”

They laughed some more. I shook my head and got out my M16 and started scouting ahead, leaving the little budgies to have fun with each other. He was getting sold soon so Killian might as well get all his laughs in. He was going to be wailing when I handed over Chally to the ugliest, most creepiest-looking elite I could find.

My eyes scanned the make-shift map that Chomper had drawn for us, which looked like useless scribbles but the landmarks did their job. I had a plan as to where we would sleep tonight and which hotel in Mariano would be the safest for us to stay in once we arrived.

Unless we walked into the wee hours of the morning we would be sleeping in the basement or bedroom of an old rancher home. Most towns were closed down for the night anyway so chances are we wouldn’t be allowed in. Giving the kids a good night sleep would be worth spending the night out in the barren greywastes, even if I didn’t like it. I would be the only one to keep watch so I wouldn’t be getting much sleep tonight. I certainly wasn’t going to trust Killian or the mute kid to keep watch that was for damn sure.

I climbed up a small incline that was still being held back from the road with a grey concrete barrier, though it had a large fissure slowly splitting it in two. I then hopped onto a median and scanned the greywastes around us.

Same landscape, rocks sticking out of the grey ground with the occasional twisted tree or spindly bush. Sometimes when I would spend days out here it would confuse me once I came back to my basement, came back to blue water jugs and my red Coca Cola signs. You forget colour exists out here sometimes.

I remember how blue his eyes looked compared to the grey.

"Killi?" I turned around and called.

Killian, who had been learning signs from Chally as they walked, looked up at me. "Yes, hun?" His blue eyes just as vivid as I remembered them in my head, like deep blue pools of water. They contrasted the area around us to the point where they looked like fallen stars. He held the only natural colour around us right now.

I just felt like seeing them for some reason.

"Nothing," I smirked and turned back around to scale the other side of the incline. He didn't answer back, but I knew he was probably signing something to his new friend.

We spent an uneventful day following the road. During the last two hours of daylight I led the boys off the pavement and down a steady incline into a small valley. Sure enough, Chomper's map was right and there was a small little ranch house surrounded by grassy flatlands.

I tucked the kids behind a woodshed like they were cougar cubs and crossed the yard towards a closed door. The door to the inside of the house once had red paint on it, but it had all been chipped and sloughed off, only laying as crinkled ruins against the bone-dry wood.

But the chips were not disturbed; they had been there long enough to gather a good amount of greywaste dust so no one had been here for a while. Still though, a radanimal or something could've snuck in, so I kicked the door open.

The door swung and half fell off of its hinges. I grabbed it and made it stand upright before I froze my movements and listened.

No heartbeats and the smell inside was of the thick must and sour that all old houses had. No animal stink or rotting carcasses.

I let out a whistle, and sure to their cue, the kittens peeked their heads out from behind the shed. How did I end up with two timid blond kids? I swear with my luck I would find out he was a long lost brother or something and then we would be forced to keep him.

I walked in, my boots crunching against plaster. I quietly walked into every room and surveyed what would be our safest spot.

"The kitchen is clear, see if you can find us some food. If this place is this desolate I'd rather we sleep on the second floor than the cellar. I want to be able to see shit, not just hide from it," I said, glancing behind me. I pointed towards a half-crumbled wall, its dry beams sticking out and chewed on from long gone radrats. I could see the bottom of a fridge through it. "It's behind that wall."

Killian nodded, Chally beside him with his eyes wide. He was holding a flashlight even though it was still daylight outside. He seemed to be sticking pretty close to Killian.

I started testing the stairs and wiggling the railing as I climbed up. These stairs seemed shoddy at best but they were supporting my weight. If they could support me the two marshmallow fluff boys would be able to walk up here.

I coughed into my sleeve as the disturbed dust tickled my nostrils. The walls had shed all of their plaster but the insulation had remained in their partitions; though it collected dust like a magnet and it seemed even the slightest of movements was making it fly.

I walked into a bedroom and saw an old crib pressed up against the wall and a soiled mattress on the ground. I saw a skeleton with a rat-chewed blanket draped over top, and though the black stain on the mattress made it hard to tell, I think I saw the kid's skull tucked under her arm. Poor ol' bitch probably died during a winter. If she had been killed there would be no way her body would've been allowed to go to waste, or the kid's – kids tasted great.

I closed the door and checked out the next room, but it was just a bathroom with a rust-streaked tub and a cream-coloured toilet without a lid. We could piss in that tonight if we needed to, the floor looked decent enough.

No mattresses to be found besides the one that had the years old bodies rotten on top of it. The master bedroom's mattress shredded under the kicks of my boots so I knew once our weight was on it the springs would be digging into us. But we were more than used to sleeping on the ground and the mute kid would be too.

I walked to a warped window frame with glass long since broken, laying in shards underneath the sill mixed in with the ground-in dirt of the carpet. This room hadn't seen a living soul in a long time from the looks of it; even before the Fallocaust it seemed to have been an older home. It still had wallpaper on the gyprock, peeling down in long ribbons one layer after another. I counted five layers of wallpaper, all different floral patterns.

I scratched my finger against the thin paper and stripped off a few to see the bright blue pattern underneath. I tossed it into a corner and coughed again into my sleeve.

"Alright, come up stairs now. I want us in one room before night falls," I called down to them. I laid my M16 against the door and walked down the stairs. I wanted to push an old couch I had seen against the door to the outside.

Killian appeared with two cans of mystery food, the label faded and already falling onto the floor with even his gentle touch. "I think this might be beans." He coughed too and tapped the can as I pushed the couch.

The mute kid appeared and gave me a hand which I appreciated, though I think it was more to suck up than to be useful, but who's to know.

When night fell I turned on one of our flashlights and put it underneath the blankets. We didn't have a bluelamp to call our own anymore so this would have to do. I didn't want to waste the batteries so I fed the kids as quickly as I could. The can wasn't beans however, it was beets but whatever, those tasted alright though it stained all of our fingers. Chally was just thrilled to get something other than Ratmeal so he didn't bitch, or sign a bitch anyway.

I wonder if he could do that.

After Chally curled up with his thin blanket, I brought up a chair to the window and watched the dark moonless landscape around us.

When I heard rustling, I looked over and saw Killian drape his blanket over Chally. I sighed and shook my head though I bit my tongue.

So caring and so sweet… but this wasn't Skyfall, this wasn't Tamerlan…

"Come here." I motioned him over and shifted back on the chair.

Killian gave me a shy smile and sat down on my lap. I put my arms around him and kissed behind his ear.

He tilted his head back to try and kiss me with a pucker of his lips. He couldn't reach though, which he giggled about, so I craned my head and did the rest of the work.

"You're such a dumbass," I said to him sweetly.

Killian shifted his body so he was leaning against me before grabbing my arms and tightening them around his waist.

"Are you okay?" he asked.

I furrowed my brow. "Why wouldn't I be?"

Killian paused for a second and I felt him let out a breath. "I just want to check in… make sure you're… you know."

"I'm fine," I said flatly, but that just made him make a noise in his throat.

"In relationships people check in with each other even when nothing is apparently wrong… I'm checking in."

"I'm just fine… even more fine now that we have some time to ourselves, without dipshit and dickweed always causing trouble."

Killian, of course, laughed at this. "They're not that bad. See how well-behaved Perish has been? He's been trying really hard, and Jade too. He's a bit… feral, but he's a nice guy."

"I just want it to be us again… and Reno." I sighed and leaned my head against his. "I can't believe it's been this long and I haven't been able to tell Elish where he is. What if I'm too late? All because we turned on the fucking power in Kreig and alerted… *them*."

The boy was quiet for a moment. We both stayed in our silence as I surveyed the empty land in front of us, tinged blue with a silver hue, even darker now that the moon was gone.

"Do you think he'll stay in Skyfall now? Since he's engaged to Garrett?"

Immediately my body tensed. "I won't let him."

"But Garrett seems to really love him…"

"I don't care. Reno belongs to me and he knows it."

I wondered if he was going to argue with me, but to my surprise, he just squeezed my hand. "I know, love. I'm sure it will all work out."

A flicker of jealousy smouldered my gut, and though deep down I knew it was stupid, I didn't want Reno to love anyone. It was immature and it reflected badly on me but… I was comfortable with the relationship we had. He loved me and was devoted to only me, even if I was with Killian now.

Nothing wrong with that.

"Can I ask you something though?" Killian's voice raised an octave and I knew I wasn't going to like what he was going to say next.

"Nope."

"Reaver!" Killian tugged on my hand. "That's not what you're supposed to say next."

"Then if you're going to ask anyway, why ask permission?"

He huffed a breath out of his nose.

I rolled my eyes. "Alright, ask away. I'll prepare myself to tell you to shut up."

"You knew Elish before you met him in Aras, didn't you? You said he went as James and Jade went as Michael, right?" Killian said.

I nodded. "Yeah, now that I think back, I have been seeing him since I was a kid, but he always altered his appearance slightly or avoided me. I remember Leo and Greyson going off with him to the bunker or the East House. I mostly just remember when he started coming with Jade. I dangled Jade over a deacons' den, did he tell you about that?"

"I've heard him complain about it a few times," Killian smirked. He shifted into me more. "The thing is… Elish was the guy who fired my father. I had met him previously too, he came to our house and Jade was right behind him. Jade gave me some rum and told me I was going to be going to the greywastes soon."

Huh, I didn't know that. "Well, I guess we owe him for us meeting, huh?"

The boy was silent for a second. "That's the thing, I don't think it was a coincidence. I think he sent me to Aras because of you. I think Jade maybe did his aura reading and saw us as a match."

I shook my head. "Maybe. Weren't you ripe to get sold off to a chimera? Maybe you're a chimera magnet and Elish wanted you far away from the family," I smirked. "So he sent you to the baddest of them all; my own little sacrificial lamb." Feeling playful, I leaned over and gave his neck a mock-bite. He squealed at me and scrunched his neck.

"Chimeras do seem to like me for some reason… Perish loved me, Jade likes me, you love me, even Elish has always been kind to me… I mean he got Biff for us and he was patient with me when I barricaded myself in my bedroom back in the greyrifts shelter." Killian's voice was full of wonder; I think he saw the prospect as fascinating. "Maybe it's my blood? Hey, even Leo liked me, until… you know I threatened his secret. Maybe I am a magnet!"

"Hmm, I'll need to watch you then. I might catch you trying to sleep with Jade."

"Ew, Reaver. He would shred me to bits. Do you see the scars he and Elish have? They go at it like wolverines!"

"Mmm… do they now? Show me…" I let that trail as I gave his neck a small lick before I put my mouth over it and gave it a long suck. I broke the seal with a pop and rubbed his new hicky. Killian scrunched his neck and I could see his jaw tighten as he smiled.

I wasn't done though; I brushed his hair away from his neck and kissed him again, before my hands started to trail down the rim of his pants.

"Chally is sleeping ten feet away from us, mister. Not tonight!" Killian hissed.

But my hands were already down his pants and he didn't stop me when I grabbed his dick, still soft but hardening with my roaming touch. "And? He won't hear us."

"He's mute not deaf!" Killian said exasperated.

I smiled as I heard a soft moan escape his lips a moment later. He raised his hips and started rubbing himself against my hand. My free hand slid down my own pants and I started to unbutton them.

"Come here," I whispered.

Not another protest left the boy's lips; he turned around before giving the sleeping lump in the corner of the room a nervous glance. Then, as I pulled my own dick out, he slid his pants off and straddled me.

Always prepared, I dug out a small bottle of lube out of my cargo pants pocket and prepped myself, and slid a finger inside of him as he started to kiss my lips.

"You…" He grabbed my chin and made me look at him, his eyes were narrow. It was so cute when he was trying to be dominant. "I get to be in control. I don't trust you to not make me cry out. Got it, Mr. Chimera?"

I smirked at him and kissed him deeply, opening my mouth and taking him in as he positioned himself over my dick. He then grabbed my member and started to push himself down on it.

Just because I was an asshole, I jerked my hips, roughly breaking into him. He cried out, and of course, I laughed, before he hit me really hard on the shoulder.

I kissed him again, though it was hard through the smile, then found my teeth clenching as he sunk my entire length into him.

I leaned back and let him lead, his beautiful body rising and falling on top of me, the greywastes in the distance framing his thin body perfectly. If it wasn't winter, I would have stripped every shred of clothing off of him so I could see those angelic, slender lines in all its perfection. He was beautiful, every last detail of his body engineered to the point where if I didn't know better I'd say he was the genetically-enhanced one.

He was perfect and finally being alone with him in my element, without people around to disturb us, made me appreciate the flawless creature he was.

Killian's breathing was in sync with his movements, small little puffs of winter air every time I would sink back into him. Soon I had his dick in my hand, slowly stroking and playing with it.

We were two fugitives, one a chimera and another the chimera-magnet, far from what was no longer our home, but for now, together and safe.

I shouldn't take him for granted… and I wouldn't.

I put my hands on his back and held him against me; his fingers gripping my shoulders as he rode me. I moved my hips up and down with his movements and closed my eyes. I could stay like this forever and I wanted to. I could forget everything… I could forsake my revenge; I could… give everything up just to make sure he was still safe.

I couldn't lose him, not even at eighty years old.

With my mind elsewhere, I was taken by surprise when, after a while, his moans started to get louder. Leave it to me to be off in my own head and not even enjoying that I was in the middle of sex with him. That happened more than I cared to admit, but I was always one to go inside my head at inappropriate moments.

I started stroking him faster, and when his heartbeat reached its quickened rhythm, I put my free hand over the head of his dick. I loved him to pieces but cum was really hard to get out of dark clothing and we didn't have any water to spare.

He groaned and started making short but higher pitched noises. I closed my eyes again and started thrusting myself into him as he came in my hand. I pulled him into me and started rapidly pushing in and out of him as my own pleasure multiplied. This made his moans increase and I came to him shooting the last bits of his cum into my hand.

Afterwards we laid together on our last remaining blanket; he was still out of breath and I was just starting to catch my own. He would fall asleep now, and when he did, I'd go back to sentrying, but for now I wanted to give him the comfort I knew he missed.

"I love you." I could hear his smile even though I couldn't see it.

"What is this love thing? Chimeras can't love… I tolerate you though." That got me a smack; I laughed and kissed his neck. "I love you too, Killibee, now go to sleep. We have a long ass day of dealing with greywasters tomorrow."

"Mmhm, I will. I won't even ask if you're going to let me take watch." Killian yawned and nestled himself into me before falling silent.

I brushed back his blond hair and sighed to myself, thinking thoughts inside of my head that I could never share with him. I wish I could, but I couldn't scare him… I couldn't tell him how close I was to not going back to Hopper's caravan. How close I was to saying fuck it and finding a town for us to live in forever.

But Jade had said they would find us, no matter what. If not Silas, than Elish… who had been pulling strings and controlling our lives for longer than I had previously thought.

Had he really sent Killian to attract me? I scowled at the thought, in a way it made sense if he somehow knew Killian would even me out.

The thought that Elish had been controlling what entered and left my life filled my mouth with an odd taste… I know it was in his nature to do as such, but I didn't want a chimera controlling my life. I was my own person now.

No… I was his weapon.

And I had to kill Silas, not just for revenge and for killing my fathers, but because he would kill Killian and continue to seek me. I was made for him and he wouldn't give me up.

I didn't have a choice.

This wasn't my life anymore.

My life was now keeping Killian safe.

He was all I had.

"Alright, what do you want your name to be?" The small town of Mariano was only a half an hour away now, just a small town with a shoddy fence and lots of smoke billowing out of the small structures. Besides a few dogs tied to stakes, it didn't look like they had any protection from the greywastes. Before the Fallocaust this might've been a town. One of those ones that you drove by on the way to a bigger city, where if you blinked you would miss it.

Now it was small, maybe a hundred or so people, but it was on the main road so I assumed most of their income came from travellers or caravans. Not the ones heading to Falkvalley though, but for all I knew, there were other towns further south or west.

"Lance? That's my middle name and it was my Grandpa's name too."

I shook my head. "No, I'm going to say I'm Chance. It rhymes and it'll make us look stupid."

Killian passed our water bottle to Chally and gave me a half-smile. "It sounds cute! Chance and Lance!"

I gave him a look. We had been together long enough that I didn't need to tell him that I was not cute.

He rolled his eyes at me. "Fine, how about… Jeff, like my dad?"

"Sure, why not…" I could see a man sitting on a wooden chair beside a derelict house. He was holding a shotgun in his hand. I was to assume that's our welcome party. "Okay, *Jeff*. We're travellers and we bought Chally from an abusive master out of pity and now we're pawning him off. I want to stop in some bars to scout for info after we hit the store. We're staying the night and an hour before daylight we're leaving, okay?"

Killian nodded but I saw the sadness in his eyes over us having to sell the kid, behind me Chally's face darkened too but he didn't say anything.

Heh.

Say anything.

I adjusted the pack of our supplies, including the Ieon and remote phone. Jade had stopped bitching about not coming with us to the town but he had refused to hand over Elish's laptop and the hard drives. The remote phone would be good enough, it had Elish's number programmed into it and a cell phone was better than that shitty buffering network anyway.

The dogs barked at us, making the shotgun man stand up slowly on what looked like a sore back. He gave us a nod and was immediately backed up by a lady with short black hair.

"We usually only get merchants here. Unfortunately, since it's winter, we can't give handouts…" The old man seemed polite enough; we were off to a good start.

"We have money. We're here to sell a slave, have a few drinks, spend the night and get some supplies," I said, crossing my arms over my chest. "Nothing else."

The man gave Chally a shifty look and then Killian. "Those are arians; you know that's illegal…"

I stared at him. "And you know this ain't Skyfall?"

He laughed and raised his hands in the 'you got me' type of motion. He let them drop. "We don't ask too many questions here. We get slavers every once in a while, but this is the greywastes you got us there. Okay, welcome to Mariano."

I gave him a nod, wishing Killian had a collar on that I could grab onto just to make sure he stayed safe and near me. I wondered if he would be too overly oppose to that one, Jade's had come in useful many times when I had to deal with him. I could see why Elish still had one on him.

The three of us walked down a single-lane street; buildings repaired with pressboard, tin, and sheets of plastic, giving all of it that patch-work look our buildings in Aras had. Though this town was worse off but all normal towns and settlements were. The good thing about a block was that we got perks for paying taxes to Skyfall, the cat-subsidy alone paid for our Ratmeal, mostly since Greyson and Leo treated them like fluffy little kings and queens. So since Skyfall, when it came down to it, paid for our rats we had taxes from the residents left over to buy oil, gasoline, medical supplies, and the big machines we needed to clear roads or tear down the houses that collapsed in the occupied areas.

Mariano had no such luxury. Piled up beside what looked like a small shop was a collapsed house that looked like its exterior had been chewed on by radrats. There were also a lot of cars still on the roads; some with ramps going up and down them, which I guess was easier than trying to move them. Even the people here looked more starved and sunken in, and most of them were carrying around bottles of swill that smelled like turpentine.

But they left us alone, or they didn't talk to us at least, everyone seemed to be watching us. Physically we didn't stand out too much compared to the usual greywaster, but I suppose since I was a dominant-looking guy leading two cowering little blond boys… perhaps I stood out more than I thought I would.

The first thing we did was duck into one of the shops, a shitty looking shack with 'Bill's Place' writing in green on a sun bleached board of wood. With Killian beside me and the mute kid trailing behind, we entered the store.

It smelled like cigarettes and mould and was only lit by the winter sun coming in from the stained windows and a single bluelamp that had seen better days. I saw black flecks stuck inside the light, some of which had legs.

Bill wasn't who I expected him to be; it was a younger chick with badly dyed hair, smoking a cigarette with a baby on her hip. I assumed that was either Bill's wife or daughter or something.

She put the baby on top of a makeshift table that had a cash register resting on it and gave us all nods of recognition.

"Browsing? Or can I point you in the right direction?" she asked. She raised her cigarette in the air just as the baby raised a fat little pink hand to grab the ember. Kids are so stupid.

"Water purification tablets, goggles, warm blankets and jackets, and…" I tried to think of anything else we might have on the list. "5.56mm ammo and .357 magnum." I checked my cargo pants pocket and felt for my wallet. Elish had given me free rein over his cash supply and I had taken full advantage of that. I was glad I had, we weren't supposed to have ventured away from Kreig so in all senses we didn't need money… but I was a greywaster and I never turned down the opportunity for free cash.

The chick nodded and took a drag of her cigarette. Then she looked down and I saw that another little brat was grabbing onto her jeans. "Go get Uncle Pete and tell him to bring the ammo. We have customers." She glanced up at me as the little boy ran past us and out the door. "We keep our ammo under lock and key, everything else we can help you with. How long are you in town for?"

"We'll be leaving before the sun rises," I replied, watching Killian and Chally out of the corner of my eye. Killian was taking intense interest in something, and as I turned to see what it was, I gave an internal eye-roll. It was a stack of bar soap.

Of course it was.

I decided to be the nice boyfriend I was. I reached over and grabbed a bar of the smelly soap and saw they had a few tubes of toothpaste and a toothbrush. I grabbed some of that stuff too and put it on the counter. "And this shit, I guess."

Killian's heartbeat jumped behind me but he kept quiet, which I gave him credit for. I might be getting lax on showing affection around my brothers but it was still not allowed in front of people we didn't know.

A few minutes later, after our supplies were sitting in a bag (Hopper's goggles had pink frames which I thought was just great), an older man who I assumed was Uncle Pete, came in with the little boy trailing behind.

"Well, don't you look like a man not to fuck with." Uncle Pete gave me a nod. He had a scraggly greasy beard and his breath smelled like a cat shit. "Where are you heading?"

I opened my mouth to tell him to piss off and stop asking questions when Killian cut in. "We're just heading north, that's all. Does Porchlight have any rooms open?"

Pete looked past me to the boy and shook his head. "No, Porchlight burned down last summer. You'll be looking for Little Eight, it's an actual hotel we finally were able to make safe. Just follow the main road until you see it."

Killian nodded his thanks and I started sifting through the bag of ammo that he had brought with him. He had my M16 ammo and the Magnum ammo I needed. Not a hell of a lot but it was all bonus anyway. This town trip was just a perk. I had packed enough ammo for me and Killian, and Elish had more than enough spare ammo for the AK 101's the other two had.

"I want this, how much?" I asked laying out the worn-out cardboard boxes.

"Forty bucks for the ammo, fifty for the supplies."

I snorted. Fuck that. "That's not going to happen, that's double what it was in…" I paused catching myself before I said Aras. "Tintown." Well, that was the only thing I could come up with.

Uncle Pete crossed his arms, so I did too, burning holes into those beady little eyes of is. You would think with this toothpaste and shit he would use some to brush his fucking green teeth. "We're far away from Tintown, my friend, and–"

"We're not frien-"

"Ninety is fine," Killian cut in. He put a hand on my shoulder and took my wallet. Strangely enough, he hadn't burst into flames which I thought he would considering the fucking death glare I was giving him.

"I'm also selling a slave. Not this one, the blond kid with the grey eyes." I motioned behind me towards Chally who was standing as quiet as a mouse. "Put the word around. We will be at the bar this evening."

Before they gave me an excuse to argue, Killian paid him and I took my wallet back. Then, with a forced exchange of farewell pleasantries, we were off and on our way.

"You know arguing like that is going to make them remember us," Killian hissed at me, dropping his voice low enough so only I could hear it.

"They're ripping us off!" I hissed back, looking ahead to scout for the hotel. I thought I could see it in the distance.

"And? We'll be gone tomorrow and it isn't even our damn money! Elish literally has all the money in Skyfall." Bah, I hated when he was right; it was more the principal of it though.

He continued, "We're not… home, these aren't our people. I know it goes against–"

"Yeah, yeah, I got it," I said bitterly, before muttering under my breath. "When I'm king I'm going to get back my forty bucks, mark my words."

We checked into our hotel room without incident. The man there was cordial enough and he had a pretty face which I got glowered at when I pointed it out to my boyfriend. After having a couple cold water showers, and an hour to rest our feet, the three of us headed towards a bar we had walked past.

I sat down with a beer and a couple shots of whiskey and found a dark corner for the three of us to sit down in. This bar was even shittier than Melpin's back in Aras, dimly lit with just bluelamps plugged into extension cords and LEDs. We had left the remote phone and the Ieon back in the hotel room getting charged, hidden under a radrat-chewed mattress though there were two guards watching over the hallways which made me a bit more comfortable with this place.

Hell, maybe tonight I might actually get some sleep. I didn't need a lot of sleep but I wasn't a machine. Donnely had been a nice reminder of that.

I gave Chally a shot of whisky. "You ever drink before? Want me to get you a glass of milk?"

Chally gave me a look before he grabbed one of the pens Killian had on him and a scrap of paper Killian had stuffed in his pockets. My boyfriend laughed when he saw it.

Just because I can't talk doesn't mean I'm not a real greywaster. No talking doesn't = soft idiot. I'm mute not stupid.

Really now? I gave the kid a look. "You've gotten bold."

He started writing again. *No, I've gotten my collar off.*

Killian laughed again but I just shook my head. It did make me think of the little asshole a bit differently though. I suppose when you had half a dozen metal prongs just itching to dig into your neck you behaved yourself. Not being able to talk would only add to that, if you don't defend yourself against people's insults people just assume you're soft and easy to kick around.

I let the dog have his day and watched him take down the shot of whisky without so much of a mouth twitch. I ordered him another because it would be funny get him drunk, then relaxed myself with an opiate cigarette.

I noticed a man looking at us; he had been here for about half an hour before he finally got up with his drink. He casually walked over and pulled up a chair.

I stared at him as he took a swig. “I heard you’re selling a young arian boy?”

Killian’s heartbeat jolted and so did Chally’s. I pointed to the kid. “That’s him. I want a hundred and fifty for him.”

The man with short blond hair and a square face looked Chally up and down. “What’s he good for? Can he suck cock good?”

I shrugged, and as Killian withered in his seat, I looked at the kid. “Well? Can you?”

Chally’s little owl eyes looked up at the man and nodded, before signing something to Killian.

“He says he can.” Killian’s voice was flat and edging on the tear-zone.

“What he can’t talk? Why the fuck are you charging so much for a retard?”

“You want him to make conversation or do you want him to be a good fuck? You don’t need to speak to lick cock, buddy.” I shot him a glare. “Are you interested or not?”

The guy reached out a hand and lifted up Chally’s chin, before moving it from one side to the other, then his fingers trailed and he drew the kid’s shirt down to glance at his pasty chest.

“Virgin?”

“He’s a slave, what the fuck do you think?”

The man’s mouth twitched from one side to another. “I want to try out the goods.”

No, you want a free fuck. “Fifty dollar non-refundable deposit if you’re actually serious. I’m a slaver not a pimp.”

The man narrowed his eyes at me but he didn’t have anything else to say. He dug into his pocket and slammed two twenties and a ten on the table.

I checked them out, the only currency of value here were Skyfall dollars, which were Canadian dollars but they had to be cycled through the Skyfall Mint first. So if you just found a stack of money in the greywastes you were shit out of luck, they had to be documented and stamped and only with that stamp did they actually become money again.

I checked out the bills, and sure enough, they had the dried leaf stamp that all Skyfall money had. I nodded and looked to Chally. "Well, he isn't that ugly. Go do your job and you won't get your throat cut in Melchai."

Chally leaned over and took the whisky shot Killian still hadn't touched. He downed it and got up.

Killian gave me a soul crushing look as Chally and the man disappeared out the door; I had my money though so I was just fine. I tucked the bills into my wallet and ordered another drink.

"What!?" I said when fifteen minutes had gone by and he was still on the verge of tears. "This is going better than you thought it would, right? He's not being sold to some fat old man. Why are you so upset?"

Killian exhaled from his own opiate cigarette he had been smoking. We'd been cutting down on the heroin and were now down to just inhaling pills and smoking Skyfall quils.

"I'm just going to miss him… you know if I hadn't been sold to a factory that could've been me, right? You wouldn't want–"

I put up a hand. "Don't start that shit with me, Massey. You're manipulating me right now and I've given in enough to you. Chally won't die, you can't fucking expect me–"

"I am not manipulating you!" Killian sounded aghast but the writing was on the walls. I took a drink of my beer and ignored him. I was done with this conversation and his ways of trying to tug on what little empathy I had. My empathy was solely focused on Killian; it did not extend to mutes.

"Well?" Killian said, his temper getting short.

I looked at him. "I'm done talking and I dare you to keep poking me. Now just shut up, you're giving me a headache."

Killian glared at me before he crossed his arms over his chest and decided to act like a five-year-old by giving me the silent treatment. There wasn't a single fuck for me to give though; I enjoyed the silence all the way up to when Chally came back with Mr. Blond Hair.

The kid sat down with a sullen and forlorn look on his face.

I glanced up at the guy. "Well?"

The man nodded. "He'll do. Bill's shop is closed now. Give me until daybreak to sell a few things and I'll give you the rest of the money."

I wanted to leave an hour before dawn, but if I could ditch the kid this easily I would stay later. “Daybreak, no later. One hundred bucks.”

“Can I have him for the night?”

“No.”

After he left Killian slunk further in his seat, and Chally just stared into the shot of whisky the bar man had brought him. So since this party had died, and I hadn’t heard any mention of the Legion from any of the sunken-eyed fucks around me, we made our way back to the hotel room.

It was chilly and dark. I was happy for the heaters that were in our hotel room, though we were paying out the nose for the luxury. This was the first hotel room I had ever stayed in and so far it wasn’t that bad. The armed guards had been a nice touch that was for sure.

“Reaver…” Killian’s voice whined when I was digging the remote phone out from under the blankets, I was pleased to see it was charged. “Chally doesn’t like him.”

“I don’t care,” I replied and sat on the bed with the charged Ieon beside me. I unplugged the remote phone but frowned when I pulled off a little device that was supposed to be secured under the antenna. I fiddled with it to try and put it back on.

My heart gave a bit of a jolt when I saw the signal got stronger without the device, not overly strong but instead of no signal it was giving me one bar. Perhaps I would get lucky and actually get that blond fucker on the phone.

I started scrolling through the numbers until I found Elish’s. I pressed it and held it up to my ear.

I could hear the echo in the remote phone but a moment later there was static and a pissed off beeping noise. I sighed but tried again, lighting another cigarette.

I leaned against the window while I kept trying the phone, ignoring Killian talking to Chally as he wrote his responses on whatever scraps of paper those two could find. His new master would have to fucking find him a Magna Doodle or something.

After a couple hours of me trying to call out on the phone, Killian came over and put his arm around me.

“I’m sorry,” he said quietly. “You are already doing a lot for him and I got caught up in it.”

I put my arm around him and offered him the last drag of my cigarette. "If this was all happening in Aras, I would have given him to Reno or something… but we don't have control over our own lives anymore… and I can't handle another kid to look after. You're all that's important." I stroked his hair back and he leaned his head on my shoulder.

"You're the most important… you being safe," Killian said quietly. I had to smile at that comment.

"I'm immortal, I'll always be safe."

But he shook his head. "We need to keep you from Asher…"

Even calling him that made my blood start to simmer. He wasn't Asher and he never was Asher. Asher didn't exist. All of the drinking times, the time with the ravers… everything was fake, a put on, a fucking show…

Killian found my hand and squeezed it. "You're the most important person in the world… you're going to kill him and make us safe again."

"Yeah," I whispered turning away from the window. "Apparently that's the only reason I was born."

I glanced over at Chally sleeping on one of our two beds. I got an idea; one that I thought might make him happy.

"How about this? A middle ground… the blond guy seems okay, not kinky-freaky or anything. Why don't we let him buy Chally and once Elish picks us up… we'll double back and slit the guy's throat and take back Chally."

Killian looked at me before his mouth dropped open. Sensing the cry machine was revving up, I pressed on. "Elish can probably find him a job as a slave or a cook or something in Skyfall, where he will be safe."

My boyfriend's face dissolved. I caught him as he leapt into my arms sniffing and crying. "You mean it? Thank you, baby. I love you."

I let out a breath through my nose and rolled my eyes. "Still with the tears? You're too old to cry." I patted his back. "You'll be eighteen soon, right? I'll make this your birthday present."

Killian pulled away and gave me a long, drawn-out kiss. I took him in and smiled at him when we broke away.

"You have so much power over me, Mr. Massey. I hope you appreciate just how much you've wormed yourself into my heart." I kissed him back. "I love you, just don't use my love against me."

The boy blushed. "I don't know what you're talking about. I'd never use my power over you to promote my own agenda." He gave me a crooked smile.

Well, he might cry too much, but he was a crafty little shit.

We sat together for an hour before I finally resigned that I could use some sleep. I yawned and stretched and decided to make his day even more.

"I'd like to catch two hours. Why don't you keep watch?" I took off my M16 and handed it to him.

Killian's face brightened like he was his own little solar system. "Really?" he squealed and held my gun like I had just presented him with a new puppy. "Okay, go to sleep! I'll take care of this."

He let me sleep three hours and I gave him a good glare because of it, but I didn't pitch too much of a fuss. After he went to sleep I leaned the M16 up against the windowsill and took my usual place on a chair. Tonight we were warm though, comfortable and guarded, so it wasn't as stressful as it had been the previous night.

I sat back with an opiate cigarette and relaxed. I got out the remote phone to occupy myself and kept trying to dial Elish, but it still gave me that long pissed off tone whenever I would try. Like everywhere, it seemed the cell phone reception was non-existent. But why wouldn't it be? Why the fuck would there be reception in the middle of nowhere hundreds of miles away from Skyfall? I bet me, Jade, and Perish were the only chimeras for miles.

With the lamps off in the room, I was able to see below me a bit clearer, but the windows looked painted shut so I couldn't hear worth a damn. It was quiet though, just the occasional grey-faced waster milling around or taking someone home. This place seemed quiet and sleepy, it didn't look like much happened here.

I wonder if a place like this would be where Killian and I would eventually settle down. If it ever came to that, before, you know, I decided to take back Aras.

I wasn't giving up on my town and I never would… Merrik's founded Aras and I was a Merrik, no matter what my DNA said. I was their kid; I was a Merrik not a Dekker.

This brought a tightness to my chest, which I dimmed down by taking a hit of opiate powder. The alcohol had already made my chest warm but it should be far enough in my system that the Dilaudids wouldn't interfere. I was missing the heroin already, but that brick wasn't going to last forever and I'd rather be weaned before it ran out.

At about four in the morning I saw something that caught my eye. Not just one embered cigarette moving along the street… it was five of them.

I stood up and tried to open the window but I was reminded that it was painted shut. I crossed my arms and leaned against the window frame and watched the group, or watched the cigarettes anyway; the people to who they belonged to were nothing but shrouded figures. Dark shadows in a backdrop that held no form from where I was standing.

Still though, my eyes never left them. They seemed to be walking down the street slowly, like they hadn't a care in the world. I wondered if perhaps they were a gang or something like that. A group of street punks like they had in Moros; I suppose that would make sense.

The group disappeared for an hour and I went back to my usual silent vigil, mulling over things in my head that had been plaguing my thoughts for the past several months. Mostly how I ended up here and how much I was pissed off about it.

And also the many ways I was planning on killing King Silas, that I thought of whenever I needed cheering up.

Then the embers appeared again. They were coming up the road, closer this time. I killed my own cigarette and watched them, feeling an uneasy prickle in my gut when I saw that two of them had the blue-embered cigarettes in their mouths.

And what the hell were they wearing anyway? It wasn't legionary clothing, it seemed like normal greywaster attire… wasn't it? I looked closer and was able to make out some of them. They were all male, burly-type men… one of them… I couldn't see but…

The blood drained from my face as I noticed this one had a cape on.

In that second, as my heart rose to my throat and the extinguished cigarette fell to the floor, the man turned around, and as his eyes scanned the hotel room, they fell on me.

Eyes that could see me – blue-violet eyes.

Nero Dekker.

No fucking way… how did he…

"Killian!" I suddenly yelled. For the first time in my life, I felt an incomprehensible swell of panic. I ran towards Killian, and as he screamed from shock, I grabbed him and pulled him from the bed.

"Rea- what!" Killian cried out. I started pulling him out the door.

But as I put my hand on the knob, I could hear the hotel's squeaky door. There was only one exit, only one fucking exit…

This couldn't be happening. How? How did he find us? No one fucking knew we were here.

As the chaos swarmed and destroyed my brain with spasm after spasm of panic, I whirled around and pulled Killian towards the window. Without thinking, I punched it out with my fist and pushed him towards it.

The boy turned around, his eyes full of panic and fear, but he didn't have the time to look at me. I didn't have the fucking time to tell him Nero was coming for us.

"Get out, get out and run, run!" I screamed at him. I spun around as I heard the sound of a dozen boot steps hitting the dry boards of the hotel stairs. They were coming slowly… but they were coming.

The kid's face was pale and stricken with the same fear that I was feeling inside of my gut. I cleared away the rest of the glass with my now bleeding hands and pushed him towards the window.

"Run!"

"Reaver… where do I…" Killian was cut off when a gun blast sounded; I heard it ping off of the hotel roof. There were people down there… ready to fucking shoot all of us. Why wouldn't they? I was immortal and they wouldn't give a fuck about Killian.

"Chally, get up!" Killian cried. He tried to move away from my hand but I clenched him hard. My mind going like a thousand cylinders, unable to form a proper plan, unable to know what to do. I was cornered in here, they couldn't… fuck, they couldn't…

They were coming closer.

My eyes fell on Chally who was on his feet; he was holding a knife in his hand. His owl eyes were wide and looking at both Killian and I in horror. He wasn't moving, he was standing steady; the cowering nature seemingly disappearing in our new reality.

Chally…

Blond-haired, grey-eyed, small Chally.

I turned to Killian; his eyes looked back at me with such agony I could feel it press up against my heart.

Immediately and swiftly, the fear drained from my body, replaced with a grim understanding and a reality as to what I had to do. No more did I feel scared, no more did I feel my mind slip into the fractured insanity that only pure panic brought.

It was all replaced by black… though it had no colour.

"I love you… I love you so much," I whispered to him as I heard a door slam; they were searching the rooms for us. "Get into the closet and don't make a sound."

He stared at me; my beautiful boy stared at me. "We'll shoot them… we can take them I…"

"Killian…"

The boy shook his head, tears streaming down his pale cheeks. "No, don't you dare, Reaver. Don't you fucking dare make me hide. I'll–"

I spun around so he was in front of me, his back against my chest, then I wrapped my arm around his neck and held his arms down. I wedged his neck between the crook of my arm and squeezed.

I cut off the oxygen going to his brain, and as he started to gasp and struggle, I closed my eyes, feeling them burn.

The light that only he fuelled inside of me dimmed as I whispered into his ear, "No matter what happens, I will come back. I will find my way to you. Never forget that; never forget that, no matter what. I belong to you… and I love you. Go find Jade and Perish." I felt his pulse start to race, and I counted each heartbeat as they started to slow.

Killian managed to free one of his arms, it immediately went to the one wrapped around his neck. He clawed it and started thrashing. I walked backwards with him and opened the partially-ajar closet door with my foot and walked inside with him.

His breathing started to slow and I knew it would be over soon. I had done this sleeper move on Bridley; I had done it on Reno… I had even done it on ravers I wanted to keep alive.

Just slow down little heart, slow down and go to sleep. When you wake up, it'll be quiet again.

Fuck, I'm sorry, Killi Cat.

I'm so sorry.

When his arms went limp and dropped to his side I put my M16 beside him. I had just closed the door when the door to the hallway got kicked open.

The blood rushed through my ears as I saw Nero Dekker; he beheld me with a grin that told me he recognized me and knew exactly who I was. He held up his AK 47 and pointed it at me.

"Where did you get that remote phone, puppy? Steal it from Perish's lab, did we? Now who were you trying to call? Don't tell me you miss the king that much."

You've got to be fucking kidding me... you have seriously got to be fucking kidding me...

Then it hit me.

The device that strengthened the signal when I had accidently knocked it off.

It was a tracking-blocker, you stupid fucking moron. You piece of shit, you just doomed yourself.

Nero grinned. Five legionary were behind him, every single one of them pointing guns at me and Chally.

Chally... I glanced over at the kid who was still holding the combat knife. I hoped beyond hope he wouldn't throw it down and start pointing to the closet but I wouldn't put it past him. Though maybe he knew he would be fucked either way. Maybe he wanted to save Killian; he had been the one to save him from Melchai.

But Chally was staying still… and for now, he would be my Killian.

"Let Killian go and I'll go with you peacefully," I said, glancing towards Chally. I knew they wouldn't, I wasn't an idiot, but I had to make it look real. When Nero had seen Killian in Aras it had been dark and there had been activity all around us… he wouldn't recognize him.

I hoped he wouldn't recognize him.

Nero smirked and shook his head. He walked up to me with that cock-sure swagger his master had perfected. I could now see he had Silas's lips.

Nero glared down and grinned before putting a hand on my shoulder and rubbed it. "How about I fuck your little ass in front of him instead?" He grabbed my crotch and the last of my restraint broke.

I grabbed my combat knife and took a swing, slashing Nero's face with an agonizing yell of a cornered animal. I saw the fissure appear before Nero snarled and gave the orders.

I didn't hear what the orders were but I felt them.

Popping. Chally letting out a single scream, and the feeling of my body snapping back like half a dozen people were punching me, one after another, hit me.

Then red… the red haze and the same feeling I had felt so long ago: a roaring inside of my ears, a hot heat that sent flames throughout my body, searing my blood vessels and shredding my internal organs with a white hot pain. I knew all of these feelings but it was different this time; I knew they weren't rubber bullets.

I fell to my knees and keeled over, blood squirting from my body and painting the floors around me.

But I was okay… I would be okay.

Stay asleep, Killian.

Stay asleep.

I'll find you.

I promise.

CHAPTER 26

Reaver

I STAYED FOR MANY HOURS IN MY IMMORTAL LIMBO. A place that I first thought I'd only been once but had quickly realized this white fire of immortality had been flaring inside my soul since I was a child. Not just a night terror that brought you full-body paralysis, not just a bad dream to which you woke up gasping, I had been dead each and every incident, biding my time and my patience for the white flame to slowly rebuild my cold body.

I was starting to notice how my body changed after death shut down my internal organs and the outskirts of my brain. At first I would go cold. I could dance on the very fringes of oblivion before the flame would draw me back with hands of boiling ice. Then I would become heated, hot to the point where I wanted to scream and thrash my paralyzed body. I felt like I was burning alive, every blood cell, every piece of hardened bone. Even my blood felt like it had been touched by the sun.

But, after several lifetimes in the pits of hell, my body would cool and the pain would dissipate. Like I had been planted in the arctic, everything would freeze. My entire body would become stiff and rigid like I had fallen into rigor-mortis. This state was the longest and it was there my thoughts and memories would slowly trickle back to me. Life would trickle back, my warm blood would trickle back. That is where the Reaper would meet me, and the outstretched hand that told me with a laugh that I would never meet him on that sun bleached porch.

Then light… candlelight. I found my mouth gasping open, and with that, I took my first conscious breath.

I opened my eyes to see where I was, only to realize my face was shrouded in some strange see-through fabric. I lifted my hand up and touched it, my mind still in a foggy haze.

Automatically, I sat up, and the soft fabric spilled off of my head and onto my chest. I realized as I looked down that I wasn't in my greywaster clothing anymore; I was dressed in silk black pants and a dress shirt, like fancy pajamas.

But why? Where was I? How the fuck did I get here…?

I squinted my eyes and held my head, trying to massage some sense into my brain. I couldn't grab a hold of what reality was in that moment. Everything was still strange and unexplained, but for the most part my emotions were null. There was no mad awakening that filled me with anger; there was no thrashing or fighting, everything inside my brain was gone.

Perhaps this was the other end of the spectrum. When I had woken in Elish's greyrifts apartment I was insane with rage, now it seems the opposite had happened.

"Good Morning, Reaver."

My head jerked towards the voice, one I didn't recognized.

My eyes fell on a man, he was standing beside a black dresser with several candles on top. He was tall man with brushed back black hair and vivid copper-coloured eyes. He was standing with a satisfied smirk and a lip ring in the corner of his mouth. Immediately I could see he had King Silas's eyes and his face shape as well.

Another chimera, great.

The first pangs of anger started to burn my throat. I shot him a look and tried to rise to standing. "Where the fuck am I?"

A smile started to spread on his face and as the corners of his lips rose. Like Sanguine and Jack, he had pointed teeth.

His name was Thelonius but they called him Theo.

Elish had said he was crazy. A military chimera who sometimes shadowed Jack.

"I have been waiting for you to wake up. I have had to take the place of our Grim. I will tell you, your description does not do you justice. You are a stunning specimen."

"Where's Killian?" I ripped the silks off of me and stalked up to him. More anger burned inside of me as I heard the sounds of chains rattling, and finally my ankle snapping back. I was chained. Of course they would chain me… they weren't stupid.

The man's shiny copper eyes twinkled before becoming small slits as he smiled. He seemed like a slippery bitch this one, just like Elish had warned me when he had shown me Theo's photo.

"He is somewhere… last I heard he was being kept in quarantine. Interesting little thing that one… he hasn't found his voice, hm?"

Oh thank fucking god… they hadn't found him; they hadn't found my Killian.

And with that flood of relief, I felt the first strands of myself start to shine through the anger and the confusion. I gave myself a pep talk in that moment and I decided I wouldn't snap. I wouldn't turn myself over to insane rage. I would play this as calm as I could.

No matter what, Reaver Merrik... they cannot kill you, and since they didn't find Killian you would be okay. Killian is probably already back with Perish and Jade, maybe Elish is even there.

As long as Killian was okay, I am okay. Like Greyson said: stick to the basic truths. That asshole might be the reason I am here, but he did have his moments of wisdom.

"He stopped talking after Leo and Greyson died and after your king raped him, fuckhead," I snapped at him, yanking on my ankle chain, trying to find any weakness in it. "He has nothing you fucking want. Let him go."

The man chuckled; his bronze sparkling eyes reflecting the candles around us. I had no idea what type of room I was in, everything smelled off but the walls were concrete. It was a fort I think, I must be in a fort… even though this room, with its iron rung candle holders and weird drapes, looked like something more medieval.

"I will let King Silas decide that."

The mere mention of his name brought acid to my throat. "Bring him in. I want to fucking see him." I had a few things to say to that asshole. I would give anything to have a face-to-face with that blond-haired fucking coward. Bring it on… I owed him for killing Leo and Greyson and I owed him for raping Killian.

No... no... The anger in my throat rose but I pushed it down to the void. *Remain calm... remain calm.*

Do what you will to me; I am a fucking god now.

Both me and the chimera turned our heads towards the door as the knob rattled. A moment later, there was a heavy banging.

Theo gave it an aloof but very unimpressed look and walked towards it, though when he unlatched the door he jumped back as it slammed open.

"Where is he, Theo?!"

Then more chaos.

This one I recognized right away, and I knew from the look he gave me alone that he not only knew who I was, but that he knew what I had done.

Without mincing words, Kessler stalked up to me; a burly man with a buzz cut and a pissed off face. I opened my mouth to tell him to go fuck himself when he laid a punch right on my chin.

It threw me off of my feet. Fucker was strong and that punch was meant to shatter bone. I fell backwards onto the bed I had woken up on, and smacked the back of my head against the concrete wall.

With a bellowing yell, he grabbed my shirt and slammed the back of my head again into the concrete, screaming something I couldn't understand over the blood roaring through my ears. I couldn't even defend myself; my head had paralyzed my arms and my legs. I could only close my eyes in the red daze his hits had rained down on me.

"Get off of me! HE KILLED MY SON!" Kessler screamed, before with a sickening *thunk*, he landed a blow on my jaw. I felt it snap inside of my head, a sickening crunching noise that I knew I would never forget.

"He strung him up... he... he took his fucking heart!" Kessler was choking through tears. This realization brought a small silver lining to the fact that he was beating me to death right now.

"Kess! Get off of him..." another male voice sounded, then the blows stopped coming.

I spat blood and tried to pull myself up to the sitting position, but my head felt like it was electrically charged. I managed to sit up though and looked up at him.

Kessler's face was dripping with agony; his grey eyes wide and his stance that of a man using every bit of his restraint.

My hand trailed down and I found my jaw. It felt funny though, and as I tried to shift it a blinding pain shot through me. It was broken, dislocated or something; either way, it was fucked.

"He tasted good," I whispered, holding my face. I glanced up at Kessler as another man tried to coax him away from me.

Kessler's face didn't change. "What are you trying to say to me, you fucking greywaste piece of shit?"

"That's the Raven to you. And I'm saying your little boy screamed like a girl when I split open his rib cage and ate his heart. And there was nothing better than watching you drag Calig-"

Kessler ripped himself from the man's arms and raised his fist. But in a flash, the man grabbed him, and to my surprise, Theo did too. They pulled Kessler's thrashing, shrieking body away from me.

"Get out of here, Theo. He's alive so your work is done!" Kessler roared. He shoved him away and glared at me. "I want him strung up in my interrogation room. Now. NOW!"

As Kessler was dragged away from me, half a dozen legionary filed into the room. With my jaw screaming in pain and my head still feeling like an untuned radio, they handcuffed and shackled me.

I was taken out of Theo's room and led down a hallway, blood drops falling from my face. I could taste it in my nose, but I knew there were several other injuries on me that were currently leaking their despair onto the white tile floors.

Killian was okay though… Killian was okay.

My boots started to drag along the floor and I realized I was starting to lose consciousness. I tried to stay awake though, scanning the corridors I was being led down to see if I could spot an exit.

I was definitely in a base; I don't think I was in Skyfall. From the descriptions I had gotten from Jade and Perish, all the military bases were in the greywastes. In Skyfall there were just skyscrapers or regular buildings. I think I was still in the greywastes.

I looked to my left to see two metal doors with an exit sign hanging above them, no windows though… there seemed to be no windows in this tomb.

The only old military base I had seen was what was left of Greenbase, and it was the same makeup. No windows, only concrete and brick, and long winding hallways that you could easily get lost in.

It didn't matter though, I just needed one exit… or one room that I could find guns in and I would be out of here. Even if I was deep in the greywastes I would find Killian. Nothing would keep me from my boyfriend – especially not a bunch of chimeras.

I looked down at my handcuffed hands and immediately they started getting drops of blood on them. Ahead of me was the man that had held back Kessler, I think that was his non-chimera husband Tiberius. If I could get him alone I might be able to negotiate my own release. Surely Kessler wouldn't risk him after I had already eaten his little son.

Or Caligula… I really didn't care what shit I would get in with Elish if I killed 'Clig'. If it meant my escape I would kill all of them, family or not.

I looked to both sides of me but all I saw were legionary carrying really big guns. I was chained from the wrists and the legs with my jaw either broken or cracked, and my left eye starting to get blurry. Should I snap and try a manic escape right now or bide my time?

The younger me would go manic and thrash until they killed me, and even though a large part of me wanted to, just to satiate my inner bloodlust, that would accomplish nothing. I wouldn't be able to get to Tiberius, and even if I did, I wouldn't be able to use him as my own little ransom, not before they showered me with bullets.

If I thought I was a mortal I might try anyway… just because I might believe they won't shoot me because King Silas wanted me. But I am immortal… they'll shoot me on the spot.

So I let them carry me down a flight of stairs. On the way down I did see a window in the stairwell, it looked like we had been on a second floor and were now descending to the first. This was important, I'd jump from a window if needed be.

Then I was brought to a dark, uncomfortable room; only lit by a single recessed light in the push tile of the ceiling. Beside that light was a metal plate embedded in the ceiling, with a chain and hook hanging down.

The interrogation room.

Killian is safe, you're immortal… you'll be fine.

You've been through pain before… you've been in an explosion. You've been chewed on by ravers. You've been strangled to death.

You'll be fine.

That hook hanging down looked rather grisly though, drawing a long and ominous shadow over the grey-speckled concrete. It reminded me of the best parts of a horror movie. It looked like I was going to be in my own horror movie soon.

I let them lift up my arms, and a moment later, I heard the metallic sound of the hook going through the metal rings; then the sound of steel scraping as they winched the chain and the hook until I was dangling off of the ground.

"Bring it on," I said quietly. I tried to make eye contact with Kessler but his husband kept turning his face from me. He was the weak one, the submissive one, trying to hold back his brute commander of a husband so he wouldn't get set off again.

"Remember what we talked about? Remember this is Silas. Don't engage him."

"I fucked Tim… hear that Kessler? I fucked him," I called, feeling a bit mad in the head as I grinned at him. "I fucked him until he liked it."

Kessler's teeth gritted together. I could almost hear the squeaking but his husband came to his rescue. "You know that's not true, Kess. They checked, you know he's lying."

"He called me Daddy. You kinky fuck."

Kessler roared and charged towards me; he raised his fist and another crack hit my jaw. I spun in place this time like a chimera piñata before receiving a blow against my gut.

Then I felt him grab me, his fingers digging into my shoulders as he shook me. "Alright, you piece of shit. I'm done playing your fucking games. Where's Perish?"

Perish? So he did want something out of me; he wanted the non-chimera back, our other born immortal. Well, he could pull out my fingernails and rip out my eyes because he wasn't getting a word out of me. Killian was with Perish.

"Perish is long gone." My voice choked on my own blood. I spat it and smirked at him. "He left long ago, *brother*."

Kessler shook his head at me. "Bring Killian in."

I chuckled, wondering if I should pretend to be upset or not. "Go ahead; King Silas will never let you kill him. If you want to torture him in front of me, have at it. Please monitor my heartbeat though, so you can see just how little of a shit I give."

The two men stared at me, two different looks poisoning their brute faces. The husband was suspicious, but Kessler stared at me like he wanted to call my bluff.

Go ahead, kill the slave.

Kessler brought out his radio and talked into it. I heard Killian's name.

My body swayed back and forth, my hands held over my head. I felt the handcuffs, tight and restricting on my wrists, already becoming chafed. It was wrenching my shoulders in an uncomfortable position, but I knew I wouldn't be alive for very much longer.

I stared at him as he lowered the radio and realized that if I got them to kill Chally quickly… not only would Kessler be in trouble, but I could make sure Killian was safe forever.

"Bring him in, Daddy," I whispered with a smirk. "See how fucked up of a clone I am. I would love to prove to you just what came out of Kreig's lab."

The looks, it was the looks they were giving me that filled my body with adrenaline; it was what was giving me the drive to egg them on.

Sorry, Chally, but my boyfriend will always be more important than you, more important than anyone.

The two men stood there with their arms crossed, glaring hatred into me. If looks could kill their razor blade-filled glares would eradicate every immortal in existence.

A few minutes later, the steel door to the room opened.

Chally was badly injured which I was surprised at, but I guess they'd probably been interrogating him too. Though he was a mute and I didn't have to worry about them torturing secrets out of him. Obviously they didn't suspect that this wasn't Killian if they were trying to bait him against me.

When Chally saw me his large owl-like eyes widened. He lifted his hands to sign something at me before dropping them. I couldn't understand him anyway but it made me wonder if he really was playing into my plan for passing him off as Killian.

They had been friends but his loyalty towards my boyfriend was odd to me. Chally hadn't known him for that long, why wouldn't he turn him in in hopes for some leniency? Was he that loyal towards my boyfriend who had freed him?

I wonder if Chally knew they were about to kill him.

Chally turned his eyes from me and looked over at the man who had brought him in, but he had already closed the door.

We were alone, the four of us in this interrogation room. My fake boyfriend, my chimera brother, and the husband that Silas let him have.

"Well?" I raised an eyebrow and spat out another mouthful of blood. "Go torture him a bit; he might have stopped talking for me but he can still scream."

The Imperial General glared at me, before in a desperate attempt to call my bluff he stalked towards Chally.

Chally backed away from him until his back hit the wall. He cowered as Kessler raised his hand and shrieked when he hit him several times in the face.

Then he pulled the boy to his feet, grabbing him the same way that he had grabbed me. "Where is Perish?"

The boy's entire body was trembling; he let out a weak whimper and shook his head before clasping his hands over his face.

Kessler hit Chally again and yanked him to his feet; he gave him a hard push and pushed him in front of me. The walls echoed from Chally's screams as Tiberius kicked him in the ribs; I saw his hands claw the concrete from the pain. Everything about this thin and frail kid was giving them what the predators wanted; my only wish for him was that they made it quick.

Tiberius kicked Chally until he rolled onto his back, his nose bloodied and his left eye staring to become rosy pink from bloodshot. He stared up at the ceiling in a daze before his eyes fell to me.

I made eye contact with him and gave him a small nod, not knowing what else I was supposed to do.

When Kessler grabbed him again I saw Chally's hands move, and before the others could notice, he signed Killian's special hand signal name, before mouthing *safe* to me.

I stared at him and nodded again, then with a frustrated growl Kessler threw him across the room; Chally's head hit the wall with a crack. Kessler then grabbed his blond hair and wrenched his head up. The big tough chimera slammed the scrawny kid's face against the concrete before pulling him up again.

What a badass, beating on a kid less than half his size.

Chally's glassy grey eyes stared off into the abyss, blood streaming down his nose and mouth, then he disappeared as Kessler slammed his head back down to the concrete.

"Beating kids… how manly of you," I said with a smirk, looking down from my dangling chain and seeing the pool in front of Chally's head start to grow. I could hear his choking noises, and finally a sad little gurgled sob.

"He isn't even flinching!" Kessler roared. He turned angrily to his husband and pointed towards me. "His heart isn't even fucking fluctuating! He doesn't care… just like Elish said. He's a monster, a fucking monster. We're not–"

"Not in front of him, you idiot!" Tiberius found his balls and snapped at his husband. "Just call Silas and get him here; he can deal with this fuck. What he's about to spend a lifetime in can atone for him killing Timothy."

Kessler glared at me and I glared right back, feeling a darkness start to descend on my head. A smooth blanket of cold energy that was almost tangible on my body; the Reaper in me that had been edging my conscious. The same motivation that made me want to torture Kessler for everything that he had ever done to me.

"Yes, call Silas. I would love to see who I am supposed to be with… forever. Especially since you just killed my boyfriend." I smiled thinly. "When me and Silas are married I'll become king, and just think of what fun I'll have when that happens. I really cannot wait; I have plans for you and your entire legion family."

The Imperial General got another good hit on me, making my body spin back and forth. To my left, Chally was whimpering and groaning but he was still moving. I was surprised he wasn't dead yet.

I lifted my head up though when I heard a flick. I cocked an eyebrow at Kessler as I saw him take out a switchblade.

"Silas doesn't even know we have you, and I won't tell him until I decide I have gotten enough out of you," Kessler said in a hushed voice. He put the knife up to my neck before slowly trailing it down my silk clothing.

"And if you think this -" He looked around before locking his eyes with me again. "- is all the Legion has… oh, my boy, we're just starting. I know your weak spots, because I know King Silas's, and before the end of our special time together – you'll sing like a canary. No matter how many times I have to kill you."

My smile only widened and I decided then to be the biggest asshole in the world.

I puckered my lips and blew him a kiss. "Bring it on, Daddy."

I clenched my teeth as he dug the knife into my stomach. I tried to take a breath but the blade kept pushing, pushing… pushing.

I tensed my body when he broke through the skin and steeled myself as I felt the cold metal break into my gut. I looked down and saw the entire switchblade get pushed into my stomach, a flow of blood starting to stream down his hand and onto the floor.

He twisted the knife and I heard his hot breath in my ear. "Where's Perish?"

With every ounce of my restraint, I tried to hold back a grunt of pain. I managed to get it down to a sharp inhale as he wrenched the knife up my gut.

My entire body started to tremble from shock; though I adamantly tried to stop it, it was something I couldn't control. My mind might know I was coming back, but my body didn't.

"He left… long ago," I said through clenched teeth, grunting as he twisted the knife again. My head was starting to go light, and when he withdrew the knife and a quick flow of blood coated his hands, I knew it wouldn't be long until I died again.

Then he slid the knife down lower and pressed the blade against my crotch. "I will give you one last chance, Raven. Tell me where the scientist is or else I will break you… my way."

The blood was flowing quickly from my stomach, the knife blade he stabbed me with tapping against his dark green cargo pants.

Tap, tap, tap.

"Gone."

Kessler nodded; his face sculpted steel holding a burning anger inside of his grey eyes that told of a hatred only a chimera father could have. I think he was done with me at that moment but I knew his head must not be in the right place. There were so many fun ways to torture someone, I had gotten quite creative when I was torturing Bridley.

Was this really all he had?

I was disappointed.

My vision got blurry; I blinked it away and shook my head. Besides Chally groaning to my left, I could hear my own blood splattering on the ground. It was a fast stream, he must've known which of my organs to pierce. I heard the pancreas bled like a bitch.

I coughed and saw more blood.

"Bring him to Nero, I'm done with him," Kessler said after several moments had passed.

I tried to snap myself out of my blood loss-induced haze. I looked up when the door slammed and was surprised to see Caligula looming over me.

Then I was on the floor. They must've unchained me, or he did anyway. I think we were alone in the room.

Caligula pulled me to my feet, though he struggled under what I knew were shot legs. He had some stamina on him, or else chimera medicine was more advanced than I thought.

Indeed Caligula was a tough son of a bitch, his odd mercury-like eyes hard and stoic.

Good ol' calm and controlled Caligula… but I had heard him screaming.

I had seen his agony and I had feasted on it.

I wonder what state of mind he was in right now. Far far away in the greywastes with his boyfriend locked up with Reno. Locked up and probably getting…

My eyes widened. As Caligula pulled on my arm to walk me out of the interrogation room, I stopped.

"Nico." I was surprised that my voice had left me; I was losing blood faster than I thought.

But it got his attention. Caligula paused and stared at me like I had just uttered black magic.

"What?" he said cautiously.

"Reno…" I coughed but the force of the cough brought me to my knees. I didn't think I was going to make it out of this room; I was dying and quickly.

"Morse code on the ransom tape. They're in Cypress sewers… Cypress sewers, understand?" I rasped, trying to make eye contact with him so he could tell I wasn't lying. We may not be on the same side but if he loved his boyfriend… where he was, Reno was.

"Cypress sewers?" Caligula looked behind him to make sure no one was listening. "What do you mean there was Morse code?"

"His blinking… he blinked it." My head tilted forward, and this time it felt like it weighed a thousand pounds. I wasn't able to lift it, and I wasn't able to grab onto the bits of reality that were helping me maintain consciousness. I fell forward onto the concrete and it was there that I died again.

CHAPTER 27

Reno

IF I WAS ASKED BEFORE, I WOULD SAY PAIN DIDN'T have a colour… but it did. It was a bright, uncomfortable colour and no matter how tight you closed your eyes you couldn't escape it. Not only a colour though, pain had a taste, a sound and a smell… it had systematically become all of my senses and it seemed to be my life.

There were no pain killers, no doctors, and no help… I was stuck in another room, however this one had streams of blinding light shining on my bloodied and dirtied corpse.

Because I was no longer in the sewer. I was locked in a shed with a single padlock, a crazed Crimstone with red hair keeping a constant guard, and Trig the cicaro, whimpering useless beside me.

I was shot, I was badly injured, and every time I woke up to this cold room I was surprised that there was still breath inside of my lungs. How I was still living I didn't know, but I ran with it and kept the image of Garrett, Reaver, and Killian at the forefront of my muddled and hazy mind.

My sore eyes shifted to Trig, a small waif that the darkness had swallowed up long ago. He had his knees tucked up to his chest and his dirt-stained arms wrapped around them. The boy barely spoke anymore, and when he did it seemed he needed hours to recover.

And what would he speak?

Ares will come for me.

Over and over.

You poor little wretch, no one is coming for us. I sighed and hated myself for the dark turn my thoughts had taken during the last several days, since we had escaped from the sewers. Where hope had once reigned and grown like well-watered weeds, only bitterness and dark conclusions could be found.

Reaver had come for Killian, as soon as he had realized the boy was missing he had gone out and into the greywastes to find him, vowing to not return until he had that boy beside him.

Before he even knew Killian, he had risked his life for that little blond boy. By the next day he was walking with Killian in his arms, his ear blown off and his back a shredded mess.

I was engaged to a chimera, a ninety-year-old chimera, the second born prince. Why hadn't he come for me? Garrett had the world at his disposal, and yet it had been weeks and here I still was. Beaten, tortured, raped, and now shot. Where was my hero?

There are no heroes… there never had been. Reaver had said that to me over and over and I guess he was right. But there were still lovers, still people who were supposed to care for you.

Did Elish tell Reaver I was missing? Maybe Reaver would come and save me.

No… he would never risk Killian here, and he for sure wouldn't leave him in the greywastes. Killian was his sole concern now.

Not me.

I slowly inched my hand over and took the water bottle that Kerres had tossed for us, filled with irradiated sludge that made my Geigerchip vibrate over top of my collarbone. I brought it to my lips and drank down the cold metallic liquid before motioning it over for Trig to drink.

The kid took it with a trembling hand; his eyes glassy and his hair now dark from the dirt and oil stuck to his forehead and his neck. It made his ears stick out, but even they hadn't escaped the shit we had gone through; his earrings had become infected and I could see pus leaking through the gemstone studs.

A silence crept back into the already void-like atmosphere around us, broken up only by the occasional mumblings of Kerres. The crimson-haired man was on the other side of the door, though what he was doing or what his plan was, was lost on me. He just sat out there with his gun, rambling on to himself about Jade and Elish, and how he would eventually get his chimera boyfriend back.

My back was leaning against the exterior wall of the shed we were locked in; we were almost back to back with each other.

I wiped my nose with a greasy sleeve and looked down to check the wound on my leg.

A cold trickle of dread formed inside of my gut when I saw the dried blood framing the black bullet wound. But that wasn't the worst of it, my gut had started to darken and what little piss my body produced was rosy pink. During the escape the healing bullet wound I had must've ripped open inside of me and something was going wrong. My energy was leaving me to the point where every time I closed my eyes I wondered if I would ever open them.

"Ker? Do you have any food? It's been days, man," I said weakly, rubbing the back of my head as the splinters in the shed prickled my scalp.

There was shifting before Kerres's own rather weak voice responded. "I'm not going back inside of there, they'll kill me. By now they'll be looking for Meirko."

"And… what did you do with Meirko? You know his meat is still good, right? Bring me some Meirko." My mouth salivated at the thought of some meat, even raw; I didn't care at this point.

There was a pause like he was considering it, before he replied back, "He would've turned by now."

Who cares? "I've eaten some pretty shifty shit in my day, dude. I don't care. Hack me off an ass cheek or something, that's got some pretty tender bits on it."

Trig's eyes, barely visible in the dark corner he had shut himself in glanced up, his expression turning to one of distaste, though I challenged him to be picky right now. It had been the same amount of days since he'd eaten too, and even then the Crimstones had barely fed us.

"I hid his body, in case the Crimstones came looking. He's rotten and in the back room of a Burger King. We have no food," Kerres replied back stiffly.

Even in my starving misery I felt a surge of anger course through my body. "Then what the fuck is your plan, Kerres? We're fucking starving!" I snapped, and at my tone Trig started to cry.

I shifted over to Trig and put my arm around him as big tears ran down his face. I shushed him like I had seen Reaver do to Killian and pet back his hair. I had never had a soft type to do this to. I was the soft one in both my failed and never-was relationships, and with the man I was engaged to now. All I had to go on from experience was what I had seen Reaver do.

"What I am planning on…" He stumbled as he spoke, and I realized then he had no fucking idea what his plans were. "…on doing is none of your fucking business, chimera lover."

You love a chimera too, you fucking asshat. Luckily, I wasn't stupid enough to say that to him.

Trig whimpered, I tried to draw him further into my arms but my gut gave a jolt of pain. I settled for leaning his head against my shoulder with an arm around his back. I hugged him close to me and he seemed to relax under the embrace. I wondered if Ares had ever held him like that, he never seemed like the type.

There was silence after that, except for more mumbling from Kerres that seemed to intensify when the winter darkness fell upon us. Once it started to get colder, I laid down with Trig and held his body against mine, trying to get as much body heat as we could between us. I had no idea how we hadn't frozen to death yet, sometimes during the night I swore the kid had died he was so cold.

But we didn't die… not yet anyway. I was still very much alive when, in the middle of the night, Kerres opened the padlocked door and jumped inside, an air of desperation around him.

I tried to rise myself, giving the red-haired Crimstone a look of confusion as he quickly shut the door and pressed his back against it. His wild brown eyes were shooting off in all directions and his chest was heaving.

"Wha-" My own voice cut itself off when I saw the first flashlight glare sweep through the cracks in the shed.

Garrett? Oh please, oh I am begging you, please be Garrett. I fucking don't think I can make it through another night… please, please…

"The Crimstones… they're looking for us," Kerres's voice was thin and strained; he looked stricken with a fear so vivid it was radiating off of him. "Be quiet, you have to be quiet or they'll kill all of us."

I narrowed my eyes at him, the greywaster mentality seeing a fault in him I wanted to exploit. "So what? We're going to fucking die here; why not take you down with us?"

Kerres's eyes shot down to me. "Because they'll rape and murder you in front of the entire city of Skyfall, that's why. Do you want to get raped again, Trig? Huh?"

The young boy let out a wheezed whine. "No." His voice was small but full of desperation.

I ground my teeth as another flashlight beam illuminated the boy's deathly thin face. His eyes were so big I could see that he would rather die than go through that again, and I knew my heart felt the same thing.

Yes, it might not be much but being in this room was a step up from having a gun to my head and a cock in my ass inside the sewers.

And I could… yes, I could overpower Kerres; he was a wreck right now.

But a dangerous wreck, the bullet wound in my upper leg was a testament to Jade's ex-boyfriend's current mental state.

Another flashlight beam. When it swept over the crumbling plaster and loose wires of the interior of the shed I saw Trig's eyes well. He started to cry so I put his face into my chest to muffle him.

"Shh, shh… it's alright, they'll be leaving soon," I whispered to him. "Just be quiet, that's all you have to do."

The boy whimpered. I squeezed him tighter, wondering how good of a boyfriend I would've been to Killian if Silas had taken Reaver. I think I would have done alright. Maybe it would've given me a bit more balls to deal with situations like this.

"Maybe it's Ares?" he whispered.

But before I could open my mouth to respond, we heard a muffled voice in the distance and it didn't belong to a chimera or any legionary. I recognized the voice as one of the Crimstones though his name was lost on me. He had beaten the snot out of me a few times, that I did remember.

Sure enough, Kerres's eyes widened. He slid his body down to the floor and put his arms behind the back of his head. He let out a groan and shook his head back and forth.

"I'm never going to see my baby again, they'll fucking hang me for killing Meirko," Kerres whispered, in a surprising moment of lucidity. "Then kill you two fucks, they're too deep in this ransom now. They want out. They're strong but they're a bunch of fucking cowards when they feel like their leverage is gone." But then his face darkened and his eyes narrowed. "It's too bad we couldn't have kidnapped someone important. Reaver or Jade, or even Juni, they would've given into our demands. I would've had Elish. Not you two worthless pieces of shit. Garrett doesn't even fucking care does he? Or Ares."

I shook my head, feeling like I had just seen with my own eyes Kerres's mind switch from calm to crazy. It looked like the brainwashing technique they did on some of the members seemed to come and go.

"Ares will come for me," the small voice murmured, still nestled into my chest. I continued to stroke his hair, too scared and too weak to tell him that no one was coming for us.

No one.

Kerres buried his face in his hands. The Crimstone looked weary, defeated – he looked done.

"Kerres… let us go," I whispered to him. "You can run, just let us go."

He shook his head, staring at the floor. I didn't think he was going to say anything to me, but as the sweeps of the flashlight stopped and the voices got lost in the distance, he spoke in a silent whisper.

"I love him so much, Otter. I loved that boy, my heart aches for him." A sad smile appeared on his dark features. "I would give anything to hold that boy to my chest again, to see those yellow eyes fixate on mine. I… I couldn't handle him when he came back to Moros, but I could now. I could make it work. I just…"

He paused, before his lips disappeared into his mouth. "I can't live the rest of my life seeing him on the television, proudly standing behind the man who raped, abused, and tortured him until Jade had no choice but to succumb to him…" There was another pause before Kerres whispered under his breath. "What kind of boyfriend would I be… to give up on him like that? To let Jade spend a lifetime with that monster? I could never look at myself in the mirror if I gave up on him."

That gave me pause. I turned his words over in my head and watched the Morosian boy stare at the floor with his shoulders slumped.

I think I saw Kerres for the first time there.

The former boyfriend of Jade Dekker, before he became a Dekker and a chimera. The man who had taken care of Jade for years, only to lose him to an intimidating and powerful chimera. Jade had been captured, and during his captivity as a pet, he had fallen for his captor, leaving Kerres with nothing, absolutely fucking nothing.

I understood him… and though my thigh hurt like it was on fire and my gut was a twisted mess of gnawing pain, I felt my heart break for him. Kerres had nothing. His boyfriend was now the chimera husband of Elish Dekker, and Kerres was still just a boy from the slums, unable to let go, unable to give Jade to the evil he saw the Dekker family as.

"You really love Jade, don't you?" I whispered to him.

Kerres looked up at me, and I saw his eyes were full of unshed tears. He nodded, and as he did, the first tear broke free from its prison and slid down his cheek.

I wanted to wipe that tear from his face in that moment, and give him a hug like I was hugging Trig. It was in my nature to soothe, to kiss and make better, it was what had made me me.

Kerres's heart still and would always belong to a man that belonged to another, and in a way mine had belonged to another too. But through a lot of internal tears, I had let my evil greywaster go, because I saw how happy he was with Killian. I saw how much of a better person Killian made Reaver, and it made me feel good to see that happen to him.

Kerres didn't have that in him though, and maybe it was because he didn't see the best in Jade get brought out by Elish, or at least what Kerres would see as the best in him. He saw Jade become the ankle biting little serial killer he was now. A chimera with pointed canines, a dangerous attitude, and an arm always hanging off of his blond elegant master and protector.

How would I have felt if I saw Reaver doing the same to King Silas?

The thought made my gut feel sick, and it made me sympathize even more with this poor lost Morosian.

"I'm sorry," I said to him simply. "One sad fuck who fell for a chimera to another… I'm sorry, Kerres."

He nodded but after that it was silence. A silence that seemed to sync itself with the biting winter air, becoming one continuous muted landscape that, even though it would absorb and exploit even the slightest of movements, was bringing nothing to my ears but internal static.

Finally Kerres spoke; a low tone but one that made me automatically fix my eyes on him.

"I won't give up… I'll find him one way or another," he said, more to himself than to me. "This plan might not have worked… but I'll find him."

Will you let us go? I wanted to ask so badly. *Just let us go.*

Kerres rose to standing and turned around. He looked out the thin cracks of the shed and I heard him sigh. "I have nothing left to live for… I'll find him or I will die by his hand. I have nothing left… I gave up my life to save him."

What do I say to that? I felt like getting up and putting an arm around him, but I was too weak, I could barely sit up. "You will, bro, I'm sure… I mean when shit is at its worst just remember – something's gotta give."

Kerres nodded and to my surprise he opened the door. Without another word, he walked out into the cold night, and I could hear the padlocks lock behind him.

I heard him sit back down in front of the door, and with a weighted sigh, I closed my eyes. I held the cicaro against my chest for warmth, wondering in my tired thoughts if Kerres would ever get the resolution he so dearly needed.

The next day Kerres was nowhere to be found, and we were all alone.

I called to Kerres a few times when I had been woken up by Trig's crying. My whole body was aching, and what sparse bits of energy I did have had been spent just being able to find my voice.

He didn't answer but I'd been hoping he was asleep, or had gone out to find us food. But when afternoon hit us and I still hadn't heard so much of a shuffle, a deep foreboding had started descending on me.

I managed to crawl my body towards the cracks in the shed and I looked through them.

And there was nothing. Everything was gone. His gun was gone; the crate where he'd sat was empty.

Kerres had abandoned us.

My teeth clenched and ground, in a fleeting moment of false hope I managed to stand on weak legs to try the door. But no, Kerres and I might've had a fleeting moment of understanding last night, but he was either thoughtless or he didn't want us to come after him once I was free… because the padlocks were still on the shed.

I closed my eyes and leaned my forehead against the door in defeat. I inhaled a deep breath and pulled on the handle, but I was so weak the wood didn't even bend under my strength. Even though this shed had wood as old as the Fallocaust, it was still too strong for me to break through.

Kerres had sealed us into our tomb,

I turned and looked around the small shed he'd stuffed us into but there was nothing in there I could use to break out of here with. Only crumbling plaster, insulation full of dirt and debris, and thin strips of wood that might've been wood paneling at one point. Besides that, the room had been cleaned out, we had nothing.

This is where we're going to die.

"Is he gone?" Trig's voice was so weak I almost couldn't hear it. The boy had shifted himself to sitting and was slowly rocking himself back and forth, his glassy dark eyes half open but dead.

"Yeah… he's gone." I almost felt too defeated and done to feel the fear from those words. I had no idea what was in store for us now, and the fleeting hope that Kerres had just gone to get food or something was becoming dimmer by the passing second. It was late afternoon now and I had been on and off awake since the morning.

The kid wasn't coming back.

And unlocking the shed would've been too dangerous for him. Kerres was really ready to sacrifice anyone and anything to get Jade back, or at least get him away from Elish.

Motherfucker…

My back slid down and I leaned against the door. I stared forward and ran my hand along my hot and blackening stomach, before it went father down to the hole in my upper leg, now clogged with dried blood and from the smell of it… becoming infected.

Then there was silence, but this silence had a different air to it. It wasn't thick or full of emotion like some of the quiet moments I'd experienced. It was cold and thin, like it had been stripped naked and exposed to the elements. A sober tranquility with nothing more to say, for its presence was enough for you to know why it was there.

There was nothing more to say, and I had no warm words of reassurance for the little cicaro. I would die in here with him, and soon.

Trig sniffed and huddled in on himself, shivering from the cold. His jacket doing nothing to warm that stick-thin body. What would Reaver have done in this situation if that were Killian? I didn't know; I had never been in this position and right now my only instinct was to curl up against the door and die.

Even when Trig started to cry I didn't move. I sat with my back against the shed door and just stared forward, feeling every ounce of pain wash through me again and again every time I struggled to get breath.

At that silent admission, I took in a deep inhale and realized it was starting to get hard to breathe. I lifted up my shirt and knew why; the black on my stomach that was hot to the touch seemed to be crawling up to my chest. I wondered of my lungs were going to start filling up with blood or something. I didn't know how it worked… I just knew it wasn't good.

The next thing I was conscious of was Trig's muffled sobs. I opened my eyes and looked ahead, shocked as hell that it was dark out.

"W-what's wrong?" I mumbled. My voice was a scratching rasp that sounded like sandpaper scraping together.

The boy's head jerked up, his face tear-stained and gaunt; I could see his lips turning blue. "They're back."

Sure enough, a beam of light shone through the cracks in the shed. I swore inside of my head and made sure my back was leaning against the door. The door was metal and it didn't have cracks for them to see my outline in.

"Shh," I whispered to him and I tried to motion him over to me but he was too petrified. "Just be quiet and they will go away."

"I can't let them take me again." Trig's words were muffled; he had his hands over his mouth as if trying to stifle the sobs breaking his lips. "They raped me so many times in there. I can't… Otter, I can't let them take me again."

"Shh… they won't, we just have to be quiet… I'll… I'll fucking think of something," I whispered. My heart was slamming against my ribcage with such a ferocity I was sure it was going to bust out of my chest and hit the wall.

A single flashlight beam slowly swept over the shed and I heard more muffled voices, men's voices who sounded just as authorative and dominant as the Crimstones. I didn't recognize these ones, but I knew they were probably the reinforcements. No doubt trying to look for Kerres, and to a lesser extent, the prisoners he doomed to slowly starve to death.

If my own injuries didn't kill me first.

It was a tense half hour after the last flashlight swept over the shed. When he was finally confident that they were gone, Trig managed to crawl over and lean beside me, careful and considerate enough to not touch my aching stomach or my leg.

He wept beside me, long mournful cries that I tried to stifle by directing him to my chest.

"Why won't Ares come for me?" he cried softly, pulling on my shirt in his own inner turmoil. "Why won't Garrett come for you?"

That hit me where it hurt… I wanted to give him false confidence that hey, maybe they were coming for us, but it had been too long and I had accepted the fact that no one was looking for us anymore. Besides the Crimstones, of course.

"I don't… I don't know…" I was surprised that my own voice cracked under my emotion. "I thought Garrett would have found me by now." I tried to laugh it off, but I was in too much pain to laugh.

"I don't want to go back into that fucking sewer." Trig clenched his teeth and let out another small cry; his grip on my shirt a small window into the internal agony he was experiencing. I could relate. "I'd rather die than go back in there. I can't… they can't just kill us, they'll torture us just to feel like they won."

I swallowed. "Yeah, I know."

"They'll find us, won't they? The Crimstones?" I saw Trig's eyes looking at me but I couldn't look back.

My teeth once again clenched together. Though to my absolute surprise… I found myself getting angry.

"Yeah, yeah, they fucking will," I said bitterly, my breathing started to become shorter. I didn't know what was going on inside of me, but I think the last ounce of restraint, hope, resolve, the last ounce of fucking *everything* left me.

"They're going to find us, rape us, and kill us. And Garrett is going to sit in his fucking skyscraper as everyone does his dirty work for him!" I suddenly snapped. "Because that's what these chimera assholes do. We aren't important to them. Who the fuck cares if Elish is exchanged for us? He's… he's fucking immortal! Isn't Jade going to get all immortalized too? Do that trick on him and hand him over and we can get him back. But no, fuck us, they don't care. They're a bunch of heartless animals, just like Reaver!"

I suddenly burst into tears; I buried my face into my hands and sobbed. My strength had left me; the funny, charismatic Reno had left me. I was done and I knew I was done.

"Ares isn't coming for you, and Garrett isn't coming for me. We're on our own and we'll either die in this shack or the Crimstones will take us back to the sewer. That's the life of mortals unlucky enough to get caught up with chimeras. We're expendable to them, Trig." I sniffed, my hands soaking wet with my own tears. "I was stupid to think Garrett would care. I'm just another human to him, another mortal he will see live and die. He might love me as much as a chimera is capable of loving, but you can see as well as I do… the writing is on the fucking walls. We're expendable."

Trig dissolved into tears; he shook his head and I saw a hand reach up to grab a tuft of his hair. From what I knew was stress alone, he pulled on it hard. "No, Ares is coming for me… Ares loves me. He WILL come! I know he will. Ares and Siris… they'll come, and joke and call me names. He will, Ares will–"

"ARES ISN'T COMING!" I suddenly screamed.

I rose to my feet, even though my legs were buckling, and slammed a fist against the wall. Then I fell to my knees with a painful cry and gave the door another slam.

"Ares isn't coming! NO ONE IS!" I grabbed the kid and shook him, his tears falling against my face. "We're fucked, okay? We're done! The

Crimstones will find us and what they'll do to us will be ten thousand times worse than us dying in this shithole."

Trig cried even harder; his small thin body was trembling hard under the weight of my harsh words. I couldn't believe such anger was coming out of me, but with that same thought, I knew why it was.

Because it was true. Everyone had left us and now we had nothing. I was going to die, if not tonight then tomorrow morning. Already it was getting hard to breathe and it would only get harder.

Trig suddenly let out a large wail. I let go of him and felt my own tears run down my face, but they weren't from sadness, they were from anger, betrayal, and devastation.

Reaver would have come for me.

I stared at the boy as he sobbed long drawn-out wails into the cold night air. A devastating sound I had heard come from Killian when Redmond had shot me.

Maybe you could come and get me, Tinkerbell?

Someone?

Please?

Suddenly Trig's face was illuminated, but in his own despair he didn't notice. Immediately my eyes widened and the anger left my body.

The Crimstones had come back.

"Trig… be quiet… be fucking quiet!" I said desperately. We might be fucked in this shed but I'd rather die here than go back into that sewer, back into that fucking pit to be raped and beaten and I knew he felt the same way.

But the kid was too deep in his own emotions to hear me. He continued to cry loudly, and as another flashlight joined the one on the shed, my heart rose to my throat.

I grabbed Trig, and though my chest and stomach screamed from the pain I held him to my chest like I had done yesterday.

"Be quiet, Trig, you have to be quiet!" I pleaded desperately. I held the back of his head and shut my eyes tight. I stifled my own desperate cry and said through locked teeth, "You need to be quiet!"

"I see something!" a voice suddenly sounded. "Bring the light!"

Panic rushed through me; a cold wave of dread followed by such an overwhelming flood of fear I felt myself temporarily fall into madness. I clutched the back of Trig's head to muffle his sobs and bit my tongue to try and suppress my own.

No, no, no... they won't take us... they won't take us! I groaned as I heard another voice, and another one. I clenched the kid's head and steeled myself; the minutes seemed like hours.

"Yeah, someone's in there! We fucking found them!"

No, no!!!! I squeezed Trig harder, ignoring his hand clenching and digging my side. I rocked the boy back and forth to keep him quiet; he was so loud but his sobs muffled as his face pressed into my chest... *Shut up, Trig, shut up, Trig!!*

They won't find us... they won't take us back there... Oh fuck me... no... no.

Please, no. What did I do to deserve this? Where was my house on the hill? Where was my Reaver? My drug nights in the basement?

I cried out when I heard them rattle the door, and kissed Trig's forehead. He had stopped struggling, he was limp in my arms. The poor kid had resigned himself to our fate, just like me.

He had no fight left in him, and neither did I.

Then the door was kicked open and a wave of winter air rushed in. I looked up and saw a silhouette in the door, with a blue embered cigarette hanging from his mouth.

"Hah! Looky here! Motherfucker!" a happy voice sounded.

I stared, not believing who I was seeing.

It was Ares.

"What, seriously?" Siris appeared beside his twin brother. His eyes widened and he let out a barking laugh. "Well, holy fuck! He has Trigger too! Hey, Tiggy-Wiggy!"

My mind went blank, and with my mind, my body drained of its last reserves of energy. I felt my arms go limp, and with that, I released Trig from the protective hold.

His body fell limply to the ground, and for a moment, all I did was stare at him.

Trig's eyes were open and so was his mouth; a soundless scream on his lips and an expression on his frozen face of pure unaltered fear.

Trig was dead.

I had smothered him.

CHAPTER 28

Jade

"GET UP! FUCKING GET UP, YOU GOD DAMN…" I WAS fast asleep which was saying something considering I was having a fuck load of trouble falling asleep recently. Well, they didn't give a shit about that because I was being yanked out of my bedroll.

My instincts kicked in though and I pushed whoever it was away from me. "What the fuck?" This is the second time this had happened, but Reaver was off charging the Ieon and the remote phone so who was pissed at me now?

I looked at his grubby fingers, with dirt-caked into his untrimmed nails, before yanking my arm away from him.

It was Hopper. What the fuck was up his ass?

"What the fuck? What the fuck!" Hopper yelled. He pushed me backwards so hard I almost lost my balance. "Jimmy is fucking dead, that's what! What the hell… that's it… I've had enough… get out, get out of my caravan and if you dare–"

I had barely woken up; if I couldn't smell that damn slaver I would have assumed I was still dreaming.

I shoved him away, and as my slum-pride dictated, I advanced on him with my arms spread wide. "I didn't do shit, Hopper! And I didn't kill that old man either."

Hopper shook his head; his lip clamped down over his teeth. "Look, fucking chimera shit…"

"Did you see me? Did you fucking see me!?" I snapped. My eyes went towards a strip of daylight that suddenly shone on me. I was cautiously relieved to see Perish coming in, one of our guns strapped to his back. Mine was beside me, but if I needed it…

"What's going on?" Perish blinked and looked at the two of us. "What's everyone upset about?"

"The dark-skinned dude is dead and apparently this is all coming back on me," I said angrily to him. "I was sleeping the entire time. I didn't kill anyone."

"He ran off the damn cliff!" Hopper's eyes were wide, and though when he was at his best he was a calm and charismatic soul, now he was pissed off and frustrated. I knew we had overstayed our welcome now, even if it wasn't me.

I picked up my AK 101 still in its holder and belted the strap around my chest. "Well, instead of fucking assuming it was me, why don't you actually try and find out who did it?" I said bitterly. "I didn't kill that old man, and I didn't kill Jimmy."

"I just want to get the fuck outta here and you can leave too." Hopper glared at me, all three of us walked out of the tent. Sure enough, I could see Churro and Tabbit talking in hushed but rapid voices, their own arms crossed over their chests. They were standing beside a median, and below their feet, I could see skid marks.

No doubt, like the old man, Jimmy had been chased.

When they saw Perish and me they gave us the most threatening glares I could imagine, ones that told me they would crucify me and burn me alive if they weren't so fucking scared of us.

However, Reaver wasn't here anymore… I swallowed at that realization. Maybe we were no longer safe with these slavers. Perish wasn't threatening at all and I was still only seventeen years old, at least for a little while longer.

"We aren't leaving…" I looked over at Perish and saw his unfocused eyes looking from Jimmy to the tent I had just emerged from. "Reaver and Killian will be coming soon and we must wait for them."

"You can wait for them…" Hopper said lowly. "I've had about enough of having chimeras for guards. Obviously you little mutants can't control your urges. We're done, deal's off."

I suppressed a growl and looked over to the tunnel that we had camped beside. We had been trudging uphill on a cracked road all day yesterday, and it had taken a lot of work getting the caravan through some of the fissures in the road. Hopper had been right, it had been slow going but we made it.

"That's not going to happen."

My head snapped towards Perish. I almost wanted to do a double take at the serious and rather unmanic look he was giving Hopper. The scientist, dressed in a black duster and Garrett's bowler hat looked every bit a greywaster right now. He had changed a lot over the past several weeks. He even had a thin brush of facial hair over his face and no longer spent hours grooming himself like he used to.

Hopper raised his hands and let them fall. "It ain't up to you! This is my caravan, buddy. I hired ya and I can fire ya."

I rubbed my head as those two fought; it was pounding with a headache now. The only thing I had to try and dull the pain were some of the pain killers Reaver had in his drug suitcase. He'd left it behind but had left out the combination of course, so I just had what he'd left me.

"You hired us to help you get to Falkvalley, and we are. If you have any proof that Jade did this, I'd like to see it." Perish glanced at me. "Is your head aching, Jade?"

I nodded, giving it more of a rub, though, of course, it never helped. "Yeah."

"Come, come, pet… we'll get you food." Ignoring Hopper swearing at the two of us, Perish led me back to the tent.

"We're having a meeting," Hopper called as we disappeared into the tent. "All you guys, come to the covered caravan and we can decide what ta do."

I ignored him, not giving a shit about their meeting, and sat down on my bedroll. I glanced down at my fingers that had been scratching behind my head and scowled at them.

My fingernails had dried blood caked into them. I scratched again and this time I could feel the scab on the back of my head.

This wasn't really anything new though. I once had over a dozen small pock mark scabs in my skull from the surgery to prevent me from using my empath abilities, but they had healed long ago. As long as my ears weren't bleeding I didn't worry too much about it. I knew when I was in the danger zone, it had happened to me before.

"There you go, eat it all." Perish presented me with a bowl full of canned peaches. I looked at them hungrily, my mouth giving me a sour jolt as if anticipating the flavours.

"Thanks, Per." I wasn't used to the scientist treating me nicely. He usually reserved his affection for Killian, but maybe that meant he was on my side. He would've seen me if I had snuck out of the tent.

Though it wouldn't be that hard for someone to come into the outskirts of camp. We were short for night watchmen since Reaver had taken off, it was just Perish doing patrols.

I played with the idea that perhaps he was the murderer, but watching that guy sit down and stare off into space as he chewed on a piece of jerky made me reconsider that. Perish was a scientist, he wasn't a fighter, just like Lycos never was a fighter. Science-oriented chimeras excelled in brains not brawns; I couldn't see that guy doing any joy-killings. Even if he technically wasn't a chimera, he had still jumped into the role of one for the past seventy years; he just didn't have that bloodthirsty nature in him.

I finished off my peaches, noticing Perish's eyes continuously looking through the empty tent flap. No doubt watching for Killian and Reaver even if we were miles from the dirt road they were supposed to be using. Dude seemed devoted to that kid; I wonder how Reaver could stand it. Anyone who showed any affection to my master was on my shit list, it already annoyed me that Elish had been nice to Killian.

Eventually we emerged out of the tent and saw everyone packing up their stuff, most of them giving us weighted glares as they did.

I shook my head as I heard the crunching of boots behind me. "I don't know, Perish. We're at a high elevation now, far away from Kreig. Maybe it wouldn't be a big deal for us to just go off on our own. We're dancing a thin line with these fucks now."

Perish wrung his hands. He leaned up against a rusted out car and looked up over the rim of his hat. "No, we should stay with them. A few more nights maybe."

I didn't like the idea but the only person who could override that decision would be Reaver. Then again, he was the first guy to pin these murders on me.

Maybe I should just branch out on my own… eventually Elish would find me. I still had my tracking chip imbedded in my head.

No… not only would Elish kill me and never trust me again with a task, I couldn't leave the remote phone and the Ieon behind.

I stayed near Perish as we continued up the pass. To my left was a rough cliff, completely crumbled and blocking off the road in some areas. To my right was a sheer drop off, where Jimmy's crippled remains were.

So who had killed Jimmy though? I had been so worked up defending myself that I never stopped to have a think over who it could've been. When the old man had died I just assumed he had made a mad dash for freedom or something, as dumb as that sounds. Now that Jimmy had made his leap of death – who could it be? I know it wasn't fucking me that was for…

My hand lifted absentmindedly and I scratched the back of my head, where I had felt the blood. I started to move my fingers over the scab.

"What a pretty view," Perish said happily beside me, rubbing his hands together as he looked to his right. The drop off was fifty feet down but it led down to a valley below us. Off in the distance we had rolling hills speckled with trees and yellow brush, acres and acres of black tree forests, coated with the blowing grey ash to make it appear like a sand-washed painting more than an image in front of me.

My eyes travelled to Perish, and for the first time, I looked down at the bag he was always carrying.

Perish never had any possessions before. Of course Leo and Greyson had given him none when he was captive; everything he had on him now was borrowed from the lab in Kreig.

"Have you ever been up here before?" I asked him, not taking my eyes off of his rapidly jerking eyes, always trying to take a thousand things in at once but only a quarter of it was ever processed in his brain.

Perish shook his head. He bent down and picked up a rock before throwing it over the edge of the road; it flew down to the valley below never to be seen again. "No, no, I haven't, but I may afterwards. This is such a quiet, nice place. I can't wait to show Killian."

I drew up his aura as he talked; the fractured aura with thousands of small cracks, each one holding behind those fractures little splinters of his–

Holy shit.

No. I peered in deeper, watching him like a hawk as he picked up another stone to throw over the edge.

I couldn't believe what I was seeing. The cracks were almost gone; it was like they had knitted themselves back together. This wasn't the same aura I had seen in the greyrifts apartment… it was repairing itself.

But how? I know I had seen who he was before that brain piece had gotten cut from him and put into the O.L.S, but we weren't in Falkland yet. There is no way this could be happening to him without the god damn piece.

The realization came to me slowly, but once my mind even hinted to the fact it started to become more and more a reality. I found myself looking at my hands, at the blood crusted in my fingernails, and the scabs behind my head.

As Perish jogged ahead, climbing up rocks and walking on top of medians, I reached into my own bag and pulled out the velvet case which usually held the claw rings that were my trademark weapons. Something I wore to my battles, or when I felt like I needed extra protection.

I watched the scientist and opened the case.

The colour drained from my face, and I could feel my knees start to wobble like they had been turned into jelly.

Blood stains… there were blood stains on the claws.

I had done this.

I had been killing them… it had been me all along.

What the fuck was that mad scientist doing to me?

The apprehension and fear filled me to the point where I found my legs almost pivoting to turn around, to just get the fuck out of here and make my way back to Kreig. I could, I really could… the family didn't know I was aligned with them I could… I could make up a fucking excuse as to why I was there.

I wanted Elish – Why the fuck was I here? I had been sent here to get the information I needed out of Perish's head, and it looks like I had gotten more than I bargained for.

Something was happening with Perish, though I wasn't sure what. Why after all of this time would his mind start to come back? He was

Silas's age, and he had been the manic man he was for at least seventy years. It didn't make sense.

Though at this point I really did want to take off and run, I knew I couldn't. I wanted to know what was happening to Perish; Perish was the key in finding out how to kill King Silas. Perish's brain was the reason why we were in this caravan, going up a mountain to reach Falkvalley. When it all came down to it, I had a job to do.

Tonight I would stay awake. I would watch Perish like a hawk and I would find out just what the fuck he was doing with me. And if he gave me the chance, I'd go through that damn bag of his and see just what he was hiding. If he was slipping me scopa, like Killian had said Silas had been doing to Reaver, I wanted to know.

Then I could at least have some damn proof when Reaver came back with Killian. To not only clear my name, but hogtie that fucking scientist until Elish came and then he could decide what to do with him.

"Look!" Perish came jogging up to me, and to my own chimera amusement, like a strange dog running up to a cat, I immediately felt apprehension in my chest to the point where my entire body tensed up.

But he was only coming to show me a wristwatch. "It was on a corpse. It doesn't work but I've always like repairing things. If you see any other corpses please look out for watches I may need parts, okay?" His voice was still that fast-paced tone, like he was speaking without commas or periods.

I nodded at him, adding a smirk and a shake of my head. He might be a born immortal, but like Silas, he'd had enhancements added later on. I knew his hearing was good. "Sure, I'll keep an eye out."

Perish gave me a smile and looked towards where we were walking. The road snaked up the hill at a slow incline, gradually making its way up the summit like a grey ribbon or a smooth scar. Though, to my dismay, I could see another large rockslide about two miles away, another delay. I hoped Reaver and Killian weren't waiting on us; Reaver hated being left to wait.

"Killian and Reaver will be back soon. I'll give it to Killian as a present!" And with that he ran off to check more of the cars.

Sneaky… sneaky Perish.

Things were tense around the campfire that night. I swear if I got one more heated glare from these slavers I was going to burst into flames. No one trusted us, no one liked us, and I knew as soon as we got Killian and Reaver back we were going to have to find our own way. Even though it looked like they decided to keep us around at their slaver meeting, our time here was winding down.

In all respects, they'd been right all along. It hadn't been a young carracat or just accidents… it had been me. I had been killing them.

Or Perish had anyway.

At this metal note, I shot the scientist a sideways look. He was sitting beside me chewing on a piece of tact with some half-cooked Jimmy on top. He looked normal enough; it was only when I drew up his aura that I understood he was turning into a different person.

No… he was turning into what he had used to be, before the Fallocaust and during the early years of Skyfall. Before the piece of his brain had been removed and made into the O.L.S we were trying to find.

But would we even need it now?

I puzzled over this, chewing on my own Jimmy-tact and half-listening to the conversation taking place around me.

I sighed and popped the last bit of tact in my mouth before wiping my fingers on my duster. I got up wordlessly and walked past the slavers.

"Going to rest up before another night of killing, boy?" Churro said acidly. He held out his leg like he wanted to trip me. Everyone laughed, thinking that was the funniest thing in the world.

I ignored him; if I didn't ignore him I'd rip his ugly face to bits right there and they had more guns than the one strapped to my back.

I walked into the tent Perish and I shared and kicked my bedroll a few times to make sure nothing crawling had gotten into it. I sat down on it and drew my knees up to my chest.

Perish's blue bag was resting on top of his bed. He wasn't overly protective of it which I would have suspected a normal person to be if it harboured some sort of secret. But even if his own mind was knitting itself back together, perhaps his logic hadn't changed yet.

I eyed the flap of the tent and paused, listening for the low-toned male voices and the sounds of water bottles crinkling under firm grips. I wasn't sure if I should do this now or when Perish was asleep.

Well, he might not technically be a chimera but he had the enhancements of one. All you needed was a good surgeon and immortality and they could fill any chimera with the basic perks. I had my hearing permanently improved during my surgery last year. An enhancement I was implanted with as an embryo but had never developed successfully.

At this mental note, I tuned my hearing to Perish's voice and his movements. Then I quietly reached my arm over to Perish's bag and picked it up. The scientist had his own hearing and I had to do this as quietly as I could.

I hated my hands for trembling at this moment but they were. I don't think I was scared, I didn't get scared anymore. I think I was just stressed out and edging the end of my rope. Though I had been raised a Morosian and now a chimera, being in the greywastes was new to me. I was tired and drained from all of this. I just wanted to go home.

I looked down at Perish's bag and saw a crisp white lab coat. I gently took it out and rested it beside of me. I then glanced down and started moving things off to the side.

It didn't take me long to find what I was looking for.

I swallowed the tightness in my throat and gave myself a small nod. I drew up a Ziploc package of syringes and stared at them.

There were three of them that were full, the rest empty. The full ones contained a clear liquid, and as I glanced down into the bag, I could see clear vials which I assumed contained the same liquid.

I put the Ziploc back into Perish's bag and tried to read the writing on the vials.

Scopolamine…

Yep, I bet that was short for scopa. Liquid scopa.

Immediately I felt a surge of anger go through me. I clenched my hands over the bottle and resisted the overwhelming urge to throw the vial against the tent wall. Even more so I pushed down the twitching in my body to lunge at Perish and rip his windpipe out of his throat.

Why was he doing this? For fun? He wasn't achieving anything by drugging me. Jimmy hadn't done anything wrong, the old man I could see but not Jimmy. Perish was making me kill them for fun, but why?

Does he even need a fucking reason, Jade? He's a mad scientist and you're an empath chimera with a trillion little talents inside your head.

I was a fucking gold mine to him.

I had to know more, I couldn't call him on this shit… not even with Reaver here. I had to wait for Elish to come and get me. I would tell him everything then, calling Perish out on it now would just put me in a lot of danger.

I jumped and my heart gave an anxious jolt as I heard Perish laugh outside the tent. I had been so focused on his voice the switch from low tones to high pitch laughter jarred my head. I took it as a sign to cover my tracks and started putting everything back.

Then my hand grazed something. I looked down and saw one of my water bottles full of water.

It might not be the most well-thought-out of ideas but right now it was really all I had. With the scientist exchanging campfire stories with the slavers, probably trying to remain in their good books, I unscrewed the cap and started filling syringes.

In an act of intelligence that surprised even me, I didn't dump out the scopa he had filled in those syringes, I pocketed those needles and filled up the empty ones. We had empty syringes in our own medical supplies, the ones Elish had packed for me to use on the others.

Even though my hands were trembling and shaking the entire time, I managed to re-fill the syringes with water. The scopa was clear, and once I was finished everything looked in its place.

My heart was pounding when I laid in my bedroll that night. I pulled my brown blanket up to my chin and tried to calm it down. It was too late for my body though, I was already shivering underneath the blankets. The adrenaline and the prospect of remaining conscious during Perish's next control over me had filled my veins with ice water.

The scientist came into the tent an hour later, when I was half-asleep and in my own head, pretending that the weight behind me was Elish, and not just the bag I had been packing around.

Perish yawned and I heard rustling before, without a word, there was the sound of blankets shifting.

At least I was sleeping on my stomach; he wouldn't be able to hear my heartbeat.

But then again – it meant the back of my head was exposed to him.

I resigned myself to sleep and prepared myself for what was to come.

The sharp prick in the back of my head came sometime in the early morning.

My eyes snapped open and I gasped from pain and shock. Immediately I felt a hand on my mouth and the calm voice of Perish.

"Shh… it's okay," he soothed before driving the needle further into the base of my skull. I cried out as he wiggled the needle into the small pin-sized hole in my head, the pressure and pain was overwhelming.

Then he broke through with a soothing noise on his lips, and I felt the cold water flow into my head.

I groaned and clenched my teeth, and though I knew nothing was going to happen, I still felt apprehension inside of me. I didn't know what was supposed to happen next but I knew scopa took away all of your free will.

He was going to make me kill again, but I didn't know who.

"Sit up, Jade."

My chest filled with a thousand small charges as Perish said those words. His voice had dropped. His tone was different. It was still Perish's voice but his run-on sentence way of speaking had disappeared. He sounded normal; he sounded like he was in control of every corner of his brain.

This wasn't… this wasn't right.

I had known Perish was having slip-ups, telling us truths about his origins without him even realizing it, but this was different.

It wasn't just his aura…

It was him.

"Sit up, Jade."

I felt a drip of snot run down my mouth as a blinding headache started to coat my brain, whether it was from the water he had injected or because of my realizations, I wasn't sure.

I shifted and sat up, wiping the snot absentmindedly from my nose. I gathered myself and found the chimera bravery I was born with, and looked Perish right in the eyes.

Perish Fallon stared back, his jaw tight and his eyes taking in every bit of me with a coldness that rivalled my master's.

He put a hand on my chin and drew it up, before tilting it off to the left and then the right.

"You are of good quality, aren't you, Jade?" Perish murmured. He traced a hand down and slipped it underneath my shirt. I tried not to recoil and I tried even harder not to look into his eyes. "Valen had so many errors in his coding… but it looks like I did a grand job with you."

You made me?

Perish narrowed his eyes before slipping a hand to the back of my head. "It's a pity you will probably be dead before Elish can fulfil his dream of you becoming immortal."

He wouldn't let me die, asshole.

"Now, draw up your aura."

I stared at him, trying to look as vacant as I could and drew up my aura reading abilities.

My own flares of purple, black, and silver started to ripple off of my body like heat waves; coating my arms, my torso, every inch of my body in its opal-like glow.

"That's it… now look at me."

I drew my eyes back up to Perish, and with that, I saw his once fractured aura.

Still repairing itself; still knitting the small hairline cracks together. I could see colour coming back to it too. A thousand different hues of blue, twisting around the fragments and sticking to the cracks like super glue to porcelain. The auras around people had no physical shape, no light, and no substance, but in my own mind I could work them like they were physical objects. They were real inside of my own head, and held such a presence I used to play with the strands as a child.

"There we go…" Perish whispered, then to my horror he tightened his grip on the back of my head and drew me into a kiss.

My eyes widened and my heart jolted. To my further shock, I heard Perish's pants unzip.

"Take off your clothes."

What… the… fuck…?

What the fuck are you supposed to do now, Jade?

I swallowed the lump in my throat and started undressing myself, knowing that I wouldn't be able to let him fuck me; knowing that at any moment the chimera inside of me would kill him.

My eyes travelled down and I watched my hands absentmindedly undo the buttons on my shirt; one button after another, exposing my pale chest to the winter air.

Before my mind could come up with a way to get him off of me, Perish, with his shirt still on, discarded his pants.

I stared at him, my mind going a mile a minute trying to figure out a way out of this. What the fuck could I do? I was stuck. Elish had told me to do whatever I could to find a way into Perish's mind, to find out where the O.L.S was, but–

But this wasn't fucking Perish, and Elish giving me permission was beside the fucking point. I had been raped before and I had no control over the beast that emerged when I was under that sort of stress. I was going to kill Perish the moment I felt the pressure between my legs.

I blew out a plume of cold air and watched him take his hard penis into his hand. I pulled off my pants still sitting down on the bed. I waited for my next command but my hand was twitching towards the assault rifle beside me.

"A pity you need the ressin to make it hard…" Perish murmured before his head disappeared between my legs. I sucked in a breath as I felt his warm mouth start to lick the crown of my flaccid dick. He took all of it between his lips, then withdrew his mouth and started to flick the tip. "Scopa boys make the most useless of sex victims… but ressin and scopa… well, I've heard things, let's leave it at that."

His mouth went back to my dick and I felt him make a suction with his mouth. I groaned and leaned back on my hands, electricity shooting through my chest and centering around my groin. I was angry, more than angry, at what he was doing to me, but my body responded the same. It had happened hundreds of times during my first year of being Elish's pet. No matter if they were raping you, your dick would still get stiff and you would still cum. So the hardness growing in Perish's mouth was no surprise to me.

Elish is going to fucking kill you, Perish. But I am not Killian; I won't cry because I'm getting a blowjob right now. But the moment you try and stick that fucking thing in me I'm gouging out your…

"Ah…" I moaned. Perish drew his head back, releasing my dick from his suction with a *pop*.

"There we go… nice little slut, aren't we?"

How did you get this way without that O.L.S, Perish Fallon?

As soon as I was aroused enough for him, Perish stopped sucking me off. He looked up at me with a smile, running his hand up and down my shaft. His blue eyes sparkled in the darkness. The man looked like a ghost in that moment, a phantom, a spectre, something not from this world but yet he was someone who had been in it longer than anyone.

The third immortal chimera… though if he was older than King Silas–

–he could have been the first.

Perish drew his face back up to mine and kissed me hard on the mouth. He then separated my lips with his and I felt his tongue. Knowing what he wanted, I met my tongue with his and we kissed deeply, my stomach lurching and churning with every caress of his tongue.

To my confusion, he started to climb onto me. I shifted myself back to get away from him, but he once again started *shh' ing* me like when he'd injected me.

My jaw locked; I waited for him to grab my legs. But with a crack of a small lube bottle and the smell of silicone, to my confusion… he started to lube *my* dick.

They usually fuck me…

I hid the shock on my face as he grabbed my dick and started sinking himself onto it. I closed my eyes and steeled myself, trying desperately to remind myself that I was supposed to be drugged right now, but I was a horrible fucking actor and I knew it.

I rarely got the chance to be the one doing the fucking. Obviously Elish and I had a very one-sided sex life. The only time I got the chance was when he brought me home presents in the form of borrowed cicaros and other chimeras, or the occasional virgin a brother had given us as a gift. When Elish was in the right mood he loved to watch me fuck them; he loved to watch me make them scream at his command.

I tried to avoid eye contact as Perish rode me, his hips rising and falling on my dick, in sync with the moans he was trying to stifle. I stared up at the ceiling and tried to pretend I was somewhere else.

"Keep your aura up," he commanded. He leaned his head down and let out a loud groan. "Relax your whole body, relax and let it take you."

Let it… take me?

Perish's entire body enveloped me. I felt his hair tickle the sides of my cheeks as he lay on top of me; his torso moving back and forth. I resisted the urge to start moving my own hips but I wasn't sure if that had to be commanded.

Thank god I'm not a prissy little bitch like Killian, or a normal person. This wasn't scarring me, it was disturbing me but I was okay, just confused as fuck over what he was doing.

I was no stranger to rape or sexual abuse. I had gotten gang fucked by Ares and Siris; they had massacred my body until it was nothing but blood and pulp. This was a full-body massage compared to what I had been through. Elish had told me to do what had to be done; it would be him punishing Perish for this.

"Relax," he whispered into my ear. I felt a hand on my forehead. "Fall into me… let me see what's inside that head."

What?

Suddenly I felt a rip of pain go through my brain, centering around Perish's fingertips. But as quickly as it erupted from his touch, it was gone, replaced by a darkness… a shrouded cloak that seemed to coat my mind like a thick blanket.

I had felt this before… last year…

Silas had done it to me. He had thrown this darkness over my head in front of Elish, taunting him that he could make me go mad right now. Did he have the same mind-tinkering ability that Silas had supposedly been born with?

Of course he did, he's a born immortal…

Then like my mind was a machine, Perish flipped the off switch. Everything went black, every lit corner, every hive of buzzing bees quieted and were silenced.

Alarms went off inside my head and immediately I tried to resist whatever he was doing to me. Inside my own head I steeled myself and erected every fortress I could to keep him from accessing whatever it is he wanted.

"What are the passwords to Elish's laptop?"

Passwords on Elish's laptop? I don't know them and I certainly wouldn't tell Perish.

A new voice inside of my head seemed to growl at my own inner thoughts. He was angry I didn't know the answer.

There was silence, though the silence was as tangible as the apprehension growing inside of my chest. Perish physically on top of me had seemed to disappear, but the pleasurable sensation was still burning inside of my body. It was like he was hypnotizing me, lulling my physical body into a forced relaxation and encouraging my own mind to follow suit.

I started to feel my mind slip from my fingers. I squinted my eyes and tried to force his voice from my head, but he kept whispering to me. I could feel the heat on my neck. It wasn't cold anymore.

"Jade… I know Elish has my old notes about sestic radiation. He knows the right exposure and the timing needed to make greywasters immune to it." Perish's voice inside of my mind was so calm… it was different.

"He never told me… he never told me any of this," I whispered.

Couldn't Perish hack into it? In the dark parts of my mind I brought up the image of Elish's laptop.

"No, I can only access parts of it, not the notes I need to find. I need to know how much radiation I have to expose him to before he becomes immune to it. I need to know the dosage… the timing… I can't fail him."

Who?

"You don't want to know what I'll have to do if you don't tell me," Perish said. "I don't want to give him any more power."

I grunted but Perish kept pressing his own aura against mine. I tried to push him off but it was like pushing off liquid. It kept surrounding me, permeating me. Every bit of me… I had to escape.

"Think, Jade."

"I don't know how to make greywasters immune to the radiation… Elish never mentioned anything like that."

My mouth opened. I gulped a breath of winter air and used that to try and push my mind back into reality, away from this overbearing darkness that Perish had pushed on me. This is what Perish had been doing… he had been getting information out of me, but I didn't know what answer he was looking for. Elish had no reason to give me those passwords and I bet that part of his laptop was protected for a reason.

Who did he want to make immune to the radiation?

My jaw clenched and I started to feel my fingers, like wading through tar I managed to regain control over them.

I put them on Perish's shoulders and tried to push his body off of me.

Though as I pushed, his hips continued to rise and fall. He had never stopped riding me, and without even realizing it, I was brushing the fringes of my peak.

I pushed harder, grinding my teeth together as I did, but moments later my hands clenched and a cry fell from my mouth. The burning tension in my body summited, and with an intake of breath and one last push of his shoulders, I came.

Then colours.

Lots of colours.

I was in pain, overwhelming pain. My entire body was on fire but my head hurt most of all. It throbbed and pounded like a hammer hitting an anvil, splitting my head in half and spilling its contents onto the linoleum floor.

White floor, blood and dirt-stained, with boot imprints making a thousand mosaic shapes. It sticks to the bottoms of their boots now; the sound was rooted in my brain. I had heard it for weeks now, like the sound of Velcro being quickly torn in two.

I sniffed and tried to protect my head. But all that I had to protect me were my bruised and cigarette-burned arms. I don't even know why I bother to protect myself, I'm caged and they do to me what they want.

They cut my fucking head open, Master, they cut open my head.

"You're still crazy. How long does this usually take?"

Lycos? I recognized that voice anywhere.

"I don't know!" I cried.

Automatically my body tensed up, the breath leaving my chest as anxiety claimed my muscle movements. Like expected, I got dealt a kick to my side, making me cry out and scrunch myself up tighter.

"Maybe you did it wrong?" another voice sounded. I didn't recognize it.

"No, Doc… the device was working. Like all fucking Skytech technology, green means working. I just don't know how long it's supposed to take. I've killed him seven times already."

"Just keep trying. If you're sure this should work – you know more about this than I do, Leo."

"That's not his name," I croaked, before coughing into my hands.

I yelled out as Lycos gave me another hard kick, digging into the soft flesh of my side. I whimpered and rubbed the area before burying my face back into my knees. I had tried to escape. I had tried to negotiate. I had even tried reasoning with Lycos. I had known him, I had taught him at the college. But he was a greywaster now; he wasn't the blond chimera scientist I had trained.

"Well, break him open. If anything we can see if the O.L.S frequency has changed. Perhaps the position is wrong? It's not like we have Sky to compare him to; he's the only person now with an implant."

Break me open again?

I started to whimper, shaking my head back and forth. *No, no, don't break open my head. Or at least kill me first – it fucking hurts, you fucking maniac.*

Then the sound of a saw. Like a bell to Pavlov's dog, my stomach brimmed with anxiety. I pressed my arms down on the back of my head and felt a sob break my lips.

Reality hit me like a ton of bricks, reality in the form of Perish hitting me repeatedly in the face.

I hollered and pushed him off of me, the cold winter air stinging my naked body. I looked around trying to get my bearings, feeling my mind half in Perish's head and half clinging to where I was now.

I put up my hands, but when I felt the next attempted blow to my body I grabbed Perish's hand and twisted it back.

Perish glared at me; his cold blue eyes searing my flesh with a newfound hatred. I raised my free hand and punched him in the face.

He flew back and hit the side of the tent with a holler, but as he started to rise I saw movement in the corner of my eye.

"What the fuck? Lover's quarrel?" Hopper ripped through the entrance of the tent, the first glow of morning framing his silhouette. "For fuck sakes ya chimeras fuck like Klingons. Shut up we is trying ta sleep!"

"He fucking attacked me!" Perish suddenly cried. My head snapped towards him and I felt a growl rise to my throat. He was back speaking in his manic, quick-paced tone.

Fucking fraudster.

Hopper threw his hands up into the air. "I don't give a fuck who fucks who or who chews on who when it comes to you four. Just shut up while–"

"PERISH!" a familiar voice suddenly screamed.

My mouth dropped open, and at the same time, so did Perish's. All of a sudden what had just happened seemed unimportant.

That was Killian and he sounded like he was in physical pain.

I jumped to my feet and quickly put my pants on. I ran out, still buttoning up my shirt, looking around the abandoned rest stop for where his voice was coming from.

"JADE!" Killian screamed. I looked towards where the dirt road was and saw Killian stumbling down it. His face was pale but his eyes puffy and red; his hair was messed up and he was covered in dust and dirt. I could hear his heavy breathing from where I was standing, mixed in with the stifled sobs that continued to roll from his lips.

I ran to him and he collapsed in my arms, hysterically sobbing. I put a hand on his head and looked behind me where Perish and Hopper were running towards us.

Perish slowed down as he approached us; his crazy eyes shooting from Killian to behind him.

"They got Reaver… they got Reaver didn't they?" Perish whispered.

Oh… fuck.

Killian cried harder. He held onto me like I was his life-preserver. I held him, though at this moment I felt like I was going to collapse myself.

Reaver was fucked.

"The Legion found us. Nero got him. Nero got him," Killian sobbed.

Yeah, Reaver was fucked.

We were all fucked.

CHAPTER 29

Reno

"TIGGY? TIGGY??"

The blood rushed to my ears, a heavy pressure that seemed to push my own mind out of my body. Like my head was doing everything it could to not hear what was going on around me.

But it was real, the voices were real, the frozen air, so thick with emotion, was real. The dead boy in my arms was real.

Trig stared at the ruined ceiling, his eyes wide in a shock I could only imagine.

I had killed him… my arms clenched him to my chest to hush his terrified crying. Because none of us wanted to be dragged back to the hell underneath our feet.

"Knight… get the Falconer… we… we got them." I felt Trig get taken out of my arms.

My eyes travelled up to Ares's face, but I could no longer lift my head. I didn't want to lift my head, there was nothing happening around me that I wanted to see. Only a thousand images that I knew, once I saw them, would burn themselves into my mind.

I didn't want to see Ares and Siris; I didn't want to see Trig dead in Ares's arms. I didn't want to see that Ares had come for Trig. Just like the cicaro said he would all along.

"Garrett?" I croaked as Siris lifted me up. I tried to raise a bloodied hand but it fell limp to my side. The cold winter air stung my body and the bright light made my eyes automatically close.

Why wasn't I happy? I was free… I was safe…

"He's back in the skyscraper, bro. We'll bring you to…" Siris sucked in a breath. I winced as I felt his hands brush my side and my stomach. "Wow… Ares we need to get this chicklet to a doctor. He's been shot… did… did they shoot Trig?" They were running with me now. I could hear a rumbling plane in the distance. Where did they land? I hadn't heard anything.

A grey building with the side of it a crumbled mass of dust and brick passed by me, a car was overturned in front of it with its tires deflated and hanging off of the rims. All of this passing rapidly in a blur of grey as they ran with me.

"I don't know, he's cold… he has some pretty bad injuries on him," Ares sniffed. I shut my eyes and tried to tune out what I knew was his stifled emotions.

Ares had come for Trig.

My fiancé was warm in his skyscraper. Not a media appearance in over a month, not a single negotiation for my release. Ares had come for Trig.

No one had come for me.

"Holy shit… holy fucking shit… I… I just radioed Mom. She's meeting us in Sidonius's skyscraper." A male voice was shouting over the noise of the Falconer, it was a low roar that I could feel vibrate my chest cavity. "Did you see any Crimstones?"

No, they left us too. Kerres left us.

They put my cold body onto the floor of the Falconer, my back hitting the metal bench. My head flopped down but someone caught it, the one who had mentioned he had a mother. That could only be Knight, Ellis's son. I had never–

"I'm sorry." I suddenly burst into tears, like my own stunned mind had finally caught up to the horrible thing I had done. The hot tears streamed down my face and onto the rusty-red stains dried to my shirt and pants. I put my hands behind my head and pressed, trying to keep in the hysteria I could feel crawling up my throat. Like a thousand little insects they filled my mouth, just edging me to the point of madness.

I didn't know what was happening to me but I had seen it happen to

Killian. I knew I was witnessing my own mind breaking; the end of my rope finally being felt by my own frozen hands. Why was it always the feeling of safety that brought you to the fringes? I had been on auto-pilot and now… and now…

I felt a hand on my shoulder, and at that point I broke down again. The man I didn't even know made a sympathetic noise and put his arms around me.

"Poor little guy. We really need to get him to Sid's. I don't even want to imagine what he's been through." Knight clicked his tongue and patted my back as I tried to push down the agony and horror I was feeling.

I had killed Trig. I didn't mean to! I didn't fucking mean to I just needed him to be quiet!

The plane took off and another hand was on my shoulder. "It's okay, Otter. We'll drug you up good and get Sid to look at those wounds," Knight reassured.

"Trig… Trig's dead," I stammered. I felt him try and put his hand in mine but it was shaking too hard. "Nico's dead, fucking… all of them are dead."

To my surprise, the half-chimera, a man with short black hair and royal blue eyes, gave me a sympathetic smile. "Nico's alive. It was Caligula who figured out the code you left. Smart thinking, Mother is quite mad at herself for not figuring it out sooner."

Nico's alive? Someone got out alive besides me?

Caligula came for Nico.

The rest of the plane ride I sat beside Knight, too stunned to say anything more than a few simple sentences. They asked me where I was shot; they asked me where Kerres was. I answered them as best as I could but the gears in my mind seemed to have rusted. I was tired and defeated. I should be jumping up and down but instead I felt a pit in my gut that I couldn't shake, no matter how many times I reminded myself that I was safe.

I was safe and I was going to be back in Garrett's arms soon.

I hadn't even realized I had passed out, actually I don't even know if I had actually passed out. All my mind decided to make me aware of was that I was now in a small room with light blue walls, lying on a hospital bed with many beeping things around me.

I was warm… I was on strong opiates from the feel of it and…

My heart gave a jolt.

There he was.

Garrett was sleeping. His head resting in his arms which were crossed on my bed, a leather chair pulled up close to where they had laid me. He was sound asleep, with his usual slicked back hair messed up and his once smiling face troubled and creased. My fiancé looked tired… but we were all tired.

I was tired.

I reached out my hand and touched his stiff gelled hair. My hand was wrapped in a clean bandage, and as my body shifted in the hospital bed, I could feel many other places wrapped too.

So here you are, Reno, you've been rescued, you're back with the chimeras. Why don't you feel relieved? Why don't you feel ecstatically happy like you thought you would?

Because I killed Trig, because Garrett stopped looking for me. Because I was just a mortal human engaged to an immortal chimera and no matter what… I was just another person to him. Someone who he would see live and die, then eventually get over.

I felt nauseas… and I hated myself for it. I should be happy but instead I just felt numb, sad and numb.

The tears started to come again. My mind just wanted to dissolve, to… disappear completely. This place wasn't offering me the calm, warm blanket I had so sorely needed. I felt homesick and sad. Stuck here with people I didn't know, when my friends were in the greywastes so far out of reach. I bet they didn't even know what had happened to me.

Garrett stirred and I withdrew my hand. I couldn't take my eyes off of my fiancé in that moment, though the love I felt for him was mixed in with my confusion.

He lifted his head and I saw those light green eyes widen with shock. He pursed his lips and gave me a smile, heavy with sadness.

"You look beautiful," Garrett said to me. "Are… are you in any pain?"

I shook my head; my mouth turning to liquid, unable to form even the simplest of words.

Garrett's face softened, but he looked like he was on the edge of tears. My instincts told me to comfort him, but I was the one in need of comfort.

"We had Sidonius sew you up. You're in my medical wing… you're home, lutra." His face crumpled as he said this, but he managed to hold back the tears I could see brimming in his eyes. "I finally have you home."

This was my home? I had no home – I was a greywaster without a block, just a stupid mortal idiot who would end up being nothing but a blink of an eye to Garrett.

Maybe I was just nothing then…

No.

I was a murderer… I had that going for me. Sure, I had killed before, but never someone innocent. Never a little cicaro who held onto the hope, until the very end, that his heartless, sadistic chimera of an owner would come for him.

And he did.

My chimera never did – but Ares came for his toy.

"Knight told me that you know Nico is alive. We got most of our information out of him, so don't worry… no one will pester us. I have sent them all away. We stopped the internal bleeding and we have the best antibiotics for you and - and…" Garrett was looking more and more anxious with every word he said. I saw him clench the sheets underneath his hand before he stopped speaking altogether. He took a moment to gather himself and managed to press on. "And… I brought up a wheelchair for you. Can I take you down to our apartment? I'd just… like you to be safe and home."

I looked at him and he stared back at me. He looked so tired, so defeated, but relieved. I could understand the first two but the third…

"I want to go," I whispered to him.

My fiancé smiled back and rubbed my hand. "Okay, let's go home."

I shook my head and pulled my hand away. "No, I–want–to–go–home. I want to go to where Reaver is."

Only the steady beeping of the machines around me broke the thick silence that fell on the room. They were our metronome, our only signal that time was still passing by; that time didn't stop the moment Garrett realized what I was saying.

"Lutra..."

"My name is Reno," I whispered to him. I started to try and get up off of the bed. "Reno Nevada from Aras, and I want to go home – Find Elish and tell him I want him to bring me to Reaver."

"But... why?" he choked. Garrett stepped back as I put my feet onto the floor. He didn't stop me either when I started unplugging myself from these machines.

Why? Because I spent a long time being locked up by terrorists and in the end it was the Morse code I gave that led them to find me. Garrett had stopped looking for me weeks ago, not a single media announcement, no negotiations, nothing. Garrett had resigned me to my fate.

Chimera love.

I stood up and tried to take my first step, but with a teeth-clenching cry of pain, I sunk to the ground. Garrett put his hand on my shoulder, but for some reason the moment he touched me my mind flared with anger.

I shoved him away and felt the area behind my nose burn. "Don't fucking touch me!" I screamed at him. I tried to crawl my way towards the wheelchair he had waiting for me.

"You... you're sick, love. Please, let me help you get up. You're just exhausted," he said hurriedly. Garrett ran over and grabbed the wheelchair, his hands trembling so much they rattled the steel arm handles of the chair.

I glared at him, pursing my lips tight to hold back the meltdown I knew was coming. My eyes stung, my body ached. Why was I here? Why did I even fucking exist if I didn't belong anywhere?

"No!" I screamed again when he tried to help me up. "Just get out of here, just fucking..." I tried to rise to my feet but I collapsed again; this time my head hit the floor. I saw stars and a bright aura-like haze in my vision. I groaned, but the next time he grabbed me I had no strength to pull him off.

"What's going on?" an unfamiliar voice sounded. "Why is he on the floor?"

A numbness came to my body, flowing up my fingers before sweeping through my battered and bruised frame. When it found my head it coated it with a heavy shadow, and with that, I passed out again.

I woke up with Garrett's familiar smell around me. The smell of his skyscraper apartment, on the highest level with the grass and flowers on the roof. A place where I had once felt safe and comfortable, a place I had spent with my fiancé.

My eyes blurred as I opened them, and I realized as I tried to focus them that something had woken me up. Two voices I knew very well. One cold and calm; the other in absolute agony.

Though I still felt the cold hollowness inside of me, I was still human. I had never heard Garrett this upset before.

"Why would he want to go to the greywastes?" Garrett cried. I heard the tinkling sound of a glass. "He was so cold… he screamed at me not to touch him."

Then Elish's frozen tones, still a ribbon of tranquility, such an odd contrast against Garrett's voice. "We have no idea what he went through in those sewers. I think you ask too much of him."

"No, it wasn't just that… he hates me. I saw it in his eyes."

"I have seen worse hatred in Jade's eyes and he loves me all the same," Elish replied.

"Jade's a chimera."

"And Reno is a greywaster whose best friend is a chimera. Yes, he is a cheerful one but, brother, you are expecting too much from him. If he leapt into your arms and sobbed from happiness I would be more alarmed by that."

"You don't understand…" I could hear a fresh flow of tears take Garrett. His voice choked as he continued to speak. "I think he hates me."

"The boy is traumatized. Trig died in his arms. Sid says he was raped and he was obviously terrorized and in a constant state of fear. Really, Garrett, get a hold of yourself. You are a chimera and you must start acting like it."

"He hates me, Elish."

"Give him time." There was another pause. "I must take my leave; I have a meeting with Ares and Siris now. King Silas has granted you your several weeks off. Apollo is more than happy to take over your duties."

"I really love him, Elish." Garrett's voice broke again and I heard a sniff.

I stared at the muted TV, Elish and Garrett behind me where

Garrett's bar was. His words reached my heart but I was too confused to know what to make of them. The Reno I was when I came here would have held him and loved him but… I just…

I don't know. I don't know anything. My friends were supposed to tell me how to feel about things, I didn't know what I was doing. I just knew I was cold, tired. I just knew I felt uncomfortable in this place.

No, I felt uncomfortable in my own skin. I felt uncomfortable with my life. And the life that I was okay with didn't exist anymore. It was gone and… and this was where I ended up.

I didn't hear Elish's reply, only the door closing and Garrett sniffing behind the bar.

My own eyes burned, and like the chimera hearing that I had come to rely on so often with Reaver, Garrett heard.

"Lu- Reno?" Garrett whispered. He kneeled down in front of me and gave me a small smile. "Do… you want me to leave you alone?"

"No," I whispered. I winced as I tried to sit up. Garrett set his glass of brown liquor on the table and helped me sit up on the couch. "I'm sorry about earlier… I–"

"No, no, don't apologize. I know this is a lot on your poor little mind."

I gave him a weak smile. "It's not little, asshole."

My fiancé stared at me for a moment, before, with another whimper, he started to choke up. I made a sympathetic noise and pulled his hand. He sat beside me and when he put an arm on my shoulder and drew me in, I didn't protest.

"I'm sorry, we will find all of them, I promise. You will have front row seats to me personally killing the remaining ones in Stadium. This will never happen again, that I will promise." I felt him kiss my forehead. "Oh, my Reno. I will spend the rest of my life making this up to you. I'll buy you whatever you want; we will do whatever you like."

I sighed, hearing more behind those words than I wished I had heard. My fiancé thinks that gifts and vacations will make me happy. When really all I wanted was my life back in Aras.

With Reaver, with Tinky…

Reaver would've come and got me. Reaver would've found a way to get me out of that sewer, like Ares had found Trig.

My eyes burned.

I wanted to go home.

Garrett brushed my now silver and black hair and tucked it behind my ears. "I was so worried about you. What a smart boy you were for using that Morse code. I will never forgive myself for not seeing it. None of us did. We will make our own codes from now on. Though, of course, this will never happen again." He kissed my forehead. "My brave little Reno."

He's speaking to me like I've heard Reaver talk to Killian. I was his Killian and he was my Reaver. But Reaver would've…

I pushed the thoughts from my mind. It wasn't doing me any good. I had to be present, where I was now. No matter how much my mind was in the greywastes.

Garrett brought my hand up to his lips and kissed it. "I bought you all your favourite drugs, amor meus, and I shall purchase you a pet, and we will buy twice as many games as Elish has purchased for Jade. We will–"

"Why do you think that buying me shit will make all of this better?" I said to him in a dead voice.

My fiancé paused, his mouth open, ready to promise me the world. He closed it and looked at me with those emotional green eyes. "I, ah… well, I just want to make you happy."

"I lived off of half-rancid meat and two hundred-year-old candy for twenty-two years, Garrett. Material shit doesn't make me happy. I don't care about that stuff so stop… stop assuming you can buy me presents to make this okay. This isn't okay."

"What isn't okay? Tell me." Garrett rubbed my hands in his but all I could do was shake my head. I didn't want to break his heart; I didn't want to be an asshole to him. I just… I don't know.

"Would you like to speak to Elish? You know he is our councillor, and he also acts as our therapist too since Mantis took his leave. He may be able to help you… with what you have gone through. I can be there for support if you wish or you can go alone." His voice was so supportive. I felt my lips press and my head nod. Maybe that was what I needed.

"Is there anyone besides Elish? He's a bit of a dick."

Garrett laughed at that comment and I felt his lips press against my cheek. "Oh, lovely boy, I know Elish is cold but he is very intelligent and he will listen to you. We will bother him once he returns. He's going to Kreig soon to fetch Jade and the information he sent your friends to find."

My head rose from Garrett's shoulder. "What then? Did he say? Is he going to take Reaver and Killian back to the apartments?" Could I see them?

Garrett nodded with a smile. "Yes, that's what he says. Apparently our dark chimera murdered Tim Dekker, Kessler and Tiberius's chimera son. They had to flee Kreig because Jack, well, I told you Jack's job. They had to run to a town on the outskirts and Elish lost contact. He's gathering that once Kessler and Jack left that they took shelter back in the labs or several surrounding towns. Either way, Jade's tracker will alert Elish as to where. Once they're in the greyrifts I would love for my little Otter to see them."

See them… I wanted to be *with them…*

Garrett continued. "Once you're healed we will both visit them. I met Reaver for a–"

"You saw Reaver?" My mouth dropped open; a shot of adrenaline went through me.

Suddenly I started to feel almost alive again. Just the mention of my friend seemed to bring the colours back into my memories. I hadn't seen Reaver alive since the deacon ripped his throat out. The last I saw of Killian he was being dropped off in the greyrifts apartment. Everything back then was so chaotic, so grisly. "How is he? How's Killian?"

My fiancé smiled at me, he leaned over and handed me a small baggy. I think it was opiate powder. Well, at least he knew what I liked. "They were just as anxious to know how you were doing. Reaver a little less polite about it of course."

Of course.

"They looked well, both of them. They were more worried about you; they knew you had been kidnapped. They are fine, lutra, do not worry about them. Just concentrate on your own recovery." He gave me a metal sniffer. "There, this will help your heart. It is about to hammer out of your chest."

I wanted to see them. I wanted to see Reaver and Killian. They were the ones who needed to be worried about… not me.

Well, maybe me a bit. I sighed and closed my eyes for a moment, before picking up the sniffer and sticking it right into the bag. I inhaled some powder into each nostril and rubbed my nose.

Garrett put his arms around me and rested his head against the side of mine. I heard him give out a long, drawn-out sigh before he kissed my ear.

"I love you… so much do I love you."

Will you love me when I tell you I killed Trig? Or when I tell you that I might not be coming home with you when I am finally reunited with Reaver and Killian? Will you love me if this vision for us that you'd been imagining for years, turns out to not be all you had thought it would be?

"I know," I said instead, and accepted another kiss to my ear. I may not know what the future brought, but I did know what I felt in my heart. "I love you, Garrett."

CHAPTER 30

Reaver

NERO HAD A CIGARETTE IN HIS MOUTH WHEN THEY pulled me off of the plane. I was chained, shackled and gagged. They had to do all of these things because every bit of freedom they gave my body I exploited. I twisted, writhed, snapped, and yelled when they took me out of the military base. I even took up screaming at the top of my lungs in a fleeting hope that a chimera might hear me.

A chimera so they could tell Elish they'd captured me. So that fucker could get his blond ass down to this fucking mansion and take me back to where I belonged. Unless Theo said something, that stupid fuck wouldn't even know I was down here.

The brute chimera's face split into a grin when he saw me; his teeth a vice against the shredded filter of the cigarette. He looked pleased with himself.

Kessler pushed me out of the plane. I stumbled, and because my legs were shackled, I fell onto the greywaste ground. A large mansion was in front of me, surrounded by fence and barbed wire.

I inhaled a sharp breath and smelled the damp dirt. It must've rained recently; I could smell the rain on the dirt and the parking lot in front of me.

I missed that smell.

"There you go. Do whatever the fuck you want to him. Just make sure you wipe that fucking smirk off of his face." I felt Kessler put his cigarette out on my shoulder, but I didn't flinch. "I want to know where Perish is."

"I want that little blond twink too," I heard Nero say.

I saw the cigarette fall to the ground; it bounced once, smoke still trailing from its crushed body.

"Clig says that's not Killian. We don't know who he is and he's a mute. He ain't talking," Kessler replied.

Shit… Nero might've forgotten what Killian looked like but Caligula hadn't. He was right there for the prisoner switch; he had seen Killian plain as day.

"Well, kill him and fucking find me the blond shit. I want both of them!" Nero grabbed me by the chains around my neck and pulled me to my feet. I growled but remained still.

"No, I don't care where he stashed Killian, I just want Perish. Soften him up for me, I'll be back for him in two weeks," Kessler said. I heard the scraping of boots, and with no more exchanges the sliding door of the Falconer closed.

There was a low chuckle behind me, then Nero rattled my neck as we both watched the Falconer take off into the steely-grey sky. "There he goes, the only other man who knows you're here. You're mine now, hunny-bunny. You're all fucking mine."

Suddenly I heard the sound of a Taser, that ear-itching electrical snap. I clenched my teeth and braced myself for it.

My whole body tensed and my legs froze in place. I stumbled as my body got thrown out of whack and found myself back to smelling pavement.

Then half-lucid darkness, spasming muscles, and jolt after jolt of pain. My body was being dragged across the ground, then I hit pavement, followed by carpet, and then finally: a bedroom.

Back and forth. Back and forth. Back and forth.

I was shredding my wrists, they stung and I encouraged every chafe, every throbbing wave of pain. They could cause me as much discomfort in the world; I would welcome every painful percussion that the synapses in my brain decided to grant me.

Back and forth. One twist, two twist… red twist, blue twist.

I was naked, completely naked and chained to a bed. The bed frame was iron rung which held my cuffs, a single pair that were on a thick chain that looped behind me. I could move my cuffs back and forth. The sound was like a saw slowly going through a tree. Back and forth, back and forth, and one twist, two twist.

Blood dripped down my wrists, both of them. I had twisted them back and forth for so long I could see my tendons pop out every time I clenched my fists; they were bulging like worms trying to escape from something rotten. It had always been about the worms. My flesh may not rot but for some reason they always found me. I think I had my boyfriend to thank for that.

My eyes swept the room, going over the black furniture. The dressers, the credenza and chairs, all of these things in the shadows. The only thing lighting this room were candles; over a hundred fucking candles. They made this whole room uncomfortable; I didn't like the light and I didn't like the flickers of panic I was getting in my chest. Panic that warned me of realities that I was in no way prepared to process right now.

I twisted my body back and forth, the wet from the cuffs doing little to help me slip out of them. They were on tight and they were strong, the chains twice as thick as the cuffs the enforcers had back in Aras. I had tried, tried and tried but I couldn't slip out of them.

But that didn't stop me from continuing to try. I took a deep breath and pulled as hard as I could on the cuff. My hand was white and pasty; the fingertips going blue from all the trauma I had been putting them through.

Nothing.

They can't kill you, Reaver. Just remember that. They can't kill you.

My eyes shot to the door as I heard the latch unlock. To my surprise, a growl vibrated the back of my throat. Never in my life had I made a noise like that, I had only heard it from Jade.

To further the confirmation of my current mental state, I shifted my body back on the bed until my naked back was being stung by the cold iron. Like a caged animal as soon as its abuser came into view.

When I saw Nero I lunged, my wrists snapping back with a ripping pain that I paid no attention to. I growled and tried to stare him down, locking my eyes with his as he shut the door behind him and beheld me with a smile.

"You're not doing yourself any favours, sweetcakes. I love them biting. I love them thrashing." Nero's face split into a grin and he started to walk towards me. I refused to move, though I wanted to back away from him as far as I could. "I love them cumming as I split them in half."

I chuckled and shook my head, trying not to recoil when he reached over and ran a finger down my shoulder and arm. "You can bluff as much as you want. Your master would boil you alive if you fucked me. Don't make me laugh. He wants me a bottom-virgin and you know that as much as I do."

I smirked at Nero and stayed steeled in my position as his finger traced down my side to my groin.

I let out a grunt when he roughly grabbed my balls. I gritted my teeth together with such force I heard a crack go through the back one. My mind was screaming in the pain but I held it back.

"Silas doesn't even know you're here, baby. You think Kess is gonna let him bring you to Skyfall so he can crown you? Please. You're all mine." He squeezed my balls tighter, and with that, a cry of pain escaped my lips. I swore, my body frozen and rigid.

"No one knows you're here. You're all mine, bro-bro. All mine."

They can't kill me.

A gasp of relief came from my lips as he released my balls from his hand. "You can't hide me forever. And the moment I see him, I'll be sure to mention that I am no longer–"

Nero raised his fist and punched me right in the gut, knocking the wind out of me. I took in a gasp before feeling my wrists snap back as I automatically tried to grab my stomach.

Nero chuckled; he brought a hand up to my face. When he withdrew it I could see it coated in gleaming blood. My nose had started to bleed.

He brought it up to his mouth and licked it. "I remember the first time I saw you. Hot as shit with that cigarette in your mouth, looking like such the little hard ass."

Nero leaned over to kiss my neck. I took that opportunity and sunk my teeth into the side of his neck. I bit down and hard.

To my shock, he didn't even flinch. As I bit his flesh, slowly pressing my teeth through his neck like I was biting bread… he continued to calmly speak.

"I wondered to myself: What does his face look like while he's getting fucked?"

I pulled the chunk of flesh away, watching the last string of skin stretch before snapping back to the rest of his body. I held the piece of neck in my mouth and watched him.

Nero's smile widened, blood running down in thick bands onto the white bedspread underneath my body. Not once did Nero Dekker wince or show any sign that he was in pain. He only stared, with a hunger on him that made the panic in my gut grow.

"I bet he's just a big badass on the surface… but the moment I put my cock inside of him, he's going to just melt in my hand."

I glared at him, his flesh dangling from my lips.

"Are you gonna eat that or not?" Nero smirked and got on his hands and knees. He leaned down until we were face-to-face and took his own flesh into his mouth.

He ripped it out of my teeth, and a moment later, it disappeared down his throat.

"You have no idea what a sick fuck I am, Reaver. You have no idea what I am going to do to you." He licked his bloodstained lips and put a hand on my cheek.

I was too angry to move. I continued to glare at him as he stroked my cheek; his face only inches away from mine.

"You are going to die many times, my friend," I whispered to him. "And many more after I am king."

"I fuck kings." Nero pressed his lips against mine, his weight making my body fall back on to the bed. Immediately I opened my mouth to bite him.

Like he was waiting for it, I felt something wedge between my teeth. I tried to spit it out but he shoved it so far back into my molars I couldn't move my jaw.

Nero chuckled and freely licked my lips with his tongue. "I always liked it when they had sharp teeth. Oh, you should see my body after Sanguine gets finished with me, last time it took me a week to recover."

The brute chimera slipped a hand onto my stomach, before to my surprise, he glanced behind him.

"Tie his legs back."

I saw a black-haired boy behind him, doing his best to avoid eye contact with me. His hands were shaking and he looked scared. I wonder how many times he had been torn in half by Nero.

I heard the shifting of chains, but when the boy touched my leg I tensed it back and delivered him a kick right to his chest.

With a scream, the boy fell backwards, skidding on the floor and taking a good amount of the area rug with him. Nero laughed at this before snapping his head away from me as I lunged to take another chunk out of him. I could hear the boy whimpering on the floor.

Nero let out a barking laugh. "Get back up, you whiny little shit. I said fuckin' chain him!"

The kid got up again, rubbing his chest which was already forming the red outline of a welt. He sniffed and grabbed the chains again.

This time Nero grabbed my leg. I already had a thick iron ring around both of my ankles. Without effort, no matter how much I twisted and kicked, the brute chimera held my leg as the boy clicked the chains to it. With a slew of spat curses and oaths that I would one day fulfil, he chained my other leg back.

Okay, Reaver, what now? How are you going to handle this? How are you going to stop what he has every intention of doing?

No, he won't do shit to me. Silas wants me pure and clean for him. He was intently interested back in Aras about the extent of my sexual exploits. He wanted my first time taking it to be with him. No fucking way he would let Nero take that prize from him.

The chimera held out his hand and immediately the black-haired boy gave him a cigar, before, with a struggle, the boy managed to flick the flint of the lighter. He lit the cigar for Nero and quickly walked back into the shadows of the room.

Nero took an inhale of the cigar and removed his shirt. He lay down beside me, though all I could see was his frame in the corner of my vision. I was still staring forward, freezing my body in its state, not allowing my brain to shift a single muscle out of place.

I am a chimera. I am a clone of King Silas. I am the Reaper; I am better than all of them.

A plume of sour-smelling smoke reached my nostrils. He blew it up and down my body before dashing the ashes on my chest.

Nero put a finger on my stomach and traced a circle, but I didn't move. I stayed still, even when he started rubbing the cigar ash into my chest. He wasn't speaking and neither was I. Not even the boy in the shadows breathed a breath out of place.

Another suck of the cigar, then I heard a hand start to fumble with his belt. Nero removed his pants and I heard them fall to the floor. The faint smell of cologne mixed itself in with the cigar smoke filled the room, and the blood from both of our fresh wounds.

"You know what to do," he said to the boy.

My own restraint surprised even me when he brushed a taunting finger over my dick. He picked it up and chuckled to himself. "They even spliced the cut-gene into you, eh? Perhaps Lycos knew just how much fun we have chewing off that foreskin." Nero's finger traced down even lower, and to my surprise, I heard the chains tighten.

My leg rose and the chain on my knees made it bend back, exposing myself to him.

When I felt his finger push against my hole, I completely lost my mind.

Every ounce of hastily gathered restraint snapped and crumbled as he put pressure on his finger. My cold countenance and steeled self-control was lost as a rage inside of me erupted that I was in no state to control. No pursed lips or clenched fists could win me back my sanity. They had left me the moment his finger confirmed his intentions.

Nero laughed, and as I bellowed out a loud threat, he pushed the digit inside of me.

My jaw set and I tried to thrash my legs, but with another jingling of chains, my binds became tight. The boy in the shadows was controlling my body like a puppet. This wasn't just an ordinary fucking bedroom; this was some sort of fucked up sex dungeon.

And I was stuck here.

Nero moved his finger in and out of me with a low chuckle, before I felt the pressure of a second one enter me.

"Such a tight little bitch," he purred, "and here you are just wrapped up and hand-delivered." He put a hand on my other leg and pushed it back. I saw his two fingers moving in and out of my ass.

Then my eyes fell lower, past his fingers to his own rock-hard cock. Thick and long like all chimeras, rigid and holding a drip of precum on the tip. I looked away from it, my jaw tight and my eyes a blaze of anger. My mind racing at what I was supposed to do, if there was anything I could do to get out of this.

There were limited options inside of my head and most of them I quickly dismissed. I was a greywaster, a chimera, and an immortal. And because of that–

Nero positioned himself over me; he put a hand on my chin and made me face him.

I will not beg.

Nero chuckled and shook my chin, trying to get me to look at him but I refused eye contact. I smelled lube, I smelled blood… I smelled him.

I will not cry.

An ear-splitting scream rose unbidden from my throat as an overwhelming pain and pressure shot and pulverised every single one of my senses. At my display, Nero Dekker laughed and pushed himself further inside of me; fully penetrating me.

I will not beg.

I will not fucking…

… fucking cry.

I am

I am a chi-

Another scream. Nero roughly ripped himself out of me, only to plunge himself back into my ass. My teeth gritted and ground roughly against one another; my hands clenching so hard my fingernails broke and sunk into my skin.

No, no, no… why aren't you obeying your master, you fucking son of a bitch. Silas will kill you… you fucking piece of shit. Fuck – fuck – FUCK!

My chest convulsed, my body contorted and twisted in my binds as I thrashed like an animal. I was unaware of my movements or what I was trying to do. All I could feel was the blinding pain as he drove himself in and out of me, and the madness that it brought to my body and mind.

I was thrashing, yanking, and pulling my bound arms as I tried to hit him. Shifting my body away from him to try and get relief from the intense pressure and pain between my legs. But Nero had me pinned and he had my arms chained. No matter how hard I pulled or moved I remained in the same spot, stuck underneath this brute chimera as he skewered me like a fucking animal.

Nero was laughing; he had never stopped laughing. He had a hand on my forehead, pressing down to escape my gnashing and snapping teeth. His other hand was holding back my leg, pushing it back so I had full view of him ramming his bloodied dick in and out of me.

Shit… I was bleeding, look how bad I'm bleeding. In my madness I had to stop and stare at it roughly being drive into me, glistening and glassy with my own blood. It was all over me, seeping out of my backside, sticking to my inner thighs and his pubic hair.

"All virgins bleed," Nero's voice whispered in my ear, deliberately he pushed my knee up higher as if wanting me to see every bit of what he was doing. "Whether it be a tight little cicaro whose voice is still cracking, or a twenty-year-old chimera too manly to let his little boytoy fuck him. They all bleed the same."

I had no words; I was in no state to form them. All I could do was attempt to breathe, attempt to force myself through the pain and shock.

Nero's mouth rose in a smirk; he grabbed onto his cock and positioned himself to re-enter me. With a wry grin he got the angle, and as he broke his cock back in, I stifled a scream.

To my further horror, he leaned into me and locked my lips with his, his purple-blue eyes closing and his hand clenching around the side of my head.

I opened my mouth to take him in and indulged him until the right moment presented itself.

As soon as I felt the flesh of his lips, I bit down and sunk my teeth into his bottom lip.

But Nero didn't stop. I swore angrily, my own inner thoughts more desperate than I wanted to admit. He didn't even flinch, I thought I could even feel him pull my mouth closer to his lips as I chewed and ripped at them.

It fuelled him, it only fuelled him. As the blood spilled into my mouth he started to ride me harder, pushing himself in and out of me with long jabbing thrusts, made easier for him by the influx of blood spilling from my body. I chewed and ripped more, if only to ease my own pain as he mercilessly fucked me.

Nero pulled away with a rough, gritted moan. I opened my mouth to try and get breath and looked up at the damage I had done.

His lower lip had been almost completely chewed off. It dangled from his face and dripped red onto the white sheets underneath us. He was completely unphased; he only looked at me with a fresh hunger.

Nero rested his forehead onto mine and his remaining lips pulled into a smile, his minty breath hot against my now blood-covered face. He kept his face there, away from my teeth but still dangling over me like a baited hook tempting a shark.

I closed my eyes and tried to focus on my own breathing. I tried to count my breaths but each breath seemed to be perfectly synced with his thrusts. In the end that was all I was counting, each thrust of his cock inside of me, followed by each spring of agonizing pain as he ripped me inside and out.

The blood churned in my veins, heated to the point of boiling. I felt like a beast trapped in his own skin, unable to break free and escape from the horrors and madness that were happening all around me. How did I let it get to this? The question to which I had no answer for.

Was this what my dads had wanted for me?

"Pretty little bitch," Nero groaned. I felt his words vibrate against my ear but I didn't open my eyes. The smell of blood was so thick in the air and on his body, I could almost see his outline through my closed eyelids. I knew his head was bowed and I knew he had my knees so far back my ass was off of the ground. He was thrusting himself in and out of me without pause, fucking me hard with the same stamina I had once admired in Donnely.

Karmic justice, you fucking bitch. You laughed when Perish got raped now look at you.

My jaw ached from clenching it so hard; I kept trying to count his breaths… no, my breaths… no, I was counting his thrusts.

One, two, three, four –

I screamed again, for no new reason other than my own manic

frustration. I once again thrashed and tried to pull him off of me, but with a snap and a painful jolt in my wrists, the beast inside of me was reminded that he was chained. I didn't care though. I couldn't let this happen.

I couldn't let this happen.

"Let me go!" I suddenly shrieked. I bellowed so loudly my vocal cords broke under the strain. I drew my knee back to try and kick him but it was tight and bound in its prison. So instead I twisted and contorted my own body to try and get him out of me, anything to unjoin our bodies. This wasn't fucking right… this wasn't fucking right.

"What was that? Scream louder, Reaver," Nero hissed before I heard the popped sound of him breaking the seal on his lit cigar. I smelled the sour smoke again before he gave his hips several hard thrusts.

"Fucking let me go! SILAS WILL FUCKING KILL YOU FOR THIS!" I screamed in my own delirium. I balled my fists and thrusted them down, trying to fit my hand through the cuffs.

My mind was leaving me. I screamed a third time and tried with all of my strength to hit him.

But Nero only moaned; he put his face just out of the reach of my teeth and started to fuck me harder.

"Yeah, what will he do, baby? Tell me again," Nero purred.

"I'll fucking murder you! And you will fucking stay dead!" I screamed. I clenched my teeth and let my head drop onto the back of the bed. My chest crackled, the fire inside of me burned like an inferno. It seared every lucid, sane memory I had in my head. I felt like I was going to go crazy. I had to escape; I had to get out from under him.

The pressure in my head grew, boiling my brain inside of its shell. It felt like my ears were going to burst from the blood that was roaring behind my eyes. I had to do something. I had to do something.

He sped up and drove himself roughly into me; one hard painful jab after another. He was moaning loudly, his voice mixing itself in with the roaring inside of my head. It was all one continuous flow of sensations; one baseless and formless pressure inside of my mind, pressing and pressing waiting for that final snap.

Then flesh, I could smell his flesh. I didn't even need to open my eyes; I could smell and feel the warmth of his neck near my mouth. Like a leech to heat, a wolf to a fresh kill, I opened my mouth and clamped down on his neck.

Nero cried out and his thrusts increased, but a moment later, he pulled away.

I looked up at him, at two neck wounds now dripping cruor onto the bloodied sheets. In response, Nero looked back down at me, his face sweaty and clammy.

I thrashed my head as he lowered his mouth onto my neck. I swore and tried to pull him off of me as I felt his teeth against my windpipe. Then, when he bit down and broke my own flesh, I opened my mouth to holler again – but the air got sucked from my throat.

I could hear rough breathing through his nose, stifled moans as he started to fuck me harder, his hips slamming against me in a sporadic pace that told me he was orgasming.

His teeth tightened, my windpipe pinched and was sealed. I gasped, hearing a high-pitched wheeze come from my throat as my lungs started to scream for air. My body was thrown into the manic spasm that only came when death was only moments away.

My eyes dimmed, my pounding ears picked up nothing but the moans that spilled through his clenched teeth. I died to him cumming inside of me, and he came to me dying.

A blue ember pierced the sea of shadows that swirled around my vision. I watched it as it rose to his mouth, before brightening. A moment later, with a puff of silver smoke, he lowered it.

My eyes adjusted, and the light from the candles started to bring form to the shadows around me.

His hand offered me a cigarette. I stared at it.

"Take it," he urged, before moving it towards my mouth. I opened my lips and heard the flick of a lighter.

A small comfort from the throbbing pain that had lay claim to my body. I inhaled the soothing smoke and blew it out of the corner of my mouth.

"Do you do drugs?"

"Heroin."

Nero chuckled; he shifted and leaned against the back of the bed. I saw his thumb raise as he flicked the ash from his own cigarette. "Get him some ciovi, Kiki. Prepped and ready." He looked at me. His now fully healed face losing none of its menace.

"So? Enjoy your first time, brother?" Nero's lips split into a grin.

I had no answer for him, I only stared forward. My backside was raw and bleeding but everything else, every other injury, was gone.

Nero must have been able to read my thoughts. "I fucked you when you were dead; then I fucked you when you started to breathe. You know you moaned when you were breathing? Moaned like a little whore."

My eyes remained fixed, though the rage was starting to bubble under the surface again. I tried to push it down, into that dark void; the one that was overflowing with my own suppressed feelings and emotions.

"Ah, calm down. If you work yourself up into a rage I'll have to pound you back down to earth." I jerked my head away from him as he tried to play with my hair.

The black-haired boy, named Kiki, came back holding in his hand a small tray with what looked like a crack pipe and a lump of white powder.

Nero put the full pipe to my lips and lit his lighter again but I spat it out. He laughed at the gesture and lit the pipe himself.

To my anger, he took an inhale of the smoke before, in a flash, he locked his lips back with mine.

I opened my mouth in an automatic response to snap at him, but in turn he breathed the hot smoke into my mouth before withdrawing. I coughed and hacked, it tasted like pure chemicals.

A warmth started to sweep my body. Nero took another hit beside me before drawing Kiki onto him. With a grunt and a high-pitched gasp from who I assumed was his sengil or cicaro, the boy started to ride him.

I closed my eyes and let my only fleeting comfort ease my body into a false relaxation. It was the only thing I could hold onto, the only sliver of light in this eclipse I had found myself in. A small dose of medicine that my body eagerly devoured.

Kiki moaned with the rhythm, Nero grunted. I took that distraction and tried to find my shattered mind. Though nothing was making sense to me; I had no solid thoughts and no plans. My vision could only see red and my thoughts only the carnage I so badly had to inflict on my captor. My chimera mind and my greywaster mind commanded it. The fiber that knitted who I was demanded nothing short than torture and murder for what Nero had done to me.

For what Nero had taken from me.

Immediately my jaw tightened and I pushed that thought from my head. I was no fucking damsel needing to keep her virginity intact. Fuck those thoughts. It was just… a physical action, it was nothing… nothing besides torture. Nothing else.

Nothing… else.

Kiki giggled and I opened my eyes to see him framing Nero's face in his hands, kissing him on the lips as the brute chimera smirked back at him. An odd couple if you would call it that but they seemed rather happy with each other.

I stared more intently at Kiki, and for the first time I noticed his unnatural orange eyes. He was a chimera, a sengil or a cicaro I wasn't sure. I wouldn't be surprised if he was a plant from Elish. Another lover set to be used as a carrot for Elish to sway a brother. Like he had done to Garrett with Reno, and as he had told me in the greyrift apartment: to Joaquin and his pet Jem.

Then my captor reached a hand over and traced it along my cheek. I didn't move; I didn't bother to snap at him because I knew that's what he was waiting for.

"You wanna taste his dick, Kiki?" Nero's voice turned to a low, sensual purr.

I narrowed my eyes but I still didn't move. I wanted that kid on me; I wanted him close to me.

There was no need to explain why.

Kiki's orange eyes slowly travelled over to me. He bit his lip but laughed when Nero raised his head and licked his ear.

"He'll eat me alive," Kiki said cautiously.

Nero put a hand on Kiki's head and started sucking on his neck. "He can't reach you, puppy. Go on, I'll get you a new ring if you can make him hard," Nero said in a voice dripping honey. I noticed then that Kiki had several silver rings on his fingers, including one that looked like a raccoon. "Go on, do it."

Yeah, come a little closer Kiki.

The boy gave me a cautious eye. I gave him a look back that could melt steel. He cautiously took my dick into my hands and started to stroke the flaccid organ up and down. I saw that his hands were shaking.

The drug Nero had given me had soothed the live wires that he had frayed the first time he'd fucked me. I tried to force my body to relax, and with my self-control, resisted the urge to snap at the young chimera. Though if I wanted to get him to do what I wanted, I couldn't give in that easily.

I mock advanced towards the boy, and sure enough, to prove just how frightened he was of me, Kiki recoiled back with a sharp gasp.

My ears rang as Nero dealt me a punch to the head. I swore and saw white followed by a sick haze that dripped down my eyesight like plasma.

I decided to play to it; I let the white noise take my head. As I let my head drop, I submitted my body to the boy's roaming tongue.

And it roamed. Nero separated my legs, the chains slacked, only his own strength holding my knees back. I felt a heaviness in my groin and a burning pleasure that made my throat go dry. The warm tongue travelled up and down my shaft before, with a murmured command by Nero, he put his mouth over it.

I growled, and with that, I got dealt another blow, this time to my cheek. My mouth immediately started to fill with blood; I let it drip down my chin and onto my chest.

The white noise came back; not only illuminating my vision in a thousand sunbursts but filling my ears with the same roaring that had taken me during my first round with Nero. However this time it was mixed in with the intense feeling of pleasure centered between my legs.

Nero talked to him and I felt a cold air hit my hard cock, then another mouth. Nero was sucking me off now. I opened my eyes to see them both passing off my dick between them like they were sharing a popsicle.

"Go on… get on top of him," Nero urged. Kiki's tongue lapped the head of my cock, now fully hard in his mouth.

I closed my eyes and clenched my jaw, trying to push the image of my boyfriend far away from my head. I wasn't thinking about him on purpose; I was making a point to exile his face from my mind.

He would understand, and that was all I needed to justify what was about to happen.

Nero put his hand on my jaw; I felt his grip tighten as Kiki got on top of me. For good reason, my teeth were grinding together.

Nero nipped my ear and growled into it. "If you behave yourself, I'll let you cum in his ass. You want that, sweet cakes? I sure do want to see what you look like when you cum. I bet you make the cutest faces."

Unable to control myself, my head snapped to the side and I tried to bite him, channelling Jade my feral brother. But, of course, Nero was waiting for me. He jerked his head back with a laugh and grabbed my cock.

I closed my eyes and tried to force myself outside of my body as I felt the boy's tensed opening on my cock. I ground my teeth and called the kid every name I could think of as he lowered himself onto me. Breaking my dick into him; he was already full of Nero's cum.

The boy let out a soft moan before he started to ride me.

"Ever have another ass squeeze your cock, Reaver? Or just your little Killian?" Nero taunted. I could smell his breath on my neck, he gave the side a long lick before hissing in my ear. "When I get a hold of that little twink, I'll fuck him until he shudders and dies."

I sucked in a breath but I didn't lash out. I stayed perfectly still as my body responded in ways I didn't want. My dick throbbed and pulsed inside of the kid. It felt good. I fucking hated it, but it felt good.

My body was going numb, the roaring inside of my ears travelling through my blood stream, tensing and coiling my body like I was a snake ready to strike. Every muscle seemed to harden and become like steel, resisting the pleasure that filled me with humiliation and shame.

But there was no time to feel those emotions. It was what it was.

And at that admission I stifled my first moan.

Nero laughed, and at his order Kiki started to ride me harder. Sharp, small moans breaking his lips, steady and in rhythm to his body bouncing on top of me.

I opened my eyes and saw the slight and tawny boy riding me. His hard cock moving up and down as my own sunk into him. He had his body far away from my reach; one arm half-raised to steady himself, the other on his side.

Up and down he moved. Black-haired, orange-eyed little shit. Probably from Tim's generation though a little older.

Nero laughed though it was ragged. I could feel the movement beside me which I knew was him pleasuring himself to the scene unfolding.

"Come on… make him cum, Kiki," Nero growled. "Make him cum."

The boy licked his lips and started doing me harder, like he had probably been trained to do by Nero for fuck knows how long. He knew his work though, every time he slammed his hips down on me I edged closer to my peak.

I closed my eyes and relaxed my body. Only my hands clenching the sheets drew a light on the mental state I was in. I took in a deep breath and let the pleasure overwhelm me.

When I let out another moan, Nero, as he loved to do, laughed at me. He commanded the boy to take me in deeper and he did; Kiki not too far away from cumming himself.

Then the chimera boy let out a loud cry, slammed himself down on me again and again until, like an earthquake rippling through my body, he brought us both to orgasm.

As I came my eyes snapped open, like a predator eyeing his prey they focused on Kiki. His own eyes closed and his mouth open and crying out in ecstasy, cum shooting from his hard cock. Beside me Nero was rapidly stroking himself, quick and rapid moans telling me I had him where I wanted him.

I had never been one to waste an opportunity.

I clenched my fists and pulled on my handcuffs. I used the taut chains as my leverage as I pulled my arms down and moved my body up, shifting me into a sitting position.

With my body I brought the boy into my range, and even better, the jerking of my body threw him off balance. Kiki gasped as he lurched forward, his face coming within inches of my own.

There was a shriek and a flash of blood and skin, I ripped the flesh away and opened his face up from lip to ear. A huge split, one that brought ripples of fat and the gleam of white bone.

Before Nero could pull him off of me I went for the neck next. I sunk my teeth into the soft, white flesh and clamped down as hard as I could.

Nero bellowed and grabbed the shrieking boy, he pulled Kiki away from my teeth but he left a good amount of flesh behind in my jaws.

Blood spilled from the kid's neck, he was shrieking and screaming as Nero pressed a hand against his wound. He turned around and yelled out the door. "Sid! I fucking need Sid!"

Nero shot me a single dangerous look as the blood continued to gush out of his hand, before his attention turned to the door swinging open.

A man with chin length black hair and burgundy eyes burst in; his face paled when he saw Kiki.

"Now, now… hurry!" The door slammed shut as everyone ran out.

I drew the chunk of Kiki's neck further into my mouth and started to chew, slowly and deliberately, enjoying each bite.

Back and forth. Back and forth. Back and forth.

I started twisting my wrists in their shackles, watching the door, waiting for him to come back. The skin had healed when Nero had killed me and my soft, new flesh was thin. My skin broke easily.

Back and forth.

I looked down and saw my own cum, covering my soft dick, and the chimera boy's on my chest before he was ripped off of me. The boy's blood was all over me too, dripping to form small rivers down my stomach and legs.

Back and forth. I chewed the flesh, feeling the tough skin start to get stuck in my teeth. My hands rhythmically twisting back and forth. Watching the door. Watching the door.

Then, after what seemed like a thousand lifetimes, the door flew open. As expected Nero's face was red, his indigo eyes wide and holding the fires of hell inside of them.

It was my turn to chuckle. With my tongue I centered the remaining flesh I had ripped out of Kiki's neck, and spat it at him.

Nero had a knife in his hand but he didn't slash my throat like I expected. Instead he backhanded me hard against my face. My head snapped under the force of the blow and I heard a ping. Immediately blood filled my mouth and I felt several gaps in my teeth.

He hit me again and I saw the walls get sprinkled in my blood.

I coughed and he grabbed my chin, pulling my face up to his.

"Dead yet?" I tried to raise my lips in a smile but my face was paralyzed.

Nero's eyes burned me, violet-blue sapphires that held a small sun in each. "No, no, you little cunt. He's going to be just fine." Another hit but I only felt the force of the blow; I couldn't feel anything in my face but a cold numbness. An overwhelming feeling that crept itself up my nose and centered in my brain. Like growing mould it coated the folds, ravaging and destroying my senses.

Then pain. Real pain.

I screamed before I could even think of stopping myself, immediately tensing my body to struggle to get away from what was happening. Alarms rang in my head but were silenced by the agonizing pain over what Nero was doing.

Nero twisted the knife; it sank deeper inside of my ass. I screamed again, thrashing my wrists as he dug it in, my own struggling movements slicing me further. I swore and tried to force my fucking body to calm down but my instincts were overriding my self-control.

Nero pushed the knife in up to the handle, then, with his own teeth clenched in anger, he ripped it out of me.

I gagged and started choking on my own vomit.

Then the pressure, made even more painful with the huge gouge that was now between my legs. He pushed himself easily into me, the blood and the knife wound giving little resistance.

He fucked me. The rage encapsulating him and giving him a thirst that seemed to bring out a beast I had yet to see in him. The chimera brute at his worst, and me, shackled and chained, on the receiving end.

Nero grabbed my head and slammed it against the iron rungs behind me. Then he grabbed my shoulders and twisted my body so I was face first in the bed. Automatically, as I lay on my stomach, my knees tried to raise my body, and with that, he thrusted himself back into me.

I let out a frustrated scream and grabbed onto the iron rungs, I pulled them towards me before slamming them back against the wall. Doing anything I could to distract myself from the overwhelming pain.

Nero didn't stop and he didn't slow down. Like I had admired in Donnely, Nero had stamina in him that I had never seen before. The brute chimera mercilessly fucked me, every once in a while grabbing my head to slam me into the iron rungs of the bed, usually when he was orgasming.

In that time I was lost to the world, the pain even dissipated as I went into full-body shock. Each blow he delivered to me, every face slam into the iron rungs, every hard thrust was nothing but pressure to me now. As time went on my senses left me, pain in the forefront. The only thing holding me up was my hair clenched firmly in his fist.

When he finally dropped my head I fell onto the bed gasping for breath. My breathing getting short and my heart a rapid and uneven beat.

Nero was gasping too. I felt a weight of his body, then with a shift he laid down beside me on the bed.

I tried to move myself onto my back so I could breathe better. I cringed as I felt his hands firmly grab me so he could help with the move in position. The sheets underneath me seemed to stick to my body.

Then I looked down.

I didn't know what I was seeing at first; my automatic reaction was that he had stabbed me in the gut. But the red swollen mound of flesh, followed by intestine, all of it coming out of my backside, told its own story.

I felt light-headed and nauseas. I gagged on my own vomit and bile as my own rectum lay on the sheets, surrounded by a large stain of blood.

Nero chuckled beside me, I began to feel cold. My body started to shake and then my muscles started to seize and spasm. The white light claimed me not soon after.

CHAPTER 31

Killian

WHERE THERE ONCE WAS LIGHT, THERE WAS NOW dark. Where there had once been dark, there was now nothing. Parts of my mind, once lit up with his shadowed presence had become dormant, like they had never existed in the first place.

My temples throbbed. My head felt like it was slowly filling with blood to the point of bursting. I wanted to scream, tear out my hair and cry but I couldn't. I knew I couldn't.

I knew I had to be strong. Even if knowing and doing were on two opposite ends of my world.

My boyfriend… my raven-haired sentry, my dark chimera, Demon of Indifference, Scourge of the Greywastes.

Reaver Merrik.

My baby.

Perish rubbed my arm, he had barely left my side since I had reached the camp. A half of an energy bar crept into the corner of my vision. "Eat, eat."

I shook my head but he urged the Dek'ko bar into hands. "No, you gotta eat something. Come on. Please?"

We were riding in the back of the cart; I had barely walked in the last several days, mostly because it was so hard. I had ran most of the way to the dirt road and running down it especially had strained my knees and had covered my feet with sores and blisters.

So my crazy scientist had taken to being my nurse. He was glued to my hip now, coaxing me with food and bandaging my feet. Perish never left me alone to the point where it was kind of smothering. But I was too anxious and overcome with worry to tell him to stop. Every part of my mind was pre-occupied with my worry regarding Reaver.

At the mention of his name my heart hurt. My whole chest ached to the point where I was surprised I couldn't see a bruise. I was so worried about him.

Was he in Skyfall now? Was Elish going to get him? Elish must know. He was Silas's councillor and Silas had no idea that Elish was plotting against him. Elish would hear about it and he would rescue my baby.

I turned my gaze to the steep ridges behind us, the part of the mountain that we had already managed to trudge up. Sharp cliff edges, some of which seemed to have been shorn right off of the mountain. Combinations of greys and browns mixed in with thousands of black trees, some so large I didn't think I could wrap my arms around them. These were different trees than the ones we had in Aras, or they looked like it. Their bark was thicker and they clung to the slopes with strong roots that didn't look as dead as ours. It reminded me of how a cat clings to a windowsill as it tries to climb. They even had the same air of desperation.

Everything around our caravan was overwhelmingly large. I had never been up so high, at least not while still keeping my feet on the ground. The surrounding mountains were vast, rolling, and overlapping into each other; just ashy greys getting darker and darker until the haze swallowed them for good.

I craned my neck and peeked past a median only a foot away from our cart. It was a steep drop off and I couldn't see the bottom. I wonder how many cars were down there, desperate families fleeing their burning cities only to speed off the road to their cold crypts below. I wonder how long they were airborne, and further more… if they had any last thoughts.

I wonder what Reaver's last thoughts were when they opened fire on him. Maybe it was of me?

Perish laughed lightly beside me and nudged me with his shoulder. "You're holding it, now you just need to eat it, silly boy."

Oh, right… the energy bar. I raised the Dek'ko bar and took a bite. I chewed the dense, vitamin-filled bar to appease my caretaker, and as my reward Perish patted my arm.

There was a crunching of boots behind me. I managed to give Jade a smile as the yellow-eyed chimera approached our cart. "Want some energy bar? It's blueberry flavour."

Jade took the candy bar from me and chewed off a piece. "If I ever go back to Skyfall I'll get you a real chocolate bar. We have some pretty good bakers in Olympus." He handed the energy bar back and looked behind me where the rest of the slavers were leading the slaves and the bosen. Without Reaver to tell him no Jade had been acting as the new sentry. A job he seemed to have taken to. Perish was more than happy to stay close to me. "We're almost at the summit now, then it's all downhill. Hopper is just–"

There was a crack of gunfire in front of us. My heart leapt into my throat and immediately we all went to grab our guns.

"Killian, stay in the caravan," Perish said hurriedly. But he wasn't Reaver and I wasn't helpless, so I grabbed Reaver's M16 and followed Jade to the front of the caravan.

Hopper was scratching his head and Tabbit was jogging in front of him, his shotgun smoking. All of the other slavers were circling in too.

"What is it?" Jade asked.

Hopper turned around, his brow furrowed.

"Last thing we need, that's what it is. It's a raver and as we know they usually don't venture off alone." The slave captain turned back towards Tabbit. "Go up on that ridge, see if you can spot their den."

A ravers' den? I swallowed down the fear that brought. I hated ravers. I not only had gotten chased by them when my family was on our way to Aras but Reaver had almost gotten killed by them too – or well… whatever temporarily killing an immortal was called.

"What… what happens if there are ravers?" I asked, trying to force down my anxiety. I clutched Reaver's gun to me, feeling my eyes burning. Not because of the ravers though, but because I wanted him here with me so badly.

Elish… get Reaver soon…

"Ah, well there's a resort down a few miles off. We'll have to take a detour to camp there but it'll protect us a hell of a lot better than the rest stop I had planned." Hopper poked the rim of his hat up with the barrel of his gun. "We didn't have any last year, or the year before, but they migrate. It's been a warm winter for mountain weather so maybe they stayed. Not much snow in the Fallocaust but the mountains still get some sprinklings and the ravers hate it."

Perish hissed as I jogged towards the raver but I carried on. Beside me was Jade with Elish's briefcase forever in his hand.

"Wow!" Jade exclaimed, like he was a child seeing a new toy for the first time. Then I remembered this was his first time seeing a raver. "How do they not die just from their injuries?!"

I stopped when I got to the raver. It was a male with half of his jaw gone and yellow, broken teeth showing through his radiation burnt skin. He had stringy brown hair that fell to his neck, completely covering what looked like a half-severed ear.

"The radiation I guess, maybe it's the same reason why so much of our scavenged canned food is still edible. Sestic radiation screws up the bacteria and preserves things." I shrugged. I watched as Jade broke a stick off of a nearby black tree and started poking the dead raver in the arm. I didn't know what was with grown men and having to poke dead things with sticks, Reaver had never been any better.

Jade poked it a little harder before twisting the stick in his arm; I could see bits of flesh start to tear under the pressure. "I guess that's what we're eating tonight. At least if we're stuck in the resort town we won't use up any extra food." Then his eyes travelled up to the sky as they so often did. He let out a sigh.

I knew why he was looking so longingly up at the sky. "Maybe he'll come why we're there…"

Jade nodded and said quietly, "With Reaver. I know the reason he's taking longer… is because he won't come and get us without him."

Immediately my heart gave a pang. I took a slow deep breath to try and stop the tears gathering behind my eyes but Jade wasn't stupid.

The cicaro patted my shoulder. "They can't kill 'em, Killian. Elish will find him; Reaver's too valuable to him."

I sniffed and nodded and we both turned away from the raver.

"Stop making him cry, stupid pet," Perish snapped when he realized I had started to cry again. He went to take my hand, when to my surprise, Jade put his arm out in front of me.

"You stay the fuck away from him." My eyes widened at Jade's tone. I had heard him pissed at Perish before but this seemed harsher. Less little-brother-getting-bullied-by-bigger-brother and more… serious. Since I had come back he had been really short with Perish. "I don't like you sticking around him so much. He's fine."

I blinked as Jade shifted himself in front of me, almost like he was protecting me from Perish. He had been sticking close to me too when he wasn't patrolling but I thought it was just for support.

Perish's eyes blazed; he glared at Jade and I could see his fists clenching. "Watch your mouth, pet."

"Yeah, I'm not a fucking pet. Do you see a master around? I'm a chimera, unlike you, Fallon. So shut the fuck up." My mouth dropped open as Jade said these words. I immediately separated the two of them, feeling the atmosphere around us suddenly become hostile and static.

"Enough! Both of you. We have enough to fucking worry about, stop acting like fucking children!" I snapped. The first tear rolled down my face. "Just get along, alright? Please?" I started to cry again; the empty feeling inside of me growing.

Please… Elish… get him before Silas does. Don't let Silas take him.

Jade put an arm around me, but to my surprise, Perish slapped it away. Instead he took my shoulder and helped me back to the caravan; my feet were starting to ache.

As soon as I got inside the safety of the cart I broke down again. I welcomed Perish's arm around my shoulders, and even more, I welcomed the baggy of Dilaudid powder. I took a good amount into each of my nostrils as the caravan started to move again.

"Killian…" I looked over in surprise, noting Perish's tone had gotten serious. "You need to watch out for Jade. He's been acting kind of weird lately. I think he's been slipping back into his old ways without Elish. When he was in Moros and killed all those people, remember? Be careful around him, okay?"

My eyes shot to Jade who was standing with his arms crossed, watching Tabbit start to skid back down the cliff, a trail of dust following him down.

"What do you mean? He seems fine…" I said.

Perish shook his head. His eyes travelling around the covered caravan, always unable to make eye contact unless he really tried. "While you were away, you know Jimmy's accident? Hopper almost kicked us out. He thinks it's Jade and and…" Perish nervously wrung his hands and took a deep breath. "I am not sure but I think one night he was trying to get me into his bed. He was touching himself outside the blankets but I just pretended to sleep… it was strange I think he wanted us to have sex. Just watch out, okay? Killian… okay?"

I stared at him and felt the air get sucked out of my lungs. I tried to talk but ended up stuttering out a response. "W-what? Jade? He's married to Elish, he–"

Perish hissed at me to drop my voice. "Jade's addicted to sex. Elish and his sex life… well, he's missing it I bet. I know his engineering. He's taking out his frustrations by killing and I… I don't want you alone with him anymore. For your own safteys, be close to me."

I… I couldn't believe it. A thousand thoughts filled my mind followed by a million more fears. I watched the cicaro, now helping Churro drag the raver towards the second caravan.

Jade had told me all his stories. How he had been the Shadow Killer; how he had felt so empty and abandoned when Elish had left him to go back to his life in Moros. He had lashed out; he would kill and then have rough sex with Kerres. Jade had said it was like sharing a smoke after sex, something that just felt right.

Had Jade been falling back into that state of mind? Did Elish's absence bring out the chimera beast that always seemed to be just under his surface?

The prospect made my head flush with nervousness. Perish sensed this and rubbed my hand. "I won't let anything happen to you, sweety."

I nodded and swallowed. "I'll keep an eye on him. I'm sure he's just homesick… he would never try and hurt us. That's just not him."

Perish dragged his teeth over his lower lip and started tensing his hands. "I am sure too. We will both keep an eye out." He looked behind him towards the front of the cart. "The turn off is soon, for the resort town. I guess Tabbit saw more. I'll go check, stay here and rest your feet. I'll change those bandages."

I drew my knees up to my chest and sniffed, then took more of the Dilaudid powder. I watched Jade a bit differently now, hating myself for being wary of the cicaro. I couldn't help it, he had freely told us about his past and what he had done. He didn't feel bad about killing all those people in the slums. What if the same breakdown was happening again?

I sniffed again; I really didn't need this. I was useless right now, waiting for my Reaver to come back, hoping that Elish would come with his plane and bring him. I didn't want to have to worry about Jade; my thoughts were completely with Reaver.

Sure enough, as Perish had suspected Tabbit had seen a ravers' den off in the distance. They made their presence known at least. The ravers who had higher brain activity liked to collect things that were bright colours, spray paint especially. They decorated their 'dens' usually abandoned apartments, large buildings or plazas, with crucified people, staked heads, and lots of flashy colours.

I stood up on the back of the cart as we travelled down the winding road into the valley below us. The slaves behind us being led by Chomper; all of them murmuring nervously to each other. I could relate, without Reaver near me everything was a threat.

If it wasn't for that asshole boyfriend of mine I would be with him right now… but he had to protect me, the only way Reaver knew how. He had put me in a sleeper hold because he knew I would never let them take him alone.

Not alone… Chally was me at least to the Legion. I wonder if they've found out… I wonder if they've killed him.

Poor guy, if I hadn't begged Reaver to stop him from being sold to Melchai…

After several hours of travelling down the winding road we finally stopped. I got out to study our new hideout.

The resort was made up of several structures. The smallest one and the one we had parked against had a faded sign saying *Lobby*, with the paint all chipped off and only the faded black outline remaining. It was leaning against the building, made of warped wood that hid dusty, badly decaying bricks. Around that first structure was a large parking lot and an overhang that was leaning badly, the same overhang became the roof as it went on and that seemed mostly intact.

Past the lobby I saw the biggest structure. One that looked like a large hotel with rocks imbedded in the brick and tall pointed roofs with big, broken picture windows. Before the Fallocaust I bet it housed rich people, it looked magnificent, even what surrounded it showed off its wealth. A curved driveway that looped around a fountain, and beautiful rock walls that once held raised beds but now only cradled twisted black bushes. Even though everything was cracked and broken now, even caved-in in a few places; I couldn't help but be taken by its beauty.

I started to walk down towards the resort hotel to get a better look but Perish grabbed my arm.

"No, we aren't going near there. It's too dangerous; we're sleeping in the lobby."

I frowned and looked at the resort. Reaver would have loved to explore it, maybe not with me but he would at least tell me what was inside. I bet there was a lot of neat stuff in there; we were so high up in the mountains that I bet it had barely been scavenged.

As everyone else around us started to check out the lobby, I gazed longingly at the hotel. I really didn't like that Perish was telling me what I could and couldn't do. I was almost eighteen years old now, I could go wherever I wanted. No matter what it seemed someone was always more than willing to boss me around.

But because I knew Reaver would never want me to go into that hotel alone, I didn't press the issue. Even though I was tempted just to make a point to Perish that he wasn't me keeper.

That night half of us would be on guard. Jade volunteered to spend most of the night outside, perched in the tall, thick trees that surrounded the resort. The cicaro had a stealth to him that made him extremely agile and he could scale up and down those tree tops faster than I bet even Reaver could. From Hopper's experience with ravers they couldn't climb well, so Jade would be safe up high.

I was going to be taking the 3 am shift with Churro for four hours, then I could sleep in the cart as we made our way back to the road. My shift wasn't nearly as long as the others but I didn't argue. The more I slept the less I time I had to worry myself about Reaver. I'd take it, I hated being idle with my own thoughts.

We fed the slaves and put them all into an old conference room. We chaining them to large pieces of furniture and shut the door with a fire poker that Perish had found. This lobby was full of big pieces of furniture: chewed-on couches, many conference chairs, and large, heavy wooden desks that still held treasures inside.

That evening, after I spent a lot of time scavenging around the lobby, filling up my satchel with forgotten office supplies, I slept in my bedroll waiting for my wakeup call so I could take my shift. Jade left with his assault rifle and his Game Boy Advance and found a snarled tree hanging off of a cliff face that gave him a good view of the valley around us.

The hand on my shoulder came too early. I yawned, but remembered I was trying to prove to these slavers that I was a man, so I got up looking as alert as I could.

It was Churro who I was taking shift with. I lit a cigarette and belted Reaver's M16 to my back. Then with my pockets full of opiate powder I followed Churro off into the night.

I was surprised to see snowflakes starting to fall. They swirled like disturbed ash, matching the bright moon that peeked through the towering trees around us. I found it almost magical in my mind. I had never been in a real forest, and in the dead of night I almost couldn't tell we were living in the Fallocaust. To me it just looked like snow falling in a forest.

I stood to admire it, the faint hints of a smile on my face. Tranquility and peace were two things hard to come by in this world, and even with my heart full of worry and my surroundings full of danger… I took a moment to appreciate it.

Churro though didn't care. I jogged to close the distance between us and we quietly walked to our location: a thick concrete fence that edged the strip of road that led to the hotel. We were taking the hotel watch in case anything came out of it or the area surrounding it.

The hotel looked all the more ominous in the night, the moon's glow highlighting and coaxing out every detail and texture. If I didn't know better I would say it was haunted. Though in this world ghosts would be a welcome sight. Ghosts couldn't kill you but a dozen ravers or a hungry carracat could. People before the Fallocaust lived so comfortably they made up shit to scare themselves.

Idiots.

"I wonder if this snow will get worse." Churro sucked on a cigarette and looked up at the sky. He blew out the smoke and shook his head. "I bet you it will. Snow clouds all around us… I told Hop we should be thankful we have this area to hide out in if it ends up dumping on us. Better here than the rest stop I guess."

I rubbed my gloved hands together and hugged the blanket I had wrapped around me. "Why do you do this trip so late in the year?"

Churro dashed the cigarette and sat down beside me. He had his own green blanket over him to try and keep warm. It was freezing up here.

"Melchai sacrifices the slaves during the spring. Crops and shit. Also they want some extras for the Man on the Hill," he replied.

Man on the Hill? Churro shook his head slowly when I asked him who that was.

"Some freaky dude who lives in a black house a half-mile up from the town. Do not even get me started on that shit. The town is a bit fucked up, lots of superstition." Churro shrugged. "They pay us great, that's all we care about. Mostly because no other slaver is stupid enough to make the journey, especially not this time of the year."

Well, I guess the money was worth the danger. Even though we had lost the old man and Chally they still had a decent amount of slaves to sell.

And Hopper hadn't complained that we had never replaced Chally like Reaver had promised. I was planning on telling him we would pay the slavers for Chally, the same rate this Melchai town would. Elish literally had all the money in Skyfall and I am sure he wouldn't mind if I asked nicely.

I liked Hopper more for that. For a slaver he was a good guy, he had been patient with us – *very* patient with us. I think he understood that what had happened in Mariano had caught us all off-guard. He wasn't like the slavers Reaver had warned me about.

As the night went on the snow started to fall harder, and by the time our shift was over it was starting to stick to the ground.

Hopper and Perish relieved us for the evening, both of them didn't look happy.

"I ain't going to bother…" Hopper said in a low voice. He looked up over the rim of his hat. "I ain't bothering, Churro. It's sticking now…

unless it slows down; we're camping here until it stops."

Churro sighed and brushed off some snow that had stuck to his blanket. "We're in the mountains; we have to keep trudging down. At least it's downhill now. We might break a couple bosen bones but we can get the slaves to pull the caravans if the bosen die. If this snow comes, it's staying. I say we break for it."

Hopper's mouth pursed, then moved to the side as he mulled over Churro's suggestion. "Nah, we had the same thing happen a few years ago and the rains came. I mean this whole damn area usually has its week or two of rain or snow then it disappears until next year. The raver we killed will feed all of us for a few days and if we run out of food we can shoot another one. I want to wait for at least a bit o' rain, this snow won't last."

I could tell Churro wasn't liking his boyfriend's idea but he nodded anyway and patted my back. "Well, that's Cappy's orders I guess. We'll get some sleep then."

I gave Perish a smile and started walking towards the lobby. On my way, my eyes swept the trees to see if I could spot Jade. I couldn't see him though, even with the moonlight highlighting the trees. I ended up just waving in a guessed direction. He was probably watching me and I wanted to say good night.

I doped myself up on not only some Dilaudid pills but the medication for my night terrors that Elish had given me; the same stuff he used on Jade. Then, feeling as okay as I could given the circumstances, I fell asleep.

Even though I no longer screamed and thrashed in my sleep, the nightmares were still there. This was a nightmare of a different sort however.

Reaver and I were lying in bed together, naked. We had just made love and we were facing each other, talking and laughing. The heaters were on in his bedroom and the lights from the living room illuminating every beautiful curve of his body.

So perfect. My engineered beauty. I reached out a hand and ran it up his side, up his chest and I cradled his face. By now I knew every detail of that face. His eyes, his little nose, and his little ears. I knew where each of his scars came from. I knew their stories. I knew him.

Reaver smiled at me, a smile that made the edges of his eyes crease. His real smile, the one only reserved for me; the relaxed tranquility on his face that came from hours of sex and endless stupid pillow talk.

I jerked awake suddenly, gasping and exhaling a plume of frozen breath. Then before my mind could wake up I felt someone take me into his arms.

"Reaver?" I sobbed.

"No, no… it's Perish. You're crying, poor thing. It's okay. You were whimpering in your sleep." Perish? What was he doing here? He was supposed to be patrolling; why was he in here, near enough to hear me?

I let him hold me, because I was more upset by my dream than I was that he was close to me. Perish was understanding and he was my friend. He seemed to have accepted that Reaver and I were a couple, and he hadn't tried anything inappropriate with me since the incident in the greyrifts apartment and that was months ago now.

I whimpered into his jacket and he made soothing noises, petting my hair back.

"What's Silas going to do to him? Please tell me Elish will save Reaver… I… I can't stand not knowing. It's been so long since Nero took him," I said through sobs. I grabbed onto Perish's jacket, it was all I could do to relieve my own agony.

Perish shushed me and kissed my forehead. "Oh, sweety… it might take a long time. Silas will try and get information out of Reaver, and since Reaver won't say anything…" Perish stopped as I let out another wail and squeezed me tight. "I'll protect you… from Jade… from everyone."

I was really lucky to have him. In all of this danger around us, I could count on Perish to keep me safe. He might be a bit on the crazy side but I knew him, I knew his quirks and I understood him. Perish would keep us all safe, and soon… soon…

"… Elish will rescue Reaver soon, right?" I whimpered.

Perish sighed. "I hope so, but until he does and until he takes Jade back… we'll make due; just the two of us."

I lifted my head up. "Jade isn't dangerous. He's a chimera and I can handle chimeras. Please don't talk like he's a threat or not a part of our group. He's my friend, Perry."

Perish looked down at me, and for a moment, I saw a flicker of something in his eyes, like he didn't want to believe me, but in the end, he nodded. "I'm more careful because I'm worried about you. That's all. Now… why don't you go to sleep more. I'll be here."

He wanted to keep holding me while I slept… but I wasn't comfortable with that. Perish had been really good with me and the boundaries we had to have, I didn't want to entice him or anything. So I shook my head and started to get up. He didn't look too pleased with that, but well… we weren't in Donnely anymore and he wasn't my boyfriend, or captor. I had started to stake my claim of dominance, at least a little bit, and this would be a good time to enforce it.

I was older now. I wasn't a baby anymore and I wasn't useless. I was a man and the boyfriend of the most important chimera in existence. When Reaver came back to me… I wanted him to see that I was growing up, that I wasn't scared anymore.

I bundled myself up in my clothes and brushed my teeth before making my way towards the front of the lobby.

Perish, Jade, and I had taken up a room away from the slavers, a den-like area in the back of the lobby. It was a good size room covered in a film of dust so thick it coated everything in a monotone blanket. There were boxes, couches, and chairs pushed into corners here but I couldn't even guess their state or colour. Some of them looked so fragile I wondered if they would hold my touch at all; maybe they were just casts of the furniture the dust once laid on, with the real furniture now disintegrated underneath.

I went out the door and started walking down the hall, putting my gloves on finger by finger.

But I paused when I saw the unnaturally brilliant daylight coming through the windows. Immediately my eyes shot up to the front of the lobby.

Everything had become white overnight.

"Yeah, and? You fucking jinxed it by mentioning snow!" Tabbit sounded pissed off. Snow flew off of his beard as he shook his head.

Hopper let out an annoyed noise. "There ain't no such thing as superstition. You're just nervous because we're getting near Melchai."

"Yeah, well, the town is overgrown with crops and they use

superstition… so who's to know. I just know you mentioned it hadn't snowed and here we be. Good one, Hop!" Tabbit kicked the snow, sending it up into the air then back down to join the foot of snow underneath their feet.

I rubbed my nose; it started to run under the fresh, cold air. I decided to play to my skills and act as a mediator. "We can't help the weather. Even if you had listened to Churro… that would only mean we would be on the main highway in the snow, right where the ravers are."

It seemed to have helped. Hopper gave me a thankful but slightly smug smile; Tabbit still didn't look happy.

"Thank you, Killian," Hopper said before shooting a dangerous look at Tabbit. "I don't want to hear nothing about fucking jinxing shit. It'll rain soon just like it had before a few years back. We can just hunker down, rip some paneling off the walls and off the hotel walls too. Make a big ol' fire if the chimney works and we can all be warm and happy as pigs in shit. You should be fuckin' thanking me for the break. Now go get some warm clothes and a fire on those damn slaves before our investments freeze to death."

"Hey… isn't that Mikey?" Chomper suddenly called.

Mikey? Most of them still called Jade that name even though they all knew our real names since the legionary incident. I looked towards where Chomper was carving up the raver just as he let out a barking laugh.

My eyes fell to the ridge, above the road we had travelled down to get here. On top of the sharp, snow-covered incline I saw Jade, dressed in black.

Sledding down the hill.

I rolled my eyes but smiled as Jade hooted and hollered, two large rooster tails of snow trailing behind him as he picked up speed and raced down the ridge. He was getting some good speed on him, I guess he must've found a highway sign or something to use as a sled.

Jade put a hand up in the air as if he was trying to perform a trick. Sure enough, I gasped from nerves as he raised another hand and stood on top of his sled. He stood up as the slavers hollered and cheered, egging him on and obviously loving every moment of this.

Then I started to get nervous. He was approaching at an extreme speed and the trees got thicker past the resort and he could easily hit one, and that was if he didn't accidently hit one of the concrete barriers hidden like pitfalls underneath the snow.

But he had it under control. As Jade skidded onto the parking lot he jumped off of the sled and easily landed on his feet. He then quickly turned around as the sled careened into one of the concrete walls that surrounded the lobby.

Then a sickening crunch. I brought my hand up to my mouth in sheer shock as the sled slammed into the barrier and exploded, or the top did anyway… no, not the top… the head.

Jade had slid down on a corpse! I ran up to the make-shift sled and couldn't help the laugh on my lips. It was a raver; he must have found another stray one. My god it had crashed headfirst into the barrier. Its skull was a ruin now and the skin of its back was all sheared off from the sharp rocks Jade had sledded over.

"Elish would ring my neck if he saw that!" Jade jogged up to me out of breath; he had a smile on his face a mile wide. "Did you see me? We need to find some fucking sleds, man."

I laughed. How could Perish think this guy was dangerous? He just seemed like a normal guy to me. "I saw. You almost gave me a heart attack, but I saw."

"Well, I see you're starting to make up for all the people you've murdered." I just paused and stared forward as I heard Perish say that very icily behind us. Jade paused too and I saw his jaw lock into place. He turned around, seemingly more than willing to ignore Perish's quip.

But Perish pressed on, "I suppose since we're stuck here, we should all be sleeping with one eye–"

"Perish!" I said to him sharply. "Stop fucking picking a fight. You don't know Jade did that, no one does."

"It's obvious he–"

Jade wordlessly turned around and started walking to the slavers; his happy mood now gone. I looked angrily at Perish; he stared back at me, his cold, blue eyes firm but distant.

"Stop upsetting him," I snapped, before shoving Perish in the chest. "I'm fucking sick of always having to worry about you two. Just get along, alright? Jade's homesick and sad, if you want him to stop doing crazy shit stop making him worse."

A hard look crossed Perish's face, immediately making me stop shoving him. I swallowed a bit as I remembered myself and remembered the state Perish could easily slip into. The crazy and unpredictable state of mind that made him murder the rest of his splices and the captured arians.

Shit, Killian, the moment you get comfortable with him you forget this.

"You… you're not afraid of Jade? After everything I told you he tried to do with me? After we think he's killing people?" Perish blinked as if not able to comprehend what I was saying.

"I understand chimeras. I see past their actions and their quirks… like I did with you, Perry." I sighed and glanced behind my back. "I understand Jade and he's my friend. I'm not scared of him; I have no reason to be. Whatever he may be doing it's because he's going through a lot. He is in a strange land with strange people away from his soul mate. Cut him some slack. He won't hurt me or you, I know this."

The scientist's brow knitted but he didn't make eye contact with me, instead he looked up at the snowy clouds then shook his head. "You should be afraid of him, Killian. Just you see, he's dangerous."

I wasn't going to win with him, and I didn't have the mental energy to try and convince him he was wrong. My heart and my mind were with Reaver, at all times. Jade and Perish, Hopper's caravan, even going to Falkland to find the piece of Perish that would make him whole, our entire mission was insignificant, all that mattered was getting Reaver away from Silas.

And back home to me.

CHAPTER 32

Reno

GARRETT PUT HIS ARMS AROUND ME AND BLEW A raspberry on my cheek. I scrunched my face and giggled like an idiot before pushing him away. For the past several weeks he had been doing such stupid things to make me laugh, and when I did he saw it as a victory and was happy the entire day.

Sure enough, Garrett hissed his win and gave me a playful slap on the butt. I retaliated by aiming a kick at his, which he dodged.

He was sucking on a lollipop which he offered me. I popped it in my mouth. For me he had been making an effort to cut down on the cigars, but because he always seemed to be having to do something with his hands he had taken up to sucking on lollipops or chewing gum.

My fiancé had been so supportive since I had come back to his skyscraper. He had been cuddly and kind, loving and attentive, exactly what I needed to thaw out the ice that had formed on my heart.

I had been feeling better. Not just pretending to feel better because I didn't want to hurt him. The past few weeks have been the therapy I needed to start recovering from my ordeal.

And I was recovering; I was a resilient greywaster. Recovering from shitty experiences was a part of our life and I had surprised myself with how quickly I had been bouncing back. The large cloud of depression over my head had been breaking and it was all thanks to my little sunbeam.

Garrett circled back after my missed kick and kissed me on the lips. Then he weaved his fingers inbetween mine and brought them up to his lips. Our matching engagement rings shining in the lamp light.

"I love you, I'm so happy you've been feeling better," Garrett said with a smile. "Waking up next to you… every morning I think it is just a dream and you're still gone."

I kissed him, a quick peck, but as was my nature, one small kiss wasn't enough. So I took him for another one. A long drawn-out one this time, one that made my knees weaken.

But always being Mr. Restraint, once it started to get heated Garrett pulled away with a light chuckle.

"Come here, love, why don't you show me how to play Spyro. Come, come, I'll get you some drugs and we'll order up some cheesecake with our dinner," Garrett said happily, walking towards our order-a-sengil phone which was screwed into the wall beside the kitchen.

I rolled my eyes. In my slowly improving mood I had been edging towards… my old ways. With my time under Cypress fading into the distance, I was starting to get a bit of a drive again.

I was only human.

"Alright." I rolled my eyes and gave his butt a pinch just to show him I wasn't amused. "Make the cheesecake like a fruit I haven't tried yet though. What about blue raspberry or something?"

Garrett blinked at me, holding the sengil phone in his hand. "Love… there is no real berry called blue raspberry."

I snorted incredulously; he was a smart ass chimera with all the fruits and vegetables at his disposal, grown in fancy hydro-whatsit-powered greenhouses and he didn't even know what a blue raspberry was. "Yeah, right. I once found a big cardboard case of Jolly Ranchers and my favourite was blue raspberry. Call Elish and ask him; he's smarter than you, he'll know."

He stared at me for a moment longer before smiling at me. "Well… you certainly do learn something new every day. Okay, well, why don't we get strawberry this time and I'll send away for some… blue-coloured raspberries. Just for you."

Sweet.

When he was done ordering Garrett sat beside me. He put his arm around my shoulder and pulled me close and watched me start to control the little purple dragon as he found his friends.

I kept dying though and no matter how bad I tried I couldn't concentrate. After many failed attempts the food came and we both sat on the couch with the TV on in the background. Garrett carried on talking about his day and the phone calls he got from Apollo who'd been taking over as Skytech president during his days off.

"King Silas called me as well. He would love to see you since you've gotten back. Master is quite happy you survived, everyone does love having you around," Garrett replied.

I choked on this information a bit but managed to swallow my mouthful of food. Garrett sensed my apprehension and continued on. "I told him that would be fine and I think it shall be. He will not hurt you and the longer he is in Skyfall… the less time he is in the greywastes looking for Reaver and the others."

This didn't make me feel any better. "Is he close to finding them?"

Garrett shook his head, taking his pickle off of his cheeseburger and giving it to me. In exchange he got my tomato. We had this stupid little routine we went through every single time we got hamburgers. He also got my toothpick that was skewered through the burger so he could double skewer his, since he liked to eat politely, and I kind of just… shoved it all in my face and hoped for the best.

"No, I don't believe so. We're doing everything we can to subtly mislead him," Garrett continued.

We should be doing more than just subtly misleading Silas. I had gotten the keycard for Elish, so why isn't Silas dead yet?

I let out a sad sigh. I wished I wasn't so in the dark… I might not be able to be with Reaver and Killian just yet, but I wanted to at least know how they were.

"Oh, Otter…" Garrett sighed, reading my face like the open book it was, "don't be sad. Come now, lutra." He reached a hand up and cradled my chin with it, stroking my stubbly chin with his thumb. "Do not worry for Reaver and Killian. Elish has hidden them well."

"I'm just worried, Garrett. I know Elish is like super computer smart but… man, shit was so easy this time last year." I let out a long breath and took a bite of my pickle. I had come to find out since being in Skyfall that I fucking loved pickles. "It's hard trusting him to keep Reaver and Tinky safe. I'm not used to trusting people besides my core group, especially not Elish."

Garrett nodded, still holding my chin in his hand. He brushed my lips with his thumb and looked at me longingly.

So I brought his hand to my mouth and kissed it, then as he smiled at the gesture I leaned in and kissed him. Kissing was all he allowed, and granted, since I had been seeing the light at the end of this Crimstone Horror Tunnel… it had been getting harder to leave it at just kissing.

I broke away the kiss and smirked at him. "You know… I bit one of their dicks off. Clean - fucking - off."

Garrett stared at me blankly, like the words I had just spoken were so unexpected that they failed to register in his mind.

"W-what?" He stared. His reaction caused me all sorts of amusements. I chuckled at this and gave him a playful shrug.

"It was the dude who got with me… I snapped a bit while he was doing it and well…" I clipped my teeth together.

I expected Garrett to laugh with me, but instead I saw his lower lip quiver.

Aw, man. How can he be a chimera? He was so… emotional. It was just so cute and sad in a way. I think these chimeras had to be hard asses just to survive in this family, but Garrett just wasn't.

"Aww," I made a sympathetic noise. "Garebear… my poor boy. I was trying to make you laugh not cry."

My sweet fiancé stared at me, his eyes full of sadness. He must have swallowed a lot of sadness in his long life. It was amazing that he hadn't turned stone-cold like Elish.

"I'll kill him…" he began, but I shook my head and kissed the corner of his mouth.

"Kerres put him out of his misery. He's dead, hun," I replied. "I paid him back for what he did and… after that no one touched me. They beat the shit out of me and made me feel like crap but… nothing sexual."

But the reality had already been brought to what had been a quiet evening. I had successfully ruined the best night we'd had in a while. I cursed myself out inside my head and kissed him again. Garrett reciprocated but his hand crept into mine, I knew he would never let me be far from him ever again.

And I was okay with that.

After we ate and enjoyed a couple of drinks together, I laid down on a day bed he had beside a window and watched my fiancé's fingers gently press down on the ivory keys of his grand piano. So soft and delicate, gently coaxing each note out of the keys like he was touching silk. It was beautiful and almost hypnotic to watch.

He was playing *Moonlight Sonata* even though I had asked him to play me Metallica. He was trying to show me what real music sounded like, though I knew he just wanted to show off his skills.

Garrett looked over at me and his face tensed, followed by just the slightest amount of blush.

No, my fiancé was too shy to ever be able to show off to me. He became flustered so easily when I asked him to sing or play me a song. He was ninety years old and still he was so…

"Oh shit!" Garrett hissed sharply as his hand slipped and hit the wrong note.

… he was so Garrett.

I smiled and rested my chin on my hands. "It was beautiful."

Garrett made a noise and raised a hand up in the air to showcase his dismissal of my comment. I laughed and rose to my feet.

I went up behind Garrett and put my arms around him. Then, with my head swimming with liquor, I proceeded to jump on his back.

To be a jerk I smacked his ass like a horse. "Okay, Mr. Neigh Neigh, take me to… Disney Land!"

Garrett adjusted himself and grabbed onto my legs. "I could take you to mars, you're so light. Has all that ice cream and potato fries I've been feeding you done nothing? I shall start force feeding you sticks of butter soon."

I smacked him again on the butt, making him *ouch* out loud. "Horses don't talk! Don't make me sell you to the circus, talking horse. Now bring me to…" I looked around the apartment and pointed to the bar. "To the watering hole!"

"I didn't catch that… you should probably smack me again," Garrett said with an air of mischievousness in his voice. So I decided to be a bit of a tease and smack him again. Though always having to take it a step further, I kissed the nape of his neck.

"Oh, bad Reno!" But I kissed him again, and at that point he slid me off of him.

The alcohol sure did wonders for us. It was helping us get back to who we had been. We had been such playful idiots before the Crimstones. Smacking, chasing, and howling with laughter like a couple of kids. It was our personalities and being able to act like goofballs around each other was what made our relationship unique. Elish, Reaver, all of the others would've rolled their eyes and called us morons… but around each other we were free to act like ourselves.

And *ourselves* were usually immature teenagers who fed off of each other.

So as Garrett turned around to give me hell for kissing his neck. I instead grabbed him and gave his neck an obnoxiously slobbery lick.

Garrett squealed and struggled to get away from me. "Nope, I'm a pet. I'm grooming you," I said. I licked him again and my ninety-year-old fiancé dissolved into giggles. I grinned; it was always such a victory when I could make people laugh.

"You're not a pet anymore, you're my fiancé!" Garrett laughed, slapping me away but I didn't let go of him. Instead we both sunk to the floor of the living room. I crawled on top of him.

"Stop that!" Garrett laughed. "You're like a giant Great Dane."

"Woof!" Instead I wrapped my mouth around his neck, and knowing he was going back to work soon, I started sucking on his neck, in hopes of giving him a huge hickey.

And he knew what I was doing. Suddenly he started struggle-howling and trying to push me off. But I kept the seal until the end, then let my lips break away with a pop. A giant red welt was my reward.

"You shit! You shit! I have a meeting tomorrow, you!"

I grinned and went to give him another one.

But he deflected me. Instead he grabbed my chin and locked my lips with his. To keep me from pulling away, he wrapped his arms around my chest and drew me in close to him.

It felt nice… and the alcohol only intensified and fuelled it. My lips separated and we kissed deeply, but as we started to make out on the living room floor I could feel something harden underneath me.

I don't know what came over me, though the past two weeks being around my fiancé had done wonders for me. So before I could convince myself I wasn't ready… I started to lightly grind my hips into his.

Garrett allowed himself a single moan before he started to shift himself out from under me, but instead I slipped a hand down and started unbuttoning his pants.

"Ah-ah! No!" Garrett gasped. "Reno… you're drunk, stop."

I drew down the zipper of his trousers revealing his boxer briefs underneath. I felt another warm rush go through me as I saw the outline of his hard dick showing through. To my own surprise, I felt a jolt of heat go through me. Suddenly I wanted him and badly.

"Reno…"

"It's okay." I unzipped my own pants and ran my hand over my own dick. I adjusted it just slightly so the very tip of my penis was showing through.

Garrett's face paled; he looked like he was going into shock. His green eyes stared at my briefs, well… the general area. He was looking at it with a hunger in his eyes that lit a fire inside of me.

"We need to wait…"

I leaned back down and kissed him again. Then, to be sneaky, I pressed my groin up against his, only our underwear separating us, and started to grind into him.

"Reno!" Garrett tried to shift away from me again, before to my inner-joy he let out a moan. "S-stop… fuck." He put a hand on my backside and clenched it, before another, much louder, moan broke from his lips. The sounds he was making were only driving me to stimulate him further. Suddenly I wanted all of him, in every way I could. I wanted him inside of me; I wanted to be inside of him. Lick every inch of his body, taste his cum, rim him, have sex for days… constantly. Fuck, I wanted him.

"Reno, I - said - STOP!" Garrett suddenly yelled.

The tone made me freeze on the spot. He sounded angry; I had rarely heard him angry and had never heard him pissed at me.

Garrett shoved me off of him, his face flushed and sweaty, not just from drinking. Quickly, he stumbled to his feet and did up his pants.

"I… I'm going to go to the office for a few hours," he mumbled avoiding all eye contact.

"Fine, whatever. I'm going to bed," I said bitterly, feeling more embarrassed than shot down. I didn't know what had gotten over me but I wanted to get away from him as much as he wanted to get away from me. I swallowed through my parched throat and disappeared into my bedroom.

After I heard the door close I locked mine. Then, because my body was on fire and swirly from the alcohol, I took it out and started rubbing one out by myself. I mean, I was still Reno and though I was pissed off and embarrassed... my body wanted what it wanted. I would be extremely surprised if Garrett wasn't in his office doing the same thing.

So in Reno fashion I fell asleep, half-naked and baring it all for the world. But it didn't matter either way, I woke up the next morning alone.

I yawned and rubbed my eyes. I quickly showered and dressed myself and made my way to the main area of the apartment to face Garrett.

My ears went hot just thinking of having to see him. I was kind of embarrassed over last night.

But when my hand was outstretched to turn the handle on the door, I heard Garrett's voice outside.

"Well, this is it... it will be weird for a few days but we're nice people. At least the two of us are."

What? Garrett had someone with him? What the hell?

I opened the door and walked out.

Garrett was bundled in a jacket and gloves like he had been outside, even though his office was just a few floors below us. He was walking in with... with a blond young man.

The kid was a bit shorter than me, with short dirty-blond hair and big grey eyes. Immediately I could tell he had been beaten on recently, and from the way he looked wide-eyed at the room, it was obvious that he was a bit shell-shocked.

"Who's that?" I said flatly. I didn't realize I was wary and perhaps a bit offended until I spoke those two words. I think my mind was jumping to the assumption that he was bringing a boy home for me to fuck just so he didn't have to touch me.

Garrett took the boy's jacket, he was skinny and twiggy. He actually reminded me a bit of Killian. Small with that terrorized look to him, the kind of look that a cat got when its fur went all poofy.

"Caligula called me and asked me to get the boy from his and Nico's apartment. Apparently Kessler picked him up from the greywastes from a couple slavers they killed. Kess wanted to give him to Nero but Clig managed to smuggle him out. He'll be staying with us, and if it is alright with you, I want him to start shadowing Luca so he can become our sengil. He's… he can't go back to the greywastes, he's a bit… disabled."

The boy scowled at this. I guess he wasn't disabled in the head… he could understand us perfectly well.

"How?" I walked up to him with my arms crossed and looked him up and down. He still had all of his limbs but I knew chimeras and I knew legionary, the kid had probably been beaten and raped, that was enough to fuck any boy up.

Garrett put a hand on the boy's back and led him towards the couch. "He doesn't talk. I'm not sure if it's psychological, or he has something physically wrong with him, but he doesn't speak words."

The kid looked at me before he moved his hands. Garrett saw this, and oddly, a big smile appeared on his face. "He knows sign language, well perfect! So do I. What's your name?"

The kid flashed some hand gestures at him.

"C-H-A-L-L-Y. Chally? Well, that's a cute name. How old are you?" Chally held up ten and then nine. "Nineteen? Wow, you look like you're eleven." That earned him a look, and to both of our amusements he held up the only sign language sign I knew: the good ol' middle finger. We both got a kick out of that.

"He's the typical sengil build. We choose sengils that are small, cute, and obedient. He seems to at least have two of those features. I think he will ease right into training and Luca wouldn't mind the company. He's so bored without Jade to occupy him, that poor cat never gets a break." Garrett poked him like he'd just brought us home a hamster. Chally responded like a hamster too and kept flinching away.

"I'm just happy to give him some shelter. Nero wrecks any young man he gets into his possession, he'll be safe here." Garrett patted Chally's head. "Well, enough talk. We'll get some food into him and I'll start a file on him too. I have access to greywaster records on my laptop;

I'll mark him as dead and create a new file in the sengil registry. Reno, show him his room and perhaps make some calls to Luca so we can get him some proper clothes."

I could do that. Though I took a moment to look over this new little greywaster.

Oddly he seemed to be looking at me too, but in a much more subtle way. Chally kept giving me sideways glances and when I looked back at him he started paying a good amount of attention to the picture windows around us.

I shrugged it off and started making calls as Garrett click-clacked away on his laptop. Luca was thrilled at the idea of having a friend, from the sounds of it he was still alone in Olympus. He talked on the phone with me for fifteen minutes about Biff and how he was starting to sew a sengil outfit for the cat.

An outfit.

For the cat.

He and Killian would've been best friends. I really hoped one day Reaver would get to meet this kid just so we could have a laugh about these boys. Sengils were a breed of their own; I couldn't get enough of their odd nature I swear

Chally stood around looking uncomfortable as Garrett and I did our thing. By the time evening was coming and we had settled down with a couple drinks he was starting to relax.

With my drunken actions forgotten with Chally coming, I laid my head on Garrett's shoulder and he played with my hair.

The greywaster boy was still eyeing me, though he hadn't signed anything to me directly. He seemed to just communicate with Garrett. I wish I was ninety so I could learn a thousand different languages.

I watched him as Garrett doted on me, both of us watching *Friends* on TV, one of our favourite shows together. I kept turning to try and tell Chally why parts were funny, since he wasn't laughing, but then I remembered he was mute not deaf. I was glad I stopped before I made an ass out of myself.

But there was something I couldn't shake. The kid kept watching me, maybe that's why he didn't get the jokes… his grey eyes were always fixed on me and Garrett.

Finally when Garrett fell asleep, his head resting on a throw pillow on the couch, I rose to my feet and motioned Chally to get up.

Because chimera hearing was what it was, and Garrett was a light sleeper when he wasn't drunk, I pulled Chally into Garrett's study and closed the door.

I expected the kid to be wary of what I was doing, but he let out a breath like he knew what was coming.

"Why do you keep looking at me? You know I'm a greywaster or something?" I crossed my arms, standing in front of the door so the kid couldn't escape my interrogation.

Chally stared at me and nodded. Suddenly he looked really nervous. He wiped his face with his hands and looked behind him, to Garrett's desk.

The greywaster took a piece of loose paper and a pen. Smart since I couldn't speak sign language. He wrote something down on it and handed it to me. Oddly… his hands were shaking.

Kligula and Neeko sent me down. We need you to come with us.

I stared blankly at the piece of paper, trying to process the words. My eyes rose to his face, a face that was tensed and creased with worry.

Caligula and Nico?

What the hell?

Why did they need me and why couldn't they come and get me themselves? I hadn't seen Nico since he'd made me leave him in the sewer. I would have been thrilled if he and Clig dropped by for a beer and a few lines.

"This makes no sense. What do they need me for? They can come here and–" I stopped talking when Chally shook his head. "Then what is it?" I demanded, starting to feel my chest tighten with apprehension. I didn't know what was going on and it was frustrating and a bit intimidating. This new kid knew something and his way of communicating it was driving me nuts.

Chally got the piece of paper again and started to write. But halfway through he stopped and closed his eyes for a second. By now the anxiety was starting to eat my stomach, a cancerous pit was starting to form.

It was like he abandoned what he was writing. Instead he took my hand and started leading me out the door. I followed him until he got to the doorway.

"No… no…" I shook my head. "I ain't going anywhere with you. I don't know you and the last people I was alone with kidnapped me and held me for ransom. I'm waking Garrett."

"Ah!" Chally actually made a noise. He shook his head vigorously and swept the room with his paranoid gaze. He inhaled a shaky breath and pushed the note into my hand. Like this was causing him pain, he held my hand before snapping it away.

I opened the note, more confused than ever.

Nero has Reaver.

"WHAT!" I exploded. The paper fell from my fingers. "Who are you? What the fuck? How do you know? TELL ME!"

"Reno?" Garrett's surprised voice suddenly sounded but I didn't care.

I turned to Chally. The kid backed away from me until his back hit the wall. He held up his hands and clenched his teeth.

I turned around. "Nero has–" Suddenly the kid put his hand over my mouth, jumping on my back as he did. I spun around and grabbed his hands to try and pry him off but he was like a spider monkey.

Faced with this odd scene, Garrett looked at us both bewildered before he ran over and pried Chally off of me. The kid squawking and thrashing, talking in a variation of tones like he so desperately wanted to talk. "Calm down, little thing. What's going on?"

"Ah-ah!" Chally protested. I stared at him, wondering why he didn't want Garrett to know… Garrett was on our side.

And I would need him. "He just told me that Nero has Reaver. That Caligula and Nico want me to go with them… to…" I looked at Chally. "To save him? They want me to help save him?"

Chally stared at me, his arms being held back by Garrett. He stopped struggling and nodded.

When Garrett let Chally go he started to quickly sign to Garrett.

My fiancé watched him go at it, then started to swear.

"Is he telling the truth?" I demanded.

Garrett paused and shook his head. "No, no he isn't." My heart fell. "It must be a trick of Silas… just go to bed, love."

Despair washed over me, but the more I processed Garrett's words the more I didn't believe them. "Garrett… you… you're lying aren't you.

They caught Reaver, didn't they?" Where was Killian then? Fuck… fuck. Oh god, they better not have hurt him.

Garrett ignored me and grabbed his remote phone. I paused, wondering if he was calling Nero.

"Yes, Luca… send a car, you'll be picking up Chally–"

"No!" I grabbed the phone out of Garrett's hand and closed it. "You're damn well lying to me, aren't you? Garrett, tell me the truth!"

But he was ignoring me. The knowledge of what was going down around me brought me more panic. Like a thousand loose strings had been dropped around me and I had twenty seconds to tie them all back together.

I had to know.

Garrett's eyes were heavy. He looked at me for a brief moment before he held a hand up to his mouth. Garrett swallowed hard and I could tell he was thinking of every reason not to tell me.

But I was his fiancé.

"They…" Garrett looked over; I did too and saw Chally continue to sign to Garrett. The kid's face a photo of anxiety and his hands a trembling mess. Each sign was just a blur of movement to me but Garrett seemed to understand.

"Reaver was caught when he was taking Chally to a town to sell. Chally pretended to be Killian, and Killian, he thinks, escaped. The last thing Chally heard was Kessler giving Reaver to Nero, without Silas knowing. This was a couple weeks ago. Caligula told Kessler Chally wasn't Killian and took Chally him-himself."

Then my fiancé paused as Chally continued to sign. His mouth twisted like he was physically trying to stop himself from saying what he was going to next. "It was Reaver who broke your ransom code, not Caligula. He told Caligula where to find you, before he was given to Nero."

My jaw hit the floor. My temples hammered and a white light seemed to creep into my vision.

It was true? It was really true? There was nothing else to say then. Wordlessly, I turned around and grabbed my jacket.

"NO!" Before I could register the desperate cry from Garrett, he was grabbing my hand and yanking it away from my jacket. "You are not going! NO!"

I tried to keep my emotions in check, I really did. But hearing Garrett's voice break in front of me made my eyes burn. Especially because I knew – I was leaving.

I wrestled with him for the jacket, and when he pulled it from my grasp, I grabbed my thick leather one instead. "I gotta go, love."

My fiancé shook his head back and forth. "No… no, no. You're not leaving. You are not going, it's too dangerous! I forbid it!" He jumped in front of me and blocked the door.

I pushed down the shock at his actions. He seemed on the verge of mania with how he pressed himself against the door. His panicked eyes burrowing into me, begging and pleading.

"I have to save Reaver!" My voice broke as I said those words to him. "Come with me if you must, but I am going."

Garrett shook his head back and forth. I saw tears glistening in his eyes as they swept the room. Like he was looking for something that might help plead his case.

"I can't go. If they catch me I'll lose everything and so will Elish. You… you know that. I can't go…" Garrett screamed, his teeth clenched and his face tight. "They will kill you if they find you. I can't lose you again. I CAN'T! I can't go through that again. Please, Otter, NO!"

"I… I'm sorry…" I whispered. My body was shaking so hard I thought I would fall down. I didn't know how I was still standing when my world was crumbling beneath my feet.

There was nothing to be said, nothing to be done. When it came to my Reaver there was no room for discussion. I was Reaver's friend first, I was his fiancé second.

"I love you, Gare… I'm sorry."

I grabbed the handle of the door to open it.

To my shock, Garrett grabbed my hand… hard.

"I said no."

I was momentarily stunned as I heard a sharpened edge to his voice. "I said no, and you will obey me."

What? I looked at him, his face only a foot from mine.

Holy shit.

Garrett's eyes were two slabs of emerald lit on fire. They pierced me and burned me alive with just one hard, scathing look.

I had seen that look before but not on him. I had seen that on his king and master the night I told *Asher* I didn't want to have sex.

"You… you can't–" My tone turned to mush as his eyes ripped me apart. I could taste the atmosphere changing around us. The high-strung mood quickly turning dark and hostile.

"I am Prince Garrett Dekker, and a greywaster will not tell me what I can and cannot do." Garrett's tone dropped to a threatening dark level. I found myself backing away as he moved from the door and started slowly stalking towards me; his movements holding the same terrifying grace that his master's had. "Until I say my vows to you, you are my cicaro, and I say you will not leave this apartment."

I yelped as he grabbed the collar of my shirt and pulled me close to him. His hand twisted my shirt as his face blanked. The emotional eyes dark and dead, but at the same time I had never seen them so brilliant. They were overflowing with energy, a caustic acid that could burn your skin like he was some sort of Titan.

He was a chimera… he was Silas's creation.

My head swam and suddenly the only thought in my mind was to get away from him. Get away from this chimera. I wasn't safe in here with him; if this was a rare state he might not know how to control it. I have seen crazed chimeras before and people died when they let their bloodlust take them.

Another twist of my shirt, this one starting to restrict the air in my throat. I struggled, but as soon as he saw my hand reach up to grab his, he snapped it up first and crushed it in his grip. "If I have to break your legs, Reno, I will. Do not test me. If you think I will let you go into a chimera and legionary-filled base to get him… you do not know me. If I have to hurt you to protect you… I will."

All I could do was stare back at him, stare back in shock and terrifying amazement as I witnessed Garrett in this rare form.

I nodded and at that recognition he dropped me. I stumbled and watched Garrett as he took a step back. He looked over at Chally. "Tell Harvard to take you to Olympus. Get out of my fucking sight."

Chally, who had been staring dumbfounded at us, nodded before he turned and fled out the door. Garrett went into his bedroom.

I stood there just staring, not knowing what to do with myself. Not knowing if I should make a break for it.

I started to make plans to leave once Garrett fell asleep when I heard a distinct click.

I jerked away when I felt something on my neck. "Stay still," Garrett said, his voice acidic and biting.

He belted the leather collar on me and secured it with a lock. Then, with a chain leash still in hand, he led me to my bedroom.

"If you're going to chain me like the fucking Crimstones did, at least have the dignity to put me in a room separate from you," I said to him.

Wordlessly, Garrett led me to my old bedroom, before he chained my collar to the foot of the bed.

I wanted to say volumes to him in that moment. I wanted to ask him if he was proud of himself for doing this to me, but all I could do was stare; drinking in the dark side of my fiancé, but at the same time – ready to fake it until he unchained me.

Because once he did I was gone.

Reaver had come for me.

In the only way he could, Reaver had saved me. And I had to save my best friend, the man who, if it wasn't for Killian… might've been my fiancé one day instead of Garrett.

I had been joined to that man since he was two years old. I had grown up with him. He had been my first friend, my first kiss. We shared between us first kills, as well as first sexual experiences. I was bound to that man.

The moment I had a chance… I would come for him and I would save him.

The words started to come to my lips to plead my case, to tell Garrett I would stay put. But as soon as he secured me he turned and left the room. I heard a slam and in the background the television turned off and then the lights.

And I was alone. All alone.

I fell into a troubled sleep that night. Nightmares slipped in easily but they didn't leave with the same grace. They stayed and sunk into my brain like poison, and my distraught and anxious mind soaked up each thought like a sponge.

My eyes opened when I heard the rattling of a door knob. Immediately my brow knitted and my eyes hardened. Though I was still half-asleep, I mentally prepared myself for a fight. Because if he let me out and assumed everything would go back to normal… he was going to taste what being engaged to a greywaster really meant.

Then the door opened and I shut my eyes, wondering if I could play possum just so I wouldn't have to talk to him. I liked that idea so I relaxed my body and started to play pretend.

"He's in here. Keep your voice down."

I opened my eyes. That… was not Garrett.

I jumped up quickly, the chain on my neck pulling as I stumbled to my feet.

At first my heart froze in shock and fear as I saw the two masked intruders in my doorway. The Crimstones and my abduction still the first line infantry of thoughts in my head.

They must have known where my mind was going because one of them held out his hands in a *calm down* gesture. But it wasn't until the second one took his mask off that the fear turned into a flood of relief.

It was Nico. Without a word, he fumbled with a set of keys, beside him Caligula also drew his ski mask up.

"Here to break me, eh? Again?" I smirked as Nico started unlocking my collar. Caligula pulled something black out of his pocket and handed it to me. My heart jumped when I realized he was giving me a gun. It had been too long since I handled a gun, too long.

"Chally told us right away… about how Garrett reacted." Caligula tossed me a jacket. There was the sound of shifting chains as Nico dropped my collar onto the bed. "We're here to bust you out. Nero's had Reaver for too long and eventually King Silas is going to find out."

I quickly put my jacket on… but I paused halfway through. "Wait a moment… Elish never told us you were on our… our side."

Caligula pulled his ski mask back down over his face. "It was Reaver who saved Nico's life. I repay debts, I don't make them."

"But…"

Caligula held up a hand. "I have my reasons and they're my own. Follow us, we have a Falconer waiting."

That was good enough for me. I slipped and laced up my boots and followed them towards the door.

But as my hand touched the door frame I paused. I turned around and looked behind me at the apartment.

He would understand… and if he didn't understand…

I turned from Garrett's apartment and followed Caligula and Nico down the hall.

My engagement ring on the table.

CHAPTER 33

Jade

I SNORTED IN MY OWN CRUEL AMUSEMENT AS DEEK looked around confused. The snow falling lightly around him, covering his grey coat in white dust.

The deacdog looked at me. And because he was the trusting, friendly dog he was, he wagged his tail.

So I did it again just to be a jerk.

I picked up some snow, the snow cooling my hot, flushed hands, and formed it into a ball.

"Okay, fetch!" I said, trying to sound as excited as I could. I chucked the ball into the parking lot where it fell into the two feet of snow, never to be seen in ball-form again.

Deek lurched up on his back legs before running after it, kicking up snow into the air. But once he got to where the snowball was he stopped, his tail cautiously wagging.

He looked behind his shoulder at me; I looked away and glanced at the sky, watching him look at the snow, perplexed.

I loved this dog; he was such a happy dumbass. I whistled him over and gave him a raver finger as a treat. Then I grabbed some wooden boards from the stack we had made in front of the lobby and made my way inside to find some warmth.

We had been hauled up in this lobby for at least ten days now and it had been the most stressful, aggravating days of my life. It wasn't just me, no one was really happy, everyone was getting cabin fever, itching to get back on the road. No one could believe the snow had lasted this long, it was unusual for Fallocaust weather.

So I took as much time as I could during the day to play with the dog, or go with the scavenging party to pry boards off of the interior of the hotel; anything to keep me occupied and to try and sway Killian away from Perish.

I hadn't told Killian… I hadn't told Killian what Perish had been doing to me.

I just – I shook my head as I walked through the entrance of the lobby and towards the back room the three of us slept privately in. *I just couldn't put that on the kid right now.*

What could Killian do? We were stuck here in this lobby, and there was nothing we could do about it. If I told Killian I knew he wouldn't be able to keep it from Perish, he would confront him, and right now that was too dangerous.

I closed the door behind me and swept the dimly lit room with my gaze. I saw Perish and Killian in the corner playing Pokémon together.

Right now Perish was only seeking to control me; to use my own empath abilities against me. He wasn't hurting Killian, and I was afraid if I confronted Killian with proof, then Perish would start hurting the boy. I knew I was walking a dangerous tight-rope with these two, but I felt like I had little choice. Elish would know what to do when he found us, when he came to get us with Reaver.

Was it the best of ideas? I didn't know. Perish was constantly on me, constantly picking apart everything I did, and he never missing a chance to belittle me. He liked pulling Killian aside to talk to him, warning him about me probably, but…

I think we were okay as long as we were in the lobby. The scientist knew it was unsafe for him to do his by-proxy killings right now, not with his precious Killian so close by. If the slavers turned on us we were trapped here with them; no place to escape and no place nearby, save the hotel that we could shelter in.

At least Perish was smart enough to know he couldn't do his scopa control of me right now. I had that going for me, and I think that was the push my mind needed to justify keeping my mouth shut.

I think this is what Elish would have wanted me to do…

Killian looked up at me with his bright, sunny smile. Though I knew it was fake, like all his smiles were lately. His aura was as toxic and dark as it had ever been, barely any of his bright sunshine yellows to be seen.

And Perish's had been continuing to heal.

Lycos… Lycos, you idiot. Why couldn't you have told Elish what you had done when you saw him?

I knew that answer though.

"Catching lots of Pokémons?" I put on a smile and pulled up my bedroll so I could join the group.

Perish, of course, gave me the stink eye before turning back to the Game Boy. I laid down and bundled myself up in blankets and stuck close to the fire. I always got cold easily. I had been enjoying my life as an inside pet.

The dog came over and laid beside me, and as the evening went on we were treated to the smell of not only wet dog, but singed dog fur. Once he was dry though he made a great pillow. I had been using him as a pillow and a heat source since we had started on this journey.

Tonight would be a rare night for us. It wasn't often that all three of us got an evening where we weren't taking sentry shifts or on wood gathering duty. It was thanks to Hopper. He had decided that since we were all snowed in that the slaves might as well start helping. They were wood gatherers now which lessened the load on us.

So we got to be comfortable and warm in this back room. Even though the insulation was sparse it was closed in and also windowless, so it kept the heat in good. It was frozen enough outside for us to keep the fire on all night too. It was the most comfortable I'd been in a long time.

But no matter how comfortable I was my ears were always listening for the Falconer. For Elish to come and find me and take me into his arms.

Even thinking about my master brought a twinge to my heart. I missed him and I missed his protection.

I watched the wooden boards burn in the fireplace; snapping and crackling as it consumed the over two hundred-year-old wood. I shifted closer to the small blaze and rested my head against Killian's satchel.

Before Elish left… after I had jumped out of that plane with a parachute, he had reminded me how joined we were. He showed me our matching wedding rings before taking me into his arms for the last time.

Out of earshot of the others, he whispered to me, *"I love you and you know this. Now you must be strong and prove to me you are the chimera I know you are."*

He was making a point to be affectionate with me and I knew now it was because Elish had known he would be gone for a long time. My master and my husband knew that dangerous times were ahead for both of us.

"I love you, Elish. Please... come back for me soon."

"I will."

I could count the number of times he had outwardly said *I love you* to me. It hadn't even been a year since the first time he had said it. This relationship, something that had grown beyond master and pet, had been new to him too.

I swallowed down the restricting feeling in my throat and closed my eyes as my heart gave a throb. Would he be proud of me that I wasn't telling Killian about Perish? Would he have advised me to do this? I hope so.

Everything I was doing now was for him; it was for his end game, and I would die before I disappointed him.

This thought put a pressure on my brain. I squeezed my eyes and held my head, feeling the first signs of a headache. To try and dispel the pain I knew was coming, I buried my face into Killian's satchel and drew the blankets over my head.

After a few minutes in blissful, silent darkness I heard Perish snort out a laugh. "All that pet does is sleep. Fucking lazy."

"Perish!" I heard Killian snap. "I fucking told you to lay off him a thousand times. If you keep doing it I'm not playing Pokémon with you anymore."

Great threat, Killian. But I guess that's all Killian could really threaten… I appreciated the gesture all the same. I ignored Perish and tried to shut my ears off, though every time he said something his voice seemed to tweak and annoy the inner registers of my mind. I managed to push all outside stimulus away though, and with the fire warming my body, I fell asleep.

Sometime in the night I was woken up by a needle in my skull.

Once again my body spasmed from the sheer surprise of it, before I felt a hand against my mouth.

"Shh, shh," Perish soothed. He clenched my face in his hand before pushing down on the plunger. I groaned and bit down on Killian's satchel as I felt the liquid get shot into my skull. Though it thankfully had no taste to it, it was still the water.

"There we go…" Perish whispered. I shifted my face away from his hand to get a deep breath. I inhaled cold air, the fire beside me burning down to smouldering coals. It was deep in the middle of the night and I could hear Killian snoring beside me.

"Go lay down!" Perish hissed and my mind picked up another sound. Deek growling. But with Perish's dismissal I heard the dog patter away.

My face twisted when I felt his lips kiss my neck. I stared forward and tried not to show the disgust on my face. I wished for this to be nothing but a nightmare that I couldn't wake up from, but here he was… doing it again.

Now what did he want? What questions did he have now? Each kiss he laid on my neck left behind its own imprint of acid. Once again I asked myself how far I would let him go before I snapped.

"There we go… let it take you, you little whore." I laid there limp and lifeless as he crawled on my back. I fixed my eyes on the back of Killian's head as he lay there asleep. Even when I felt his hard penis grinding into my ass I didn't shift or move. He hadn't given me an order yet and I knew until the controller did… you didn't move.

You stared off into space, you were helpless; a puppet on strings.

The scientist commanded me to lie on my back and I did. Then he proceeded to remove my pants and then underwear. I lay there exposed to him, soft and cold.

Perish trailed his tongue along my earlobe, before whispering into it, "Get on top of me."

He wants me to fuck him again? If that was the worst thing I did tonight I would take it. As I had deduced before, I wasn't a goody-goody. Elish would understand.

So Perish took my place and I straddled him. He drew me in and kissed me, then I felt his warm hands start to tug and rub my cock.

"Yes, get hard for me, little slut," he whispered with a low growl to his voice. Like before, he had transformed into the normal, sane Perish. I was starting to think he was just pretending to be crazy most of the time now. Maybe it wasn't something that came and went.

He growled and smiled at me, blue eyes brilliant and bright, holding small glows inside of them from the dying coals. "Now, draw up your aura."

My aura? No… if I do that he'll do that immortal trick, the same one that Silas had. The dark smoke that fucks up your mind – No, fuck you, Perish. I'll play your little game; I'll let you molest me but I won't say a fucking word to you about Elish's plan or this sestic radiation shit you were asking about.

And as soon as this snow melts, I'll show Killian my evidence I have on you and we'll tie you to a fucking tree for the ravers to eat.

But until then… until then…

"I can't anymore…" I leaned down and started rubbing my hardening dick against his hand. "My headaches…"

Perish stared at me for a moment, his brow furrowing. Then he drew me in for another kiss.

"Just a… hint for next time. People under the influence of scopa, do not talk back."

My body froze as Perish kissed my lips, then suddenly he screamed at the top of his lungs. "KILLIAN!"

What!? Ice, more frozen than the landscape around us, coated and sunk into my body. I felt like I was going to throw up at the sheer horror of what I knew was about to happen.

Here I was naked from the waist down on top of Perish, grinding my hardening penis, not in his hands, he had withdrawn it… I was grinding myself right into his groin.

Perish pushed me off and screamed again. "Get off of me!"

Then Killian… Killian was shouting… a lump of sludge formed in my stomach because all I could do was stare at the two of them, paralyzed in shock as they threw me down onto the floor.

"Why!?" Killian cried. "Jade? Why!?"

Perish was crying… what a great actor. He had crawled backwards until he hit the edge of an old couch we were dismantling for firewood.

Tears were streaming down his face, he was going to win an Oscar for this one.

"Killian, Killian… make him go away. Killian, Killian… he's going to rape me like Nero."

Oh fuck… fuck me.

"He's going to rape me!"

The anger coiled in my stomach like I had swallowed snakes; I couldn't contain it. The serpents crawled to my tongue, and with that, I spat my poison.

"He's lying!" I screamed. I grabbed the blanket I had been using and wrapped it around myself. "He's fucking lying, Killian! We… we have to go. We have to get the fuck out of here. His mind is back; he's been fucking faking it for weeks now!" I took a deep breath. I ignored the shocked looks Killian was giving me and tried to press on. Not wanting to admit to myself I was probably sounding crazier right now.

"Killian!" Perish sobbed. He put his hands behind his neck and started sobbing. "I want him gone."

Killian stared at me like he didn't know what to do. "I… Jade… Jade, why did you do this? What's happening in your head?" Showing the sensitive patience that was so unique to Killian, he put his hands on my face. "Is it your headaches? Are you hearing voices?"

"Killian, I want him OUT!" Perish screamed. Obviously upset that Killian wasn't kicking me out into the cold night.

"Perish, enough! He's sick!"

I loved that kid, fuck, I loved that kid. He was forgiving to a fault; no wonder Reaver loved him so much.

I grabbed onto Killian's hand and looked at him straight in the eye. "Listen to me, Killian. Perish is–"

Suddenly Perish came out of nowhere and shoved me away from Killian. I lost my balance and fell down onto the ruined couch, a billow of dust rising up around me as the springs dug into my naked waist. "Get out!" Perish screamed.

My temper suddenly snapped and the chimera stirring underneath my surface sprang forth. Anger took over my resolve, and my anger at Perish broke through my countenance. I announced my fury with a scream of boiling anger and jumped onto Perish. I swung my fists and started hitting him as hard as I could, feeling my emotions rage as the reality of his trickery lit like a beacon in my mind.

"Jade!" Killian's voice was far away in another world. Plunging its pleading tones into the deep ends of my mind where my self-control could not hear it. I felt him try and pull me off of Perish, but I shoved him back and continued to punch Perish in the face.

Then a ripping pain shot through my body. An electrical current that I knew came from Perish's hands; the chimera talent that Elish also possessed. It automatically made my jaw clamp shut and, taking this opportunity, Perish shoved me off of him.

Fucker, he never had this ability before. What the fuck did you do, Lycos?

I groaned on the floor, hearing Perish's manic sobbing and Killian's sniffling attempts to calm him down.

I had to get out of here, away from them… too much… too much in my head. My eyes closed as I felt an intense headache start to gather behind my eyes. With nothing more than a mumbled mention that I was going for a walk, I grabbed the rest of my clothes and ran out of the room.

Killian called after me but I couldn't… couldn't… I had to get out of that room, away from them.

Fuck, my head. I put on my clothes and my boots. My brain felt like it was swelling inside of my skull, pushing itself against my eyes and filling them with a white, blinding light. So much pressure…

I groaned and stumbled outside into the darkness. I picked up a handful of snow and pressed it against my left eye, trying to soothe the clustering pain.

It seemed to help a bit. I walked further into the snowy night towards the winding road that eventually led up to the highway.

I found comfort in the high trees when I was keeping my watch. I loved heights and I felt safe up high. So I climbed up my favourite twisted black tree and perched in a spot I found myself in during most of my sentry evenings. I gathered more snow from adjacent limbs and tried to ice down my head.

The snow was swirling around me like soft feathers, calm and silent. It fell to the earth and covered the trees and pavement in its own sound muting blanket. Sounds ceased to exist when it was snowing heavily, and what noise did break through had to struggle to reach your ears. It was beautiful in this forest, and though I loved the snow in Skyfall, there was something unique about watching it in the dead of night, surrounded by hundreds of miles of forest. I almost felt alone, and tonight that was what I needed.

I lit a cigarette and watched the soft flakes fall down to earth, breaking up the black silhouettes of the trees and making them just shadows of static grey. I inhaled and blew the smoke out, seeing if I could melt the snowflakes with just my breath.

Yes, this is what I needed in this moment, a break from my friends and a break from this mission. Even if it was only for a few hours with a cigarette as company I would take it. When I was with my master things were most often quiet. Elish was tranquility encompassed, a man of silent grace and an aura about him that made you stare in hushed awe. He was a cold but calming presence and one that told you to shut up.

I took another long drag and felt the pockets of my jacket, just to reassure myself I had more cigarettes if I wanted them. I knew by the time I climbed down this tree that I would probably burn through half a pack.

At least we had a lot of smokes. Killian was going to need the cigs and the drugs for tomorrow.

Because before dawn broke… we would be gone. Just me and him on our way back to Kreig. No more Falkland, no more O.L.S. It was too dangerous for both of us now. I had to get me and Killian away from Perish.

He would believe me. Perish was crazy and he had experienced that first-hand. He would believe me, and if he didn't, I had Perish's scopa to prove it to him that Perish had been drugging me.

I flicked my cigarette out of the tree and tucked my fingers into my jacket for warmth. Then I closed my eyes to try and will this fucking headache out of my head.

Sometime later I was jarred out of my partial sleep by the sounds of voices. I looked down and saw Hopper and Chomper walking together, sharing a smoke between the two of them.

They stopped underneath the very tree I was perched in; I stayed still and tuned in my chimera hearing to catch their conversation.

"I really was expecting the snow to melt now and I apologized for it, alright?" Hopper dashed his cigarette and leaned against the tree. "I didn't think we would have to deal with the little shits for this long either."

Oh, they were talking about the slaves.

Chomper brushed the snow away from his beard. "Tabbit is ready to blast a hole in the yellow-eyed one. Always spouting off like a fucking wild animal. I highly doubt we can get anything for him when we get to Melchai. Killian maybe, the other chimera probably… but Mikey is a wild fucking thing. I really just think we should put a bullet in his head and make it look like an accident; his meat would be nice."

What? My body jolted like I had just got a static shock. I was sure I had just had a stroke. What the fuck was going on?

"Nah, I think Man on the Hill might have some use for him. We have a fucking treasure trove right now that fell into our fucking lap. And Melchai has the people in it that would pay good money for not only the little blond shit, but the wild one as well. Fuck, I ain't letting them go for no less than four hundred each."

So we had gone from being mercenaries to fucking slaves ourselves? I guess the plans to bring us to Falkvalley, the town next to Melchai, was completely bullshit. I wonder when they decided that.

My eyes narrowed and I quietly bit off the end of my cigarette to mask the illuminated ember. It must have been that group meeting after I had killed Jimmy. That was when they decided we were more trouble than we were worth.

"I would have let them go. I fucking swear on all that is holy… but I am just through with their shit. I know Mikey killed Jimmy," Hopper said, and as if to confirm my suspicions he added: "Churro was right, if we can fake it till we make it to Melchai… we can put collars on 'em before they even realize we turned."

Low, muffled laughing sounded underneath me. "I gotta say, we're going to need to bind and tie them before we get to Melchai. The crazy one will rip out our throats the moment they realize what we did. What a bunch of fucking idiots. I swear though, I tried to be friendly, I fucking tried."

Shit. Shit. Shit.

"Yeah, me too. The world will be a better place with a couple less chimera scum," Hopper said through laughter. I heard him break away from a cigarette and then exhale. "Fucking chimeras and their bullshit. I wish life was easy enough for me and Churro to have drama like that. Too bad we're too busy fucking surviving. Well, whatever. Let's scope out the road."

I felt dizzy; nauseas and dizzy. As the wool over my eyes slowly drew back I thought for sure I was going to throw up. We had been tricked and we were still being tricked.

I had enemies all around me.

That's it… that's it. I'm done.

With my mind sifting through a thousand thoughts a second, I waited for Hopper and Chomper to disappear. Then when the two slavers were out of sight, I scaled down the tree and ran back to the lobby.

My chest was so tight, it constricted my heart and my lungs making it hard to breathe, and on top of that, my headache was coming back. But I had to push through it… I had to tell Killian. I had–

I yelped as cold hands grabbed me in the lobby; one immediately covering my mouth. I opened my mouth to scream when I felt a needle go into my neck.

"This isn't water, this is real scopa," Perish hissed into my ear. I felt a burning, bitter taste in the back of my throat. I thrashed my head, not to tell him to stop but to tell him what Hopper had done.

"Perish, Hopper… Hopper's lying…" The hand cupped my mouth again and I heard his low, sinister laugh. No quickened tones, no hand rubbing madness – just a cold, dark chuckle.

"Let it take you, Cicaro. Let it take you." Cold lips pressed against my cheek. "You will not feel your own mind free… for quite a while."

The light inside of my mind started to fade, like a dimmer on a light switch I watched the colours around me start to burn away to a charcoal grey. It smouldered and swirled until there was nothing left to see and nothing left to hear. All of it static, just static to my ears.

That rhymed.

I stood there, my eyes fixed forward. Seeing a tipped over desk in the corner with a broken computer monitor, all covered in thick dust.

Thick dust…

"Jade."

My eyes lifted and I saw Perish. I sniffed as I felt a string of drool start to run down my chin, my nose was running too and my eyes. Everything was turning to liquid, like my mind, like my brain.

Hands on my cheeks. My heartbeat hammered each nail into my coffin, pumping the drugs through my system. Faster, faster.

Dust on everything… liquid, dust.

I outstretched my arm so I could feel the dust. And even though it was on the other side of the room… I could feel it so soft underneath my fingers. It stuck to the tips and in my own head I rubbed my fingers together. It fell to the floor like ash.

Ash.

Fell to the… floor.

… like ash.

"Now tell me, Jade. What did Hopper say? Tell me everything."

Killian

I huddled by the fire and squeezed my eyes tight to fight back the tears. Perish had left to get more firewood and I was here alone, wringing my hands so hard that my joints were aching and sore.

What was I going to do? Everything was just falling apart. Now Jade was acting this way… I didn't blame him, I really didn't. I had been around Perish and Reaver, I knew chimeras and I knew even though they were genetically engineered… they seemed to fall into madness more easily. I don't know if it was a side effect of their coding, a fault or what, but I knew they were susceptible to it, so I understood Jade.

I just wanted to help him…

I knew Jade and he didn't care for Perish any more than Perish cared for him. He would have never tried to have sex with him… that just wasn't Jade.

Right now I felt like I was responsible for these two chimeras. It was like I was walking two rabid dogs on short leashes. I had to keep spinning and contorting myself to try and stop them from ripping each other apart.

I couldn't even control my own chimera well… let alone his brother and his fellow born immortal. What if Perish killed Jade?

What would Reaver do?

Reaver…

It had been three weeks now since they took Reaver. I had been apart from my boyfriend for almost a month. I had to hold onto the hope that Elish already had him and they just hadn't found us yet. If I didn't… if I let myself believe that Silas had him, I wouldn't be able to cope. I would tip into madness just like Jade was.

So Elish had Reaver… that was my truth. They were looking for us right now.

Maybe tonight… maybe tonight Reaver would come. I would hug him so hard his ribs would break. I would make love with him all night, until the sun rose and after.

No… I didn't want sex, I just wanted to hold him, and make him like it.

I whimpered and closed my eyes, trying to pretend I wasn't here. That I wasn't alone in this room with a dying fire, hundreds of miles from Aras, a town that was no longer my home, and a hundred more from my boyfriend.

I picked up Reaver's gun and ran my finger up and down the barrel, my biggest connection to him.

I glanced over at Jade's briefcase. The fact that it had been left behind in the closet Jade had been using was a testament to how quickly he wanted to get away from Perish. That suitcase was to Jade what Reaver's gun was to me. A physical reminder of the men we were missing.

Suddenly an ear-piercing scream cut the tranquil night and my solemn mood. I shot up to my feet, quickly attaching Reaver's gun onto my holder and went to run outside.

I almost crashed right into Perish speeding in.

"Follow me, follow me… come, come you must come now!" Perish was breathless, his hyper voice several octaves higher than usual, and his left hand holding the iron poker we used to bar the slave room. I watched his eyes sweep the room before he quickly grabbed our satchels. "Now. NOW!"

"What's going on? Where's Jade?" I demanded, though the energy Perish brought in the room immediately had me grabbing the rest of our stuff. "What was that scream?" It wasn't Jade's tone of voice, it sounded like…

"Ravers are coming." Perish grabbed the belt of my gun holder and pulled me out of the room we had been staying in. "We're going to the roof. I know an easy way up. Come!"

I followed him, passing Tabbit as he raced through the debris-strewn hallway we were sprinting down. He didn't even look at us.

I glanced behind me. Perish took me into their old public bathrooms, and to my surprise, I could see a shelf of snow that had collected in the far corner. I looked up and saw snowflakes falling through a gap in the roof.

"Climb!" Perish pushed me forward. He closed the door behind us.

"What about Jade? And Deekoi?" I dug my boots into the mound of snow and started to scale it towards the opening in the roof.

"He has trees and the dog can outrun them easily. Just you, we need to make sure you're okay. Hurry!" Perish started to climb right behind me. I managed to pull myself through the collapsed concrete and wiggle my body between two thick metal beams. Snowflakes were landing on my face now, immediately melting under my heated skin.

Then another scream broke the night; this one filling me with a new sense of urgency. It was closer, closer than the last one. A high-pitched and manic shriek, one of a radiation-crazed subhuman that was smelling the sweet aroma of human flesh.

I pulled myself onto the roof and took a cautious step back as Perish followed behind me. I drew my gun and started looking around the courtyard and forest.

Immediately I saw the slavers, they were shouting orders at each other. Chomper and Hopper were running down the winding snow-covered road, and Tabbit and Churro were talking loudly to them as they did. Everyone had their guns out and Churro was holding a lit torch that added orange and yellow to the snowy night.

They looked like villagers from the ancient times, wielding torches and pitchforks to hunt down some great beast. Gathering together for strength in numbers to seek out and destroy the monsters in the woods. Monsters that were shrouded in the heavy snowfall around us; nothing but crazed shadows who only gave away their shapes once it was too late.

And then they would make it rain little red rubies onto the ground, white and red, the grey buried underneath the snow. I wondered, in a mind too used to morbid thoughts, just what blood-soaked snow we would leave behind for the next traveller.

"Get down," Perish whispered behind me. He pushed on my shoulders and I fell to my knees. The scientist wrapped an arm around me and pushed Reaver's gun into my hand. "Do not let them know we're up here, the roof is too fragile to hold all of them and we'll come crashing to the lobby."

I stared at the slavers. Churro was passing around torches. "We need to find Jade."

But before he could answer back there was another scream, and as soon as the last shrill octave got swallowed up by the winter air, another one took its place.

And another.

And another.

Then I saw them. A flicker of movement where the road bent out of sight, but no sooner did I focus my eyes on the brown creature did three more appear beside it.

My heart gave a panicked jolt but Perish held me to him. "Shh… not a word."

Then something happened. I could see the ravers looking behind them in their own desperation. I couldn't see them well, but from their own jerking movements and backwards glances I could tell they were upset over something. They were looking behind them only to start running again. All of them trudging down the almost two feet of snow on bare feet so light they could almost walk on top of it.

Then another scream from the raver in the front of the pack. I saw his mouth open in a gaping yawn, and with that, he clamped his hands over his ears. He clawed at his ears so hard I could see his blood start to ooze down the side of his head.

I stared at him curiously as he shook his body… then started to run.

And they followed him, all of them.

Fucking dozens of them.

"Hopper!" Tabbit yelled.

"Get into the fucking slave pen. It's secure… bar the fucking door! NOW!" Hopper's voice was shrill and broken with unimaginable panic. The slaver looked behind him as the ravers all started to run down the road, screaming and clawing their heads like they were in physical pain. All of them were running as fast as they could, with snow being kicked up around them. They were in a frenzy, driven crazy by a source I didn't understand.

It was like they were being… were being herded.

"Churro!" Hopper screamed. "Quick!"

My eyes flicked to Hopper. He disappeared into the lobby and I heard a door slam.

Then Chomper's voice. "This door won't shut properly, the fire poker's gone. Hop… we need to make a break for the hotel. I can't find the… we can't…"

"They're right behind us!"

Perish's hot breath was on the nape of my neck. He was mumbling reassurances to me but all I could do was switch between the manic voices of the slavers and the ravers running down the hill. They were getting closer and closer to the lobby, clawing their heads as they ran and leaving gouges so deep I could see bone. They were ripping their own ears off.

Why?

Then I saw a new shadow.

I shifted away from Perish and rose to my feet; the slavers now all inside of the lobby. I took a step to get a closer look as I saw a silhouette dressed in black walk along the bend in the road. He was walking in such a smooth way it was like he was treading on pavement.

It was Jade.

In the white backdrop I could see his face perfectly. Jade's yellow eyes were reflecting like a beast's in the full moon above us. He was walking down the road, a demonic grin on his face and blood running down his nose and eyes.

"Jade!" I screamed. Perish grabbed me and pushed me back into his arms. I struggled, a new, fresh panic coursing through me like lightning. "Jade! He's… he's controlling the ravers. How?" I demanded.

Perish clutched me close to him. "The whistle we know, maybe? Or maybe he's tapping into some new tricks he has. He's luring them towards us. Jade's trying to kill us, Killian. I told you. I warned you."

Another shadowed figure appeared beside Jade. It was my dog; a plume of vapour rising from his mouth as he breathed in and out. He stood beside Jade, their matching yellow eyes watching the group of ravers run down the final bend of the road; only the parking lot and courtyard now separating them and us.

Jade looked down at the deacdog. The Shadow Killer mouthed something to Deek and the dog took off running, closing the distance between the ravers and him. Then, to drive the radiation-crazed creatures into further frenzy, the dog started to snap and growl at them, luring them closer and closer to the lobby.

Then the first gunshot of the night rang. I saw a raver, climbing over the concrete fence that surrounded the fountain, fall to the ground in a mosaic of blood. Soon a second one followed, and a third.

Jade then ran. As he ran down the road I could see his lips slightly pursed as he made the high-pitched noise that only chimera hearing could pick up. He sped, still stepping lightly on top of the snow, down the ridge, before branching off to the left to help heard the ravers.

I wanted to see, I wanted to fucking help the slavers, but whenever I jerked my body away from Perish he held me tight to him, unwilling to even give me an inch.

I watched as Jade ran out of sight, the crazed ravers screaming and running in front of him.

Then the ravers reached the slavers.

I muffled a cry of despair as I heard Tabbit scream. He was shouting at the slaves to get back. Why weren't they in the slaves' quarters? Why couldn't they bar the door? Every evening they used a fire poker to slip between the two…

I looked down–

–and saw the metal rod I had seen Perish bring up with him. It wasn't a metal bar at all. It was the fire poker.

What… what was going on?

A desperate scream… a hysterical scream. I closed my eyes and clamped my teeth down on my lip as the sensory scrambling shrieks of dozens of ravers and terrified slavers filled the winter air, breaking through the peaceful milieu that a snowy night brought.

Then gunshots, so many gunshots.

Unable to stand it anymore, I broke away from Perish's grasp and crawled my way over to the edge of the roof, near where the hole Perish had found had been. I held the M16 to my chest and shifted over to see if I could help.

"Killian!" Perish said angrily. He tried to grab me but I kicked him. He might not care but Hopper and the others had been nice to us. If I could help shoot the ravers I would. I wasn't a coward and I would prove it.

The screams were constant, the panic lighting flares of electricity that clung to the atmosphere. I got to the hole in the roof and looked down. "Hopper! Hopper, up here. Up–"

I gasped in surprise as Perish grabbed me again, this time more forceful. I screamed and tried to bite down on his hand as he dragged me back to the center of the roof. His grip was hard and the anger clear by his forceful movements.

"Killian? The boy's on the roof!" Hopper was outside… another several gunshots sang in the air, followed by the screeching of injured ravers. In my line of sight I saw three of the crazed subhumans, one of them dragging a dead Tabbit by the leg as the other two ripped large chunks of flesh away from the soft areas of his stomach.

I froze; the sight temporarily robbing me of my senses. I gaped, my mouth dropping open in shock, as they pulled out his entrails, chewing on them as their necks jerked back and forth like they were rubber bands, digging fingers into his stomach and widening the hole.

Like Cholt the mercenary, the one who'd been eaten alive on my family's journey to Aras.

Transfixed, I stared. Every sound around me becoming lost in my own stunned stupor, my eyes only saw the carnage that being in the center of the roof had saved me from.

There was movement in the gap in the roof behind me, and once

Perish saw it he temporarily let me go.

I rose to my feet and walked to the edge of the roof.

Tabbit's blood had saturated the now slushy snow around him, sinking his body down into his own white and red coffin. Surrounding him were pieces of his flesh and his clothing, stuck to the white or hanging on spindly branches like flags of surrender. He was his own art project; a collage of red organs, tainted snow, and four brown worms, heads down, that vibrated from excitement as they consumed his flesh.

A slave ran out, its shackles gone but the slave collar remaining. He sprinted out and into the woods; a raver followed him, hunched over with a snarl rimming his lips. As the raver ran to claim him, another slave sprung forth and made a break for the road. Two ravers closed in on that one.

They went down quickly, and with the maddening shriek, the desperate tenor that only showed itself during the most grisly and painful of deaths, I saw the blood start to dye the snow.

Then the black figure, distorted from the falling flakes. Still frozen in shock, I watched Jade casually walk past the ravers who had just taken down the slave. His walk an assured saunter like he was on a Sunday stroll.

Jade brought a cigarette up to his lips and kept it in there as he inhaled, then he started sprinting towards the lobby. Deek was behind him, the dog's hackles raised and his muzzle drenched in blood.

The Shadow moved like a cat. With a stealth unheard of, especially in two feet of snow, Jade grabbed onto the trunk of a black tree and started clawing his way up. His claw rings on his fingers, and the canine teeth he had implanted glinting in the moonlight.

I could hear Perish behind me but I didn't move; my eyes were focused on Jade.

The chimera cicaro climbed up until he was at an even level with the lobby roof. Then, without effort or even a glance to see where he was going, he jumped and drew himself onto the roof and stood.

Immediately he turned his back to me and gazed out onto the madness he had created. Gazed out and looked upon the bodies that littered the snowy forest, the red stains like blemishes on porcelain skin, and the infected subhumans he could now control.

"Jade? Perish?!" I looked over and saw Hopper and Churro's heads, both trying to pull themselves up on the leaning carport not ten feet from us. Churro had a knife in his hand, a large chunk of flesh missing from his wrist.

"They're fuckin five… five… inside, FUCKING HELP US!" Hopper screamed. Behind him I saw two large male ravers closing in on them. Their boney fingers outstretched and clawed; a wild, crazed look on their scarred and now earless faces.

I was frozen from fear, only able to watch as Jade turned his head away from the chaos and sauntered up to the carport.

Help them, Jade…

The cicaro flexed his fingers as he beheld the sight in front of him, Churro desperately trying to climb up on his injured wrist and Hopper trying to push him up.

"What the fuck you lookin' for! HELP!" Hopper screamed. He looked behind him and let out a desperate noise, then looked back. "Get Churro first. Get Churro first!"

I saw Jade shake his head once, then, to my horror, he withdrew his combat knife… and stabbed Churro in the hand.

Both the slavers screamed, and as Jade withdrew the knife, Churro fell onto the ground. Hopper let himself fall beside him, grabbing Churro's jacket to try and drag him to safety.

But it was too late. I watched in horror as the two male ravers attacked Churro. Sinking their broken and shattered teeth into his neck and his face, chewing and biting as the slaver's skin shredded in their mouths.

The screams were horrific, the scene more morbid and heinous than I had ever witnessed.

Churro was crying out. Hopper was silent, his face drained of colour but his body grabbing the raver in a desperate attempt to get his teeth away from Churro's face. He wrenched the raver's head away and tried to stab him with his knife but ravers couldn't feel pain.

Spurts of blood squirted from Churro's neck, gushing into the raver's mouth as his chewed, shredding the slaver's clothes apart with his sharpened fingers, revealing tallowy, white bone underneath that soon became coated with blood.

Then Hopper. The slaver leader was screaming his despair, but not a moment later his pain was ended. Filled with a bloodlust of his own, I watched my own dog jump on his back and rip Hopper's head off with a single vicious bite.

I turned at that moment, unable to watch it anymore.

But no sooner than I had torn my gaze away from the carnage below me, my eyes went to Jade's face.

I couldn't believe what I was seeing.

The Shadow Killer's eyes were fixed forward, blood running down his nose and mouth. But it wasn't just blood; it was also drool and snot. It was trickling down his face and down his neck, a slippery river that drenched the entire front of his jacket.

I had seen that look before… I had seen those glassy eyes.

Immediately my eyes shot to Perish. He was standing behind us, his gun in his hand, watching with me the scene below us. He was even-faced, calm, and collected.

"You gave him scopa…" I whispered to Perish. "You made him do this, didn't you?"

Perish's eyes darted to mine and he looked at me.

My mouth went dry. I watched as he stared me down, his ice blue eyes cold like the snow falling around him.

Then I saw Perish's features subtly change. His tense face softened, his brilliant, crazed eyes focused, and the hyper-manic Perish that I had once known disappeared. He was now replaced by a doppelganger, though in my heart I knew it was the doppelganger that had left his mind.

"How did you find that O.L.S, Perish?" I asked.

The born immortal, quite possibly the oldest man in the world, smiled. A smile that drew with it a sinister grimness, a smile so dark and foreboding it made me want to jump off of the roof and run.

It was no manic smile of a crazed scientist, it was one of a shifting spectre; a man with such an eerie darkness to him I felt my knees weaken. It was darkness. It was a phantom. It was a man broken apart, who had just found the final piece to put himself back together.

"It was beautiful, wasn't it?" Perish said quietly, gazing back at the horrors below us. "Did you enjoy it?"

Then he looked over to Jade and walked up to him. I watched as he put a hand on Jade's back and rubbed it in an almost caring manner. "And you… well, I don't have any more use for you now, do I?"

Suddenly I saw a flash of black. I screamed and put my hands out to stop Perish as he raised the fire poker and swung it at Jade.

It connected with Jade's head with a sickening *crack* and the cicaro went down. His body twitching and his chest gasping like a fish out of water, a pool of blood quickly appearing behind his head.

I screamed and ran to him.

Jade's chest was rapidly rising and falling, his glassy eyes seemingly transfixed to the sky. There was so much blood coming from his head. I petted his hair back, my mouth opening in a soundless scream.

"He was too dangerous to keep alive; his powers are extraordinary," Perish whispered behind me. "We really had no choice."

I kept petting Jade's head, not knowing what else to do; all I could do now was soothe him.

"And now we must go, we must leave these greywastes," Perish said behind me. "Let's go, Killian."

I jerked my head around, almost unable to talk under my own agony. "You fucking killed him! Perry… Perry, I know you're in there somewhere. You need to… you need to fight your way out."

But Perish only smiled at me, before drawing up his hand.

He was holding a slave collar.

CHAPTER 34

Reaver

I SWALLOWED THE WARM WATER AS KIKI BROUGHT it to my lips. His hands shaking so badly it spilled over my mouth and neck, mixing in with the blood and leaving rosy stains on the sheets underneath me.

The young chimera stared at me like I was an atomic bomb, a row of stitches starting from his right lip and ending by his dark sideburns. Twenty stitches, all of them with dried blackened skin stuck to them. They were unbandaged and showing off their gore to the world; though the wound on his neck was heavily bound.

When I was finished he pulled the glass away quickly, then ran to the shadows where he had been since he had returned sometime in the past.

I no longer knew what time was, there were no windows here and Nero came and went on a sporadic schedule. It must have been weeks though, but it felt like years.

I took in a long inhale, my blackened chest forever protesting for more air. I had four broken ribs that had been unable to heal. Death had not reached me yet, not during this session.

It had been seven times now that I had woken from the death Nero had put me in, well, six from him and one from Kiki once he returned. He let the boy cut off my dick and balls, then they watched me bleed to death as they fucked on top of me.

I no longer cared. I no longer had the capacity to care anymore.

When I first woke up here, he raped me.

The second time he literally raped me to death.

The third time he suffocated me while he tried to make me give him head.

The fourth… the fifth… sixth, and seventh…

All just… images that swirled into each other. Patterns without patterns, loose thoughts and partial memories that all blended into one never ending string of pain. Pain and humiliation, that was my existence; what I had been outside of these walls now nothing but a badly painted picture that currently lay crushed underneath Nero's boot.

Perhaps I had been here for a year.

Maybe I had never left and this had always been my life.

Like a tracker, my eyes followed Kiki as he refilled the glass of water for himself. He gave me a cautious eye and took a sip.

I moved my wrists in my binds, the thick scabs chafed against the metal. The scabs were thick, brown shells that wept fluid freely as they cracked under my constant movement. I stared at my wrists before I looked back to Kiki.

The boy never took his eyes off of me, orange eyes that peered at me from the shadows like the alley cats in Aras. Nervous and forever shifting, wondering if I was nearing the time when I would snap these chains off of me and bomb this entire mansion.

When I am king I would spare that boy though. I had too many chimeras on my kill list and many of them deserved fates worse than death. That little thing still had redeeming parts to him, his submission mostly. He could be my sengil. Perhaps I would give him to Reno.

Reno… I wonder if they got him. I wonder if Killian–

My brow creased as I immediately pushed their faces and names from my head. I purged their memories and hardened the areas that they had softened. Thinking of them would only cause me pain and I was in enough pain as it was.

Sometime that night I felt the weight of the bed beside me. After some fleeting taunts and insults from Nero, he commanded Kiki to adjust the chains holding my legs, then he proceeded to fuck me like he so often did.

My hands were on the iron rungs; they were holding me up as my body rocking back and forth. The sounds of chains knocking against the iron drowned out Nero's moans. I tried to focus on them most of all.

It was all I could do not to lash out and try to kill him. Not to jerk my head back and try to take in any bit of warm flesh I could grab. It was useless, and all it would do was drain my energy; he was waiting for me to attack him.

That's what he wanted after all. My captor wanted a reason to kill me again and I was done giving him one. I was immortal, and from that immortality drew patience. I would get my chance and when I did…

It would be wonderful.

So instead I pushed down the fire and brimstone that crackled underneath my surface and stared at my shackled hands. The scabs were now worn through, loosened and ripping away from the red flesh underneath. There was white tendon showing through, I had worn the shackles into my skin so much they were starting to sever my hand from my wrist.

Severing my hand from my wrist.

Severing my fucking hand from my wrist.

Nero groaned and I felt his breath on my neck. "You break so easily, I'm disappointed, Reaver." I kept staring as he licked my earlobe, before thrusting himself into me several times to finish himself off. I felt his cum inside of me, mixed in with the blood. Even the smell of it made me want to throw up.

I hadn't been able to shower or bathe myself. The only time I was cleaned was when Kiki bathed me with a sponge and a bucket of soapy water. I let him without trying to tear his face off. I felt filthy and disgusting, I felt like an animal.

I was an animal.

Nero rolled off of me and stretched out on the bed, naked and baring it all. Blood was staining his half-hard cock; it was glistening with sweat and his own remaining cum.

I laid down too, and as was the norm, he lit me a cigarette. I took it without complaint, not to be obedient but because it was the only highlight of my day now. I took whatever he offered me whether it was the muscle relaxing ciovi, mind numbing heroin, or the bumps of cocaine he enjoyed taking off of my back.

Mostly it was the blue-embered cigarettes, the fancy Skyfall kind called BlueLeaf. I had a taste for them now.

Nero watched me smoke; I saw he was smirking at me. “If I could trust you not to chew my face off, I’d have real sex with you. I bet you fuck like a steam engine.”

The blue ember brightened as I inhaled. I ignored him as I so often did.

I guess he wanted me to answer him. Nero hit me right across the face, the cigarette getting smacked from my lips and falling onto the bloodstained sheets. It started to smoulder.

“I told Kessler you escaped, just so you know. So if you think he’s going to come and throw you into a comfortable cell away from me – think again,” Nero said. He wiped the blood from my lips but I still didn’t move.

This made him laugh. He motioned to Kiki and I felt him unchain my legs. “Stunned and dead to the world. It’s always amusing when they get to this state. I can just feel the mania seep off of you. It makes me wanna fuck you again.”

He picked up the cigarette, which had now started burning a hole through the sheets, and put the ember out on my cheek. I still didn’t flinch, even though my legs were unshackled I didn’t swallow his bait.

Once again, this made him angry. He was a man who thrived off of reactions. I had seen how much he enjoyed tormenting Perish, and had seen first-hand how much he enjoyed tormenting me. So to appease his thirst, he proceeded to beat me, and to top it off, before he left Nero fucked me once again.

I didn’t move, I didn’t scream; I was too numb. The world was far away, out of my grasp and out of what had become my own inner reality.

He left unsatiated, the door closed with a bang and Kiki following close behind. I was surrounded by snuffed out cigarettes and cigars. All of them put out on my face and what was between my legs.

When I was convinced that he wasn’t coming back, I shifted my sore body up to the sitting position, a fresh streak of red blood following my movements. These sheets had been changed so many times but my body was like a paintbrush. Forever painting and contaminating everything I touched.

I looked over at my cuffed left hand. I twisted it around in the shackle as I most often did to occupy myself. Though this time I bent my wrist back to see just how deep I had chafed it.

My insides stirred, the first reaction sans violence that I had managed to pull from myself in quite a while. Soon after, adrenaline followed, or perhaps it was the cold reality of the task ahead of me.

My wrist was worn down, a bloody swollen ring filled with sticky clear liquid, broken scabs, and tendons that flexed and twinged like the strings of a guitar. Seeing the flesh so damaged, so worn through, had given me the most transgressive and morbid of ideas.

Without hesitation I put my teeth to the inflamed flesh of my wrist…

… and I started to eat through it.

There was no second-guessing my decision, no inner debate over what I was doing. This pain was nothing compared to what I had been subject to for the last several weeks. This was Sunday fucking dinner.

So I chewed, like a wolf with its leg caught in a trap, I chewed through the warm flesh, ripping and swallowing any good chunks of meat I got. There was barely any flesh to bite through though; it was all mostly ropey, stringy tendons and blood.

I left the larger veins I saw intact, but I chewed through every tendon I found. The white ribbon that gave my fingers movement was chewy and tough but I severed them. Each finger twitching and tugging as I nipped the white string before they fell into paralysis.

Blood was flowing quickly from my wrist when I finally chewed the flesh away from my bone. The red pulsing veins just waiting for the last sever. My hand and wrist looking like a chewed apple, the bone its core.

I took a deep breath and sat on the bed facing the wall, taking a moment to get used to sitting up. I had lost a lot of blood and my head was swimming, wave after wave of dizziness doing their work on my already battered body.

But I was the fucking Reaper and pain didn't control me. Pain was nothing but a discomfort for a mortal to remind themselves they're only human.

And I was a chimera; I was not human.

I wedged my hand into a tight space between two of the iron rungs, palm down, and leaned back, then I shifted myself so my feet were pressing against the head of the bed

Then, with a stifled scream, I pushed my legs into the iron rungs, and pulled my arm.

I clamped my teeth as the pain overwhelmed me, but I pushed through it and twisted my arm. I could feel the bones snapping more than I could hear them. A sickening sound that travelled up my arms and centered in my brain.

Then, with a gasp, I felt my hand detach, and with that, the cuff whipped itself behind the rung it had been looped over and fell onto the bed, bloodied and still holding my severed hand in its steel mouth.

Overcome by pain, I laid on my back gasping. I wanted to stay there to catch my breath but blood was squirting out of my severed veins.

So I rose, before collapsing onto the floor. I crawled over to the dark corners where Kiki hid and opened one of the dresser drawers. I took out a sock and quickly, with only my remaining hand and my teeth, tied off my arm.

I was free. I managed to put on a zippered jacket that had been draped over the chair and in the pocket I placed my severed hand. I zipped it inside and looked around for something to defend myself with.

There was nothing, everything had been taken out of this room. Not a gun or a knife to be found. I ground my teeth before tightening the makeshift tourniquet and walked towards the door.

The door opened; they never locked it, they had no need to. I walked through the thick wood door and saw a long hallway in front of me. I wasn't overly conscious when they dragged me into this room; but all I needed was a window.

I managed a few steps before I sank to my knees. I swore under my breath and struggled to rise, craning my ears to try and listen for Nero or Kiki coming back. All I could hear though was the adrenaline rushing through my head and the steady trickle of blood from my severed stump.

I looked at where my hand had used to be. My two arm bones were poking out, like snowy glaciers in a bloodied sea. Absentmindedly, without even knowing what I was doing, I bit on the end of the biggest bone and crunched down on it as hard as I could. I heard and felt the familiar snap of bone and then the sound of splintering as I ripped the tip of the bone off.

I could see the red marrow in the center, but what I was more interested in was the actual bone. I'd done what I had needed to do. Instead of a rounded edge, the piece I had bitten off had made the blunt end sharp.

With a half-sane smirk, I struggled to my feet again. I put my good hand on the wall to help balance myself and started trying to find a door.

Back and forth. One foot in front of the other. I pushed the stump of my arm into the crook of my other arm to stem the flow of blood, and concentrated on walking. I tried to ignore the intense pressure in my chest from my broken ribs, and the dizzy consciousness-ending delirium that was creeping to the forefront of my mind.

Then I reached the end of the hallway, filled with furniture of the highest standard all arranged like the photos in magazines. I swept it with my gaze and started walking towards a door to the right.

I opened it and stepped through.

A legionary was standing guard at the door.

He looked at me, and for a split second all did was stare at me in shock. I must have been a sight to see. Too bad for him that split second hesitation was my opportunity.

As he reached behind him to grab his gun, I jerked back the ruined remains of my arm. Then, with as much force as I could muster, I stabbed him in the neck with the chewed and sharpened bone.

The legionary let out a gurgled scream. I ripped out my arm before stabbing him again in the neck, blood squirting from the wound and showering me in red.

I fell to my knees as he dropped to the ground, another nauseas wave of dizziness claiming my head. I bent over and tried to catch my breath as the legionary died beside me.

I took his handgun, knowing I wouldn't have the strength to roll him onto his stomach to get his assault rifle. I wouldn't be able to hold it properly with one arm anyway, so I grabbed the pistol and held it in my good arm and staggered to my feet.

But my position had already been uncovered. I looked up as I heard the scuffling of feet.

"Stop right there!" one of them shouted.

Why do they say things like that? I raised my gun with a trembling hand and shot the legionary. To my luck, I managed to hit him; he flew backwards and landed on the ground. Dead before he even hit the floor.

I stumbled past him, seeing a pool of dark blood start to gather behind his head, and staggered on. I knew my clock was winding down, guns were loud and this mansion, I believed, was swimming with chimeras.

I needed to find a quad, a dirt bike… I had to find so many things before I died and I wasn't sure if I was going to be able to.

No, failure couldn't be my option.

With this in my mind, I put one foot in front of the other, leaving a trail of red behind me. All I could hear was the sound of blood roaring through my ears, and my bare feet scraping up against the carpet. I was naked, save for the jacket on my back, holding my severed hand.

I rounded another corner and breathed a small, cautious sigh of relief. I was in what looked like the entrance to a hanger or a storage room, and chances are those rooms held doors to the outside.

I closed my eyes for a brief moment to try and find an adrenaline store, before taking a step into the large, box-filled room.

Then I heard the familiar laugh… and my heart sank.

"Smart. I would've never thought you would sever your own hand. I underestimated you," Nero chuckled. I heard boot steps behind me but I refused to turn around. "You were so close too. The hanger for our vehicles and planes is just behind those walls. I'm tempted to give you a bike just so I can hunt you and fuck you again."

I didn't know what to do; I was too light-headed from blood loss to do anything but keep walking. Several stacks of boxes were in front of me and I thought I could see windows behind them. I kept walking, squeezing my bleeding stump in the crook of my arm.

When I felt his hand take my shoulder and pull it back, my mind broke.

I whirled around and took a swipe at him with the sharpened bone of my severed arm. Like what my teeth had done to Kiki, I slashed his face to the bone. Opening up a large gash from his ear to his nose. It ripped half of his nose clean off.

With a desperate cry, I raised the gun and shot him in the chest. He stumbled back and hit a stack of boxes behind him.

I heard a loud *thud* and I realized that the kickback had made me drop the gun. I reached down on trembling, weak knees to try and pick it up, but he was already on me.

Nero pushed me to the ground and fell on top of me; the blood from his face dripping on me as he pinned me down with his body.

I clenched my teeth but a scream of frustration and anger sprung to my lips. As he shifted himself into position and took his cock out of his pants, I twisted and hollered with every last ounce of energy I had.

My mind was thrown into insanity as he pushed his already hard cock into me. Once again, I felt desperate and trapped, made worse by the fleeting taste of freedom now dissolving into nothing around me. I screamed loudly; I no longer cared to save the dignity he had been systematically robbing me of for weeks now.

Nero grabbed my chin and pursed his lips at me, laughing at his newest plaything, one that I knew must've tickled every single transgression he had inside of him. I wasn't an obedient sengil or the spineless scientist Perish. I was a toy that fought back, screamed obscenities back, and raged as he plucked at the last strands of my pride.

And as if Nero knew that he was finally breaking past the greywaster-born pride I had been raised with, he smiled, the corners of his mouth rising and seeping self-satisfaction. He knew I was edging my rope and he knew, if only just for now, just for tonight, that he had Chimera X in his hand.

"I ain't gonna stop fucking you until you call me baby, hunny-cakes," Nero growled. In an act that only solidified his state of smug pride, he leaned down and kissed my mouth, licking the upper and lower lip with his warm tongue.

I snapped at him but he held me down easily. Then, with a groan from his mouth, he started to drive himself into me, hard.

"I will kill you. I swear on Killian's life you will be the first immortal I kill!" I snarled. Words were all I had now. Until I could escape, words were all Nero had left me. "I swear I will put your rotting skull up in my skyscraper as a warning to ALL OF YOU that I AM THE FUCKING KING!" I screamed. Desperation swept through me, taking me to places I never thought I would be. I was trapped; I was trapped and I wasn't in control and it was literally driving me insane. Every thrust, every toying word stripped my nerves and my resolve bare. All I wanted in that moment was to burst out of my skin. Kill them. Kill all of them!

I screamed and thrashed my arms, his cock mercilessly pounding into me, his voice laughing and bringing me sweet taunts that fell on ears blocked out by my own mania.

Then behind Nero a silhouette appeared, a man with a black ski mask over his face and a buttoned up duster. Before I could deduce whether he was real or not, he raised an assault rifle and shot Nero several times in the side of the head.

The side of Nero's head blew off and immediately he collapsed on top of me. I could feel his cock go flaccid inside of my body as the crater on the side of his head oozed blood and pureed brains onto my chest and neck.

Two of them were there now, pulling Nero off of me.

But my mental state won out over the notion that these two were here to help me. As soon as they pushed Nero off of me, I snarled and stared them down.

One of them held out a hand. "Reaver, we're here to free you. Can you walk?"

The low vibrations rumbled in my throat. I stared them down and didn't move.

"Just grab him, he can't do very much damage to us," another one whispered. That voice… I think I had heard it before.

Before I could snap my limbs away from them they both grabbed me. Immediately I thrashed and howled. My head automatically filling me with dire warnings that they were going to take me back to Nero's room. And with that alert blaring inside of my head, I hollered and screamed as loud as I could. I knew there was little sense to it but my mind was gone. All that was left were the primal instincts of a wounded, wild animal.

They both carried me and were soon joined with a third waiting by the door. I tried to keep twisting and thrashing my body but within seconds I was exhausted. When they took me out of the storage room and into the one next to it, I was too weak to do anything more than growl.

My bare feet dragged against the floor, I couldn't even hold my own head up to see where they were taking me.

I realized as we passed through the doors though that I could hear a plane in the distance. Were they taking me to Skyfall? Why were they masked?

I managed to raise my head just as they were stepping onto a Falconer, and saw the third one take his mask off.

Reno?

"Oh, baby…" he sobbed.

Reno's face was twisted in despair. He looked different. His hair was half silver, half black. He was skinnier too, but I think his face had changed the most.

I wasn't used to seeing him so upset.

Though as much as I wanted to greet my buddy, all I could do was stare. I didn't even have the strength to hug him back when he took me into his arms and squeezed the life out of me.

I heard him start to sob, and as I lost feeling in my legs, he sunk down to the floor with me.

Reno was crying; he was crying so hard. I tried to look around, feeling dazed and confused.

A moment later, the two masked ones appeared again, carrying what looked like my pants and several other articles of clothes.

"We got everything; let's get the fuck out of here before Sid or Kincade realize what just happened." The door slammed and the man who just spoke turned around. As the plane rose into the air, he took his ski mask off.

It was Caligula, and beside him also removing his mask, was his boyfriend Nico.

"Nico, drive the plane." Yet another familiar voice. This one I could only stare at, wondering just how he managed to sway Kessler's son onto our side.

Elish appeared in the doorway of the cockpit and kneeled down in front of me, Reno sobbing and squeezing the life out of me.

"You're safe. I am going to give you an injection to put you out of your pain." Elish brought out a needle and took my severed arm. He didn't even flinch when he saw the mess of flesh and tendons that had used to be where my hand was. He just put it down and picked up the arm that still had my hand attached. Reno though groaned. I could feel his face press against my neck and a sniff.

Elish stuck the needle into the crook of my arm. “Hold him up, Reno. He’s going to fade soon.”

Wait… where are we going? We need to find Killian… and the others.

I opened my mouth to speak but a burning took me, and a moment later, the darkness.

End of Volume 1

A NOTE FROM QUIL

Hey, everyone! Did you miss me? You did? Great! (This isn't Choose Your Own Adventure, you have no choice but to say yes). I'm happy to be back, and I hope you enjoyed Book 2 Vol. 1 of The Fallocaust Series. No worries, Vol. 2 is right around the corner and will be released November 15th 2014. Thank you for all of your continued support, and thank you for visiting my world. I spent a lot of time here as you can probably tell, and being able to tell my boys' stories is a dream come true. I mean that literally too, being a writer has always been my dream, and I am seeing it happen thanks to you.

As usual: for updates on book releases, to view excerpts, or to watch me act like a complete nutjob follow me on Twitter @Fallocaust, and also find me/befriend me on Facebook, which is under /quil.carter. I also have my own website now www.quilcarter.com.

And thank you for reading. I mean it. Your time is valuable and I appreciate you spending some of it reading my work. I hope it was worth every minute (and if not… haha, stole your time).

Sincerely,
Quil Carter

Made in the USA
Middletown, DE
16 October 2023